The Malign Alliance

PENN ADAMS

THE MALIGN ALLIANCE

First edition. April 20, 2020.

Copyright © 2020 Penn Adams.

Written by Penn Adams.

Edited by Simone Ford (IPEd).

Cover Design by Rob Williams, ilovemycover.com.

ISBN: 978-06488080-1-5

DEDICATION

For my beloved daughter, Caroline.

Chapter One

It was a cruel and sudden twist of fate that only three days after her twenty-first birthday, Linnayen Genara lost her beloved father and, as a consequence, gained his throne. On the third day after Yenshar Genara's death she became the Lady of Light, the Ki of Altan, and whilst she inherited much of her father's wisdom and guile, she had yet to discover within herself his natural warmth and tolerance. However, her calculating mind stood her in good stead for, most important of all, she inherited his war.

The conflict with Earth had plagued Altan for over twenty years. Its people fought to stay out of the Union of Planets, the body of like-minded sovereign worlds of which Altan was currently the elected convenor. Whilst the Union had long since ceased its efforts to enlist Earth, prejudice remained, and Union trade and research outposts were often attacked by Earthan fighters without warning. The continuing conflict with its endless skirmishes had saddened and angered the old Ki for many years. Now they had become the death of him. The injuries he had received on board the battlecraft *Sur-Lenes* in the latest battle were too many and too severe. He would not survive the night.

Inside the Genara palace, in a high room overlooked by the snow-tipped peaks of the Ksas Mountains, now shadowed by the purple evening gloom, Yenshar lay still and calm. He was no longer in any pain and, although the succession was secure, he could not leave without saying goodbye. He called for Sen-Beoraan, his most trusted privy counsellor, and beckoned him to draw close.

'There are many things and people in this life that I have loved, my old friend. You are one of them. Thank you for your good advice all these years.'

Genara's voice was ragged as he struggled to form the words, but there was more to be said.

'Your friendship … I could not have governed – I wouldn't have achieved anything – without your friendship.'

Beoraan shook his head, a lock of his long greying hair fell and hid his welling eyes. 'No, my lord. You were the one, always strong, always wise. I was nothing.'

'That's the first truly stupid thing I have ever heard you say, Beoraan!' Genara broke into a faltering grin. He laughed weakly and Beoraan smiled back through a film of tears.

'Is there nothing they can do for you now, my lord?' Beoraan pleaded.

'Nothing,' the Ki replied, patting the old counsellor's hand. 'But there is one last favour I would ask of you, my old friend.'

Beoraan looked up expectantly. 'Yes, my lord. Anything.'

'Bring my daughter to me.'

Beoraan had not needed to ask which daughter. Although older by two years, Evica was not the one – could never have been the one. Rumbustious and loud from her earliest years, a whirlwind of a child, Evica Genara had never displayed any of the decorum that the position of Ki demanded.

The younger daughter, Linnayen, was different. Even as a baby, the variance in the temperaments of the two sisters was striking. Little Linnayen never laughed out loud like Evica. She showed her pleasure with small smiles and quick hugs. When brought to sadness, tears would well in her eyes, brimming like an overfull cup. But she never sobbed out loud as most children did.

Linnayen questioned everything, as did Evica, but she would wait patiently for the answer, hands folded neatly in her lap, whereas her sister's mind would have already wandered off along the hidden trails of a child's imagination.

Then there were the many portents surrounding her birth. Dar-aak's Comet – a once-in-a-hundred-year visitor – flared through the southern skies, its tail appearing twice as long for the first time in recorded history. But strangest of all was the sudden disappearance of the Bastimi Falls. For thousands of years the waters of the mighty Bastimi River had fallen over a three-hundred-metre precipice. The noise of the great falls could be heard from kilometres away and their spray had created a unique miniature rainforest in the river's gorge.

The people in the nearby tourist village of Bast-ra woke up on the morning of the Lady Linnayen's birth to an unexpected and eerie silence. No birds sang, no movement of any sort. All was quiet. Gradually, in small murmuring groups, people made their way to the lookouts over the falls only to find that the river had gone. They stared at the never-before-seen back wall of the falls, silky smooth and still wet in places, with small puddles and pools drying out in the warmth of the morning sunshine.

It was, of course, soon discovered that the river had not actually disappeared but had instead diverted itself down through a collapsed fault in the escarpment some two kilometres back from the precipice. Now the torrent poured into a dark gaping fissure, only to re-emerge some five kilometres further downstream from a gash in a wall of red rock. Even so, taken with the comet's appearance, it was perceived as a portentous event and a sign that this day would long be remembered.

On that day, the Lady Li-el Dacas, consort to Yenshar Genara, the most powerful mentante and matriarch of the noble family Dacas, was delivered of her second daughter in the peaceful surroundings of a dayroom adjoining the palace's inner garden. Linnayen's birth was almost painless and mercifully quick, another sign that she would be a placid soul, not like her older sister, who was a two-year-old fireball of boundless energy.

But nature and powerful portents were not enough to ensure that Linnayen, and not Evica, would be the successor. There would be many tests and examinations by the holy men and women of the Altaniskaran and, many times in their childhood, Evica and Linnayen were sent to various monastic retreats for instruction and observation.

It was not all learning and religion though. So that they would always appreciate the privilege of their birth and learn the value of hard work, they spent their summers working in the farms and fields, helping to the care for livestock and bring in the grain harvests. It was hard, physical work, and although both girls would groan at the thought of having to again go through the pain of those first calluses, once in the farm commune and seeing the many familiar faces of old friends and workmates, they soon loved being back. They would return to the palace in the first days of autumn, tanned and supple, bragging to their father of their new skills and knowledge. Yenshar would revel in observing their animated, laughing faces, and the way they would trip over their words in the rush to be the first to tell their proud father of their adventures.

But, on Evica's fourteenth birthday and upon her return to Genkarah after her final year's examination, the Altek, Altan's holiest man, pronounced that despite her many attributes – strength, joy, bravery, to name but a few – the Lady Evica was not Yenshar's natural successor.

That honour was to be Linnayen's, and the Altek had confided to Beoraan early in her twelfth year that she showed all the signs and had all the right attributes to become the next Ki. She was an adept mentante and was grasping all the complexities of high-level administration and statecraft with relative ease. Indeed, her serious nature and ability to examine and synthesise even the most complex problems was exactly what was needed in a future leader.

When Beoraan reported this news to Genara, he was not surprised at the Ki's reaction. Yenshar had nodded. 'I knew it would be so. I knew we would not have to look to another family to inherit the throne. She will be a great Ki!' he had concluded proudly.

It took less than two minutes by windshifter for Beoraan to reach Linnayen's apartment in the northern tower of the palace. He knocked swiftly on the door, which was opened by a pale-green-skinned Huthon servant. The man lowered his head as a gesture of respect to the Sen as he ushered him into the anteroom.

'I wish to speak to Lady Linnayen at once. Please fetch her,' he ordered.

'I am here already.'

Linnayen Genara pulled aside the muslin curtain that separated the anteroom from the rest of her apartments and stepped forward. The princess royal, just twenty-one years old, was dressed formally in a long, high-necked yellow coat that was tied at the waist with a cummerbund of silver cloth. Her waist-length, almost black hair was twisted in a simple curled strand and worn over one shoulder. Her large green eyes, usually bright and clear, looked dull tonight, Beoraan noted. She was almost as tall as her father and possessed a natural beauty that needed no enhancements. Linnayen's figure showed only a trace of womanhood and her face, with its full mouth and aquiline nose, still bore the softening fullness of youth.

'It's time?' she asked of Beoraan.

'Aye, my lady,' the old man replied, fighting hard to keep the tears from pooling in his eyes.

'Don't be sad, Beoraan. He'll never be gone in our thoughts. You know that, don't you?' She was trying to comfort him and, in truth, he would never forget the girl's father who had been a strong and wise leader.

Linnayen moved closer and took his head in her hands. She placed a kiss on his forehead both as a mark of respect and affection, then took his hand and walked with him to the door.

'Come. My father is waiting.' Her command was a gentle request and, in that moment, Beoraan knew that he would follow her anywhere.

Father and daughter. Teacher and student. Friends. They knew each other so well. Linnayen could not remember a time when she could not hear her father inside her head and he, too, could read her thoughts almost from the moment that she was born. They were both mentantes, born with the ability to read minds and communicate without words, a telepathic ability found only within a few Altani families.

Linnayen looked down at the supine form of her father and smiled, recalling the memories they shared. Even in his weakened state, Genara managed to smile too as she reminded him, with not a word spoken between them, of the time they got caught in a tropical downpour on the planet Hutho. She had been five and, forgetting all rank and ceremony, they had danced in the puddles, laughing and giggling until their faces hurt.

Yenshar Genara's laughter became too much for him and he suddenly began to cough and clutch at his throat.

'Oh! I'm sorry, Father,' she cried, kneeling beside his bed. She lay her arm lightly across his frail body. 'I didn't mean to hurt you.'

The slight figure of Dr Em-sin Mai, the family's retained physician, moved from the shadow behind the bedframe and she laid a hand on her shoulder. 'It's all right, my lady. You've done no harm.'

Linnayen turned to the doctor and Beoraan. 'Stay close by. But please, let my father and I have a few minutes alone.'

When the pair had retired to chairs on the other side of the room, Linnayen sat on the edge of the bed. She turned to her father and spoke quietly yet urgently.

'I'm not ready, Father. I don't feel at all confident.' Unbidden, tears came to her eyes. 'How will I cope without you? I just can't do it. Father, I'm scared.' Her head sank into the coverlet.

Genara touched her hair with his hand. For all her apparent maturity, she was still a child, he thought. But not after tonight. Hard as it must be – for both of them – there was a greater duty and she would rise to meet it, as had countless other Genaras and Dacases before them.

'Look at me,' he ordered, and she lifted her head to meet his eyes. 'You are the Lady of Light.' He spoke slowly and deliberately, his words hammering in her ears like iron bells as the familiar litany began. 'Bring light where there is darkness, hope where reigns despair, peace where discord rules, love where evil festers.

'This is your sworn promise. Remember?'

Linnayen turned her head away, trying desperately to deny the impact of his words, but his eyes held their grip, forcing her to look back.

'You *are* our Lady of Light! You can be no other thing!' Genara rasped out these last words.

She knew what he meant – only too well. The years of testing and training had taught her that there would be no other role for her. Linnayen took a long, steady breath and swallowed to clear her throat. She looked deep into her father's sunken face and, putting aside rank and formality, spoke in a small voice that held infinite sadness.

'I will miss you, Father … I love you!'

Linnayen could not hold back her tears, and Genara knew that he must let her have this time, for it would never be allowed to come again. Once he was gone, once Linnayen succeeded him, she could never allow herself to show such emotion or else she would be unable to function as the Ki. The very essence of their role was detachment, clarity of thought and purpose. Emotion played no part in statecraft.

Waiting for her sobs to cease, he spoke softly. 'Linne, child …' His voice was fainter now and Genara knew he didn't have long.

'In my garden … my arbour …you'll find my last journal. It contains news which you must act upon to secure peace. Our mission to bring Earth into the Union must not fail!' His words were urgent but his voice was weakening. He coughed again, fighting to control his breathing and his voice, then stopped to take more air.

'I will hear it, Father.'

In the face of these explicit instructions, Linnayen regained her composure, her emotions now fully under control. Genara appreciated the effort this took and was grateful. He focused his thoughts once more.

'Tell Evica,' and here he smiled, 'that she brought me much joy. I love her and I am so proud of her. Look after her.' Genara had said his farewells to his elder daughter earlier that afternoon and recalled with painful poignancy the looks of both fear and sadness in her clear jade eyes.

'I will. But I think it is I who will need her courage,' she replied.

'You are wrong. She is brave, but not steel. She will always need you.'

Genara took another long breath but struggled to fill his lungs this time. Linnayen clasped his hand and held the palm to her cheek.

'Linne!' he called out suddenly. Then, in a softer, almost inaudible tone, he whispered, 'I am sorry. I wish we had more time …'

Yenshar Genara closed his eyes and, after a few more moments, his breathing finally stopped.

There was no movement. Linnayen's tears fell silently over her father's hand, still clutched to her cheek. All was quiet in the room. With gentle precision, Linnayen laid Genara's hand onto his now unmoving chest. Sniffing back her tears, she stood up and, as she turned, saw that Beoraan and Dr Mai had come to stand behind her. Linnayen raised her chin, almost defiantly.

'Thank you, doctor, for trying to help my father. And thank you, Beoraan, for being a good and faithful counsellor. I trust that you will continue to serve me as well as you have my father.'

It was not a question but a statement. Beoraan nodded his assent.

The Ki's aide, the nobleman Sen-Vinca, who all this while had stood at the back of the room almost hidden in the folds of the heavy drapes, now took his place in the centre. He carried a long metal rod known as the Staff of Vidoka that was carved in the Mayaran style. He banged the end of the staff onto the wooden floor of the bedchamber three times and, as the sound reverberated around the room, all heads turned to him.

'Ki-Yenshar Genara, Lord of Light. Go in grace!' he cried out in deep tones. There was complete silence for a full minute. Then his voice rang out once more.

'Hail the Esteemed One, Ki-Linnayen Genara!'

And all in the room, bar one, dropped to their knees in homage.

Genkarah sparkled under a velvet evening sky. It was a magnificent city, known throughout the Union for its ancient wonders. Spires of stone and turrets of carved woods from all the known planets had been used in its buildings, creating a topsy-turvy skyline of strange, abstract pinnacles. When sunset colours touched the towers, turning them indigo and gold, it was breathtakingly beautiful. Down below the spires and the raised walkways that connected them lay pristine fields and forests. They were the playgrounds of the Genkarans and helped to keep the air sweet and clean. It was not the biggest city in the Union – at least ten others stood ahead of it – but it was the traditional home of the Forum of the Union of Planets, and of the Genara family, for whom the city had been named.

Evica Genara had always loved her home city, especially seeing it from here, her apartment's private parapet, and bathed in early evening colours of sapphire and gold. In all the hurly-burly of her life, this was the one place where she could be quiet and still. She laughed to herself. 'Quiet' and 'still' were two words that no one, not even Linnayen, would use to describe her. It both amused and angered her that most people saw only what was on the surface.

Like the city today. *It looks the same as ever*, she thought. *Yet deep down it mourns, just like me.* She had been so sure that her father would recover. He had many wounds, it was true, but the doctors and medications were so good these days – they could fix anything, anyone. Look at the number of times they had put *her* back together again after her many accidents and fights on the training ground. But not this time.

Evica, elder sister of the new Ki, was twenty-three years old. She was tall, like her sister, and possessed of a lustrous mane of wavy auburn hair, whereas Linnayen's was almost black. They shared the same eyes, though – a pastel mint green, like the clear waters of a rainforest stream. Her mouth easily broke into the broadest of smiles, giving her a flirtatious look. Her body had long since matured and she had been favoured with a shapely figure, much complimented by other women and, somewhat less openly – for she was still the daughter of a royal house – coveted by many men.

Men. Now there was a subject she found perplexing. Not that Evica's opinion of men was derogatory, but she was well aware that most men could not see past her body and her face. She could think of only two men who did not positively gape when she passed by: her father and Sen-Beoraan. As a consequence, her distrust of men and their motives had left her lonely and, so far, unattached, despite her obvious charm.

There was now no one in Evica's world in whom she could confide. Her father's untimely death had taken away the only one who listened to her fears and comforted her. As for Linnayen, Evica felt that her little sister was too young, too serious and too wrapped up in thoughts of duty and service. They had so little in common and it was the same with her imperious mother, the Lady Dacas, who had little time for anyone but herself – not that she was ever there, anyway. Her mother stayed away from court, having chosen many years ago to closet herself with the Holy Order at the Arbour of Serenkiraah in the Ksas Ranges. Evica and Linnayen had not seen her for over two years and it was unlikely that she would make the arduous journey down from the mountain, even for her former consort's funeral.

Since her father's passing late last night, it was as though an icy river flowed through her veins and she could not seem to get warm. This was more than grief. Although her mentante abilities were not as acute as Linnayen's, she shared enough of her family's prophetic gift to know that dark days were ahead: some evil was coming and it would change them all irrevocably.

Linnayen felt it too. The feeling was even stronger inside her than for Evica and, as she looked across her father's funeral pyre to her sister, standing on the opposite dais, she prayed that she would recognise the moment when the evil threatened. Perhaps, then, she would be able to stop it, to turn back the black tide of despair.

Today was my father's funeral. There was much joy in the gathering as we retold his story and celebrated his many achievements. Evica and I took comfort from the surge of love and respect the people displayed, although we could not smile or sing or dance, having not partaken of fre-gath. Even had we done so, I do not think it would have worked – our hearts were too heavy.

The final part of the ceremony started in the late afternoon, after the heat of the day had passed. Once we had reached the banks of the river and heard the eulogy, which was read by Sen-Beoraan, I watched my father's body set aflame. Within minutes, just as the flames reached their height, there was a loud crash of thunder and it began to rain very heavily. Lightning also danced around the skies, which became black and overcast, and the water fell in sheets from the heavy clouds. To me it was as though the world could not contain its tears. But they were not enough to put out the pyre.

My father is dead. I have become the Ki. But all I want is for the world to stop, for time to stand still, so that I can catch my breath – and catch up. It is all happening too quickly. Too much to do! My task is so great and I am scared to death.

Chapter Two

The funeral ceremony for the dead Ki would have appeared to the people of Earth uncommonly light-hearted, filled as it was with music, dance and, sometimes, even wanton behaviour. It was traditional for Altanis to celebrate a person's life by singing about them or reciting poems and performing dances and plays, which re-enacted scenes from their life. Funeral parties often went on for many hours and could become raucous affairs. This was largely because a narcotic drug, known as fre-gath, was added to the food served at funeral banquets. Tradition dictated that this was one of the few occasions when Altanis were encouraged to relax their formal behaviour and make free with their emotions.

For most of the people of Earth, though, the abandonment of moral codes at such a sombre occasion as a funeral was considered disrespectful. It was just one example of the differences that existed between the two species and was added to the list of reasons why they resisted the onslaught of the Union of Planets with such force.

Their ways are too different, too heathen, thought Sheikh David Bashir. *They want to eliminate our culture, take away our gods and our religions, founded on beliefs that have held true for millennia, and give us only their pagan ways and their supernatural meddling.* It was intolerable and, by the breath of Allah, it would never be tolerated whilst he or his son lived.

David Bashir al Fahrazad was an imposing figure. At just over two metres tall, wide-shouldered and well-muscled, he towered over most men. He was unusual for his race *and* for his family, as past Bashirs were known to possess smaller builds and finer features. It was rumoured that the family had originated from the Pathans, a tribe from the Afghan highlands known for their greater size and fairer skin tones. Bashir women, on the other hand, tended to be delicate and almost elfin of look, and David's mother, the Princess Roxanne, was just such a one. Petite and with ridiculously large eyes, it seemed impossible that she could have given birth to such a giant of a man, and David's son took after her.

Although he was going to be tall like his father, the young Kevor Jax Bashir's body was slim like his grandmother's. Most strikingly, though, he had inherited something else from her, a most unusual feature that appeared in his family only once in a generation: his eyes. They were large, like Princess Roxanne's, but it was the colour upon which people commented. They were a deep, clear midnight blue – 'starry-night eyes' his mother, Thea, often called them.

'Kevor may be a handsome boy. He might even be a clever one. But he has little else about him that inspires my confidence!' Bashir complained to Professor Marcus di Luca, Jax's teacher and mentor.

'Give him time, sir. He's only twenty-two. Hardly a man!' The professor, usually of good humour, was losing patience with his employer. *This must be the twentieth time I have had this conversation with him*, he thought, *and* still *he does not believe in his son. The boy has such talents!* Out of loyalty to his student, and with no small amount of professional pride, he tried once more.

'Trust me, sir. He will blossom one of these days into the finest flower of manhood, and you will be rightly proud of him.'

'Blossom? Huh!' Bashir was not impressed. 'You've been saying that for months … years, professor! But I see little improvement. Even after three years at the military academy he still drifts around, mind in the clouds half the day. When is he going to learn to fight, eh? That's what he should have been learning all these years. That's what this planet needs – fighters, not poets!'

Professor di Luca could see that no amount of words, however true or well spoken, would change the sheikh's mind. Bashir wanted a son just like himself, a son with his physical strength and mental acuity. He could not discern what di Luca had perceived years before, that Jax was intelligent, sensitive and with an uncanny ability to focus on the heart of the matter. *Kevor Jax would never be the man his father was*, thought di Luca. *But he could be much more!*

'Is he here yet?' the sheikh asked.

'I'll see,' returned the professor, and he went to the door of the anteroom, hoping that by now the young nobleman had been found. Not for the first time, Jax had wandered off, going where his thoughts led him, and the professor had had to send servants searching for him. He sighed resignedly and opened the door.

'Thank God!' he said under his breath as he took in the shape of the sheikh's only son lounging on a daybed, feet up, reading a book.

Kevor Jax was what most people would describe as a lanky youth. He appeared taller than he was for his twenty-two years, because his body, somewhat disproportionately, had not yet developed the muscles of full manhood, thus giving the impression of lankiness. This was as much due to the fact that Jax preferred to spend his time exercising his mind rather than his body as it was to his genetic heritage.

His well-defined cheekbones made him look a little gaunt and his dark auburn hair was generally an unruly mess. Caught halfway between youth and manhood, Jax's face held a promise of attractiveness, though with his family's status and wealth he had little need of good looks to secure his position in life. He was a most fortunate young man, bright enough to realise it and well brought up enough not to abuse it.

'Look at this, di Luca!' he exclaimed, not turning his head but stabbing a finger at the book. 'It says here that people used to believe that there were pixies and fairies and the like. Nearly every culture had them, you know – the Irish had leprechauns, the Scandinavians had trolls, and we had magical spirits called genies and djinns. A bit like the beliefs of the Altanis, eh?' Jax's interest quickly turned to amusement. 'Whoops! Better not let my father know about that. Mustn't condone anything heathen, eh?'

Di Luca scowled at the disrespect the boy's words held.

'Enough, Kevor!' he barked back. 'Your father is in no mood for your jokes today. Get in there.' When he saw that Jax was in no hurry to raise himself from the daybed, he fired off, *'Now!'*

Jax raised an eyebrow in mild surprise, taking no offence. His tutor did not often lose his good humour. His father must have given the old teacher a hard time this morning. He pushed his shoulders back and, taking a long, resigned breath, he strode into the sheikh's chamber.

At the sound of the door closing, Bashir turned and saw his son already in a low bow of respect. A document in one hand, Bashir gestured to Jax to wait while he finished the page, using this time, covertly, to espy his son.

Jax was an enigma to him, much as his mother was. Tall, slender and with a mop of dark auburn hair that – much to Bashir's annoyance – always fell into his eyes, Jax was, he imagined, rather handsome. The large dark eyes, the fine cheekbones and the wide mouth with its too full lips so like his mother's, he thought, too feminine for a man. *But who can tell? Perhaps di Luca is right and he will grow into a fine young man. Just make it soon!*

'Kevor. I have some news for you,' he began.

'Good,' Jax replied. 'And how you are today, Father? Well, I trust?'

David Bashir was caught off-guard. Jax always did this, wrong-footing him with his infernal good manners. It made him uncomfortable. Who was the senior around here, him or his son? He stammered slightly as he replied, 'Er … yes, well … I am well. Thank you for asking. Now, my news.'

But before he could continue, Jax interrupted, a hint of a smile playing along his lips. 'As I am, too, Father. Well, that is. Indeed,' he continued with a flourish, 'I feel very positive about the future. In fact –'

Bashir jumped back in and took control of the conversation.

'Yes, I'm sure you are and I'll be happy to hear about it some other time. But right now I have to tell you that I've enrolled you in the Diplomatic Corps. You recall I discussed the possibility with you some months ago? You've done well at military school but ... Well, your mother and I have looked into it and we agree it's the best thing for you. Time you started to learn how to be a leader, eh? So you'll start your training when the next semester begins in four weeks' time.'

Jax was taken aback. His father had finally done it; Di Luca had warned him that a spell at the Corps was on the cards. Although he didn't really object, it was all happening a little sooner than he would have liked.

'I suggest that you use the next four weeks with the professor to go over the history of the council. You must expect that there will be little time for flying or poetry once you are at Corps,' his father instructed.

'Of course, Father,' he agreed. Then, raising an eyebrow and with a hint of mischief, he went on. 'I am sure that the world of politics and diplomacy will throw up many more *new* delights and amusements.' Jax could not resist teasing his father.

'You are not going there to have fun!' Bashir barked back. His face was dark and his brow furrowed. 'You know how to fight with weapons. Now you will learn how to fight with words! And I expect great things of you. There's still a war on, despite what some in the council would want us to believe. I will *not* be disappointed.'

Jax saw the steely glint in his father's eyes and knew, as di Luca had pointed out earlier, that this was not the time for light-heartedness. His father was deadly serious. With a suddenness that surprised him, he felt a rush of affection for this bear of a man. Perhaps the depth of his father's feelings had for an instant touched his heart and, although he could not yet share them, he could appreciate their purity and strength.

'Father, that is something that I vow I will never do. I know full well my birthright, my heritage and what our people expect of me. I will not fail you or them.' Jax's gaze was steady, flint-like as it locked with his father's and, for the first time since his son had become a man, the sheikh felt an inkling of pride and wondered if he might yet have bred a true prince of the house of Bashir.

The Bashirs could trace their history back over nearly two millennia. It was a history containing stories of poverty and wars, of commerce and trade when times were good and great suffering when disease or natural disaster struck. The family's earliest ancestors were warriors and Sheikh David often regaled guests with the fact that there was even a Bashir fighting the invading Crusaders in Jerusalem in 1192.

But it had only been in the last one hundred and fifty years that they had really risen to prominence. Their ancestor the astro-engineer Tomas Bashir had been a member of the United Democratic Nations Scientific Forum. He had begun as a brilliant student of astrophysical engineering and spent five years at the head of a research team into quasar-pulse genesis and morphology, the results of which brought about technology that quadrupled the maximum speed of most of the craft in Earth's space fleet. After becoming a member of the Scientific Forum he continued his research and, at the tender age of twenty-eight, and with his scientific career blossoming, Tomas became the forum's president. From there it was a short step only seven years later up to the governorship of the entire UDN Council.

From that time to the present day, there had always been a Bashir in one or more of the UDN's many committees and forums and others at the head of some of the largest commercial operations on Earth. Tomas had had the good luck (or was it the good sense?) to marry an equally brilliant scientist, medical doctor Cathleen Jaxson. Her family connections – gained through her father's enormous pile of inherited wealth – secured his entry into most, if not all, of the finest houses in the world.

Tomas's children inherited those two ingredients vital to the establishment of a dynasty, political power and vast wealth, and six generations later David Bashir had relished taking up his family's mantle. He thrived on the cut and thrust of politics and, like Tomas all those years ago, he had through sheer hard work, determination and inspired leadership been appointed to the highest position, that of president of the council.

Whether his son would follow in his footsteps remained to be seen. But the old man was not confident that Jax (named after his renowned ancestor) would amount to anything. Although the boy was intelligent – indeed, his father conceded that he was an exceptional classical scholar and possessed excellent reasoning skills – he had not yet shown any signs that he could be a strong leader. He had similarly excelled at military college and had turned out to be a proficient fighter pilot, but it annoyed Bashir that his son preferred poetry and philosophy to more useful and serious subjects like politics and economics. He was in no doubt that if Jax were ever to amount to anything, the training he would encounter at the Diplomatic Corps would be the key. Thus it was with a happy and purposeful mind that Bashir signed him up for the full year away in New York, during which time he would learn all the wiles of negotiation and the protocols that were the backbone of the council's day-to-day operations.

His only sadness – and it was but a passing concern – was that his wife, vowing that one politician in the family was more than enough, hated the idea.

Thea Bashir smiled warmly. In the distance she could see her son's wetsuit-clad frame as he quickly sprang up onto the surfboard. Finally, he had caught a good wave, around two and a half metres. She hoped that he would stay up this time instead of taking the usual tumble into the foam. A few days ago Jax and Duncan McCrae, his best friend, had suddenly decided to learn how to surf in the middle of their final holiday before Jax went to the Corps. Thea had not meant to come, knowing that the young men would have had a perfectly good time without her, but instinct got the better of her. She had had to put up with hardly ever seeing her only child for the past three years and now David had signed him up for another bout of seclusion. It was too much and a week in the

Cornish countryside, a quiet corner in a bustling world, seemed ideal.

Jax had not minded. He enjoyed his mother's company as she was usually relaxed and easy-going. His father on the other hand … Jax could not quite put his finger on why there always seemed to be tension between them. He was extremely proud of his father and bore great affection for him – love, really. But his father wanted him to be a paragon – of everything: his studies, his behaviour and indeed every aspect of his life. David Bashir had exorbitantly high hopes for his son and he made sure Jax was aware of it. It was hard enough learning to be a pilot at military school and then how to steer his way through a life lived so much in the spotlight without the added burden of becoming something he was not, just to please his father.

Duncan McCrae, Jax's friend since they met at school nine years earlier, was a born flirt. He had been endowed with classically good looks: honey blond hair that waved like a field of wheat, warm hazel eyes, a straight nose and a smile that had the power to melt ice. Without doubt, the young McCrae was a heartbreaker in the making. Thea's only concern was that he kept his aptitude with women to himself as she did not want her son to treat women in such a cavalier way. She had always impressed upon him that everyone was worthy of respect, no matter their station in life, their race, their religion *or* their gender. It was, perhaps, just as well that Thea did not see what the young men got up to in town each evening.

Thea squinted against the harsh glare of the light on the sparkling water. Jax had ridden the wave well enough and managed to stay on his board the whole time. He jumped smartly from it and waited at the water's edge for an equally triumphant Duncan to coast up next to him. The young men walked up the beach towards her, laughing and talking as they came.

'That looked like fun,' Thea said.

They smiled back and Jax dropped down on the fine yellow sand beside her while Duncan fixed the boards upright to dry.

'Sure was. Did you see me take that last wave?'

'What can I say?' she said, with the barest trace of mockery. 'You were fantastic!'

'Oh, come *on* …' Duncan pretended to gag and Jax leaned over to flick some sand at him.

'You're just sore because I'm better than you … as ever!' Jax teased back.

Duncan looked down at him in amazed disbelief.

'At surfing maybe. But that's it. In all other things, I am the master!'

Jax laughed, not minding the implied criticism. He was used to Duncan's banter and bravado.

'You know, with all that talent for self-appreciation, it's probably just as well you're not coming to the Corps, humility being something of a requirement.'

'I can do humble,' Duncan protested immediately. 'I *am* an actor, after all. And if I can't do it now, I'll practise till I get it right.'

'I think it's a shame you're not interested in joining up, Duncan,' Thea interjected. 'I'm sure it needs someone like you around to liven up all those stuffy diplomats.'

'Diplomacy's loss is the theatre's gain, eh?' said Jax.

'Absolutely. If I'm going to spend all my days talking, I'd much rather do it in front of an audience – and get paid for it!'

'Pay you to shut up, more like,' Jax joked back.

The bantering between the two young men was both typical and familiar. They had slipped very easily into their friendship. As two thirteen-year-old boys packed off to boarding school by their equally high-ranking political families, they had a great deal in common. They were both only children and their fathers were both council members, although Duncan's father had retired a couple of years ago. They both had an interest in athletics and shared a love of literature, Duncan being increasingly drawn to plays, whilst Jax was more interested in poetry and novels.

At eighteen, Jax had gone away to military college to begin pilot training. He loved flying. One of the rewards he had earned for devoting time to his mother's charitable causes had been a course of flying lessons and, as soon as he had sat in the soft calfskin seat of the tiny aircar, he knew that this was where he belonged. From then on he had held no other dream than to fly. The year at the Diplomatic Corps was going to be hard for him. He knew his mother sympathised, but she had still supported his father's decision.

'It's only a year, Kevor. Let him have that,' she had said, referring to David. 'And honestly, it won't do you any harm to have another string to your bow.'

'Yes, but diplomacy!' Jax had retorted.

'I know it doesn't seem likely that you'll use it now. But you have a vast future ahead of you and you just don't know what it will hold,' Thea persisted. 'Please, for me, try …'

He could see her reasoning and certainly appreciated his father's ambition for him. But it was not flying.

The yellowing sun began to drop closer to the horizon and Thea shivered in a sudden breeze. The next day would be their last of the holiday and, reflecting that she would not see her son for many months to come, Thea felt it was important to have a good last night out.

'Come on, you two. It's getting late and I'm cold. Let's get back.'

'Okay, Mum.' Jax looked knowingly across to Duncan, who nodded a response. 'Just one more wave and we'll be right behind you.'

She smiled and sighed. They would make their own way back to the hotel, of course. They did not need her. After all, they were not boys anymore and the sudden thought of their lives stretching away into a future filled with possibilities – that would not necessarily include her – both saddened and excited her. Her job as a mother was virtually done, she thought. But her place in her son's life was enduring and the knowledge gave her comfort.

As it turned out, life at the Diplomatic Corps proved to be far more interesting than Jax could have imagined and, far from railing against his father's heavy-handed decision, he soon felt rather pleased at the outcome. The courses covered political science, constitution, media and communications and, inevitably, negotiation and conflict resolution, something he wished he had studied long ago as it might have helped him get along better with his father, he thought ruefully.

The Corps was based in the vibrant, bustling city-state of New York, which had been the home of the UDN Council's progenitor, the United Nations, over a thousand years earlier. Whilst the tradition of international relations continued in the establishment of the Corps some two hundred years ago, the council's headquarters had long since been decentralised to a variety of other cities around the globe. With the coming of vidscreen technology back in the twenty-first century and the implied security risks of having senior officials physically in one place, it was only logical to disperse the council geographically. Consequently, many council meetings were held simultaneously in places as far afield as Murmansk, Santiago and Shanghai and many councillors' offices were in fact at their homes.

The decline in face-to-face conversation combined with a corresponding increase in the volume of communications that had been facilitated by the speed and reliability of commweb had led to some remarkable developments, not the least of which was the globalisation of language. The more familiar and most often used words from a variety of languages had become incorporated into a base language, which due to its ubiquity had been English. Upon this matrix, French words sat alongside Chinese, Greek expressions mingled with Malay and, fuelled by the omnipresent media, vocabulary was constantly on the move. Thus, 'Talk', as it was simply called, was a dynamic language that was ever-changing.

However, although people from all parts of the world could better understand each other, they did not necessarily communicate with better understanding. Conflict and misinformation still occurred and diplomacy and the art of negotiation became much prized skills.

To Jax, it still seemed an odd paradox that with the greater understanding of words and the increased ability to speak to each other came a propensity for dispute. It reminded him of something his teacher, di Luca, had said many years ago.

'Hearing is not listening, Kevor. And listening is not knowing. And knowing is not understanding. *That* is found in the spaces in between.'

This was what he now knew he had come to the Corps to learn. He was beginning to find those important spaces and, to his surprise, he was discovering that the keys to it were humility, compassion and empathy, traits he had never associated with his view of himself. Indeed, he had never spent too much time at all on introspection. He was, essentially, an observer. But now he was being forced to participate – or so it seemed. For it would be only through these basic human traits that he would begin to succeed at diplomacy and it was important to him to do this thing well.

Then, one warm afternoon in late spring, life as he had known it changed irrevocably.

He lay on the soft, pampered grass of the college's inner grounds trying to read a weighty paper comparing the civil rights movements in what was once the United States of America with the republic of Sud-Africa. The smell of freshly mown grass and the buzzing of insects were making him drowsy and, irresistibly, he found his eyes drooping and the rushing sound of sleep surging through his ears. He fought to stay awake and the thought crossed his mind that probably nothing of what he had read in the last half an hour had sunk in, so he might as well give in. His eyelids closed and through them he could make out the wavy dappling of light and shade as the leaves of the tree above him danced in the sunshine.

The peace was suddenly shattered by a burst of high-pitched laughter that dissolved into an infectious giggle and was followed by woman's voice – very clear and with an accent that was unmistakably upper-class English.

'I don't believe a word of it. You're making it up.' The woman's voice was both derisive and amused.

There was a murmuring of a voice in response, but it was too indistinct to make out the words.

'Simon wouldn't have the nerve – or the cash.' Her voice rang out again and Jax could not resist opening his eyes to look at its owner.

She was a few metres away walking briskly along the path, her arms swinging. Her companion was a young man who carried a large pile of books and seemed to be walking half a pace behind her, though desperately trying to catch up. Jax's mouth dropped open. She was young – early twenties, he guessed – and she wore her bright red hair in a short neat bob with a low fringe. The skin of her face was milky white, as were her bare arms and legs, and she was very slim – almost too thin, he thought. But, by her pace and the straight way she carried herself, she struck him as being robustly healthy. She spoke again in response to something the young man said.

'No. I won't. Doesn't interest me.'

'Please, Harrie,' the man pleaded. 'For me … It'll be fun.' He placed a hand on her arm in an effort to pull her back.

She stopped dead and made a show of tugging herself free of his grip, loose as it was. She looked down at the offending hand then faced him, her hand resting firmly on her hip, as if to reinforce her meaning.

'I've already said no.' Her tone changed. There was an edge of anger to it.

'Bull! You used to like it … You know you did.' He was goading her now, almost threatening.

The girl tried to make light of the situation again, but her voice still contained an element of warning. 'If you don't stop going on about it, Colin, I swear I'll drop you – for good! You're becoming very tedious.'

The man grabbed her wrist to stop her marching away.

Jax saw his chance. He had to speak to her – like his life depended on it! He jumped up and called out.

'Hey! Need some help?' It was pretty weak, he knew, but he could think of nothing else.

She turned around, squinting in the sunlight to see who had spoken, and took in the tall, handsome young man walking languidly across to her. The slightest of smiles reached her eyes.

'Thank you. Yes,' she called back. 'My companion is being a pain in the backside and I need rescuing from his obnoxious company.'

Jax smiled directly into her blue eyes. 'Then allow me …'

He walked around to the now timid Colin.

'The lady no longer needs your assistance. Thank you. Goodbye.' Jax stood a full fifteen centimetres higher than Colin but the smaller man stood his ground.

'Go to hell! And *she's* no lady.'

'How dare you!' Harrie chimed in.

Jax had heard enough. Whatever the relationship between these two, the man had no business to speak like that. He leaned forward and spoke closely into Colin's face.

'You have under five seconds to remove yourself from this place before I remove you from this world.'

The girl added, 'Go on, Colin. Clear off! You're not wanted here.'

The pairs of eyes trained on him were too firm in their intent to bother continuing the argument and, muttering something under his breath, Colin finally walked away.

The girl looked up at her new champion. She had to squint against the sun, so her grey-green eyes appeared calculating rather than appreciative. There was a small smile on her perfect face.

'That was neatly done. Been trying to offload him for days. Follows me around like a puppy. Fun at first. Then not. Still, tells funny jokes. His one advantage.'

She spoke in the same way that she walked, briskly and with purpose. Jax was spellbound and could only stare back. A noise and a movement broke their mutual concentration. The retreating Colin had thrown some of the books he had carried onto the ground. Harrie sighed resignedly, shrugged and went with Jax to retrieve them.

'Some gentleman, eh?' she said, shaking her head.

'We're not all like that,' he replied.

She tilted her head to one side as though sizing him up. 'Yes, you are – we all are when pushed. Sorry,' she said, holding out her hand. 'Harrie Whitton.'

He shook the offered hand. It was his first touch of her silky pale skin and he vowed it would not be his last.

'Right … Kevor Bashir. But my friends just call me Jax.'

'Son of David Bashir, council president, yes?' she queried with a slight furrowing of her eyebrows.

For Jax it was unavoidable that his name was well known, but inwardly he cringed and hoped that it would not spoil anything. He did not want this girl to slip away before he got a chance to know her purely because of his family connection.

'That's right.'

'So you drop the al Fahrazad? Bit of a mouthful, eh?'

He laughed and, in turn, her features softened.

'Me too. Right Honourable Harriet Sophia Oenone Whitton-Blake in real life. You can see why I prefer Harrie.'

He grinned at her self-deprecation. 'And me – Jax.'

'Well, I shall call you Kev. We're special, you see. We'll go well together – lots in common.' As she spoke, she nodded her head as though she were well satisfied with the day's work. In Harrie Whitton's book, to have dumped the tiresome, no-name Colin and acquired the well-connected, rather handsome president's son was indeed a job well done.

Chapter Three

The day after the funeral, Linnayen went to her father's garden to listen to the journal entry he had made. Her heart was still heavy and her thoughts consumed by the tasks ahead of her. She was worried by what she would find in her father's journal and wondered what he had discovered that was so important. Perhaps it was the fear that whatever her father had to say would alter the course of her life. *Not that my life could be any more changed than it is right now.*

Genara's death had taken its toll on the girl. Whilst her mind was the rival of any elder statesman or woman in the Union, the impact of her father's death and the weight of her accession to the Ki-ship showed in the slump of her shoulders and the empty, lifeless look in her usually bright green eyes.

At the smooth metallic door to the arbour, which was framed by a trailing lei of bright orange magori flowers, Linnayen placed her fingertip on the soft fabric of the entrance pad, feeling a familiar tingle as a microscopic sample of her skin was analysed for its genetic code. The door panel slid open.

The arbour walls were awash from floor to ceiling with moving graphic images of the countryside near Mayar. Sweeping vistas of deep green and gold fields of grass swaying in a light breeze were broken only by tree-lined rills and the whole framed by the distant, snow-capped mountains of the Ksas. The images were three-dimensional and Linnayen felt as if she had stepped into the very landscape itself. As the door sealed behind her, the image was complete and the rural scene enclosed her.

In the centre of the arbour was a low chair. She sat down, arranging her skirt as she did so, and spoke a command.

'Access journal entry YG31774.'

Within seconds, her father's familiar voice was talking to her.

'Welcome, Linnayen.' There was the hint of a smile behind the words. It was every ruler's duty to record a journal, which was kept as a historical and personal account after the Ki's death. While they were alive it could be heard only by the Ki's heir and was a vital tool in training for statecraft. Linnayen had been privy to many former Ki's journals before as part of her education, but listening to her father at this time was one of the hardest things she had ever had to do. Of course, when he had recorded it, Genara could not have known it would be his last. His voice, its tone now formal and businesslike, continued.

'I am aboard the *Sur-Lenes* and, by Commander De'gath's reckoning, we are two hours away from where we will engage the Earthan fleet. I am going to try one last time to persuade them to stand down and I have ordered De'gath not to fire under any circumstances unless fired upon.

'Sadly, I inherited the conflict between the Union of Planets and Earth from Ki-Orak Dacas. Had I known then what I know now, I would gladly have given my life to bring peace years ago. Two months ago, Dr Ullan Ropar of the Huthon Institute of Endogenetoteric Research came to see me. He was excited because, in the course of his research into the human species, he had discovered a startling and irrefutable fact.'

Linnayen's interest was sparked and she furrowed her brow in an effort to concentrate on what came next. Her father's deep voice resumed.

'As you know, Linnayen, Altanis and Earthans are, as a species, virtually identical. Our planets being so alike in climate, geology, size, atmosphere and so on, it was inevitable that we would evolve species that would adapt to our environments in comparable ways. But Dr Ropar had discovered that the similarities between humans and Altanis might not be coincidental.

'He has developed a new genetoteric displacement test called EP dio-sequencing. He's used it on various species' blood and cell samples. When he tested Earthan blood, the samples examined contained an endo-protein dio-sequence that was identical to a sequence found in we Altanis. The doctor felt most emphatically that this could not have happened by chance.

'Dr Ropar assured me that the test proves conclusively that in some way, and at some time in the past, Altanis have either mated with Earthans or have in some way had their blood lines mixed, or perhaps we share a common ancestral heritage. He was convinced that there could be no other explanation. Obviously, how, why and when our two species came together, or whether we originated from the same source then were separated, we do not know. But the fact remains that we were a linked species – from the same evolutionary tree, so to speak. This, of course, would explain how there has been successful interbreeding between us, too. Our similarities are more than just skin deep – we are of the same stem species.'

Almost as though he knew Linnayen would need a few moments to digest this information, Genara's voice paused, giving her time to collect her thoughts.

'Naturally, I examined the doctor's evidence and it looks accurate in every detail. Did protohumanoids evolve here on Altan, then somehow travel to Earth? Or vice versa?

'Space travel has only been possible here – and on Earth for that matter – for the last thousand years or so, and we did not even know about Earth until two hundred years ago! Thus it is a complete mystery.

'Since the failure of the last armistice and the cessation of talks, I will, of course, try to convey this information to the Earthan commanders as soon as they are within range. I hope that they will postpone our battle, at least, to allow time for the data to be examined by their own scientists. Who knows? This may be the key to unlock the gates of peace!'

Genara's voice had been hopeful and enthusiastic at this point. He had genuinely trusted that the Earthans would be open-minded and willing to listen. Desperate to avoid another bloody conflict and the resultant loss of life, he believed that the Earthans would put a stop to the skirmish. It had, as she knew only too well, not gone according to plan. His words had been interpreted as a sly tactic, a ploy designed to lull them into reducing their weapons' strength and they had duly opened fire. The *Sur-Lenes* had been forced to defend itself and then limped back to Altan, badly damaged and with many casualties. Her poor father had paid with his life and no peace had been achieved.

The impact of her father's news began to sink in. *We are the same – Altan and Earth … We are the same!* The thought drummed inside her head. *We should not be fighting. We are killing our own kind!* Her father was right. This news must be acted upon immediately and the challenge would be to use this information wisely. The temptation was to announce it from the rooftops, but caution, born of years of training, told her that knowledge of such importance must be managed carefully. Not everyone would be pleased by this news.

On a practical level, there was the matter of how to impart this knowledge to their avowed enemies. How would she reopen discourse with the stubborn Earthans without raising their suspicions again? It was too large an issue to think through alone.

Linnayen jumped up from the chair, her look of sorrow replaced by one of determination. Whatever the obstacles, she had to act on the knowledge and there was not a moment to lose. Instantly, the fields of Mayar dissolved and the door slid open, allowing in the sweet, warm air of her father's garden. She did not notice the fragrance of the flowers or the warmth of the sunshine on her limbs as she raced into the palace, calling out Beoraan's name at the top of her voice.

It had not taken long for Beoraan to arrange a meeting between Linnayen and the reclusive Dr Ullan Ropar. He had tracked him down within hours of her rushing from the old Ki's arbour, but Linnayen had been forced to wait some weeks to meet him in person until the doctor returned from a field trip to the distant planet Autabron, where he had been giving a series of lectures.

Thus, Linnayen had spent the intervening time trying to understand the basics of gene science and genetoteric testing, in particular. Much of it, she admitted, was beyond her understanding and the few scientists she had questioned on the subject made even less sense to her. She was desperately hoping that Dr Ropar would be able to explain his findings simply and eloquently.

As it turned out, she had no need to worry. Ropar's hermitic behaviour was more a product of his work environment than his nature. Many long hours spent in the laboratory had led him to be a solitary soul, but once in the company of an appreciative audience that wanted to know about his work he became fluent in the extreme.

'It's like this,' he explained, unbuttoning the neck of his tunic, as though settling in for a long session. 'Theoretically – well, it's my theory, actually – if you go back far enough in time, all life in the universe is connected. Has to be. All planets, all asteroids, moons, and everything on them – all mineral, elemental and bio-organic substances – are linked from the time of the creation of the universe. The substances that were produced at that time and the compounds they have since evolved into are, perforce, connected at some indeterminate base level. Way down at the genetic level – beyond it – the very proteins that bind our genes therefore have the potential to possess similarities. They don't always, of course. That would make it too easy. Wouldn't need people like me then.'

He laughed at his own joke and Linnayen, making a supreme effort to follow his train of thought, smiled weakly at him in encouragement.

'Let's face it, if we could spot the protein similarities between your average Altani and, say, a Dasnirian wafrig beetle, my theory of cosmic interconnectivity would be proved overnight. But we can't. So it isn't.'

'Hmm … Perhaps that's just as well,' Linnayen had added, as the unbidden image of the repulsive twenty-legged water beetle entered her mind.

'Ah, but it's not. You see, they *are* connected! At least, I believe so. I haven't proved that particular link yet, of course, but it's only a matter of time. The new dio-sequence test is just the first step.'

Linnayen brightened at the mention of something familiar.

'My father mentioned your test in his journal. What exactly is it?'

Dr Ropar raised his eyebrows in surprise.

'Now that's a question and a half, so stop me if I lose you.' His smile and the mischievous twinkle in his eyes dispelled any hint that she might have felt that he was being patronising.

'I start with a bio-sample. You can use pretty much anything, but I've been working with blood mainly as it's so easy to obtain and transport. Then you break it down to a cellular level. Next I isolate the genetic strands. You know that every cell in the matter of every living thing contains its entire genetic code?'

'Yes,' she said. 'I learned that at school.'

The scientist nodded his approval. It was good to know that their future leaders were given a well-rounded education and weren't just mindless heads of state.

'Next, we split the strand – like dissecting it, chopping it down the middle – and bombard it with lyfardic radiation. That serves the purpose of divesting the genes from the proteins.'

'I understand – so you have the genes separated from the proteins?'

'Well, yes,' he replied, with some hesitation, knowing that she was being too simplistic in her understanding. 'That's close enough. But now the real work begins.

'Most scientists have looked at the genes themselves and have analysed DNA sequences to produce formulas for each particular biota. You've heard these referred to as gene maps, no doubt. But the test *we* devised looks at the proteins. And there is one protein – just one type of stem protein – that can be broken down into what's known as an endo-protein. The dio-sequencer – that's a machine we made for the job – takes care of that. Now although the chemical makeup of stem proteins differs between species, when we analysed them at the endo-level we found amazing correlations between quite diverse species.'

The doctor was well in his stride now and his enthusiasm for his subject was infectious. Linnayen found herself quite engrossed.

'Actually, not just correlations … well, not always. In some cases – about twenty percent, in fact – the endo-proteins were identical. The question was, could this be mere fluke? Happenstance? Or was there a definite link?'

He was getting ahead of her and there was something else Linnayen wanted to ask about before they went on to discuss the possible explanations for these occurrences.

'Wait … Doctor, my father recorded that you found identical endo-proteins between Earthans and Altanis, particularly those of Latis-Mei ancestry. But did you find similarities between other species too? Did you test other species?'

'Oh my goodness, yes! Of course. We tested a whole range of things. The Autabroni gunsa-hog has stem endo-proteins that are identical to the Altani kareek – yes, kareeks! Imagine it! Another example is the srillik, the seabird from Dasnir, and the nelumuk worm from Huthon – both the same. The ypa bee from the Ksas highlands and the allinia polyp from the Sea of Kir on Dasnir – again, the same. Quite amazing, eh?'

Linnayen was both stunned and confused. This did not seem possible. The species of animals the doctor was talking about were immensely different – surely too different to have any connection. Genetic connections between humanoids were understandable, but what the doctor was describing was virtually unbelievable.

'Are you sure about the test? This seems incredible.'

Ropar looked momentarily offended, then remembered who was in front of him. The Ki of Altan's position and rank demanded respect and obedience and, on a more self-serving level, he had no wish to offend a potential benefactor.

'The test methodology is sound. The dio-sequencer is just a device to break down stem proteins and the chemical testing applied to the product is standard stuff. We all use them,' he ended, referring to his fellow scientists.

'So you are quite sure of your results?'

'Absolutely,' he replied without the slightest hesitation.

'Then what this means …' Linnayen struggled to gather her thoughts.

'What it means is that my theory of interconnectivity is right. All life is related. I believe that if we keep on testing we'll find even more evidence to link all life forms in the universe.'

Linnayen was not so convinced. 'But you said only a fifth of your tests had shown identical results. Surely that leaves room for doubt?'

'So far, my lady, yes,' the doctor nodded. 'But it's early days. More testing will bear me out, you'll see.'

She was no longer listening as her mind turned over the possibilities. If the doctor's tests were authentic and robust then there were, as far as she could tell, only two ways of thinking about it. Either Dr Ropar was right – all life was connected – and eventually his tests would prove this to be the case. Or – and she felt this to be more likely – only *some* life was. And if this were so, why? This she felt was the more interesting and intriguing question. Why *not* all life? If all matter in the universe had come from the same source then the doctor's idea should be correct and it was just a matter of digging deep enough to find the links or patterns. But had some other guiding process been at work?

The religious instruction she had received during her upbringing had always accepted the existence of greater powers, forces that were beyond knowledge and understanding. Shapers. Creators. Gods, she supposed. Could this be a factor in the doctor's discovery? Whatever the answers – if there were ever to be answers – she knew that she would not find them here today. She needed to consult with people who were far more expert, and not just in the scientific aspects of this revelation. There were the political ramifications to be considered and how they were to use this knowledge in the conflict with Earth.

'Dr Ropar, thank you. You have explained things very well and I begin to understand. We will need to talk again but, for now, I have heard all I need to.'

She straightened up her lithe frame and lifted her chin, ready to take her leave. The doctor bowed as she turned away, wondering if he had said enough and worried that he had said too much.

'So Harriet is arriving when, did you say?' Thea asked her son.

'It's Harrie, not Harriet. She hates Harriet,' Jax replied. He knitted his eyebrows and laid a hand on his mother's arm. 'Don't call her that, will you?'

Thea stared in amazement at her son. This was a side of him she had not seen – at least, not since he was eight and had his first crush on a girl who used to take tennis lessons with him. It was endearing when he was eight, but now, when he was nearly twenty-three, not so much.

Raising one eyebrow, she looked at him sardonically. But he was not paying her any attention. His eyes under furrowed brows were staring intently out of the kitchen window to a point in the distance from where he expected Harrie and her father to fly in.

The Bashirs were spending a week at a restored farmhouse in the Provence region of southern France. It was a rare chance for them all to be together and, even if Jax and his father were not exactly thrilled to find themselves at such close quarters, Thea was delighted. The only thing that niggled at her contentment was the fact that they would be having house guests. She had wanted to have her husband and son all to herself just for once.

David Bashir was pleasantly surprised when Jax announced that he would like to invite Harrie Whitton and her father along for a couple of days. This was not because the presence of guests would provide a diversion from the constant company of his son but more because it showed a maturity of thought in the young man that he had long searched for. Jax had had girlfriends before, of course, and those that David had met seemed nice enough. They never lasted very long though, and that lack of commitment to developing relationships was, to David's thinking, a perfect example of his son's fecklessness.

But this one was different. Jax was serious about the girl, and the fact that she was from a good family and eminently suitable only made matters better.

Jax had been seeing Harrie for nearly three months and he was more in love with her than he could have believed possible. She was funny one minute then searingly incisive the next. She read people. At least, that was how he described it and that was what made her so good at diplomacy. She understood human nature instinctively and with an accuracy that bordered on clinical. He often joked with her that she should have taken up psychology rather than communications and called her 'Doc' when he wanted to make fun of her. She retorted that there was no difference, that one could not succeed at diplomacy without being a psychologist and, as ever, he had to admit that she had hit the nail on the head.

That was another thing he loved about Harrie. She was intelligent – super intelligent. Nothing got past her. Whether it was a snatch of music or an obscure quote or a little-known fact of history, she would know it, or where it came from, or who said it. It was quite remarkable to him, but Harrie passed it off like some inconsequential, sleight-of-hand parlour trick.

'I'm not brainy, Kev. Really. I have a photographic memory, that's all. Family trait. Dad has it too.'

'Dad' was Sir Anthony Whitton-Blake, about whom not much was known, except that he was currently head of defence policy development for the Eurotanian government. He was a widower, having lost his wife, Lady Edwina, in an aircar accident some two years earlier. He was also the third and last son of the Earl of Lindrick. Thus, Sir Anthony had had to find his own way in the world by joining the army, where he had served honourably for nearly twenty-five years before becoming a high-powered civil servant. Bashir suspected, though, that he had been a highly trained operative and that Whitton-Blake's military service had comprised more espionage than soldiering.

Standing together on the stone-flagged balcony, the Bashirs watched the Whitton-Blakes' small convoy of aircraft descend to the field below the farmhouse. Bashir had sent a bodyguard to escort them from London but Sir Anthony had also included his own detachment, which indicated that his role at the defence department was more sensitive than Bashir had realised.

'Kev!'

Within seconds of landing and above the fading whine of the engine, Harrie jumped out of the aircraft and called out her greeting. As she ran over the grass, her red hair swept across her face and Jax could not see if she was smiling. He ran down the balcony steps and swept her up in a big bear hug as she fought to stop the strap of her bag from falling off her shoulder.

'Okay, okay … You can put me down now.'

'I have missed you so much,' he began before she stopped any further conversation with a kiss.

'Come off it, Kev. It's only been five days.' Her rebuke was delivered with a giggle. Harrie was happy – happy to be adored, happy to be worshipped, if need be, by the handsome young man. He *was* rather special, she thought. Good-looking, clever, funny and oh so well connected. She was occasionally tempted to scold herself for thinking such mercenary thoughts, but if she waited a few seconds it soon passed and she could once more revel in her amazing stroke of good luck in having found Kevor Jax Bashir, who was everything her father had ever wanted for her.

'Careful, Harrie,' he had warned her on the flight down. 'Don't stuff it up.'

'Dad! I'm not stupid. I know what to do.' Her retort was swift and sharp.

'And what *not* to do, my dear.' Her father raised a cynical eyebrow.

The look she had given him would have wilted a lesser man. But Whitton-Blake had met far nastier characters in his time and he was not intimidated.

'You know what I mean,' he warned.

'Yes, Dad. Now enough!'

She had spent the rest of the flight in silence with her arms folded across her chest. He did not need to harp on about it. She was being a good girl these days – relatively. And he must know that she would never do anything to jeopardise the family's interests.

The two days passed far too quickly for Jax's liking. Luckily, the weather had been warm and sunny so he and Harrie had relaxed by the pool, driven to picturesque villages perched on rocky hillsides, walked through groves of ancient olive trees and, on one evening, flown to the Côte d'Azur to the large resort city of Cannes. There they had enjoyed a romantic dinner at an exclusive hotel restaurant followed by a walk on its private beach away from the prying eyes of the media, who were already alerted to the presence of a new woman in the young man's life.

Jax was beginning to feel that Harrie Whitton was the one. She enthralled him with her quick humour, her enthusiasm and her style. She had an air of confidence and surety so much in contrast to his often gauche manner that he felt himself to be completed by her. Whatever shortcomings he possessed in his character were more than compensated by her attributes, of which he felt there were many and all positive.

Harrie Whitton's thoughts were of a slightly different nature. She liked Jax. He was open, honest, charming, intelligent – all the very best traits, she knew. He was good-looking, too, and that helped enormously. But Harrie had much of her father in her. She only truly thrived when she lived close to the edge; she needed that sense of freedom and unpredictability like she needed oxygen. So, whilst she liked the idea of having a prince for a boyfriend, when she thought about her situation with the increasingly lovesick Jax she began to get a little uncomfortable. She had never envisaged a future for herself where she was a companion, attending charity functions, ceremonies and embassy balls and being constantly in the spotlight.

Unfortunately for Harrie, her father was an ambitious man and the future that worried her was exactly the one he sought for himself. He already had a degree of power and influence but the salary of even such a high-flying civil servant as he was not immense, not compared to what he had always desired and, he felt, deserved. The Lindrick family fortune had gone to his eldest brother and its lands to his second one. So what better way to restore his personal wealth than by marrying into one of the richest families in the world? Harrie had presented him with a golden opportunity and he was not about to let her squander it. He knew what kind of trouble her behaviour had got her into in the past and he was not going to let it happen again.

It was their last night together. In the morning, Harrie and her father would be returning to London.

'It's been amazing having you here, you know,' Jax began. 'I think my parents have really taken to you.'

Harrie scoffed affectionately. 'Don't be daft, Kev. They hardly know me – just like you.' Her smile softened the hard edges of her words.

'What do you mean? I know you very well and I like what I know – very much.' He tried to sound affronted but it was hard to keep the warmth out of his reply.

'Well, thank you. I'm rather fond of you too. Or hadn't you noticed?'

He laughed and combed his fingers through the tangled fringe of her hair. Their lovemaking had been, as ever, vigorous. Resultingly, Harrie's hair was a mess and her cheeks were flushed with her exertions. He leaned over and cupped a hand around her naked breast.

'Oh, I noticed all right.'

His voice deepened. He kissed her fully on her mouth and she began to writhe underneath him.

Suddenly, she broke free and pushed him off her. 'Enough, tiger,' she giggled. 'You may have the stamina of a bull but I'm worn out – for a few minutes anyway.'

She lay on her back and stared at the ceiling.

'Truly, darling, about us ...' Her voice became serious, introspective. 'I know we're close, which is amazing. But it's been only three months, Kev. Do you think that's long enough to know someone? I mean, really *know* them? Know if you want to be with them – long term?'

He did not answer. The trace of uncertainty in her voice set off alarm bells. Just small ones, but enough to give him pause. She went on.

'I mean ... Well, we're getting pretty serious, aren't we? I just want to know if it's what you want ... If I'm the sort of woman ...'

'I could love?' He finished the sentence for her.

'Well, yes.'

He raised himself up on his elbow and looked down into her grey eyes, now darkened by the evening shadows.

'Harrie, I'm surprised you even need to ask. What's not to love? You're smart, gorgeous, fantastic ... And more.' Suddenly he smiled and stroked her face. 'Or are you just fishing for compliments?'

She lowered her eyes. She knew she was running close to the wind now and that her own concerns about their relationship could end up destroying it. If that happened, her father would be livid. She had to stop herself.

'Oops ... Found me out.'

'So that's it,' he said warmly. 'It's not like you to feel insecure. You must know how I feel about you. Or do you want me to say the words?'

'No, Kev.' Her response was a little too quick. She took a breath. 'Not unless you really mean it.'

'You know I do. I always will. Till the day I die.'

His kiss engulfed her and drained away any willpower she had to resist – either him or herself.

Chapter Four

Linnayen felt like slumping across the desk. Oh, to close her eyes for just a couple of minutes! Had she ever been this tired? *We've been at this all week and still nothing. We're no nearer to nailing this damned treaty than we were four months ago when these infernal talks began!*

Outwardly, the young woman gave no sign of her fatigue. She sat firmly upright, keeping her back straight and her shoulders square. Her face was losing the roundness of youth, due in large part, she felt, to the draining nature of the peace talks. But, like a true professional, she appeared interested and open to the discussion that was taking place around her – a discussion that was becoming increasingly tiresome.

Beoraan's patient but firm voice broke her reverie.

'We have shown you the evidence not once but on many occasions, and we admit that we do not have all the answers to the mystery of how and why our races came to have contact with each other.'

The counsellor was trying once more to entice the Earth representatives with an insistence on logic.

'The evidence itself, though appearing conclusive, *may* have been misinterpreted, we're prepared to admit that too. But what kind of peace, what kind of relationship could our two planets have if we do not start out as equal partners in the investigation into our shared past – if we truly have one?'

'Yes, counsellor. I know what you are saying and, believe me, I appreciate your sentiments,' the Earthan ambassador, Hal Byers, replied. 'But you have to understand that there is more to this than scientific conjecture. Your people have inflicted great damage on us over the years. Dear God, man! Many thousands have died and I'm telling you now, their families, their *children* are not going to just roll over and say, "Hey, it's okay. Let's all be friends now." Forgiveness doesn't come that easily!'

Byers' voice had risen towards the end of his speech. *He is obviously too close to this issue,* thought Linnayen. *Has he lost a loved one?* She made a mental note to have a more thorough investigation done on Byers. If there was something in his past that was influencing him, it must be dealt with and overcome.

'Please, Ambassador Byers, won't you at least consider putting aside – just for now – the issue of reconciliation?' Linnayen asked.

Break the problem down into smaller pieces. She heard her father's words inside her head. *Get agreement on the little things first, on the things you can agree. Then, slowly, giving no offence, use the example of what you have agreed to show that you can do it again. If you can find the common ground on just one issue, you have found the place to start your journey!*

'I suspect that no one in this room is unaware of or insensitive to the suffering of our respective peoples. We must all, eventually, find a way to apologise and atone,' she continued placidly, and with as much sincerity as she could express. 'All I ask is that for now we concentrate on the matter of our shared heritage. Can it be proved? If so, what are the implications? Will you at least think about this?'

The question was aimed at Byers directly, not the whole gathering. She knew that there were already sympathetic rumblings in the Earth delegation and some members had already been won over on this point.

'Oh, I'll think about it. That I can guarantee!' shot back Byers. 'But I must tell you, my lady, that all we see here is just another way for you to win this war. You can't do it by force. That's obvious. We've been damaging your fleet badly, and you know it. So is this is just a new, more subtle way to get under our defences?'

Beoraan's hackles rose, but he tried to keep his mind and body calm as once more he attempted to deal with the ignorance and prejudice of the Earth representative.

'Ambassador Byers, you know we have declared a truce – albeit a temporary one – while these negotiations take place. We have absolutely no desire to continue this conflict.' The old man shook his head and looked up. His eyes met the Earthan's steely gaze before continuing. 'What can I do, Ambassador Byers? What sacrifice can I make to prove to you that this is no ploy, no scheme, no connivance? The Union wishes peace between us and an end to the killing. That is all.'

'Sacrifice', Beoraan had said. Linnayen repeated the word in her head. *Sacrifice. Yes, that's the key. We have to make a grand gesture, a sacrifice of some sort that would be big enough to convince the Earthans of our commitment to peace but would not leave us vulnerable. They think they are defending themselves from wanton aggressors. Surely they must know they have much to gain by exploiting the Union's riches too. But do I trust that they would not take advantage of our acquiescence?*

She made a mental note to talk this through with Beoraan after the meeting.

Byers was talking again, assuring Beoraan that there was no sacrifice big enough to convince the people of Earth that the Union meant them no harm. Linnayen was sure now that he was speaking purely to hear his own voice. *Doesn't the man ever get tired? Or hungry?*

She felt a strong rumble in her stomach. She had to put an end to this. Waiting for an appropriate break in Byers' diatribe, she pushed back her chair and stood up. This was a signal to all the Altanis and other Union representatives that the meeting was now over. But in order not to give offence to the Earthans, Linnayen nodded her head towards them, awarding them priority in her closing remarks.

'Honoured emissaries from Earth, representatives of the Union, I wish to thank you once again for taking the time to come to this forum today. The hour is now late and I am sure that you are all tired. But I hope that, like me, you feel we have progressed in our understanding of each other. These matters are weighty and, because of their importance, we do no justice or service to our people to deliberate them with tired minds and bodies. Let us retire, enjoy a late supper and reconvene in the morning. Thank you.'

She turned and walked away from the desk, closely followed by Beoraan and Nen, her personal assistant, who had arrived some twenty minutes earlier ready to escort her home. She could feel rather than see Byers and the other Earthans muttering their disapproval of how the day had gone.

No matter, she thought, *however long it takes, however much talking we do, I will have peace!*

'Ha!' Evica's strong tone hammered home her triumph over her sparring partner. 'Relent!'

'Not while there's breath in my body and blood in my veins!' Tariik Min laughed back at her, gasping with exertion. '*You* will give in to me!'

Evica threw back her head in a gale of mirth, her fiery curls tumbling down past her waist. She was straddled across the breathless young lieutenant, having just pinned him to the dirt floor of the training arena. It had taken her months to perfect the body-slamming move, but finally it had paid off. She had Tariik Min just where she wanted him: flat on his back and at her mercy.

But inside, silently, in her dreams, she admitted that she did not have the thing she really wanted from him – his heart. How could he be so wonderful, so perfect in every way, yet so totally blind to her affection for him? Her reverie lasted no more than a second as, feeling her body stir, she snapped her mind back to the present.

'I will never give in to you, Tariik,' she said, smiling. 'I beat you fair and square. Admit it!'

Tariik looked up at Evica's flushed, animated face and could not help but laugh. 'Very well, I admit it. You did well, my lady. Now let me up.'

Having won the point, Evica was happy to remove her leg and allow him to get to his feet. Was it just her imagination that he lingered a moment longer than he needed to?

Tariik was relieved to be out of Evica's grip – not because he didn't like her, or because he felt humiliated by her. No, her nearness provoked an altogether too strong response in his body. He had long since fallen in love with the bright, vivacious young princess. But his feelings brought him little joy. She was so far above him and, despite his best efforts to break free from his emotions, he knew that he was in danger of losing his heart to her. *Don't be such a fool,* he thought. *You can never have her. Just get it out of your head!*

Lieutenant Tariik Min was well aware of his station in life. Born on the watery world of Dasnir into a sea-farming family, he knew only too well how lucky he was to have got this far. He had done well at school in the community where he lived with his parents and three sisters. He was bright and had studied hard and he dreamed of one day travelling to all the other planets. There was so much to see, to learn, to experience. He loved the farm and his family – they were good people – but he wanted adventure. At the age of just fourteen he applied to the Cadet Corps on Altan and, from then on, his dreams had all begun to come true.

After graduation, his first tour of duty, at the age of twenty, had been on board the spaceracer *Sur-Kabanash*. At twenty-two he was promoted to deputy head of security on board the battlecraft *Sur-Dacas* and spent a couple of exciting years patrolling the Union's outer reaches, dealing with the Earthan skirmishers. Now twenty-five, having attained the rank of lieutenant, he had been posted to the academy at Genkarah for six months to train the young Ki's elder sister in the use of hand weapons and bodily combat and, in the moment when he first saw the Lady Evica, his simple world was turned on its head. He was irretrievably, overwhelmingly in love – with the one woman, apart from the Ki herself, whom he could never have. *Farmers' sons do not marry princesses!*

Tariik dealt with his dilemma in the only way he knew how. With typical Dasnirian restraint, he buried his feelings as deep as they would go and covered the mound with a thick top layer of friendly reserve.

'Now, that you've completely humiliated me, my lady, can I take it that I am free to go?' he asked, brushing the dust from his clothes.

'If you must,' conceded the still grinning Evica. 'But only on one condition!'

'And that would be?' he enquired.

'That you will partner me in the Dasnirian reel tonight at my sister's birthday feast,' she fired back, her eyes shining with mischief. 'You know I'm hopeless at it, but I've got to do it for the sake of our guests. Go on, Tariik. You can get me through it. Say yes.' Her tone was too compelling for him to resist and, smiling fondly at her upturned face, he acceded.

'I would be honoured. We'll dance till we drop!'

Evica clapped her hands together with pleasure. The day was going perfectly and, with just a little luck, the night would be even better.

Laughing and chatting affectionately, the two young people walked across the training arena and entered the cooler shade of the cloisters. There Tariik took his leave of the lively young noblewoman and, as he walked towards his quarters, he wondered how hard it was going to be that night to feign indifference when, in his mind's eye, all he could see was his mouth upon hers and his hands stroking her beautiful face.

'Sacrifice.' The word played inside Linnayen's head as the shower water trickled down her body. Pondering the word – and the concept – she was not really concentrating on washing herself, or on the coming night's birthday celebrations, a milestone that brought unhappy memories of her father's death a year earlier. No, what she would wear and how she would look were at this moment quite inconsequential. Her thoughts were entirely wrapped up in the idea of sacrifice and the lack of progress – yet again – in today's peace talks. She was coming close to despair but she knew that she could not give up. The promise to her father was binding.

The shower compartment was decorated with living plants to make it look like a forest bower and, as she stepped out, the reflected green light framed her slim physique. She saw Nen, her assistant, quietly humming and busying herself about the room, laying out a selection of opulent dresses and their attendant jewellery from which Linnayen would make her choice. At her approach, Nen looked up and smiled.

'I thought you'd be in there all evening, my lady,' she said with genuine warmth in her voice. 'Now then, what do you think of this?' Nen held up a deep blue brocade gown, which was trimmed with gold fur and studded with tiny gold glass droplets.

'Mmm,' said Linnayen absentmindedly. 'They are all lovely, Nen. You choose.'

'Lady Linnayen, I can't make that decision! It's not my place. Besides, I wouldn't want to offend you.'

Nen pretended to be slightly shocked at her mistress's informality, but she was, of course, secretly pleased at Linnayen's trust in her.

'You wouldn't offend me. Besides,' she insisted, 'you have excellent taste, Nen.'

'Yes, but…' Nen was searching for a way to put this without riling her mistress. 'You'll want to look your best, my lady. I mean… Every eligible man in the Union will be here tonight.'

'Oh, Nen! Really!' Linnayen admonished her somewhat shortly. 'That's the last thing on my mind right now. I have far more important things to worry about than whether tonight's the night I'll meet my husband!' The very thought of it! She was only just turning twenty-two, for goodness sake. *There's plenty of time to get married – one day.*

Suddenly, a tremor coursed through her body and caused her to gasp. *Sacrifice! That's it! Not a sacrifice… a marriage!*

Jax whistled a tune as he flew. The controls of the small but powerful fixed-wing aircar responded instantly to his touch and he was having the ride of his life. The craft was as light as a feather, a major advantage of the new series of Airdancers.

Far below the steel blue-black waters of the northern Atlantic were broken by white specks, which he knew to be icebergs. Many were massive – they had to be in order to be visible at this great height – and he was tempted to descend. But were he to do that he would have even less time with Harrie in New York. As it was, one evening was pretty meagre. He was determined not to waste a minute on the journey.

They had spoken every day while he had been seconded to a residential course in Oslo over the previous two weeks, sometimes twice, but he had still missed her dreadfully. When he scored a day off from the interminable lectures due to his earlier strong test results, he thought he would take the opportunity to surprise Harrie in New York. She would probably be out, he figured, as she was still as sociable as ever; dating the president's son had not curbed her fondness for parties and dance clubs. But if she was not at home, Jax had a pretty good idea where to find her. All he had to do was make a few calls.

He parked the aircar in the stacker on the roof of Harrie's apartment building. It was now half past nine, so chances were she would already be out as Harrie liked to dine with friends most evenings before hitting the club circuit. So he was surprised to find that, when the door to her apartment slid open, the lights were on and music was playing.

Excellent! She was home after all. The music was coming from the bedroom and Jax wasted no time in going straight there.

He did not register the crumpled bedclothes at first or the muffled noises coming from a place out of sight on the floor, hidden by the mattress. And Harrie did not register that anyone other than she and her lover was in the room. She continued to grind herself on top of the man's naked torso and it was only when she sat up fully and flung her head back to let out a deep, satisfied moan that she saw Jax staring at her. His face was ashen, his eyes disbelieving.

'Oh God! No!' She pulled herself off the man and, grabbing a sheet to cover her nudity, ran to follow the fast retreating Jax.

He did not speak – could not speak. He stumbled through the rooms of the apartment, tripping over furniture, seeing nothing but Harrie's head thrown back, her tousled hair, her eyes closed, her mouth open, the beads of sweat on her flushed cheeks. The way he had seen her a hundred times before – with him.

From a distance he could hear her voice calling out his name, then begging him to stop. *Stop? No.* Stopping would mean having to look at her– having to see that beautiful, ugly face. Stopping would mean that she might convince him that it was all a mistake – that it meant nothing – that she was his, would always be his. *Ah, but she wouldn't be.* She would never be entirely his ever again.

'Kev! Please! Not like this! Let me explain …'

He was at the door and, in his agitation, could not focus on the exit code. He punched numbers on the keypad but the door did not open. She caught up and laid a hand on his arm. He flung it away. Her touch was a scald.

'Please! He's nothing, I swear. Just fun. Not like you.' Her words were slurred and thick.

'Get away from me!' His voice was a low growl.

'Darling, please, listen to me …' She was having trouble sounding out the words, as though her mouth was paralysed.

Jax pushed her away and she tottered backwards. Then he saw what stood on the table by the door. He'd seen the same paraphernalia at the homes of other people – not friends, acquaintances, people who liked escaping reality.

'Oh, Harrie … Not you.' The despair in his voice was almost tangible. She followed his glance.

'No, Kev. It's not like that. Just once in a while …'

Suddenly he was calm. He could hear Harrie still talking, pleading, but her voice was just noise. He was conscious, too, that the man, Harrie's lover, was emerging from the bedroom, but he made no move towards them – he just stood there, leaning against the doorframe, watching the scene, engrossed in the drama, the flicker of a smile at his mouth.

Their eyes connected and, in that moment, he knew Harrie Whitton-Blake – knew everything about her, who she was and what she was – and he vowed that this would never happen again. Not to him.

He punched in the code again. This time the door slid aside and he left without a backward glance.

Hal Byers and the Earth delegates looked uncomfortable. They were seated at a low table on Linnayen's right – a place of great honour – but they did not seem to be enjoying the Huthon dancing troupe or be aware of the high position they had been accorded. Granted, the Huthons' slow and exaggerated movements appeared awkward, but it was all down to having a genuine passion about their art. That was the Huthon way, thought Linnayen. They were a sober people and it showed most strongly at times like these in their precisely measured dances.

A smile played around the corners of Linnayen's mouth. The torpor brought about by the protracted negotiations had lifted that afternoon when she had had her brilliant idea. *That was the only word for it,* she thought, *brilliant!* The more she thought about it, the less she could find that was wrong with it and she could not wait to talk it through with Beoraan. A union brought about by a marriage between Altan and Earth. Not a marriage of minds, although that might well come in time, but of *people* – two people, and she was to be one of them. All that remained to be done was to find the appropriate other half. It would be no sacrifice if it could seal a lasting peace and fulfil her father's dying hope.

'What a wonderful birthday celebration this is, sister.' Evica was seated on Linnayen's left. Her smile was wide and her eyes laughing. She had been looking across at Tariik Min, seated on the Dasnirian table. He looked very handsome tonight in his dress uniform; the crisp white linen showed off the darkness of his hair and brought out the blue of his eyes. She forced herself to look away from the young lieutenant. 'Can it be that the talks have gone well? You look almost radiant!'

'I beg your pardon! Take a look in the mirror if you want to see someone shine,' Linnayen replied, smiling. 'So, what have you been up to?'

Evica's laugh tumbled into the air. 'Nothing – yet. But the night is still young.'

'You still have to make it through the Dasnirian reel. It's exhausting,' Linnayen warned.

Evica got up and sashayed away. 'Oh, I'll make it. You'll see. Must go. Have fun, sister.'

Linnayen and Evica had drawn closer to each other since their father's death and it made her heart glad to see her sister so animated. She had known of Evica's affection for the handsome if solemn Lieutenant Min for a little while. Not that Evica had said anything openly about her feelings. It was just that she never missed an opportunity to slip his name into the conversation. *He makes my sister happy*, she reflected. *But why does he not respond?* It tugged at her heart to see Evica so besotted with the man and he so cool and unaffected around her. Was he in love with someone else? Or maybe had he no liking for females. It was at times like this that she wished she could break with mentante protocol and scan the young lieutenant's mind to see what he felt, if anything, for her sister. But, of course, that was strictly forbidden. The reading of a person's mind without their permission was taboo and considered most rude.

The music suddenly got louder and there was a crashing of Dasnirian cymbals and bells. Linnayen smiled. This would be fun, she thought. Dasnirian reel-dancing was enormously energetic and exhilarating to watch. Brightly clothed dancers, adorned with shells and sea-feather ferns, entered the room. Evica and Tariik were among them, both resplendent in their shimmering robes and dazzling headdresses. Beoraan leaned across the table.

'Your sister looks wonderful, my lady. She does us great honour,' he said.

Linnayen acknowledged the compliment with a curt nod then gave her attention to the dance. The music was uplifting. Though, judging by the grimace on Byers' face, possibly a little loud, Linnayen thought. Evica and Tariik and the other dancers swirled between each other, each pair stamping their feet to the vibrant rhythms. At the appropriate parts in the music, their voices lifted in cheers and whoops and there was much handclapping and laughter. As the dance progressed, the tempo quickened and Linnayen could see the sweat breaking out on the dancers' skin as they tried to keep pace. The Dasnirian reel was a love dance; its purpose was to bring couples together both in competition and in a celebration of life. Whoever was left at the end, whichever couple lasted the pace, would win a prize, and tonight the prize was a private midnight supper on the Ki's royal barge.

Evica was determined that she and Tariik would be the last couple standing. Although she could have a trip on the royal barge any time she liked, she could never have got Tariik on it by any other means. Given their respective positions in society, it would have been most inappropriate, and then there was Tariik's natural reserve. He would never agree to go with her if she just came out and asked him.

Sure enough, their physical stamina and Evica's determination ensured that they were the last couple left in the reel. With a crashing and clashing of horns and cymbals, the penultimate couple collapsed and Evica and Tariik were declared the winners. They were exhausted. Breathless, their chests heaving from the exertion, but very pleased, they hugged and the watching guests let out a round of cheers for them.

Linnayen looked across to Hal Byers and his party and was pleased to see some smiling faces at last. It looked as though her sister's madcap dance had worked a little magic. She hoped that her own performance in the forum tomorrow would be equally effective.

Chapter Five

Beoraan and Linnayen sat on the terrace that encircled her tower apartment, their eyes on the sparkling lights of the city spread far, far below. The intricately woven balustrade was made of a light metallic alloy which, at the touch of a sensor, emitted a protective, invisible force field that was impervious to all weapons and blocked all sound and vision from the outside. She and Beoraan could see beyond the field but no one would be able to spy on them or eavesdrop on her discussion. Once the old man was settled in a tapestried armchair, she began.

'Thank you for coming at such a late hour, Beoraan. Be assured I would not have disturbed your rest had it not been important.'

'Oh, please don't worry, my lady. I don't sleep much these days, anyway,' he sighed, acknowledging the fact of his increasing age. 'How can I help you?'

'Firstly, I want you to have Ambassador Byers' history researched more thoroughly. I know we have a career biography on him but I want to know about his personal life. Something is influencing his negative reactions and we need to know what it is. Will you see to it for me?' she asked directly and he nodded his assent. It was late and she wanted to let the old man get back to bed as soon as possible.

She continued. 'Next … I have had an idea that I truly believe will seal the peace once we can get past the ambassador's objections. You gave me the clue, actually, Beoraan, when you asked what sacrifice you could make to prove that we were serious about peace.' She paused, both for breath and to let her words register. 'Well, Beoraan, there is no sacrifice I would ask or expect of *you* or our people. But there is something *I* can do, although I do not see it as any great sacrifice, given the prize of lasting peace.'

The old man's brow furrowed and he went to speak. Linnayen raised a hand to halt him.

'I want to offer myself in marriage – to an Earthan.'

Beoraan's eyes opened wide as the full import of her words sank in.

'Marriage! Are you sure, my lady? And to an Earthan!'

His could feel his heart pounding inside his chest. It was the last thing he had expected her to say.

'Quite sure, Beoraan. A political marriage. A union with the sole aim of forging two nations as one. It's not such an unusual idea, you know,' she went on, trying to allay the look of concern on his face. 'Although we have had no use for it on Altan, the Autabronis and the Huthons have both used arranged marriage in their histories. So have the Earthans. In fact, it was quite common for nearly two millennia, although that was a long time ago,' she admitted.

As she spoke, Beoraan began to digest the implications of what she was proposing. The more he pondered it, the more he began to see that the idea had some merit.

'Just think of it, Beoraan. If I were married to an Earthan – of an appropriate rank, of course – it would be the supreme gesture. Altan would be showing how much importance it places on attaining peace by giving something – or someone – it holds dearly to Earth.'

Linnayen continued to explain her idea and her enthusiasm was becoming a little contagious. 'We would also be – as the Earthans say – practising what we preach. Dr Ropar has proved that our species share a common ancestry. What better or more fitting way to reunite our people?'

'You might be right, although I can see obstacles too.' Beoraan's brow furrowed in concentration as he focused his mind. 'By offering them our own royal princess, they will have to appreciate that we are serious in suing for peace. I would be loath to place complete trust in them though. You could be in personal jeopardy if something went wrong. There must be no danger to you.'

'I don't see that there would be any real risk,' she retorted. 'In fact, I would negotiate to have my prospective husband come here to live – well, for most of the time, at least. Thus, Altan will remain the seat of power –'

'With an Earthan consort helping us to govern,' Beoraan finished the thought for her.

'Exactly. But as we know, Earthans don't have our skills in statecraft, so we should be able to keep my future spouse busy with seemingly important affairs of state while you and I get on with running the Union. How hard can it be?'

She raised an eyebrow and stared into his eyes. Beoraan could not help but be proud of the way her mind had been trained.

Beoraan rubbed his chin. 'My lady, I think your plan might just work!'

Linnayen laughed and the old man was rewarded with the sight of her lovely face lit up with pleasure. *A far too rare sight,* he thought.

'I think so too, old friend. But,' and here she leaned forward conspiratorially, 'there is one more rather important consideration.'

Beoraan looked at her quizzically.

'Whom shall we pick for my husband?'

Lieutenant Min held out his hand to the Lady Evica to help her into the barge. Her eyes were bright and full of intent, though in the shadowy darkness he could not see the way she looked at him.

'Thank you, Tariik.' Her voice was warm and her eyes locked onto his as she stepped into the vessel and chose a place on a low pile of cushions in the stern. The boat master took his place at the helm inside the wheelhouse, having assured Tariik that they would have complete privacy. All he had to do was sit back and relax.

Relax! How in all the heavens can I do that, thought Tariik. The boat master released the cable and cast the barge off and, within a minute, they had moved far enough away from the lake shore to be in near darkness.

'Tariik.' Her voice came softly to him as she patted a silk cushion next to her. 'Please, sit next to me.' He had never heard Evica's voice so soft and low and it rather surprised him.

'Is that appropriate? I mean ... Is it allowed?' he asked hesitantly.

'Probably not,' she answered with the trace of a smile in her voice. 'But *I* won't say anything. Come on.'

He moved to the stern and sat beside her. To keep off the chill night air, she placed a large fur pelt over their legs. He helped her to pull it higher to better cover her arms and shoulders.

'There, my lady. That's a little better. That will stop you from getting too cold.' Tariik felt in danger of babbling nervously and forced himself to keep his mouth shut.

'Oh, I'm not cold, Tariik. And please, you don't need to call me my lady when we are alone. I'd like you to use my name, actually.'

'Evica?' he asked incredulously. 'I'm … I'm not sure that would be wise.'

'Wise!' she retorted. 'Who wants to be wise tonight? In fact, I want to be most *un*wise.'

Her shoulders sank. Had she said too much? Been too forward?

Tariik was eager to calm her. 'Very well … Evica. It *is* a nice name. I like it very much.'

'And I like Tariik. I've always liked the way it sounds. Very strong.'

She could not bring herself to say the word 'you'. Evica's chest rose with the pounding of her heart. He was so near, so warm. Her nostrils filled with his scent and her eyes drank in the perfection of his face in silhouette. She traced the long line of his straight nose and then followed the curve down to his lips. They were full and sensuous – and they looked soft. She wondered how soft.

Tariik broke her reverie. 'Would you like something to eat, my la – er, Evica? There is fruit and some cheeses, or biscuits …'

He leaned forward, examining the spread of foods that had been left for them. Evica interrupted him, impatient for his full attention.

'I'm not hungry. Thank you.'

'A drink then?' he enquired again.

'I'm not thirsty either.' Her voice was low and quiet.

'Right.' Tariik tried to settle himself next to her. He was desperately trying to calm his body and control the sense of weightlessness in his stomach. It was hopeless. The nearness of her, the scent of her, the warmth emanating from her body all served to stir every muscle and sinew into tight knots. He could feel his blood rushing in every vein and artery and he fought to keep control of himself.

Evica, too, was excited. But, unlike Tariik, she wanted to let go of the feelings, to let them take flight. Suddenly, Tariik's profile turned towards her. He caught her gaze in the reflected lights from the shore. Her jade eyes sparkled. They searched his face, looking for a sign that would tell her the truth. Did he love her? Did he have any feelings at all towards her? If only she could be sure! And now, tonight in this darkness, it was still impossible to tell.

There was no mistaking the look in Evica's eyes. *So, it was true!* He had suspected – even dreamed and prayed – that her feelings towards him were more than those of a friend and colleague for some months. He looked away, his head downcast. Regardless of her feelings, he could only ever be her teacher, maybe her friend – one day. *If only she wasn't who she was,* he thought for the hundredth time. *A pauper may look at a prince … but only look.*

'We danced so well tonight, Tariik. It was wonderful. It seems we do many things well together,' she said, her voice thick with emotion.

'Aye, we do,' he agreed. 'You've been an excellent partner … I mean, student. It's a shame I'll be leaving in a few weeks for the *Sur-Dacas* and my new posting. I'm going to miss you.'

He heard her catch her breath. 'Yes, I'll miss you too, very much.' Her voice wavered. 'In fact, I really don't want you to go. Perhaps I should ask my sister to have your orders changed?' Evica forced a smile with these last words, trying to sound light-hearted. But the thought of his leaving left her desolate.

'You know that wouldn't be right,' he replied.

'Yes, I know. But sometimes it's right to do the wrong thing … Can't it be so?' she pleaded, hoping that he would, for once, be selfish and agree with her.

'How can what is wrong be right?' Tariik replied with great seriousness. It was at that moment that he noticed a tear on her cheek, caught in the reflected light.

'Oh … my lady … Oh no, Evica, don't cry.' His voice was almost a whisper.

He lifted his arm and wrapped it around her shoulders, pulling her body closer to his. Evica could not help herself and she seized the opportunity to snuggle in closer to Tariik, placing her own arm across his chest. Nuzzling her head against his neck, she felt his other arm go around her, holding her ever more tightly.

Her voice was a low whisper. 'I can't help it. I don't want you to go.'

Had there been a moment when he could have stopped this from happening, Tariik wondered. If so, it was too late now. He could hold back no longer. His body surged and he felt himself melt into her. It was as though they were becoming one. Slowly, inch by inch, their faces came closer until, hearts hammering, almost bursting, their lips met.

Evica reeled. There was nothing but this moment, no world, no light, no reason, only his mouth on hers. Their breathing quickened. Their hands began to move, slowly at first, caressing faces, then ever more urgently exploring new parts of their bodies. Tariik could not stop. He had dreamed of this moment for so long. He had touched her before – many times their bodies had made contact in the training arena – but never like this! He found the cords holding her bodice and loosened them. Evica sighed in pleasure as his hand pushed inside her blouse and found her naked breasts. She needed to say his name, 'Tariik. My love.'

It was as though her words had let loose some sudden, unstoppable action. Tariik's body, hard with the tension in his muscles, pushed at her and she rose up for him. Again and again, she pushed her body into his, as if they could truly become one. Her hands sought his skin and pulled at his tunic, clawing to remove it. Their mouths did not cease and there was no sound except for their breathing and moaning as their excitement mounted.

Evica felt his warm bare flesh on her exposed breasts. Tariik by now knew that his body could not be halted and he moved one hand down to raise the hem of her gown. Grasping at the folds of material, he pushed them aside until he found what he so desperately sought. For Evica, the touch of his hand between her legs was electrifying and she gladly opened herself to him. All she wanted now, all she had ever wanted she now knew, was Tariik, inside her, filling her. The moment came. He was there. Her breath and his by now were ragged and gasping. Their hands clawed at each other, mouths locked together in a kiss that never ceased. Their bodies were as one and, as the glorious chasm came ever closer, they rushed towards it willingly, breathlessly. And they plunged down.

Beoraan had been busy in the last few days. Before any decision about Linnayen's plan could be made there was some homework to be done. It would be foolish to rush before the Earthan delegation without ensuring that the idea was feasible and would be acceptable to the other Union planets. There was also the matter of re-investigating Hal Byers' background and Beoraan had set a team to work on this as soon as he had left Linnayen on the evening of the banquet.

He and Linnayen spent the days after her birthday subtly probing the delegates from Huthon, Autabron and Dasnir about their views on developing ties with Earth other than those purely for trade purposes. For one thing, they wanted to get an idea of how the other planets might feel about an Earthan holding such high rank in the forum. They also talked about how there might be in only one or two generations hence the first mixing of the species. Had they even considered that genetically they were all so very similar? If Earth finally joined the Union, would this be seen as an opportunity or a threat?

Dasnirians and Huthons had been living on each other's planets for the last five hundred years and already at least a fifth of their mutual populations were of mixed race. The Autabronis were more insular in their dealings with other Union planets; they were in the Union for trade purposes only and their religion, known as Nuonabat, forbad them to marry non-believers anyway. The Dasnirian ambassador told Linnayen that their scientists had already made a study of the genetomorphology of humans and were prepared for the consequences of, as they put it, 'muto-speciesism'. They rather thought that the physical strength and size of the humans would be an asset to their bloodline, whilst humans might benefit from their ability to breathe underwater, an ability they believed humans might have actually possessed once in their presentient form.

As for the idea of a political union through marriage, the Huthons and Autabronis were surprised at the possible revival of the somewhat outdated strategy but thought it just primitive enough to appeal to the Earthans. The Dasnirians were less impressed by the idea, and Beoraan suspected that they were worried about the political bond between Earth and Altan at such high level. Would this give the Altanis too much power? Would a dynasty ensue that would be loath to relinquish its position if the time ever came? Above all, would the good governance of the Union suffer as a result of the proposed action?

Whatever happened and whatever decision was made, both Beoraan and Linnayen knew that all these fears must be put to rest and all issues resolved before such a union as the marriage could take place. When they took the proposal to Hal Byers and the other Earth delegates, they had to present a united front. Finally, after a week of discreet talks with the Union representatives and feeling confident that the plan could work, Linnayen summoned Hal Byers. She wanted to speak with him in her private garden.

She was meditating to a chorale from the Mayar Book of Prayers when Byers was shown through to the summerhouse and, although she heard him coming from some way off, she feigned surprise at his approach.

'Ah! Ambassador Byers. I'm so glad you could join me. I hope I have not inconvenienced you by asking you to see me at such short notice?' she enquired solicitously.

'Oh, no inconvenience, my lady,' he replied, then shuffled uncomfortably and cleared his throat.

Oh, how gauche the man is, thought Linnayen tersely. *He is twice my age yet he's lumbering around like an embarrassed schoolboy!* For the proud young Ki, suing for peace with these naïve people sometimes felt like trying to reason with a child. She had to make allowances and, although she tried hard to control her impatience at their lack of statesmanship and their flurries of emotion, she could not help but feel galled by it sometimes.

'Please, do sit down. Would you care for a cold drink?'

Byers looked around, saw a velvet-covered daybed under the open window and sat. 'No, thank you. I don't need anything to drink.'

'But you *do* want to know why I have asked you here, don't you?' Linnayen smiled, hoping this small gesture would lull the man's nerves.

'Well, yes. I admit to being intrigued,' he confessed. 'What is so important that you couldn't discuss it in open forum tomorrow?'

His rudeness is as annoying as his lack of finesse!

'It is a sensitive matter, ambassador, and I will be raising it at the forum tomorrow. But, to put it plainly, I do not want you to hear of it first in front of the other delegates because the import of it will, I believe, cause you some surprise. You will need time to think about the matter, compose yourself and decide your reactions accordingly.' Linnayen's manner had now become very formal, though she tried to keep her tone friendly, as she knew the man from Earth would feel reassured by this. *These heathens don't realise that voice and tone are just tools! Or weapons …*

'Ambassador, over the last week I have been thinking hard about how we in the Union of Planets can convince you of our commitment to peace, despite our past aggressions. You have asked for assurances – quite understandably – that we are not intending to trick you or lull you into letting down your defences. In other words, a gesture of sincerity is needed, a gesture of so much importance and weight that there can be no mistaking the Union's desire for peace between our warring worlds. I am about to make such a gesture – to offer you something we consider to be priceless, something the Union will think of as irreplaceable and *our* holy people believe sacrosanct.'

Linnayen spoke clearly and deliberately. Her eyes locked onto his.

'I am offering a union by marriage – a royal marriage, if you like, to seal the peace. I offer myself as one half of the union. Naturally, I would expect the prospective husband to be a man of equal or near-equal rank on Earth.'

Byers' mouth fell open and his eyes were two saucers. He could not believe what he was hearing. Royal marriages for political reasons were just not done anymore. Earthans believed in free choice. No one was forced to marry on Earth – not nowadays.

What the Ki was suggesting was so unorthodox it was almost barbaric!

Linnayen soon gathered from the expression on Byers' face that he was shocked and appeared genuinely angry. Had she misjudged the Earthan nature? Surely, with their less sophisticated beliefs and behaviours, they would see the logic in a political marriage – especially when the reward would be a lasting peace.

'Ambassador Byers, you seem nonplussed by my proposed solution to end this dreadful war. Do please remember that it is a suggestion only, a proposal for you and your delegates to consider. My only purpose tonight in telling you of my idea is to allow you time to compose yourself before I raise it at the forum.'

Byers could barely control his emotions. He felt anger and confusion as he desperately tried to find the sting in the tail. *Where's the trick,* he asked himself. *What's she trying to pull?*

'At the forum?' he cried. 'You can't do that!'

Linnayen kept a tight rein on her voice, trying to hide her growing irritation with the man.

'I confess I am a little surprised by your reaction, ambassador. You seem to have already formed an objection to the proposal. Have I offended you in some way? Do tell me if what I have said has angered you.'

Byers did not know what to say. He was uncomfortable with this whole situation. Then, as he looked at the young girl's face, her dark brows drawn together in a look of concern that appeared to be more for his feelings than the situation in which they found themselves, he realised that she was genuine. Perhaps her offer of marriage was just that – an offer to help achieve peace. He relented slightly and brought his emotions back under control.

'No, my lady. You've not offended me. I apologise for the rashness of my reaction.' Judging from the look of confusion on Linnayen's face, he felt he needed to explain further. 'I was just taken aback by your suggestion. You see, I don't think we have had so-called "political marriages" on Earth for over a thousand years. This is all a bit out of the blue for me.'

Linnayen smiled and nodded. 'And for me too. We have never had them on Altan, although the Huthons and the Autabronis used the practice of mating partnerships to forge trading and wealth unions in their pasts.' She paused. Then, feeling tired of the conversation, she continued. 'My own people may well find this a strange, perhaps uncomfortable resolution to our troubles. But I say again, Ambassador Byers, the Union desires peace – a *lasting* peace. We have already proved to you that there is a genetic link between our races, although we do not know how or why this has occurred. What I am suggesting is a reengineering of that link, both in order to settle a peace now and to bring our people together in harmony in the decades to come.'

She could almost see the wheels turning inside the man's head. The furrows on his forehead smoothed. *Good! He is beginning to relax about it. If I keep homing in on the end goal – the attainment of peace – he will soon come to terms with the means. And I will have my way.*

'Perhaps your idea has some merit, my lady. Whatever the outcome, I thank you for warning me of your intentions. I will brief my colleagues. However, there is one further matter to consider,' he concluded.

'And that is?' she enquired.

'If your proposal is accepted, who do you intend to marry?'

'Ah. Well, that's where I was hoping you would help....'

Linnayen stood up, putting her hand out for Byers to stand. Together they walked, heads bent together, under the curved arch dripping with clusters of white sinnsey flowers in the direction of Beoraan's apartments.

Largely due to their preparation in raising the concept with the Union delegates beforehand, there was little open consternation in the forum when Linnayen put up her suggestion for the marriage between Altan and Earth. Byers had obviously spoken to the members of his team, judging by the calm, mannered reaction to her statement. But it was obvious that they had spent the night preparing a list of objections, the main one being that the people of Earth would never assent.

'Your proposal, my lady, is I believe just too radical for the people of Earth. It's too foreign a concept,' Hal Byers explained. 'We did away with arranged marriages hundreds of years ago. People choose their own life partners now. I'll wager that even your own people will find this proposal difficult to accept.'

'Ambassador Byers, you know as well as I that the path to peace is rarely straight and easy,' Linnayen replied. 'There will have to be some concessions in people's thinking, of course. People must be persuaded to the idea gently, and I agree with you that if we put forward this idea too quickly, or as a "fait accompli" as you like to say, we risk alienating everyone.'

Byers' face was a stone wall.

Linnayen continued. 'Thus, our one chance for peace could be lost. Neither of us wants that, do we? But can I ask you this: are you prepared to at least explore some likely scenarios with us? Maybe if we can get a more concrete idea of how such a union might work in practical terms we might see how best to present it to our people. Or even involve them in its execution. Well, ambassador? Can we at least talk it through?'

Byers turned to look at the other Earth delegates, his face asking the unsaid question. Can we – *should* we? How badly do we want peace? And is this a price worth paying? There was complete silence in the forum while this interchange took place and Linnayen used the time to scan the faces of the other delegates. She could see no outright opposition. All had had their turns to speak and, for the most part, were open to the idea. But the air could be cut with a knife as all waited for Byers to speak.

'Very well. I guess we have something to talk about,' he finally conceded.

Linnayen felt like jumping up and clapping. Instead, she coolly nodded her head in a gesture of both thanks and acceptance.

'Excellent. I had so much hoped that you would agree to discussions that I have taken the liberty of asking Sen-Beoraan to find an appropriate envoy to work with you on my behalf. I hope you do not mind this presumption?' she asked solicitously.

Byers' attitude was one of resigned defeat as he replied, 'No, my lady. We will be happy to work with whoever you choose to represent you.'

'Good.' Linnayen replied, her voice sounding just a little too self-satisfied for Beoraan's liking.

Careful, my lady. Don't push it too far. Remember – show humility.

'In that case,' she said, turning towards Beoraan, 'all that remains is to ask you, Beoraan, if you have found someone suitable from our diplomatic corps. Who is to be my envoy?'

Beoraan cleared his throat and, making it clear that he was addressing both Linnayen and the Earth delegation, he spoke the words he had memorised the night before.

'I have selected a young Altani captain. He is possessed of high intelligence and sensitivity. But of note is that he has studied Earth – its peoples and cultures – and has expressed a sincere interest in and liking for all things Earthan. I think we will all find him a most suitable ambassador and representative. His name is Captain Durroc Navarr.'

With this pronouncement, the meeting was brought to a close and Linnayen rose to leave the room. Inside her head, thoughts were spinning like a thousand tops and it took all her self-control to stop from laughing out loud. *I've done it,* she thought. *It was almost too easy!*

Chapter Six

The forest planet of Hutho had long been a favourite retreat of the Altani reigning families. One hundred and fifty years before, Sen-Cadal'baran, the then leader of the Altani delegation, had asked the Huthon Council for the right to purchase a small tract of land by the River Utieku. With thin soils and devoid of trees, it was considered by the Huthons a place with no purpose, bleak and barren. But in Altani eyes, the grassy meadow which swept down to the banks of the river was a delightful spot and Cadal'baran wasted no time in building a fine lodge on the open site.

Raised on low pillars of granite, the lodge was a confection of materials. To honour the Huthons, the outer walls of the lodge were made of living trees after the local fashion. These were trained as they grew, forming tall twists and braids. But the inside of the building was in the Altani style of smooth lines and soft colours. The walls were stone inlaid with burnished bronze panels that curved around a central double-storey atrium, which was open to the sky. In the middle was a deep pool of crystal clear blue water.

The pool had been chiselled down into the rock below and was fed by a warm spring at its base. All main rooms of the lodge faced into the atrium, which had been planted with green shrubs and flowering plants of many colours. The aura created was one of calmness and purity and, given that the sole purpose of the lodge was for relaxation, spiritual enlightenment and to pleasure the senses, it served its purpose well. It was an ideal and much-needed retreat for any burdened Ki and his or her senior counsellors.

It was to this place that Linnayen retreated some three months later, once the peace negotiations with Earth had been adjourned and she had won over all the planetary delegations to the royal marriage proposal. She felt completely drained and in need of a break. Statecraft, though often inspiring and fulfilling, was also extremely hard work, both on the mind and the body. It was good to get away, if only for a few weeks, and although she hoped she would not have to, she could always work from here if necessary. Sen-Cadal'baran had had the foresight to build into the lodge complex a fully equipped state office, with links and communications to all parts of the Union.

She was floating in the atrium pool, her mind drifting freely, when the lodge manager, Sen-Kilas'ab, came to tell her that Sen-Beoraan had arrived. Linnayen had been expecting him the day before with news of Captain Navarr's briefing. The young officer had been undergoing training in diplomacy over the last two months as well as some intensive Earthan history, geography and sociology instruction with a top professor from the University of Genkarah. She was both relieved that Beoraan had arrived safely and annoyed that he was late. But no matter, he was here now and she was eager to hear his news. She asked Sen-Kilas'ab to show him through to her straightaway.

It was as she stepped from the pool, her bathing tunic of pink muslin clinging to her wet body and squeezing the water from her long black hair, that Beoraan entered the atrium. But he was not alone. Behind him stood a man – a strikingly handsome man – and, at the sight of him, Linnayen froze. Her heart seemed to stop and her breath cease. Though only a few seconds passed, she felt as though minutes had sped by. Her eyes were wide and unblinking as they locked with his. Suddenly, aware of her situation, she regained her composure. She felt her chest heave as air rushed back into her lungs. She was finally able to speak again and she turned her gaze to Beoraan's smiling face.

'Welcome, Beoraan! It is good to see you. And who is this you have brought with you?'

'Forgive me, my lady. I should have warned you that I was bringing a visitor. This is your envoy on the Earth mission, Captain Durroc Navarr.'

Beoraan stood aside in order to let Navarr step forward. Linnayen took in his features. Short, sun-blond hair topped his broad forehead. His ice-blue eyes were as clear as the pool's watery depths, though narrowed as he squinted in the brightness of the atrium's light. She noticed that there were creases at their corners where the sun had darkened his skin, leaving whiter cracks deeper down. His nose was straight, of medium length and its tip was angular, but not sharp. Lastly, there was his mouth. It was wide and his lips were full and one corner of his mouth curved in a brief smile, as though he had sensed her discomfiture and was enjoying it.

He bowed to her, but protocol forbad him to speak unless spoken to. Thus, he was forced to stand while she took the measure of him.

'So, Captain Navarr, I hope you are well and have had a pleasant journey?' she enquired. She moved across to a chair at the side of the pool to retrieve her wrap, acutely aware that the wet cloth was displaying her body's curves, although thankfully not its detail.

'Thank you, my lady. I am very well and our journey was excellent,' he replied.

His voice was strong and deep, his manner was courteous and confident, and she could not help but notice that he was taking in her appearance. He hid it well, but there was no doubt that he was studying her under his long lashes. She wondered if he liked what he saw.

'I was not expecting you, Captain Navarr. But you are, of course, most welcome,' she said with a formality intended to hide her embarrassment. She knew that she needed to stamp her authority on this man as soon as possible and she certainly did not want him getting any ideas above his station.

'Oh, my lady,' cut in Beoraan. 'I am so sorry. I should have explained. The captain joined me for the journey only. He had leave due to him and was coming to Hutho to visit his sister. I asked him to postpone his family visit for a couple of days in order to let you meet him and, if you wish, brief him personally.'

'Of course,' Linnayen replied. 'But rather than brief *him*, I am more interested in what Captain Navarr has learned over the last couple of months. May I ask you some questions, captain?'

'Of course, my lady,' he responded. 'I would be honoured to answer them and I thank you for sparing me some time.'

'There is no need to thank me, captain.' Her tone contained a hint of warning. In strictest formality, she continued. 'Finding out what you know and making sure that you will speak properly for Altan and the Union when the time comes is part of my duty.'

Navarr bowed his head in deference to her. 'Of course, my lady. I meant no impertinence,' he said. 'Only I know that you are here on Hutho to take a short break from your duties and I do not wish to intrude on your leisure time.'

'If the success of your mission secures a permanent peace between the Union and Earth, it will hardly be an intrusion.'

'Indeed, my lady, and I vow that I will do my utmost to succeed. I am very aware of how much is at stake,' he said earnestly.

'Are you?' Her thoughts swiftly flew to a memory of her father. She still missed him, missed his good counsel and his friendship. But she could not allow herself the luxury of drifting at that moment. There was work to be done. 'Yes, Captain Navarr. I am sure that the importance of your mission has been impressed upon you. However, you would be a strange man if you did not still have questions about what lies ahead. Come to my rooms this afternoon and I shall do what I can to answer them.'

To Beoraan, who knew her so well, it was obvious that this was the end of the interview and no further words need be said. But Navarr had no such advantage and, as he dipped his head, he made the mistake of speaking once more, just as Linnayen had turned to walk away.

'And should Sen-Beoraan accompany me?'

She stopped in her tracks and turned her head to send him a withering look. 'If I had wanted Beoraan to be there I would have said so.' Her voice was ice cold. She spun on her heel and promptly walked away.

Navarr knew in that moment that this was no pampered princess, no insubstantial figurehead. He would be dealing with a forceful leader, someone spirited and intelligent. But still, she was a woman and that fact would make all the difference. He smiled inwardly as he left with Beoraan to prepare for his next encounter with the beautiful Ki.

Durroc Navarr had come a long way from the alleys of Silbaraz-Re, the largest city on Altan. He was twenty-nine years old and even he was amazed that he had got this far. There was a time – most of his childhood, in fact – when he would not have gambled on making it alive to adolescence, a circumstance due largely to poverty and the things his mother had had to do to keep he and his sister, Balisel, alive.

Merani Lanil, Durroc's mother, had not deserved her fate. She had been delivered to her parents nine months to the day after her mother's egg had been fused with her father's sperm. For forty weeks, she had been grown in an artificial womb in Birth Centre 74 until the day came when her parents got the call to come in and collect her. Like most new parents, the Lanils were thrilled to have a new baby. Merani grew strong and happy. But when she was six years old, her father lost his job at the gesallica processing plant. He had never been a particularly enthusiastic or ambitious worker and his poor references, combined with a self-pitying and aggressive attitude, made it hard for him to get another job paying the same salary. An ensuing string of temporary jobs led him into depression and life in the Lanil household became increasingly tense. Merani's mother tried to be encouraging and brought in a little money to meet the family's bills. But her father escaped with the drug derantel and began to pass his days in a stupefied haze.

One afternoon shortly after her seventh birthday, Merani came home and found her father stretched out on a low couch, seemingly asleep. Ignoring him, she made herself a snack and returned to the room to do some drawings, unaware that her father was watching her. She could never quite remember how it happened that first time. Durroc guessed that she must have blanked it out. But Merani never drew again.

It took her mother a year or so to realise what had been going on; Merani's father was a manipulative man who covered his tracks well. Her mother thought about leaving him but by then he had regained his confidence and got a good job. They were prosperous again. This and the thought that it was good to have someone else to divert his voracious attentions away from her made it easy for her mother to ignore the horror that was being inflicted upon her child.

One day when she was fourteen, in a biology class Merani read about the toxic properties of the little known hitarr palm. The powerful hitarr toxin had the effect of halting muscle movement but was effective for only an hour or so, more than long enough to stop the muscles around the heart from contracting. She decided to poison her parents. Her mother deserved to die, too, thought Merani. In her view, they were both as evil as each other.

There were some samples of the palm in the city's botanic gardens. So one afternoon when she was supposed to be revising, she went to the gardens instead and, when she was sure no one was looking, swiftly pinched out a single leaf of the deadly plant. It was a simple job to clone the leaf in the school laboratory and a mere two months later she had a propagated a healthy specimen.

Merani waited until the middle of the night, when her parents were fast asleep, before tiptoeing into their room with a small pressurised canister that she had made for her science project. Inside was a distilled concoction of hitarr gas that she expected would do the trick; it was her own unique recipe and she sincerely hoped that she had made it strong enough. The breathing apparatus and tank of air she wore protected her from inhaling the deadly gas as it hissed out of the canister directly above her parents' faces. She stood and watched them as they died. Two pairs of eyes flew open as their bodies seized. Her father locked a stunned accusatory gaze on her while a single tear trickled from her mother's right eye. Merani marvelled at how cool and calm she felt observing them and, for the first time in six years, she laughed – *really* laughed.

With money she stole from her parents she bought a pretty new face and identity – Navarr – from a reassigner in distant Silbaraz-Re, who asked no questions and worked only for cash. She heard the tragic death of her parents reported on the news and the police's fears for the missing fourteen-year-old child. Despite a month-long search, the girl had disappeared off the face of the planet. The investigation had remained open for many years but it was never solved, and in the meantime, Merani tried to earn a living as best she could.

Not having finished school, and with her parents' money having run out, she turned to the one thing she knew how to do. She was surprised at how calm and detached she could be and how eager her clients were to experience actual physical sex rather than visit a stimulator. The life of a love-maiden suited her. She made good money, worked hours to suit herself and had a smart if small apartment in a nice part of the city.

There came a time, though, when her looks started to fade and getting work proved more difficult. As the years went by and, with her client numbers dropping, she began to fall behind with the payments on the apartment. To add to her troubles, she became sick. Her head pounded, her joints ached and, worst of all, she vomited every few hours. After a month or so, she began to feel a little better and put on some weight. But she soon realised that she had become pregnant and cursed herself for not noticing it sooner. So few women these days undertook their own pregnancy, she had been unfamiliar with the signs, and now the pregnancy was too advanced for the foetus to be removed safely.

By the time she went into labour – three weeks prematurely – she was sleeping in a five keks a night women's hostel in the ancient quarter of the city, where she was delivered of healthy twins, a boy and a girl. She named them Durroc and Balisel.

Men came and went over the months and years. Some stayed for a day or two, some longer. One or two hit Merani and there were often fights. Then some days little Durroc and Balisel would try to shake their mother awake from whatever drug- or drink-induced stupor she was in.

It was inevitable that the twins would grow up to fend for themselves – it was all they knew how to do – and their angelic faces were masks that served to hide their growing inhumanity and immorality. They fought and clawed their way through life, begging, stealing and kicking to get what they needed. The backstreets and alleys were not so much their playground as their territory and the pickings were usually good.

Then a strange and uncalled for salvation came in the form of a police detective named Andranusi who, in the course of reviewing unsolved cases, came across the Lanil case. Convinced it was murder, he felt that the key was the missing daughter and set about finding her. It took him many months before a journal belonging to a dead facial reassigner gave him his first clue.

Andranusi followed the trail assiduously and it led him to Merani and the twins, now ten years old. It did not take many questions before the drug-hazed Merani told him the whole story and, although he was sympathetic, there was no statute of limitation on murder. Merani was arrested and removed to the Sheng women's prison, there to enjoy, finally, and for the rest of her life, a comfortable bed and three meals a day. The twins were taken to the Silbaraz-Re children's centre and their care and education became the responsibility of the city authorities. No more could they run riot or get what they wanted by bullying and intimidation. The new regime involved proper schooling and discipline imposed by severe, sour-faced teachers. Not that the twins brought out the best in people. Their belligerence was well entrenched and their apathetic behaviour to everyone save each other was enough to try the patience of a saint. Even so, as the years passed, something must have got through. Their teachers noticed a softening in their demeanours and they began to be well behaved. Durroc especially seemed to thrive in this new environment once he had learned to read, and overall their teachers were pleased with their progress.

When they were sixteen years old, the principal felt that they were ready to move on and called them in to talk about their respective futures. When asked what she would like to do, the forthright Balisel was clear – commercial college. She wanted to learn how to make money, lots of it. Durroc smiled at the memory of the principal's face. The old man was almost frightened at her determination. His beautiful blonde sister, eyes as icily blue as his own, made her demands quite clear, leaving little doubt that she would be capable of turning ruthlessness into an art form.

As for Durroc, he wanted to carry on studying and, rather fortuitously, he had done well enough in his exams to win a scholarship. The principal suggested pursuing an academic path but Durroc had determined on military college; he felt it would be a perfect outlet for his inner aggression and an excellent training ground upon which he could hone the skills he had acquired during his early childhood. These methods had always got him what he wanted and nothing he had learned since had disproved their efficacy. He did not mention these reasons to the old principal, who was surprised at his choice but happy enough to put him forward. It would, he thought, be somewhat of a relief to be rid of the Navarr twins, for there was something a little cold and unsavoury about them. Despite their intelligence and near perfect manners, it was hard to warm to them.

Before they set off for their respective futures, Durroc and Balisel visited their mother in Sheng prison one last time. Merani had mellowed over the years in jail, but she had never warmed. She could no more give her children the love they had once needed than she could have forgiven her parents for their betrayal. Her final words were engraved on their memories as they left.

'Get out of here. I don't want you … Never did. Leave me alone.'

They smiled ironically at each other. It was as they expected. No one cared about the Navarrs. No one ever had. They had only each other and it would always be that way. Their loyalty to each other, their loneliness and their oneness was an unbreakable bond.

Durroc was looking forward to seeing Balisel again before he set off for Earth. In the twelve years since they had left the children's centre, she had excelled in her chosen profession, taking higher degrees in business management two years ahead of all the other students. She had been headhunted by the Altan Ministry of Interplanetary Trade just prior to her final examination and had risen through the ranks to junior ministerial level at the age of only twenty-four. Then she received an offer she could not refuse: third vice-president in charge of finance of the Huthon company Gunashey Kuth and Dor, the single largest manufacturer of cosmonic bioengineering systems in the Union and its tenth largest company overall. Balisel had no other interest but her work. Romance played no part in her life – she had no time for it as she was too busy making money.

By the time of Durroc's visit to Huthon, Balisel Navarr was a multimillionaire with a personal wealth estimated at 37 billion keks. She had risen to become the financial controller of GKD, owning some twelve percent of its shares, and was listed in the 3328 edition of the Commercial Directory's Top 100 Most Powerful People. It made him smile inside to think that his sister shared a place on that list with Ki-Linnayen Genara, one coming from a gutter and the other from a palace.

He pictured Linnayen again, seeing her body outlined as she had stood by the pool. Her curves were quite delicious and he felt a small surge of pleasure in his loins at the memory of her nipples outlined through the cloth. She was a beautiful woman but still had the look of a girl. He had always liked his women youthful. But they did not have to be particularly eager – he could always make them want him, eventually.

This one will be no different.

He was smart enough to realise that the Ki was the ultimate prize that would guarantee his future. He did not want to just take her and move on. Acquiring her would mean that he would be set for life. He laughed at the thought that the Navarr twins, born and raised in hell, were well on their way to a heavenly future.

Linnayen was just finishing an entry in her journal when Sen-Kilas'ab tapped on her door to tell her that Captain Navarr was waiting outside. She was pleased to see that he was punctual and hoped that his skills as a diplomat would be equally impressive. She thanked the Sen and asked him to show Navarr in.

Although she had her back to the door, she knew the minute he walked into the room. Surely his eyes were on her? When she turned, however, his head was downcast and he stood with his hands clasped loosely in front of him.

'Thank you for coming, Captain Navarr,' she began. 'Please take a seat and make yourself comfortable.' She gestured to two armchairs across the room on her left.

'Thank you, my lady,' he said, and walked unhurriedly to the first of them. She could not help but notice that he looked very smart in his uniform. The severity of the tunic enhanced his muscular body and the dark blue colour contrasted well with his close-cut blond hair and slightly bronzed skin. Her cheeks flushed as she suddenly realised that this was the first time in her life that she had been so physically attracted to anyone.

She sat down in the other armchair, facing him. 'Captain, I would like to ask you about your preparation for the mission to Earth. You have now finished your induction, I understand?' Her tone was measured and formal, a useful trick in hiding the confusion she felt inside.

'That's right, my lady,' he replied. 'As you know, I had already been studying Earthan history, society and customs over the last two years and I am well informed on these matters. The bulk of my briefing has concentrated on people, personalities and recent political changes.' He looked directly at her as he spoke, never breaking eye contact.

'And Ambassador Byers and the Earthan delegates have been helpful in this?'

'Very much so, my lady,' he answered enthusiastically. 'Indeed, I could not have hoped for more cooperation.'

'It seems, then, that they have become a little more accepting of the proposed marriage solution. Perhaps your personal enthusiasm has helped to convince them?'

His smile in return was quite disarming. 'Oh, I wouldn't think so. But most people like to talk about themselves, don't they? Maybe it was more to do with that.'

'If what you say is true,' she countered, 'then you won't mind telling me about yourself. I want to know the person to whom I have entrusted my peace mission… *and* my future. What is your story, Captain Navarr?'

He had not expected this. He had prepared a review of his briefing and what issues had been covered. He had not planned to speak about himself, and the fact that he did not know what Linnayen had already been told about him made him uncomfortable.

'Well, it's not much of a story, my lady. I fear you would be bored,' he replied.

'I'll be the judge of that,' she answered rather firmly. 'Begin, please.' Even though it contained a request, there was no doubt that this was a direct command. Navarr had no choice.

'Well, I have a sister, as you know. We're twins. We were orphaned, you might say, when we were ten. Our mother was taken into an institution.'

Linnayen interrupted, a puzzled look on her face. 'I thought she was taken to prison?'

She had obviously been briefed more fully than he thought and Navarr was faced with the discomfiting prospect of telling her everything – well, nearly everything – about himself.

As he spoke, Linnayen listened intently, both crosschecking his words with what she already knew and to discern the manner of the man. He had had such an appalling past. It was a wonder that he had come through such disadvantage to shine so brilliantly at military college. And his sister had done so well too. He spoke of himself and his background succinctly and with little emotion. But Linnayen could not work out if this was due to his feeling nothing or because of his self-deprecation. Yet he did not strike her as a humble sort of person.

'You appear to have overcome much adversity, Captain Navarr,' she commented. 'These experiences must have left their mark on you. What scars would you say you have?'

Though her question was meant to be probing, by now Navarr was well in control. He smiled again. 'No scars, my lady, just memories. And you're right, they are not all happy ones. But if I have learned anything from my experiences it is to appreciate how lucky I am now to be doing what I love best.'

'And you wouldn't want to jeopardise all that, would you?' she finished for him, but it was a rhetorical question. 'What about your sister? You must be proud of her.'

She expected that he would have smiled at this question too, however his expression was blank and she could not help speculating that there was a hint of defensiveness in his response.

'Balisel has worked hard to get where she is. She is very clever, and she loves her work.'

Linnayen noticed that he had not quite answered her question – a useful trait in a diplomat but it was not what she wanted now. She needed his complete honesty. She needed openness, not this hedging around the question.

'That's not what I asked, Captain Navarr. I asked if you were proud of her.' Her tone was frosty, leaving him in no doubt that she had seen through his doubletalk and was the measure of him. He would have to be more careful, he resolved. *This one will need delicate handling.*

'I apologise, my lady.' He appeared contrite, but his next words still did not leave Linnayen feeling that she had scored the point. 'Yes, I am very proud of her, as she is of me. And I am looking forward to catching up with her before I leave for Earth.'

'Ah yes, your mission. Let us return to that,' she said, and proceeded to ask him for a full briefing on the current political issues.

Navarr was on home ground now and, as he talked, he showed how well he knew his subject.

'As you know, my lady, Earth is a planet made up of many disparate nations and races and, although its people have different appearances, they are in effect the same species. These physical and cultural differences and the amounts and nature of the resources each nation holds has led to the planet having a history of internecine war and racial or religious aggression. It has only been in the last couple of hundred years that Earth has united under the banner of a single governing body, the Council of United Democratic Nations. But, even here, tensions often run high as many national representatives seek to further their countries' status.'

Linnayen knew all of this already but allowed the man to continue so that she would have more time to make her assessment of him. She had to confess also to rather enjoying the sound of his voice. It was smooth and strong and easy to listen to.

'At present, the council is led by Sheikh David Bashir al Fahrazad. Bashir is violently opposed to the Union, mistrusting our motives and believing that our ultimate aim is domination. He maintains, and I quote, that they "will not have peace at any price". There is, though, significant opposition to Bashir's stand, coming mainly from the countries on the American and Asian continents. Their people comprise the majority of the troops in the Earth Combined Forces and, after all these years, they desperately want an end to the war. They also want peace so that they can start to trade.'

'If these nations are so powerful within the council, why is their call for peace not being heard?' Linnayen asked. Again, she had knowledge of the situation but wanted to hear Navarr's version of it.

'There is a hard core of opposition, led by Bashir among others, which speaks for the religions of Earth. The main religions – although not the only ones – are Islam, Catholicism, Judaism and Hinduism. The four have formed an alliance, which is odd considering their traditional hostility to each other. The main aim is self-preservation against what they see as a common foe. Between them, they control the hearts and minds of billions of Earthans, including those in positions of great power and with great wealth. Their argument is fundamentally that the cultures and customs of the Union's member planets are too alien, and they prey on peoples' concerns that their own ways would be swamped by our new ideas. They are, of course, using the fear of change strategy to keep their power base.'

Navarr knew his subject all right, but Linnayen was still unsure of his character and decided in that moment to take a little more time with him. She felt she needed to know this man as much as it was possible before turning him loose on the forthcoming delicate negotiations. But not right now. The time had flown while they had talked and she reminded herself that she was here to relax.

'Thank you for your insights, Captain Navarr. The time is late and I have kept you too long already,' she said, sounding solicitous. 'We shall resume this discussion tomorrow morning. You and Sen-Beoraan shall join me on a short river trip. Good afternoon.'

Navarr had learned enough by now to know that he had been dismissed and he got up out of the chair. As he stood, he looked down and for an instant Linnayen felt his ice-blue eyes upon her, almost like a caress on her skin. She felt a sudden rush of warmth in her cheeks and cursed herself for blushing. Navarr gave no sign that he had witnessed her discomfort.

Bowing, he said, 'Good afternoon, my lady. I look forward to tomorrow.' With that he walked across the room and Linnayen would have been mortified to see the knowing smile on his lips.

Navarr knew he had to go slowly. If he rushed, he could lose her – lose everything – and he would only have one chance at this. He explained all this to Balisel that night on the secure vidlink. Not that he needed to say much. Balisel knew what he meant and knew that the stakes were high. She and her brother would have plenty of time to see each other in the future, once he was established in the forum – and he would be. With the Ki's help, if not with her knowledge, it was just a matter of time. And then the Navarrs would be a force to be reckoned with.

I met Captain Navarr today. He is the man
whom Beoraan has chosen to be my envoy in the
negotiations on Earth. I have to say that I do not
yet know what to make of him. He is handsome

and hugely self-confident. I found him intelligent. But I did not feel at ease with him. I felt that he was hiding something. Of course, I did not dare to probe him. I trust that Beoraan has chosen well, but I have my doubts about this man.

We are entrusting him with one of the most important missions in our history and yet what do we really know of him?

I can't help but wonder if I am doing the right thing – not about the marriage. That is the way forward, I have no doubt. But perhaps I should send Beoraan to Earth instead?

Chapter Seven

The next morning saw a thick yellow-green mist hanging over the meadow surrounding the lodge. The air was heavy with moisture and still cold. It did not look good for the river trip Linnayen had planned. But, as Sen-Kilas'ab and his staff hurried about the business of preparing food and equipment to load onto the boat, it was obvious that the weather would not be halting her plans.

Navarr watched the servants scurrying around in the central atrium from where he stood on the small balcony of his room and inwardly sneered at the scene below. *Privilege! All these people, fetching and carrying and kowtowing to a spoilt 22-year-old brat, just because she had the good fortune to be born into a rich family.* It would not be like that, he thought, when he was running things. Navarr would ensure that people would be rewarded for their achievements and their skills – not their birthright. Privileges needed to be earned, like he and his sister had earned them, through hard work and dedication.

He snapped his attention back to dressing himself. The river outing was going to be an informal occasion so he did not need to wear his uniform, but he wanted to look smart enough to impress the young Ki. He had picked up the signals. She was nibbling at the bait. But he knew he had a long way to go before he had her hooked.

Navarr chose a white shirt with loose sleeves tucked into an old but still smart pair of tan breeches; these, he felt, outlined his muscular legs. He covered the shirt with a longer ivory waistcoat. The neutral tones all served to highlight his lightly tanned skin and blond hair and he knew he looked good.

Suddenly, the sounds from below got louder and he stepped briskly to the balcony to see what the fuss was about. Linnayen had arrived and she appeared to be running through a checklist with Sen-Kilas'ab. As he watched, unseen, Navarr noticed that she was, like him, dressed in tight-fitting leggings and sporting a pale green tunic over the top. It was a shame that the tunic hid her breasts, but at least the leggings showed off her long legs to perfection.

She was nodding her head and then, hands on her hips, was looking around as though searching for something. She said something to Sen-Kilas'ab, which he could not quite make out, and instantly the manager barked an order to one of the servants. This was loud enough for him to hear and, grabbing his boots from the foot of the bed, he made a dash for the door in order to be downstairs before the servant reached him. It wouldn't do any harm though to let her think she had put him at a disadvantage.

As he rushed into the atrium, boots in hand, Linnayen's look of astonishment turned to a small smile. *So, the perfect captain can be caught off-guard.* She was pleased with herself that she had thought to bring the trip forward by fifteen minutes. It was somehow reassuring to know that the exemplary and efficient captain was just as fallible as anyone else.

'Good morning, Captain Navarr,' she called across to him. 'I'm glad to see you are ready. Come along.' With that she turned on her heel, giving him no opportunity to reply, and walked quickly towards the outer doors of the lodge. Sen-Kilas'ab and a small retinue of servants followed behind. Navarr was forced to bring up the rear as he had to stop and put his boots on.

By the time she got to the landing stage where Beoraan was already waiting, Navarr had caught up.

'A very good morning to you, my lady, and to you, Captain Navarr!' Beoraan was in a good mood. He had slept well last night and had enjoyed waking up to the gentle sounds of birdsong rather than the urban hum of Genkarah.

Linnayen smiled back at the old man. 'Morning, Beoraan. It's going to be a good day.' She, too, was in a good mood, but for different reasons. Linnayen was looking forward to the little tests and challenges she would be putting the clever captain through today and was especially pleased that he knew nothing about them. She had made Beoraan swear to say nothing.

'I'm not so sure, my lady,' the old counsellor replied. 'This mist is very thick.'

'It'll lift. Don't you think so, Captain Navarr?'

'If *you* say it will, my lady, then I have every faith it will be so,' he quipped back, a half smile on his lips. He was teasing her and not many people dared to do that. Linnayen enjoyed the jest and laughed out loud.

'Come. Let's get going.' She stepped aboard the sleek cruiser that was to be their transport today and was met by the boat master who showed her to the upper cabin. This was a sumptuous room decorated in swathes of brightly coloured fabrics and padded sofas surrounding a central low table. The front and side walls comprised panels that appeared to be completely open to the elements but were, in fact, shield walls. They both protected and contained the space, allowing in only the sounds of the river.

Once Linnayen and her party had been escorted to the cabin, the boat master and his staff left them to enjoy the scenery, although there was little yet to see through the fog. A simple breakfast had been placed on the central table. Linnayen sat on a sofa covered with a brightly woven tapestry throw and invited Beoraan and Navarr to join her.

'This looks delicious,' she exclaimed, her eyes taking in the array of Huthon fruits and pastries spread before them. 'I take it that you have not had breakfast yet, captain?'

He was aware that this was a reference to his earlier tardiness. 'No, indeed, my lady. But I'm rather glad of that now, seeing all this,' he said in reference to the food.

'Well then, you'd better eat,' she retorted, a little annoyed that he seemed to have bettered her. Linnayen did not join in; she had breakfasted in her room an hour earlier. Instead she used this opportunity to talk to the two men who would be so instrumental to her future.

'Before we get to our destination today, I wanted to discuss my expectations for this mission,' she began. 'Firstly, and most importantly of all, I expect you to select no less than three appropriate candidates for the marriage. As you know, they are to be men of high rank and influence, but not necessarily of noble birth. Their standing, their popularity and their influence in the global community are the most important factors. They need to be able to command respect and sway opinions, but not necessarily form them for themselves.'

Navarr was puzzled. It sounded as though the Ki was only interested in a figurehead for a husband.

She continued. 'My future husband's age and appearance are quite irrelevant. However, I feel it is important that he should be in good health and have a strong genetic record, in case the need falls upon us to produce heirs.' Her tone was matter-of-fact and her delivery of these words was formal. Beoraan knew her well enough to know that she had selected every word well in advance and knew exactly how she would be saying them – for Navarr's benefit.

'May I ask something, my lady?' Navarr interjected. She nodded her consent. 'Would you not, though, as a woman, prefer that we selected candidates who were, at least, of a similar age and perhaps of pleasing appearance?'

Linnayen glared back at him, then tried to cover her irritation. 'Captain Navarr, whilst I appreciate your sentiments, may I remind you that my female sensitivities are *not* your consideration. I have outlined my main criteria. Have you made any progress in identifying suitable candidates?' Although the question was aimed at both of them, Beoraan thought he had better be the one to answer.

'Yes, my lady, we have. The list now stands at six,' he responded, conscious of the need to mollify the young Ki. 'I have prepared background notes on all of them for your consideration, but I have to say that there are three that really stand out.'

Linnayen asked him to describe them and she listened in silence while Beoraan continued, with only occasional additional comments from Navarr.

'Firstly, there is Louis Charles Lombard, a 44-year-old self-made businessman and, almost certainly, one of the five richest men on Earth. He has a reputation as something of a lady's man, though how he finds the time …' Beoraan shook his head, recalling the list of mistresses he had seen the night before. 'He has made his money buying older, under-resourced companies, revitalising them and then selling them off for large profits. He invests these in huge amounts of land and property and is said to be Earth's largest landlord. At any one time, it is estimated that he owns or controls around twenty percent of the net worth of all commercial enterprises on the planet.'

Navarr added, 'His vast wealth also buys him access to the top political leaders. Thus, he is a man of great influence. As to his popularity, I expect to investigate this once I am on Earth.'

Beoraan nodded his appreciation of Navarr's comments and, turning to look at Linnayen once more, went on.

'Next is James Toyotomi, the 26-year-old son and heir of an ancient noble family of the ancient country known as Japan. The Toyotomis have a distinguished history, having been one of the ruling families in both the second and third millennia. Again, wealth plays its part here as the family has a large fortune. However, of greater importance is the fact that Toyotomi's great-grandmother is one of the loudest voices for peace in the UDN Council. The old lady, Kumiko, would most likely be happy to see her great-grandson married off in the cause of peace. For his part, the young James is a doctor of medicine and has built a reputation as an eminent research scientist.'

'He sounds very clever, Beoraan,' Linnayen interrupted.

'Quite so, and his dedication to his work has helped him to become very popular – both in the community and within his profession,' Beoraan replied.

'Last but not least is the 24-year-old Kevor Jax Bashir, son of Sheikh David and Lady Thea Bashir al Fahrazad. As you know, my lady, Sheikh Bashir is the president of the UDN Council and our opponent. Kevor Jax is his only son and he is grooming him to step into his shoes.' Beoraan continued, 'The young man is known as plain Jax by both the media and his family and he's currently studying at the UDN's Diplomatic Corps. He was previously at the military science academy where he was trained as a fighter pilot and, we are given to understand, a rather good one. Yes, the family is wealthy, but two factors are almost more important here. Firstly, he is the son of one of our most outspoken opponents, and secondly, his youth points towards his naivety in the ways of statecraft. One suspects that he would be easy to work with.' Beoraan finished his summation and Linnayen looked across to Navarr.

'Do you have anything to add, captain?' she asked.

'Only that this Jax, like the Toyotomi candidate, is popular with the public.' Here, Navarr paused and looked almost apologetically at Linnayen. 'But frankly, my lady, our chances of persuading the sheikh to part with his only son are just about impossible.'

'Only "just about", captain?' Linnayen smiled slightly, raising one eyebrow. 'But what a coup to win over the son of our enemy. If we could demonstrate that two such opposing entities can be brought together in the spirit of peace, think how significant that would be in keeping it.'

'You're right, my lady,' cut in Beoraan. 'That would be quite an achievement. But in the face of the sheikh's opposition, Navarr would have his work cut out for him.'

'Nothing our capable captain can't handle, I'm sure.' Linnayen was being both mischievous and challenging.

'Quite so, my lady,' Navarr said. 'Whichever candidate you finally select, I will pursue him with the utmost vigour.' He bowed his head in acknowledgement of her authority.

They were interrupted by a knock on the cabin door and the boat master announced that they had arrived at their destination.

'Thank you, master,' said Linnayen, and she stood to smooth the creases in her tunic. 'Come along then.' She said this to Navarr, ignoring Beoraan who, feeling the rumble in his stomach, had reached across to the spread of foods. Navarr sprang up and Linnayen enjoyed the look on consternation on his face. He had no idea, of course, what was about to happen. *Did he honestly think this was going to be just a boating trip?* She secretly smiled.

'We need to get kitted out down below, captain.' With this she strode across to the door and left the cabin. Navarr followed quickly after her, wondering what in the name of heavens was going on. He joined her below in a smaller room that was lined with all manner of tackle and equipment.

'I hope you enjoy rapid riding, captain?' she barked over her shoulder to him. 'Have you ever done it?'

'Yes, I have, my lady. But, sadly, only on a couple of occasions,' he replied.

'Ah, so you liked it then?' Her question was rhetorical and she continued. 'Good! Because I think you'll enjoy our sport today, in that case.'

As she spoke, servants began fitting them protective wetsuits to go over their clothes plus boots and a variety of belts, straps and clasps. They also brought helmets fitted with face shields and communicators. The final piece of equipment handed to them as they prepared to leave the cabin was a pair of thickly padded gloves, each possessing a corrugated lining on the palm to improve grip.

'This seems rather excessive, my lady,' Navarr ventured to comment. 'So much equipment for a rafting trip?' He also thought that it was rather a shame to cover the Ki's delightfully lithe body in an ugly wetsuit.

Linnayen turned and, with a deadpan expression, said, 'Oh, that's only the first part of the trip.' She was about to say nothing more, then changed her mind.

'After three klix we'll come to the Gutokoroc Falls. Perhaps you've heard of them?'

He certainly had. The Gutokoroc sequence was a series of four waterfalls on the Utieku River, each one a sheer drop and increasing in height as the raging waters fell over two thousand metres from the high plateau to the forested lowlands of the Hutoriaku Plains.

'And? When we get to the falls?' he asked, his voice sounding just a little concerned.

'That's where the fun comes in. We're going over them.' Linnayen could not resist laughing out loud at the look of horror on Navarr's handsome face.

'Please tell me you are joking!'

'Oh, come on, Navarr. Don't tell me you've never done any gliding?' Linnayen continued to explain as they waited for the flexi-raft to be lowered into the river waters below the cruiser. 'Well, this is fall-flying. We raft to the edge of the falls – the first fall, that is. Then, on my signal, we jump and dive down the falls. When you're about halfway down, squeeze the fingertip panels in your gauntlets and your pressure shield will kick in. This will slow you sufficiently and allow you to steer yourself back to the raft using the flaps in your wetsuit and your paddle. The idea is to touch down on the raft and continue the journey.'

Navarr sucked in his breath and raised his eyebrows, his earlier look of alarm being replaced by one of admiration. 'And you do this to *relax*, my lady?'

Linnayen smiled and said, 'Not to relax. But I can't think about affairs of state when I'm fall-flying. I find it's a useful exercise in focusing the mind.'

'I can believe that!' Navarr replied. 'And have you been doing it for long?'

'Since I was sixteen. My sister taught me. She's *very* good at it. I've never seen her miss the raft.'

The raft was now ready and, despite his apprehension at what lay ahead, Navarr could not help feeling excited – and more than a little surprised at the young Ki. He had not marked her down as a daredevil.

The early morning mist had now mostly burned off with the warmth of the day, and a pale green-gold sky could be seen. They paddled one klik downstream when they came to the first rapid. It was about two hundred metres long and an almost perfectly symmetrical S shape, enclosed by towering granite columns that the raging waters had carved over many eons. All the while, Linnayen, who sat in the stern using her paddle as the rudder, barked out commands to Navarr. Over the length of the rapid they had dropped a vertical height of fifty metres, which was quite enough to give them a stirring ride and get their adrenalin pumping.

Their bodies were by now in tune with the twisting-turning movement and had loosened up. They entered the next rapid, which was only half a klik ahead. This time the river shot through a long, steep stretch that was dotted with dangerously jagged rock outcrops. Linnayen dug the paddle hard into the gushing water to turn the raft first this way then that in order to get them safely past each rock pillar. As the solid banks of the river channel narrowed at the far end of the rapid, the overall effect was of relentlessly mounting volume and velocity and, sure enough, the raft shot out of the end of the gorge at twice the speed it had entered.

Navarr let out a loud cry of excitement as they left the rapid and Linnayen raised a bemused eyebrow at his obvious enjoyment.

'That was terrific!' he called back to her, a wide grin lighting up his face.

'Not bad, eh?' she cried back.

For the final stretch before the first of the Gutokoroc falls, the water slowed and the noise lessened and they enjoyed the sudden calm in silence. But only a few minutes later they heard the first sounds of the water's roar.

'We're approaching the falls, captain. This is our last chance to turn back. Are you ready to do this?' Linnayen felt she should offer him the opportunity to pull out at this stage. Although he was not aware of it, even if he had chosen to not continue, it would not necessarily mean he had failed her test.

He looked back at her unsmiling face and, matching her expression, he replied, 'We've come this far, my lady, and I've never been one for turning back.'

'Good. In that case, let me explain what you need to do once more.' She recapped the procedure, calmly back-paddling as she talked to give them a little more time before the drop came.

'And don't forget,' she concluded, 'your pressure shield will only slow your descent, not stop it. It will protect you from any impact with a solid object, but not the water. As soon as you land it will switch off, thus breaking your fall. So if you miss the raft, you'll get wet!'

He nodded his understanding and, once he pronounced himself ready, Linnayen steered the raft into the centre of the flow, calling out final instructions.

'Remember! Keep a tight hold of your paddle. You can use it to steer even in the air. Be ready to spring up on my command!'

Ahead, Navarr could clearly see the edge of the water as it disappeared over the precipice into nothingness. Beyond was nothing but pale sky. He tried to breathe deeply in order to focus, as Linnayen had advised him, but he could feel his nerves tingling and heart racing with anticipation. Then they were within seven or eight metres of the drop and Navarr estimated they had about six seconds to go. All too soon, the distance between the raft and the edge of the fall was down to three metres, then two, then one. He gripped the paddle and prepared to jump. Suddenly, Linnayen's voice rang out, strong and clear.

'Now!'

As the raft tumbled away over the edge of the drop, his knees uncurled and he sprang into the open air. His hands clutched the paddle, which he held up high and in front of him. He was looking straight ahead, seeing only sky. He realised that he had not exhaled since he jumped. But now that the pressure on his stomach had kicked back in, he let out the stored air in a deep rush. It was at this point that he looked down and saw the river and surrounding land rushing towards him, getting ever larger in his field of vision. He realised that he was veering a little away from the fall's plunge pool and that he needed to squeeze the pressure tips in his gloves to activate the pressure shield and slow himself down to get back on track.

He pressed his thumb and forefinger together and, instantly, his fall was slowed. As Linnayen had instructed him, he used the flaps in his wetsuit and the broad blades of the paddle to steer back towards the river, where he saw that the raft had already cleared the falls and was meandering in the calmer water downstream.

It was at this point that Linnayen dropped past him a couple of metres away. She had a wide smile on her face and was obviously enjoying herself. Navarr was horrified that she was still falling and hadn't used her pressure shield yet. She was already well below him and he was about to call out to her when, suddenly, she slowed down. He watched her steer over to the raft and land feet first in its centre. He tried to follow her line. It was not as easy as she made it look and, sure enough, as he had suspected would happen, he landed short of the raft, which danced ahead.

He could hear Linnayen's full laughter as he floated in the water, waiting for her to turn the raft and come back for him. He climbed into the raft and, although a little humiliated at his drenching, he felt very happy.

Linnayen, too, felt exhilarated. She loved this sport and was pleased that the captain had negotiated the first fall so well.

'Not bad, Captain Navarr. I hope you enjoyed it?' she asked.

Navarr smiled back at her. 'That was brilliant!'

'Good, because we've got three more to go – and each one gets bigger.' She threw back her head and laughed. Navarr, noticing her long slim neck and white teeth, had to admit that she was indeed a beautiful woman. Which would, of course, make his task so much more pleasurable.

Navarr had never experienced such a rush before. His body felt truly alive. Each drop had got longer and, even though he did not manage to land in the raft each time, he did, like Linnayen, leave it as long as possible before activating the pressure shield. He soon realised that this was what the competition was about. Skill in falling and targeting the landing were important, but the sport was in who got there first. By the third fall, he and Linnayen were landing at almost the same time, except that *she* was dry.

They had already descended over a thousand metres since they had entered the first rapid and had only the last fall to go – a heart-stopping, near vertical leap of nearly a kilometre.

Linnayen's eyes were sharply focused on the approaching line of water, a view broken only by the outline of Navarr's strong shoulders and the silhouette of his handsome face in profile. Brushing away her thoughts and trying to control the small surge of inner warmth that she felt below her stomach, she took a deep breath in through her mouth.

'Here we go again, captain. Ready?'

He looked over his shoulder to where she sat in the stern and nodded firmly. Inside her head, Linnayen counted down the seconds. Three, two, one …

'Now!' she shouted and, a split second behind Navarr, she leapt up, punching the air with gloved hands that gripped the paddle.

It was a good fall and her face broke into a broad grin as she took in the immensity of the drop below her. At this height the river looked like a thin, twisting silver ribbon draped across a swathe of dark green cloth, and the forested plains disappeared into a distant, hazy mist. Navarr was a metre ahead and she could hear his whoops of delight and excited laughter.

They were about a hundred metres away from the bottom of the falls when Linnayen noticed that the raft had just cleared the plunge pool, but it was inverted. It would still be their target and, neck and neck, they fell towards it. With only fifty metres left to go, Linnayen could take no more and pressed her fingertips together. Her body shuddered for a moment as the shield took effect and her fall slowed. But Navarr had gone beyond her, leaving it till the last thirty metres before he slowed. He also looked on course to hit the raft for the first time and Linnayen was pleased for his achievement.

She watched him land safely on the slippery underside of the raft and cheered out her encouragement.

'Well done!'

He had time enough to look up and wave back before she, too, landed. But the wet surface and the speed of her impact made her stumble forward, straight into the kneeling figure of Navarr. His arms caught her as her body crashed into his, knocking them both over and nearly tumbling them into the swirling waters. For a few moments, as they tried to get their breath back, Linnayen lay on top of Navarr, staring into his clear blue eyes, her face only inches from his. Her mouth was parted as she fought for air, as was his and, as she looked down into his eyes she could not help but wonder what his lips would feel like against hers.

Navarr was thinking much the same. The slight weight of her body on top of him and the soft yet excited look in her green eyes made the blood course through his body. One of his hands was wrapped around her, holding her firmly in the small of her back. But the other was only a fingertip away from one of her breasts.

Linnayen felt Navarr's body stir beneath her and knew she had to move – quickly. She broke away and sat in a kneeling position whilst he remained sprawled underneath her.

'Well, that was fall-flying. What did you think of it?' she said briskly, trying to cover her embarrassment.

Navarr's smile widened into a grin and his chest shook with laughter. Then he stilled himself and looked directly into her wide eyes.

'Unbelievable! I can honestly say that I have never felt anything quite so amazing before,' he answered.

But the gleam in his eyes made her wonder if he was talking about fall-flying or some other experience entirely.

Balisel Navarr's normally expressionless face flickered with a trace of happiness at the news that her brother was waiting in the foyer of GKD's new head office in central Mulakush. Her assistant, Jeremiah Danforth, had been instructed to interrupt her no matter what she was doing as soon as he arrived. Thus, all the softly spoken Earthan had to do was touch a companel on his desk and she knew that Navarr was outside.

She was in the middle of a satcom conference with the company's representatives on Autabron, which had been going for over an hour. Usually she enjoyed these conferences but this morning she had found it difficult to concentrate as her mind intermittently switched to images of her brother's handsome face. She touched the conference convenor pad on her desk, which signalled to all parties that she needed to interrupt them. Instantly, the conversations ceased and all heads on the wall screen turned towards her.

'My apologies, everyone. I have to go now.' Her announcement was cool and formal and she went on to give her last orders to the conference attendees. 'Mr Genkaar, please have the bergussian output figures for the last period ready by the time we meet again. And, Sen-Bikash, may I remind you that the report on future staffing levels in the processing core is overdue. Would you see to it, please? We will reconvene in two hours. Good morning, everyone.'

Without waiting for their farewells, she turned away from the screen, which faded to black just as the door to her office slid open. A grinning Durroc Navarr entered the room and Balisel jumped up from her desk to run to him. He caught her up and swung her around in an affectionate hug while she laughed her appreciation.

'At last!' she cried. 'I thought you'd never get here. I take it the young Ki is more charming than I've been told?'

'Sister! You know full well you're the only woman in my life – who matters, that is.' He pulled back to better see her face then lightly stroked her cheek and smiled into her eyes, exact replicas of his own. 'Oh, I've missed you. It's so good to see you.' His voice was low and husky.

'And you, little brother,' she replied fondly, referring to the fact that she was the firstborn by three minutes. 'You look well. This mission agrees with you, eh? All that responsibility …'

Balisel spoke with obvious pride. Her brother had done well to come so far.

'Seeing *you* agrees with me. I've been looking forward to this for months,' he answered.

Balisel smiled. Vidlinks were all very well, but nothing compared to the joy of being with him again. It was a twin thing, she supposed. The feel of his skin, his warm smell, the softness of his hair – all so familiar to her – made her feel complete. When

Durroc was with her, she was whole once more, as though her body had retrieved some missing part.

She stepped away from him but took his hand and pulled him after her.

'Come on, Durroc. Let's get out of here,' she said, leading him towards the terrace where her personal windshifter stood waiting. They climbed inside and Balisel spoke an instruction into a control panel. Instantly, the windshifter rose into the air and flew in a smooth, wide arc away from the GKD building towards a line of low wooded hills in the distance.

As he looked out through the vessel's clear shield walls, Navarr felt again the strangeness of this planet. The depth and quality of the green Huthon sky varied with the weather, from the very palest hues of a tropical lagoon to the crystalline richness of emerald. Today it was fresh and clear, the colour of Altani apples, and it imparted a clean brightness to the landscape below.

'This is a truly beautiful place. You must enjoy working here,' he commented.

She raised one eyebrow on her near perfect face.

'It's just a place.' She shrugged off his observations then continued, 'And the only thing beautiful about it is that it's good for making money. It's a trader's paradise!'

Navarr laughed. There was no swaying Balisel from her course. 'So is it still your ambition to be the richest woman in the Union?' he asked.

'No,' she replied, then laughed at the puzzled look on his face. 'I want to be the richest *person* – man or woman. And, my darling brother, you're going to help me achieve it.'

After only a few more minutes, the windshifter touched down at the Kushaan Canopy Park. The recreation complex set high in the tops of the trees was one of the strangest structures Navarr had ever seen. Wooden platforms extended in every direction and at a variety of levels, all interconnected by moving walkways and cylindrical tubes, some of which were horizontal and others almost vertical. Enclosed buildings and structures stood upon some of the platforms while others remained empty and open to the skies. All were partly shrouded in drooping foliage in shades of green and gold and festooned with flowers, and Navarr guessed that the whole complex must have covered a vast area. It was a small city in the trees.

It was to an apparently open platform on one of the highest levels that Balisel led him via a series of near-vertical lift tubes. Once there she stood in its centre, instructing Navarr to stand at an exact spot next to her. At a touch on a depressed panel in the floor a domed shield wall rose up and over them, and sections of the floor slid away to reveal sunken seating areas beneath. They both rose and went down a small flight of steps into the sanctuary.

There were trays filled with all manner of food and drinks set on a low table between two sofas, upon which they both took a seat.

'This is very nice,' he said, reaching across for some fruit from a tray. 'Very secluded. I take it we're quite protected here?'

'Absolutely. No one can see us or hear us, and no one knows we are here,' she replied.

'Why all the secrecy? Surely you and I are not that important?' he asked.

'Trust me, Durroc. It pays to be cautious,' she countered. 'I've learned that along the way, especially here at GKD.'

He was concerned to hear this. 'Why? Has someone tried to hurt you?'

Balisel smiled ironically. 'Little brother, no one hurts *me*. But it's not been through lack of trying. In this business, you don't trust anyone.'

'Even me?' he parried, trying to look hurt.

'Even you. Not because you'd ever harm me, of course,' she explained. 'But, because you're clueless without me. I can't trust you to keep on track. You need my guidance.'

Navarr laughed out loud. 'You think you know me. But I am totally focused on my present mission – find the perfect husband for our cherished Ki. This will involve securing a marriage agreement to some malleable but high-ranking Earthan. I will then return to Altan, make myself indispensable to the esteemed lady by successfully achieving every task she sets me – quietly, modestly. She will come to trust me, to respect my opinion. Perhaps I will even seduce her and make her my lover – she's beautiful, you know. She will come to depend on me so much that she will, ultimately, share her power with me. In effect, I will control the Union through her.'

Balisel's smile grew as he spoke. 'Very good, Durroc. You *have* come on. But you've forgotten one thing.'

'Impossible! It's consumed my thoughts for weeks. I've got it all worked out,' he replied.

'The royal marriage is intended to secure a peace between Earth and the Union. True?' she asked. Navarr nodded his confirmation. 'But peace will not bring us profits. And by "us" I don't mean my employers. There's far more money to be made while the war goes on.'

'How so?' Navarr was genuinely intrigued as to what his sister was scheming.

'Well,' she began, 'I've been making one or two investments over the last year or so – not just in Union companies but in a couple of Earthan ones too.'

'What!' he exclaimed. 'That's not possible. There's no way the Earthan authorities would allow it.'

'Oh, brother, sometimes you can be so green! Do you honestly think I would let a little thing like that stop me?' As she spoke Balisel occasionally popped small titbits of food into her mouth. 'Mmm, these careno plums are delicious. Would you like one?'

'No, thanks. You were saying? About your investments?'

'Ah, yes.' She swallowed the last morsel of plum and continued. 'You're quite right, of course. If the authorities knew I was the owner of certain shares there would be an outcry. Probably jail. However, Jeremiah – you met my able Earthan assistant – *can* buy into Earthan companies. He shouldn't be here, of course, but he's one of those conscientious objectors, absolutely opposed to the conflict, so the Union welcomed him with open arms. Through him I covertly control two organisations: one supplying advanced mili-comp systems to the UDN Combined Forces and the other providing seventy percent of the fuel for its spacefleet.'

A smile spread slowly across Navarr's face. Balisel was so focused on her goals that he knew nothing would stand in her way and he admired her for it. She was accomplished, beautiful and no one would suspect the shark inside. Sitting there, in her flowing pastel pink dress, blonde hair held loosely at the nape of her neck, she looked an ingénue, hardly capable of controlling commercial empires.

'Of course,' she went on, 'I also have shares in some Union-based operations too. So it hardly matters who wins or loses as long as they keep fighting.'

'I'm impressed,' he replied. 'But what about Danforth, your assistant? How do you control him?'

At this, Balisel allowed herself the tiniest of smiles. 'Ah … Young Jeremiah, whilst being eminently efficient and level-headed in many ways, has one little flaw. It's a common Earthan failing. He's in love – with me. Or perhaps I should say obsessed. He will do anything for me.' She rolled her eyes. 'It's a little tedious at times.'

Navarr was surprised. Although he knew that his sister was beautiful, he had never thought of her being in any relationship other than the one she had with him.

'Anything, eh? And how do you manage that?' His tone was brusque.

'Trust me, little brother, I have my ways. Earthan men are slaves to their bodies. You just have to know how to handle them.'

Her smile was knowing and Navarr suddenly realised that he did not really want to know how she controlled Danforth. The thought was a little too uncomfortable.

'Isn't that all a little risky? What if he falls out of love or gets tired of you?'

Raising an eyebrow in surprise, Balisel smiled at her brother's naivety. 'Brother! I'm ashamed of you. Do you honestly think I would allow that to happen, or that I haven't planned for that eventuality? I have only one more step to take with Jeremiah to ensure that everything he owns is mine and then, sadly, we will part – for good.'

Balisel's face was now quite without emotion of any sort and Navarr became acutely aware that she was talking about murder as plainly and simply as if it were an everyday business transaction. This was a side of his sister he had suspected existed but never seen in action, and he was taken aback. Was she really capable of murder, he wondered. And given their closeness, if *she* was, could *he* ever do that too? Was this their mother's dreadful legacy to them? He pushed these thoughts to the back of his mind and snapped his attention back to their conversation.

'What's the final step with Danforth?' he asked.

'Marriage – in secret, of course.' At this point, Balisel laughed out loud. 'And you thought Linnayen Genara's wedding to an Earthan would be the first, eh? Sorry, little brother. I think I'll beat her to it. Of course, it won't be as grand. But it *will* be legal and that's what counts, doesn't it?'

'You can't be serious, Balisel! You can't just marry the man then ... dispose of him,' he countered.

'You're right. It'll be a terrible waste of a good assistant. But ...' She shrugged her shoulders, 'I'm prepared to make the sacrifice.' As the end of her sentence hung in the air between them, the full import of his sister's plans started to register with Navarr. Balisel slapped her knees in a businesslike gesture and moved on.

'Now, back to your mission, Durroc. Peace is unthinkable and I expect you to ensure that it is *not* achieved.'

Navarr threw back his head and guffawed. 'And how in blazes do you expect me to do that?'

'Only time and circumstances will tell. But once you are in a position of power and influence, my darling brother ...' She purred almost seductively then continued, 'I'm sure you'll know what to do.'

He leaned across from where he sat on the couch and reached out his hand to touch her cheek. 'And I suppose you'll be there to help?' he asked, his voice low and deep.

She responded to his touch by lifting her face and stretching her neck in a feline motion. His hand dropped to her breast as her eyes locked upon his.

'I will always be there – for you.'

Chapter Eight

Much to his own surprise and despite the disaster that had been his relationship with Harrie Whitton-Blake, Jax had enjoyed his year at the Diplomatic Corps. He had made a handful of good friends who he would be sad to leave behind. Getting out of New York, though, and its memories of Harrie, gave him a sense of lightness, and the knowledge that he would be entering a new phase of his life was something to look forward to.

The fanfares and speeches of the graduation ceremony now over, he bad a cheerful farewell to the small group of graduates and staff who had gathered on the crisp green lawn of the Corps' grounds. They would all be going their separate ways, although some of them would, no doubt, meet again at their various postings around the world. Thankfully, he was due a few weeks' break before he took up his posting to the United Democratic Nations embassy in Dublin as assistant secretary. Due to the embassy's proximity to the first-class Boyle Air-dock and the chances it would offer for flying, he was quite looking forward to it.

His mother, Lady Thea, was already in the state shuttle jet, which was parked outside the stadium as he arrived. Jax climbed in next to her as the jet's engines roared to life and lifted them swiftly into the air. As he smiled fondly across at her Thea was instantly aware of how handsome and manly he had become. At twenty-four he was still young in years, but he had developed an air of maturity, though he was still a little too trusting in some respects. Thea thought that he seemed more at peace with himself. Not quite sure, perhaps, of where he was going in this life, but quite certain that he could deal with whatever came along. *Perhaps David and I have done a good job after all,* she thought.

'The ceremony was excellent, Kevor. And you looked very handsome!'

'Well, I'm glad you enjoyed it,' he answered warmly. Then she saw his eyes turn suddenly cold as he continued. 'Shame father couldn't come.'

Thea felt the kick his words delivered. Outwardly, she gave no sign.

'You know he would have been here if he could. The visit to the Makassar Republic was crucial to maintaining stability in the region. You do understand, don't you?' she enquired, trying to make her voice both formal and solicitous at the same time.

'Yes, I understand,' he sighed then, seeing the frozen look in her eyes, he added, 'Sorry, Mum. I know he can't always be around. It's just that I'm never going to graduate again, am I? There are some things you only get one crack at.'

Thea secretly agreed with him. But she loved her husband and had always been a loyal partner.

'No one knows that more than your father!' she snapped back. After a moment, a sigh escaped her. 'Kevor, you know the pressures he's under. How does he choose between people who might be plunged into civil war at any moment and his son's graduation? Accept it. This is our life. I know it's not of our choosing – *your* choosing – but it's who we are. It's what we do.'

Jax shook his head in resignation. Then, seeing the worry in his mother's eyes, his apology was not long in coming. 'I'm sorry. You're right.'

Thea tried to lighten the moment with her next piece of news and said brightly, 'Yes, well, enough of that. Actually, you'll get to see your father quite a bit over the holidays … If you want, that is.'

He was intrigued. 'Oh? Why's that?'

'David has asked if you would like to take a temporary position for a few weeks as his assistant, a sort of aide-de-camp. He rather thought that you might like to see what goes on every day in the council. You know, how the business of government happens. He also wants your help on a rather sensitive diplomatic matter. The Union of Planets is sending an envoy to finalise the peace proposal Hal Byers' team brought back from Altan. The Ki of Altan, Linnayen Genara, has suggested that she marry someone from here – someone of appropriate rank, of course – and he wants you to assist with the envoy's visit and all the meetings it will entail. What do you think?'

Jax was stunned. *So, the rumours were true.* There was to be a royal marriage! Even more surprising, in all these years his father had never once suggested that he come anywhere near his office at the council, let alone act as his assistant. He took a minute or so to gather his thoughts. *He wants me there … with him!*

'Well …' He stumbled through his words, as though searching for hidden obstacles. 'Yes … That would be good. But why me? I usually only irritate him.'

'Oh, that's unfair, Kevor!' she replied, brow puckering. Jax knew that she was not really angry with him. She tried to explain. 'He's like most fathers. He wants you to be just like him. But he doesn't realise – yet – that you're your own man. Really, he's very proud of you and what you've achieved. I also think he genuinely wants to spend some time with you – get to know you a little better.'

'Wants to see if I've improved, you mean,' Jax replied, somewhat cynically.

Now Thea really was losing her patience with him and she spoke firmly. 'Not at all, Kevor! Give him a break. He's a man with the cares of the world on his shoulders. But he's also a father who for too long has missed out on his son. He wants to spend time with you. And he really *does* need your help with this envoy.'

Jax could not help being a little intrigued. 'I didn't think we were *that* friendly with the Union.'

'We're not, and we may never be if the discussions break down. The idea of a political marriage is extremely unusual. It'll need a light touch. Anyway, they're sending a Captain Navarr as their representative on a special mission and we have agreed to offer our hospitality. As a gesture of openness and friendship, it would be good of you to escort him, show him around … that sort of thing.' She could see Jax's interest was growing. 'The captain is something of a scholar, too, we are told. Your father thinks that you might enjoy sharing ideas and finding out about the Union – from the horse's mouth, so to speak.'

He had to admit that he liked this idea. He had learned much about the four planets that made up the Union both at the academy and from his tutor, di Luca. And he had seen a great deal of archival material on them. It would be quite different, though, to hear about them and their people from a native. He began to think of the many questions he could ask of the envoy. Was the sky on Hutho really so green? And the two suns of Autabron – what must they look like and how do people cope with the heat? *Maybe spending time with father wouldn't be so bad after all.*

'Perhaps you're right, Mother,' he said, smiling. 'So when does the captain arrive?'

'In about two weeks, I believe. Just enough time for your father to fully brief you on your duties.'

Thea's smile was as self-satisfied as Jax's, but hers was tinged with a hint of pride too. He had grown taller now, his chest had broadened and his body possessed the solidity of manhood. She was pleased to see that his mind had also taken on the mantle of maturity and had no doubts whatsoever that he was assured of a bright future, if he used his talents well. Perhaps Captain Navarr's visit would make certain of it.

On Hutho, Navarr had spent a further three days with his sister, enjoying many more meetings and outings with her before reporting to Beoraan back at the lodge. As soon as the windshifter lifted away from Balisel's apartment building in Mulakush, he felt as though he had left a part of his body behind. It was always this way when he had to say goodbye to her and he knew that she would miss him with the same intensity.

There was no time, though, to think about such sensitivities once he was back at the lodge. For one thing, Beoraan wanted to go over his engagement schedule for his first two weeks on Earth and decide on the format for these important initial meetings. Then, as he discovered within minutes of his return, the Ki wanted to see him before he departed for Earth and had left instructions that he should join her for dinner that evening. Sen-Kilas'ab also informed him that the Lady Evica Genara had arrived at the lodge and would be joining the dinner party.

He gave careful thought to what he would wear that night. After speaking to Balisel he realised how important it was that he secure the affections of the Ki as soon as possible. He would be on Earth for the best part of three months so he wanted to make quite sure that she would be thinking of him – and only him – while he was away. Once the marriage pact was signed and sealed, he might only have a few weeks to entrap her before the wedding. Whatever happened, she would have to be his – emotionally and, perhaps, physically, too – before her new husband had any time to influence her.

Navarr was very sure of his charms. He had never had a problem attracting women; his sun-blond hair, ice-blue eyes and clear, fresh looks were irresistible. His strong, well-toned body and a well-practised boyish grin added the finishing touches to his magnetism. But for Navarr, a woman was merely a mirror in which to view his reflection and he never tired of watching them admire him.

Depending on the circumstances and the woman, of course, he hid his vanity well behind a mask of charm and good manners. There were some women, though, for whom such behaviour was not necessary and he did not waste any effort on these. Whores and harlots. But Linnayen Genara would be different. She would need a gentle touch and he would have to win both her trust and her friendship in order to claim the ultimate prize. He knew he could only do this by being a consummate professional. The better he undertook his mission, the more she would like him, respect him – and then desire him.

These thoughts filled his mind as he waited for the other dinner guests to arrive in the lodge's atrium. He had decided to wear dress uniform after all and he was not the only one conscious of how handsome it made him look.

From the cover of a carved screen, which hid the door to her room, the Lady Evica Genara took a few seconds to study the dashing captain she'd heard so much about from her sister. *He's certainly handsome. But not as good looking as Tariik.*

At the thought of her lover, Evica felt the warmth radiate in her heart. She and Tariik had managed to snatch a few hours here and there over the weeks left to them before he had taken up his posting on the *Sur-Dacas*, hours when their love was allowed to grow and flourish in quiet corners, and through soft kisses and silent glances it had deepened and strengthened. They kept their affair secret from everyone, knowing full well that discovery would spell disaster for them both. Evica would be forbidden to associate with someone of such low rank – maybe not by Linnayen, although she knew her sister's beliefs well enough to know that she would not be too pleased at any serious association with the low-born lieutenant. But the holy men and women of the High Altek would be furious with her and Tariik would probably be discharged from the force for such a breach of protocol, his career ruined. By the time he had left Altan to join the battlecraft, they both knew that they were meant to be together for life, although how this would be achieved they did not know, and it was the source of much anxiety for them both.

Her reverie was broken by a sudden noise. The door to Linnayen's apartments opened on the other side of the central pool and she saw her sister enter the atrium and walk towards Captain Navarr. She, too, chose this moment to move forward and, as the two women approached him from different sides, Navarr was caught off-guard.

Linnayen was pleased to see that, albeit unwittingly, they had wrong-footed the all-too-competent captain. He turned his head this way then that, trying to honour both women, but it made him look clumsy. Seeing him suddenly fallible, it made her feel more confident that she was doing the right thing in sending Navarr to Earth. The emotional Earthans would appreciate someone with a more 'human' face, without the usual formal Altani manners. She had not been sure about sending him until after the fall-flying experience. He had handled that well and she had had the chance to see real emotions under the captain's stony façade.

She strode purposefully up to him. 'Good evening, Captain Navarr. It's good to have you back.'

He bowed his head respectfully. 'Thank you, my lady. It's good to be back.'

'Let me introduce my sister, the Lady Evica Genara.' With this, she gestured to Evica and, once more, the proud captain bowed.

'My lady, I am honoured,' he replied.

'I have heard much about you, Captain Navarr. Mostly good.' Evica's voice was barely polite.

'You are very kind, my lady.'

'No, I'm not,' Her voice held a hint of reproach. Then, more softly, she continued. 'I say as I find. I have yet to form an opinion of you.'

Navarr nodded. 'Then I shall endeavour to ensure it becomes a good one.'

Linnayen interjected. 'You can only do that, captain, by doing a good job and making a success of your mission.'

'Which is exactly what I intend to do, my lady – both for the Union and for you.'

Nicely caught, thought Evica. *He is indeed a good diplomat. Perhaps a little too good?*

All during dinner, Evica reserved her judgement on the handsome captain. Already smitten by Lieutenant Min, she was not susceptible to Navarr's cool charm and, having grown up surrounded by courtiers, was not overly impressed by his fine manners. However, she was a little perturbed to see that Linnayen responded to him in an almost friendly manner. This was most unlike her sister, who was not given to familiar behaviour with anyone except her and Beoraan. It rang alarm bells deep inside her.

The old counsellor had joined them for the meal and, because of this and the fact that Navarr was due to leave in two days, much of the conversation revolved around the plans for the Earthan visit. Linnayen wanted to ensure that Navarr's diary included meetings with all the right people, as it was important not to give offence.

'So, captain, when will you be meeting with Ambassador Byers?' she asked.

'I understand that he will be in the welcoming party on my arrival. But I have asked if we might meet in private as soon as the ceremonies are over. We need to check the parameters of the mission and I need to find out how much the shortlisted candidates know of our purposes.' His tone was serious and businesslike.

'I would be surprised if these men have been told nothing of why we are sending you. Surely Ambassador Byers has briefed the council of our plans?' She addressed her comments to both Navarr and Beoraan.

'Yes, the full council has been told the purpose of Navarr's mission,' Beoraan responded. 'But they have not been given our list of potential bridegrooms – yet.'

Navarr joined the discussion. 'I rather thought we would need Ambassador Byers' more precise advice on the matter before any of the candidates were approached. I think it is important to involve him every step of the way, don't you?'

'You're right,' Linnayen replied. 'But the final choice is mine.' She was quietly emphatic.

'Absolutely! Everyone should be able to choose the husband they want,' Evica interjected. This was her opportunity to sow a seed.

Linnayen looked at her sister, a slight furrowing of her brow the only sign of her concern at the remark. 'You know, Evica, that is not always possible for people like us. We must, sometimes, stifle our own wishes for the good of our people … or for the Union.'

'Then lucky you won't have to do that, sister. For you'll be choosing your husband,' Evica countered.

'Yes, but I'll be choosing the best person to bring about peace, not someone I might love. You know as well as I, love doesn't come into it. This is politics.'

Evica felt as though she had been chastised and knew that she should hold her peace. But there was something devilish in her tonight.

'Yes, but as a woman, Linnayen, surely you would prefer to marry a man you *could* love too?' she persisted. The use of her name informally in front of a relative stranger such as Navarr only served to anger Linnayen.

Linnayen's neck stiffened as she shot a dart into Evica's eyes. 'My marriage is a matter of state, sister. Love is not important.'

The sudden cool stillness was broken by Navarr's smooth tones.

'Love is always important, my lady.'

His voice was measured and calm, ignoring the looks of surprise on the women's faces.

'And if my mission results in you finding your soulmate, then so much the better. However, in the greater scheme of life – and statecraft – one's emotions are of little importance.'

'Then you will not let the looks or youth or other charms of my sister's future husband sway your recommendation, captain?' Evica asked.

'My lady, the Ki has been most precise in the criteria I am to employ,' he replied, nodding with respect towards Linnayen, who sat impassively. 'Attractiveness and a pleasant disposition are not on her list. I will, of course, keep to my brief.'

'See that you do, captain.' Linnayen's tone was firm. 'Never forget that peace is our prime goal and we must succeed!'

Navarr could not help but remember Balisel's words. *Peace is unthinkable. It hardly matters who wins or loses as long as they keep fighting.* All he had to do to help his sister achieve her ambitions was to ensure that the seeds of mistrust were kept viable and, although he still did not quite know how he was going to do it, he knew where to start. He had to pick the right husband – or, rather, the wrong one.

But for now, the tentative truce of the last six months was holding. Both the Union and the Earthan spacefleets were on standby, patrolling their mutual border zones. The only active combat either force was now seeing were occasional skirmishes with Earthan guerrilla ships and Union pirates. For the diplomats on both sides these continual raids by either the idealistic rebels of Earth or the self-serving trader-pirates of the Union were irritating obstacles to peace. The peace would be hard enough to win as it was without the interference of these protagonists. Navarr wondered how he could use the situation to keep up the tension whilst appearing to secure the peace and he was uneasy with the thought that the Union might eventually capitulate and accede to the Earthan terms. In that situation, it would be difficult to stir up trouble and keep the conflict alive – and Balisel would be furious.

The dinner finally came to a close and Linnayen rose to take her leave. The parting look she gave to her sister told Evica that she wanted to talk to her privately, and so she too bad farewell to Beoraan and Navarr.

Once back in the seclusion of her room, Linnayen turned to Evica and asked the question that had been at the back of her mind all evening.

'Well, sister, what did you make of him? Is he the right one to send? Or should I postpone and send Beoraan instead?'

Evica studied her sister's face. She noticed the furrows on the usually smooth brow and Linnayen's green eyes staring at her in avid concentration. A great deal was riding on this venture and Evica knew that Linnayen would never get a better chance at bringing about the peace settlement that was so dear to her heart.

'Honestly? I don't know. He's very smooth, very polished. He obviously knows a huge amount about Earth.' By listing what she knew about Navarr, Evica hoped to clarify her thoughts, for both of them. 'He's very skilled at diplomacy too.'

'Yes, perhaps too much. That can so often make one appear insincere, can't it?' Linnayen pondered.

'True, and maybe that's a risk you'd run with whoever you send. The fact is, you can't go yourself. You've got to send *someone*. So it might as well be him. After all, he is good at his job. He seems to know exactly what he's got to do.' Evica hoped that her words were helping Linnayen, who was still frowning, staring at the floor and obviously concerned. 'He's also very good looking …'

Linnayen looked up sharply and saw the knowing look in Evica's eyes.

'You like him, don't you, little sister?' Evica asked, a teasing smile playing about her mouth.

Linnayen looked back down to the floor, trying to think of what to say to counter her sister's observation. *Do I? Has he affected me that much? Is it so obvious?*

Her retort came quickly and in clipped tones.

'No, I don't like him, Evica. Not in that way. But if his appearance wins us friends on Earth then so much the better.' She spoke decisively, trusting that her tone would put a stop to any suggestion that she had feelings for Navarr other than those of a leader towards their loyal subject.

Evica accepted what her sister said with a nod but she knew Linnayen well enough to perceive that she had just used her skills in statecraft to cover up her true feelings. It was better, though, to say no more and she went to take her farewell.

'It's late. Time to sleep,' she said.

'Yes, of course. I'm sorry to have kept you, but I really wanted your thoughts,' Linnayen replied.

'I know. And for what it's worth, I think your captain's the right man for the job.' Evica kissed her sister on the cheek and turned away. Linnayen's hand on her arm stopped her.

'And your lieutenant's the right man too – for you.' Linnayen spoke quietly and kindly. 'I'm sorry I was a little hard on you earlier. It wasn't what you said. It was saying it in front of strangers.'

'I know. I'm sorry too. I don't know what came over me,' Evica admitted.

'You're missing him, aren't you?' Linnayen asked. 'Are you really that fond of him?'

Evica gave a small smile and shrugged her shoulders, trying to dismiss the question. It was too soon to let Linnayen know the full depth of her feelings for Tariik Min, but it was an appropriate occasion to hint at them.

'Fond? Yes … He's likeable enough, good company and all,' she said with a shrug of her shoulders. 'But that's all. He's just a man.'

Linnayen wondered how and when they had become so good at deceiving themselves. Why could they not just admit to each other that they both had strong feelings about these two very different men?

'Of course,' she replied. 'Just a man.'

Thoughts trailed through her mind like a wisp of morning mist. Then suddenly the haze cleared and Navarr's face appeared. Linnayen flushed at her body's quick surge of warmth and, trying to hide her anxiety, she turned to Evica.

'We'd better rest,' she sighed. 'Goodnight, sister, and thank you. I needed to know what you thought. It's helped me so much.'

Evica's smile was warm and soft. 'Good,' she said. 'And whatever you decide, it will be all right.' With a final hug for Linnayen, she turned and left the room.

Three days later, on a bright, fresh morning, Navarr left for Earth. The air in the shuttle dock was still cold as Linnayen and her small entourage watched the craft take off to rendezvous with the larger spaceliner, which was in orbit around Hutho. A sudden shiver went through her body and she pulled her cloak more tightly around her. Was it just the cold or her anxiety?

As the shuttle lifted away, she realised that she would not be seeing him for at least three months – possibly more – and the prospect did not please her. Once again, his features filled her mind and she thought back to yesterday, when they had spent nearly the whole day together talking about the finer details of Navarr's task and reviewing the candidates in more detail. She recalled how she had studied his features, trying to memorise his expressions, the curve of his mouth and the shape of his eyes. She noticed that he had a small pale brown mole on his neck just behind his right ear and she had blushed at the unbidden mental image of her lips upon it. Luckily, neither he nor Beoraan had picked up on her sudden unease and the discussion had continued.

It was finally ended by Beoraan's suggestion that they all take a break to get some fresh air and stretch their legs. Only then did Linnayen realise they had been talking for nearly four hours and the old man was obviously uncomfortable and tired.

She decided to call it a day. She was now sure that Navarr could be trusted and was confident that he would be able to identify an appropriate consort for her. The sooner he got started the better. It was well over a year since her father had died and she had begun the first steps towards settling a peace treaty. She was impatient to see the end of the process and hoped that Navarr's time away from Altan would pass quickly – and not just because she wanted to get the wedding underway.

Durroc Navarr was thinking much the same as the shuttle lifted away from the dock. He could see Linnayen Genara standing next to Beoraan. She stood tall and stiffly in a formal pose, her eyes fixed in a determined stare at the porthole behind which he sat. Their eyes met and he knew, in that moment, that he had her. He had worked his quiet charms well and he could see that she wanted him as much as he wanted her.

His mouth formed a slow smile, but it did not extend to his eyes. *By all the planets, let the mission go well and get me back here swiftly to take the prize!*

Chapter Nine

An hour after Navarr's shuttle craft docked with the spaceliner *Kuttashansi*, the sleek vessel moved out of orbit around Hutho. Navarr watched the lush green planet fall away as they moved into free space, gathering speed all the while, until they were just beyond the Huthon system.

A vast tract of open space lay before them until they came to the inhabited sectors of the Bargassi Demi-galaxy, wherein lay the planet Autabron. They would then cross a further uninhabited tract before entering the Jarunei Strand, an arm of the spiral galaxy known on Earth as the Milky Way. It was from here that the spaceliner would use the naturally occurring ionic wave pulses to boost it out of the plane of the galaxy, thrusting it far up into free space before it powered back down into the Ngoro Cluster, wherein lay the solar system. They would reach Earth in only ten days.

Navarr pondered that these enormous distances could only now be covered due to the advances in cosmonic engineering brought about by conflict with Earth. Balisel was right when she said that war was good for business, but it was also very good for technological and scientific advancement. The necessity to be better, smarter and faster in order to beat your opponent forced the pace of discovery and innovation. Thus, new fusion-propulsion systems had been designed so that Union craft could get to Earth and Navarr had no doubt that the impetus of conflict had spurred on the Earthans too.

Having time on his hands during the journey, he reflected on their history, searching for a hint or clue to explain the genetic connection between Earthans and the people of his own planet. Their story began some two hundred years earlier when an Autabroni scout ship in search of new planetary mineral sources had come across the Earthans while mapping life-free planets in the Jarunei Strand. By chance, an Earthan UDN Institute of Technology scientific research ship had also been in the Strand analysing the io-pulses, and it was inevitable that the two vessels would detect each other's presence.

Within minutes of the Autabroni scout's arrival in the sector, both vessels had picked up each other's signals and both captains put their ships on emergency standby. Being so far from their home planets, neither vessel could summon support. They were on their own; two lots of foreigners, neither knowing the other's language and uncertain of how to communicate.

The captain of the Earthan vessel had clear instructions on the procedure to follow in the event of first contact with an alien species. They had long hoped to find other sentient life forms – had long reflected on the appropriate protocols that should be followed when first encountering an alien species. Consequently, the discovery of a technologically advanced species was the realisation of the Earthans' greatest hopes and fears all at once. The approved, nonconfrontational method of communication was to use the ordered sounds and cadences of musical notation, the only truly universal language – or so they thought.

As luck would have it, though, they had encountered the Autabronis ahead of the more cultured Dasnirians and Altanis, or the more spiritual Huthons. So, as the rhythmic melody of Strauss's 'Blue Danube' waltz reached the ears of the no-nonsense Autabroni crew, their anxieties grew. And by the time the Earthan captain had switched the music to a ballad by the popular performer Etosha Leo, the Autabronis were so agitated that they put their weapons on standby and were ready to go down fighting for their planet.

Thankfully, the Earthan captain, having received no signals of recognition after some five minutes, decided to switch to transmitting simple sequential chrono-pulses instead, overlaid with a simple vocal message stating who they were. Almost immediately, the Autabronis calmed down. Here was a mathematical rhythm that they could relate to and obvious vocalisations, although they knew nothing of what the sounds meant. Within seconds they were sending their own messages back.

Over the ensuing minutes, hours, then days, the two vessels tentatively got to know each other and both took to exploring the other with great enthusiasm, the original purposes of their missions now put aside. The first steps were made to interpret each other's language and learn about each other's home planets. The Autabroni captain was delighted to discover that the planet Earth contained a huge variety of minerals, some of which were so rare on Autabron and other known planets that she could become a very wealthy woman if she could find a way to exploit them.

The Earthan captain was equally happy and amazed to discover that Autabron was only one of four inhabited planets, and that life forms like his own existed on all of them. It was as he and millions of people on Earth had imagined for so many centuries. They were not alone! And he would be the hero who would return home with the absolute and incontrovertible proof that there was humanoid life in space.

From this stumbling and almost childlike first contact, a more in-depth communication and a sharing of languages, histories and cultures grew over the next few decades. Ten years after first contact, an early exchange – three years in the planning – took place whereby an Earthan delegation travelled both to Autabron and Altan, and a combined gathering of scientists and diplomats from all four planets of the Union travelled to Earth on a reciprocal visit. The fledgling relationship between these alien yet similar beings was off to a good start. Honest exchanges prevailed and the sharing of scientific knowledge undoubtedly was a key factor in the advancement of technology. The honeymoon lasted a mere thirty years before fear and greed replaced openness, and the planets set about warfare.

In those early days the journey had to be taken in stages, with rest stops at space stations that were built along the route, and it took nearly three years to complete the first journey from Earth to Altan. With the work of leading cosmonologists in the Union and visionary scientists like Tomas Grigor Bashir, the current president's forefather, along with the boost provided by the astounding Jarunei ionic wave pulses, fusion-propulsion systems were now so advanced that the journey time had been reduced to slightly over ten days.

It was still a long time, though, when one was a passenger and not a crewmember. So it was that Durroc Navarr busied himself with a comprehensive study of the reigning families of Altan. When he had exhausted that subject, he turned his thoughts to the players in the continuing skirmishes between the Union and Earth. Using the higher security clearance he had been awarded for the mission, he accessed intelligence files concerning the Earthan resistance forces and the pirates of the Union planets.

He reasoned quite sensibly that he would need to know the strengths and weaknesses of all the parties in this dangerous political game if he and Balisel were to play successfully and acquire both immense power and wealth. After all, this was not a rehearsal. There would be no second chances; he would have to get it right first time and he had little doubt that he would.

It was on a rain-drenched afternoon in early summer that the space shuttle containing Navarr and his small entourage of civil servants touched down at the City of London Spacedock. The craft descended slowly, colourful clouds of gases from its exhaust portals quickly dissipating in the wet air. Through a wide window Navarr could see both tall, smooth, metallic buildings and lower, more ornate structures that appeared to be made of stone. From what he knew of the history of this ancient city, the stone structures were ancient churches and public buildings that had been preserved for over two millennia. This alone alluded to the fact that the Earthans were a species with a keen sense of history and an awareness of how precious the past can be. He would be dealing with a sophisticated people at least as civilised as his own kind. The only difference was in the expression of their culture and beliefs – and there they were worlds apart.

Jax's thoughts were running much along the same lines. The Altanis were said to be the most advanced, most civilised of all the Union's races, and he was about to meet them in the flesh for the first time. Although he had read about and studied the various races of humanoids from Altan, Dasnir, Hutho and Autabron, he could find no way of describing adequately his feelings about meeting one for the first time. He was about to meet someone so foreign, yet so familiar. About to find out what it was like to grow up on a planet with three moons, a pink sky and mountain ranges whose peaks, ascending over twenty kilometres into the lower stratosphere, were nearly three times higher than the highest mountains on Earth. It was the stuff of dreams.

The outer doors of the spacedock closed and, amidst the noises of engines powering down and the shuttle's portways being released, Jax tried to contain his excitement. His stalwart friend Duncan McCrae stood next to him and perceived his nervousness. Jax had asked his father if Duncan could join him here today, not because he felt he needed support but because he didn't want Duncan to miss out on this historical event.

Suddenly, the portway closest to the shuttle's bridge slid open and the two young men could clearly see the Altani envoy preparing to disembark. The shuttle's captain led the envoy and his entourage out onto a steel mesh ramp, which had only moments before been extended across the gap between the craft and the reception lounge.

Hal Byers stood impassively at the end of the ramp, waiting to greet Navarr. Although he could not hear what passed between the two men, Jax watched as they shook hands firmly, obviously exchanging pleasantries. Then a smile broke out on the usually dour Byers' face and, still talking, the two men began walking towards them.

Duncan and Jax took in the envoy's appearance. It was evident immediately that here was an imposing man: tall, golden blond hair and looking every inch an ambassador in his navy-blue dress uniform. His eyes locked onto Jax's as he and Byers approached and, ignoring Duncan altogether, he bowed very formally in front of the younger, leaner man, keeping his head dipped until Jax spoke.

'Welcome, Captain Navarr. I am Kevor Jax Bashir al Fahrazad and I am very pleased to meet you,' said Jax, holding out his right hand in greeting.

'The pleasure is very much mine, Prince Bashir. I am honoured by your presence.'

Jax smiled at the old-fashioned formal compliment and at the fact that the envoy knew who he was. He had obviously been well briefed.

'Thank you, but the honour is mine,' he replied. 'My father, the president, and all members of the Union of Democratic Nations welcome you here today. They send you every good wish and have asked me to escort you to the council chamber so that they may greet you in person. I hope that is convenient for you and that you are not too tired?'

'Of course!' Navarr declared. 'I am very much looking forward to meeting them and I have rested well on the journey.'

Then he remembered to smile, recalling that this was considered a polite and friendly gesture by most Earthan cultures. Only Duncan, an accomplished actor and trained to notice – and mimic – the smallest changes in facial expressions and body language, picked up on Navarr's smiling afterthought. He filed away the impression for later reference but, in the meantime, thought it might be a good idea to keep a watchful eye on the new envoy.

Jax led the way from the spacedock's reception lounge to traverse the short distance along a glass-encased moving walkway to the council chamber on the other side of the river. From this vantage point, Navarr got a fine view of the spiralling city towers and the dark, swirling waters of its river. *Impressive, but not remarkable.*

The reception awaiting him in the chamber comprised at least one hundred council representatives. They were seated in a huge amphitheatre, all clapping his arrival as he entered. He lifted his head and grinned back to the gathering, waving his hands in the manner he had seen portrayed in the archival material he had studied. The gesture felt strange, but he was gratified to notice that it seemed to please the crowd even more. Then the unmistakable frame of the president came towards him, smiling. David Bashir's arms were spread wide and, with something approaching horror at the gross informality of the behaviour, Navarr realised that the man intended to hug him. His grin froze as he allowed his body to be encased by the huge man's arms. He supposed that if this was the way these people showed their friendship and it was what was needed to get the job done, he would have to get used to these grand gestures – and quickly.

'Welcome, welcome!' Bashir's voice was strong and booming. 'We are so pleased to have you here with us, Captain Navarr. We have much to talk about, eh?'

'Indeed, Mr President. I am most touched by your generous welcome. You do me too much honour though.'

The sheikh brushed away his remarks in an uncommon display of humility and Jax knew that his father was enjoying the diplomatic game that had begun between them. Underneath the façade of welcome, though, Bashir remained cautious. The envoy was here to talk, yes, but peace was still uncertain.

'Now, before you meet some of the other members of the council, I want to formally introduce my son, Kevor.' David gestured to Jax to step forward from the position he, Duncan and Byers had assumed to the rear of the envoy. He continued, 'I have asked him to be your aide while you are with us and you must feel free to call upon him for every assistance and advice. He will be delighted to help you.'

'Indeed I will, captain,' confirmed the smiling Jax.

'Thank you so much, Mr President. I have heard many good reports of your son and, without doubt, I look forward to getting to know him.'

Something in the look he shot across to Jax as he said these words worried Duncan McCrae. Did it penetrate too deeply? Was it ever so slightly calculating? Duncan noticed that neither Jax nor his father seemed to have picked up on the envoy's silent communications or the stiffness of his body. The warmth they were displaying to Navarr, though, as they took him off to meet the first cohort of council members, seemed very genuine. But as Duncan watched the historic scene in front of him, he suddenly found himself suppressing a shiver and knew instinctively that it had nothing to do with the cool spring weather outside.

After two months on Earth, Durroc Navarr felt he knew more about these strange people and their unusual planet than he could have known from a lifetime spent in the research library back in Genkarah. For the most part they appeared friendly and welcoming and far too trusting by Altan standards, which rather suited his purposes. But he felt that for all their attempts at civilisation, there was still a discernible tendency towards the primeval. They seemed to allow their emotions to influence their decisions so easily and this was the fundamental reason why they continued to be so belligerent. This was a planet where competition and war seemed to be endemic in both behaviour and thought and Navarr could now understand why it had been so hard to sue for peace with them. They still equated the possession of territory with survival and had not moved beyond this primitive tenet.

It was, though, immensely exciting, and everything had happened so quickly. He had met hundreds of new people, seen strange, colourful landscapes and weird, unimaginable creatures, digested the oddest tasting foods, and tried new sports and entertainments, all mostly in the company of the young Bashir.

Jax had proved to be an excellent aide. He was courteous, well informed, intelligent and he could not help but display his genuine interest in and enthusiasm for the planets in the Union. He was always asking questions or making comments about aspects of the Union's politics or conventions, trying to engage Navarr in more informal conversation. However, this looser style of talking was not something with which Navarr was familiar and it took some weeks before he began to feel relatively comfortable in Jax's company.

When he was not in meetings with council members, or private talks with the marital candidates, Jax had taken him to sporting events or theatres and galleries, even to private dinners hosted by all manner of talented people ranging from artists and musicians through to industrialists and academics. His family's influence and connections meant that Jax was welcome in nearly every home, studio or institution on the planet. It also helped that everyone was more than a little intrigued to meet the imposing envoy from Altan. Once word spread among society hostesses of the envoy's good looks and his charming if somewhat reserved manners, it became a task in itself to reply to all the invitations.

Naturally, Navarr had become a hit with the planet's media and he soon found that everywhere he and young Jax went, a bevy of reporters followed them, documenting their every move. Jax, of course, had grown up surrounded by these bands of followers and knew how to keep them at a distance whilst retaining their good humour. His style with them was easy and natural, but he never gave away too much about his personal life or feelings.

So far, Navarr had not raised the question of marriage to the Ki with Jax or with his family – and he did not intend to, despite being quite certain that Jax would make the ideal husband. He was confident that the only way to secure the naïve young prince for his

Ki, especially in the light of his father's probable opposition, was if the suggestion came from Jax himself.

For most of the last two months though, it had not entered Jax's head that he could be a potential candidate, especially as all the discussions had focused on such eminent and wealthy people as Louis Charles Lombard-Jenks and Dr James Toyotomi. Even Prince Oleg of Kessler-Lichtburg, the mining magnate and heir to the vast Kessler fortune, had been examined and, for a time, was a highly favoured candidate. In such elevated company, even if he had considered himself a contender, Jax would have felt quite humbled. However, the more time he spent around Navarr, the more chances he had to learn about Ki-Linnayen Genara. And the more he knew and saw of her, the more he wanted to know.

She was beautiful and fascinating, mysterious and intelligent. Jax had had some opportunities to both see and hear her when he had viewed archival footage taken to meetings with the candidates or their representatives. The footage was of very formal occasions and he wondered what she was really like when she was not on duty. In his mind he imagined that she was quietly spoken and kind. He also envisaged her smiling and laughing, or enjoying conversations with her friends, or going to sporting events or the theatre. Over the weeks he built up an image of the exotic young Ki as a woman he would very much like to know. He did not yet dare admit it, even to himself, but he was falling just a little in love.

Linnayen and Navarr spoke at least once a week to discuss his progress with the various candidates. Their conversations were always formal and businesslike, Linnayen giving no hint of her developing feelings.

Then one day, and at the specific behest of the Ki, Navarr asked Jax to sit in on one of their meetings for a few minutes. Linnayen had thought it was time to take a closer look at her intended husband, having now decided that the young and malleable Kevor Jax was the best choice. She wanted to get the measure of the man, for although it was her duty to marry the right man no matter his looks or personality, it would, she felt, be some comfort if he were a likeable individual. It would make the task less irksome at the very least.

Jax had been reviewing the day's schedule in the small anteroom that adjoined Navarr's office when the envoy asked him to step through to the main room. The council had allocated the envoy space in a new government building that completely spanned the River Thames.

At the sound of Navarr's voice command to the computer, the sweeping view of the grey-blue waters and the city's complex skyline faded and the window took on the milky appearance of a blank vidscreen. Within seconds, Linnayen Genara's visage appeared at twice life-size on the opaque wall and Jax's eyes widened as though he was trying to take in more of her beauty. He had, of course, seen many images of her before, but he was not prepared for the effect seeing her like this would have on him. Her eyes were the colour of crystal peridot and the lashes that framed them thick and black. She wore no makeup and her shimmering black hair hung loosely around her shoulders. Suddenly he realised that he was staring at her like a lovestruck schoolboy. He swallowed and composed his features.

Sitting at her desk in her private office in Genkarah, the young woman soon made him feel at ease with the warmth of her first words.

'Greetings, Prince Bashir.' Linnayen spoke carefully and clearly. 'I am very pleased to meet you at long last. I have heard only good things about you from Captain Navarr and I would like to thank you for assisting him so well.'

Jax bowed his head in reverence and then looked up into her clear green eyes, trying to concentrate on his reply.

'My lady, I need no thanks for undertaking a duty that has been nothing but pleasurable. I have enjoyed helping Captain Navarr in his mission and I have learned much about the Union and your beautiful home planet from him. It sounds …' Jax wanted to say more but, at the sound of Navarr clearing his throat, he realised that his opinions were not required to be expressed at such length. He concluded, with a little embarrassment, 'Ah … amazing. I trust that you are well?'

Navarr nodded his thanks to Jax for his compliments and his brevity and Linnayen resumed speaking.

'I am in good health, thank you,' she replied in as friendly a manner as she could muster. 'But I am eager to know how the discussions are progressing. Prince Bashir, I take it that you know the nature of these talks?'

'I do indeed, my lady. Captain Navarr has confided in me that it is your wish to marry a man of rank from Earth, thereby pledging your commitment to peace between our planets.'

'That is correct,' she replied. Then, her brow furrowed in concentration as she continued, 'What are your thoughts on this approach?'

'I think it is a supremely noble gesture, which the majority of the people on my planet will see in a good light.'

Her eyes widened in anxious surprise. 'I don't want it to be regarded purely as a gesture, you know. I am quite serious in my desire for peace and I am more than committed to this marriage.' Linnayen spoke clearly and deliberately. 'I intend that this union be for life and that it will create an environment for harmony between us, both at the political level and between individuals, for generations to come.'

Jax was warmed and enthused by the strength of her words. *If only some of the council members could hear her directly. Then there would be no doubting her, no doubting the Union's desire for peace.*

'My lady, your words and your intent gladden my heart. No one would be more pleased than I to see the growth of friendship and trust between our planets. It behoves us all to strive to make a successful marriage arrangement for you, my lady, and I will do all I can to assist your envoy.'

'Thank you so much and for taking the time to talk with me today,' Linnayen replied, softening her voice in an effort to sound warm. However, time was pushing on and she needed to talk to Navarr. She concluded, 'I hope that we will talk again soon.'

Navarr watched and listened to this exchange with great interest. The boy handled himself well. Not too flowery in his compliments and he had thought about the words he should use most carefully. He was obviously skilled in diplomacy and this was a little disconcerting, for it did not suit his or the Union's purposes to have too clever a husband for the Ki.

He noted that Jax had something of a moonstruck look about him while speaking with Linnayen. His eyes had been wide, pupils dilated and his mouth had been slightly open the whole time – all signs that the prince might be taken with the young Ki. Navarr wondered, would it suit his purposes to have the intended husband in love with the bride? How could he use this knowledge? Otherwise, it was all going as he had planned.

A few days later, Jax and Navarr travelled to Hokkaido. *Another candidate to meet!* All worthy men, thought Jax, but his frown as he stepped into the steaming water of the onsen tub was more one of disquiet than pain. *They were all so old!*

Jax gasped as he gingerly lowered himself into the water. Navarr was already settled and seemed to be luxuriating in the hot water, as was their host, James Toyotomi, the famous medical research scientist. Both men seemed at ease with the heat and the situation. But Jax was a little discomfited by conducting their meeting in such circumstances *and* by his nakedness in front of the two older men. Finally he managed to sit down and the conversation they all had started in the dressing room continued.

'Of course, Dr Toyotomi, the suggestion of marriage to Ki-Linnayen is just that – a suggestion – nothing more. It is one of many possible ways to cement the accord,' Navarr reiterated, anxious to allay the doctor's obvious concerns.

'I understand,' Toyotomi replied. 'But I am puzzled that you should approach *me*. I am a scientist, not a career politician.' He spoke quietly but with distinct authority and self-assurance.

'It is precisely for this reason that the Ki asked me to approach you,' Navarr countered smoothly and swiftly. 'She is desirous of a partner who is serious and thoughtful, someone who is well-respected in his field and who has no thought for personal gain but only good wishes for peace between our planets. Your family has long supported a resolution to our troubles –'

At this point Toyotomi interrupted, nodding his agreement. 'Yes, my great-grandmother has spoken in council many times on the need to put aside our differences.'

'Exactly so,' Navarr replied. 'Perhaps then you can see how a union between two noble families, one on Earth, the other on Altan, both strong voices for peace, both highly regarded, could be the answer to our prayers? The demonstration of commitment by both parties would surely impress even the most hard-bitten of our opponents.'

'Oh, I do not doubt the reasoning behind your proposal. I just wonder at your lady's choice. I am, after all, a quiet man. I do not involve myself in politics and I am not used to being in the public eye,' the doctor restated.

'So much the better,' Navarr said. 'A gratuitous publicity seeker or a career politician would be far from appropriate for this undertaking.'

Toyotomi's broad face remained impassive as he stared down into the water. Then, suddenly, he looked up at Jax, who could not help but show his discomfort with the situation. This was all too much like a business transaction for the young prince's liking. Toyotomi wondered if his demeanour was due solely to the hot water.

'I will think about what you have said,' he replied, still looking at Jax but speaking to Navarr. 'Now, let us finish here and take some refreshments.'

They stepped out of the hot tub and Toyotomi led them through to another room with a deep tiled bath of cold clear water in the centre. This room's walls comprised hand-painted panels depicting snow-crested mountains and tall fir trees, except for one that opened onto a solid wooden veranda with a stunning view across the forested slopes of the Hidaka-Samiyaku ranges. They had come to the Toyotomi ancestral home in Nippon-ko to meet with the last of the short-listed candidates. All the others – the playboy billionaire Lombard-Jenks and Prince Oleg of Kessler-Lichtburg, who apparently had uncommon sexual proclivities – had by now been dismissed as unsuitable. Only the eminent doctor and researcher James Toyotomi remained and, as far as Jax knew, it was Navarr's job to persuade this final suitor to the marriage.

Toyotomi gestured to the two men to follow him into the pool. The icy water caused Jax to gasp, but within seconds a tingling sensation coursed through his body and the feeling of relief from the former heat was terrific and very welcome. Navarr and Toyotomi gave no indication of any pleasure they might have felt at this sudden change of temperature. Jax could understand this in Toyotomi, who would have been brought up to bathe this way, but he could not fathom Navarr. Did the man really not feel anything? Was his self-control so good?

When they had cooled down, dried off and dressed again in loose-fitting house kimonos, the doctor led them along the veranda to an area laid with floor mats and low cushioned seating. There waiting for them in an intricately carved wooden chair was an old woman whose silver-grey hair was streaked with stark white. She was dressed in a pale blue kimono embroidered with delicate pink cherry blossom motifs and held at the waist by a silken lilac obi. Her long hair was coiled behind her head and fastened with pins, which were hidden by a single creamy frangipani flower.

It was not until the three men had sat down on the cushions that the old woman raised her head and they saw her dark eyes, as black as the night sky. It was hard to believe that Kumiko Toyotomi, matriarch and consummate council politician, was a hundred and five years old. Although her skin had the appearance of softly crumpled rice paper and the whites of her eyes were now a dull yellow, it was obvious that she had been a beautiful woman in her youth.

'Good morning, Great-Grandmother,' said Toyotomi, bowing his head in deference.

'Good morning, Great-Grandson,' she answered. 'I hope that you and our visitors feel refreshed?'

'We do, Great-Grandmother. May I present our guests to you?' James Toyotomi asked in his quiet voice. Noting her nodded assent, he continued. 'This is the special envoy from the Union of Planets, Captain Durroc Navarr from the planet Altan.'

At the pause, the old lady spoke. 'You are most welcome, captain.'

'My thanks, madame,' he replied, following Toyotomi's lead and bowing his head.

'And this is Prince Kevor Jax Bashir, Great-Grandmother.'

'It is good to see you, Prince Bashir. You are so much like your dear mother.' Kumiko spoke kindly to him. But he could not help but notice that she had not included his father in her greeting and he remembered that this harmless-looking old woman was no friend to the Bashirs.

'Thank you, madame. You are most kind,' Jax replied.

'Now then,' said the old lady, as she looked back to Navarr and Toyotomi. Her tone suddenly changed from the subdued warmth she had used for her greetings to a brisk, no-nonsense manner. 'I take it that you have discussed the marriage idea? So, James, what do you think?'

'I am very honoured to be considered for this important position, Great-Grandmother, and I am flattered to think that I could help bring about peace. However, I have told Captain Navarr that I would like some time to think about the proposal,' Toyotomi responded succinctly.

'Yes, of course. That is wise,' she replied. 'But do not consider too long, eh? Or you may lose your chance altogether, James. I am sure that the Ki of Altan has other suitors to choose from.'

'Indeed, madame. But my lady is entirely happy to wait – for the right husband. These matters are delicate and should not be unduly hurried.' Navarr wanted to reassure her and give her the impression that her family was important enough to warrant delay, if necessary.

'True. But is my James the right husband?'

Navarr looked into the old woman's dark, piercing eyes in surprise and puzzlement. *What is she saying? Surely she wants him to be the chosen one?*

'Please do not misunderstand me, captain,' she began. 'No one is more conscious than I of the honour the Union brings to my family by considering my own great-grandson for this unique role. I myself am very aware that a royal marriage is the best way to seal a fledgling peace. But by marrying James, this would become a pact of like minds, of friends. It would hardly be likely to convince the opposition that the Union is serious in its intent.'

She waited for a few moments to let her words sink in before continuing.

'Surely your lady would do better to marry an outspoken opponent to show that you were truly holding out an olive branch. Would this not bring most of the dissenters over to our side?'

Navarr pretended to think about what she had said. He had, of course, already worked out the strategy with Linnayen months before. Thus, his task was purely to manipulate the protagonists rather than set any agenda himself.

'What you say, madame, is of course true,' he agreed. 'But given the early and delicate nature of our relationship with Earth, I hardly think it is a practical course of action. I cannot see that opponents of peace would take kindly to allowing one of their own to join with a supposed enemy.'

Kumiko looked across at Jax who was seated on her left. He had been concentrating on the interplay and was caught off-guard when the old woman's eyes drilled into his.

'Is that true, do you think, Prince Bashir? After all, your own father speaks out against the Union all the time.'

Jax knew enough of the ways of politicians to see the danger in this question. Consequently, he took a few seconds to gather his thoughts.

'Madame, there are some matters that are above politics and religion, above personal allegiances or gain. These matters must be decided purely on the grounds of what is fundamentally right and best for the majority.' Jax had not intended to make a speech, but he found himself rising to defend his father and so went on. 'My father's job and that of every member of the council is to analyse the facts of the situation and, using their skill and knowledge, make the best decision for the majority of people, regardless of their personal preferences.'

Kumiko fired back. 'Agreed. But it is hard to be impartial when the decision affects your own family, don't you think?'

'Only if you place them – wrongly – above your constituents. My father is a man of honour. He would never do this.' Jax felt that he had defended his father well against Kumiko Toyotomi, little realising that he had stepped into the old woman's trap.

'Then I presume he would not be averse to seeing his own son joined to the Altan queen, if, of course,' she added slyly, 'it could be proved beyond doubt that this would be the best union for lasting peace?'

The question shot through the air like a bullet and the ensuing silence hung heavily in the warm spring air. Out of the corner of his eye, Jax could see James Toyotomi writhing uncomfortably and he was aware of Navarr's shocked expression. But then the import of the old woman's words registered in his brain. He and Linnayen Genara married? *Impossible! Couldn't happen … Could it?*

'Madame, I appreciate your logic,' Jax began, trying hard to keep an impassive expression. 'And I maintain that my father would still act in the best interests of the people, no matter what the personal sacrifice. But I think you must know that I am not an appropriate or worthy suitor to the Ki of Altan. I hold no high office – my career has hardly begun and I am not involved in council business. Therefore, with respect, your argument is irrelevant.'

But Kumiko Toyotomi, after nearly a lifetime spent dogfighting in international committees and the council chamber itself, was not a woman to be easily quieted.

'Is it?' she asked lightly. She turned her attention to Navarr. 'Is it, Captain Navarr? Surely you considered our young Bashir when selecting appropriate gentlemen to marry your lady? After all, is he not well connected? From a good family? Is he not of the right age? And rich, too. How could he not be considered?'

Navarr, the supreme diplomat, felt himself too clever to be tricked by the old woman and he smiled across at her as he answered. 'Indeed, madame, Prince Bashir *was* considered in our deliberations. But knowing of his father's outspoken opposition to the peace treaty, it was felt that to approach him might be thought wilfully antagonistic and, therefore, counterproductive to our purposes. This, of course, bears no reflection on the suitability of the prince who, as I already believed from my studies, and now know for certain, is an excellent young man with exceptional qualities – as is your great-grandson.'

With this verbal flourish, he bowed his head to both Kumiko and to Jax, whose eyes were wide. Thoughts raced inside his head. *I was considered! She thought of me!* Then the reality of where they were and what they were here to do hit home. Jax had to face the fact that James Toyotomi was the chosen one, not him.

As suddenly as she had begun, Kumiko Toyotomi relented. She lowered her head, signifying that this part of the discussion had ended, then turned to a servant who stood in a recess of the veranda to order their food be served. Only James Toyotomi was surprised. He could not understand why his great-grandmother had chosen to disengage from her attack at the very moment when she could have won and seen off this ridiculous envoy with his half-cocked proposal from the Altani upstart. Did he really think that the Toyotomis, a family of imperial status going back nearly two millennia, honoured and respected throughout the world, would soil its bloodline with the seed of a barbaric alien? Preposterous!

As the tiny platters of food were placed in front of the gathering, the silence allowed each to digest their thoughts. Navarr was a little disconcerted that the old woman had precipitated his plot and was trying to work out how he could regain control of the outcome. Jax was dwelling gloomily over the thought that, but for his father's opposition to settling, he could have been the one to have the young Ki, not just in his dreams, but for real.

And Kumiko Toyotomi recalled the conversation she had had on the vidlink with the fine-looking old Altani gentleman who had suggested that she engineer these events. He had struck her as an honourable man with a genuine desire for peace. Could she, perchance, steer the conversation or plant certain thoughts? The old man had explained to her that whilst her great-grandson was a worthy young man and an eminently acceptable suitor for the hand of the Ki, how much better it would be for the Ki to marry her enemy's son. He hoped she would not be offended but would support him and the Ki in their quest for peace and an end to these ridiculous, terrible hostilities. Kumiko had been more than happy to oblige him in his request. Rather than sully her family, let the Bashirs be saddled with the alien whore. And if it brings the beginning of much lucrative trade for the Toyotomis then so much the better.

Chapter Ten

*T*oday, *I spoke again to the Bashir prince. He is a pleasant enough young man, but very naïve. I can see in his eyes and by his body language that he is becoming infatuated with me; he has a dazed look about him. This will not, of course, harm the situation and should add to his fervour for the marriage. But I hope it soon passes. I can think of nothing more intolerable than having this young man mooning after me like a lovesick kareek.*

As for Captain Navarr, he looked very well. His skin has darkened since he has been on Earth – the ultraviolet emissions from their sun are very strong and the skin of many Earthans becomes thus tanned. But I have to say that the shade suits the captain. It makes him look even more handsome.

I wish I could talk to someone about the feelings I have. Beoraan cannot help, of course. Evica suspects, I think, but she is too wrapped up in her own feelings for Lieutenant Min to be objective. And that's another problem brewing – and I do not know how I will deal with it either. Father never told me how to properly separate my personal feelings from my abilities to govern. I suppose we ran out of time.

Milos Visnivic had no doubt that what he was about to do would, one day, go down in history, because he would be a hero. He alone would be responsible for halting the takeover of Earth by the despicable Union of Planets.

In his mind's eye, he saw his statue in town squares, his image on every front page and vidscreen, his story told in museum exhibits and libraries. They would examine his life and tell of how the great rebel hero grew up in a sad and sorry shanty in the mangroves of the Amazon Basin, where his family eked out a living processing fish oil for the cosmonogenic parts plant in Macapa. He heard an imaginary newsreader explain how his traditionalist parents, albeit of mixed Slav and Amazon Indian descent themselves, had fostered in him a belief that the purity of the races was all important and bloodlines should never be tainted. He recalled how his father, a fervent member of the Unified Nation Party, would thump the table in anger, roundly cursing Hispanics, Jews, 'Polaks' and all other races he could think of, blaming them for all the troubles in the world, and for taking the best jobs at the plant.

Once grown, Milos moved away from the dank, stifling heat of the mangroves and went to the city. He studied at college and he travelled in the holidays, taking in the beauty of his home continent. After graduation, he made his father proud by joining the armed forces. They trained him to be a fighter pilot and he relished his new skills. Learning to fight using such refined and well-honed weapons fulfilled his most fervent wish: to save his planet from invasion by the Union and its despicable alien species. It was ridiculous that his instructors and superiors could not appreciate his ideology – why else train him to kill? He had had to keep his thoughts private, of course. He reasoned that if they didn't want him to fight for them, there were others who did, and he lost little time in finding them.

His eyes were glassy, consumed by his fantasies and his memories. Suddenly, the voice of the onboard computer broke his reverie and reminded him that he had a job to do.

'Target craft, *Brutus*, is now within range.'

Visnivic had selected a voice for his raptor's computer system that sounded like a sexy young woman. He often passed the time in the cockpit imagining what she might look like, enjoying his body's subtle but sublime response to her deep voice.

'What are the coordinates of the micro-smelter?' he asked the computer.

'Zero one three, zero zero two,' came the reply. Visnivic turned his head to the left, reading a display of figures on a lighted panel.

'Stand by,' he said, concentrating hard on the panel. 'On my mark, detonate smelter.'

'Standing by.'

A few seconds passed during which Visnivic looked up out of the cockpit window only once. He did not need to see where he was going; the comp-system took care of the flying. But he could see the jagged peaks of the mountains now no more than ten kilometres away and was pleased that when *Brutus* went down – as it so surely would – there would be no chance of survival for the passengers. If they weren't killed in the impact, the sub-zero temperatures would soon finish them off.

The panel finally showed him the information he needed – all the coordinates reached zero.

'Fire!' he cried, and the computer duly responded.

The honeyed voice responded, 'Micro-smelter detonated.'

Visnivic smiled broadly as he took over the controls of the raptor. He turned it towards the north and the bulk of the mountains, searching the skyline for his target. He would not only get the scum alien envoy but the traitor president's son as well. *Two for the price of one! This'll show the lily-livered son of a bitch not to go pandering to the Union freakos.*

Senior pilot Celeste Malone had been flying for twelve of the twenty years she had been in the Special Services Corps. She was a good pilot with an exemplary record and, importantly, she knew how to address the senior diplomats and politicians with courtesy and professionalism. Her skills brought her a variety of commissions all over the world – even a long-hauler to one of Jupiter's moons, Ganymede, escorting the director of gas mining to his new post.

It was only now that she was in her forties that she had begun to think about retiring from the force to raise a family. For all the advances in science and the ability to create babies in artificial wombs, there was still no better way of raising children than inside the loving confines of a family. Retirement, though, would be a quiet affair after such a high-flying lifestyle and she was still in two minds about whether to give it all up or not.

This next mission, to fly the Altani envoy and the president's son back to Nairobi from their meetings in Hokkaido, would be straightforward enough. It would also give Celeste the chance to see the isolated northern island, which she had heard had a raw rugged beauty. That was one of the perks of the job, she thought. She got to see so many different places, landscapes, even space-scapes, and she never tired of their beauty.

Considering what the planet had been through in the last couple of millennia, with warfare, terrorism, mass deforestation, species extinction, famines and global climate changes, it was amazing that anything lovely survived at all. It had all but become a wasteland, where the majority of people scraped a living out of barren soils between bleak, forbidding cities. Thank God for the United Democratic Nations Council, which had fought hard to bring countries together and restore environments.

Celeste waited patiently next to the aircar outside the massive wooden door of the Toyotomi residence. She had already been notified on her transceiver that the envoy and the young prince were making their farewells and would be with her in about two minutes. She opened the panels of the aircar, making the vehicle ready to receive its occupants. Suddenly she felt a small pricking sensation on her right cheek and put her hand up to rub the affected area. Pulling her hand away, she noticed the smear of blood and the squashed remains of the mosquito that had bitten her. *Just what I need,* she thought. But the bite was not itching. In fact, when she looked in the aircar's mirror, she could barely see the mark at all.

The weather down from Hokkaido to the northern edge of the great Himalaya Mountains was clear and bright and Celeste was enjoying the flight. Jax was dozing fitfully in a reclined seat in the rear cabin of the small but luxuriously fitted turbocraft, and Navarr was listening to recordings of last week's council meeting. Apart from the pilot, Navarr and Jax, only Count Joseph Aramikov, a high-ranking SSC aide who had been assigned to look after the personal needs of the envoy, was aboard the craft, making the manifest four in all.

With time now to reflect on their meeting with the Toyotomis, Navarr was rather pleased that the old woman had raised the suggestion of Jax being the chosen husband, if only for the expression on the boy's face. Jax had been surprised at first, then almost wistful as he had ruminated on the idea. Did the prince have a secret longing for his beautiful mistress, he wondered. And, if so, how smitten was he? More importantly, did Navarr really want him to be in love with Linnayen, or would that cause unnecessary complications?

He looked out of the window. They had entered a remote, mountainous area. Jagged peaks pierced through unblemished caps of snow and ice, which lay like a pale gold cloak in the late afternoon sunshine. Despite his unease with Earthans and general dislike of their casual manners, he had to admit that they possessed a remarkable planet with exceptional natural resources – one that the Union would do well to bring into its fold as soon as possible.

Back in the cockpit, Celeste Malone tapped the enviroscope and asked the computer, once again, to run a system check. It had been playing up since they left Hokkaido. She had run diagnostics on every piece of equipment on board and there was absolutely nothing wrong. The scope was now showing that the unstable chemical hyproxichlorazine was present somewhere within a ten-metre radius. But this was impossible. Hyproxichlorazine was not only extremely rare – one of its component chemicals was found only on the gas giant Neptune in minute quantities – but was also a banned substance, held only in the most secure laboratories on the planet or on its home world. No, the scope had to be picking up something with a similar atomic signature and reading it skewed, she thought, and she mentally noted to get it recalibrated when they got to Nairobi.

'Micro-smelter detonated.'

At that very moment, in response to the signal received from the raptor, a transpondic emitter fired a tiny explosive charge that pierced the membrane, separating the two halves of a microscopic bicapsule. The bicapsule, one half of which contained a droplet of the dangerous chemical hyproxichlorazine, had travelled through Celeste Malone's body from its entry point on her right cheek and nestled in the aortic muscles close to her left ventricle. The chemical reaction that took place resulted in an instantaneous emission of heat at around 550 degrees Celsius, propelled initially at a rate of fifteen metres per second. This speed depended on the density of objects it met and could be reduced to a mere five metres per second when up against certain metals such as lead or iron.

The human body being of a soft and light composition, most mercifully Celeste Malone was dead before the nerve endings near her heart got a message through to her brain that she was in extreme pain. Her lifeless eyes did not see her flesh as it dropped in syrupy ripples away from her cream-coloured bones, which, in their turn, shattered and powdered – all in the space of three seconds.

The reaction continued relentlessly downwards, pulled by a force even greater than itself, gravity, towards the floor of the cockpit. Melting through cables and conduits on the way, it met the titanium alloy shell of the craft and, finally, the force of its genesis fully expended, the reaction ceased.

If the micro-smelter had not had enough force to melt through the floor of the cockpit, there was every chance that the craft's autopilot would have continued to keep them flying and the passengers might never have known their predicament. As it was, the sudden increased pitch of the engines and the even more worrying dip of the turbocraft's nose instantly alerted Navarr and the SSC aide, Count Aramikov.

Navarr shot up out of his seat and ran towards the cockpit door, while Aramikov shook Jax, who was, in any case, already coming out of his sleep, his body's senses sending subconscious danger signals to his brain.

'Quick, sir! Wake up!' Aramikov cried desperately.

One look at the sticky remains of the pilot and the gaping hole in the cockpit floor was enough to tell Navarr that they were in serious trouble. He did not know enough about the Earthan craft to know how to fly it, so he turned back into the cabin to look for emergency parasuits, reasoning that their only chance of survival would be to evacuate.

Jax quickly shook off the remains of his nap and, in a split-second, his brain switched into military mode. His years of training at the academy came flooding back in an instant and he strode purposefully to the cockpit, almost pushing Navarr out of the way.

The pilot's chair was virtually non-existent and he tried hard to put aside his queasiness at the oozy concoction there that had once been a living human being. Settling himself into the co-pilot's chair, he took control of the joystick and began to assess their situation. He ran through the quickest key systems' check he had ever done whilst pulling back on the stick to raise the craft's nose. The mountains were looming ever closer and he prayed that they would begin to level off and regain some height soon.

At that moment, Navarr came back with a parasuit for him.

'Here, put this on,' he commanded.

Jax did as he was told, wriggling his arms one by one into the bright orange jacket. He recognised the logic in Navarr's thinking – there was no need to reply.

Gradually, the turbocraft began to fly level, although Jax could not get it to climb, no matter how fiercely he pulled back on the joystick. Now, at least, they were not heading down into the mountains. But they were leaking fuel and Jax was aware that a prolube fluid line somewhere must have been damaged because the fuselage was tipping from side to side. He was barely able to control the sway and knew that he could not keep it up for too long.

'What's happening?' Navarr called out to Jax above the screeching whine of the engines.

'Fuel leak, hydraulics gone, losing height,' Jax shouted back, not daring to take his eyes off the instrument panels, which were flashing in front of him.

'We can't go down in this country,' Navarr cried back. 'We'll have to jump.'

Jax ignored the comment and focused on the job at hand – keeping them straight and aloft.

Within a minute, Jax had the turbocraft under as much under control as he was going to get it. He had already sent out an alarm call and, luckily, the still-functioning computer was able to tell him that there was an unmanned but serviceable airdock at the small mountain town of Pokhara about a hundred kilometres away. At that speed, slow as it was, they would be there in only five minutes. He looked over his shoulder at the serious faces of Navarr and Aramikov.

'We can make Pokhara in under five minutes,' he called out.

'No!' answered Navarr. 'Let's get out now, while we can.'

'Never survive. Minus forty.' Unconsciously, Jax had reduced his speech to the bare minimum needed to communicate. It was as though his body had made the decision to divert all his mental strength towards keeping them alive.

Aware of the silence behind him, he turned his head and gave a quick, reassuring nod to the two men.

'Don't worry. We'll make it.'

In the raptor, Visnivic was slightly irritated to see from his sensors that *Brutus* had not gone down yet. He knew that the micro-smelter had done its job because he had intercepted the emergency transmission – and blocked it, of course. It was tiresome, but he was going to have to go in and finish them off.

The course he steered brought him into range in less than two minutes and he was gratified to see that the turbocraft was pouring smoke from beneath its fuselage. Its flight pattern was unsteady, wings tipping continuously. Visnivic guessed that whoever was at the controls was taking it towards the airdock at Pokhara.

'Oh no you don't,' he muttered to himself, and swung the raptor's joystick gently to the left, bringing the craft onto an intercept course with its target.

As soon as it was in sight, Visnivic armed his weapons array and made ready to fire. He was going to enjoy this. But he wanted to see the face of whoever was flying the plane. That look of sheer terror just before he killed someone always turned him on.

He brought the raptor up on a parallel and level course with the turbocraft and held it steady some fifty metres off to its left. He saw the stand-in pilot and smiled when he recognised the traitor's offspring. *How apt*, he thought. *Your father will want to know how you died. Now I can tell him.*

Out of the corner of his left eye, Jax became aware of the shape of another craft. For a split-second he entertained the hope that it might be a rescue plane. But the grin on the face of the pilot was, somehow, disturbing. He was instantly on his guard. The fact that it was a raptor was also worrying. It was a hunter-fighter craft, not commonly used for rescue or patrol flying. Something was wrong.

The raptor dipped away, below and aft of the turbocraft.

'What's going on?' asked Navarr. Jax was about to answer when the computer emitted a warning siren.

'Shit!' he said under his breath, frantically touching lighted pads on a control panel to his left. 'He's firing at us.'

No sooner had he finished speaking than the first of Visnivic's missiles rammed into the stern shield that Jax had just engaged, jarring the craft but not significantly damaging it.

'What was that?' Navarr asked urgently.

'Felt like an aerojammer,' Jax replied, trying to get the computer to lock them into an evasion course programme. For now, he was faced with having to fly the craft manually. 'Damn! Look, I'm going to try –'

Wham! Once again, a missile from the raptor slammed into the shield, unsteadying Navarr and Aramikov, who toppled back into the main cabin. Navarr got quickly to his feet and returned to the doorway leading to the cockpit, leaving the count to crawl into a passenger seat.

'Try to what?' he asked Jax.

'Fly manually,' Jax replied quickly, shouting above the increased noise of the engines. 'We've got to get down. The shield can only take two more hits and that bastard hasn't missed yet.'

'You're mad!' Navarr called back. 'You can't land in this terrain. Let's jump while we can.'

Jax dismissed the suggestion once again. 'If we jump he'll pick us off one by one. Our best chance is to stay in here as long as possible.'

The craft was swaying and turning wildly in its efforts to evade the raptor as Jax regained more control. Visnivic let loose another missile, but due to Jax's expert piloting it missed and whooshed past, churning up the air ahead. The resulting turbulence nearly threw Jax from his seat and Navarr had to hold on tight to the frame of the cockpit door.

Jax had been steadily bringing the craft down since the raptor's attack began and he tried to keep it at a height of about a thousand metres while looking desperately for somewhere to land. There was nothing. The peaks jutted out hard and sharp against the cobalt sky and, although the snow-covered slopes looked soft, Jax knew that the inclines were just too steep. Land there and they would slam into the rock beneath.

'Look for a landing area, Navarr,' he called over his shoulder.

The craft continued its mad, zigzag course as it dodged the raptor, which had now begun small weapons fire. Jax felt the shudders as a couple of fission lasers ripped through the flank sections of the hull at the back of the craft. Warning lights flashed in all the companels and the computer voice monotonously warned of key systems' failures, until Jax felt ready to punch its keypad to shut it up. Amazingly, they kept aloft. But so, too, did the raptor and Jax was beginning to realise that he could not evade it much longer.

'There!' Navarr's voice cried out and he shot an arm forward. Jax saw it instantly: a level snow plateau about six or seven hundred metres long, only a few kilometres ahead.

'It'll do!' he called back. 'Hold on.'

Navarr dashed back into the cabin and threw himself down into a seat, grabbing frantically for the safety harness. The turbocraft suddenly lurched and plunged as its speed decreased in preparation for landing. In the cockpit, Jax made frantic efforts to control the craft, his body shifting and jerking around in the seat. All the while he was aware of the fission laser emissions blazing past the window, and he knew that they were only missing them by a few metres. The raptor's pilot was good. But this was what Jax had been trained for at the academy – combative air action – and he had proved to be one of their most gifted pilots. Now that he was into his stride, his senses took over and he was a hard man to beat.

They would have only one shot at landing on the snow plateau, just one kilometre away, and Jax focused all his energies on lining up for the landing.

Suddenly there was a hammer blow to the rear of the craft. They had been hit and a whole section of the hull blew away in a shower of sparks and flames. Jax hoped the smoke from the strike would blind the raptor pilot for a few seconds as it homed in on them, giving Jax the time he desperately needed to drop to twenty metres above ground level. They were within seconds of landing in the snowdrifts of the high plateau almost directly beneath him.

The controls were now dead and Jax knew that all they could do now was hope that the hull would hold together long enough after impact to allow them at least a chance to survive. He closed his eyes and his mouth formed the words of a silent prayer.

There was a sudden smacking impact on the underbelly of the hull, followed by the grinding noise of metal upon rock as the momentum of the landing carried them forward. The fuselage twisted and slithered wildly and, even within the confines of the safety harness, Jax's body was thrown around like a fallen leaf in a raging mountain stream.

Back in the cabin, Navarr and Aramikov were faring no better and, with every crunching sound and shuddering smash, Navarr wondered if these were to be his last seconds alive.

Finally, all movement stopped. Whirling blasts of snow filled the broken craft, dampening the crackling sparks and smothering flames. Jax ripped open the clasps of his harness and bolted for the cabin. Navarr, too, was already out of his seat and moving towards the frightened Aramikov to help him.

'Come on!' Jax called, noticing the showers of embers falling around them. Half the fuselage on the port side was missing and clouds of steam and snow were beginning to fill the space, making it difficult to see. Navarr finally got Aramikov to his feet and led him towards the opening, where Jax was working at the catches of a depressed storage panel. As they pushed past him into the freezing air, Jax got the panel cover free and reached inside. He took out two Fox 49 atomic rifles and handed one of them to Navarr.

Without a word, Navarr took the weapon and slung it over his shoulder. They could plainly hear the raptor's engines. It seemed to be veering back around to the crash site.

'Jax! Look!' Navarr cried out, pointing to his left with the end of the rifle.

'I see it,' Jax called back. 'Run!'

In the swirl of snow and debris they could just make out a small outcrop of tumbled black rocks that would give them some cover. It was not as far from the smouldering wreckage of the turbocraft as Jax would have liked, but they had no choice. The raptor had circled above them and the screeching whine of its engines was clearly getting closer. They would be lucky to make it to the outcrop before the determined pilot was on them once again.

They had just made it, flinging their bodies down, when the first crashing explosions of the raptor's weapons hit, sending shards of rock into the air. Jax did not know if the blood-streaked scratches on their faces had come from the crash itself or from the splinters of rock thrown up by the raptor's fire.

It was coming around again, but this time Navarr and Jax had time to ready their rifles. They managed to get off a few shots, none of which hit the speeding fighter, when there was a huge shattering of the rock around them. One of the raptor's missiles had struck home and their cover was blown into a thousand pieces. The impact threw Aramikov into a snowdrift some ten paces away. Jax and Navarr were unhurt, but with their protection gone, they knew they had to run. It seemed obvious that one of them was the assassin's target; at least they could lead him away from Aramikov.

'This way!' Navarr called across to Jax, and they began running as fast as they could across the icy surface. Ahead of them a swirling wall of wind-whipped snow blocked their view and, at any other time, it would have been madness to plunge into it. But, Jax reasoned, if *they* could not see through it then neither could the raptor's pilot. Besides, it was the only cover they had.

Suddenly the ground dropped away and they began to fall. In the whirling whiteness, just as his stomach began to catch up with the rest of his body, Jax felt his hand being gripped tightly while his legs swung in open space. Navarr had him. But as Jax could see once the air cleared around them, he was barely holding on himself. Navarr's right hand was clenched around a small, sharp protrusion of frost-covered rock, which jutted out from a narrow ledge. His left held Jax's wrist like a vice.

They had fallen only a few metres down the cliff face, but it was enough to confuse Visnivic and put paid to the strafing run he had been about to commence. As he flew past the cliff edge he saw the mountain drop sheerly away to an enclosed valley some five hundred metres below and he realised that the two men must have fallen into it. He swung the raptor to port to come around, figuring that he might still be able to see the bodies either falling or already smashed on the white valley floor.

'Climb!' Navarr spoke through gritted teeth as blood trickled from a cut on his cheek into his mouth. 'I won't drop you.'

Jax did not need to be asked twice. He was amazed at the strength of the man. Were all Altanis this strong? Navarr's arm slowly bent, muscles straining, as he pulled up Jax's dangling frame until he was within reach of the ledge. Once he had found a handhold, Jax hauled himself the rest of the way up, trying not to use Navarr's dangling body for leverage. Once securely on the ledge, he turned his attention to Navarr.

'Give me your other hand. I'll pull you up.' He croaked the words out, struggling for breath.

Below them they heard rather than saw the raptor flying in tight circles, obviously searching for them. They were not out of danger yet. Navarr had just reached the safety of the ledge when the whine of the raptor's engines increased as it turned in the air and came towards them.

Visnivic laughed as he took the fighter in towards the cliff face and the two scrambling figures. He wanted to get a little closer before he dispatched them to see the look on their faces. His body was already excited by the battle, adrenalin pumping, blood coursing. He was almost giddy with anticipated pleasure and had to force himself to focus as he pushed the joystick forward.

The raptor came at them, straight and level, not yet firing. But Jax knew they were done for. The mad pilot had seen them and was coming in for the kill. Out of the corner of his eye, though, Jax saw Navarr move. In one swift action, Navarr swung the Fox 49 down into his hands, took aim and began rapid fire – straight into the oncoming cockpit and the pilot's icy eyes.

The raptor suddenly plunged down and slammed into the rock wall about thirty metres below them. It exploded in a slow-motion fireball and the cliff vibrated in response to the impact. In a flurry of falling rock and snow, the ledge crumbled beneath their feet. But instead of falling, as they had expected, a rush of hot air hit the soles of their feet and they were thrust up into the clear, crisp sky. The shockwave from the explosion carried them about five metres above the plateau where they had crash-landed before they fell back in a rolling tumble on the soft, deep snow.

When they came to some minutes later, Aramikov was kneeling next to them, his eyes turned up to the sky. Next to him was the turbocraft's emergency emitter, orange lights flashing. Aramikov was watching the approach of two rescue hoverplanes.

At first the whirring, whining sound of the engines unsettled Jax and he thought it was the raptor coming at them. Then he remembered what had happened. He glanced across at Navarr, who had just regained consciousness. The two men looked into each other's eyes and knew in that moment that they had forged an unbreakable bond. They had shared a common danger, fought a common foe, and the adventure they had just lived through brought with it a mutual respect. For Jax, it was a bond of comradeship that would be hard to break. For Navarr, it was a grudging admiration for the young prince and the knowledge that, for his tenacity alone, you would not want this man for your enemy.

'Your plan failed and the Order wants to know what you intend to do about it.'

The female voice issuing from the implant behind his ear was smooth and deep with only the slightest trace of an accent. But Hal Byers knew only too well that its owner was not a woman to cross. He had never met her, did not even know her real name. But he had seen the results of her handiwork, mostly in the headlines of every journal and vidnews outlet on the planet – and it was never pretty. He knew her only as Oleander and in her quiet but forceful way, she insisted on an answer.

'I know.' His voice was low and controlled, and he hoped it suppressed the nervousness he was feeling. 'And I want you to assure the Order that I have the situation under control.'

'May I remind you that you are being paid handsomely for your assistance?' Her tone was clipped and efficient. 'We expect results.'

'I know that – and they'll come.' Byers was irritated by the veiled threat in Oleander's words. He did not need reminding of the objectives of his commission from the Order of Sumere.

'The Order does not doubt you,' she replied, 'but it is impatient and concerned that this peace treaty may succeed if you do not act *quickly*.' The emphasis she gave to her final word contained a hint of danger, enough to make Byers aware that the sweat on his upper lip was not only brought about by the wet heat of the Nairobi afternoon.

'The downing of *Brutus* was just one option,' he countered. 'I have others. But I want to be sure this time. Don't forget, the Order wanted a fast response to the problem – *against* my advice.'

'Understood and noted.' Oleander sighed. She was tiring of the conversation. 'But I am not here to have a discussion with you. The problem remains: fix it before *you* become the problem.'

Oleander's voice was replaced by a single toned beep, signifying that the transmission was over. Then there was silence. Byers turned away from the animatronic primate exhibit in the Royal Environmental Gardens that he had been pretending to study whilst he spoke with Oleander. He looked around, checking once again that he was alone. Satisfied that he had not been observed, he meandered down the small tree-lined incline towards the exit gate, wondering all the while how in hell he was going to stop this infernal peace treaty.

Chapter Eleven

As it turned out, the one who suffered the worst injuries from their encounter with Milos Visnivic was Count Aramikov, who sustained a broken arm and three fractured ribs. He was forced to stay in the hospital at Delhi while Jax and Navarr resumed their journey to Nairobi. Remarkably, they had acquired only superficial cuts, bruises and stiffness in their limbs. But the incident, and their survival of it, left a lasting impression on Jax. He was now more determined than ever to ensure that the envoy's visit met with success.

Clutching a Special Services Corps report, he touched the access panel on the door to Navarr's apartment and waited for it to announce him to the occupant. The door slid open and Jax entered the room.

'Envoy Navarr, I have the final report,' he began.

'Ah yes. Our assassin. Who was his target? You or me?' Navarr asked. He sat at his desk and stretched a hand forward to take the report from Jax.

'Actually, both of us,' Jax replied. 'The pilot was one Milos Visnivic, a radical right-winger, member of Labyrinth, a terrorist organisation dedicated to keeping Earth free from – pardon me – 'contamination' by alien species … their word. As an Altani with a supremely important mission, you were an obvious target. I was chosen because Labyrinth believes that my father is collaborating with the enemy by continuing the peace discussions.'

'I see,' Navarr said. 'So your death was meant to be a warning to your father?'

'Correct. Had they succeeded it would probably have worked. You know my father has his doubts. Our deaths would certainly have caused him to stop the peace talks.'

'That would have been terribly disappointing now that we have come so far.' Navarr let his brow furrow in a look of concern and sorrow. 'My lady is impatient to have an answer from Dr Toyotomi, if only because it means that we can get the marriage underway. Now that we know the strength of the opposition, it is even more important to move quickly.'

Jax was nodding in agreement. But he could not help but squirm uncomfortably at the mention of the Toyotomi name. Since their meeting with Kumiko and James Toyotomi, he had thought of little else but the old lady's words. '*His own son joined to the Altan queen … If it could be proved beyond doubt that this would be the best union for lasting peace.*'

Then Navarr's response: '*Prince Bashir* was *considered in our deliberations.*' But he had been rejected due to his father's expected opposition. What if his father did not object though? What if he could prove to his father that a marriage between the houses of Bashir and Genara was the best possible resolution for peace? Would the proud and beautiful Linnayen Genara still have him for a husband?

Jax knew that he could not keep his thoughts bottled up for much longer. He had seen and spoken to her again shortly after their escape from the raptor's attack and, once more, was almost struck dumb by her beauty and regal bearing. When she spoke, her velvet voice made him shiver with pleasure and he avowed silently that a man could joyfully drown in the clear pools of her green eyes – crystal green, not grey and clouded like Harrie's. Slowly, the pain of his first love affair was receding – thanks to the beautiful alien queen – although he suspected that he would never quite be free of the images in his head. Harrie and her lover. He thrust them away.

The more he saw of Linnayen Genara, the more he thought of her, the more he could not stop thinking of her, and the agonies of indecision were churning him up inside.

'Navarr … May I put something to you?' he asked hesitantly. Navarr, who had been skimming the pages of the SSC report, looked up and noticed that Jax was unusually nervous.

'Yes, of course. What is it?'

'I've been thinking about what the old lady said … Kumiko Toyotomi. About how it would make for a more secure peace if the Lady Linnayen were to marry a husband from an opposing house, rather than a friendly one …' Jax wanted to set the scene very carefully. He did not want his suggestion to sound ridiculous or too forward.

'Yes. And?' queried Navarr, keeping a puzzled expression on his face. *The little fish is biting!*

'Well, I think she's right.' Jax's statement brought a look of surprise to Navarr's face and, seeing this, he hurried to correct any misunderstanding. 'I mean … Well, no offence to Dr Toyotomi, who is an admirable man, but a marriage with him might serve only to alienate your opponents – people like my father.' Now that he'd started, the words began to come more easily and, because Navarr had not interrupted him, he felt encouraged to go on.

'Surely that would be disastrous both for Earth and the Union of Planets? And, as you said, we have come so far. So can I respectfully suggest that you, or rather the Lady Linnayen, look at an alternative candidate?'

'I see your point.' Navarr gave the appearance of carefully considering what Jax was saying. He shook his head ruefully. 'But our negotiations are well advanced. Unless you have someone special in mind …' Navarr let his words hang between them.

Jax cleared his throat and swallowed. 'Me.'

There. It was out now. He could breathe again. At the look of near shock on Navarr's face, Jax thought he had better qualify his statement in some way. 'You told me yourself that I had originally been considered and that I'd only been rejected because of my father's presumed opposition. But what if I could persuade my father? What if I could make him see that this would be the best – the *only* workable solution to our problems? Do you think the Ki would reconsider?'

'Maybe. You *were* a highly regarded candidate,' Navarr conceded, drawing his eyebrows together in a look of concentration. 'But what about the Toyotomis? What if Dr James says yes?' he asked.

Jax's eyes searched about the room, as if he could find the answer there. 'I honestly don't know,' he replied, then, after a few seconds of quiet thought, he went on. 'But shouldn't you ask her? After all, it's immaterial if she is totally against having me anyway.'

'Yes, but then there's your father, Jax,' Navarr countered. 'He would never permit it, no matter how forceful the argument. I don't know if the Ki would want to risk alienating him even further.'

'He can be a tough old bird, true. And I'm not saying it would be easy to bring him round,' Jax admitted. 'But if the Ki is willing to have me, I am willing to try. It's like Kumiko said, if it can be proved that this is the best union – for the peace treaty, for *all* our people – then we must make sacrifices. That's if you think of this as a sacrifice, which, actually, I don't.'

Navarr sat back in his chair, pondering Jax's words. Things were going perfectly. The old Toyotomi woman, without knowing it, had done his job for him very well indeed and he had the foolish young prince eating out of his hand – his and Linnayen's. Navarr had picked up the desperation in Jax's words. Though he had tried to make himself sound cool and detached, it hadn't worked. Navarr saw through him. The boy was infatuated and this was making him more determined to marry his Ki. Surely, given the apparent strength of his feelings, he would prevail over the stubborn father?

'Very well,' Navarr replied. 'I will bring your idea before my lady – in confidence, of course. And we will take it from there, eh? I'm sure we will have an answer for you by the time I join you in Cairo.' Smiling as affectionately as he knew how, he stood up and reached across the desk to shake Jax's hand.

As he turned to walk back towards the door, Jax could hardly believe what had just happened. He had done it! He had put himself forward to become the husband to the most amazing woman in the universe! Navarr did not seem horrified or insulted by the idea, which was encouraging. But how would the one who mattered most react? What would be Linnayen Genara's answer?

His face was solemn and studious, hiding a whirlpool of thoughts as he returned to his rooms. It was only when he closed the door behind him that he let out the large sigh that he had been storing inside. It was quickly followed by a wide grin.

The compact vidscreen in Navarr's day case flickered into life. Instantly, Balisel Navarr's icily beautiful face appeared and, as soon as she saw her brother, her feline eyes widened and she smiled.

'Durroc.'

'Balisel.' An uncommon warmth filled his eyes. 'I have good news. Everything is going well. I should be able to leave for home in less than two weeks.'

'I'm pleased to hear that, little brother,' she replied. 'I've missed you.'

'Me too.' His voice was low and his face became intense. 'And I want to see you as soon as I can after my return. That's one of my reasons for calling.'

Balisel's eyes widened as she gazed into his.

Navarr continued. 'The fish is hooked at this end but not at the other, and that's where I need your help.'

'Whatever I can do,' she returned. 'Although I'm surprised. I wouldn't have thought you needed my help.'

'Perhaps I won't. But I'm a great believer in insurance.'

Balisel smiled again. She loved intrigue and the thought of manipulating events to help her brother and, ultimately, herself held no fears for her, only excitement.

'So you would like me to …?' She waited for his reply.

'Gentle persuasion will take too long. But the threat of danger can be an effective inducement, don't you think? If her life, or maybe her honour, was at stake – and a loyal protector was there to save her in the nick of time – she might be very grateful, eh?' he asked, a sneer curling the edges of his mouth.

'She would be indebted to her rescuer,' Balisel concurred. 'She would want to keep him close by at all times.'

'I knew you would understand.' Navarr laughed, confident that his sister understood very well what was expected of her.

'Leave it with me, brother. I will find a tame shark to frighten your little fish into the net. Now, when can we get together?'

'Why not take some time off and join me on Altan when I get back?' he asked, his voice softening, deepening.

'I'll be there,' she promised.

The screen went blank. Navarr leaned back in his chair and closed his eyes with a satisfied smile.

Jax had left Navarr in Nairobi finalising the details of the treaty with Ambassador Byers while he flew to Cairo to see his father. It had been two days since he had put his suggestion to Navarr and he was both surprised and relieved to have heard back that morning that Linnayen Genara was giving it her full consideration.

At least she had not totally thrown it out of court, he thought. He was in with a chance.

As the small turbocraft flew low over the parched brown plains of the Nubian Desert, Jax reflected on what had passed. He still could not quite believe that he had made the proposal. He did not even know if he was ready for marriage yet and the strangeness of making a home on another planet. But he *did* want the peace treaty to be finalised and the alien woman *was* stunning and just as dedicated to its success. Would it be so different to the arranged marriages of his own race's past? Those parents had made the choices usually to improve the family's status or increase its wealth. Often love had little to do with it. The only difference now was that *he* was making the choice. His family's fortunes and standing would be much enhanced by a union with the Altani queen and, whilst it may be a formal marriage, a strategic alliance, who was to say that she may not come to love him in time?

These thoughts were still fresh in his mind as he landed at the Garden City airdock in the ancient quarter of Cairo. There to meet him was his mother.

Thea Bashir's darkly beautiful face wore a worried look and there were dark circles under her eyes. She had wanted to race to Delhi where Jax and Navarr had been kept in the hospital when she first heard about the assassination attempt. But Sheikh Bashir had asked her not to go. He felt that it would signify to the terrorists that they had partly achieved their aims if the Bashir family or the council reacted hurriedly. No, he had explained, better to play it cool. Better to give the appearance that the terrorists' actions had not got to them. Jax was unharmed, so Thea must wait until their son returned to Cairo.

Even so, she could not hide her relief at seeing him, tall, fit and with his bruises and scratches healing well. With no words of greeting, she took him in her arms and hugged him, pausing only to lean back and take in the features of his face. He had come so close to death, her only, most precious child. And he was alive!

'Mother,' he said, returning her hug and kissing her on the cheek. 'How are you?'

'Never mind me. How are you?' Her voice wavered a little with the emotional release of the moment. 'I wanted to come to you. But your father said we mustn't give in to terrorists by showing how much they affected us. And you weren't too badly hurt after all. But I wanted to come …'

'I know, Mother, I know. It's all right.' He tried to comfort her, stroking her hair as she stayed in his arms. 'Father was right – and I was fine. Just a few cuts and bruises.'

'Yes, but you could have been killed,' she countered.

'But I wasn't, was I? We are all fine. Even Aramikov will be out of hospital in two days and back at work in a couple of weeks,' he reassured her again.

'Even so, I was worried.'

Jax smiled down at her. 'Well, thank you. It's nice to have someone who cares, eh?' he fondly teased her. 'Now then, come on. I want to see Father. Where is he?'

'Stuck in a prograin budget meeting,' she replied, and Jax grimaced sympathetically. He knew how much his father hated the humdrum, bureaucratic meetings, but even he acknowledged that they were a necessary part of the democratic process that kept the nations from fighting once more. Thea continued, 'But I've sent a message to tell him you've arrived. He'll be home by the time we get there.'

'Good, because I've lots to tell him. Well, both of you, actually.'

Thea raised her eyebrows in mild surprise. 'Sounds intriguing. What's this all about?'

'Wait till we get home. I only want to say it once.'

Once will be more than enough, he thought and, in an instant, the euphoria he had felt over the last couple of days withered and died.

'Kevor!'

David Bashir got smartly to his feet as his son and wife entered the room, which also doubled as his office when he was at home. 'There you are. It's good to see you, son. Are you well now?'

David moved across to encircle his son in his arms. Sheikh Bashir was more than relieved that Jax was safe. Despite their differences – or maybe because of them – he treasured his son. It was just so difficult to tell him that he loved him.

'Yes, Father, I'm fine. Only a few cuts and they're healing well,' Jax replied, pulling back from his father's warm hug.

'Those swine!' Bashir exclaimed. 'I can't believe what they tried to do. Needless to say, we've put Covert Seven onto it and they are trying to track down the members of Labyrinth.'

Covert Seven, or C7 as it was more commonly known, was the name of a specialist anti-terrorist squad comprising secret agents from the seven super-nations: Antipodea, Amerimex, Nippon-ko, Eurotania, Africana, Indi-Chine and Latinia. Its agents were highly trained in various forms of assassination, espionage and survival and they were used to combat internal threats to global security. In recent years, though, they had also operated off-world on the various moon colonies of the solar system and it was widely believed – though never confirmed – that some of its members, on the pretext of infiltration, were actively engaged in the resistance movement. It was a short step from being an officially sanctioned planetary guardian to becoming a rogue resistance fighter, defending the Earth against all comers, and it was a line that Bashir knew some C7 operatives had crossed, even though he could not prove it. Still, commissioning them was the best they could do in this instance; if anyone could get inside Labyrinth, they could.

'They'll have their work cut out for them. From what I've read – and there's little enough of it – Labyrinth is deep undercover,' Jax returned. 'Besides, the threat might now be over. That little operation to remove Envoy Navarr and I would have cost a packet. How could they afford a second attempt?'

'That's not the point,' Bashir countered. 'Firstly, we don't *know* that they won't try again – they may be very well funded. And, secondly, we – and by that I mean the council – can't be seen to be at a disadvantage to a bunch of bloody terrorists, however much some of our members might sympathise with their cause. They must be found and dealt with. Otherwise it would open the door to every crackpot outfit who thinks they could have a pot shot at us and get away with it.'

As he spoke, Bashir guided his son to a couch set in the centre of the room. Thea, who had been pouring drinks by the cabinet, came over to join them.

'Your father's right,' she said, placing the glasses carefully on the table and sitting next to her husband. 'This Labyrinth – and whoever is behind them – must be caught. I won't have my family put at risk.'

Jax smiled. His mother's motive was solely to protect her family. From her perspective, they were all vulnerable and any loss would be devastating.

'Don't worry, my love, they'll be found and, in the meantime, we will carry on. Business as usual,' Bashir replied, laying a hand gently on his wife's knee.

'That's right, Mother. You've no need to worry. Byers and Navarr are in the last stages now. Then nothing and no one can stop the treaty.'

Bashir cleared his throat. His son had reminded him that, for better or for worse, they would soon have to deal with these wretched aliens. He still did not like it. For so many years he had been implacably against a peace deal of any sort, mistrusting the Union of Planets and finding their ways and customs – what he had heard of them – distasteful, heathen and downright suspicious. It had not been until Hal Byers returned from his visit to Altan with the news of the Genara queen's offer that he began to concede that there may be some substance to their words of peace and friendship. She was indeed an important prize. Byers had also told him that the Union was offering selected mining rights on the mineral-rich planet of Autabron and reduced trading fees for a ten-year period from the signing of the treaty. They were, without doubt, offering more to Earth than Earth was giving in return – for now. But was this cause for concern? Was there some subterfuge going on that was not apparent? Bashir could not help but wonder if they were doing the right thing. Or would the price of peace be far higher in the long run than the cost of continuing the conflict?

Bashir's thoughts occupied his mind to such an extent that he hardly noticed Jax had continued speaking.

'But something could help to make it better,' he said.

'Eh? What?' asked Bashir, a puzzled look on his face.

'Look, you'd better know,' Jax began hesitantly. 'I put a suggestion to Envoy Navarr. What I mean is, I sounded him out first and he seemed to think it was good … that it would help and, well, might be acceptable. So we agreed to put it to Lady Linnayen and she's thinking about it, which is amazing, of course, because I never dreamed that she would ...' Jax was babbling now and he knew it as he saw the puzzled looks on his mother and father's faces.

'Think about what, Kevor? What are you talking about?' Thea's calm voice cut through Jax's torrent, allowing him time to breathe and gather his thoughts.

'Yes. What's all this about?' his father asked directly, his knitted brow darkening his features.

Jax's intense face turned to them as he began speaking. 'I've asked if *I* can be the bridegroom – husband – whatever ...' There was silence. Jax felt an overwhelming need to fill the gap it made. 'I've asked the Lady Linnayen to marry me – to consider *me* – and not the other candidates.'

Thea's mouth hung open and her eyes sank to look at the floor. David, on the other hand, continued to stare blankly at his son, still trying to come to terms with what he had just heard.

'Think about it,' Jax went on. 'I'm well born. I'm politically well connected. I mean, our family is one of the most prestigious on the planet. And because everyone knows that you have been an opponent to peace, this would be a real and solid union, bringing together two old enemies. It wouldn't just be a marriage of convenience. It would create a lasting resolution to our troubles. More than that – it would bring friendship and trust.'

Still there was silence. Still his father's face gaped at him.

'Father ... Mother ... Say something,' he pleaded.

He waited anxiously for their response, any response. His father was the first to speak.

'Say what? What is there to say?' Bashir let his head drop. 'Oh, my son. What have you done?' He closed his eyes and shook his head.

'Done?' Jax replied, puzzled. 'I've done the right thing. This is the best option. By marrying me – if she agrees – we'll be uniting two of the most powerful families on our planets. We'll be bringing peace to our people for generations to come. This *has* to be right.'

'It does not!' Bashir had got over the initial shock and was moving towards anger. He stood up and began to pace towards the window. 'Whatever were you thinking? What possessed you?

Didn't you think what this would do to our position, *my* position, in council?'

Jax had feared that his father would react poorly to his news and so he steeled himself against the barrage.

'Improve it, I would think,' he rounded. 'Show them what a statesman you are by putting the planet's needs above your own family.'

'Improve it! It's been hard enough to get some of the members to believe in these talks. Especially when I've hardly been convinced myself. Now all they will say is that I have engineered this to increase my family's wealth and status. That I've sold my own son.'

As the full implication of what Jax had done began to register, Bashir found more and more reasons for dissatisfaction. 'I'll be hounded out of office for this. Forced to resign. How will we face the scandal?'

At these words, Thea Bashir jumped up from the couch and went to her husband. She laid a hand on his arm and, rather forcefully, drew him around to face her.

'Now listen to me. There will be no scandal. You will *not* have to resign,' she stated emphatically. 'First of all, this is only a proposal. The woman has not agreed – yet – and she may never do so. Also, *we* know the truth and, if it came to it, you would tell the truth. That this was Kevor's decision, nothing to do with you. There is nothing in this that can't be salvaged if it is handled properly.'

Both Jax and Bashir looked at her, surprised by her command of the situation. She was thinking like a political strategist, not a mother.

'I still don't like it. It could be disastrous,' cautioned Bashir.

'Yes, it could be,' Thea agreed. 'But it could also be wonderful. Our son could be right. The joining, in lifelong friendship, of two enemies – for the sake of their people. It would be hard for the resistance to find support for their cause if the peace was so securely based, wouldn't it?'

David's eyes searched his wife's face for the truth. *Would it? Is my son right?*

Thea turned to face her son. 'As for you, Kevor, how *dare* you put us in this position without consulting us first! I thought you were a *man*.'

The censure in her voice hurt more than all his father's angry words. He had hoped for his mother's support but it looked like she was against him too.

'Mother,' he began apologetically, 'I'm sorry. I didn't think. I just wanted to do the right thing. And it seemed so obvious.'

'The right thing? No! You didn't think!' She threw up her arms in resignation. 'Whatever … It's done now and it can't be undone.'

David collected his thoughts once more. 'You said that she is thinking about your …' He searched for the appropriate word. 'Suggestion. Is she seriously considering it?'

'As far as I know, yes,' Jax replied. 'I suppose she might just be being polite. But Navarr said that I had originally been on her shortlist.' David's eyebrows shot up in surprise as Jax went on. 'I was rejected because they thought you would never agree.'

'They were right about that. I wouldn't have,' Bashir concurred.

'But *I* might have. She's a wonderful young woman, Father. Very dedicated. Serious about peace. She sees it as a vocation. I'm sure you would like her once you got to know her.'

David did not notice the slight change in his son's voice as he spoke these words. But Thea did. Jax's tone was different somehow. There's more to this than politics, she thought. *He has feelings for her. Is he in love?*

'Well, depending on the lady's answer, we may never find that out, eh?' Bashir finished.

Then again, thought Thea, they may learn only too well.

That night, Jax had a dream, which in itself was not unusual. But this dream, unlike so many others that faded with morning wakefulness, he remembered vividly both the next day and for a long time to come.

He had been at a grand ball. There were hundreds of people, all finely dressed, dancing and talking in a huge hall, which was decorated in long billows of multi-coloured fabrics hanging from the rafters. There were strangely carved wooden panels on the walls and the floor was paved with stone slabs of a shimmering green rock he had never seen before. It was a scene filled with music and laughter and the clinking of glasses. It was brightly lit, too, and Jax recalled that he had been leaning causally against one of many smooth marble columns that ran the length of the hall on both sides. He had felt happy. He looked down to find that he was dressed in strips of black cloth, like an ancient swathed mummy. Every part of his body was covered by the black muslin except for his mouth, and even though his eyes were hidden by a fold of the material, he could see through it.

He was smiling as he began to walk into the crowd of swirling dancers. He tried to see their faces but they were masked and moving so fast that it was all a blur. Then, in the space of only a couple of seconds, the lights began to dim and the hundreds of dancers moved away from him towards the sides of the hall, their faces fading in the lowering light. When it was nearly pitch black, a single vertical shaft of brilliant light pierced the darkness before him and, standing in its centre, as if trapped by invisible bars, was Linnayen Genara.

She was dressed in a golden gown adorned with thousands of tiny diamonds and pearls, and Jax could plainly see the rise and fall of her breasts with every breath she took. She was frowning and it was obvious that she was anxious and scared. He wanted to comfort her, to reassure her. But she did not see him. It was as though the boundaries of the spotlight formed an impenetrable barrier, through which she could neither pass, nor see, nor hear.

He walked towards her, stretching out his hands as he slowly closed the space between them. One of his hands went to cup the back of her neck whilst the other encircled her slim waist. She reacted as though she felt his touch but still could not see him. He was so close! She should have been able to feel his breath on her cheek. But nothing! She stared straight through him as though he was a ghost. He bent his head down to her at the same time as tilting her head up to meet his and he placed his lips upon hers.

The reaction was instantaneous. A shiver of electricity passed through their bodies causing each to gasp. His lips moved over hers, gently exploring their softness. He felt her body stiffen and she resisted for a few seconds. Then her mouth opened to receive him and her tongue tasted his lips. Jax could feel her relax and meld into him as her arms went to enfold him.

He felt an overwhelming surge of love and lust and passion all rolled into one. There was nothing for him in this moment but this woman, only this woman, and they were as one.

Suddenly, her eyes flew open and, with a look of both terror and terrible sorrow, she was pulled out of the column of light into the surrounding blackness. Her hands, white and reaching out towards him, were the last things he saw before waking up in a state of high anxiety.

He threw back the sheet and stumbled out of bed, making for the open window that led onto the balcony. It was still the middle of the night and the evening breeze helped to calm him. Regaining his breath and waiting until his heartbeat had dropped back to normal, he reflected on the dream. What could it have meant? Did it signify that he almost had the Altani queen in his grasp, only to lose her immediately? Or, worst of all, did this mean that his proposal was to be rejected?

He could not get the feeling of foreboding out of his mind, or the look on Linnayen's face as she had been pulled away from him. She had not wanted to go, he felt sure. She was frightened. Yet did he imagine that there had also been a look of resignation? Was she resigned to some fate that he could perhaps have saved her from, yet had done nothing?

He remained confused and ill at ease for the remainder of the evening and could not get back to sleep. Sitting on the balcony staring at the glistening lights of the city, his thoughts churned until, finally, the eastern sky turned a paler shade of dark blue, and he went inside to wash and dress. Somehow he knew that this would be the day he would discover his fate. And now, since the dream, he felt quite certain that it would not include the woman who had consumed his imaginings last night.

Chapter Twelve

Navarr smiled knowingly at the vidscreen image of Linnayen Genara. She was dressed today in a riding outfit of white shirt, tan jodhpurs and brown knee-high boots. She looked quite magnificent, he thought, a worthy and, in all probability, willing bed mate. As she spoke to him, he watched her mouth and was surprised to find himself thinking of what it would feel like to have those red lips on his body. It brought on an instant reaction and he was glad he was seated.

'I think that I would like to give young Prince Bashir the news myself. Don't you think that would be best, Captain Navarr?'

'I do indeed, my lady,' Navarr replied, forcing himself to concentrate on the conversation and trying to ignore his body's urging.

'But before you bring him in, I would also like to congratulate you on a job well done.' Linnayen smiled and her voice softened slightly. 'I trusted you with a vastly important mission and you not only succeeded but also proved to be highly dependable and efficient. On behalf of the forum and our people, thank you very much, captain.'

Navarr was surprised to find himself blushing. Could he be touched and pleased by her words? Perhaps he had a sentimental side after all, he thought.

'I was only doing my duty, my lady. But I am pleased to have been of help,' he replied. 'I hope that you will allow me to continue to serve you once I am home again.'

Linnayen had not been expecting him to say anything along these lines. Indeed, she had given little thought to what would happen to Navarr once this mission was finished. She supposed that he would re-join his combat unit and take up a posting on board one of the Union's battlecraft. *But then I would never see him again* ... No, that must not happen. She was not ready to give him up – yet.

'If that is your wish. Perhaps we can find something for you to do. I will speak to Sen-Beoraan.' Regaining her composure, she continued in a more formal tone of voice. 'Could you ask Prince Bashir to come in now, please?'

Navarr got up from the desk and went to the door. Touching the panel to open it, he saw Jax standing by the window staring out across the ancient city's skyline, apparently deep in thought. He had not heard Navarr's entry.

'Kevor Jax? Could you come through? My lady would speak with you.'

Jax swirled around, impatient to get this over and done with. He had prepared himself for the disappointment he was about to face and steeled himself to make a good show of it. *At least her refusal will please my father*. He walked into Navarr's apartment, one of the finest the Hotel Qattara had to offer, a concoction of silken drapery and low padded couches in rich reds and purples. It had been made ready at short notice when the envoy announced he was coming to Cairo yesterday evening with important news.

Linnayen's face was smiling across at him on the vidscreen, the clear green eyes looking deep into his and he found that he had to catch his breath.

'Hello, Prince Bashir. Thank you for waiting,' she began.

'Good morning, Your Highness.'

'I asked to speak to you personally, rather than through Captain Navarr. I hope you don't mind and that this is within the bounds of protocol on Earth?' She sounded genuinely concerned not to give offence or cause embarrassment. Jax, in his nervousness, assumed that she wanted to let him down gently.

'Yes, that's fine,' he replied, somewhat glumly.

'Good. First of all, may I say how very honoured I was to receive your proposal.' Her tone was businesslike, although she tried to ameliorate it somewhat. 'I was most impressed by your solid reasoning and fine grasp of statecraft.'

'Thank you, Your Highness.'

Linnayen nodded to indicate that she had heard his words, then turned to Navarr.

'Captain, would you please leave us? I would like to speak to Prince Bashir alone.'

Navarr had not been expecting this and it was with some surprise and a little indignation – albeit swiftly concealed – that he left the room.

That was kind of her, thought Jax, to not let anyone else witness his disappointment and humiliation.

'I hope you don't mind me dismissing Captain Navarr? I rather thought that this moment should be just between us,' she said, a touch conspiratorially and with the hint of a smile in her eyes.

'Not at all, Your Highness. You are very thoughtful,' he replied, now more than ever convinced that she was going to reject him.

'Quite so. Now, I have given your proposal a very great deal of thought ...'

She paused to take in the countenance of the young man before her. He was, she admitted, quite handsome, if a little pale and nervous right now. Given the circumstances, this was understandable. But it plainly showed how naïve he was and reaffirmed her feeling that he would be easy to manipulate.

'As you know,' she continued, 'I originally considered you long before my envoy came to Earth to take up the marriage negotiations. But I discounted you on the grounds that your family would be antagonistic and I had no wish to – as you Earthans put it – stir up a hornet's nest. This treaty is too delicately poised to risk upsetting, don't you agree?'

Jax had not expected to be asked a question and was caught a little off-guard. He cleared his throat. 'Um, yes. You're quite right.'

'However,' Linnayen resumed, 'I had to re-evaluate the situation when Captain Navarr told me of your proposal. Your willingness to become my husband put matters in a new light, for you always were a strong candidate.'

Jax was surprised to hear her say this and his eyes widened. He had not thought he was held in such high regard.

Linnayen continued. 'My prime concern was your family's reaction. But, if you can assure me that your father will accept a union between us, I will most happily accept your proposal of marriage.'

His mouth fell open and silence issued forth. His eyes took in that she was smiling. Then, after what seemed like an eternity, he started to breathe again and the full force of her words hit home. But, still, he could not speak.

'Prince Bashir?' she asked with concern. 'Did you hear what I said? I said that I would –'

'Yes!' He interrupted her with a grin that split his face from ear to ear. 'And it's just … wonderful! Wonderful news. Thank you, my lady. You do me the greatest honour.'

'I hope that your father will feel the same way. Remember, my acceptance is conditional upon his approval,' she warned.

'I fully understand, my lady. I will speak to him immediately.'

He could not believe it! She had said yes, and in a matter of only months they would be together in person and she would be his. He would be able to hold her, touch that fine skin and feel her next to him. He could not wait. His dreams were coming true. All that stood in his way was his father's temper. Thus, with more words of thanks delivered and a subdued yet obvious happiness, he bowed, took his leave of her and hastened to his mother's rooms at the Bashir mansion in old Cairo.

'That was nicely done, my lady. Your plan has worked well.' Navarr's smooth, quiet voice interrupted Linnayen's thoughts as she watched the retreating figure of Kevor Jax. Instantly she focused on Navarr, and the trace of the smile she had shown to the young Earthan prince was replaced by a furrowing of her brows.

'You make it sound like some sort of devious plot, captain,' she snapped. 'I am only doing what is right for the Union. I mean no ill will towards this young man.'

'Of course, my lady. My sincere apologies.' Navarr quickly bowed his head in submission. He remonstrated with himself for forgetting that, though a desirable young woman, she was first and foremost a royal leader, not only by birth but also by training. Every fibre of her being was dedicated to what she saw as her duty and she was not to be underestimated. He still had a way to go before she would become more malleable to his charms and, remembering this, he made a mental note to call Balisel before he left Earth. It was time to speed things up and, besides, he was looking forward to seeing the proud, arrogant young queen reduced to a lovesick ninny.

'Your apology is accepted, captain,' she replied. 'Now, please set up a meeting between myself and the Bashirs. I think he may need a little help.'

Navarr nodded his assent. 'At once, my lady. And … Perhaps I could start making the arrangements for my return to Altan?' he added.

'You are eager to get home?' she asked, slightly puzzled. Was this a new, softer side of Durroc Navarr, she wondered. 'I had expected that you would travel back here with Prince Bashir?'

'If that is your wish, I will, of course.' Navarr feigned the merest hint of sadness in his tone, enough to do its work. She picked up on his hesitancy.

'But?' she queried.

Navarr lowered his eyes and allowed his features to take on a look of nervous discomfort, as though she had made him reveal something he did not want to confess.

'But, well … I miss …' He gave the appearance of being about to speak of his true feelings, but then remembered his professional duty. He continued stiffly. 'That is, I thought that with such an important wedding to organise, you might want to use my skills back at home. I would very much like to continue to serve you, my lady.'

Linnayen studied the man before her, trying hard to read his true motives. Naturally distrustful, she could not quite believe his display of dutiful dedication. But his attention to her and the approving looks she caught him giving her from time to time were flattering. No man had looked at her in the way that Navarr did. For once, it would be nice to feel the warmth of such adoration, a feeling she had not had since her beloved father had died. She made her mind up there and then.

'Very well, captain. I am sure that Sen-Beoraan will appreciate your assistance in planning the ceremony. You may return home as soon as the marriage is approved by Sheikh and Lady Bashir and the treaty is settled.'

A small smile brushed across Navarr's face. 'Thank you, my lady.'

Their business done, Linnayen concluded the transmission and, once out of his sight, allowed herself a most private smile.

Two weeks later, as the orbiter shuttle lifted off from the London Spacedock carrying Durroc Navarr towards Jupiter orbit, where he was to rendezvous with the spaceracer *Sur-Kabanash* for his journey home, Jax and Duncan McCrae stood on the deck of the Bashir family's hydroplane. They were drifting in the bay off the floating city of Elidian. The two friends took in the full magnificence of the city skyline in the early evening glow, its spiralling towers and sweeping bridges highlighted in the low rays of the sun, casting long purple-black shadows far out to the east.

Elidian: a dream-like word for a city of dreams. Floating in the crystal azure waters of the Red Sea, it was the culmination of one woman's dream. Dr Kathleen Jaxson had wanted to create a place of beauty, harmony, self-sustenance and, most important of all, healing and learning. The building of Elidian and its educational institutions took a chunk of her family's money, but she judged it well spent indeed as it attracted the finest scientists and most formidable brains on the planet. The returns had been worth it. Elidian became the centre of a new renaissance in all the sciences, arts and cultures. It showed humanity a way to live that was above petty desires and individual caprices. Kathleen had wanted the city to exist solely to serve the people and set it down in the city's charter that Elidian would strive to be an environment where people worked for the common good. It was a city of hope and imagination and its unique and surreal structures reflected its values, as Jax's ancestor had intended they should.

Jax felt the weight of guardianship for Elidian that his illustrious ancestor had passed on to him. Somehow, he felt that she wanted him to watch over it, and every time he looked at Kathleen's beautiful city he glowed with pride and love and respect. He wanted to bring his wife here one day.

'I still can't believe it, old man,' Duncan said fondly. 'You! Married. And to a beautiful, exotic, alien queen!' Duncan stood at the hydroplane's rail shaking his head in disbelief. 'If I'd known you'd get up to this as soon as my back was turned I would never have taken that part in the new Barani production. Methinks there's a bit more than politics going on here.'

'I don't know what you mean,' Jax replied, trying to sound haughty. 'I'm doing this for our planet. My own feelings don't come into it.'

'Oh, suddenly self-righteous, eh?' cracked Duncan. 'There's definitely something going on. Have you got the hots for the Altani love goddess?'

'Must you?' snapped Jax disdainfully, for once losing patience with Duncan's flippancy. 'She's a very serious, well-intentioned young woman. She only wants to do the right thing – as do I. This is entirely a political match.'

'And the vision of that dark-haired, green-eyed stunner with the curves of an angel has nothing to do with it, eh?' Duncan sarcastically replied, raising a sandy-coloured eyebrow.

'Of course not!' Jax threw back, annoyed more with himself than Duncan for being so obvious about his feelings for the young queen.

'Oh, go on! You can tell me. We're friends, after all.' Duncan would not let it go and was determined to tease his friend.

'There's nothing to tell. Linnayen Genara is noble and dedicated. Her hopes for peace and unity match my own. We will marry and our planets will stop fighting. Many thousands of lives will be saved. What more do you need to know?' Jax returned. He was obviously getting annoyed and he turned away from Duncan, walking towards the hydroplane's control panel.

Duncan sighed. Had he gone too far? If there was a breach in their friendship it needed to be sealed. He walked behind Jax and placed a hand on his shoulder.

'I'm sorry,' he began ruefully. 'I shouldn't have started it. I know what this means to you. It's just that … Well, it takes a bit of getting used to. You getting married. Leaving me behind. A week ago you were just Jax – my pal. Now you're going to be one half of an interplanetary ruling family. I mean, really …'

'Put like that, you make it sound a bit overwhelming,' Jax smiled. Then, with quiet determination in his voice, he added, 'But we'll still be friends. That won't change.'

'Friends, yes, of course. But things *will* change,' said Duncan, and he could not hide the sadness in his voice. 'After all, you'll be living on another planet most of the time.'

Jax stared at the control panel, his brow furrowing. As Duncan's words sunk in, he realised that his friend was right. His life would change forever. By marrying Linnayen Genara he would be fulfilling a dream but losing a large part of the way he was now. He was leaving his youth behind.

'You're right.' Jax shrugged his shoulders resignedly. 'It'll be like a new life for me – very different to the one I always thought I'd lead. But, like I said to my parents, it's as though this was meant to be. Destined, somehow.'

'How was your father when you told him she'd accepted your proposal?' Duncan couldn't wait to hear how old man Bashir had reacted. Not good, he suspected. *There've been quieter volcanic explosions – but not many!*

'Ah … He was just about the maddest I've ever seen him in his life.'

Jax winced at the memory of the scene he'd had with his parents a week ago in the Cairo house. Linnayen had said 'yes' and his father had been so angry that he'd been speechless at first. He had blustered and whirled around the room, making almost incomprehensible sounds, whilst his mother sat calmly on the couch, her silent, knowing eyes fixed on Jax the whole while. Finally, his father could not contain his bile and the words shot forth like bullets.

Did he have *any* idea of how stupid he was? Did he know what he'd done? He'd handed Earth to the Union on a plate. What had the last twenty years fighting to keep our freedom been about if it was to be thrown away on the whim of a brainless boy? How would he explain this to the council? How could he! How *dare* he!

It went on for many long minutes. The harangue was relentless and both Jax and Thea knew that when he was like this, they could only wait for him to exhaust himself. But it was very hard to hear his father's words. His mother's eyes told him to ignore the insults. David would not mean them when he had calmed down. But Jax had to admit that, seeing it from his father's point of view, he had done a pretty reckless thing and deserved much of the ire that had been flung at him.

Finally, with a resounding slap of his hands on his thighs and a sinking of his wide shoulders, his father had run out of steam. He had turned to face Thea and Jax and they could see the moisture reddening his eyes. His anger had brought him to the verge of tears.

'I just don't know what to do,' he said, sighing. His voice disclosed the absolute despair of a man so used to knowing everything, having all the answers, suddenly floundering as he struggled to find a solution.

Jax shuffled his feet, about to speak. Quickly and with a sudden scowl, Thea motioned to Jax to say nothing. She had risen and went to stand directly in front of her husband, taking him in an affectionate hug and kissing him on his cheeks.

'My darling …' Her voice was barely more than a whisper. 'It will be all right. He's a foolish boy. But he's our son and we love him.' She spoke quietly and slowly and fondly stroked the huge man's hair.

'And you know,' she went on, 'when he is married to the alien queen,' Thea felt his body wince at these words, but she kept up her caresses and continued, 'he will be more than just her consort. He will be the joint ruler of four planets. Imagine that! A Bashir – leader of an interplanetary empire!'

Her voice almost shook with the emphasis she gave these words, and her hands moved to cup David's face. Smiling and looking deep into his eyes, she completed her manoeuvre.

'How hard will it be to convince the council that this situation also presents perhaps the greatest *opportunity* in history for Earth to dominate the known universe?'

David's eyes searched her face – for truth, for reassurance that it was so. His mind was a maelstrom; Thea could almost see the wheels turning. She was right. Presented in the right way, the council could be won over. Perhaps something could be salvaged from this God-awful mess.

'You're right! Thea, my clever, wonderful wife!' he exclaimed, his enthusiasm tempered only by the need to think through his strategy. 'It can be turned around … from disaster to success.' Then, with a final withering glance at the still silent and humbled Jax, he took his parting shot. 'But with no thanks to you, boy!'

Jax had squirmed. But, as his father's mind raced through the possibilities, Jax saw that his mother's sharp brain and quick thinking had got him out of a tight spot and he was grateful.

Later that afternoon, he tried to thank her for her intervention. Entering her studio on the top floor of the old stone residence, he saw her standing in front of the yellowed carved screen that hid the view of the rooftops of the grand houses and embassies of Garden City. She was as still as the ochre sandstone of the terrace and did not move even as he approached.

He began hesitantly. 'Mother, I wanted –'

'What? What did you want?' Thea's voice ripped through to his heart like an icy blade. 'To thank me for getting you out of trouble? For making it all okay with your poor father – again!' she sneered.

He hung his head, staring fixedly at the brown tiled floor.

'I'm sorry. I know how much you did for me back there.'

'Sorry doesn't begin to cover it!' Thea snapped back. Despairingly, she shook her head. 'You're not a child anymore. You're a grown man now and you more than most should know that politics is not some simple game you play whenever the fancy takes you. Every move, every action, every thought, gesture and utterance for people in our position must be thought out beforehand. Offering yourself to this woman without even stopping to think about talking to your father – or me – was stupid and disrespectful.' Her anger was deep and it took all her effort to stop her body from shaking.

'I know that now, Mother, and I am truly sorry.' Jax lifted his head, trying to make her look into his eyes to see the truth of his apology.

'Don't you *ever* do anything like this again!' she spat out.

'I won't, I promise.' His response was genuinely contrite and Thea's attitude began to soften. He was, after all, her only son and she adored him.

'Next time, I won't help,' she warned, 'and I wouldn't have this time, if only you weren't so stuck on the girl.'

Jax's eyes widened in astonishment. *How did she know?*

'All I will say to you, son, is that you had better be right about your feelings for her and *she'd* better feel the same way, or we'll all be in more trouble than you can possibly imagine.'

Jax flicked a switch on the hydroplane's control panel and the vessel's engine gently hummed. The metal hull lifted away from the water's surface, suspending them gently above the slight swell of the waves, and they hung there, motionless.

'But he came around in the end, thanks to my mother,' he finished, turning his wide smile towards Duncan's intense hazel eyes.

Pushing a small lever forward with his right hand, the hydroplane rose a hundred metres into the air and shot forward towards the sparkling lights of Elidian, which was fast becoming a silhouette against the pale purple sky.

'Welcome home, Captain Navarr, and congratulations on a job well done!' Beoraan's old voice wavered, but his tone was genuine. He placed his hands on the captain's shoulders in the formal Altani style, then took a step backwards in order to bow. Navarr was not unaware of the honour Beoraan was doing him. This display was most unusual for one of his rank and he was rather taken aback.

Linnayen looked down on the scene from high above in the foyer of the Genkarah Transit Tower. The massive columnar structure of burnished metals rose a thousand metres above the city, dominating the skyline. Many platforms and landing docks jutted out at various levels from each of the columns making the whole look like an enormous coppice of tall spindly trees, bedecked in flashing lights and beacons.

Navarr's shuttle had just docked and Beoraan had gone down to the landing bay to greet the captain. Linnayen saw him bow to the tall blond figure, who stood rigid and strong, the only deference to the honour Beoraan was doing him shown by the slight lowering of his head. At that moment, without meaning to, she willed him to look up and was horrified to see his face turn up to her. His eyes did not search the faces of the people around her – they did not need to, her thoughts had told him where to find her. She was locked in his gaze and her mind conjured up an image of a long, sticky silken thread travelling between them, growing slowly shorter, drawing each ever closer to the other.

Suddenly aware of her surroundings and her duty, she brought herself back under control and snapped the connection. He was no mentante, she was sure of that. Not like her father had been, or her mother, come to that. But he had some strange quality, something compulsive that drew her to him inexorably and it both frightened and excited her.

She took her place facing the foyer's entrance just in time for Navarr's arrival in the company of Beoraan and the Earth emissaries. Having had time to compose herself, she assumed a high level of formality now.

Addressing the whole party, she began. 'Welcome home – and welcome to our friends from Earth. I commend you all for your efforts as my envoy to Earth and in fomenting a solid peace. I am pleased and proud that these efforts have met with success. The contribution you have made to finding a lasting peace between the Union and Earth is immeasurable and, on behalf of the entire forum, I wish to thank you.'

She paused for a few moments, watching the gathering's reaction to her words. As she expected, they stood stiffly, looking straight ahead, hardly acknowledging her presence. They had been well trained. At least they had not forgotten how to behave after nearly three months with the uncivilised Earthans. How much of that was down to Navarr, she wondered.

'In recognition of this sterling work, I am pleased to inform you that the forum has awarded commendations to you all.' Then began the first stirring among the crowd. Linnayen went on, 'And I hope you will join me in congratulating your captain who has been promoted to the rank of commander.'

He stared in amazement at her, but her eyes remained impassive. He could feel the smiles of his team members behind him and one or two voices murmuring their congratulations. This was truly unexpected. However, as the news sank in, he quickly realised that this was the first of many inexorable steps he would take to achieve supreme power. The vision of a glorious future suddenly filled his mind – him, Linnayen, Balisel, palaces, important meetings, banquets, people doing his bidding. It all looked so good and, now, so attainable.

All it needed to make it all come true was a little extra effort and he made a mental note to talk to his sister as soon as possible.

At the sound of the approaching footsteps, the newly promoted Commander Navarr looked up from the vidscreen and a slow smile travelled across his still bronzed face. She was here at last and he could not believe how good she looked. Her long, slim legs were displayed well by the clinging black fabric and her full breasts were outlined by the dark, handwoven Dasnirian sea-silk that draped in a deep V between them. She wore no jewellery except for a wide bronze belt encrusted with gemstones that accentuated her slender waist, and she had let her luxuriant hair fall simply around her shoulders. As she walked, she sashayed her body ever so slightly and her nipples danced to a rhythm all their own under the thin fabric.

Navarr's body reacted in a way that was both delicious and forbidden. He stood up from the desk and went forward to greet her.

'Balisel … Here so soon,' he said, enfolding her in his arms, conscious of the way her body fitted into his.

'Oh, I didn't want to miss this,' she replied with a smile, letting her lips stray to his neck just below the ear. Navarr's reaction was instantaneous. Pulling back, he placed a hand under her jaw and drew her face to his.

The kiss was forceful and passionate; his tongue pushed into her mouth and she drank him in. Pressing her body into his, she felt him harden beneath his breeches, wanting her, desperate for the sweet relief that only she could give. This was no time for such behaviour though – not in the Genara palace, where they could be discovered any minute. Regaining her senses instantly, she pulled sharply away.

'No! Anyone could be watching.' Her breath was coming hard and she fought to regain her composure.

Navarr reeled from the separation, as though an electric shock had zapped him, and drew in his breath sharply.

'My quarters are secure. I've checked them myself. Besides, no one would dare disturb the new commander.' He smiled arrogantly and stroked his sister's cheek.

'Ah, yes. I was forgetting your promotion. But even so, we don't want to make any mistakes,' she replied. 'The stakes are too high and we still have much to do.'

'Speaking of which, dear sister … The next act in our little drama? Any news?' he enquired, gesturing for her to sit in one of the chairs near the veranda where a light breeze fanned the muslin drapes.

Balisel curled her legs under her and sat cat-like in the soft chair. Smoothing out the folds in her black silk pants, she began to tell him of her plan.

'His name is Margog Delgar. He's a loyal operative from our ore processing plant at Euta Makaan on Autabron who won a trip to Altan in the staff lottery, staying at the five-star Adhana Island Hotel. I had my assistant, Jeremiah, find him and bring him to my office so that I could congratulate him personally.'

Sitting across from her, Navarr watched Balisel coldly deliver the report of how she had charmed the young worker, offering him a drink, then another, until he passed out. With Danforth's help, she had then injected a microscopic programme-capsule into the cerebral matter just above the Autabroni's hypothalamic cortex. Delgar would never know what he would soon do, just as he would never see Autabron again. But his actions would help to change history. Quite an achievement for an ordinary fellow, reasoned Navarr.

'When he came to, of course, he had no idea of what had happened. We told him that he seemed to have drifted off for a few seconds. Perhaps the excitement of the day?' Balisel threw back her blonde tresses and laughed boldly. 'This is all so easy, my little brother.'

'I'll only be sure of that when it's over,' he retorted cynically. 'Meanwhile, how will it work? When will – Delgar, is it? – spring into action?'

'Whenever we choose. He'll respond to a synchro-pulse that I will send at the appropriate time. But I'll need from you the necessary intelligence about the lady's diary engagements. Where, when and so on. We'll need to find an appropriate opportunity.'

'I can get that for you. We may need the secure codes for entry to the lady's inner chamber. That'll be tough,' he said, and a fleeting look of worry passed across his face.

It was all business now between them, the flaring of their unseemly passion firmly put away for another time, another place. Instinctively, Navarr drew his chair nearer to hers so that they could lower their voices while they discussed the plan. Nothing too elaborate, figured Balisel, as that would arouse suspicion. A simple night-prowler with theft on his mind, suddenly consumed with lust for the Lady of Light and risking all to take the ultimate prize? Or, perhaps, an attempted assassination in front of witnesses?

Navarr could not be too far away. He would have to be quick in saving his queen, because once started, Delgar's programming would not allow him to stop until he was brought down, terminally. They were assuming that if Delgar attacked at close quarters, the fit young queen would likely put up a good fight, giving Navarr time enough to pull the rogue off her. But Autabronis were possessed of much greater physical strength than all the other races. Thus, her brother would have to engineer events to be within earshot of the lady's cries for help. Between them, he and Balisel went through a number of likely scenarios.

They were deep in conversation when the companel announced that Jeremiah Danforth was seeking admission to the room. Navarr looked at his sister, his features questioning.

'I asked him to come,' she said and, as the carved wooden door slid open and Danforth walked towards them, she explained. 'Jeremiah has been so very helpful.'

'Hello, Commander Navarr. A pleasure to see you again, sir.' The tousled-haired young man held out a hand in greeting and Navarr, now so familiar with Earthan customs, took it and they shook. Danforth was a little nervous and out of breath, as though he had run to get there, perhaps afraid of being late for an important meeting.

'Mr Danforth. Please take a seat,' he said formally, then, keenly watching the excited Earthan, he resumed his own.

Balisel, who had not risen to greet the young man, continued, 'You see, Jeremiah knows all about how we plan to use Delgar to obtain Haranshay's secret extraction process, don't you, Jerry? He helped me implant the sonochip and, when we get that formula, we're going to be very rich indeed, aren't we, darling?' She smiled fondly at Jeremiah and stroked his cheek. He beamed in return.

'You bet, angel!'

Navarr felt both nauseous and angry at the unfamiliar use of the endearment by this complete stranger. How dare the man use such terms to his sister. Why, he wasn't fit to shine her shoes!

'And we're going to need it, too, aren't we, my love? It'll pay for the most fabulous honeymoon, a quaint Earthan custom – a luxury cruise through the Floating Gardens of Dasnir.'

Danforth gushed like an excited schoolboy, looking all the while at the feline smile on his fiancée's lovely face, seeing nothing but her stunning beauty. He did not notice that Navarr had got up from his seat and walked away from them towards a small table at the other side of the room.

Every muscle in his body was rigid and it was all he could do to control himself. Rage surged inside Navarr at the thought of this imbecile laying with his sister. *How could she?* How could she bring herself to do this? His fists clenched tight. It sickened him to his core. Balisel knew what he must be thinking, of course. Had she not gone through it too? The thought of her beloved brother touching, holding and more with other women. But they must rise above it. Put aside their feelings for now. Do what must be done and then one day, when they had it all, they could do whatever they liked – and no one would dare gainsay them.

'Durroc,' she called to him. 'Jerry and I know how extremely busy you must be. But we have a small favour to ask, don't we, darling?' she said, looking adoringly at Jeremiah's open face.

'Absolutely!' Jeremiah agreed.

She stood up and crossed the room. Standing next to the hardened frame of her handsome brother, which was still turned away from young Danforth, she put both her arms around his waist in a fond hug.

'We want you to witness our wedding – tomorrow afternoon,' she said and, just as the bottom was about to fall out of his world, one of her hands moved slowly downwards, out of Jeremiah's line of sight, and cupped his genitals in a fond, demanding and intensely exciting embrace.

'Of c-course.' His voice broke and Jeremiah was moved to see the affection this man held for his sweet sister.

Chapter Thirteen

'Sister!'

The delicate mei-mei lace curtains were still swinging in a frenzied motion behind Evica's leather-clad frame which stood, arms stretched wide to greet Linnayen, at the entrance to the formal meeting hall. Evica's delicious laughter filled the ancient, hollow space, bursting the silence within the stones like a popped bubble. Linnayen could not resist grinning.

'How good to see you, Evica,' she said, standing up from the Receiver's Chair, the Ki's throne of office. The last of the supplicants had left only minutes earlier and Linnayen, in the unaccustomed quiet period after the formalities, had been reflecting on her forthcoming marriage – and him. He invaded her thoughts and dreams and if she was not so sure that he was *not* a mentante, she would almost swear that he was putting his visage inside her mind deliberately.

'How did it go with mother?' Linnayen asked. 'Did you manage to speak with her?'

'Yes … But she didn't like being interrupted.' Evica winced at the memory of her mother, the Lady Li-el Dacas's reception.

Evica, at Linnayen's request, had travelled to the high Ksas Mountains to the Arbour of Serenkiraah, wherein their mother had been a student for some years. The journey itself had been a trial. The arbour, home to a handful of reclusive, higher-order Altaniskaranis, was meant to be as difficult to find physically as it was spiritually. It could not be reached by air as the winds in the high passes were often whipped up to alarming speeds and twists of direction by the sheer walls of the crags. Even soarcraft could not manoeuvre safely. Anyhow, the dense woodland on the lower slopes made access by any means other than foot virtually impossible. There was a road that had been roughly excavated some hundred and seventy years ago. But it became nothing more than a dirt track for the last twenty kilometres where it wound through a stunted primeval forest, overhung by trailing shackle-vines. The road was also said to be haunted by the spirits of long-dead high 'Karanis, who would send unworthy visitors along a false path deep into the hidden side of the tangled trees, never to be heard of again.

Evica recalled how easy it was to believe those stories as she trudged upwards along the dark, unfriendly road, dodging around the tiresome vines, accompanied by her small retinue of guards and servants. *Trust mother to live here!*

'You know, Linnayen, for the life of me, I can't see why she stays there,' said Evica with a hopeless shrug of her strong shoulders. 'The place is miserable. Cold most of the time. Damp, dripping in squelchy moss. Crawling with insects. No habitable buildings to speak of – just huts and lean-tos. No decent food – just flat bread and vegetables. No wonder they all look so thin and ill up there.'

Evica's description was, perhaps, a little coloured by her own enjoyment of the finer things in life. She loved good food, music and dancing. She adored the theatre and, best of all, she revelled in her prowess at hand-to-hand combat in the arena. The life of a recluse such as her mother had chosen four years earlier would never have suited the spirited young woman.

'Anyway, we got through – finally. Mother made me wait, of course, but only for a day this time,' Evica continued, settling herself on the carved stool next to the Receiver's Chair. Linnayen motioned for an aide to bring a plate of refreshments while they spoke.

'How good of her,' Linnayen scoffed, a smile hovering about her mouth. 'She must have already known why you were there.'

'She knew all right,' Evica replied with disdain, then continued. 'And went on to tell me, in no uncertain terms, that it was hardly necessary for me to have been sent, disturbing the tranquillity of the arbour, destroying the 'Karani's aura. Blah, blah, blah ...'

Evica recalled the meeting. After spending a cold night in a musty, moss-roofed hut, an attendant had brought her a meagre breakfast of grey bread and a bowl of lukewarm porridge. The pale green dumplings it held were a complete mystery and she thought it best not to know what they held. She could eat no more than a few mouthfuls anyway before she felt the bile rising from her stomach and decided she needed air.

Outside, in the early morning mist, her eyes took in the scene. A deep green glade of no more than a hundred and fifty metres across, confined by an almost impenetrable wall of ksarpi trees, contained similar moss-clad wooden dwellings, some with lazy wisps of smoke rising from simple chimneys, others raised up on seemingly flimsy tree trunks. Some of the huts, like the one in which Evica had spent the night, had cloth-covered doorways or windows, which afforded some privacy. But the majority had nothing more than an opening in one wall, allowing access to both the elements and the arbour's inhabitants. It was a rough, ramshackle hamlet and the whole had the appearance of having been haphazardly thrown together, which, in fact, was not far from the truth.

For the high priests and priestesses of the order, their physical surroundings were of virtually no importance as they had given their minds, bodies and souls to the search for philosophical and spiritual enlightenment. The very fact that they still had need of the physical body was for some quite galling and a definite hindrance to the attainment of ultimate grace. Indeed, their founder, the Most Holy Serenkiraah, had nearly three hundred years earlier finally abandoned his for good. He was the first individual – though not the last – to have achieved this and still exist as a cognisant being in the ether world, his aura having been 'received' by many adherents. But, after nearly three years at the arbour, Lady Li-el Dacas was beginning to despair that she would ever reach the state of ultimate grace, and the awareness did not improve her already crotchety humour.

In the midst of all this apparent squalor, Evica could not help but wonder at the sight of the Pillar of Peyjaan. Towering over the centre of the glade, surrounded by a low circle of sitting stones, rose a magnificent structure of polished ambicinite. The sheer single column of the precious, translucent pale blue stone stretched upwards for sixty metres. Unsupported, it grew straight out of the ground like a huge needle, tilted at an angle of 25.75 degrees, thereby matching the tilt of Altan's planetary axis. This unique and natural phenomenon had been discovered by Serenkiraah himself as a young acolyte while wandering in the high mountains on one of his first spiritual quests. He took it as the confirmation of his faith in the higher state of being and vowed to make the place a site of learning and fulfilment.

Over the years, Serenkiraah brought others to this place – his arbour – and the small community grew untrammelled by the outside world and, for Serenkiraah himself finally, unattached to it. He lived on in the ether world. But at sudden and unforeseeable times, the pillar, infused with his spirit, swirled with flashing pastel hues that danced deliriously. It was a miraculous sight and all who saw this spectacle swore that they received their own private communication with the Most Holy One.

Li-el Dacas, dowager consort to the late Ki-Yenshar, counted herself blessed that this had happened for her on two occasions now. It had, though, been over two years since the Most Holy's last message and she was beginning to doubt that she would ever receive his grace again. Thus, when faced with the impending arrival of her eldest daughter and the knowledge that she was going to be called back into the outside world, she was both displeased with the interruption to her devotion but also felt guilty that she was secretly looking forward to the break.

'I know why you're here,' she had said abruptly to Evica, not getting up from the low day-cot in her hut as her daughter entered. 'I suppose you want me to come back with you?'

'That's entirely up to you, Mother,' Evica replied somewhat shortly. She had always had a hard time liking her mother. Something to do with her being so self-absorbed, she figured – and for having left them and her father when Evica had been only eighteen – a time she had sorely needed a mother's help and guidance.

Li-el grumbled her disapproval of her daughter's manner. 'You're quite right – and whilst I'm sure you're not enthusiastic about my coming with you, I'm going to anyway.' Then, noticing the grimace on Evica's face, she continued, 'Oh, don't look like that! The thought doesn't fill *me* with joy either. But the community has suffered enough intrusion with your visit without having to put it through the upheaval of my departure at a later date.'

Evica had tried to smile but gave up the struggle when it became clear that her mother had just about finished her audience.

'I think that will be for the best too,' she began. 'But don't you have any curiosity about Linnayen and her situation? Don't you have any questions of me?' Evica found it hard to believe that her mother was not the least bit interested in her sister's forthcoming marriage, or in the resultant peace treaty.

Li-el had looked down to her finely wrinkled hands, a look of concentration fixed on her face.

'What's he like, this young Earth man she's planning to wed?' she said suddenly in the midst of her reverie.

'Um … I really don't know,' Evica had replied, stumbling over her words. 'Very well connected, very pleasant, I'm told. A little – unworldly, I think.'

'Must be to fall into this trap!' Li-el had barked back. 'Was it her idea? The marriage?'

'Yes.' Evica's voice could not hide the trace of defensiveness. It was not fair of her mother to rubbish Linnayen's plan, even if it did have its limitations. After all, what had their mother ever done for the girls? What right did she have to pass judgement?

'Just like her father,' commented the older woman. But Evica could not tell whether this had been meant as a compliment. Without warning, her mother rose to her feet, sighing, and Evica knew it was time to leave to damp, cramped hut.

'We'll leave in an hour,' Li-el had announced. There was to be no discussion. Lady Li-el would expect Evica and her escort to be ready and, if they were not, she would start without them.

'I can tell you, little sister, no one was happier than I to be getting out of that soggy hellhole,' Evica recounted to Linnayen, chewing the remains of a small kokoseed muffin. The late afternoon light had caused the shadows in the long hall to sweep across the flagstones. Evica stifled a yawn.

'How was she on the journey?' Linnayen enquired. 'Did she give you much trouble?'

'Quite the contrary,' remarked Evica. 'You know how imperious she used to be, barking orders all over the place, nothing being the way *she* wanted it?'

Linnayen remembered well. Her mother had never been an easy woman. Her position as consort and, even before that, as sestriarch of the House of Dacas had caused the young Li-el to grow up in an atmosphere of favour and wealth. She had got used to having her own way. Linnayen's father, Yenshar, had found her quite a handful, strong-willed and demanding. But, because of the dynastic succession and because Li-el had been possessed of such higher level mentante powers, he knew their bloodline would be formidable. It had never been an easy marriage – for either party – and even before Li-el had left for Serenkiraah's arbour, they had rarely lived together, which was a relief for them both.

'Well,' continued Evica, 'there was hardly a peep out of her the whole way back.' Linnayen's eyes widened in surprise and disbelief. This was not like their mother at all. 'At first I thought it was the mountains – you know, having to concentrate on the trail. There's not much incentive to talk for anyone who has to travel that awful road,' Evica recalled. 'But even when we were out of the high country and on the soarcraft she was still quiet. Mind you, I suppose I didn't really encourage her to talk either.'

'You mean you clammed up?' Linnayen gently pried.

'Well, you know how she is. Open your mouth and she always finds a way to criticise you or put you down,' Evica admitted.

'Not just verbally either!' Linnayen agreed, remembering the number of times her mother had invaded her mind as a child and even across the distance from the arbour when she was a grown woman.

Although mother and daughter had rarely seen each other in person for the entire twenty-two years of Linnayen's life, they knew each other well. Just as her father had been able to talk to her telepathically and read her thoughts, her mother had the same powers. The only difference was that her father had always sought her permission first whereas Li-el felt it her right to enter her daughter's consciousness any time she wished.

'That's something, thankfully, I have never really had to put up with,' said Evica ruefully. She was not a full mentante, having inherited only a minimal ability to communicate telepathically. Luckily for her, Li-el Dacas considered anyone with less than full powers to be hardly worth the effort and had, for the most part, kept out of Evica's mind, for which she was eternally grateful.

'Ah, well,' Linnayen said resignedly. 'She's here now and, no doubt, she'll seek me out in her own good time.' She stood up, holding her hand out to Evica to join her. 'In the meantime, I have an audience with Cap – I mean Commander Navarr to prepare for.'

She tried to keep her features and her voice as composed as possible when she said his name and, probably, anyone other than her sister would never have noticed the infinitesimal change in her tone. What was that, Evica wondered. Linnayen seemed different. Unable to fathom her sister and too tired to even try at that moment, she let it pass and, with a small kiss on the cheek, bid Linnayen farewell.

The ceremony that married his sister to the love-struck Earthan Jeremiah Danforth had been short, civil and unbearable. Navarr hated the sham, loathed the bridegroom and tried hard to detest his sister – but could not. She had looked stunning in a cream silk dress, tight in the bodice, full in the skirt, that clung to her every curve, wearing, as was her habit, no jewellery save for a swathe of delicate, glittering skin-stones above her breasts. Her hair had been swept up into a light concoction of curls, one or two of which had been allowed to fall and had found their way to nestle provocatively in her cleavage.

Jeremiah stared dumbstruck as his bride walked slowly through the marbled hall of the Genkarah Bonding Hall to join him on the terrace, where the bondsman waited to perform the ceremony. Navarr's eyes hardened to flint. He could hardly bear to look.

She drew near and her heady perfume reached his nostrils, reminding him of the intimate moments they had shared only hours ago. He knew that, in this moment, he had never wanted her more than at any other time in his life. *And why not!* he thought angrily. *Why should I not love my sister? Hasn't it only ever been the two of us?*

Balisel's eyes, open and warm for Jeremiah as she looked up at him, changed in an instant when she turned to her twin. They were full of fire and veiled passion. There was no doubt – he knew that now. No ninny of a husband, or spoiled queen for a mistress, would ever come between them.

He allowed himself a small smile. The groom and the bondsman were watching and it was important to keep up appearances. The words of the ceremony passed in a haze for him as he fought to keep control. Soon, mercifully, it was over and with the barely acceptable minimum of congratulatory words and a swift kiss on his sister's cheek, he made his escape and jumped into his windshifter.

In the moments at the end of the ceremony when Jeremiah was busy thanking the bondsman, Balisel had watched her brother leave, knowing that for these few moments it was safe to lift the façade. She could see in the set of his shoulders and the droop of his head that he was in pain. A tear crept from the corner of her right eye and fell swiftly across her cheek.

Jeremiah was touched. Balisel was not one for displaying her emotions so openly. That she had cried at their wedding was, for him, a sign that he was indeed a lucky man and he looked forward to a long and happy union, safe in the certain knowledge that he had wooed and won the woman of his dreams.

Linnayen felt genuinely annoyed with herself for spending so much as a minute thinking about what she was going to wear for her meeting with Navarr. When, she asked herself, had it become so important how she looked? Since when had she cared about such matters as her hairstyle, or what colours favoured her complexion? It was both frustrating and immature. Worse! Even as a child she had never been so ridiculous! But whilst she hated herself for giving in to her feelings, the giddy whirl she felt building inside her heart excited and pleased her.

He would be here soon. She had not seen him for nine days – since she had welcomed him home at the Genkarah Transit Tower. In only a few minutes she would see him again in the flesh, no longer a flat vidscreen image but the real, whole man, and she blushed at her body's reaction to what was to come.

Nen finally solved her dilemma by pulling out from the far reaches of her closet a soft ivory thigh-length blouson, embroidered with pale fuchsia coral beads and fastened at the waist by a single glittering skystone clasp. Worn with a tightly fitted pale rose bodysuit underneath, cut just a little low to show off the rise of her breasts, Nen pronounced that she looked the height of chic.

'There! You look perfect, my lady,' she announced approvingly, and set about tidying the young queen's hair. It needed little apart from brushing and Linnayen thought it best to wear it in her favoured simple twist, over one shoulder.

Time was pushing on and she knew that by now Navarr and Beoraan would be waiting in the outer chamber of her apartments. She had asked for an early evening meeting to discuss the arrangements for the wedding as she did not want the planning to interfere with the everyday tasks of governing the Union. Although the peace treaty was now secure, Linnayen did not want to antagonise other member representatives of the Union by spending too much time on personal matters, albeit that it was a state wedding. Thus, it seemed more appropriate to hold their discussion outside of the normal hours.

At least that is how Linnayen justified it to herself. And the fact that their meeting would, of necessity, be more informal had, she told herself, absolutely nothing to do with it.

With a final glance at herself in the mirror, she turned and strode to the door. Beoraan and Navarr were deep in conversion as the panel slid open but they stopped immediately and Navarr quickly jumped to his feet. He bent down to assist the old man but Linnayen held up a hand to gesture that this was not necessary.

'Good evening, counsellor, and to you too, commander.'

'A very good evening to you, my lady,' returned Beoraan.

'Indeed, my lady. You look well.' Navarr bowed his head and hoped that she had had time to see the look of approval in his eyes. She did, indeed, look good tonight, the pale pastels certainly enhanced her dark beauty. How ironic, he thought, that she had chosen to wear the same colours that his sister had worn at her wedding the day before. *Not that she could compare!* He knew he would find it hard to summon up the required degree of passion to convince the young queen of his love for her. But his ambition was strong. He would do it – both for himself and Balisel.

Food was served and they fell to talking about the various matters to do with the wedding ceremony. The guest list, the wording for the service itself, the timing, who should comprise the bridal procession, the requirements for the groom's party, the music and, with a little confusion on Linnayen's part, the honeymoon. This was a tradition, Navarr told her, that was common practice on Earth.

'When a couple marry, they immediately depart, right after the ceremony – usually to a holiday destination. This period of time is called the honeymoon and its purpose is to allow the couple to get to know each other – in private,' he explained.

Linnayen was puzzled. 'Yes, but what do they actually *do* on this honeymoon?' she enquired.

Beoraan cleared his throat and chose this time to enlighten the young queen, feeling it more properly his place to explain the significance of the ancient Earthan custom rather than the handsome commander who, if he was not mistaken, seemed to have an effect on his young mistress. He had seen the colour rise in her cheeks a couple of times tonight and speculated that perhaps this kindling of Linnayen's first stirrings of love was more than a little overdue. He only hoped that these feelings would rightly and properly soon be directed to the young man who was to become her husband.

Linnayen tried very hard not to show her discomfiture as Beoraan described the true purpose of the honeymoon. Was procreation all these Earthans ever thought of, she wondered. She had been making every effort to put aside the notion that she would one day have to have sex with her new husband. It seemed, however, that this cursed honeymoon would bring the matter to a head rather more quickly than she would have liked. She reminded herself that she was doing it all for peace, for the best of intentions. She would have to push through the small amount of fear and discomfort she felt.

The hour had grown late and Beoraan was showing obvious signs of tiredness. They had been talking for over two hours and had covered much of the detail of the wedding. However, they had still not got onto the subject of the Altaniskarani priests' roles in performing the ceremony and how these needed to be amalgamated with the Earthan religious traditions. Noticing the old man's drooping eyelids, though, Linnayen suggested they call it a night.

'Perhaps we could discuss this again tomorrow evening?' she asked.

'Indeed,' Beoraan quickly agreed.

'As you wish, my lady,' Navarr concurred. Then, as an afterthought, he continued, 'But perhaps I might suggest we go over these last matters on the way to the Living As One opening ceremony tomorrow?'

Linnayen was to officiate at the launch of a new initiative to promote cross-species integration the next morning in an underprivileged area of Genkarah. Members of the Union's special policy unit had devised yet another community arts and cultural programme aimed at forging closer ties between newly arrived immigrant species with indigenous Altanis. It was a common part of her role to oversee such events and, although she sometimes found them tiring – and tiresome – it was important to the people that she attend. Navarr was right. It *would* free up some time if they could hammer out the basics of the ceremony's religious content on the way to the event.

'Very well, commander. We leave from my office at ten sharp. I'll expect a draft format from you.'

'Very good, my lady.'

Rising from her chair, Linnayen bad them a good evening. Navarr got up first in order to help the more unsteady Beoraan and Linnayen, as she moved towards her inner chamber, was pleased to see this display of kindness. She had never really appreciated that the proud commander could sometimes be considerate. Had she perhaps been too hasty in thinking him overly arrogant and ambitious?

Navarr was pleased with the turn of events. The launch's programme that he had seen earlier that day showed that the Ki would be meeting and greeting some of the initiative's first participants, a collection of new migrant artists from the other three Union home-worlds. The heavy-set, ruddy-complexioned Autabroni Margog Delgar would not stand out in such a crowd. Far from it, he would look just the part!

The reception hall was packed. The numbers had been swelled by a host of junior ministers and civil servants from the Office of Interspecial Relations and two news crews from the rival interplanetary networks, UniCom and Newscast, both of whom intended to feature the normally reclusive Ki on their midday prime-time slots. If the Dasnirian trade talks did not break down for the third time, or the threatening seismic shiver did not destroy the Kalinbi-Makkar Dam thereby flooding parts of the city of Silbaraz-Re, there was a good chance that the young ruler would head up the bulletin. She had, after all, become much more newsworthy since her engagement to the Earthan prince had been announced. This was celebrity at the highest level and the greedy public could not get enough of her. Consequently, what would ordinarily have been just another civic function – mostly dull, always worthy – had turned into a circus, with vid-ops jostling for the best angles and haggling with Linnayen's press officer for some time with her, or just a quote – *anything* about the wedding. They had little interest in the success or otherwise of the project itself and its aim to improve interspecial relations through the arts.

Linnayen, though unused to this level of attention, was prepared for it. She knew the approaching wedding would cause a stir; that was inevitable. Her job was to deal with the increased interest in order to highlight the positives of her actions and she was well prepared, even to the point of making a couple of jokes about the wedding within her otherwise dry speech about the worthiness of the project. The crowd loved it. Their head of state was no arrogant, spoiled brat after all! She was funny and good-natured. The Earthan prince was surely getting the better of the deal and he would be a prize fool if he did not appreciate how lucky he was.

Navarr watched the crowd. The sea of faces, from all the four Union planets, was turned towards the young Ki, happy and smiling, and, Navarr noticed with relief, there was a sprinkling of red-skinned, white-haired Autabronis. Delgar was in position close to the front of the barricade, which had been placed along the route of Linnayen's exit from the hall and he, like everyone else, wore an excited, hopeful expression. Balisel had told him that, as a special treat, he could accompany her to the royal event today if he wished. *If he wished! A chance to see the Ki of Altan, the leader of the Union! What a story this would be for everyone back home.*

So it was that with almost no effort, Balisel had got her man in place within the crowded hall. She insisted that as a loyal and hard-working employee, he deserved to take her place next to the low barrier so that he could better see the Ki. Why, she might even shake his hand! Delgar's grin almost split his face, the gleam of his teeth a fine match for the whiteness of his hair.

The speeches finally concluded, it was time for the royal party to move along the hall and meet some of the project's staff and participants. Navarr had earlier suggested that he stay close by the Ki so that he could join her in the windshifter on the way back to the palace. This would allow them time to continue their meeting about the wedding ceremony, he had explained, and Linnayen agreed that this was a good idea. The thought of keeping him close by also had a personal appeal.

A multitude of faces turned towards her, some grinning but all with their eyes fixed on no one but her. Slowly walking along the line, she nodded her head and gave greetings. The project director, a small raven-haired Dasnirian woman who accompanied her, occasionally pointed out a particular worker or participant who had made a special contribution and Linnayen stopped her progress in order to question the individual. She must have spoken to at least half a dozen people before she came close to where Margog Delgar stood, impatient to get a closer look at this icon of the Union. In his blind enthusiasm he jostled a man standing next to him but took no notice of the mutters of complaint, which were, after all, somewhat muted. It did not pay to anger an Autabroni. With their superior physical strength and ancient honour code, a legacy of their belligerent history, it was too easy to get into a fight with one. Luckily, Delgar's mind was on other matters at that moment and all he knew was that the Ki of Altan was only a few paces away from him now and ... Yes! He was certain. She was going to shake his hand!

Inside the pocket of her exquisitely tailored Anair Zoff catsuit, Balisel Navarr, assured that Linnayen was now close enough to the ridiculously grinning Delgar, touched a palm-sized console that emitted an undetectable pulse.

The expression on Delgar's mouth went from grin to grimace, but the change was barely noticeable. Only his eyes bore witness to the sudden anguish and confusion that filled him. His mind screamed. *What is happening?* He could not understand why, suddenly, he had an unstoppable desire to place his hands around the lovely Ki's throat and crush the life out of her. He could neither comprehend nor control what he did.

Within seconds he had surged forward and smashed the heavy steel barrier aside. It flew into the air and landed in the crowd beyond Linnayen. Before anyone had time to cry out in amazement or, for some, great pain, the dazed Autabroni plant worker had reached his target and had both of his huge red hands around the throat of the terrified young woman. It had all happened so quickly. Linnayen, on hearing the commotion, had turned her head and, instantly, the hands gripped her. Oblivious to the bodies that were trying to pull him off, Margog Delgar tightened his crushing hold. He watched with something approaching pity in his eyes as Linnayen's face began to swell then grow pale as the blood supply above her neck lessened with every passing second. Only a few more moments and it will all be over, he tried to say. But the words would not come out, only thoughts. *Soon there'll be no more pain – for either of us.*

Did he know that he was going to die, Navarr wondered, as he plunged the razor-sharp dagger deep into Delgar's abdomen. From his position behind Linnayen, it had been easy to reach forward with his knife and slide it into the yielding flesh of the Autabroni's stomach. For a few horribly long moments, the massive hands did not release their fierce grip. Navarr withdrew the knife and blood pumped out of the gaping wound. His hand covered in the warm, sticky fluid, Navarr swiftly moved to a position behind the dazed assassin in order to cut him again. This time he pulled back the Autabroni's hair, staining it red with its owner's blood, and sliced hard at Delgar's throat, instantly ripping the veins, arteries and muscles.

Only then, when he was half dead and barely conscious, with his lifeblood draining out of him, did Delgar loosen his hold on Linnayen. She would have slid to the floor but for the project director and her staff, who lifted her up and carried her swiftly towards the doors at the front of the hall.

Navarr, blood-spattered and shaking, stood looking down at the now lifeless body of the hapless lottery winner. His face was a mask of iron determination – he had killed, proudly, to save his leader, and this was the image that flashed across the planets' news and media conduits over the next hours, then days. But, at that moment, all that was important was to ensure that Delgar was truly dead.

A security officer knelt next to the body then looked up at Navarr and nodded. Having obtained the confirmation of a deed well done, Navarr closed his eyes in sheer relief and tipped his head back to relieve his strained shoulders of the weight of it.

Only Balisel, gazing intently at him from within the shocked, weeping crowd, noticed the flicker of a smile at one corner of the mouth she knew so well, and knew also what it signified. Linnayen had seen him! In her terror, staring fixedly over Delgar's wide frame just before she passed out, she knew very well who had saved her life, and Balisel knew that the young, imperious Ki, who was already enthralled by her handsome, beguiling brother, would be eternally grateful.

.

Chapter Fourteen

The windshifter taking Linnayen to the nearby Obani-te Medcentre had already lifted off by the time a blood-spattered Navarr pushed his way through to the hall's exit. He insisted to the few enquiries by concerned yet still stunned individuals that that he was quite unharmed. But he wanted to follow his Ki. He needed to know that she was going to recover. He demanded that a windshifter be brought immediately.

No one was going to deny the hero of the hour. Indeed, the security officers around him were still in awe, amazed at the man's quick thinking and desperately fast reactions. Without any shadow of a doubt, a few moments more and the Ki would have been dead. Commander Navarr could have anything he wanted!

Whilst the evacuation began of the outer residential towers of Silbaraz-Re following reports that the Kalinbi-Makkar Dam was likely to burst after all, Navarr's hardened, steely visage captured moments after he had brought down the would-be assassin swept along the commlinks, as did footage of the attack on the now gravely ill Ki. News bureau chiefs from UniCom and Newscast were thanking the great gods of journalism throughout the universe for giving them the foresight to cover the Living As One launch event that day. This was just the sort of pre-publicity that the forthcoming royal wedding needed to spice it up and already the subeditors were scribing the headlines that would be used for the ceremony itself. *The love that would not die. Assassin's threat to peace.* It made a great angle on an already good story.

By the time he arrived at the medcentre, Navarr's face was being flashed up on vidscreens throughout the hospital and the staff stood back, staring agog at the tall, purposeful man who strode into the reception foyer. Instantly, the attendant told him to which level the Ki had been taken.

As the elevator's doors slid open on the thirty-fourth level, the staff's reaction to him and his wild appearance was much the same as it had been in the reception foyer. A young female medicant, mouth agape, eyes as wide as saucers, tried to register what he was saying.

Navarr asked again, 'Where is the Ki? I must see her!'

'The doctor is with her now. You'll, um, have to wait,' she replied hesitantly. The man's flint-like eyes scared her.

'How is she?' he demanded, the force of his words causing her to retreat a step backwards.

'I'll g-get the doctor,' she stammered back at him and, hero or no hero, she was pleased to get away from him.

The two security officers, one male, the other female, who had accompanied Linnayen in the windshifter were stationed outside the room she was being treated in some twenty metres down the hallway. Marching purposefully towards them, Navarr scowled, his visage as black as thunder. They shuffled their feet nervously, knowing full well that they had failed in their duty to protect the Ki. The irate commander was going to give them hell for it and they were not wrong.

He strode up to them.

'What in the name of all things holy did you think you were doing?' he screamed at them, eyes blazing. 'Where were you? And how long were you going to give that monster to throttle your Ki until you deigned to jump in and stop him?'

Navarr shook his head in desperation. He rather enjoyed playing the part of the angry boss because it was not too often that he could let off steam in this way. He was surprised to discover that it was intensely satisfying and was genuinely shocked and pleased at the looks he was getting. People were frightened of him. He vowed there and then to enjoy the moment fully and, if possible, to do it more often in future.

The guards stood stock-still, their eyes wide with fear and worry. They knew only too well the terrible dereliction of duty they had committed. If the Ki had died from the madman's attack they would most certainly be expected to volunteer for life-exile, never to see their loved ones again, perhaps to die in the dreaded bergussian ore mines on Autabron. As it was, they prayed that, if there was a court martial, the judges might be lenient in view of the fact that the Ki had survived.

Navarr continued the tirade for a few more minutes until his attention was diverted to an approaching male medicant. Placing a hand on his arm as he was about to enter the Ki's room, Navarr asked again about Linnayen's condition.

'I'll find out for you, sir,' the medicant replied, not at all fazed by the questioner's obvious agitation and ill humour.

Five long minutes went by during which Navarr alternately paced the hallway or stood with his hands stretched wide, head resting against the glass of the floor-to-ceiling window. The city lay far below in a midday haze of warm air, its appearance one of a shimmering mirage in the rising thermals. The sky's natural pale rose tint, caused by the presence of jekarion gas in the planet's atmosphere, was dotted with white clouds. It was a beautiful scene – a fine, proud city, one of many in the Union that, if he played his part well, Navarr would one day control.

But, at that moment, with no news of Linnayen's condition, he began to worry that he and Balisel might have gone too far. He did not want her permanently damaged – just scared. Trust Balisel to pick an Autabroni! She should have known that he would be too strong. He had certainly been a hard man to kill. Of course, now that Navarr had made sure of Delgar's fate, there would be no one to tell any tales – which reminded him of another matter. Jeremiah Danforth. Was he a liability? He made a mental note to ask what fate Balisel had planned for her new husband.

His reverie was interrupted by the arrival of Evica with Linnayen's servant, Nen, in tow. Evica's sharp eyes took in the besmeared commander, his muscular frame silhouetted against the window and the pink sky beyond. Having heard of his brave deed while she had made her way to the medcentre, her look softened in gratitude and she cleared her throat to get his attention.

'My lady Evica!' He began his bow in reverence to her.

'No.' Evica held out a hand to stop him. 'It is I who should bow to you this day, Commander Navarr. You have saved my dear sister's life and words cannot convey the depth of my gratitude.'

Her voice was unusually soft and there was a tremble in her tone. In the windshifter on the way to the medcentre she had been drawn, silent as the grave, her eyes hard as emeralds and focused on some nearby speck, unaware of anything except that Linnayen had been horribly brutalised. The thought of losing her little sister had never entered her head before this day. Security around them both was always so tight that it was virtually impossible for this sort of attack to occur. How had the madman got past the guards, the security checks? She would get to the truth of it, even if it took forever!

'I would like to see her if I may,' he stated, simply and humbly, and both Evica and Nen were impressed by this gentle side to a man they had thought more usually arrogant and a little remote.

'I will see what can be done,' Evica acceded. 'But perhaps in the meantime you might want to freshen up a little. Your appearance is a little frightening.'

Navarr became suddenly aware of his wild, dishevelled appearance – and of the blood.

'Of course! I'll wash and change.'

He rushed away from them, not seeing the look of genuine puzzlement in Evica's eyes. What had come over the normally reserved commander? She sensed real nervousness – worry, almost – in his demeanour. Could it be that he, too, had been shocked by the possibility of Linnayen's death and, if so, she pondered, at what level did that scenario touch him? His career, perhaps? His ambitions? Or could it be that he had feelings of a more private nature for her little sister? It was intriguing, and at any other time she would have given it more thought. But now she needed to see Linnayen. She needed to know that her sister was safe.

Once he had washed and put on a fresh shirt and loose staff-issue pants, given to him by one of the medical attendants, Navarr came back to wait outside Linnayen's room. The guards were still there. The warm sun still shone over the city way below and the door to her room was still closed.

Finally, after many more minutes, the door opened and the royal doctor, Em-sin Mai, dressed in her uniform grey silk tunic, approached Navarr.

'Commander Navarr. The Ki is well, albeit very shaken and, as you can imagine, heavily bruised,' she began.

'Yes, but can I see her?' he anxiously interrupted.

Dr Mai ignored his rudeness, realising that the man was also probably in shock after his part in the assassination attempt.

'Ki-Linnayen has asked me to convey her inestimable thanks but she is not able to see you just yet. She is not well enough to have visitors other than her sister and her maidservant.' Em-sin Mai watched the handsome face fall.

He had been desperately hoping to see her. He needed to see that she was grateful to him – more than grateful. He needed to see the love in her eyes – for him, the man who had saved he life. After all, it was important to strike while the iron was hot. He had to claim her feelings, to possess them.

Dr Mai was firm. 'I am sorry. There is great damage to her neck and the Ki is not up to talking. She is weak with shock. Furthermore, as her doctor, I strongly advise complete rest. Perhaps tomorrow, commander?'

'I'll wait,' he replied shortly.

She did not want to see him! This was very bad. Why? It had all gone so well. The attack had been perfect, if a little enthusiastic on the Autabroni's part. She should be desperate to see him by now. What had he done wrong?

They had all gone now. Evica. Her mother. All gone home for a few hours' sleep. Evening had fallen hours ago and, at last, she could be alone with her thoughts.

Her mind went over the day's events: the journey to the launch event when they had discussed the religious harmonising of the wedding ceremony, then the speech and the shaking of hands. Bright, smiling faces. Then, disaster, fear, terror when the awful man had stepped out of the crowd and locked his hands around her throat. The crushing, relentless, unstoppable closing of her windpipe and the sudden surety that she was going to die looking into his eyes – not the Autabroni's but Navarr's, over the brute's shoulder. Crystal clear blue, as sharp and as scared as her own.

Then, as quickly as it had begun, it was over. She had tried to wrench the air back into her lungs but her windpipe was restricted.

The last thing she saw before she drifted into unconsciousness was Navarr's blood-spattered face with its look of horrified triumph.

Nen, before she had retired to a daybed in the next room, told her that he had waited all the afternoon and early evening to see her, despite Dr Mai's insistence that he would not gain entry that day.

Was he there now, she wondered?

There was no denying it – the truth of her feelings for this man. She had dodged the issue all along, trying so hard to put him out of her mind, out of her soul! She was in love. He invaded her every waking thought to a point where she could hardly think straight anymore. It was, she acknowledged, now impossible for her to go on without him, without knowing him – intimately. Today's incident had shown her that. She could not die without having given herself to him.

She was about to enter a loveless marriage with an immature, albeit good-natured young man. Did she not deserve a little happiness? Navarr's handsome image flooded her mind and the sudden rush of warmth it brought eliminated any pain she still felt. If they were discreet, she reasoned, no one need know. It would not affect her role within the Union, or within her marriage, she thought.

Linnayen failed to see the irony in her situation. For one so practised in the ways of sophisticated argument, she was being surprisingly good at pulling the wool over her own eyes. This was not a time when reason prevailed. She was in love – deeply, desperately in love.

She swung her legs out of the bed and sat up. Taking a few minutes to gain her balance, she slowly swept her hair back from her face and wiped the tiredness from her eyes. Her neck was sore and stiff and, had there been enough light, she would have been horrified at its discoloration. Rising carefully, she noticed her reflection in the night-dark glass window and paused for a few moments to study her features. She searched the shadowy image of her eyes for a reason for what she was about to do and, with a resigned shrug, knew that there was none. It was all instinct now and there was no stopping it.

With an unsteady gait and her heart pounding, she crossed the room and quietly opened the door to the hallway. He was there!

In the dim light he slept, reclined awkwardly in a chair too small for his frame. His head had slumped over his right shoulder, facing away from her, so that she saw little of his face, only the blond hair, the line of his jaw and his tanned neck.

From where she stood in the recess of the doorway, she could see that the guards were at the far end of the hall. One was asleep and the other was talking to an attendant. Neither of them had noticed her.

Wake up! She propelled the thought into his brain. *Navarr!* His eyes flew open and his head shot up. *Come!* Then, more softly, *Come here – to me.*

Her thoughts penetrated his unconsciousness, shaking his mind awake. Suddenly he became aware of her voice inside his head. This was it, he thought. This was the moment he had waited for. He had been stupid to worry that she would not want him, that his charms would not have worked. It had only been a matter of time. He had to work hard to suppress the smile that tried to form at his mouth.

He rose slowly, careful not to alert the guard or the medicant. As he approached the doorway, Linnayen retreated inside, into the darkness. The door slid to a close behind him. Through the window he saw the thousands of sparkling lights of the city spread out like a glittering carpet far below. Linnayen stood in front of the window, her slim silhouette blocking the twinkling panorama. Then, without a word, she slid her robe from her shoulders and let it drop to the floor.

His breath escaped in a rush and broke the stillness. He moved towards her. His body responded irrepressibly and the rhythm of his heart quickened. He stood in front of her and his gaze roved over her naked skin. Placing one hand on a soft, warm breast, he felt her hardened nipple between his thumb and forefinger and slowly, deliberately he lowered his head to taste it with his tongue.

Her body shuddered and a small moan escaped her open mouth. He put his other hand around her waist to the small of her back, drawing her barely resisting body closer to him. Then he raised his head gently in search of her lips, his mouth travelling the length of her bruised neck. She tilted her head forward and met his eyes. They questioned her. *Is this what you want? Are you sure?*

She answered him with a kiss, at first soft, the lightest touch on his mouth. Then, as the tip of her tongue caressed his upper lip, he was in no doubt. She wanted him as much as he was beginning to want her.

A tremor passed through their bodies, leaving them both gasping. Linnayen was acutely aware of Navarr's growing excitement. She could feel his firm penis through the thin fabric of the cotton pants. Its touch against her belly caused a shiver of pleasure to course through her and she felt a spreading wetness deep inside. She was ready for him and, as if he had read her mind, he moved his hand down between her legs, where his fingers pushed through her soft dark hair.

Gently, insistently, he stroked her until her breath became ragged and uneven. He could feel her hands now frenetically roving his body, tugging at his clothing and, much to his satisfaction, succeeding in their task. She dragged his shirt clear of his muscular torso and, seconds later, he felt her fingers under the waistband of his pants, doggedly pulling them lower and lower. Finally, she took hold of him and began stroking and rubbing until Navarr thought he would explode. If this continued, he thought, he would climax too soon and that would be disastrous. He needed to prolong these moments in order to give her the ultimate satisfaction. He needed to make them as powerful and memorable as he could. His future depended on how much the Ki was in his thrall.

He withdrew his hand and stood away from her. Linnayen, suddenly alone and vulnerable, looked into his eyes. She was confused and worried. What had she done wrong? Why had he pulled away?

Navarr's smouldering gaze took in the length of her body and Linnayen found herself responding again as the warm tide swept up from her soft belly towards her tingling breasts. Without a word, his ice-blue eyes riveted on her flushed face, he dropped to his knees. Then, slowly, moving his gaze down to the shadow of her mound, he placed his hands on the round cheeks of her bottom. Pulling her firmly towards him, overcoming her too slight resistance, Navarr wet his lips in readiness for the pleasure he was about to give.

The pale purple glow of dawn had taken the place of the black night sky when Linnayen opened her eyes. She took a few moments to study the pattern the morning clouds made in the clear lilac sky. Their wispy, trailing shapes matched her mood. Floating, serene, at peace. The horror of the assassination attempt less than twenty-four hours earlier was all but forgotten in her new-found completeness.

He had been wonderful. She had not expected that lovemaking could be so fantastic, could make one feel so very alive and exuberant and mellow all in one. When it was over, they had kissed for what seemed like hours until, finally, reason crept back into their night and Navarr made his farewell, promising to see her again as soon as it was possible.

She could still smell his scent on the pillow beside her and it aroused her once more. Would it always be like this? Would he always make her feel this way? So warm, so wanted, and so like a woman. She very much hoped so because, at that moment in time, she never wanted to feel any other way ever again.

Nearly three months had passed since Linnayen had agreed to Jax's proposal and he was anxious to meet his betrothed in person. To date, all he had seen of her was on vidscreen and, although they had talked many times, this intermittent contact was, as far as he was concerned, most unsatisfactory.

His anxiety was heightened by the news of the attempt on Linnayen's life, a sure sign that there were people who would do anything to stop the peace treaty. First he had been the target. Now it had been his intended bride. He was growing up fast. Although the marriage, for him, was a happy event, they must both be alert for the danger of their situation, too, and not let their opponents spoil their joy.

Consequently, he was both nervous and excited as the Earthan spaceliner, the UDNS *Lennox-Mayn*, entered orbit around Altan, awaiting its shuttle docking instructions from Genkarah Transit Tower. He used the time and the privilege of his position at the craft's viewports to take his first look at his new home and he was very pleasantly surprised.

Except for the tell-tale rose tint to the atmosphere, caused by the unique jekarion gas, Altan looked much like Earth, its waters equally as blue and its fields and forests, at this altitude, appeared just as green. There was a dark – almost black – band of what appeared to be luxuriant vegetation around Altan's equatorial zone and he imagined that these forests must be very thick and lush. The land masses of the mid-latitudes were, by contrast, a light sandy brown, similar to Earth's drier desert plains, and they were broken occasionally by jagged mountain ranges. Jax, who had used much of the last six weeks to study Altan and the other Union planets' histories and geographies, recognised these brown plains as the vast Mayaran grain fields and the source of so much of the Union's food.

Again, like Earth, the planet was topped and tailed by sparkling white polar zones. These were not as extensive as Earth's, a result of the increased degree of the planet's inclination to its sun – 25.75 degrees, as opposed to the Earth's 23.5 degrees. Despite what must be sub-zero temperatures most of the year, Jax could make out the two major conurbations of Rabakaran and Jinkat'naru. These were the famous underground cities of Altan. Only a low-level sprawl of brightly coloured filtration towers, sun-catcher arrays and power-plant bunkers were visible at the surface. The bulk of the cities reached down through the rock for many levels where they housed homes, workplaces, shops, gardens, even lakes for half a million Altanis. The cities' main source of income came from the processing of valuable dirratin gas, which bubbled up through capillaries in the rock in many places under the ice cap. Used as a propellant in the fuel systems of nearly all on-planet craft, such as shuttles and windshifters, the gas was much valued for its purity and effectiveness. Jax wondered, though, how it must be for the people who lived here, never seeing their sun's rays firsthand, never smelling the air or feeling its touch on their faces. What would such isolation do to people? He looked forward to finding out.

The *Lennox-Mayn* circled the planet three times in slightly different orbits, allowing its occupants ample time to absorb the natural beauty of Altan before clearance was given for the shuttle to dock. Jax and his entourage, which included his parents, Duncan McCrae, Ambassador Byers and Professor di Luca, took their places in the smaller craft. In the minutes before touchdown, as the shuttle glided down towards the twisted steel towers and spiralling pillars of Genkarah, he reflected on the last months and the journey to Altan.

Although the *Lennox-Mayn* was the fastest spaceliner in the Earthan fleet, it had still taken nearly two weeks to traverse the great distance between the planets. He had used the time to make a study of Altani history, culture and geography, aided by Professor di Luca. He wanted to know as much as he could about Linnayen's planet for he was intent on impressing her with his commitment to the peace treaty and to their marriage. For a young man who had appeared, as his father described it, to waste his youth on the high life, he had become unusually serious and studious in the last few months. However, if his father had taken the trouble to notice, he would have spotted an indisputable correlation between Jax's growing maturity and the first image he had seen of Linnayen Genara.

It still seemed hard to believe that he would soon be undertaking such a high-level political marriage and to virtually the woman of his dreams – a woman not only beautiful but also intelligent, thoughtful and apparently caring. He just hoped that Linnayen would, once he got to know her properly, display all these qualities. She often seemed a very serious, solemn young woman and he wondered what made her laugh, or if she *ever* laughed, for he had not seen her do so. Perhaps Duncan, with his ebullient personality and vast collection of anecdotes, would draw her out. To be sure, if anyone could it would be his best friend, soon to be his best man.

The shuttle docked. The viewport shields had been raised on the brief journey down, which allowed Jax to see the city now spread out below him. Although he had seen images of Genkarah before, he had not been able to appreciate the way it sat within the cup of the surrounding mountains. For all its many spires and towers, the city was dwarfed by the sharp, soaring peaks, most of them snow-capped. Though it was upstaged by this impressive backdrop, the city was still overwhelming, especially seeing it now, bathed in the early morning light. A thousand shafts of roseate light reflected off the metal-clad pinnacles and filtered through the crystalline bridges that joined them; the city seemed to make the very air dance with colour and form.

His anticipation grew as every minute passed. He was impatient to meet Linnayen. The shuttle's bow doors and seals slid apart with a slight rush of air and natural light flooded the cabin. The air smelt fresh and clean, though it was still a little chilly, it being too early in the day for it to have warmed up. Jax, his parents, Duncan and di Luca stood and tidied their clothing to remove the creases that had formed. They wanted to look their best for this most important meeting with the titular head of the Union of Planets – and for David and Thea, their future daughter-in-law. With Jax at the front, his head held high, his eyes shining from the warmth of his mother's affectionate smile, the party made its way to the top of the shuttle's lowered ramp.

Jax's sapphire eyes took in the scene before him – rows of people and ranks of troops, standing stiffly to attention. There was a strange chiming music coming from somewhere, followed by a fanfare of what sounded like horns or, perhaps, high-pitched trumpets. He searched the rows of faces but could see nothing. Then, walking forward from the middle of the first row, he saw Navarr, wearing a polite smile. He had been back on Altan long enough to have resumed the traditional air of formality in public. With a self-deprecating shrug of his shoulders, Jax returned the smile and walked quickly forward down the craft's lowered ramp.

'Navarr!' he cried. 'How good it is to see you again! You look well.'

The two men clasped their forearms in the traditional Earthan greeting, then, putting all formality aside, Jax held Navarr in a bear hug, which the stern commander endured with a convincing show of pleasure.

'Kevor Jax! You also seem fit. Space travel agrees with you, it would appear.'

'Hardly that, my friend. It's my marriage – or the thought of it – that agrees with me,' Jax replied with good humour.

Navarr kept the smile on his face, though he froze inside. *This man, no, not man … This boy would soon be with Linnayen, touching her, seeing her as only I have seen her, touched her.* The thought sickened him, because, like it or not, he had come to enjoy their little trysts.

Linnayen had turned out to be a willing recipient of his affection and eager to demonstrate her pleasure, a situation that was most gratifying. Why, he had almost become fond of her.

'Speaking of which, where is she? I hoped that she would be here to meet me?' Jax was anxiously looking around and over Navarr's shoulder for the face he had waited so long to see.

'Oh, she's here. Or will be in a minute,' Navarr responded. 'She watched your shuttle's arrival from the upper foyer.' He indicated the enclosed gallery high above the docking platform.

At that moment, another fanfare went up and the ranks of the armed forces slowly drew apart along their mid-line, opening up a passage that was overlain with an intricately woven carpet of many hues.

All was still and, despite the many hundreds of people gathered on the platform, no sound touched the air. Gradually there was movement at the far end of the carpet and Jax saw two figures coming towards him. The first was an old man carrying a long carved staff, whom he recognised from a couple of vidscreen meetings as the Ki's close friend and counsellor Sen-Beoraan. He was tall with a shock of white hair scything through his long grey locks, worn loose over his broad shoulders. Next to him, but half a pace behind, was the slim, slight figure of the captivating Ki-Linnayen Genara, ruler of Altan.

She was dressed in a long, deep blue shimmer-silk gown, the very colour of Jax's own eyes. The floor-length dress was simple and straight, its only decoration being a silver V-shaped girdle, which hung lightly over her hips. Her dark, almost black hair was loose, studded with crystal droplets, and left to flow down her back. Around her neck and resting above the mounds of her breasts was a heavy, ornate platinum and diamond necklace, the Cord, the mark of all female Kis.

But Jax saw none of this finery: the only point of his focus was her face. He drowned in her jade eyes. He was consumed by her full mouth and, when she drew near enough for him to lift her hand to his lips in greeting, he lost not only his heart to her but also his soul.

As Jax lowered his head in front of her, Linnayen had the chance to look at Navarr, who stood behind the young Earthan prince. Her eyes met his and, for the merest instant, a flicker of intense desire passed between them. Her body stirred in familiar response and her breast rose. Looking up, Jax took this to be the result of the kiss he had placed on her hand. It was going well.

Linnayen's thoughts took a different turn. *He is such a boy*, she thought. *He is nothing compared to Navarr – nothing!* Thoughts and images of their now frequent secret meetings flashed through her brain. Their night-time assignations were filled with a fiery passion that left Linnayen amazed and breathless and burning for more.

How can I stand this! Is it too late to stop? I want Navarr … Only him!

There was nothing she could do. The peace treaty was all but finalised. Agreements had already been signed regarding disarmament. This marriage was to be the last, most crucial piece of the procedure. Without it, the treaty would dissolve and, no matter how deeply she felt for the charismatic commander, she could not allow that to happen. Her father's dream could not be allowed to die. Linnayen knew where her duty lay.

'Greetings – at last. Kevor Jax, Prince of Earth, I am pleased to see you.' Linnayen spoke formally but hoped that she had delivered her words with something approaching Earthan warmth. She must have done well, because Jax responded with a wide, bright smile.

'And I you, my lady. Indeed, more pleased than you could possibly know.'

The look in his eyes confirmed what she already suspected. The young man imagined himself in love with her and, whilst this would greatly assist in her political manipulation of him, it could make her personal dealings with him awkward. *Look on the bright side*, she told herself, *I have the peace treaty and I have Navarr. I can do this.*

Although she could not know it, at that exact same time, Jax's thoughts were somewhat similar. He had her. He had peace. He could do this. As he held her hand, enjoying for the first time the cool touch of her skin, they made their way back along the tapestry carpet, followed by his mother, father, di Luca, Byers and Duncan. He could not hide his smile. *I am doing this!*

Jax was rather overwhelmed by his feelings during the next few days; he had never felt quite so ecstatic. He was, at long last, with the woman he both admired and adored and it felt fantastic. He began to meet Linnayen regularly, whenever her state duties allowed, and they could finally talk to each other face to face. Jax felt that they were really getting to know each other.

He told her all about his upbringing in Elidian and Cairo, of his family, his tastes in music, food, his favourite books, his experiences at the academy, though he touched but little on the Diplomatic Corps. He wanted no reminders of Harrie Whitton at a time like this. That episode was over and he was adamant that nothing like it would ever happen again.

He was full of questions for her too. What food did she like? Had she ever been climbing in the mountains around Genkarah? What were her pastimes? Did she like to read? Did she paint? He painted, he told her, mainly landscapes. What about animals? Did she have pets? Did she ride? Or do any sports? There was so much to talk about, so much that he didn't know, and he wanted to know everything about her!

Linnayen was horrified. These familiarisation sessions with the naïve Earthan prince were an embarrassing nightmare for her. He was so informal! He spoke to her as though they were old friends who had known each other a lifetime and, even then, he was still too familiar. Whilst it was encouraging that he was keen to learn – and he had asked many insightful questions about the business of government and administration, which had rather impressed her – his enthusiasm was all a little daunting and she was often relieved when the sessions were over. He left her feeling exhausted.

There was so much to learn about him and the way in which he thought. There was also so much to do to prepare for the wedding ceremony and the many delegations that would be coming from all over the Union. Luckily, Beoraan and Navarr were taking on the burden of the organisational task but, nevertheless, she had speeches to prepare and memorise, protocols to advise upon, dressmakers to see and, in the midst of all this activity, Evica was in infuriatingly high spirits.

Linnayen did not ask but she was almost certain Evica's happiness was because Lieutenant Tariik Min would be returning from his duty tour on the *Sur-Dacas* in time for the wedding. She only wished she could feel such elation. Linnayen was never more grateful for her intense formal training. *Even with all the feelings I have for Navarr and the love I bear for him, I know I can hide my repulsion for the Earthan. It will never show.*

Navarr! Just thinking his name made her glow. Thoughts of their passionate lovemaking tumbled into her mind and made her breathless. She would be able to cope with the boy, Jax. For all his irritating ways, he could have been much worse, she thought. *And, when I finally take him to my bed, I will pretend it is Navarr. Then it won't seem so bad. Then I can bear anything.*

Chapter Fifteen

It was the sixth evening after their arrival on Altan and Thea Bashir sat quietly between her husband and her son, listening to their conversation as they picked over the fruit that had been brought at the end of their meal. They were comfortably seated on couches, upholstered in the finest embroidered Dasnirian sea-silk, in the middle of a lavishly decorated dining atrium.

At the insistence of Lady Li-el Dacas and as was the Altani custom, the mother of the bride played host to the groom's family. Thus, they had been given a set of apartments in the south wing of the Dacas family palace, a short distance from the royal palace of Genkarah, where Linnayen and her sister remained at court. The south wing had not been used since Lady Li-el had retreated to the arbour so a great deal of work had been done by the palace staff to restore, clean and refurbish the rooms for the Earthan party. The result, with its polished green Utko timber floors, its walls of freshly painted murals, both abstracts and landscapes, and the tasteful arrangements of flower sculptures, was a riot of colour and panache. Every vista provided something of interest to look at. But, Thea reflected, one did not feel overawed by the variety of hues or the collection of shapes and form. It felt, she imagined, rather like being dipped in a rainbow, and the pale rose light of the setting sun only added to the illusion.

Her husband and son's voices cut through her reverie and brought her back to the here and now.

'I was amazed, Father. I honestly didn't realise how much training she had to go through. They started her when she was only two!' Jax was talking about Linnayen – as usual. 'And I thought *you* were strict!' He grinned at his father's guffawing reaction to his friendly jibe.

Her son's smile was so grown-up these days, she mused. *When did he become a man? How did I miss it?*

'Well, you shouldn't be surprised, Kevor,' Sheikh David replied. 'Think of her position! She is the head of state of four planets, with the welfare of who knows how many billions of souls in her keeping. It's a daunting role for any individual, man or woman, and statecraft and religious training are the least of the skills she would need.'

David's feelings for the young Altani queen had somewhat softened over the last few days and his tone when speaking of her was considerably kinder than it had been for the three months previous. A couple of face-to-face meetings – just the two of them, as heads of state – had allowed Linnayen to impress upon him the considered seriousness of her actions and the depth of her commitment. She had also set about reassuring him that the Union had no designs upon Earth other than to welcome it as a full yet sovereign partner to the Union – an independent member of a successful and dynamic trading entity. He had to admit that the girl – no, the woman – had impressed him. Perhaps he had been too quick to dismiss Jax's hasty proposal. He had come to believe that she was, after all, an intelligent and reflective young woman with a genuine desire to serve her people.

'But what about her feelings?' Thea quietly interposed. 'You can't train a person's heart or instil compassion. Surely this is the greatest attribute needed for good leadership?'

David and Jax smiled at her. Her words had gone directly to the essence of the matter.

'I believe Linnayen *must* have compassion. She must empathise. Why else would her drive for peace be so strong? There is a great deal at stake here if the treaty falls through. For one thing, she could lose her position as leader of the Union. The Ki-ship is not always a hereditary title. Kis have to be trained. Other families are just as well qualified. And then, of course, she *has* made a personal commitment – to me.'

'Perhaps,' said Thea, nodding. But the rise of an eyebrow told them that she was not convinced.

'Thea, you are too cynical, too hard on the girl. Perhaps you think she's not good enough for your son?' David teased.

Thea, though she appreciated the humour and affection in her husband's manner, was not to be swayed and, in a serious tone, she answered him.

'Well, perhaps she's not. High rank and breeding don't necessarily mean that she is the equal of any man – or woman, come to that. But that's beside the point.' Quietly but firmly she made her argument. 'I only speak of what I have seen with my own eyes, and I have seen no – how can I put it? There is no *kindness* in her face. She is always polite and speaks well. She's never rude. Never angry. Indeed, she's never emotional about anything. It's as though she has no passion at all. So how can she care about our son?'

The words rang in the stillness of the room. The two men were uncomfortable and Jax felt a small shiver run up his arms. David tried to restore the harmony of their earlier discussion.

'Come now, Thea, you go too far. That's just the Altani way. You know how they love their formality and protocol. We must be fair and give the girl a chance.' He smiled and winked across to his son. With sparkling dark eyes, he said, 'Besides, I'm sure that our son will help her to know passion – in good time.'

Jax raised his eyebrows and coughed in embarrassment. Thea just rolled her eyes and shook her head admonishingly at her husband's bawdiness. She could not help but smile at the play on words, but she still felt that she was right.

From a couch in the recess of her dayroom, tucked behind the maelstrom of colours in an abstract tapestry by the famous Zenkaat, Li-el Dacas watched and listened to her guests. The glorious artwork completely hid the spyhole allowing her to both see and hear through the lattice. Whilst she knew that it was very wrong to listen in to the Earthans' conversation, she could not help but justify her actions with the excuse that there were greater matters at stake here than a few behavioural niceties. It was also necessary because she had discovered that her mentante powers were virtually useless on the Earthans. She could barely pick up a single thought and it was most frustrating for her.

The peace treaty was, of course, of the highest importance and, although her younger daughter's happiness meant little to her, Li-el wanted Linnayen's ridiculous marriage plan to succeed. It would be very gratifying for the houses of Dacas and Genara to be seen as the great masters of statecraft that they undoubtedly were. The personal kudos would keep them firmly at the helm of Union politics for at least a couple of generations, and Li-el rather liked the idea that she would be remembered as the mother of a new dynasty. From what she had heard tonight, and on the other couple of occasions she had the opportunity to spy on the Bashirs, it was obvious that all was going well.

The young Earthan was besotted despite Linnayen's aloof manners and the father – who had been an implacable enemy – was coming around nicely to their way of thinking. It was a shame though that the mother was a little too perceptive. Li-el made a mental note to tell Linnayen to be warmer, friendlier. *Perhaps even attempt spontaneity?*

The hour was not late, so Li-el decided to see if her daughter was still awake. She did not have to move from the recess. A simple mind-flash would do and she instantly scanned for Linnayen's signal aura. She found it within seconds and was about to request to enter her daughter's mind-space when something stopped her dead in her tracks. All Linnayen's defences were disabled. She was completely open and permeable – an unheard-of condition for any mentante, and a dangerous one for a Ki. Anyone with higher abilities and the wrong motive could enter her daughter's mind and do untold damage to her psyche. Li-el was dumfounded. Why had Linnayen left herself so vulnerable?

Without a glimmer of a warning and leaving not a trace of her presence, Li-el slipped into her daughter's mind-space. A few seconds were enough to tell her what was going on and the experience answered all her questions. Li-el smiled. She had never imagined Linnayen would be the sort to have a passionate affair. Evica, yes, but not Linnayen. So stiff, so formal, always so correct – like her father. It was very reassuring to know that she was, as the Earthans would put it, 'human' after all.

She admired her daughter's taste. The commander, who had so fortuitously saved Linnayen's life only weeks earlier, was intensely good looking. He was obviously to her daughter's liking and Li-el could see how many women would find him attractive.

Li-el's smile was smug and self-satisfied. If only she had not wanted her daughter's plan to work she would have had great pleasure dropping hints and innuendos to Lady Thea who, if her earlier complaints were true, would be pleased to know that her daughter-in-law to be was, after all, a *very* passionate young woman. Ah, but would there be any of that fire left for her new husband?

Linnayen stood behind the embroidered muslin curtain that had been draped across the top of a long flight of yellow-carpeted wooden stairs. They overlooked the huge stone and steel atrium of the Temple of High Altaniskaran, Altan's holiest building and its spiritual centre. In the minutes before she was due to begin her descent, her solemn eyes scanned the vast space, a thousand metres long and six hundred wide. In the cool, fresh air of mid-morning, thousands of brightly coloured banners danced from the many balconies surrounding the inner temple, one trailing from each ornately carved arch of the tiered colonnades. The rainbow of billowing shapes in the breeze gave the appearance of water tumbling and cascading down the high walls. The effect was both beautiful and mesmerising.

Lining the floor of the temple, row upon row, were gathered the thousands of civic dignitaries, politicians, ambassadors, civil servants, religious leaders and family friends who had been invited to witness this historic occasion. The sea of their upturned faces was looking at the point at the top of the stairs where they had been alerted that she would make her appearance. Many were smiling, most were just curious to see – some for the first time – the legendary Ki of Altan, youngest ever ruler and first to be given in marriage to an Earthan.

Linnayen heard the low hubbub of their voices, muttering and murmuring to each other, overlain by a stately Huthon horn concerto. To her keen senses, the air seemed to shimmer in a rose-gold haze and she could detect an aural glow encasing the crowd below, as if a thousand hearts wished her well.

This is what they want. The romance, the happy ending. Although it is more of a beginning. They are happy for me, even for Kevor Jax. They are happy about the peace this union brings. And so am I … For my father.

It was what her father had prayed for, what he had inspired her to attempt and now, finally, it was all going to happen. The enormity of her achievement, embodied by the huge gathering of souls down below, suddenly overwhelmed her and she was almost moved to tears. Was it only that thought, she wondered, or the thought that she could not marry the man she truly loved and that this was all a sham? Only Evica's strong hand on her shoulder stopped her eyes from clouding and returned her focus to what was her royal duty.

Suddenly, the music stopped and the note of a single amplified horn pierced through the low noise. Within seconds, the crowd ceased its murmuring and the temple fell silent, except for a rustling caused by the wind in the banners and the occasional cough or shuffling of feet.

All heads turned towards the top of the flight of stairs, willing the curtain to part so that they could, at last, gaze upon their brave, beautiful young queen. All heads but one. Jax did not move. He stood still, facing forward, eyes resolutely fixed on the clasped hands of the high priest who waited patiently before him where they stood on the raised central dais.

He wore full military dress uniform for his wedding day and looked very handsome in the navy twill jacket with its heavy gold braid decoration. A full peaked cap covered his head, shading his blue eyes. Although he looked focused on the occasion at hand, his mind was in some other place – a place far off in the future. A place where he and Linnayen were older, wiser, a place where she had grown, finally, to love him. He was not unaware of her feelings for him now. His love had not blinded him so much that he did not sense that her well-crafted veil of reserve hid underlying feelings of apathy towards him. He wished it could be otherwise – wished with all his heart that she could feel for him as he felt for her. But, maybe, in time, that would change. Maybe, he reasoned, if he showed her how much he loved her, how much he was her friend and how strongly he was committed, she would grow to love him. For now, though, cutting silently but inexorably though to the core of his happiness like an ice needle was the fact that his future wife cared little for him while he was doomed to love her forever.

The music started again. This time it was a delicate traditional Altani air, played on sixteen Latissian harps, which rose and fell in time with Linnayen's every footstep as she progressed down the staircase.

Slowly, conscious of every face staring at her but looking only ahead to the distant altar, Linnayen moved towards her destiny – the destiny of her own making and one which, at that moment, inside her heart, she would have given everything she possessed to change.

At the bottom of the steps and with Evica trailing a few metres behind her, dressed in a superb bride-maiden's gown of iridescent aquamarine silk, she began the long walk to the central dais where, from this distance, Jax and the high priest looked like two tiny insects. The walkway consisted of opalised kalendarium panels, each one lifted some three metres into the air on a single steel column and, as the bridal party passed, each panel slowly lowered into the ground behind them. *How apt – no way back,* thought Linnayen.

Finally, at the exact second that the harps ceased their strains, Linnayen came to the foot of the dais and took her first steps up the low pyramid whereon the altar stood. On reaching the top, she waited for a signal from the high priest before slowly walking the few remaining metres to meet the young nobleman who would, before the second hour of the afternoon, become her husband and life partner.

On seeing the priest's nod, Jax turned to take his first look at his bride. He gasped and his eyes widened as he forced breath back into his lungs. Her cloth-of-gold dress was cut low over her breasts and shoulders, displaying both her soft honey-coloured skin and a superb diamond-studded gold choker.

The dress's bodice was tapered to the waist and shaped into a deep V over her flat stomach. A full crushed-gold silk skirt then fell in a wide arc that trailed for three metres behind her, the fabric dotted with pure white Timor pearls, a gift from David and Thea. Her headdress was a simple drape of fine ivory silk muslin woven into the swirls of a gold tiara and studded with tiny diamonds. Its veil was, in the Earthan fashion, left covering her face until that moment in the ceremony when Jax would lift it and look upon the face of his wife.

Jax tried hard to refrain from an outward display of emotion, as he knew it would be considered improper by the Union of Planets delegations. But it was almost impossible to contain his feelings as he looked at the misty silhouette of her face beneath the veil. He was in love. This was no time for gloomy thoughts. If she did not love him today, she surely would one day ...

His happiness and adoration seemed rather too obvious for Linnayen's liking. After all, this was a political union, no love match – at least, not on her part. This was a time of ceremony, a formal occasion demanding the utmost in Altani manners and decorum. Thus, her face, in response to him, was a blank sheet. Jax found nothing there that he so desperately wanted to see, save for a selfish flicker of pride in her flawess jade eyes at the success of her achievement.

The wedding ceremony had taken the best part of two hours. It was, of necessity, long and a little cumbersome due to the need to include customs and representative cultural pieces from all the planets that now comprised the new Union. In honour of the momentous occasion of Earth joining the original four planets, the forum had decreed that the old Union of Planets would henceforth be known as the Galactic Union. The name also acknowledged the old Union's expansion into another quadrant of the galaxy and allowed for the possibility of the inclusion of other new worlds. It befitted the importance of the moment in history and, for many Earthans, was recognised as a crucial gesture in the peace process, almost as significant as the wedding itself.

David Bashir and his entourage had been suitably impressed at the grandeur and the hospitality they had been afforded by the Altanis, and President Bashir had to admit, albeit begrudgingly, that perhaps he needed to revise his opinions after all. They were, of course, still heathens in matters of religion and he had no great fondness for the way some of them could use telepathy to read minds. That kind of mind manipulation smacked of sorcery in Bashir's opinion and it had long since been outlawed on Earth. But, overall, they were people you could, at the very least, do business with. They had a good understanding of trade and economics and they certainly possessed the rudiments of social responsibility, although to nowhere near as high a degree as most Earthan civilisations.

Overall, his son had done well. Perhaps he had been too hasty in condemning Jax's rashness. Perhaps his son had had more foresight than he gave him credit for.

He looked across to where Thea sat second from the end of the rectangular table, between Lady Li-el on her left and the silver-haired counsellor Sen-Beoraan. She was deep in conversation with the old man and they had drawn in a smiling Jax, who sat at the end of the long table. As was the tradition on Altan, the bride and groom were seated at opposite ends of the head table. Bashir speculated that perhaps an evening of being allowed to look at each other but not touch would fuel the fires of passion and get the marriage off to a lively start once it reached the bedchamber. He certainly hoped so, too, if only for his son's sake. It was hard not to notice his son's smouldering glances down the length of the table to where his beautiful wife sat in stately indifference.

Ambassador Byers was seated on Linnayen's left and, next to him, on David's right, was Evica, who was doing her best to be both intelligent and entertaining for the dour Earthan.

Evica thought that her new brother-in-law's father was hugely interesting with his stories of their family's history, which encompassed tales of wars and battles, romance and great deeds. Sheikh Bashir was charming and, as he talked about his home-world and its colourful though sometimes tragic history, she was fast becoming a fan. If Jax was anything like his father, she thought, Linnayen should be pleased with her choice – and he was not bad looking, either, in a dark, brooding sort of way. But the ambassador was a different kettle of fish altogether. Evica found trying to engage the surly, monosyllabic Hal Byers in pleasant conversation a living nightmare – and Linnayen was not helping the situation. She was unnaturally quiet, thought Evica and she speculated that this was not a show of Altani formality appropriate to the occasion. No, there was more to this solemnity and she wondered what it was.

At a natural break in the conversation, when Byers spoke across her to ask Sheikh Bashir something, Evica followed her sister's dreamlike gaze for just a second. What she saw greatly disturbed her. She was looking at Commander Navarr, sitting at the second table between Duncan McCrae and a striking brown-haired woman whom she recognised as one of the noblewomen of the Mur'ekgaskar family. Navarr was talking to the woman, who responded with obvious sexual attraction to the blond commander's good looks and easy charm.

For an instant, Linnayen's face said it all and it did not take a mentante to know what was going on in her mind. A flurry of intense emotions had swirled in her eyes – jealousy, longing, and adoration – before she had resumed her look of composure. As Evica began to understand, she felt her mother's psyche inside her head. Moving her head slowly, looking across David's body, she saw that her mother had leaned slightly forward and was smiling at her. Evica opened her mind. Li-el's dark eyes were two cold glass orbs, and their message was clear.

This is none of our business. What must be, will be. Besides, neither you nor I can change what lies inside a person's heart.

But, Mother! This is disastrous! Dangerous! We must –

Her mother's mind-voice cut her dead. *Do nothing! There is a game of fate to be played here. More than we can see.*

But Kevor Jax, her husband – does he know? This could end in tragedy – for her – for us all!

I say again: we must trust in the ways of destiny.

The tumult of noises in the great dining chamber rushed back into her consciousness and a sudden peal of laughter close at hand drew her attention. It was the young Earthan prince, his mother and Beoraan, obviously sharing a good joke. Such a shame, she thought. *He is so clearly in love with her. The look in his eyes is the same as the one I see in Tariik's when he looks at me. Such a wonderful look – both to give and to receive.*

With this Evica's thoughts turned to Lieutenant Min, newly returned from his tour of duty on the *Sur-Dacas*, and the certain knowledge that in only one more hour, when the wedding celebration was over, they would reawaken their love and begin to live again.

When the dining and dancing were finally done, Jax stood up and went to claim his bride at the far end of the table. They had barely spoken all day – not one word at the ceremony itself, apart from the vows and promises they had repeated to each other – and only a few sentences during the traditional dances they had performed in front of the wedding guests. The lack of opportunity to speak to her privately had made Jax more than a little nervous. But he tried to hide it, figuring that the best way was to breathe deeply and stay as calm as his bride had appeared to be all evening.

He approached her and, bowing his head, said, 'Linnayen, it's late. I think it's time for us to leave.' As he spoke, Jax placed his hand fondly upon one of Linnayen's. She glared at it, shocked at the informality of his gesture, then stared up into his face, instantly masking her distaste.

'Quite so,' she acceded. 'We must first say goodnight to our guests.' She turned her head away and pushed her chair back in order to stand. Jax jumped to hold her chair and, upon noticing the movement at the high table, the guests fell silent, their faces turning towards the royal pair.

Linnayen glanced an order to Sen-Beoraan who, seated at the far end of the table, excused himself to Thea Bashir, rose and turned to an aide who had been standing in attendance behind him all evening. He passed Beoraan the Staff of Vidoka, the symbol of the royal office. Coming around to the front of the table, Beoraan held it firmly in both hands and, lifting the heavy metal rod high into the air, he let it slip down through his fingers to thunder against the stone floor.

'Pray, all be silent!' he called out clearly. 'Pray, silence for the Ki!'

Linnayen nodded her acknowledgment to Beoraan and turned her face to the gathering. Jax positioned himself to her right, waiting for her to speak. Still she showed no emotion and her features were as calm as a windless sea.

'My husband, the Ki-consort, and I would like to thank you all for your good wishes and kind thoughts upon the occasion of our marriage. As you know, this union brings with it the end of war between us, a war that many would argue should never have been fought in the first place. For this reason alone, if not for many others, I know we are all thankful.'

The speech, like nearly every word Linnayen spoke on formal occasions, had been thought out carefully beforehand. She had discussed its content with Beoraan and practised it at least twice. There would be no ambiguities. She went on.

'This happy alliance – both of planets and individuals – could not have been achieved without the help and hard work of many individuals and, in particular, I commend Sen-Beoraan of Altan, Ambassador Hal Byers of Earth and Commander Durroc Navarr.' Only she was aware of the slightest tremble in her voice as she said his name. 'But all their efforts would have been as nothing had it not been for the Ki-consort, Prince Kevor Jax Bashir, whose initial proposal brought about our union and whose dedication and commitment to it is unwavering. I thank you, my husband.'

The wedding guests cheered and clapped politely. They liked this display of ceremonial warmth, which so fitted the occasion. Linnayen looked across to Jax's smiling face. He nodded his appreciation of her words. Then, to her horror, unbidden and unplanned, Jax cleared his throat to speak. He had begun before she could stop him.

'Thank *you*, my lady, now my beautiful wife. You do me too great an honour and forget your own achievements in bringing about this joyful event. I thank *you*.'

At this point, he lifted her hand to his mouth. He placed his lips to her skin in the softest of kisses. Cheering and laughter filled the air. The people loved the gesture and clapped their pleasure, one or two of them – Earthans, obviously, having had a little too much fre-gath punch – whooped in delight. Linnayen was most displeased and out of the corner of her eye she noticed Navarr, his face a frozen mask hiding his anger, only his blue-steel eyes showing his naked hostility for the Earthan. She could do nothing but bear it with good grace and feigned a surprised gasp of pleasure at Jax's gallant gesture.

She regained control of the situation in an instant with her next words, 'All that leaves for us to do now is to send you and all the people of our planets our very best wishes. Thank you and good night to you all.'

She immediately turned and found that Jax already had his arm out to escort her away. Reluctantly, she placed her hand upon it and they walked, without speaking, from the still-cheering dining hall, down the long stone corridors to the Ki's apartments and the bedchamber.

Linnayen and Jax were both deep in their own thoughts. She was dreading the ensuing encounter, whilst Jax was in turmoil. His mind raced, a million thoughts tumbling in happiness yet fearful expectation. Linnayen wondered how she would bear Jax's clumsy touch on her body, remembering now Navarr's fierce caresses and how her body warmed under the fire of his hands. The thought of Jax and what she might shortly have to do with him made her cringe and she became dully resigned to her fate.

Jax took her silence to be a case of nerves. She was a virgin, after all – Navarr had intimated this on more than one occasion – so she was bound to be anxious. Her lack of any real affection for him could not be helping things, either, he reasoned, although he hoped that would soon change. Thus, it would be his job to calm her fears. It would be better once they had got to know each other. Of this he was quite sure.

He led her into the anteroom of her apartments where they were greeted by Linnayen's maid, Nen, and Count Aramikov who, now fully recovered from the failed Labyrinth plot to kill them, had been appointed his aide and bodyguard.

'Nen will assist me to disrobe, Kevor. I will see you shortly.' It was neither request nor order – just a statement of fact, delivered, he thought, so formally that it might have been an agenda item in a forum meeting. Nen moved forward to open the door leading to the Ki's dressing room and Linnayen followed swiftly. Nen quickly closed the doors behind her mistress as soon as the last folds of her glorious dress of gold had cleared the sill.

Aramikov helped him to undress.

'I've taken the liberty, sir, of arranging a little wine for you this evening – an authentic Californian cabernet merlot. I hope that was appropriate?' Aramikov asked.

'Oh, absolutely, Joseph. Thanks very much.' He blushed a little with his next words. 'I'm sure my wife will like it very much.'

Aramikov smiled fondly. Over the weeks of working with him during Envoy Navarr's visit to Earth, he had come to like Jax and to respect him. He was a young man without guile. What you saw was what you got, thought Aramikov and, in his experience, that was all too rare a quality. He was also indebted to him for saving his life during the terrible ordeal of the assassination attempt when Jax had acted bravely and with great intelligence. From what he knew of Kevor Jax, he felt sure that the alien queen would not regret her marriage. Not if she had any sense, that is.

Jax had been lying on a daybed on the balcony staring out across the purple night sky for over fifteen minutes when, finally, he heard the door from the dressing room to the inner bedchamber open and Linnayen enter. Her eyes scanned the room and when she saw where he was, she came over to join him. He quickly sat up, swinging his long legs to the ground to make room for her. She nodded her thanks and took her place next to him, hands firmly on her knees. She, like him, took in the beauty of the evening landscape before them. The lights of Genkarah lay far below, a glittering carpet of twinkling colours overlain by a clear, deep lilac sky.

After some minutes she turned her head to look at him and noticed that the lights of the city were reflected in his dark eyes and that these were focused entirely on her.

'You look lovely,' he said.

'Thank you,' she replied quietly. 'You, too, looked very striking today. We made a fine couple, I think?' She smiled at these last words, hoping to lighten the moment.

Jax smiled back. 'I'll say! We *are* a fine couple. But I think you must be tired? It's been a long day.'

'Yes, I am a little tired. How do *you* feel?' she inquired solicitously.

'Oh, fine. I'm – fine.' Jax felt like a boy again, tongue-tied and not knowing what to say. He plodded on. 'Look, I know you must be feeling apprehensive about all this. I mean, who could blame you? But I want you to know that … We don't have to … I will be …' He searched for the right word. 'Kind. I wouldn't hurt you.'

He wanted to say more, to completely allay her fears. But she cut in.

'Oh, I know that. I've been briefed on what to expect.' Her tone was unvarnished and her features were formal and controlled, as ever.

Jax laughed nervously. 'Briefed?' Then, noticing her frown, he continued, 'Oh, I'm sorry, I don't mean to make fun of you. Perhaps it's just your choice of words.'

Linnayen was perplexed. 'Why should this be amusing? Are not young Earthan men and women taught about mating rituals and sexual intercourse as they grow to adulthood?'

'Well, yes. That is … Yes, young people *are* taught about "mating", as you put it, and human relationships. But love, you know … The more intimate things one does is – well, something one best finds out through experience.' Jax had never had to verbalise about love or sex before and he found it a little awkward. But whilst he was discomfited, Linnayen was unruffled.

'And you have had this experience?' she asked plainly.

'Um … A little, yes. Not too much, though,' he quickly affirmed.

'And I haven't, have I,' she stated rather than queried. 'I am still unmated … What you would call a virgin.' The lie hung on her lips like a fallen rose petal and she quickly brushed aside any quiver of guilt.

'Well, yes. But, then, you would be, wouldn't you? I mean … Oh God! Not that there's anything wrong with that, because there isn't.'

He felt himself stumbling into a hole of his own making and was becoming increasingly agitated about how to extricate himself from it.

'But I expect that because you're so young and, well – sheltered from all that, you wouldn't have had the same opportunities as me.'

Her eyes widened. A frown grew on her face as she tried to understand his words. Jax feared he had done or said something wrong and he wanted to reassure her that she was not unusual or different.

'Look, it *will* be all right, I promise you. You'll be fine. We both will. In fact, I'm sure it'll be wonderful … And we don't have to do anything that you're not comfortable with. I promise you.' He took her hands in his and gently squeezed them, thinking to assure her of his sincerity.

Linnayen neither needed nor wanted his assurances. And she certainly did not want his hands touching her! But she was finding it hard to maintain her aloof manner in the face of his kindness. All this would be much easier if only he could be more unpleasant. *Oh well, best get on with it.*

'Come, Kevor. It is getting a little cold out here. Can we go inside now?'

'Oh, yes, of course,' he replied, surprised at her unexpected compliance.

Inside the bedchamber and without hesitation, Linnayen removed her outer robe and draped it over the back of a chair. Nen had earlier positioned floating glow-globes around the room on shelves, tabletops and lintels, which now emitted a low golden light and displayed her mistress's lithe body very well indeed. Jax was speechless.

Linnayen was dressed in a nightgown of ivory-coloured gossamer silk, which was almost transparent. It was decorated along its low neckline with the finest, most delicate sea-green mei-mei lace, a colour that highlighted the emerald of her eyes. The nightgown was full length and, where it clung to her body, Jax saw the rounded curves of her breasts and the slight mound of her stomach. As she turned to climb the low stairs surrounding the raised bed, she lifted the hem of the gown and he saw that her legs were slim and her ankles delicate. He was completely entranced by the sight of her and, though he could feel his excitement mounting, he wanted to make these moments last a little longer.

'Wait.'

His voice was soft, barely audible. He crossed the room and stood next to her where she sat on the edge of the bed. He leaned over her shoulder and took her long braid, bringing it over her shoulder. 'Would you mind?' he asked.

'I ... Er, no,' she replied, somewhat surprised at his tenderness. Jax removed the gold straps holding the braid and shook out the coils. In seconds, Linnayen's hair tumbled around her shoulders and framed her face. Jax stood back slightly in order to take in the sight before him. His cheeks flushed with colour and he smiled.

'There ... Perfect!' He stroked her hair, letting it cascade through his fingers and fall over her breasts, then sat next to her, holding one of her hands, which she had let fall into her lap. He caressed her cheek. His eyes drank in every curve of her face, the way her lashes curled, the shape of her eyebrows and the tiniest movements of her mouth. His silence said more than he could express at that moment.

Linnayen was becoming more uncomfortable by the minute. He was being genuinely affectionate and kind. Yet she could tell by the quickening rise and fall of his chest that he was also becoming sexually excited. By now, Navarr would have been tearing at her clothing. His hands would have begun their desperate and determined exploration of her body and his mouth would have tasted her warm flesh. Yet Jax seemed content to look at her and stroke her. It was most disconcerting – not at all what she had expected.

'Shall we …?' she asked.

'Yes … If you're ready,' he said in a low voice.

He got up and, walking to the same chair where her robe already lay, he took off his white cotton dressing gown and Linnayen saw that, underneath the robe, he wore nothing. As he stood by the chair, his back, taut buttocks and muscular legs lit by the golden light, Linnayen could not help but be impressed by his sheer physicality. He was strong – stronger than he looked. His was the body of a full-grown man, not a weak boy as she had expected and assumed. He turned and walked towards her and she was surprised to find herself a little excited by the sight of his swollen manhood, unable to be concealed by the room's shadows, and his broad tanned chest with its sprinkling of fine dark down that was so different to her lover's smooth torso. An image of her hand with its painted nails moving slowly across his chest momentarily flashed through her mind and a sudden, familiar warmth kindled inside her stomach. She dared not bring herself to drop her gaze to the lower half of his body as he drew near but, unavoidably, she had glimpsed him and guiltily wondered how he would feel inside her.

Was she being disloyal to Durroc, she asked herself? How could she feel arousal at the sight of this dark man when she was so in love with her handsome, fair commander? How could her body betray her like this?

Jax sat next to her on the bed and, raising one hand, he gently took her face and turned it towards him. His eyes did not waver in their gaze; they stared deeply into her own and, without doubt, she could see the love they held. She felt a keen tug on her conscience. This man's feelings for her were stronger than she had imagined. This was not supposed to happen. He was not supposed to feel this way – and neither was she.

Then, slowly, he lowered his face to hers and kissed her cheek, then the corner of her mouth, then her neck. His lips were warm and a little moist and his kisses were delicate. Yet wherever they touched her skin tingled and she found she had no control over her response. Shivers passed through her flesh and, suddenly, without control, her lips sought out his. Their mouths joined and a blinding swirl of sensations coursed through their two bodies, binding them closer. As his tongue, soft, unstoppable, circled her lips, her eyes closed and she gave herself up to the heady rush of sexual pleasure. A mellow sensation flooded over her and, at the same time, a hot flush emanated from her stomach and began to spread through her veins.

Jax's breathing had become ragged, his mouth more insistent, and his hands began pulling down the silken straps of her nightgown, exposing her breasts. They roamed across her smooth, cool skin, found her stiffened nipples. At his touch, he heard her draw in her breath and push her body closer to his, thrusting her full breasts into his chest. She was as aroused as he and a smile passed over his lips at the knowledge that he was giving her as much pleasure as she was giving to him.

He had not dared to hope that things would go so well. He was not very experienced with women, he knew. Yet, here and now, he seemed to know exactly what to do to please this woman and, although she may not be in love with him – yet – she was undoubtedly enjoying the things he was doing to her. It was like a dream come true and Jax wanted it to go on forever.

The flimsy silken cloth fell to Linnayen's waist and, as Jax's insistent kisses forced her backward onto the bed, it was, finally, discarded with one small lift of her bottom. Jax gloried in the sight of her nakedness, wanting both to stop his kisses so that he could better look at her yet not stop, because every touch brought him closer to the final ecstasy.

Her eyes, half-lidded, questioned his hesitation. His quick response answered her as his hand slid down to the mound of dark hair below her belly. Gently prising apart the folds of her sexual centre, his fingers began to probe and stroke. The effect on Linnayen was electric. She arched her back and a low moan of pleasure broke the silence.

'Yes … Oh, yes …' she breathed into the shadowy air above them.

Jax was soon conscious that his own excitement was reaching a peak. He wondered how much longer he could hold himself back as his engorged penis pulsated against her warm thigh. He would have to break away, or it would end too soon. It was all happening so fast.

Linnayen's breathing increased in its intensity, her gasps became increasingly guttural. As his fingers teased her moist clitoris bringing her ever closer to orgasm, her hands pulled and kneaded at his body. Her mouth sought his, desperate to receive the intense pleasure his tongue could bring. In her mind there swirled a morass of images – Navarr, then Jax, then Navarr again, his sun-blond head moving down across her tight breasts and belly. Finally, it was happening. She could feel it begin to rise somewhere deep in her core. A warm, irrepressible surge …

Instantly, Jax stood up at the side of the bed and removed his hand, his chest heaved with emotion.

'No!' she pleaded with him, her eyes opening wide, begging him. 'Don't stop!'

In one swift motion, almost roughly, he spread her legs wide and, kneeling between them, he thrust himself deep inside her. Holding her hands out to either side of her body, his lips enfolded her mouth and his tongue probed its recesses in chorus with his manhood. Beneath him, Linnayen writhed and squirmed with a desperate hunger, thrusting her hips up to meet his lunges, and every touch of her skin, every movement sent waves of heat through him. Their naked bodies, rising and falling in a sea of constant motion, were beaded with perspiration. The outside world slipped away and there was no other place but here, no other living beings but they, no other sensations but these.

There was no stopping now. In the glowing golden light of the bedchamber, quiet save for the moans and breathless cries of their arousal, the young Earthan prince and his alien queen climaxed simultaneously in a glorious, tumultuous rush.

With hearts hammering and struggling to regain breath, their bodies rose and fell in the aftermath of their passion. Jax's mind fought to return from the centre of his being, which was still bathed in ecstasy. It was then, at the most intense moment of his life, that his world fell apart.

Her deep, breathy voice pierced the now still air. 'Oh, Durroc …'

Jax froze and, about two seconds later, Linnayen's body also went rigid in the sudden, awful knowledge of what she had uttered.

Chapter Sixteen

There had come a point in their lovemaking when Jax, albeit subconsciously, had become aware that his new wife was not a virgin. But the realisation that she had been taken by Navarr, a man he considered his friend, a man to whom he owed his life, was shattering. He had to leave.

Hours later, watching the alien sun unhurriedly light the purple horizon, he clasped his knees tightly to his chest. The air was still cold. He had left his wife's rooms in such a hurry that he had not thought to bring a jacket. He had thrown on his shirt and the navy pants of his uniform and had quickly thrust his bare feet into his boots. But then he had not expected his night wanderings to bring him to this empty grey beach in the hour before dawn.

His eyes stared blankly under their heavy lids. The whites were turned red both with fatigue and the tears that he had fought to stop from coming. His mind would not cease in returning to the moment, the awful moment when she had spoken the name. He had been so happy – happier than he could ever have imagined, more fulfilled than he could have believed possible. Then – emptiness. *Like Harrie all over again!* A drowning black hole, sucking him down into its hopelessness. No life, no future …

Inside his mind he saw again the look of horror on her beautiful face as the realisation took hold. It had not been *him* she had made such passionate love to. It had been Navarr! It was Navarr she had seen when she opened her eyes. Navarr had tasted her skin with his tongue, Navarr had been inside her – maybe even that night and probably many more before it.

Jax's anger grew, but he could not tell whom he hated most. Navarr? Linnayen? Or himself, for being such a fool, such an idiot. How could he have been so stupid, so trusting? He continued to alternate between berating himself and cursing his deceivers, all the time trying to force his mind to focus on what he could do to salvage something of this dreadful situation. But it was hard to concentrate when images of his wedding night forced their way into his mind, mingling with memories of the time before – red hair tousled by lovemaking, but not with him.

He saw himself leaving Linnayen, still naked on the bed, but now appearing ugly and twisted, like a surreal harpy with hair of black snakes, whose limbs writhed and reached out to him, trying to drag him back.

He had uttered no words. He had run for the door and, stumbling in the darkness of the adjoining dressing room, grabbed those of his clothes he could see. He came back into the bedroom and, as if from some far-off place, he heard her stifled sobs and pleas. They were of no import to him. Meaningless drivel, blurred noises … *Shame … Shameless!*

He remembered that she had put a hand on his arm, trying weakly to stop him from leaving and that he had shrugged it off as his eyes issued a warning to her.

'Don't ever touch me again.' His words were deep, gravely spoken, and his eyes were as black as midnight.

He barely recalled getting into her windshifter, which was on the landing dock below her balcony. He was not even sure he could remember how to fly the thing, having had only a couple of attempts over the last few days. Navarr had taken him up in one explaining that, as he was going to be living on Altan for much of the time, it was essential that he knew how to pilot a windshifter.

Navarr! The source of all his troubles. As he took off and headed into an unknown distance, Navarr's face filled his brain. That smug, knowing look in his pale eyes. The arrogant set of his chin. How could he not have seen it, Jax chided himself. His friend and his wife. Now it was all falling into place. He recalled – or did he imagine? – all the veiled words, the innuendos and the sly glances between them. How could he have missed it?

Finally, after what seemed like many hours, the windshifter had brought him to a desolate stretch of sand bordering an expanse of liquid charcoal ocean. The first hint of dawn had begun to lighten the far sky causing the light of Revishankan, the smallest of Altan's moons, to dim and the unfamiliar stars with their skewed, foreign constellations to lose some of their dazzle. A new day would soon be upon him and, like it or not, he faced a life ahead with a heartless woman, surrounded by deceivers.

The first ray of deep fuchsia light shot across the steel expanse of ocean and fell upon Jax's sunken frame. Numbly aware of its touch, he slowly lifted his eyes to take in the new day. The shriek of a passing seabird cut the silent air like a knife. The dark rose light pierced his eyes and he squinted against its intensity. At that moment, with a new world before him, and an old life behind, he knew what he must do.

'Good morning.'

Linnayen's mind fought through a grey morass towards a dull consciousness. Someone was speaking to her. She opened her sleep-clouded eyes and saw Jax standing at the side of the bed. His hands were clasped behind his back and he was dressed smartly in a clean white shirt and loose-fitting tan pants. He looked fresh and clean and she picked up traces of soap and cologne. Amazingly, given what had happened the night before, he looked remarkably cool and calm.

She lifted herself up and grabbed an extra pillow to place under her arm to give herself more height.

'Good morning,' she replied in a quiet voice.

Jax noticed that she had covered her nakedness with a nightgown – not the one from last night though. This was a simple cotton affair with no trimmings. But, damn it, it did not dim her beauty.

'I trust you slept well?' he inquired solicitously.

'No ... But I slept,' she answered. 'You?'

'Oh, I had a fine night,' he replied, his eyes never breaking contact with hers. 'Just what every wedding night should be, in fact. The opening of a door into a new life – thanks to you, my darling wife.'

His words, though said warmly, held barbs and she felt their stings. But at that very moment, he stepped across to her, bent over and tenderly kissed her cheek. Incredibly, given her lack of warmth for this man, the sensation was not unpleasant.

'Indeed, I can't tell you how much I owe to you. You've opened my eyes.' As he moved away to the companel to call for breakfast, he was gratified to see a look of confusion on her face.

Linnayen had not expected this. She thought he would be hurt, even angry. She had, after all, made a terrible slip last night. Thinking of Navarr at that surprisingly intense moment had been an awful blunder and extremely rude. But although she knew the Earthan had feelings for her, surely he could not have expected her to fall in love with him. Or that she would have been inexperienced? Mind you, she thought, up to only a few weeks ago she *was* inexperienced.

He finished ordering breakfast, returned to her bedside and sat facing her.

'Now then. I believe we have a honeymoon to get to?' His tone was a little brusque, although laced with polished charm. 'And I'm sure that you are looking forward to it about as much as I am, aren't you?'

She noticed that his smile did not extend to his eyes and it was with some contrition that she answered him. 'Of course. I'm sure that we'll enjoy a quiet period together after all the ceremony of the last few days –'

'Ah, yes,' he interrupted. 'Some quiet time to get to know each other. Just what two young newlyweds need, eh? I take it we'll be alone?'

The look in his eyes told her that he was referring to Navarr, and his blatant insolence annoyed her.

'That is the way it is done on your planet, is it not?' Her tone was clipped. Jax was pleased to see that he was getting to her.

'Absolutely! Just the two of us.' He got up from the bed and walked towards the shelves lining the far wall of the room. Over his shoulder, he could not resist the quip. 'So we'd better take plenty of vidisks. We wouldn't want to run out of things with which to amuse ourselves, would we?'

Linnayen grimaced inwardly. Who did he think he was to speak to her like that? Hadn't she apologised last night – before he stormed off? She had begged him to take no notice of what she had said. Navarr was merely her lover. *He* was her husband, a much more important position. And, anyway, this was all politics. He was a fool to think otherwise and she would not be badgered into feeling shame for her insignificant slip-up. It was his problem and he was going to have to deal with it, because one thing was for sure: there was no way in the universe that she was going to give up Navarr. Not now. Not ever.

In the midst of her reverie, a single tone sounded from the companel and the door slid open. A smiling Nen entered the room with a tray laden with food, her eyes shifting from master to mistress and back again, trying to glean how the night had gone. Whilst her mistress's face was, as ever, a mask, the young Ki-consort was all smiles. He bounded across the room to greet Nen with a booming, 'Good morning!' Then, he took the heavy tray from her to place it on a small table near the entrance to the balcony.

'My dear Nen. Why didn't you say? A heavy spread like this … I would have carried it in for you.'

Nen blushed and giggled. Linnayen stared with something akin to violence in her eyes and her mouth puckered at the way her attendant so quickly succumbed to the Earthan's charm. Nen should know better.

'Darling, look at this! Come and have some breakfast,' he called across to her. 'After all, you've got to build your strength back up.'

The corners of his mouth curled in the faintest of smiles as he lifted his eyes to meet Nen's. But it was enough – as he had meant it to be – to impress her. She could see what he was hinting at. They had shared a night of passion and the fiery glow in her mistress's cheeks was an obvious sign that she was exhausted from it. Her mistress was very lucky to have such a handsome, charming husband dancing attendance on her. He was so … How could she put it? Charismatic. Yes, that was it. And more than a little good looking too. Those velvety eyes, that full mouth … Nen sighed, a little sad at the waning of her youth, but consoled herself in the knowledge that at least she was not yet *too* old to have such thoughts.

Linnayen's thanks was rasped rather than spoken and she swung her legs heavily out of the raised bed to come over to the table.

Jax's eyes devoured the spread of colourful food. 'Nen, this looks delicious. Just what we need. Thank you.'

Nen nodded happily. 'It is a pleasure, my lord.' Her grin widened at the sight of his enthusiasm. She had chosen the menu carefully. It included such delicacies as whipped pakini eggs with aromatic sinnsey-flower dressing, a small platter of exquisitely sculpted cormander fish rolls, a basket of rare silkaan sea-berries that had been specially imported from Dasnir and a steaming pile of warm, butter-filled ribbon rolls. The repast was accompanied by a pot of freshly brewed diamre, the famous spiced tea from the hills around Patra-mikeen in the Ksas highlands.

The smells of the different foods were enough to melt away even the worst of humours, admitted Linnayen, her senses reacting to the aroma and her tummy rumbling with hunger. But she was wrong.

Once Nen had left them, Jax's pleasant veneer disappeared and his formal, polite tone, which barely concealed his ill feeling, returned. He piled some of the hot eggs onto his plate in silence. Then, as she too began to eat, he spoke.

'You know, there's an old saying on my planet: 'the condemned man ate a hearty breakfast'. It was used in relation to people who were to be executed, their last pleasure before death.' He paused to take a small spoonful of the whipped eggs and Linnayen waited in expectant silence. Then, once he had swallowed, he continued. 'I want you to know that I will not be condemned. I may have been trapped into this marriage, but it will not be my downfall, lady.'

'Trapped?' she shot back. 'Hardly that. You were the one who proposed, if you recall.'

'Yes. You engineered that very well.' His scepticism was plain on his face. 'What mind games did your lover use on me? Or were you pulling the strings behind both our backs?'

'This was no game, as well you know,' she replied, her words clipped and hard. 'There was – and still is – a peace treaty at stake here. Something a little bigger, a little more important than your bruised feelings.'

'Ah, the treaty. Of course. You've done this all in the name of peace.' His tone mocked her as he went on. 'An open, honest peace, based on truth. That's what you offered, wasn't it? Forgive me if I'm concerned about its somewhat less than perfect foundations.'

She flinched under the force of his words.

'I'm sorry,' she began, her tone almost admitting her deception. 'Perhaps your dream has been shattered. But, honestly, what were you expecting?' Linnayen got up from the table and paced across to the bed before spinning around to face him. 'This was always going to be a political marriage. Did you think I was in love with you? Of course not. I did not know you yet still you were prepared to go through with our marriage. So who's fooling who here?'

Whilst he hated hearing her words, he had to admit there was truth in them. He had been an idiot. He had wanted to believe that she *would* love him – just as he had come to fall in love with her – the idea of her, anyway. It was all an infantile, imbecilic fantasy and she was right. He had fooled himself and the knowledge only increased his anger.

Jax also got up from the table and slowly wiped his mouth with his napkin.

'You're quite right, of course. I must have known what I was doing, mustn't I?' His voice sounded tired as he continued, 'And now that the deed is done, I suppose we'll have to make the best of it.'

Linnayen turned her back on him and stepped out onto the balcony. She stood with her hands gripping the gnarled stone railing, eyes scanning the outline of the distant mountains. In silence, Jax walked over and stood next to her, unconsciously adopting her pose.

'I take it that you've been discreet? Up to now?' he asked.

Linnayen sighed with irritation. 'If you're asking does anyone know,' she left the words hanging in the warm air, then continued resignedly, 'the answer is no.'

'Good!' Jax exclaimed, almost heartily. 'That will make things so much easier.'

Linnayen turned her head and looked at him with a puzzled expression.

He spoke slowly and coldly, his eyes glittering fiercely as they drilled into hers. 'Deception was a game you played alone,

Linnayen. But now, I'll be joining you. And the game goes like this …'

As he spoke, the full impact of what he proposed began to register with her. At all times, whenever they were in the public gaze, he told her, they would give all semblance of being a tender and loving couple. They would do whatever it took to make people think that they were totally, unequivocally in love. Whether either of them liked it or not, there was a peace treaty to be upheld, one that was important to them both and which, as Linnayen had rightly pointed out, carried more weight than their injured feelings. Jax explained how it would be. Affectionate kisses on the cheek, a loving arm placed around the other's waist, the absent-minded stroking of the other's hair or hands. To all intents and purposes, but only in public, they would appear to be a match made in heaven.

'In private, of course, please feel free to lead your own life, as I will lead mine,' Jax finished sourly. 'I want no part of you, Linnayen, and it's obvious that you want nothing to do with me either. All I ask is that you and …' He still could not bring himself to say Navarr's name. 'That you be discreet.'

She nodded her head in silence. It was, after all, only courteous that she agreed to his request and it would not hurt the fledgling peace for them to be thought of as a loving couple.

Jax went on. 'There's one other thing. Given the circumstances, and although you may find this a little disappointing given your very obvious enthusiasm last night …' At this point he paused, raised a hand and turned her face towards his. To her amazement, he planted a soft kiss on her lips before continuing. 'I would rather *not* sleep in your bed again. I hope that your people weren't expecting an heir anytime soon?'

Marseille Auteuil had hoped it would come to this. She was keen to again hone her skills that for too long, she felt, had been untried. There could surely be nothing worse for a highly trained, almost gifted professional remover such as herself than to be forced to while away time and become rusty at what was, after all, her calling. The love of killing was one of the reasons she had got into this business – it was the only thing at which she truly excelled.

The buzz was tremendous. The heady rush she felt as someone's lifeblood slipped away always left her feeling invigorated. Acting as no more than a messenger to the Order of Sumere for the last few months had been both boring and humiliating; she felt she deserved better than that, given her superior skills. Now, at last, the contract had come. Byers had failed to deliver. The Bashir boy had married the alien queen, thus affirming the peace treaty and forcing the Order to find some other way to disrupt what would soon become the status quo if it did not act soon.

Of course, it rather helped that 'Oleander', as she was now known, had no great liking for the surly ambassador. In their few exchanges, she had always detected an unmistakable hint of his disapproval of her. The slight testiness in his voice, the complacency and, yes, without doubt, the arrogance – all signs that Byers was a proud, self-serving pig who deserved what was coming to him.

She had encountered his sort so many times before. As a young girl growing up in the tropical squalor of old Papeete Town on the paradise island of Tahiti, she had watched the rich tourists come and go on their private transporters. Some came by luxury hydracraft, but most arrived on sleek silver-winged rapiers that docked silently at the transit tower.

The women were sleek too. Pampered, smooth-skinned whore-wives of the rich, fat, powerful men. They had all the social graces that came with having been born into privilege and then they were 'finished' at the expensive private schools of Western Eurotania. Bred for a specific role, they knew how to coax and tease and fawn over their men, making even the ugliest feel like a rampant stallion. However despicable their actions, though, Oleander could not deny that the prize was worth it. Money, clothes, jewels, exotic holidays, secret lovers and, best of all, freedom! These women were rewarded handsomely for their talents. But Oleander knew that their masters often demanded more than ordinary sexual gratification, adulation or flattery. It was then that the island women were called upon to provide services that would make the whore-wives retch despite all their fine clothes and jewels.

Not Regine Auteiul, though, even though there was always the temptation to grab the easy money. Little Marseille often watched her mother scrub the floors in the poky, cockroach-infested apartment they shared. Regine's strong brown arms would glisten with sweat and her hands would be almost raw. But she could never get it clean enough. She had been born into a better family than Marseille's shiftless father, a family where she had been used to clean sheets on her bed every week and going to St Denis' church school every day, where she excelled at history and mathematics. She was going to go to college, too, until she met Emile Auteiul. His flashing black eyes and broad, mischievous grin reminded her of a pirate and she endowed Emile with the same dashing, fearless spirit. He spoke in poems of mystical islands and strange high mountains that only he knew of until, beguiled and bedazzled, and to her good parents' dismay, she threw away her chance at college and ran off with him.

Emile took her as far as Nouvelle Caledonie where he soon got a mundane clerical job in the bauxite mine. The money was good and went a long way towards paying for food and clothing for, firstly, their son and, two years later, their little daughter. They settled into an ordinary house – nothing grand – but, with Emile's sultry eyes to melt her heart and his strong arms around her every night, Regine was happy. Life went on in this settled if humdrum way for some years. Then one day, without warning, Emile said that they were returning to Tahiti. They had to go now, that day. And Regine, under her husband's insistent badgering, packed whatever they could carry into a couple of old valises, took the children from school and dashed to the airdock, taking the first flight out.

It was only six weeks later, after Emile and their nine-year-old son were found cut to pieces and dumped in a shallow scrape of soil covered by banana leaves, that the truth began to emerge. Emile had been embezzling money from the mine owner. Regine had not known it but her husband had used his position in the purchasing office to fake inventory records and then sell off supposedly excess stock, mainly of machine parts. The boost these activities provided to his income gave them a very comfortable lifestyle but he had explained this away to Regine with claims of promotion and company profit-sharing. She honestly thought he was just a regular hardworking man and it was a shock when the police investigation began to uncover his activities. Emile had not just been shifting machinery but also using these items to transport significant quantities of illegal drugs. The police discovered that Emile had foolishly tried to short-change one of his more aggressive customers – a Tajik hotel magnate – by supplying a substandard opiate compound. As a lesson to his other suppliers, the Tajik decided to teach Emile a lesson. It was unfortunate that he had already collected his son from the sports stadium when he was intercepted by an unmarked aircar and forced to land. The assassins did not have any option but to remove them both, and the gang boss gave them a bonus for it. The lesson was well learned as he never had any further trouble from any other supplier.

It took many long months and years before Regine could smile again. Indeed, she never really recovered. The police seized all Emile's assets and, as the house was still mortgaged and Regine could not find well-paid work, it soon had to be sold. Bit by bit over the years, Marseille and her mother became poorer and more depressed, but never so poor or down that they had to turn to the profession of some of the island girls. Even so, the constant drudge of poverty and the way it gnawed at her once beautiful mother's heart left its mark on Marseille. That would not be her fate, she vowed. *No dead-end job as a nobody!*

As soon as she was old enough, she joined the armed forces. It was the only way she knew how to get the weapons training she needed free of charge and she trained hard, fast becoming one of the force's top recruits. Her mother was proud of her achievements, even if, at first, she had been a little surprised at Marseille's choice of career. But as soon as her conscripted period was over, Marseille resigned and went in search of the Tajik magnate – not to take her revenge, but for a job. Her father had done well from him before the police took it all.

Years of working for the Tajik – and many others just like him – had honed her skills and she discovered that she had a natural ability to kill. She was able to completely detach the essence of herself from her work and she undertook her executions in a no-nonsense, professional style that won her acclaim. She became a much sought after assassin with a fine reputation. It was this that secured her the permanent contract with the Order of Sumere, which had bought her exclusivity. She did not mind. The money was excellent and Marseille did not forget her mother. She had set her up in a beautiful condominium apartment in Oahu with an allowance and Marseille tried to visit her monthly, like any dutiful daughter. The trip to Altan would upset this schedule, but it could not be avoided. It was her job and, besides, she was primed and ready to kill again.

It had been easy to gain passage to Altan. The old space smugglers were doing a fine trade in passenger transport these days since so many people wanted to go to Altan to witness the wedding festivities. As hostilities had ceased between the Union and Earth and they were on the brink of merging into the new Galactic Union, the smugglers had been forced to look at other ways to earn a living. It seemed strange that after all these decades of running border patrol ships they could now just take their craft into orbit and pick up any cargo they wished legitimately.

Oleander, posing as a freelance graphi-journalist, had arrived two days before the wedding and checked into the modest and unobtrusive Zar Guest Lodge where she proceeded to make her preparations. These included researching the layout of the Earthan embassy, information acquired for her by a member of the Order that proved yet again how useful it was to have friends in high places. That was one of the things she liked about working for the Order. It was rich, money gleaned by its members from the coffers of government departments, research projects and a host of other enterprises around the world. Resources were never a problem.

Now, at last, the Order had tasked her with the extermination of the bungling ambassador for his failure to bring about an end to the royal marriage. Besides, with the appointment of intergalactic trade commissioners, he was no longer useful to the organisation. The Order's game plan had changed. It would be easier to force a return to hostilities through corrupting trade practices and the occasional act of terrorism or, as was planned in this instance, a political assassination.

The ambassador also had an unfortunate knowledge of the Order of Sumere – not who comprised its members, of course, no one knew that. But the knowledge that it existed at all sealed his fate.

Oleander recalled from her studies of ancient barbarism that in the Dark Ages, the favoured and traditional method for executing traitors was decapitation, and she felt that this would be most appropriate under the circumstances. She had the story planned. Hal Byers, a traitor to Earth, sold us out for armfuls of Altani riches. The media would be told (anonymously, of course) exactly where to find the bank accounts in which this fortune had been amassed, although not who his real paymasters had been. Yes, Byers deserved to die a traitor's death. But how to get the incompetent ambassador to lay his head meekly on a block and, more frustratingly, how to smuggle into the embassy an object as large and cumbersome as an axe. This was not just a problem; it was an intriguing puzzle. She beamed with the anticipation of the challenge.

These thoughts consumed her mind as she sat in the well-worn armchair in her hotel room and watched the replaying of the wedding ceremony, that had taken place the day before. The ceremony had been very grand and splendid. The cameras occasionally focused in on faces in the crowd showing the mix of emotions: the grins of the Earthans, the gentle warmth of the Dasnirians, the enthusiasm of the red-skinned Autabronis and the seemingly dispassionate interest of the Huthons and Altanis themselves. Suddenly, she was looking at the close-up image of a smiling, waving camera crew atop a scaffold at the far end of the temple. What took her attention was the way they had set up their equipment on a row of tripods and the germ of an idea took root in her fertile brain.

Protocol did not allow Durroc Navarr to be present at the farewell gathering for the Ki and her new husband as they left for their honeymoon. He had no way of knowing or judging whether his circumstances had changed or not. Was he still the Ki's paramour? Or had Kevor Jax replaced him in her affections?

He hated to admit it but he could definitely detect inner stirrings of disquiet at the thought of her and the Earthan oaf in bed together engaged in pleasures that, up until now at least, only he had experienced with her. He couldn't help himself. She was both delicious and so powerful. Was it this that fired his emotions, he wondered. He was bedding the most formidable woman in the Union. She could do anything – have anything. But when she lay with him she was defenceless, and that fact alone was enough to excite him. It must have something to do with it, he thought, for it could not possibly stem from any feelings of affection for her. All his deeper emotions were reserved for Balisel and, surely, there could be nothing left over for the imperious yet immature Linnayen Genara?

Even so, images of his mistress and Jax fluttered into his mind as he watched the royal party depart in a bronze windshifter for the Genkarah Transit Tower. From his viewpoint on the balcony of his office, they were too far off to make out their features. And it was similarly impossible to read their body language, not that Linnayen would have had any trouble disguising hers no matter what she was feeling.

A honeymoon! That ridiculously pagan tradition that the Earthan delegation had been so insistent they keep. Linnayen and Jax would hardly need time to get to know each other – in *any* way – as Navarr knew for a fact that she had no intention of letting her new husband get too involved in any part of her life. Linnayen was not stupid and she had no wish for a meddling husband.

Even so, his mind clouded with images of the two young newlyweds together – smiling, touching hands, touching skin – and his brow creased. He turned and marched back towards the confines of his office, pausing on the way to hammer his fist against the cold steel architrave. His eyes and mouth narrowed into tight strips that slashed his face, ripping away all trace of his good looks. *It should be me! If anyone should share her power, it should be me.*

Li-el Dacas was at her wits' end. No matter how much mental effort she exuded she could not read the Earthan's mind. Every probe was deflected as if it slipped off the surface of a metallic sphere. There was no nook or cranny where she could penetrate the smooth perimeter and enter the sour-faced ambassador's inner being. It was a complete mystery to her. Was he doing it purposely? Or was it a feature of Earthan physiology? Surely it could not be that there was nothing to read, that the man was an empty vessel?

She watched the ambassador talking with one of his aides-de-camp across the chamber. The reception was being hosted by the Dasnirians as one of the many official functions to celebrate the formation of the Galactic Union and they were gathered in the ornate foyer of the Dasnir embassy building. Surrounded by walls of opaque blue-green swirls with high windows overlooking Genkarah's evening lights, the venue was at once stimulating and peaceful. The Dasnirians, Li-el reflected, were a people who strove after contentment and inner peace – properties she much admired though often failed to achieve. Their culture was largely based on a philosophy of the ebb and flow of life, so reminiscent of their planet's watery surface.

Briefly, her mind swung back to the events of two days ago and her farewell to her younger daughter. Linnayen and her new husband had left at midday for their honeymoon, a private week-long sojourn at the Cadal'baran lodge on Hutho, followed by a royal tour of the sea farms of Dasnir and the gas collection platforms of Autabron. Trust Linnayen to combine business with what was supposed to be pleasure. Even at a time like this her unflinchingly proper daughter had decided to use her honeymoon for political purposes.

'It will be good for morale for some of our off-worlders to see their head of state – show them that they are in our thoughts, especially at a time like this,' she had said, affirming her decision to Sen-Beoraan and the other privy counsellors.

Of course, thought Li-el, *she's right. But I wonder what her love-struck new husband makes of it all.*

'Mother.' Evica's voice interrupted her reverie. Li-el turned to see her eldest daughter smiling at her. She was accompanied by a young officer in a white military dress uniform, the silver braided epaulettes of which signified that he was of the rank of lieutenant. Li-el took a few seconds to study the man. His dark hair, blue eyes and olive skin indicated to her that he was Dasnirian, a planet of which she very much approved. Consequently, she smiled and nodded her head at the young man.

'Yes, Evica?' She turned her gaze back to her daughter, noticing the sparkle in the young woman's eyes.

'I'd like to introduce you to Lieutenant Tariik Min, a good friend of mine. Lieutenant Min undertook my weapons training here on Altan some months ago,' Evica explained.

'Then you must be a brave young man, lieutenant. My daughter is well known for her fiery nature. I doubt she made your task easy.' Li-el's face remained impassive, but Tariik took her words to be affectionate and humorous.

'Indeed, Lady Dacas. But I survived.' He smiled at Evica and she glowed in the fondness of his gaze. 'Your daughter was an excellent student.'

I see how it is, thought Li-el. *They're in love, and Evica thinks to soften me towards this low-born peasant with a show of his fine looks and manners. How can she think me so easily fooled?*

'Thank you. It is gratifying to know that my daughter was so receptive to good teaching. You must be very skilled, lieutenant.'

Evica knew that tone. Her mother's sarcasm could be relentless.

'He *is* skilled, Mother,' she countered quickly. 'So much so that Tariik has been promoted to deputy head of security aboard the *Sur-Dacas*, the youngest officer ever to have achieved the rank.'

'Really? Well, my daughter obviously feels I should be impressed with you,' she said, addressing Tariik directly. Then, seeing the rise of Evica's eyebrows, she continued. 'And of course, I am. Now tell me, would I have met your parents in my state visits to Dasnir, lieutenant?'

Here it comes, thought Evica. *Just to remind him of his place.*

But Tariik was not disconcerted. He threw back his head and laughed at the suggestion.

'Oh no, my lady. My parents are simple srif farmers. My family, though, has held domain over half of the Carrissian Basin for ten generations. So you might say that we are not without means.'

Well said, thought Evica, pleased that Tariik had stood up for himself. Li-el, though, was not to be diverted.

'Does not the Carrissian Basin suffer from the most devastating marine maelstroms? Surely this makes it a hard region to farm successfully?'

'Ah, you have heard of our storms, my lady.' Tariik was pleased that Evica's mother had knowledge of his home-world.

'Indeed, they *are* fierce and many a life was lost in the old days. I won't say that they haven't been a menace to my ancestors, but my grandfather Bedarek Min developed the grid-compact system of planting srif, which, as you may know, halves the amount of crop lost in maelstroms. Thankfully, in modern times, we have not suffered as other farmers have done.'

Li-el smiled. Peasant he may be, but at least he did not back down from a fight. Perhaps she had been too hasty in judging the man.

'Well, how very enterprising of you, lieutenant.'

'Not me. My parents deserve your praise,' he stated simply. 'And if I could have been as good a farmer as my father, perhaps I would have stayed. But my talents lie in other directions.'

'Evidently my daughter thinks so, too.' Evica shot a look at her mother that might have withered a lesser soul. Time to end this, thought Evica.

'Thank you for that, Mother. It's time for me to show Lieutenant Min the gallery now. Please excuse us.' With that, Evica dragged Tariik away towards the doors of the chamber, a faintly puzzled smile lingering on his face.

When they were out of the room Tariik pulled Evica to a halt. 'What gallery? The only beautiful thing I want to look at is in front of me right now.'

Evica blushed and grinned up at him. 'You say all the right things, lieutenant.' She grabbed the sleeve of his tunic and, stifling her giggles, dragged him along the passageway.

Li-el pushed all thoughts of her daughter and her paramour out of her mind. There were more interesting things to think about and romance bored her. She resumed her contemplation of the Earthan ambassador.

No. Still nothing. Just like the Bashirs when she had tried to read them. She got the merest traces, but nothing more. Could it be that the Earthans, somehow, had developed or evolved a natural shielding? Or perhaps they had no need of it, she thought, contemptuously. After all, their thoughts and feelings were usually plastered all over their faces for all to see. It was unfortunate, but not a disaster. They will still be easy enough to manipulate, as her younger daughter had already demonstrated, taking in the young prince with fantasies of reciprocated love. She had to hand it to

Linnayen, it was a good plan and supremely well executed. Of course, being unable to use one's mentante abilities might cause problems for Linnayen and Li-el wondered, quite academically, how they might present themselves. She had no doubt that the coming months would prove an interesting show – worth postponing her return to the Arbour of Serenkiraah, perhaps. The possibility that her daughter could end up reaping a bitter harvest from her efforts did not concern her in the slightest.

Chapter Seventeen

Hal Byers knew that his paymasters would be displeased about the marriage having gone ahead and he was not fool enough to believe that his personal standing and reputation had not been severely damaged by it. He knew he would have to repair the harm – and quickly. Consequently, he had spent much of the last few days devising new ways to cause disharmony in the fledgling treaty, thereby returning the protagonists to a state of war.

In particular, he had been very interested to hear about the attack on the Ki's life shortly before the Earthan embassy's arrival – an obvious sign of resistance to the new Galactic Union – and had made it his business to find out who was behind the assassination attempt. The assailant had been an Autabroni gas-plant worker of no known allegiance to any radical or extremist groups. Indeed, the man had been described as 'ordinary' and 'a regular man', possessing a good sense of humour. He was hardly the type to kill anyone and his family and co-workers were stunned that Margog Delgar could have had anything to do with such a dreadful action. He had not even known he was going to Altan until a week beforehand, when he had won the staff lottery. His actions had genuinely stunned everyone who knew Delgar and they just could not understand what he had done.

Everything he heard made Byers more convinced that Delgar had been a weapon controlled by some other hand. But whose? Delgar was an Autabroni. Could the puppet-master also be from the red-brown planet? The planet was so richly endowed with minerals that it would keep the Union wealthy for more generations than one could count. Perhaps someone there wanted to keep that wealth at home. That surely would be enough reason to cause havoc with Union peace plans.

Delgar had been employed by Braup-AG, a subsidiary of GKD. Byers had been trying to work out if there was a connection there. How would it benefit the mammoth GKD organisation to weaken trade links between Autabron where it had so much wealth invested and the rest of the Union? It just did not make sense.

Byers had tasked one of his aides-de-camp to work with the Altan police inspector responsible for the investigation on the grounds that any threat to the Ki was now a threat to Earth. It was a rather tentative excuse and Byers knew it. But, in the interests of keeping a harmonious relationship, Sen-Beoraan had asked the chief of internal security to accommodate the ambassador's request, which he had done as long as the aide did not interfere with the investigation. That assurance having been received, the aide was free to become Hal Byers' eyes and ears, and she had gleaned much useful information that she was now passing on to the dour ambassador.

'So he won a lottery?' Byers was not really asking a question but rather pondering the occurrence. He let his thoughts run on out loud. 'If he was merely an instrument, perhaps anyone could have done the job? Or was his physical strength important? Yet he tried to strangle her. He had no weapons, concealed or otherwise. What did the autopsy show?'

The aide responded eagerly. It was a task she had enjoyed undertaking, despite its grim nature, if only because it made a change from all the high-level diplomacy she normally had to endure.

'Nothing, sir. He was in perfect health and there was not a mark on him.'

'Which leads us to think that he was not ... tampered with, either before or after he died,' Byers finished.

'Not quite, sir. He had skim blemishes, of course. Every Autabroni has those. But the pathologist did find an area above his hypothalamic cortex that appeared to have been irradiated. There was obvious cell damage and that may have affected Delgar's behaviour. It could have been an old scar though. There was no way to tell.' The aide shrugged.

'Yes?' Byers was struggling with other thoughts and tucked away the aide's last sentence to the back of his mind. He went on. 'So, Delgar tried to strangle her and would have killed her if not for the commander's intervention. And yet anyone could have won the lottery. *Who* won was not important. Or was it? Could it have been rigged? Perhaps Delgar – or whoever it had been – was never meant to actually kill her.' Byers' eyebrows lifted in surprise at his own conclusion. 'That's it. They never meant for the Ki to be killed, only frightened. They wanted her scared off. But from what? From the marriage?'

The aide could offer no further insights and kept quiet. It was obvious that the ambassador was not looking for input, only using her as a sounding board.

Suddenly Byers had had enough of these musings. He felt he was nearly at the truth but it kept slipping away from him before he could pin it down. He was so tired. It had been a long few days – both physically and emotionally – and he wanted to leave the reception. He thanked the aide, reminding her to return to her task at the police headquarters the following day and to keep him informed of any developments. In keeping with the formalities, he made his farewells to all the important dignitaries before leaving the foyer and returning to his rooms at the Earthan embassy.

As the windshifter cruised lazily over the glittering towers of Genkarah, he tried to collect his stray thoughts and herd them into some semblance of a motive.

Delgar. Lottery. Could have been anyone. Braup-AG. Autabron. GKD. Commander Navarr – the rescuer. There had to be connections, links of some kind. But what they were and how the pieces fitted together eluded him still and, growing angry with himself, he ordered the windshifter to move faster and get him home immediately.

He was back earlier than they imagined he would be and the embassy staff were caught unawares as the burly ambassador walked briskly into the building. They rushed to greet him and attend to his needs. He was by now in such a bad mood that he barked at them to leave him alone and stomped away to his apartments. The staff were not particularly put out by this. They had become used to the sour-faced man and his moodiness and they quickly returned to their duties.

In his bedroom, finally away from the clatter and clamour of people and ceremony, he could think quietly. Or not think. Perhaps it was best, he pondered, not to think about the puzzle. *Would the answer then come?* It would have to or his usefulness to the Order of Sumere would be at an end, and he had no illusions about how that might happen. His position was now very insecure – or would be once he was back on Earth. But what if he could offer an alternative plan to destroy the new Union? Perhaps the Order would retain his services. If all else failed, though, he would have to make a run for it. Luckily he had a couple of boltholes and a means of getting to them. But not yet. It was too soon to go to ground.

He instructed the comsystem to replay that day's news items on the screen and, as he walked around the room, peeling away his clothes, the day's events flashed up. The Ki and her consort leaving for their honeymoon and royal tour was still the news of the day along with follow-up stories about associated wedding celebrations. It was to be expected; he paid little heed to it. He had been in the story himself for weeks, months and had no great wish to relive any part of it.

Other news was a spectacular storm on one of the moons of Huthon, which excited the meteoro-cosmologists from all parts of the Union. A fraud had been uncovered at a leading agriconsortium involving two directors siphoning off the profits and buying a fleet of luxury soarcraft. It was the last item of news, though, which captured Byers' attention. There had been a tragic death of a young Earthan man who had fallen overboard and drowned whilst on a cruise in the Floating Ice Gardens of Dasnir with his Altani wife.

The reporter relayed as sympathetically as was possible, considering the tantalising nature of the story, the ironic coincidence that this terrible accident should happen to yet another Altani-Earthan couple only days after the royal newlyweds had begun their honeymoon. Even stranger, the reporter went on, that this pair should be distantly connected to the royal party. At this point, the screen image cut to an image of the beautiful, sobbing Balisel Navarr being helped from the cruise ship, comforted by another female passenger who battled to keep her charge clear of the press of news people.

Byers squinted at the screen, gripped by the jerky image of the weeping widow. She lifted her chin to look at the bevy of reporters, her sad, wet, beautiful eyes scanning the faces for a sympathetic glance yet finding none.

'Mrs Balisel Danforth, formerly Miss Balisel Navarr,' the reporter continued, 'had been married for only a few weeks when her husband tragically fell overboard. He had been her assistant at Gunnashey, Kuth & Dor where she is the head of finance. Mrs Danforth is also the twin sister of Commander Durroc Navarr, who has been prominent in organising the wedding celebrations of the Ki ...'

The reporter's voice dimmed like a fading light as Byers' mind raced. GKD and Braup-AG. Commander Navarr's sister. Could *she* have had anything to do with the lottery? Had she rigged it so that the would-be assassin, Delgar, could win? And how convenient that the gallant commander was there to save the Ki from sure and sudden death. Yes! Now it was all beginning to fit.

The sister had picked the assassin, the brother had saved the target. But to what end? Had they wanted her dead? How would saving the Ki's life benefit the commander? Byers was close to defining the method. But the motive still eluded him. Finding answers, he reflected, sometimes threw up as many questions again and, with furrowed brows, he removed the last piece of his clothing and walked across the room to the bathroom.

The news of his brother-in-law's sudden death reached Durroc Navarr within minutes of its occurrence and, immediately, a broad grin spread across his face. The smile evolved within seconds into a roaring peal of laughter. His sister was just amazing!

The companel in his private quarters had sounded a pre-arranged code, a signal that he knew had come from Balisel and told him that her nincompoop of a husband had been disposed of by his ever-efficient twin. He did not really need the details. He knew she would have planned it perfectly.

That's one less problem to worry them, one less obstacle in the way of their goal. Anything Danforth knew about Margog Delgar had died with him and his grieving widow would legally inherit her unassuming husband's surprisingly large hoard of Earthan stocks and shares.

It was all coming together nicely and it would only be a matter of time before he would have ultimate control of the Union and its fabulous wealth. They were a good team, he and Balisel, and when they had the supreme power they deserved their special relationship would be of no concern to anyone, for no one would dare condemn them.

All he needed now was for the Ki to return, and soon, so that they could resume their affair and he could tighten his hold on her heart. He had no qualms now about the inexperienced Earthan prince usurping his place in the Ki's affections. She had told him as much, albeit briefly, the day after she had left on that fiasco called a honeymoon. Not in person, of course. But she had found time and opportunity to send a message to him.

'I am still yours, my love.' It was brief but said all he needed to know. The Ki would be his. Everything would be his.

Hal Byers luxuriated in the warmth and sweet scents of the deep bathwater. Its heat penetrated down into his tired muscles and soothed his skin, just what he needed after the physical and mental exertions of the last few days. He instructed the comsystem to play relaxation music and it obliged with a wispy Dasnirian instrumental that wafted through the damp air. He could not stop himself from being lulled into a light doze.

He was interrupted by a faint tapping on the bathroom door and, imagining that it was an embassy staffer, he resignedly opened his eyes and called out, 'Come!'

Oleander stepped briskly through the door, a wide grin lighting up her tawny features. She was dressed in her standard work clothes, loose-fitting overalls with many pockets and compartments. The fabric was a specially commissioned weave of microfibres which gave off a faintly opaque metallic sheen and, more importantly considering her profession, rendered her virtually invisible in poor light.

'Bonjour, ambassador,' she said brightly, savouring his discomfiture at being caught both naked and unawares.

He sat bolt upright in the bath and his hands gripped its sides, ready to lift himself out. 'What the hell's going on?' he stormed. 'And who the hell are you? Get out of here! Now!'

'Oh dear.' Oleander pretended to look crestfallen. 'Am I not welcome? And I have *so* been looking forward to this meeting.'

'Get out!' Byers was almost screaming. He began to climb out of the water, now unconcerned about his nakedness. Something was very wrong. He repeated himself. 'I said, who are you? What are you doing here?'

'So many questions. All in good time, ambassador,' she replied, shaking her head.

By now Byers was out of the bath and reaching across to grab a towel. But Oleander was quick and in one bound took the towel, playfully flicking his bare bottom with its end.

'Ow! What the … Now, look here …'

Oleander laughed. She was enjoying this sport. 'I *am* looking,' she laughed, inclining her gaze to his bare buttocks.

'Give me that towel!' he shouted, his face becoming redder with every second. 'And then get out of here.'

'As you wish,' she replied lightly and sprang back through the open door. He was forced to follow, but not before hitting the emergency switch that was hidden below the ceramic bowl of the vanity unit. That will fix her, he thought, fully expecting the embassy bodyguards to come rushing into the room any second.

She stood facing him at the base of the bed as he rushed through the door and ran to make a grab for her. Once again she leapt away laughing, leaving him to collapse face first onto the bed.

'Really, ambassador. You are making a fool of yourself.' Once again she danced away as he rushed at her. 'Why don't you just sit down quietly and hear what I have to say – what the Order wishes you to hear.'

He froze. So that was it. The time had come. Of course. He recognised the voice now, the faint trace of an accent. It was the woman who had communicated with him in the gardens in Nairobi. His shoulders drooped and his sigh of acquiescence was audible.

'That's better.' Her eyes never left him. She threw the towel to him and it dropped at his feet. Slowly he picked it up and fixed it around his waist.

'And I suppose you are here to terminate my services?' he asked, sitting on the end of the bed.

'Whatever makes you think that, ambassador?' she asked with apparent genuine puzzlement.

'Well, the wedding went ahead, for one thing. I tried to stop it. I really did. I set impossible terms. But they just kept overcoming them. The Altanis were determined to have their wedding at any price.' Byers was aware that his voice was sounding ragged, so he tried to take control of it. 'You will tell them that, won't you? You must make them understand that there was nothing I could have done.'

Oleander paced in front of him, giving the impression that she was considering his words seriously.

'Of course,' she responded sympathetically. 'You tried your best, didn't you? Shame that the plot to kill the Bashir son failed too. You've had a run of bad luck, *n'est-ce pas*?'

'Yes, yes ... I did. That's all it was, you know. Just bad luck.' Perhaps she could be fooled into believing him – at least for long enough until help arrived. *Where the hell were they, anyway?* All he could do was try to stall her. 'But that's going to change now. I think I've found some new allies here on Altan and I am sure they'll help us.'

'Really?' This was intriguing, thought Oleander, if he can be believed. She waited for him to continue, raising an eyebrow.

'Yes. They were behind the attempt on the Ki's life. Don't you see? That was meant to stop the wedding too.' Where were his bodyguards? Why did they not come? 'And I think I know who they are. No, I mean, I *know* who they are. The Order will want to know, too, eh? I could tell them.' His eyes took on a hooded, snake-like appearance.

So, he was trying to outfox her, thought Oleander, enjoying the game. 'That you could, ambassador – if you live to tell the tale. That's what you're thinking, isn't it? But, you see, there is one problem. From your point of view, that is. I am your only contact with the Order. Whatever you know you would have to tell me.'

'Yes, but you would have to report it back to the Order and wait for their instructions,' he retorted, the hint of a smirk touching the corners of his mouth.

'Ah ...' She nodded her agreement with his observation. 'Of course. And in the meantime, you would still be here.' Oleander caught the movement of his eyes as they flicked towards the door.

'Expecting visitors, ambassador?' She paused, savouring the way he squirmed slightly, then continued. 'Oh, I shouldn't think so. It is rather late, you know, and besides, I've intercepted the security systems. Right now your guards – those that are actually awake – are seeing an image of you asleep in your bed.' She watched Byers' face drop. 'We are quite alone, just you and me. So you'd better tell me what you know – now!'

'You'll take it back to the Order, though, won't you? You won't do anything until you've heard back from them, will you?'

'I wouldn't dream of it,' she assured him. 'So if you think your information is worth your life, start talking.'

Byers began to tell her about the assassination attempt on the Ki and how he had discovered the connection between the assassin and Navarr's sister and, ultimately, Commander Navarr himself. He explained how this demonstrated that there were people in high places in the Union who wished to see the peace treaty fail as much as the Order of Sumere. And he could be the go-between, so they needed him to stay on Altan to coordinate the strategy. After all, he had developed a good working relationship with the ambitious commander and they would need someone to direct operations.

As he spoke, Oleander listened intently, occasionally breaking into his flow to ask questions that were more probing than he would have liked at this stage. Consequently, he embellished his explanation. Oleander was too well trained not to notice how his body language betrayed him, although she gave no hint of seeing the holes in his story.

'Well, ambassador, it *is* a tale worth the telling after all. Very interesting.' She walked slowly towards him. He was still seated at the end of the bed clothed only in the damp towel. She stopped directly in front of him and leaned over to place her hands on his exposed knees. She smiled and looked down into his eyes, which had the all the pathos of a penitent appealing for forgiveness. 'Thank you for telling me,' she said kindly.

'Do you think they will listen?' he asked nervously.

'Absolutely,' she replied, lifting a hand to pat his shoulder in a gesture of reassurance. He felt a pinprick where her hand touched him and glanced down to see the smallest bubble of bright red blood on his right shoulder.

'What –' he began to ask.

Oleander smiled again. 'They *have* listened, you see,' she said as she drew away the fabric of her overalls from her neck revealing a fine metallic wire that lay across her upper chest. 'They heard every word. And you know what? Their decision is the same now as it was when I entered these rooms.'

Byers tried to speak but found that his voice would not come. He felt his body begin to stiffen and could not move his head or mouth. He tried to lift his arm, then to stand up. All to no avail. Nothing. His body was paralysed. Not even his eyes could move, although they took in the dark woman walking over to his desk. She seemed to be putting some piece of equipment together but he could not make out what it was.

Is this it? he asked himself. *Is this how it is to end? Oh, dear Christ! There must be some way out.* Even his welling panic could not overcome the powerful drug she had used on him. His brain was screaming at his limbs to move, to flee from the danger. But it was useless.

Finally, having completed her task, Oleander turned back to face him. Her smile was dark and her eyes mocked him.

'Okay then,' she began. 'That should do it.' She stepped away to reveal what looked like a camera mounted on top of a fine steel tripod. If he could have spoken, Byers might have laughed. *She's going to take a bloody photograph of her handiwork!* Then the question, the hope scrabbled inside his head. *Perhaps, then, this is only a warning. She's not going to kill me. This is all a demonstration. To show how easily they could get to me. I'll have to be more careful in future. As soon as I get the chance, I'll get away. The cabin in Finnlandia. They'll never find me there. No one knows about that little place.*

'Perfect! Just as you are,' Oleander said, bending slightly to adjust the camera a fraction upwards. 'Now, don't move.' Then, remembering her subject's predicament, she laughed. 'No, of course. You can't, can you? Oh well, I'll just have to snap you as you are.' Her voice was cheery, almost perky.

Byers was barely listening. He was rapidly making plans to disappear as soon as this little farce was over and done with. His eyes glared at her, willing her to finish with the game so he could get on with it.

She took a final look through the camera's viewfinder.

'Spot on!' she congratulated herself. Then, with a wide grin, she said 'Now look into the camera. Say cheese.'

Oleander pressed a small white button on top of the camera. There was a sound like the shutter opening, even a flash of bright light, and a superfine, razor-sharp sheet of fibrex, no more than twenty centimetres wide, shot across the distance to Byers' neck in a split second. The cut was so clean and quick that Byers' head remained where it was at first, the only indication that it had in fact been completely severed being the smallest trickle of blood issuing in growing beads, like a fine ruby necklace below his chin. The rest of his body was unmoving, stilled by both the drug and the complete lack of signals it had been used to receiving from its owner's brain.

Oleander stared at his face, her eyes fixed on his, watching them for some sign of what he had felt – or was still feeling. She had never killed like this before. It was quite unique. Byers had barely had any time to feel pain, which was a little disappointing.

The eyes were lifeless and glassy and she knew that he had ceased. It was over. A good, clean kill. Still enjoyable, of course, despite the speed of his demise.

She walked across to the bed to retrieve the fibrex blade from the bedhead where it had come to rest. As she approached him, Byers' body began to convulse. Muscles, now waking up to the fact that they were being deprived of blood, began tensing and contorting. Byers' right arm flew backwards as his torso toppled onto the bedcover. Oleander, surprised by the sudden movements, sprang away, and just in time. Byers' head came away from its support and the stump of his neck spurted warm blood over the coverlet.

Ugh! she thought. *Now that is gruesome.* The head came to rest on its right side where, to Marseille Auteuil's sudden discomfort, Byers' lifeless, intense eyes stared straight at her.

She suppressed the memory of who she once was, took a deep breath and summoned the professional persona once more. She quickly set about dismantling her home-made decapitator and tripod and repacking it into the pockets of her overalls, whilst the ambassador's blood gradually slowed to a trickle.

She took only one quick glance around the room before she left, giving no further indication that she had been at all affected by her dreadful deed. Only one thought entered her mind and that was enjoying a long overdue visit to her mother in Oahu.

253

Chapter Eighteen

The morning dawned grey, frozen and overcast. The low hills of the Seta Ridges were a mere five miles away but shrouded in an icy haze. Looking through the viewports of the medcentre's office in the high arctic city of Jinkat'naru, Kevor Jax Bashir Genara, Ki-consort, was not depressed. He had had a good night and the morning's gloom could not put a damper on the memory of the pleasure it had brought.

No one had been more surprised than he to discover that Kelan Koorab'aran, the assistant director of the Jinkat'naru medical centre, knew so much about Earthan anatomy. But, looking down now at her luscious figure sleeping sprawled on the daybed, he had to admit it had been a delightful realisation. The assistant director had not only been willing to share her vast knowledge of his physiognomy with him but she had been more than able to demonstrate some of her own physical abilities, much to his satisfaction.

He counted them up. Kelan would be the third woman he had been with since his marriage nearly five months earlier. There had been the fresh-faced young dancer who had entertained them – though mainly him – so well during their visit to Autabron, whilst they were on their so-called honeymoon. Her hand movements during the dance had been very descriptive of her talents, which he had discovered in their entirety when she had joined him for a private supper after Linnayen had gone to bed.

Then there had been the wonderfully funny and clever actress Jelaj Ninkatu, who they had met at a gala premiere in Genkarah three months ago. She had first charmed him with wild and funny stories about her famous colleagues in the theatre, told so expertly and wickedly. *Duncan would have loved her!* Then, when he returned to her rooms later in the small hours before dawn, he discovered she had other charms that she desired him to explore just as expertly and as often as he liked.

Jax moved quietly across the room and entered the bathing cubicle to shower and dress. It was still very early and he did not want to wake the lovely and obliging assistant director. She had had an active night and would need rest. He also had no great desire to partake of breakfast with her. She had been a delightful companion, of course, but he felt they would have little in common now that their shared experience was at an end. And, after all, he was heading back to Genkarah later that day and could not say when he would be back in the northern metropolis. It would be quite wrong to build up the woman's hopes of anything more permanent. Yet he was cognisant of the fact that in order to maintain good public relations and be assured of the lady's absolute discretion, he would have to do something nice for her. A small gift, perhaps.

Once he had dressed and left the room he called Aramikov and asked him to arrange for flowers to be sent to Kelan at her office later. He also thought she might appreciate a weekend at the exclusive Yerandak Health Spa where she could be pampered, as she so very much deserved.

Josef Aramikov was becoming used to Kevor Jax's trysts and the ensuing requests these days, although he could not help but be surprised at the necessity for them. The Ki-consort, it appeared, had an extremely good relationship with Lady Linnayen. They were always so affectionate and it was quite touching to see their devotion to each other. If something was wrong, and it so obviously was, then either his master was an absolute cad or his mistress, perhaps, was not inclined towards men. Aramikov could not believe it was the former. Kevor Jax had always struck him as a young man of high principles and exceptionally good manners. He had, after all, saved Aramikov's life. In the time that he had spent with him since Envoy Navarr's arrival on Earth all those many months ago, the young man had proved himself repeatedly to be good-natured and upstanding.

That only left one other explanation, he supposed, and it was that the Ki must lean towards an alternate sexuality. Rather a shame, he thought, given the otherwise fine relationship between the couple. But it was not his place to pass judgement; people were driven to find their happiness wherever it lay and he sympathised with the lonely plight of the young couple. If friendship was all they were ever to have, well, it was more than many people had in their lives and neither could be blamed for the way things had turned out. For Aramikov, the couple's unfortunate yet tolerable situation offered the only plausible explanation for Jax's behaviour.

As he made his way back to his rooms, Jax reflected on the last few months. The women he had taken to collecting were a welcome distraction from the frosty aloofness of his wife and he rather felt they were all that kept him sane and smiling. Linnayen had continued her affair with Navarr, albeit discreetly, as he had requested. But it stabbed at his heart. He could not make her love him, of course. He was not naïve enough to believe that he could. But the fact that she preferred a man whom he had held in such high regard – a close friend, no less, and a man who had saved his life – irked him beyond tolerance.

This unspoken bond between them was all that prevented him from having Navarr removed from court. If he could, or if Linnayen would have let him – which he doubted – he would have seen to it that Navarr was posted to one of the furthest reaches of the Union. But she was determined to keep him close by and would not discuss the matter. She seemed to be becoming inured to Jax's many sly barbs about her relationship with Navarr and either met them with her own acidic remarks or chose to completely ignore them. Both responses inflamed him further and he would often storm away to his private rooms to calm himself.

Even though the women provided a balm of sorts to his bruised emotions, his powers of self-control were fast wearing thin and he knew in his heart that the whole business was getting to him more and more. As for Navarr, he could hardly bring himself to be in the same room as the man. He may owe Navarr a debt of honour but the less time spent anywhere near him the better. *If only Linnayen would think the same!*

A shaft of roseate sunlight fell across the floor of the Genkarah Transit Tower as Sen-Beoraan's placid eyes watched the Ki-consort cross the wide space from the windshifter docking bay to where he stood waiting for him. The high metallic black walls dwarfed the figure of the young man as he sauntered confidently. Beoraan was struck once more by the young man's determined stride as he feigned interest in the goings-on around the dock before homing in on the old man's gaze. This was a new aspect of the Earthan's behaviour, thought Beoraan. He recalled that when Kevor Jax had first arrived on Altan he had been more unassuming, although he had never seemed uncomfortable in anyone's presence. He had commonly made eye contact and was always open and, by Altani standards, a little too friendly.

But a change had been wrought in the man. He was as polite as ever, he smiled as always. But his eyes appeared almost lifeless, as though they took no enjoyment in his viewing of the world. His manner had changed too. Beoraan felt that Jax had become more distant and a little surly. He was becoming more like an Altani – either that or, heaven forbid, the marriage was unstable. Beoraan wondered if he had been the only one to notice it. More importantly, would this change in demeanour affect the stability of the Galactic Union? Especially now.

Since the barbaric assassination of the Earthan ambassador months ago, the peace was once more fragile. Most Earthans had believed Byers' life had been taken by an Altani killer and they were baying for justice. After all, Byers had, after his initial objections and obfuscation, worked hard to achieve the peace treaty. Then, of course, he was on Altan when he had been so cruelly murdered. There were no more than five hundred Earthans on Altan at the time of the wedding and, although all of them had been interviewed in the subsequent investigation, not one suspect was uncovered. No one had either a motive or opportunity to kill the ambassador. *No, it had to be one of us*, thought Beoraan. *But why? Who would have gained from it? The peace treaty was settled. The marriage had taken place.* He could not work it out and it annoyed him that the answers eluded him.

Consequently, and in the light of the present tension, the Ki-consort must be kept under control at all costs. His apparent disaffection must not be allowed to further ruffle the feathers of an already sensitive situation – at least, not before Linnayen's new plan was put into action. But the Ki-consort would find out about that soon enough.

Beoraan made a mental note to delicately broach the matter with the Ki at their next private meeting. As ever, his face gave no hint of his thoughts as he bowed his head in reverence to the approaching Kevor Jax.

'Greetings, my lord. I trust you had a pleasant visit to our northern icelands?'

'Hello, Beoraan,' Jax said, smiling affectionately. Despite his appalling situation within his marriage and his slight feelings of homesickness, at least the old counsellor was a friend. He had always been kind to Jax and, more importantly, given Navarr's deception, honest. 'Yes, my journey was very good. The northern cities were most impressive.'

'I am glad you think so,' Beoraan replied. 'And what did you think about ice-harvesting?'

For many centuries the Altanis had drilled into the vast thickness of ice at the polar caps as a means of enhancing the planet's water reserves. The increased tilt of its axis compared to Earth meant that a greater proportion of Altan's available water was held as ice at the north and south poles. Consequently, where the Earthan polar winters allowed six weeks of continuous darkness, the Altani ones lasted nearly eight weeks and were extremely cold.

The mid-latitude regions were warmer and drier than those on Earth and encompassed expansive deserts and semi-arid grasslands. The equatorial belt, in contrast, endured tropical storms of nearly twice the magnitude of those found on Earth and, combined with frequent lightning storms, much of the zone was uninhabitable.

Consequently, the Altanis had developed a process whereby ice cores were drilled and fed into huge compressor tubes. Gases forced into the tubes caused the outer edges of the ice to melt and crack and the resultant slurry of water and ice flowed along a network of pipelines and flumes, many of which lay buried below ground for hundreds of kilometres. In this way, vast quantities of water were transported to reservoirs in the upper mid-latitudes of the planet. From here it was used in irrigation systems throughout the vast grain-growing regions of Mayar in the northern hemisphere and Hashaniq in the south.

Primarily a public relations exercise, one of the purposes of Jax's visit to Jinkat'naru was to inspect the ice drilling operations and to present the current licence holders with an industry excellence award.

'Very interesting, Beoraan,' he replied, answering the old counsellor's query. 'The process was most impressive. But, frankly, I had some reservations about the conditions the drill operatives have to work in. I think their safety procedures could be reviewed.'

'I will raise it with the minister at our next meeting. Perhaps you could let me have your specific concerns in writing, sir?'

'Ah, don't think so,' Jax answered with a cynical smile. 'Don't want to put noses out of joint after such a successful visit. Just a quiet word with the minister about drill clamping at sub-zero temperatures should do it. I saw for myself how easily the bits sheared away from the clamps when they're extracted. I believe they've already had some pretty grisly accidents in recent years.'

'Ice-drilling has always been a hazardous enterprise, sir. But I'll look into it. Perhaps a sensitive approach is called for. And I am sure the Ki would approve,' Beoraan replied, noticing the way Jax's eyes shifted from his face at the mention of Linnayen.

Jax shrugged. 'I'm sure you know my lady's mind.'

Beoraan picked up the unsaid words and the implication that the Ki-consort did *not* know his wife's thoughts. He was, quite frankly, a little surprised. They seemed such a companionable couple, so attentive to each other. He found it hard to believe that the royal pair were experiencing discord.

They moved towards the docking bay's exit. It was late morning and Beoraan had instructions to bring the Ki-consort to Linnayen's office as soon as he arrived.

'You know ... I have been privileged to serve the Ki and her father before her for many years. And, whilst I know her well, I cannot profess to know how she thinks, sir. That is the only thing about her of which I am ever sure,' Beoraan countered, the smallest of smiles playing at the corner of his mouth.

Jax laughed. 'You and me both, Sen-Beoraan,' he said and placed an affectionate arm on the old counsellor's shoulder. Beoraan nodded and together they left the docking bay for Linnayen's quarters in the Galactic Union offices, some thirty storeys below where they stood.

'Come.'

The panel slid open and, once more, Jax found himself overwhelmed by her physical beauty. She stood at the far end of the room, dressed in a floor-length pale blue gown that clung to her slim frame. Her black hair, left loose, shimmered in the glow of a shaft of morning sunlight, which filtered through the windows. He released a contained breath, set his chin and forced a smile. He hated that she had the power to do this to him – to make him still desire her – when all he wanted was to forget her. More reason to get away from her on official visits. The less he saw of her the better.

'Good morning, Kevor. I am glad to see you,' she said warmly. She walked slowly towards him and, holding his arms, kissed him lightly on the cheek. He winced at her touch and the brush of her lips. It sent a ripple of fire through him – and he hated her even more.

'As I am to see you, Linnayen. I missed you.' He forced the smile to stay on his face long enough for Beoraan and the room's other occupants to see.

They broke away. Lady Evica and the dowager Ki-consort Li-el Dacas were seated on a couch, waiting patiently for the meeting to begin. He nodded as he sat across from them.

'Ladies. A pleasure, as always.'

Evica and Li-el bowed their heads in an appreciation of his greeting. But whilst Evica soon turned away to look expectantly at her sister, Li-el met his eyes and continued to do so. Her examination made Jax slightly apprehensive. He had never known quite what to make of his mother-in-law. She had always been very formal with him and, as a response to her apparent aloofness, he had become adept at keeping out of her way. Their relationship had been forced upon them and both would have been the first to admit that they had no great liking for, or interest in, the other.

Linnayen's voice broke the older woman's intense gaze.

'Kevor, as you already know, my sister has for some time been in a relationship with Lieutenant Tariik Min of Dasnir, who is currently serving as deputy head of security aboard the *Sur-Dacas*.'

Jax smiled across at Evica, whose every feature was alive with anticipation.

Linnayen continued solemnly. 'Last week, Lieutenant Min asked Evica to marry him. Then, according to our custom, he approached our mother to ask for my sister's hand. This proposal being a matter of state, my mother quite correctly sought my counsel and, perforce, my permission.'

Li-el Dacas nodded towards her daughter, showing that she agreed with the summary. Although it had not quite started out like that. Li-el recalled her meeting with the moon-faced young lieutenant. He had been so very polite. Indeed, his manners – for a farmer's son – were surprisingly sophisticated. But then he had come to the crunch. Marry Evica! A daughter of the noble houses of Dacas and Genara married to a Dasnirian peasant? *What in all the heavens had the boy been thinking of?*

Had he spoken to her daughter? Yes, he had, and she had encouraged him to believe that his request would be accepted provided her mother was agreeable. Li-el had been seriously affronted by the whole business but had hidden it supremely well. She had remained courteous to the young man and had pledged that she would discuss the matter with Linnayen. After all, he was asking for the hand of the Ki's sister, the second highest-ranking woman on Altan. He did understand, of course? Of course he did. He would return to his duties on her namesake ship and wait patiently for the answer.

He was barely out of the room before Li-el blasted into her daughter's consciousness, interrupting Linnayen's early evening ablutions. She had been refreshing herself after an all too hurried but stimulating encounter with Commander Navarr and her mind was still a little unfocused. It had been over six months now since the start of her affair with the handsome commander and she was just as eager for him now as she had been on that first night. The memory of it still aroused her, as did the very sight of him. She felt she could barely last a day without seeing him or, better still, being with him privately. He touched her in a way that she would not have thought possible, effusing her with a flood of passions and emotions that she had not even been aware she possessed. She lived for the times that they could be together and the tasks associated with her position had started to bore her. It was irritating that her duties sometimes prevented her from being with Navarr, and her close attendants, such as Beoraan and Nen, had noticed a definite change in her character – mostly for the worse.

Luckily, though, Navarr's presence had left her in a good mood and she was inclined to let her mother get it off her chest. They finally agreed to talk about it later and, once she had showered and dressed, they met in the private arbour.

Li-el was still upset but Linnayen's cool manner soon smoothed the troubled waters.

'Mother … They have known each other for nearly two years and, from what I've seen, there is no doubt of their feelings for each other. It's a genuine love match,' Linnayen had begun.

'That's not the point and you know it,' Li-el replied huffily.

Linnayen recalled her own disastrous, loveless marriage. How could she allow the same fate to befall her beloved sister?

'Mother, let's not rush into this decision. I know Lieutenant Min is not of a rank that our family would normally marry into, but times are changing and Evica has always been – well – different, more independent.' Her mother was not looking any less mollified and so she continued.

'Also, Lieutenant Min's family are more than just marine farmers. They do own a sizeable tract of the Carrissian Basin.'

'But they are still not *our* sort of people.' Li-el was blatant about her discrimination. 'And he's Dasnirian! For all we know she'll have web-footed babies.'

Linnayen scowled, shaking her head with disapproval and disappointment. 'Mother! You should be ashamed.'

Linnayen turned away. In the little time she had had to think about this new development, a germ of an idea was taking shape inside her mind. She had been desperately seeking a way to patch up the holes that were beginning to appear in the new accord with Earth. Beoraan's investigation into the death of Ambassador Byers had revealed nothing useful. Indeed, the more questions that had been asked, the more it appeared that a non-Earthan had committed the murder and that it *was* politically motivated. She had had reports of disquiet on Earth. People there were far from happy with the new Galactic Union. They knew virtually nothing of the alien queen who had – as they put it – 'taken' their young prince, and it was apparent that their distrust was growing.

She had begun to think that it was about time to visit Earth in person – to show them how happy she and Jax were. All a sham, of course, but she knew she could trust Jax to go along with it. *He may loathe his situation in private, but he's enough of a diplomat to know the value of putting on a good show.*

The royal marriage had taken place on Altan. That was the way it had to be logistically and that fact could not be changed. But, she ruminated, how would it be if the Earthans were treated to another royal wedding? This time on their territory.

With the evolving thought in place, she quieted her mother and they had gone to talk it through with Beoraan as well as Navarr. With his knowledge of Earth and Earthan customs, it was essential that he be consulted.

Li-el was not altogether happy with the way her daughter had seized upon the news and was now manipulating it for her own political ends. Her main concern was Evica's marriage itself and its implications for the high standing of her family. She did not care one jot about improving relations with Earth. Finally, though, Beoraan's calm logic brought her round and, although she was never going to feel entirely comfortable about having a farmer's son as a part of her family, she accepted that the marriage might be a good idea after all. Then, of course, there was the opportunity to visit Earth. After all, she had reasoned, the mother of the bride would have to be at the wedding. And if the wedding was to be on such an exotic and interesting new planet, well, perhaps she could be persuaded to it.

Linnayen scanned their waiting faces.

'I am pleased to tell you all that this permission has been given. Congratulations, Evica – and to Tariik, too, of course.'

With a happy gasp, Evica jumped up to hug her sister, a broad grin spreading across her face. Linnayen, too, smiled widely and Jax could not help but notice how her always serious face suddenly became radiant with her beauty. He winced with a bittersweet memory of the young woman with whom he had fallen in love.

Evica then turned to her mother and, holding her elbows, expressed her thanks by kissing her lightly on the cheek.

Jax was truly pleased for her. He had only met the intended bridegroom a couple of times around the time of his wedding. But what he knew of him, he liked. Besides, the obvious happiness on Evica's face was contagious and, he quickly decided, it would have been churlish to let his own disappointment with marriage impact on his sister-in-law's feelings. He stood up and went over to her. Taking her hand in his, he smiled.

'Congratulations, Evica. I'm very happy for you.'

'Thank you, Kevor Jax,' she replied, suddenly bashful in the light of his smiling eyes.

'I think there's someone else who would like to know what has gone on here, don't you?' Li-el Dacas reminded her daughter, trying hard to keep the surly indignation out of her voice.

'Oh yes, of course!' Evica spun to face Linnayen. 'Excuse me, sister, mother. I have to tell Tariik – with your permission?'

'Of course. I've already set up an open channel for you. He's standing by.' Evica was about to race off when Linnayen stopped her. 'But before you do, there is one other matter.'

They all looked at her enquiringly and she began.

'As you know, following the murder of Ambassador Byers, relations with the Earthan members of our new Galactic Union have deteriorated. A number of skirmishes between renegade Earthan resistance fighters have been made on GU ships in retaliation for his death. Consequently, we need to find a way to restore our friendship with Earth and I would like to use the occasion of your wedding, Evica, to make a formal visit to our newest planetary member. The public relations value will be immense.'

Jax and Evica gaped at her. As ever, Linnayen's words had been carefully chosen. Jax had to hand it to her, her webs of deceit were always so finely woven.

'You mean –' Jax began.

Evica cut in. 'She means get married on Earth and, by so doing, use my wedding as a political instrument, don't you, sister?' Evica's formerly happy tone had dissipated.

'Go home?' Jax finished his thought. He could not hide his pleasure. *Home. Duncan, Mother, Father. Yes, even Father.* The extent of his homesickness suddenly hit him like a hammer blow.

'Yes. Home for you, Kevor. For the rest of us an opportunity to meet our new friends and assure them that despite the tragic murder of their ambassador, which distresses us as much as it does them, we intend to hold true to our new union and keep our promises.' Linnayen's words emphasised the message they would be taking with them and her tone demanded their compliance with it.

Evica's eyes were like steel shards.

'And this ceremony will be a demonstration that they are welcome in our planetary family. Is this not so, dear sister?' Evica could not hide the contempt that she felt at this blatant manipulation. Whilst she loved her sister, Linnayen's political stratagems, though usually clever, often exasperated her. Now this one was at her own expense and Evica was not pleased.

Jax could not contain his joy. 'Well, your plan suits me, Linnayen. When do we leave?'

'Yes, sister. When *do* we leave? I suppose you have that arranged too?' Evica was in turmoil. She was, on the one hand, ecstatic about marrying Tariik Min. The news could not have been better and she was looking forward to telling him. But she was disappointed in her sister. She had wanted a less formal wedding, not the spectacle that her sister seemed to have in mind.

'Commander Navarr will advise us when he has made the arrangements. But I expect that we shall be ready to leave for Earth in about six weeks from now.'

Navarr! Just when Jax had almost put his most hated rival out of his mind, she threw him back into his consciousness once again. He contained his anger and turned his attention to Evica instead.

'Well, sister, I'll look forward to showing you and Tariik a little of my home-world,' he concluded.

'Thank you,' Evica returned. 'I am sure we will enjoy *that* part of our journey.'

'Oh, come, Evica.' Linnayen was losing patience with her sister's truculence. 'You must know that your wedding would always have been an important event.'

'That's right, Evica,' echoed Li-el. 'You might as well make the most of it. *I'm* having to. At least this way you'll get the man you want.'

With these words Li-el made it clear and Evica realised that she had no real choice. An Earthan wedding was the price she would pay to have Tariik and there was one thing of which she was quite sure. He was most definitely worth it.

For Jax, the next few weeks could not pass quickly enough. By the time they would be leaving, he would have been married for six months and had not seen Earth for over seven. It was not such a great span of time and much had happened within it. But, for the lonely, isolated young man, it felt like years and he was impatient to begin their journey.

The palace in Genkarah was a hive of activity. Beoraan and Navarr's staff were busy around the clock organising the state visits and public appearances the members of the wedding party would be making whilst on Earth, as well as the more pressing political business of meeting senior ministers and community leaders. The list of 'essential' people to see and places to go seemed to grow almost hourly to the point where the original month-long visit had now been extended to six weeks at a minimum.

Navarr was in his element. Linnayen and Beoraan had handed over much of the logistical and diplomatic work to him and his team, and he was proving to be an excellent manager. He knew exactly what was expected of him: to have everything in place so that Linnayen, Evica, her bridegroom and the other important Galactic Union people could step into his play, speak their lines and go home. They did not want to be bothered with the detail. Well, most of them did not. Unfortunately, the Ki's husband had far too much to say about the whole trip for Navarr's liking.

There had been no way round it. With Jax's superior knowledge of his home planet, its politics, its history, peoples and cultures, there was no way to exclude him. Navarr hated to admit it but they needed his advice. He was a mine of information about the protocols involved at formal events and the historical or religious sensitivities that were involved. Even Navarr's own studies and experiences on Earth, extensive as they were, could not match the Ki-consort's. Consequently, the two antagonists were forced to put aside their differences for the time being, a situation that was somewhat helped by Jax's enthusiasm for the forthcoming journey home.

Under the circumstances, the two men almost rediscovered their old friendship. Surprisingly, they often found themselves agreeing with each other on planning matters or supporting the other's point of view. None of this seemingly rekindled friendship was of any great interest or surprise to anyone except Linnayen, who was unnerved by their behaviour together. She had been used to words of bitterness and anger from her husband whenever Durroc was mentioned, and Navarr's attitude to Jax when they were in private was one of disdain and mockery. To see them working effectively together over the weeks before their departure was unsettling. She supposed that it must have been a little like this between them when they were on Earth before her marriage, and she felt a kernel of guilt at having destroyed their former companionship.

In truth, Linnayen was not entirely proud of her actions over the last few months. For one thing, she had continued to betray her husband. Then there was her orchestration of Evica and Tariik's wedding. It was not the wedding they wanted, but what else could she do? The Earthans had to be placated. The number of raids on Galactic Union trading ships had almost doubled in the last three months alone and there were now as many GU vessels operating to contain the situation as there had been before her marriage to Jax.

Whatever it took and however much she disliked herself for doing it, she could not let it all go to waste. They had strived too long and hard to bring peace to their respective planets to watch it all disintegrate because of one assassination.

And, not for the first time, she felt angry at the grim-faced Hal Byers for getting himself killed, thereby forcing her to alienate her beloved sister.

Captain Tejarc of the spaceracer *Jensa Kadenx* watched the shuttle as it slowly approached the docking portal. The metal hull caught the reflected light of Onuak, the largest of Altan's three moons, and for a few moments the craft glistened like a brilliant jewel.

Standing tall and straight, he rubbed the knuckles of his wrinkled left hand with his thumb. Only this and the hard set of his jaw belied the anxiety he felt at his mission and he wished he could be carrying any other cargo than this. The Altani ruling family to be escorted all the way to the Earthan solar system, a journey of nearly two weeks. Two weeks during which time his crew would have to be on their best behaviour constantly and he would be judged by the arrogant commander who knew nothing about him or his ship.

Although Commander Navarr had not yet set foot on board the *Kadenx*, he had made it quite clear to the captain that he considered himself its chief officer for the duration of the journey. The captain recalled their last vidlink briefing when Navarr had given his final instructions. The blond-haired commander had issued forth with his list of what was to be done, how much fuel they were to carry, what route they were to take, where and how to accommodate the extra security officers they were bringing with them and a host of other mundane items. The long-serving captain had pre-empted all this many days since and already had his ship in tiptop order. But it was common knowledge that the overbearing commander was a favourite of the Ki and Tejarc was too old and too wise to take it upon himself to cut the man down to size. *Let him have his day in the sun*, he thought, *for every day has a sunset.*

The royal shuttle docked and Tejarc made his way to the reception area to welcome his passengers.

The craft's outer doors slid apart with a soft hiss of escaping air, then thudded securely back into the frame apertures. Next came the inner shutter and, finally, Captain Tejarc could see the Ki and her Earthan husband standing in the doorway, holding hands, waiting to step forward. He thought they made a good-looking couple. Both dark-haired, both of a proud, upright stature, although the Ki-consort was a little taller than his beautiful wife. Like many Altanis, Tejarc had had doubts about the wisdom of their Ki marrying an alien. But their Ki had been determined to marry the Earthan, not the other way around, from what he had been led to believe. And from the look of them together in all their grandeur and fine bearing, perhaps he could begin to see why.

The royal party stepped forward and greeted the captain and his senior staff members. For the most part it was a happy gathering. The Ki-consort, Sen-Beoraan and Tariik Min were smiling as they were introduced and made small talk with the vessel's crew. Tariik had been pleased to discover that a couple of his former colleagues had been posted to the *Kadenx* and he was delighted to see them again. He introduced them to Evica and Li-el Dacas, the latter making a special effort to be slightly less formal than usual.

Privately Li-el, the proud dowager Ki-consort, still hated the way things had turned out. She did not approve of Tariik Min and did not want her daughter to consort with him, let alone marry him! She did not want to go on this infernally long journey to Earth either but acknowledged that she relished the prospect of seeing the strange new planet. Then, of course, she could not bear to miss watching the play of events – a piece of theatre in which she, too, had a role. It was all just so much more compelling than going back to the Arbour of Serenkiraah, where the grace of the Most Holy had for so long eluded her. Immortality – if she were ever to attain it – would have to wait a little longer.

In the meantime, she was content to observe her younger daughter's infatuation with Navarr, surprised that the man still held any sway over her. Linnayen hid it well, she thought, but you could not fool a mentante. Li-el was adept at seeing her daughter's thoughts and getting past Linnayen's barriers and the shudder of exhilaration her daughter experienced whenever she was with Navarr was obvious. She became breathless and her stomach knotted. But whether this was an anticipation borne of love, or lust, or even fear, Li-el could not tell and it totally intrigued her.

Chapter Nineteen

With only two more days to go until they entered the Earthan solar system, Jax was getting more and more excited at the prospect of coming home. He could barely wait to see the familiar blue and white planet again and, in his enthusiasm for his homeworld, he had begun to drive even the patient Beoraan a little crazy with stories and descriptions of his life there.

Surprisingly, the one person who had every reason to hate the thought of going there, due to the shabby way she had been used, had become Jax's most avid audience. When she was not with Tariik Min, Evica would happily ask Jax to tell her more about his planet and its strange people, not forgetting the many unusual species of animals. She was saddened to hear that, in past times, humans had been so careless as to allow the extinction of many living things. She wondered how they could have been so reckless and was secretly proud that Altanis would not have behaved in the same way, placing as they did an inordinately strong emphasis on the sanctity of all life forms.

Captain Tejarc, too, enjoyed hearing about Earth. He formed the opinion that it was both colourful and diverse and, having the spirit of an adventurer, he was very keen to see if it lived up to the images the Ki-consort's words had put inside his mind. His opinions, though, were as much inspired by the storyteller as by the stories. The young Earthan struck him as an eminently likeable man. He certainly did not possess the arrogance and haughty manner of Commander Navarr, who had tried at almost every opportunity to take over his ship or give the impression – in front of the Ki – that he was in charge. It had been a very trying experience and, consequently, Tejarc would be glad for more than one reason to arrive at their destination.

On the morning of the tenth day, as had become his custom shortly after waking, Jax took his mug of hot black coffee to the bridge to check their position and status. He liked to know what had happened whilst he slept, especially if there had been any unusual cosmonic phenomena. It all went into the journal he was keeping, which was also fast becoming a historic account of the Ki's first visit to Earth.

The captain looked around as the doors slid apart and with a slight nod of his head welcomed the Ki-consort before restoring his gaze to the many light pads and sensors on the pilot's console. With his back towards him, Tejarc spoke.

'Good morning, sir. I hope you are well rested?'

'Thank you, captain. Yes.' Jax walked across to an array of controls mounted on a wall to the left of the wide viewscreen. This was the ship's eye on the outside universe, a computer-enhanced image of the space through which they were passing. Any pixel of the image could be expanded to ten thousand times its size.

Jax studied the screen and the coordinates displayed on its sides, once again looking for familiar numbers and galaxies and star alignments that would signify they were drawing close to home.

'Would you like to see it?' The captain's deep voice broke the silence. They both knew of what he spoke.

'Are we close enough yet?' Jax's response came swiftly.

'Let's see.' Tejarc was smiling. The grown man was still boy enough to be excited by both the prospect of seeing his home and by the technology that would make it possible.

Tejarc touched several light panels on the console in front of him and a single pixel in the viewscreen blew out to fill the entire space. At another touch the image zoomed up again, then again and, finally, the familiar red-orange orb of the star at the centre of the Earthan solar system was in sight. It looked like many other stars that Jax and Tejarc had seen. But, as one, the two men smiled and their eyes glowed. Neither spoke for many moments. A few members of the crew also stopped in the midst of their duties to look at the bright sphere. Some faces, like Jax's and the captain's, were smiling, others wore a look of serious anticipation. But all were quiet and only the low hum of the vessel's propulsion system could be heard.

Then the moment was broken. The doors opened and Linnayen, Navarr and Li-el Dacas stepped forward onto the bridge. All heads turned to them and, within an instant, the crew stood still and bowed their heads. Captain Tejarc, too, placed his hands behind his back and lowered his head as his mark of respect. No one moved until the Ki had spoken.

'Good morning.' Her voice was, as ever, firm and formal. The crew resumed their duties and Jax turned back to his reverie of the distant sun – *his* sun.

'Our destination, I take it?' Linnayen asked, nodding her head towards the viewscreen but speaking to the captain.

'Yes, my lady. The Earthan solar system came into viewing range about an hour ago.'

Jax turned to look at the old captain, a wry smile crossing his face. *So he had known all along.* Jax did not mind that Tejarc had teased him – he would have done the same.

'And our distance is ...?' she continued.

'Approximately sixty billion kliks, give or take the odd million, I'd say, wouldn't you, Captain Tejarc?' Jax replied.

'Sixty point three six billion to be absolutely precise, sir, my lady. We are still on schedule to arrive at Solab 3 in a little over forty hours,' the captain concluded.

'Then you have done well, Captain Tejarc,' Linnayen replied.

'No more than is our duty, my lady,' he replied, lowering his head.

'Have you spoken to the Earthans, captain? Are they prepared for our arrival?' This was the imperious Commander Navarr, once again asserting his authority.

'I have, commander. They are fully prepared and will be placing the space station on full security alert in approximately twenty-four hours.'

'Not soon enough,' Navarr barked back. 'The station needs to be impregnable for at least thirty-six hours before our arrival.'

Jax could not let Navarr bully the captain. 'That's impossible, Commander Navarr. And unnecessary. Solab 3 is a working station with many scientists dependant on it being completely operational. We cannot disrupt it sooner than we need.' On this point he was the expert authority. Navarr would have to bow to his knowledge and – however hollow it was in reality – his higher rank.

Before Navarr could be tempted to respond and openly be seen to question his leader, Linnayen spoke. 'The Ki-consort is right, commander. I am confident that the Earthans have made all the proper arrangements in good time and that we have nothing to worry about.'

Navarr bowed his head and said no more, only the twitch of a tiny muscle under his cheek belying the anger he felt at being so cut down. It did not matter. They both knew who held the reins of power. It was Navarr who had private access to the exquisite young Ki – still so passionate, so demanding that he – and *only* he – could give her what she had come to crave. Their opportunities to be together on board the *Jensa Kadenx* had of necessity been fewer. But all that would change when they got to Earth and he could, once more, take her at will.

Li-el Dacas watched the exchange between her daughter, her lover and her husband with her usual silent amusement. *Very wise, my daughter*. Linnayen had done well to place her husband above her lover in public. To have done the reverse would have courted disaster. So far, Li-el was sure that only Evica and she knew of Linnayen's affair with the handsome commander. She did not even think that Kevor Jax could know what was going on right under his nose, though his mind, like those of the other Earthans, had been impenetrable to her mentante abilities and she could intuit nothing of his thoughts.

If Linnayen wanted to keep her paramour, though, she would do well to continue such discretion, as any word of this betrayal of her marriage vows would destroy the precious peace agreement and, quite possibly, the long-standing power base of the Genara and Dacas families. There were council members who would gladly see her deposed for such a misdemeanour, if only to further their own house. Li-el made a mental note to speak to her daughter about terminating this sordid affair and get on with the business of her marriage – especially the production of an heir.

Linnayen's voice cut through Li-el's reverie. 'We have disturbed you enough, captain. Thank you again.'

Her business concluded, Linnayen turned to walk the short distance to the vatortube doors when a sudden violent shudder reverberated through the vessel's hull. The tremor stopped her in her tracks and, as her body swayed with the movement, Linnayen's eyes searched the faces around her for an explanation of what was going on.

Everywhere was motion and noise. The walls were shaking. Crew members darted across the open space to reach their workstations, trying desperately to keep their feet until they could reach their consoles and scan the screens for some clue as to what was attacking them – if it was an attack.

Navarr had been thrown against the vatortube doors and, with a natural instinct for self-preservation, clamped a magnetic wrist strap to the metal architrave. It held him firmly about a metre from where Linnayen stood, feet planted and balancing gingerly.

The noise grew to a hammering roar and the captain shouted instructions to his crew. Tejarc fought a way through to his own console and once seated, though his body shook violently in his seat, he began to run his fingers over the smooth glass panels in the armrests, still calling out questions.

'Ops! Report!'

A shaven-headed crewman shouted back to him.

'It's a psytro-ion stream, sir. We've run straight into it!'

'Strength?'

'Point six, increasing ... Rhythmic ... Lateral shift.'

'Systems! Report!' Tejarc could hardly be heard above the hammering din.

'Hull intact. Internal pressure stable ... Not for long though.'

A young crewwoman called across to Tejarc. 'Captain! Distress call sent.'

Tejarc nodded to her. 'Engine room! Report!' he shouted.

From the bridge intercom came the instantaneous response.

'FI system up four cracks, sir. Pulse drive holding. Seventy percent ops reliable.'

'Release drive. Secure!' His words, which all present knew from the many safety drills they had undertaken, were an order to hold tight onto whatever they could find.

Jax half ran, half stumbled from the viewscreen to where Linnayen stood, still trying to keep her balance and searching for something secure to hold. His arm went instantly around her waist and, using his forward momentum, he pulled her towards a wall with a metal rail. Li-el Dacas already had hold of it and she stretched out an arm to receive the stunned Linnayen.

Tejarc's voice cut through the clamour. 'Change course to zero three one seven, vector G4.'

'Ay, sir,' came the reply from the pilot, who was seated away to the captain's right. 'Zero three one seven, V-G4, sir!'

Linnayen had just taken hold of her mother's hand when there was a sudden lurch. The vessel swung sharply away to the left and downwards. Not having had the chance to grab a handhold for himself, Jax's grip on Linnayen loosened and he went sliding across the floor of the bridge, spinning on his back.

After only a couple of seconds he slammed to a stop at the foot of the viewscreen and instantly reached above his head to clasp a small metal handle before he was thrown again. His back had taken most of the impact, knocking the wind out of his lungs. But at that moment he felt nothing. From this angle, it appeared that the whole bridge was suspended above his head and tilted virtually on its side. Then he noticed that Li-el was struggling to keep her grip on Linnayen's hand. The vessel was still in its plunging dive and the frightened young woman could not fight the inertia to swing her other hand around in order to grab the rail. Her feet were almost dangling in mid-air as they could find no solid or horizontal ground to take hold.

Li-el's strength was fading. Jax knew she could not hold Linnayen for much longer. He called out to Tejarc.

'Captain! The Ki! Close the angle!'

As Tejarc looked over his shoulder, suddenly realising the danger his Ki was in, Li-el's grip finally gave out. Her face was a mask of horror as she watched Linnayen slithering and tumbling across the floor, her skirts flailing wildly around her and her hands outstretched seeking something to hold in order to break her fall. There was nothing. Even before Tejarc could bark out a course correction, the pilot, seeing the danger, was trying to level the craft out. But in the seconds before their plunge was stemmed, Linnayen had half fallen, half slithered across the twenty-metre span of the bridge and her head smashed hard into the underside of a systems console.

Psytro-ions were still crashing against the hull, like a million cast-iron needles trying to punch through, as Jax got to his feet and stumbled across the small space to where Linnayen lay. Navarr, too, flicked the magnetic lock on his wrist strap and, as much as the still shuddering ship would allow him, ran over to Linnayen's crumpled, unmoving body.

The honey-skinned woman moved across the hotel lobby with a suggestive sway of her hips. Her dark titian hair swung like a soft velvet curtain to below her waist, curls teasing the small of her back. All eyes turned to look, as she knew they would. It was what she wanted today and it made a pleasant change for her to be so conspicuous rather than her usual silent, unseen self. The knee-length emerald silk suit, with its tailored cut and short, tight skirt, enhanced her curves. The clinging fabric brushed against her thighs as she walked and it made her feel sexy. She promised herself that once her business here was concluded, she would treat herself tonight to someone young and vigorous.

She took the elevator to the twenty-seventh floor and, without any reference to the floor plan, went straight to suite three. She knocked sharply on the door and waited calmly for the response. When it came, she was prepared.

'Impressia Magazine, Miss Navarr. I'm Carri Aqua.' Her brown eyes smiled up into the comscreen. She looked like a magazine writer. Indeed, she even felt like one, knowing already so much about Balisel Navarr – not what everyone else knew, of course. No, she knew rather more than most people about the woman who had risen to be one of the wealthiest people of all the known planets. What she didn't know, though, was why Balisel Navarr and possibly her brother wanted the Ki of Altan dead. Their fate, one would have thought, especially the ambitious male twin's, was bound to hers. So why have her killed?

It didn't really matter, of course. Whatever their motives, it only mattered that Balisel Navarr wanted the Ki of Altan harmed in some way, an aim that exactly matched the Order of Sumere's current game plan. It also mattered that Balisel Navarr did not want her involvement in last year's assassination attempt to become common knowledge. These two pieces of information were Marseille Auteuil's bargaining chips – that and the certainty that she would have to kill Ms Navarr if she refused their offer.

Marseille did not want to do that though. The tailored suit was not cut for killing and she did not want to risk spoiling it through any undue exertion.

A clipped, accented voice came back to her. 'Of course. Enter.'

The door slid open and Marseille saw a tall, slim woman, her almost white blonde hair pulled back from her face in a tight bun. She wore a floor-length pale pink dress of some floating fabric that Marseille did not recognise. It was held loosely at the waist by a thin cord of white leather, giving a simple effect. But it was only when she moved forward to greet her that Marseille noticed the skirt was slit on one side to the waist – and that Balisel Navarr did not appear to be wearing anything underneath. Marseille could not help but smile. Here was a woman after her own heart and, possibly, just as dangerous.

'Thank you for agreeing to see me, Ms Navarr,' she said, putting her hand out. Balisel's eyes dropped to the hand and a look of indecision briefly flickered in them. Then, her mind resolved, she took it. Her handshake was a mere brushing of skin. She was too Altani to bring herself to actually touch the Earthan woman, especially at their first meeting.

'It was nothing,' Balisel countered. 'It is always ... interesting to meet the press. Especially now that I am on Earth.' The Altani accent sounded curiously quaint to Marseille – almost French – and she wondered if this, too, was a sign of their similarity.

'Thank you. I hope that you are going to like it here,' Marseille smiled. 'Well, I know you are a busy woman, so, I'll try to be quick.'

Balisel gestured to her to be seated and the dark woman positioned herself on a padded upright chair next to a bronze inlaid bureau of what appeared to be Indian origin. Balisel draped herself on a low couch opposite and took a sip of water as the questions began.

'This is your first visit to Earth, but not your first experience of Earthans and our ways. Your late husband was from Amerimex, wasn't he? You must miss him.'

'I do indeed. Jeremiah was a wonderful man,' Balisel returned. Durroc had told her about the dreadful sentimentality of Earthans and she knew she would have to play this one up. 'You know, he was my assistant for a long time before we – ah, fell in love.' She sighed and hung her head coyly leaving, she hoped, an impression of remembered romance.

A lesser mortal might have been entirely taken in by the display. Not Marseille.

'Indeed. I imagine he was quite dedicated to you?'

'Oh, he was. Jeremiah would have done anything for me,' Balisel purred.

'He must have loved you very much. So fortunate that you returned his affection. And such a tragedy that he died so soon after your marriage.'

Something in the tone of Marseille's voice alerted Balisel to her scepticism. She decided to tackle it head on.

'You think I did not love him?' she queried. The lightness of her tone belied the weight of the question.

Marseille countered instantly, 'Goodness me, no, Ms Navarr! I'm sorry I made you think that. It's just that it's unusual. Rare. I mean…' Marseille went on, stumbling over the words. 'Well, you were his superior and he *was* just your assistant.'

Balisel's smile was glacial. 'But you are forgetting, Miss Aqua, we were the same sort of people. From the same background. It gave us much in common.'

'Yes, of course. I wanted to ask you about that.' Marseille shifted ever closer towards her goal. 'You and your brother. You had a hard, lonely childhood. Did either of you ever dream that you would both one day be so rich and so powerful?'

Oh yes, we dreamed, thought Balisel, and more than that … *Much more!* Her eyes narrowed with the remembrance of their bleak, bitter upbringing in the dank corners of Silbaraz-Re.

'I may be wealthy, Miss Aqua. But neither Durroc nor I are powerful,' she returned.

'Oh, come, Ms Navarr. Your brother holds an eminent position at the court of Altan. Right-hand man to the Ki. Virtually indispensable.' Marseille raised an eyebrow and locked onto the woman's icy eyes.

'He is head of the Ki's personal guard, responsible for her safety. No more than that.' Balisel's softly spoken rejoinder sounded defensive and the assassin delighted in her discomfort.

'Then he must have been mortified when that brute from Autabron tried to kill her before her wedding? What went wrong there?'

Balisel did not like the way the conversation was turning. 'Nothing. These things happen. In fact, if you recall, it was my brother who saved the Ki.'

'Ah yes. His quick thinking was the Ki's good fortune, eh? And lucky that she survived and went on to marry our own Kevor Jax Bashir, who's quite a catch.' Marseille smiled reassuringly before continuing. 'The peace treaty was really in the balance there for a while. I don't suppose that would have suited *your* ends, Ms Navarr?'

Balisel was on her guard. What was this woman implying? Did all Earthan journalists assume this level of disrespect?

'I do not know what you are asking, Miss Aqua.' Balisel shifted her pose on the couch and raised herself a little taller in the seat.

'Really? I find that hard to believe. You are an intelligent woman, Ms Navarr. Can't you work it out?'

'Work what out?' She was beginning to lose patience with this upstart. 'What is your point?' Her question was more a command.

'Very well. My point is this …' Marseille rose from the chair and walked over to the couch, her eyes never leaving the blonde woman's face. She sat beside Balisel and draped an arm behind her, almost encasing her in an embrace. 'Most people desire peace. But we know better, don't we, Ms Navarr?' She paused, watching the ice-blue eyes intently. 'We know that there is more money to be made from war, not peace. And what's wrong with that, eh? We all profit, don't we?' Marseille paused for effect. 'Some of us profit more than others, of course …'

Balisel's low laugh came from deep down.

'Well, well, Miss Aqua …' She found the interplay amusing and intriguing. 'You obviously believe you have an understanding of economics, which is admirable. But this is far removed from journalism.'

Marseille countered, 'Not so far, really. I am a seeker after truth, that's all.'

'And you think you've found it?' A pale eyebrow raised in derision. 'What is *your* truth, Miss Aqua? What do *you* choose to believe?'

The dark features stretched into a wide smile. She liked Balisel Navarr. She liked her cool intelligence, her nerve. It would be a shame if she had to kill her.

'I believe what my employers tell me to believe, Ms Navarr. And what they believe,' she slid a little closer to Balisel, 'is that you and your brother arranged the assassination attempt on the Ki of Altan in order to destroy the peace treaty between Earth and the Union of Planets.'

Balisel threw back her head and laughed out loud. She stood up and walked over to a low table where she poured herself a beverage from a delicate porcelain pot.

'So the publishers of – Impressia Magazine, is it? – believe I am a would-be murderer? And my brother too?' Her laughter trilled lightly in the air. 'Oh, come now. I have money. I have power. My brother has a brilliant career and, probably, an even more glittering future, which, by the way, is tied to the Ki remaining well and happy. What do either of us need with more money, more power and a dead head of state? Your supposition is ridiculous.'

'It would seem so, yes. But when you start putting the pieces of the puzzle together … Voila! It all becomes very clear.' Marseille took her time, savouring the taste of her words like a deliciously rich dessert. 'The assassin was an employee of Gunnashey Kuth & Dor – *your* company, Ms Navarr – who, supposedly, won a lottery to visit Altan. He even travelled on the same spacecraft with you.'

'Mere chance.' Balisel shrugged her shoulders, brushing the implication aside.

Marseille went on. 'Also, both you and your brother were at the reception when the attempt occurred.'

Overlooking her own presence there, Balisel countered, 'Well, it *was* his job to be there. To protect the Ki – which is what he did.'

'Correct. And that's why we know you did not want her dead. But you wanted her threatened. You wanted her to be in fear of her life – and she was. And it was at just that point that your brother stepped in to rescue her.' Marseille was getting into her stride now. She stood up from the couch and walked back to the desk to retrieve her bag. One never knew when one might need a back-up weapon. She had learned over the years was that, when cornered, even the weakest, most unlikely people could become dangerous. *Never lose focus. Never lose control. Never become the target!* She recalled her training of many years ago.

'Again. Just doing his job.' Balisel's brows furrowed. 'I find it hard to believe that you think this is proof of some conspiracy.'

'It doesn't have to be proof, Ms Navarr.' Marseille looked absentmindedly through her bag. 'Have you heard the Earthan saying "there's no smoke without fire"? Somehow, you and your brother *are* implicated. It's not important how or why. But if enough people were to *believe* that you and your brother were involved in the dreadful attack on the beloved Ki … Well, you can see how that might affect your standing in the intergalactic community, can't you? And your brother's chances for career fulfilment? They might not look so promising.'

Balisel tried to keep the scowl from her face. But her body gave her away. She was tense. She walked a little too quickly. She sat back down on the couch a little too unsteadily.

'I see I have struck a chord. Or should that be touched a nerve?' Marseille said, relishing these moments.

Balisel's head snapped up. 'Who do you work for? Really work for?' Balisel demanded.

'Impressia, Ms Navarr. Look me up.'

It was true. The real Carri Aqua was a renowned writer with a reputation for in-depth interviews with all the top names. She was, however, at that moment enjoying a brief walking holiday in the Tyrolean Alps, unaware that she had acquired an alter ego with a penchant for killing people.

'But in my spare time I do the odd task for a group of community-minded individuals who have Earth's best interests at heart.'

'I see. And this … group wants what, exactly?'

'Ah, now … This is probably a good time to talk about that, what with the imminent arrival of the royal party.' Marseille's full mouth broke into a beaming smile. She walked back to the sofa and settled herself next to Balisel. 'The Order would very much appreciate your cooperation in a little plot to plunge us all back into war.'

Balisel eyes widened and the corners of her mouth slowly began to rise, though the smile did not extend to her eyes.

'Ah! I see you might be tempted, Ms Navarr. That's very good – and it will save us all a lot of bother.'

The vigil continued at Linnayen's bedside. They had all taken their turns – Evica, Jax, Li-el, Tariik Min. Tonight, Lady Thea, her mother-in-law, was in attendance, assisted by Nen, who had not left her mistress's side since the terrible accident on the *Jensa Kadenx*.

Thea's tired brown eyes studied her daughter-in-law's tranquil face, silently begging her to get better. Her son hid it well but Thea knew he was distraught. She knew how deep his feelings ran, even if he appeared to deny them both to others and, more surprisingly, to himself. What had gone wrong between them? She had sensed it even before she and David had left Altan after the wedding. It was as though a light had gone out in the soul of her son, leaving him floundering about in the darkness.

But, now, with Linnayen's life hanging in the balance, he could not deceive his mother. When she thought of him it was as the master of a ship sailing in a fog, rudderless and confused, sniffing the air for the slightest trace of the smell of land – and home – and safe harbour. If only Linnayen would wake up! Would that save her son? This nothingness, this waiting, was awful.

In the five days since the *Jensa Kadenx* had run into the spiralling psytro-ions which had tossed it about so fearfully and taken the consciousness of Linnayen Genara, their lives had been put on hold. Although the journey to Earth had continued, as it must, all plans for Evica and Tariik's wedding and related events had been postponed indefinitely – until they knew, one way or another, what was going to happen to Linnayen.

She had suffered a fractured skull with bleeding into the brain and had lapsed into a coma, from which, according to Dr Mai, she might take hours, days, weeks, or even longer to recover. Even then, when she did wake, there was no way of knowing how damaged her brain might be. All they could do, Dr Mai and the Earthan neuro-medicants had assured them, was wait.

That was the hardest part – the waiting, the helplessness. *For all our technology*, thought Thea Bashir, *we still cannot cure a simple blow to the head!*

But, of course, it was not simple – not Linnayen's fall, not their circumstances. Nothing was simple. Her son had spent much of his time at his wife's bedside and, to all intents and purposes, appeared to be her devoted attendant. Then there was the old counsellor, Beoraan, concerned and worried about the girl, of course, but still with one eye on the future and the succession. The stability of the Union was *his* first concern and Thea could see his thoughts churning with possible outcomes. Evica – the sister – suddenly plunged into sorrow at a time when she should be brimming with happiness. So sad, so unfair. And Li-el Dacas, whom Thea recalled as so haughty and imperious when they were on Altan, now unsure and frightened and looking many years older than she was.

Most curious of all, though, was the good-looking but surly commander Navarr. He had stopped by the Ki's room only a handful of times and had made brief, but probing enquiries as to her progress. His questions were the same as everyone else's had been. When would she wake? How would she be? Would she recover fully? But Thea noticed something more in his demeanour. There was an odd air about him. His eyes blazed when he looked at the stricken Ki as though he was commanding her to get well and to notice *him*. It was almost petulance. *Yes, that was it.* He had the look of a spoilt child about him.

Her concentration was suddenly interrupted as Dr Em-sin Mai came to check the monitors that would hopefully soon tell them how near or far Linnayen was to regaining consciousness. The grey-clad woman moved quietly around the bed, going about her business and taking no notice of Thea Bashir, except to pass her a small, hopeful smile before she left.

When the doctor had gone, Thea returned to her reverie. This frail, fragile girl held her son's happiness in her hands. She was the cause of both his dismay and his joy. Thea took a limp hand and wondered, with no small pang of guilt, whether it would be better if she did not wake up.

Navarr stepped out onto the wide terrace that overlooked the steel-blue lake and squinted against the glare of the unfamiliar yellow sun. The vista was one of water, broken only by opportune plantings of tall bullrushes, reeds and water irises. In the distance he could make out the line of tall white stone buildings that ran along the ancient thoroughfare of Park Lane. They were separated from the lake by a short greensward dotted with clumps of full-leafed trees. He found himself enjoying the sweet smells of cut grass and flowers as he strolled across to where Balisel sat at a table in the corner nearest the water. Or maybe it was just the sight of his beloved sister that raised his spirits.

The air through which he walked shimmered with an electric excitement. They had not seen each other for many long months and now, finally, here on this alien world, they were together again and desperate to touch.

He came to the table and sat on the metal chair, sliding his leg close to hers and pushing against her long limbs until she parted them enough to accommodate him. She leaned forward, taking his hands and kissed him full on his mouth, plunging her tongue deep inside, tasting his sweet warmth. He almost exploded there and then. His breathing was hard and torn. Suddenly she pulled back, sensing the eyes watching them, remembering where they were. This was too open, too public. Everything could wait until later.

He jerked back, jolted by the instant withdrawal of his life force. His eyes flew open and they met hers wherein all his questions were answered and all his protestations put to rest. *Later.*

'I have news, Durroc,' she began. 'I couldn't tell you about it over the com. But here should be safe.' She swept her crystalline blue eyes around the terrace restaurant.

He smiled slowly. 'I'm intrigued. What *have* you been up to? Apart from taking a close-up look at your wealth.' He referred to the reason for her visit to Earth: the formal acquisition of Jeremiah Danforth's portfolio of stocks and shares. Balisel had timed her trip to enable her to meet the various boards and executives who ran some of the companies in which she now held either a controlling interest or an influential portion. She was particularly keen on meeting the senior team at Hauer-Breakspere ChemCo, the company that supplied the Earthan armed forces with fuel oils and hydracants for both its land-based and cosmonic transport systems. She wondered if anyone on the board was connected with the Order of Sumere and whose eyes, if any, would be watching her performance over the coming days and weeks. It was all going to be very interesting, and the honey-coloured Polynesian woman's visit of a few days earlier had spiced it up nicely.

'Yes. That has been fun. I'm so rich that I am thinking about retiring. I'll need a lifetime to spend it!' Her laughter was genuine and the closest Balisel Navarr had ever got to self-deprecation. Navarr was a little surprised, but not unpleasantly so and he smiled indulgently.

'But the real news is that I have had a visitor. A woman calling herself Carri Aqua, though I doubt that is her real name. She represents a secret organisation of Earthan ... patriots, I suppose you'd call them. They want our help.'

Navarr's brow furrowed, a mild concern seeping slowly through his senses.

'What organisation?' he asked. 'What sort of help are they after?'

'They call themselves the Order of Sumere after an ancient tribe of Earthans called the Sumerians, who were adept at taking over civilisations and then running them – quite well, it appears. They were supremely efficient and, for the most part, they brought wealth and stability to the people they conquered. Thus, their usurpation was tolerated.'

'Don't tell me, but they were never liked,' Navarr interposed, scoffing, whilst Balisel enjoyed the joke. 'And they have a grand plan to take over the council and run the Earth their way.'

'Something like that.'

'Oh, sister, surely not. You don't believe this?' His scepticism was plain.

'Well, normally I wouldn't. But when she showed me a vidisk of the death of the old Earthan ambassador – you remember him? Byers? The one who was decapitated on Altan?'

Navarr nodded. His curiosity was aroused now and he wanted to know more.

'I was impressed,' she continued. 'It was strangely exciting to watch the old man's head come off. And quite unique. You know how I like innovation.'

Navarr grimaced and shook his head.

'Balisel,' he reproached. 'I could almost begin to wonder about you.'

She laughed. 'No need to worry. I would never let enjoyment get in the way of my mission. You know that.' She poured herself a glass of pale liquid from a frosted jug on the table.

'But it wasn't just that,' she went on. 'It so happens that their aims coincide with ours. They want disruption and conflict between Earth and the Union. Not for the same reasons as us, you understand. They just want rid of all aliens. But the result is the same. We want war. They want war. It seems logical to help them.'

'I don't know.' Navarr's brow furrowed and he shook his head. 'I'd like to know a lot more about this order before we get into anything. I mean, why did they approach you? How did your name come up?'

'Ah, that was due to the ambassador,' she replied. 'Shortly before he died, he made a confession of sorts – of things he'd found out or surmised – and he included his thoughts about you and me and how he suspected we were somehow linked to the assassination attempt on the Ki.'

Navarr jolted in his seat, his agitation plain. Noticing her brother's discomfort, Balisel reassured him.

'Oh, don't worry. Byers had only thoughts, no proof. In fact, nothing even approaching proof. But he said enough to get the Order's interest.'

'This is dangerous, sister. How do we know we can trust them – or this Aqua woman – to keep quiet? We could lose more than our jobs here.' Navarr's brain was racing with the ramifications of what the Order could do if their suspicions were made public, or even privately whispered into certain ears, like Beoraan's, for example.

'I realise that, Durroc,' she snapped. 'But working with them is our only real choice.'

Balisel turned her head and scanned the sparkling lake. Her eyes narrowed to block the glare coming from the water, making her look more tense than she actually felt.

'What else *can* we do? If we say no they will find a way to let it be known that we were involved in a plot to destroy the Ki. You know as well as I that it only needs a rumour and all we've worked for could be ended.'

Navarr shook his head and sighed.

'Damn Byers! I never liked him.'

Balisel placed a hand on his arm and massaged it gently. She wanted to do more. She wanted to comfort him and soothe him in the way that was special to them. But that would have to wait a while.

He grasped her hand and pulled it to his face, pushing the palm against his mouth where he kissed her warm skin. His tongue lightly circled her flesh and she shivered with the strength of her response.

'Durroc … No,' she commanded, reluctantly. 'We need to concentrate.'

He pulled himself back to the sunny terrace, the lake, the flowers and their predicament.

'So what do they want us to do?' he asked resignedly.

'Well, the Ki's accident may change things. But, in general, they want me to supply arms to certain Earthan rebels who have a plethora of terrorist acts they wish to commit, both here and on other planets. And they want *you* to get rid of the Ki-consort – in any way you see fit, of course.'

'Yes, but with Jax out of the way, Linnayen is a loose cannon, so to speak. Knowing her, she could just as quickly marry again to calm any discord,' Navarr countered.

'Not if she were *responsible* for her dear husband's demise. That's their idea – alien queen kills Earthan husband. Imagine the headlines! Alien murderers! Killer queen!' A slow smile expanded to the corners of her eyes. 'And as for marrying again, I don't think the Earthans would be keen to give up another of their sons to a murdering alien, do you?'

Navarr's initial surprise turned to amusement as the import of her words sank in. His mind expanded on the possibilities. *If Linnayen harms Jax, or even kills him, they would never forgive her– or the Union. We'd have war for at least another decade, and I would be the only one she could turn to. I would be her consolation and her consort in all but name … I would rule!*

'Yes, I see what you mean.' His mind spun with the expectation of his future success. 'But I can do nothing for the time being.'

'Of course. What is the prognosis for our dear leader?'

'She remains unconscious. The blow to her head caused blood vessels to rupture. She's still critical – and in a coma. Quite frankly, we don't know if she going to live or die right now.'

'She needs to survive for our plan to work,' Balisel commented.

'Right. When she wakes up – *if* – we can push ahead. But there's no guarantee. No one knows what she'll be like after this. The damage to her brain …' He left unsaid his worst fear. A dead Linnayen meant there was still a chance for him to hold onto power through Evica or whoever the next Ki would be. But a mad one meant he'd be babysitting a redundant Ki while a regent took over.

'It's been five days now …' he concluded, his voice trailing away.

Balisel's keen business mind had been working through the options as her brother spoke.

'No matter. However this plays out, my brother, you and I are going to win.' She leaned forward again and this time gripped his arm tightly. Her eyes blazed with cold fire. 'Never forget that! We *will* succeed!'

Looking up into those two orbs of icy fire, he knew she was right. There was no going back for either of them. Their future was assured and, whether Linnayen lived, died or was deranged, the Navarr twins would achieve their destiny.

Chapter Twenty

*I*t was the strangest feeling. I was there, watching all their faces, seeing their lips move but hearing nothing. Not even silence. But strangest of all was the not knowing. I did not know then who they were – not a one of them! But I didn't know then who I was either. I was just consciousness, awareness, existing but not living. I had been sat down in some foreign place and compelled to observe yet not be part of unfolding events, though it soon became apparent that I was fundamental to the whole business. I was the central character. These strangers were only there because of me and, as I drifted around them and the white room with its polished walls, I felt a kind of ridiculous self-importance. I was the reason for these events yet had no control over any of them. That was when I felt so helpless and nearly lost hope. Would this ever change? Or would this drifting go on and on forever?

They all came to watch over me. Dr Mai was there most of the time – and Nen, ever-faithful. Then there were my mother and sister, both looking very drawn and worried, never smiling. Lady Thea Bashir and Jax's father, David, were there along with Duncan McCrae. Even he could not lighten the mood. Navarr came once but he was very arrogant, barking questions at the doctor and reeling off a list of *dos and don'ts. I could not have expected anything else, of course.*

But it was Beoraan who moved me most. His eyes had seen this before with my father, although I did not know that then, and now he was living the nightmare again. It was as though his life was over and he believed it had all been for nothing. It was his despair, his tears, that fuelled my determination to come back

There was another reason, too: Jax. I remember the day I first saw him – for the second time! He was alone. Dr Mai had gone somewhere and when he entered the room, he dismissed Nen. At first, I couldn't see him too well. He stood at the end of my bed, looking at my body and his head was bowed down. I was positioned in the corner at the time, about midway up the wall and behind him. I could only really see his back and his lowered profile. I could not move. (That was one of the odd things about the experience – having no control over where I floated. I could be there, but not always where I wanted to be.)

After some minutes, he walked to the side of the bed and reached under it to pull out a stool. It was only then when he sat down that I got a better look at him. He gazed so intently at me that I could actually feel a tug on the ether that had become me and I began to drift away from the wall and closer to the bed. He took hold of my left hand and began to stroke it – so gently – unconsciously massaging the wedding ring on my finger, his eyes never leaving my face. Then, he closed his eyes and tipped his head back. A sigh heaved his chest. Then, as it was expelled, his shoulders sank back down and he turned his head towards ether-me. He opened his eyes, looking straight at me. It was like an electric shock. If I'd had breath in my body I would have lost it. If I had been in my body it would probably have trembled. His was the most perfect face I had ever seen.

'I am going to try whether you approve or not,' Li-el Dacas insisted.

'But you know how she hates it. She'll be furious with you when she wakes up.' Evica was adamant. Her mother should not, even under these circumstances, enter Linnayen's consciousness. It was strictly against the mentante's code of conduct.

'*If* she wakes up. *If.*' Li-el had made up her mind.

'I'm warning you, Mother …'

'Oh, enough!' Li-el was losing her patience. Linnayen's life hung in the balance and with it the future of the Galactic Union. As if that were not reason enough there was also the matter of Linnayen herself. Despite the distance between them growing up, Li-el loved her daughter and she could not stand idly by, waiting for her to fade from life – not when there was a chance to pull her back.

The doctors had done everything they knew how to do, both the Altani Dr Mai and the Earthan ones who, Li-el was surprised to find, were rather good.

'What about Kevor Jax? Don't you think you should at least discuss it with him?' Evica persisted. 'He is her husband, after all.'

'You think? He has hardly been her constant companion these last days. Tell me, who has been here watching over her? Only the people who truly love her, that's who. You. Me. Why even Nen has displayed more affection than her so-called husband!'

'That's not fair, Mother, and you know it.' Evica rounded on her, doing her best to support Kevor Jax who, she felt, seemed as lost and as isolated as the rest of them. Linnayen's accident had shaken them all.

Evica remembered those last two days while they were still on the *Jensa Kadenx* and the frantic rush to get Linnayen to a medical centre on Earth. Dr Mai had tried every stimulant drug they had on board, all to no avail. Her life signs had looked good at first and Em-sin Mai assured them that she would, in all probability, come around soon. Then there was the worrying drop in Linnayen's blood pressure and the stiffening of her limbs. Quietly, her face pinched, Dr Mai took blood samples and scanned the results, frowning as she fed the information through their medical databases. Finally, thirty-six hours after the accident and as they passed along one of the shipping lanes in the asteroid belt between Mars and Jupiter, the diagnosis came back along with a prescriptive menu of drugs and therapies that would be needed to cure the stricken Ki.

Navarr, she recalled, had nagged at the poor captain to go faster whilst Tejarc had tried to explain the limitations – both legislative and physical – on speeding through busy space lanes, even for an emergency. Navarr rejected it all and sinisterly promised the captain that if the Ki should die, his life, too, would be over. Tariik, always calm, always supportive, had stepped in to reassure both men that, whatever happened, no one was to blame or would be held accountable. It was an accident and they were all dealing with it as best they could. If they wanted to help the Ki in her most desperate hour of need then they had best just get on with their allotted tasks as quickly and quietly as possible.

Evica could see Navarr's body recoil from this apparent dressing-down. In rank Tariik was below the haughty commander, but he was soon to be the Ki's brother-in-law and that changed everything. Navarr's reply to Tariik had been polite, as always, but Navarr was not to be trusted. The only good thing to come out of this dreadful incident was that Navarr was removed from her sister and, for the time being at least, could not influence her. Evica could not understand Linnayen's attraction to the man. He had a level of control over Linnayen that was perhaps even dangerous and she had warned Tariik to use caution with him. He respected Evica's insight. It was a major part of why he loved her so much and it was this love and respect that was helping to contain his disappointment at having to postpone their wedding.

She was upset too. Even though she had not wanted the ceremony to take place on Earth, in the full glare of publicity, she still wanted to be married to Tariik Min and was desperate for them to start their lives together. Now everything would have to wait until Linnayen was better and Evica was certain that her sister would recover. *She must!*

Kevor Jax had, in her view, acted admirably through these awful days. Whilst they were still on the *Jensa Kadenx* and once he realised that he could do nothing for his wife, he joined the crew in making repairs to the damaged hull. Not knowing much about Altani engineering, he could do little more than fetch and carry necessary tools and parts to the technicians, but his diligence and willingness to undertake these menial tasks had won him many friends. Tariik's opinion of him had skyrocketed. Having only met him a couple of times before their journey and believing him to be a pampered prince, Tariik had been amazed to see Jax roll up his sleeves and get to work, just like any of them.

It was not true that he had paid Linnayen no attention. He had been to see her in every spare moment and Evica knew, because she had asked Dr Mai, that he had been quietly solicitous about her, asking the doctor many pertinent questions and giving her encouragement about the treatment she was giving.

Evica had caught the look in his eye, the one he had only when he looked at Linnayen, and she wondered again how her mother could even begin to doubt his feelings for her. It was obvious. Despite Linnayen's disdain for her husband, Jax was deeply in love with her. And he should be consulted before Li-el went crashing into her poor unconscious mind.

'He does care. But whether you believe that or not, he is her husband and you *must* speak with him.' Evica's tone was uncompromising.

Li-el glared into her daughter's steadfast emerald eyes. It was at times like this that she most admired her, annoying as it was to not be able to forge ahead with her plan immediately. Evica had a great deal of Li-el's own determination and, when she stuck to her guns like now, she was a force to be reckoned with.

With a sigh, she replied, 'Very well. You win.'

Jax leaned against the balustrade atop the steel and glass tower of the Santa Isabella Medical Campus in the San Gabriel Mountains. Up here, away from the pack of courtiers and attendants, away from the reporters, high above the dense yellow fog of the sprawling city of old Los Angeles far below, he could be alone with his thoughts. He could relax and give the truth of his emotions free rein.

The last six days had been a whirlwind and he felt bruised and battered. He kept reliving that terrible moment when he saw Linnayen plunge across the floor of the *Jensa Kadenx's* bridge, her eyes wide in terror, his hands stretching out to her as she fell, cursing that he had not had more time to catch her, or secure her. He should have known that Li-el would not have been able to hold her.

Images from the reality mixed and tangled with a dreamlike vision of her silhouetted in a spotlight, reaching out to him, then being snatched away. He had almost had her safe. Had almost reached her. Another second and he could have got to her and she would have been all right. She had looked only to him to save her and he had been helpless to do so. If only he had then he would not be standing here today facing the torment of a future in which she was no longer present.

He hated her. He hated Navarr. But a life without her was no life.

His family had rallied round. Even his father had delegated some of his meetings to other council members in order to be with him, although, thought Jax a little cynically, that made good political sense too. His mother had done what she always did: stood by his side, saying nothing, but knowing everything about how he felt.

Thankfully, Navarr had kept his distance, busying himself and the suddenly ancient Beoraan with altering all the carefully made arrangements and wedding plans. Jax had no doubt though that he was being kept informed of the Ki's progress – or lack of it – in the greatest detail, just waiting for the moment he could regain his former position. The thought of them together almost made him retch and he took a deep breath of the cool mountain air to shake off the nausea.

Out of the corner of his eye he saw the rooftop door panel slide open. Li-el Dacas stepped out of the vatortube and walked towards him, her eyes never swerving from his tired frame. He turned and noticed that the mountains behind were now darkly silhouetted against an apricot sky. He had been alone on the roof, protected from interruption by Aramikov, for the last hour and it had grown late.

'Kevor Jax. I need to speak with you.' Li-el, never one for beating about any bush, went straight to the matter at hand. 'I want to try to contact Linnayen and I need your approval.'

Jax's eyes narrowed. 'Contact?'

Li-el continued. 'As you know, certain of us have the ability to communicate at a deeper level. You know this ability as telepathy, although for us it goes beyond mere mind-reading. I believe that I can speak to Linnayen even whilst she is unconscious and try to help her come out of this coma. But ...'

'I know that Linnayen is a mentante," he interjected. He shook his head. 'And you want me to approve this?'

'I do. She cannot give her consent. As her next of kin, you must.' Li-el deliberately said no more than was needed. Elaboration was out of the question.

'But your code prevents you from communicating with another mentante without their approval.' Jax understood how the Altani social norms worked in this regard but wanted to hear what his imperious mother-in-law had to say about it.

'That is correct.' Li-el's face was frozen, her eyes piercing into his.

'I think that Linnayen would disapprove of such ... interference, however well meant.'

Li-el was uncomfortable with the way the conversation was progressing. She was determined to have her way – Linnayen's life may be hanging in the balance.

'My daughter has always held strong views about most things, as you well know. And, without doubt, at any other time, in any other circumstance, she would most certainly tell me to keep my mind to myself.' Li-el's voice deepened and she took half a step closer to Jax as if to hammer her words into his soul. She stared directly into his shaded eyes. 'But right now I have only one consideration – to save her life. If she does not wake up soon she will die. I am not prepared to stand by while there is a chance to save her. She is my *daughter*.'

The woman stood rigid in front of him and he knew that she would not move until he consented. Still he hesitated.

'But the dangers? Don't tell me there's no risk to Linnayen.'

'Yes,' Li-el conceded, 'there is the risk that the link will not work and she will stay as she is until she fades from life. There is also the risk that her mind will be damaged by my probing – an undefended mind can be harmed by the clumsiness of an inexperienced mentante.'

'In which case,' Jax interjected, 'she could wake up but have a brain injury for the rest of her life.'

Li-el took a deep breath and laid a hand on his arm. 'I am a powerful and highly experienced mentante. I am not inept, and I would hardly probe so deeply as to endanger my own daughter.' Li-el was running out of patience. She needed to convince him – and quickly.

'Kevor, listen to me.' Suddenly her tone softened and her eyes blinked away growing tears, although the set of her shoulders remained firm. She sighed heavily, remembering the time on the *Jensa Kadenx*. 'I let go of her. I couldn't hold on – and she fell. Now she may die and it's my fault. I have done nothing but stand by her bed and watch her fade. Please. I beg you. This is the one thing I can do that might help redress the wrong. Please let me try to help her.'

Suddenly Jax was aware of how she must have suffered during these last days and he felt more than a little guilty at the self-indulgence of his own sorrow when hers must have been similarly devastating. He looked up at the swirling roseate colours of the sunset sky above her head and tried to gather his scattered thoughts. There were three choices. Linnayen dead. Linnayen alive but changed. Linnayen alive and restored. Li-el's special skill gave them the chance to bring about two of the three outcomes. The odds were in their favour. And if Linnayen survived and was outraged at her mother's interference – well, at least she would be alive.

'Go ahead.'

Li-el's shoulders fell imperceptibly and a sigh escaped her. Her eyes, which had never wavered in their gaze whilst they spoke, suddenly dropped and she could only nod her thanks. Without a word she strode away, ready to get on with the task of saving her daughter.

Jax took one last look at the darkening skyline. A strand of magenta cloud hung across the dark city, where lights were beginning to pierce the growing gloom. The sound of the door panel closing behind Li-el Dacas reached him and, with his head held high, he turned to follow her.

Navarr was standing outside her room as Jax walked the length of the white-walled passageway. Beoraan was seated on a hard-backed chair, his head hung low. On hearing Jax's footsteps, Navarr turned to face him and their eyes locked.

Jax's thoughts were close to murderous. *Not this time. You will have no part of this.*

As he drew nearer, Beoraan stood up and bowed slightly in deference. Navarr, seeing this, did the same. Jax noted his deliberate delay and vowed to remember it along with all the other hurts and insults. But for now, his exclusion from Linnayen's sick room would have to do.

'Wait here, Commander Navarr. Sen-Beoraan, would you please come with me?' Jax's abruptness sounded more like protocol than slight, so Beoraan did not appear to pick up that any offence was intended for Navarr.

The old man nodded and followed Jax into the room. Jax could feel Navarr's glare slicing into his back, but he did not care. He was determined to have this time no matter how short-lived it might prove to be.

Linnayen lay unchanged on the bed, her features still and calm, a death mask. Evica sat to one side holding her sister's hand while Tariik Min stood behind, one hand placed reassuringly on his fiancée's shoulder. Jax went to the other side of the bed and Beoraan stood next to him. Em-sin Mai and an Earthan doctor had drawn back to the side of the room but were ready to step forward if needed.

At the foot of the bed, Li-el Dacas' tall frame, clad in a floor-length purple woollen cloak, cast a shadow over her daughter's still body. Her eyes were closed and her hands hung loosely at her sides, though she held her chin high. The silence lasted for a few minutes as everyone contemplated what was about to happen.

Li-el's eyes slowly opened as she spoke. 'I ask again: Kevor Jax, do you give your consent?'

Evica's eyes flew up to his, accusing, condemning. *Wrong!*

He responded firstly to her, his eyes speaking of his helplessness, trying to affirm that this was the only way. 'I do.' Then, turning to Li-el, he said again, 'I consent.'

Instantly, Li-el closed her eyes and placed her hands lightly on the woven blanket at the end of the bed. She emptied her mind and began the probe.

At first there was nothing. Grey. No sounds. No scent. She searched the emptiness, unsure of her direction, feeling her way slowly, quietly. To hurry into her daughter's unconscious, unprotected mind could harm her, like a needle pricking through skin, drawing blood and sharp pain. It was an approach she used commonly when her daughter was awake, however the conscious mind was naturally barricaded. Now she had to go gingerly, gently until she found a weakness, a thinning of the mind's wall where she could at first peer through, then hopefully push through.

Many minutes passed. No one moved or spoke in the white room. But Li-el had no concept of time in the ether world. It was still grey but she was aware of a thickening of the space texture, from gaseousness to something more viscous and fluid. She was drawing near to Linnayen. She knew it. She had but to remain calm and focused. She must not allow her excitement to destroy the moment. Suddenly, there it was. She reached out her hands as if she could touch the smooth walls of Linnayen's mind.

Evica shifted nervously, biting her lip. She knew what her mother's outstretched hands, hovering in the air above the bed, meant. Contact was about to be made.

Li-el slid into her daughter's mind with the softness of a mother's caress on a baby's skin. Barely perceptible, she said nothing, made no movement or gesture, thus allowing Linnayen to come to her, to find her. This she did almost instantly and like a lost child, happy and relieved to have been found, she clung to Li-el's mind, enjoying its warmth and safety. *There, you're safe now, little one. I've found you. Come with me.*

There was no resistance, only overwhelming relief. Linnayen had been regained and she was leaving the empty place where she had been lost and confused. This was the ending for which she had longed, and she knew, without any doubt of what or where it was, that she was finally going into the white room.

A single tear slid from Li-el's closed eyes as a smile graced her mouth.

The entire business had taken a mere twelve minutes before the first stirring of Linnayen's eyelids occurred. Evica and Jax gasped at the same time. Both leaned forwards, Jax grasping Linnayen's hand as he did so. Suddenly, her chest heaved upwards with an intake of breath and sank again with the rush of exhaled air.

Dr Mai stepped forward, signalling to the Earthan doctor to go to the other side of the bed. Between them they checked the screens and read-outs on the equipment that clustered around the head of the bed.

'Well?' asked Jax. Linnayen took another deep breath.

'One moment,' Dr Mai replied briskly, checking more instruments. The fact that she had moved and appeared to be regaining consciousness was not yet enough to confirm their hopes.

Li-el was still in a trancelike state at the foot of the bed, her eyes closed, her body rigid and her hands still raised in mid-air. No one dared to move or interrupt the process.

Then, after taking a sudden short breath, Linnayen's mouth opened and a low moan escaped, the first noise she had made in six days. At the same moment, Li-el's body shuddered and her hands dropped back down to her sides. Her eyes opened with a jolt and a warm smile spread across her face.

Jax, Evica and the others all looked to her and were relieved to see her nod in assent. Linnayen was back, brought home by her own mother. The relief passed around the room even though Linnayen was not yet conscious.

Jax looked to the young Earthan doctor who had been reading the monitors.

The doctor's eyes widened and he smiled as he turned to Jax. 'She's asleep!'

Dr Mai confirmed his words. 'She might wake up in a few minutes or a few hours. But she's definitely sleeping.'

Evica stood up and Tariik stretched his arms around her in a hug. She smiled happily but her eyes were glistening with unshed tears. She moved over to her mother and placed her arms around her in thanks.

'You were right, Mother – whatever the consequences.' Her throat was dry and her voice cracked. 'Thank you.'

Li-el, the sometimes pompous, always proud head of the noble house of Dacas, wiped the wet corners of her eyes. She had let go of her daughter's hand once on the bridge of the *Jensa Kadenx*. She would not do so again.

As the doctors had predicted, Linnayen slept for a little while. When she finally woke some two hours later, the room was in partial darkness. The evening had settled in and only the jagged ridges of the mountains, sprinkled with a few shimmering lights, could be seen through the windows towards which Linnayen's head was turned as she opened her eyes. She almost panicked, thinking she was back in the empty space and that the kind woman had been a dream. But then she saw him, sitting in a low padded chair right next to her. Her gaze had drifted over the top of his head. Now, as her eyes adjusted to the darkness, she could make out his features quite clearly. He was dozing, the fingertips of one hand loosely touching hers as it lay on the quilt.

She smiled, taking a few quiet moments to look more closely at him. His dark hair had fallen a little into his eyes making him look very much like a young boy, although she knew he was a full-grown man by his physique and the long legs that stretched in front of the seat. Slowly she pulled her hand away from his and instead placed it on top. Instantly his body shuddered and his sleep-filled eyes blinked rapidly.

'Oh, you're awake,' he said breathlessly. His voice was thick with sleep. 'How do you feel? Can you talk? You don't have to …' He left the sentence unfinished as she cleared her throat.

'Dizzy. Bit lightheaded,' she croaked. 'Fine, really.'

'That's good,' he sighed, the relief in his voice tangible. 'Your mother and Evica will be so pleased.'

She smiled but looked a little puzzled. 'Good.' She tried to say more but the words failed her.

'Don't worry,' he began, seeing her confusion, 'you really don't need to talk. We've all been worried, of course. But all you need to do is rest.'

'Rest? No … Water.' She shook her head weakly.

'Of course! What was I thinking?' He jumped up and brought a cup with a straw to her lips. She sipped greedily.

'Whoa! Not too fast.'

With a final swallow she relaxed into the soft white pillow, eyes scanning the room. She was indeed in the white room and she was with him, the man she had seen before.

'You've been through quite an ordeal.'

'Mmm. Head f-feels sore,' she stammered.

'Bound to. You took one heck of a crack. Still, you're going to be fine now, thanks to your mother.'

'Mother?' Linnayen was confused. Was she the woman in the greyness?

'Yes. Li-el brought you back. I wasn't sure how you'd feel about it. I know you mentantes aren't supposed to probe minds without consent.' Jax wondered whether to explain the consent he had given, hoping that she was still too dazed to be angry. 'But it really was our only hope. You might have died. Li-el hoped she could reach you – and she did.'

'Yes …' It was beginning to make a little sense. The woman in the ether was her mother, Li-el. Li-el who? Or what? And who was he? And Evica? She needed to know more. 'What happened to me?'

'Oh, no need to go into that now. I should let Dr Mai know you've woken up. She'll want to examine you.' With that he stood and made to leave the room. She tried to protest but was too weak and the words would not form. All she could do was raise her hand a few inches off the bed.

'Don't worry,' he said again as he opened the door. 'You'll be all right now.'

But will you come back? All she wanted was for him to return. She wanted to make sure she would see him again, but too late. He was gone and the door slid softly into place behind him.

In less than a minute it opened again and a bright gleam of light pierced the darkness of her room. She squinted as two figures moved towards her, one dressed in a long grey tunic, the other in blue overalls. A man and a woman. But the dark-haired man was not one of them and her chin sank.

The news that Linnayen was restored to consciousness did not reach Navarr until the next morning. He had just finished washing and dressing when Beoraan's messenger silently entered the dayroom and waited, as was customary, to be acknowledged.

Finally, as Navarr sat down and poured tea from the porcelain jug on the breakfast table, he signalled for the messenger to approach.

'Good morning, commander,' the young man began. 'Sen-Beoraan begs to inform you that the Ki has, most happily, regained consciousness, and asks if you could prepare for a media briefing.'

'What! Why didn't you tell me immediately?' Navarr demanded, furious with the now nervous young man. 'You fool! So when was this? When did she come to?'

'Sir … I-I believe it was late last night.'

'Last night!'

A whole ten or twelve hours had elapsed. Anything could have happened in that time. And he had not been informed. *How dare they!* Jax had deliberately kept the news back.

There would be no breakfast for the commander that day. Gulping a mouthful of the warm liquid, Navarr jumped up from the chair and stormed out of his rooms. He rushed to the transit bays in order to take an aircar to Santa Isabella, all the while cursing himself for not thinking to instruct one of his cohort on duty at the medical centre to bring him any news the moment it happened. He should have known Jax would do something like this. They had grudgingly pulled together on the *Jensa Kadenx* before the accident and the tentative reestablishment of the camaraderie they had once shared had lulled him into dropping his guard. But now, since Linnayen's injury, all bets were off, and their old rivalry had resurfaced.

No matter, thought Navarr. *Now she's awake, I'll soon have her back where I want her. And nothing and no one will stand in my way.*

Chapter Twenty-one

Despite trying hard not to, for fear of returning to the grey world of her dreams, Linnayen had fallen back into sleep twice more during the night. Her battered body could not keep her awake; it needed the healing power of sleep. But with each waking she was much relieved to see that she always returned to the white room and the faces that were now becoming familiar to her.

The older woman was, apparently, her mother, and it was she who had found her and rescued her. The younger red-haired woman was Evica, supposedly her sister. They had sat with her through the night. But the handsome young man had not come back.

When she woke for the third time, sunlight poured in through the windows and the room was lit with a golden radiance. She noticed that the women had been joined by an old man. She recognised him! She remembered seeing him before in the grey world and how sad and tired he had seemed. Her heart had gone out to him then and it did so now. She smiled at him and was delighted to see his face light up with pleasure.

'Good morning, my lady,' he said.

'Good morning,' she replied, not knowing what to say next. If only she could remember his name. It was on the tip of her tongue. He had been familiar to her when she had seen him before. But the name just would not come.

He turned away to address one of the women over his shoulder.

'Madam. She is awake.'

'Thank you, Sen-Beoraan,' replied her sister.

Beoraan! That was it. I know that name! But how do I know him?

The young woman came and sat on her bed. She leaned forward and stroked her forehead with warm soft fingers. Linnayen felt comforted. Almost safe. She knew instinctively that these people would not harm her, but she desperately wished she could remember why.

'How are you feeling, little sister?'

'Umm … Well. Still sleepy,' she replied.

Evica smiled at the ridiculousness of the situation. Linnayen had been out cold for six days, had slept through most of a seventh and still she felt tired.

'That's to be expected. You've had a terrible accident. You had us all very worried, you know.'

'Did I? I'm sorry. I didn't mean –'

'There's nothing to be sorry about,' Evica kindly remonstrated. 'You couldn't help it. You couldn't help anything.'

'That's right.' Li-el Dacas came to join them, standing behind Evica and, rather exceptionally for her, placing a motherly hand on her older daughter's shoulder. 'We're just pleased to have you back. You must take as much time as you need to get better. Don't worry about anything.'

Linnayen knew she must say something about her condition – and soon. These people obviously did not know what she was experiencing, and the longer she dragged this out, the worse it was going to be – both for her and for them.

'Your husband is taking care of everything. All the press and the rearranging of your schedule,' Li-el continued. 'He has been very busy and he's been doing a good job, too, I might add.'

My husband! I'm married? Oh no! No!

This was worse than she could have imagined and she needed time to think it through. If she was married, who was she married to? What about the dark-haired man she'd seen, the one who had been there when she had woken the first time? *Could he be my husband? That would not be so bad. He was quite handsome and he had such a nice voice. He seemed kind, if a little reserved.*

At that moment the door slid open and a tall, powerfully built man entered the room. He was very blond, very muscular and his eyes, she noticed as he came closer, were the most startling ice-blue. He stared intensely at her and at some place deep inside her, she trembled under his gaze.

'Ah, Navarr!' Beoraan spoke to him. 'You'll want some information for the press. We have a busy time ahead of us. We must also speak to the council representatives.'

Is this my husband, the man they were speaking of who has been busy? A ripple passed through her body. For some reason the sight of this man created an uneasy sensation in the pit of her stomach.

'Indeed. I called President Bashir on my way here. But it seems he already knew.' The tone of his voice was clipped and Linnayen sensed some bitterness. This man was angry. *But why?*

'Ah, of course,' the old man replied in acquiescence to Navarr. He had forgotten that Jax would have told his parents of his wife's recovery.

Linnayen was in a turmoil of emotions and her eyes darted from face to face, trying to make sense of it all. Her brow furrowed and she tried to speak. Evica, noticing, leaned across and placed a kiss on her forehead.

'There, there, Linnayen. It's all right.'

Was that her name? Lin-nay-en.

Evica turned to Beoraan and the others in the room. 'I think we are overwhelming her. She is upset.'

'Of course, my lady. We shall leave.' Beoraan smiled and nodded at Linnayen, then turned towards the door.

Navarr hung back for a moment and, with his eyes still locked onto hers, he said, 'I am so pleased to see you recovered, my lady. Farewell for now.'

Linnayen sensed something unsaid in his words, some message he was trying to put across to her. Whatever it was, she did not want him to come near her – and as far as she was concerned, he could keep his secret thoughts to himself.

Once the two men had gone, Evica helped her to sit more upright in the bed while her mother plumped the pillows behind, which allowed her to fall back in greater comfort. It was easier both to see and talk now. Evica also passed her a drinking tube and she gratefully took a sip of the cool water it contained. As the liquid seeped down her throat, she felt stronger and her thoughts took shape.

'Evica, Mother.' The words sounded so odd, but she must have once been used to saying them. She would get used to them again, she reassured herself. She would have to. 'There is something I must tell you.'

They settled themselves, one on either side of the bed, their friendly faces giving her the support she needed to speak.

'How to begin?' Her eyes scanned the room before they came to focus on the two women. 'I don't know who you are. I don't know who anyone is – except for the old man. I recognised him – a bit. But the rest of you – I'm so sorry.'

Slowly, hesitantly, the words came and she watched as their mouths opened in amazement and perhaps even horror, though she hoped it was not that. She told them how she did not know who she was either, or where they were, or how she had got here. And although she now remembered Beoraan's face and name, she did not know why or how she knew him. As for everyone else, it was a mystery. She had not even known her own name until she heard Evica say it just then. She rather liked it though. She knew nothing about herself – had no memory of any accident, or her life before it. Indeed, she was not even aware that she *had* a life before it. It was as though she had just come into existence and this place and these people, including the two stunned women facing her, were unfamiliar and completely unknown. She was very sorry. It must all be very distressing, but there was nothing she could do.

Li-el was the first to properly absorb then recover from the news.

'Well, that explains why you're not angry with me.'

Linnayen's face queried her and Li-el explained. 'About entering your mindspace. We're not supposed to do it – our kind of people. But I felt it was the only option.'

Evica's eyes were moist. 'Oh, you poor thing,' she began. 'Here we are, all talking at you, not making any sense. You must be so confused.'

'I am,' Linnayen admitted. 'But I feel safe – with you, anyway.'

'You are,' Li-el reassured her. 'But your condition puts a whole new perspective on things. I had better let the doctors know. They may have answers for you. For all of us.'

'Please don't tell anyone yet,' Linnayen cried. 'I feel ... I want more time – to adjust.'

'If you think so ... Let's see how things go,' Li-el conceded with a shrug of her shoulders. She got up from the bed, sighing heavily, her frown more in concern for her daughter than frustration at the turn of events.

At that moment the door opened and Jax entered the room. Linnayen's eyes opened wide.

'Kevor. There's something –' Li-el began in a quiet voice. But Jax did not seem to hear and he brushed past her, striding directly to the bed.

'Linnayen.' He smiled reassuringly and his eyes were clear and bright. 'It's good to see you looking so well.' He sat down, scooping up her hand, conscious of the fact that he needed to appear the adoring, solicitous husband again. Things would, of course, he thought sombrely, soon be back to normal.

'Now, I don't want you to worry. My father is briefing the council and the Union ambassadors and I have set up a press conference for an hour's time. I'll talk to them, of course.'

'Kevor ...' she began. *So that is his name.* Her tiredness was again beginning to take hold.

'Kevor Jax,' Evica interjected, 'Linnayen is still not well. And there's ...' She shook her head and took a deep breath. 'I don't know how to tell you.'

Jax was instantly concerned. 'What is it?'

Evica looked to her sister's drawn, pale face for the assent she felt she needed to continue. Li-el, too, had stopped in her tracks, ready for the shock that was about to befall the young man.

'Tell me,' Jax demanded, albeit quietly. 'As her husband, I have the right to know.'

Husband! It was him! Not the other one! Oh, thank goodness. It was him!

Linnayen's breathing came faster and she sighed with relief. They all turned towards her, expecting to see distress, but surprised to find that she was smiling.

'It's all right, Evica. I'm beginning to remember – I think.' Before she could say or do anything more, her eyelids dropped heavily and she was asleep once more.

'Commander Navarr?' The white-haired, red-skinned Autabroni sergeant walked smartly across the wood-panelled floor of the office in the new Galactic Union headquarters building that had been constructed only a few months earlier. She looked straight ahead, her eyes fixed on a holographic pictorial of a Huthon forest scene as she stood before the desk.

'What is it?'

'The report you wanted about the Order of Sumere, sir.'

Navarr's head snapped up. This would be interesting, he hoped. He had used his position to commission a special investigation into the Order. As he expected, no one had queried him. And why should they? He was head of security. Any potential threat to the Ki's safety was his responsibility. He was just doing his job which, on this occasion, happily coincided with his need to protect himself and Balisel.

'Thank you, sergeant,' he said. 'You may go.'

He touched a smooth square on his companel and ordered his calls to be held for the time being. He wanted no interruptions.

The dossier was not large and as he read he became more dismayed. Pretty much all that was known about Sumere was that it existed. Few names, no base locations. It was suspected of having vast sums of money, which it would have needed to finance its old arms-smuggling operations. It was also believed to contract other organisations and individuals to undertake its primary mission –

and no one was quite sure what that was either. It *was* known, however, that at the heart of the Order were certain powerful Earthans who had a vested interest in keeping the planet free of alien influence and it was supposed that this was because its members wanted to control Earth themselves.

But most of the evidence in the report was circumstantial or hearsay. There was nothing concrete. No one had ever been arrested or even questioned regarding the Order's suspected crimes. There was certainly no mention of Carri Aqua and the only names listed were individuals who were most likely members because of their known views. There was still no proof. There was one name, though, that caught Navarr's attention: Joseph Connor McCrae. Duncan McCrae's father, former senior minister in the council – now retired – and a well-known supporter of David Bashir.

Now that was interesting, thought Navarr, and he stored it away, making a mental note to tell Balisel that night over dinner.

'Not too long, sir. My lady still tires easily,' Em-sin Mai warned as she left the room.

'I understand.' Jax walked across the room onto the balcony where Linnayen lay on a daybed, dozing in the early afternoon sunshine. When she saw him approaching, she smiled and tried to pull herself up, the better to see him.

He quickened his step.

'Steady … Let me help you.' Despite her coldness towards him over the months since their wedding, seeing her helpless like this elicited a kindly response from him. She looked so pitiful and he had to admit she had had a bad time of it lately. He still felt the need to be wary, though, and he half expected her to throw everything back in his face at any moment.

'Thank you, Kevor.' She smiled up at him.

'Don't mention it,' he replied and turned away to collect a stool in order to sit next to her.

'And thank you for coming to see me,' she continued. 'I suppose you must be busy.'

It was both a statement and a question.

'Yes. Things have all rather been thrown out of whack. But nothing we can't handle.'

'I'm so sorry to be the cause of so much disruption. I really wasn't aware ...'

Her tone appeared to be genuinely apologetic. Jax could not quite believe it. Linnayen had never shown such consideration of others before.

'It's nothing.' He brushed away her concerns. 'All that matters is that you get well.'

'Yes,' she went on, hesitantly. 'I wanted to talk to you about that. I don't think my mother and sister got the chance to explain things. Properly, that is.' She looked down at her hands, which were nervously smoothing imaginary folds in her cotton gown.

'They told me that you were still confused. But that's to be expected after the knock you took.' There was definitely something different about her, he thought. Her voice, her whole demeanour seemed different. *Something about her eyes ...*

'Well, it's a little more than just confused. It's actually ...' She stumbled over the words. How to say it? How to tell him without shocking him? Linnayen decided to plunge on. 'I seem to have suffered some memory loss.'

His face was a mask of puzzlement. 'Yes, your mother told me, but that's only normal – and temporary.' His manner was too offhand. He was not taking it in – yet. She decided to get it all out while she had the strength.

'No, y-you don't understand. I only heard my own name for the first time this morning. Well, that's what it seems like. And – I'm sorry about this – I didn't know who *you* were, either, or my mother, or sister. Although I had sort of seen you all in my dreams, if that's what they were, when I was unconscious. But, otherwise, it's *all* a blank. Everything.'

Jax had not expected this. She seemed convinced her amnesia was a permanent condition. He sighed long and loud, but the look on his face was more of concern than shock.

'Maybe it'll pass in time.' His brow knitted in concern. 'Is there *anything* you remember?'

'Well, I remembered Beoraan, but I didn't know how or why,' she replied, frowning. 'The worst of it is that I seem to be – I mean, I *am* – someone important. A head of state. That was a real eye-opener! It doesn't feel right, but I suppose you all must know it, yes? It explains why everyone keeps calling me "my lady". I didn't understand that until my mother explained it to me.'

'Yes. You're the Ki of Altan. It's like being a queen, I suppose … if you know what that is?' Jax stumbled through his words, still reeling from her news.

'Right. Yes, I've a pretty good idea what it is. Evica explained it to me.' Suddenly she laughed. Linnayen *laughed*. Now Jax knew he was not dreaming and this was all real. The old Linnayen would never have laughed like that. She would never have let loose her emotions to such an extent.

'Although I don't have a clue what I'm supposed to do,' she said, conspiratorially, still laughing.

He joined in. The situation was, after all, so crazy that he might as well enjoy it. Then another realisation struck him and it was a more sobering thought.

'Then if you don't remember me, you didn't know I was your husband?' he asked tentatively.

She held back for a few moments then grimaced as she looked him straight in the eye. 'No. I didn't know that until this morning.'

Jax sucked in a deep breath as the news struck home.

'Not that it was bad news. Please don't be offended. You seem very nice.' She lurched on as best she could, searching for the right words, knowing how inadequate any would be. She continued, her voice growing quieter. 'But I have no memory of you. So, of course, you're a stranger to me. I mean, I hope and expect that, in time, I will remember more about you and our life together. Dr Mai seems to think that will happen, you know.'

Jax raised a sceptical eyebrow. 'If they do … If your memories come back, that is, there won't be much about "us" to remember.'

She was puzzled. 'Oh, haven't we been married very long?' The question was open and completely without guile.

'Well, no. Not long. Nearly seven months,' he admitted. 'But, well, you might as well know. We've not exactly had a good start, I suppose you could say.'

Linnayen frowned. This did not seem to make much sense.

'A good start,' she repeated, her dark brows knitted together. 'What do you mean?'

'Well …' Jax fumbled with the collar of his shirt and shifted his position on the stool. Slowly, uncomfortably, he looked into her eyes, seeing her confusion and doubt. He wanted to answer her questions but was at a loss to know how to do it without giving offence or, possibly, causing her pain. In the circumstances, he thought it best to just tell the truth as clearly and simply as he could and hope that she would be able to cope.

'The plain fact is that we weren't happy. We don't love each other. Ours was – *is* – a political marriage. It was made to end a war between our planets.' He did not see any point in saying too much to begin with, especially about Navarr. Then, the thought hit him. Perhaps she won't remember Navarr! He needed to use this opportunity before it slipped away, before her memories came back. Seeing her face drop, he quickly continued. 'But I think, given time, we would have come to like each other. Actually, we *did* have a lot in common. At least, I thought so. But we didn't get much time to be together, so it was hard to get to know you.'

She bit nervously at the corner of her lower lip. This was bad. This young man, Kevor Jax, was so nice. And he was easy on the eye too. How could they have not liked each other? That seemed very odd. Was it her fault?

Her sorrow was evident. 'I am sorry. Was I horrible to you?'

Jax shook his head reassuringly. 'No more than I was to you. Look, we were married for all the wrong reasons. It was politics. We were strangers. Then we had to try to build a relationship with all the world looking on.' He felt the need to say more, to fill in the gaps and set the scene. 'I guess it's hard for any couple starting out. *We* had to do it with official engagements to attend, forum meetings, state visits … I don't think our chances of success were ever going to be good.'

She sighed loudly and her body sank back onto the daybed, making her appear smaller and younger than her years. Jax was aware of how daunting all this must be. In the space of twenty-four hours she had woken from a coma, discovered she had amnesia, found out she was a planetary leader and, to top it all off, was trapped in an unhappy marriage. It would be too much for anyone to cope with.

'I'm sorry, you're tired. I'll go now. Leave you to think.'

Linnayen nodded that she had heard him. He was right. She needed some time to think – and she was, quite suddenly, very tired.

'Yes,' she said weakly. Then, as he rose and began to walk away, she added, 'But will you come and see me again soon, Kevor Jax? Please?'

How could he refuse? She seemed so lost, so helpless. Even though he hated her – *had* hated her – she seemed to need his support. Besides, it was the first time he had ever heard her ask humbly for anything. The old Linnayen would have commanded, expected, demanded, albeit in the politest language. If this was a new side to her character and if it was to last, he could almost begin to like her.

'How about later this evening?' he replied.

I may be old and tired but I'm not senile!

Beoraan closed the file on the vidscreen and shook his head, dismayed once more at the way Commander Navarr had decided to take matters into his own hands. This was becoming more and more common nowadays, ever since his promotion to commander and his ascent to the royal bedchamber.

Oh yes, I know! Did they think he was a fool? *Too old to be of any use anymore, eh?* There was very little that got past his sharp old eyes. Beoraan was happy for most people to think of him as an old, somewhat doddery but kindly old counsellor. The old Ki knew what he was really like, of course. Yenshar used to laugh at this private joke and Linnayen had kept up the tradition. The aged, trustworthy advisor in public, the wily old fox in private. That was why they could place their absolute trust in him and he in them. The partnership had worked well over all these years.

He had not spoken to Linnayen about her paramour. That would have been inappropriate unless, naturally, her liaison endangered the Union in some way. Her private life could remain just that. Perhaps, though, the time was coming close when he would have to act. Navarr was getting altogether too big for his boots. His arrogance and his pride were clouding his ability to do his job properly. That was a shame, Beoraan thought. For Navarr had always been very good at what he did – very efficient, very thorough – one of the best. But commanders, unlike Kis, were replaceable and Beoraan, even at eighty-one years of age, was able enough to train up another head of security before he retired – perhaps, finally, for good.

He stood up from the desk and walked across to the window. The view of the barren brown mountains, hidden in a mid-afternoon syrupy haze, was supposed to be uplifting – to Earthans, maybe. He found it unbearably ugly. *Mountains!* What did they offer anyone but trial and hardship? A continual climb in search of a few fleeting moments of grandeur. Was it really worth all the effort and wasn't there enough of that in an ordinary life anyway? No, Beoraan longed for the sea, or the lake near his old home outside Genkarah – the place where, as a small boy, he had dived into the cool waters on broiling summer afternoons. He remembered the silent crystal glimmer of the lake water as the ripples caught the sun's sharp rays and blinded his young eyes. Water: soft, cleansing, healing. He loved its sanctity and the promise it always brought that, in time, all things will be rounded. All things smoothed away. All things reduced to the simplicity of which they were born and the balance restored.

That's why he felt so uneasy. There was imbalance. He would have to see to it that their world was returned to harmony, and that meant dealing with the matter of the commander – as soon as possible.

He turned his mind to the matters in hand and the file he had just read on the strange, probably crackpot group calling themselves the Order of Sumere. Then there was Navarr's duplicity. *Was that too strong a word for it?* But how else could he describe it? Navarr was up to something – other than making love to the Ki.

Beoraan had made it his business to find out exactly what was troubling the Ki-consort since he had returned from the northern icelands back on Altan. Now, of course, he knew. He berated himself. He should have known that the handsome commander would have been attractive to the inexperienced young Ki. What did she know of ambitious men and their deceitful ways? He should never have picked Navarr. It was all his fault.

And now, the Ki and her young husband, who had so glaringly been in love with her when they first met, had been pushed apart. They had never got the chance to know each other, or even like each other. A wedge had come between their alliance and any threat to the marriage was a threat to the Union. Something would have to be done.

Perhaps the file he had just read could be used against Navarr in some way. He would have to find a means of discrediting the commander sufficiently to topple him from his elevated position without humiliating the Ki in the process. That was the trick. Then again, with the Ki's accident, perhaps the environment had changed. If there was anything good to come out of Linnayen's terrible fall it was that Navarr had been isolated to a large extent. Beoraan had been able to delegate duties to him that kept him out of the picture and, given the nature of the Ki's condition, it was appropriate that only her immediate family and attendants be permitted access. That, luckily, excluded Navarr and Beoraan had not been insensitive to an improvement in Kevor Jax's demeanour because of it. Ever since the accident, the young man felt that he had, at last, some control over the situation, now that his rival was at a distance. But with the Ki's recovery, things might go back to normal. Whatever he could do to damage Navarr he would have to do soon before she recovered her wits completely and took up with her vainglorious bedfellow again.

He walked back to the desk and touched a small lit panel on its surface. The vidscreen flickered back into life and the file he had been reading – the one Navarr had originally commissioned the day before – materialised on the screen.

The Order of Sumere. *Now why would you want to know about them, whoever or whatever they are?*

His eyes skimmed the words until, like Navarr's had done less than twenty-four hours earlier, they came to rest upon one name, Joseph McCrae. Beoraan knew the old minister was far too outspoken to be part of a covert organisation like Sumere. No, organisations like this comprised the silent ones, the seemingly passive ones – the people you would swear could not, would not have anything to do with terrorism, if only because they found it tacky and beneath them.

That's why another name Ennio Nori came as both a surprise and yet no surprise to the old man. Kumiko Toyotomi was a well-known and vociferous supporter of the peace treaty. She had always spoken for increasing trade and political links with the Union. She had been seen on vidscreens around the planets beaming with pleasure at the signing ceremony they had all attended after the Ki's wedding. Which was why it was surprising that her granddaughter's husband's name was on the list of suspected Order members. Had he uncovered some secret family rift? Was there a divergence of beliefs among them or was there more to discover about the matriarch's true leanings? And, if so, did Navarr know something about it? The pieces of the puzzle were scattered in his mind, their outlines beginning to take shape. He needed more time to bring them all together, to make them fit.

He shifted his position on the soft padding of the chair. It was not always easy to sit for too long in one position these days. The cartilage between his joints was not as pliable as it had once been and he often found himself too stiff to move as quickly as he would have liked. *Age! It'll be the death of me*, he thought, laughing at the pun.

It was not personal about Navarr. Beoraan had been quite fond of the young man. He had admired his dedication, his clarity of thought and his application to tasks. Given time and an abstinence from the Ki's person, Navarr could have become a valued advisor. But he could never have been trusted and, of course, that was irredeemable. He had no choice. One way or another, Beoraan had to put things right.

A light flashed on the vidscreen indicating that his assistant needed to speak to him urgently. He was not irritated by the interruption as his offsider, a female Dasnirian with a delightfully refreshing sense of humour, was not one to break his private reverie without an extremely good reason. Whatever it was, it was serious. He touched the desk's shiny surface and the door slid open.

'Asud, what is it, my dear?'

The young woman came forward. Her face, normally bright and warm, was frowning and she was plainly upset.

'Oh, sir. Terrible news from Lady Dacas. As you know, the Ki has regained consciousness. But it seems she has amnesia. She cannot remember a thing!'

Beoraan's mouth dropped open and he raised a hand to stroke his jaw. His eyes, though, belied his thoughts. They displayed no trace of worry or fear for the safety or wellbeing of his Ki. They were fixed and intent, pondering what this news would mean for the Ki, for her husband, her lover and, most important of all, for his plans to tumble Navarr from his rickety throne.

Ah yes, this will change things nicely. And to the young aide's surprise, the old man, her respected superior and a kind man not given to taking pleasure in others' misfortune, smiled.

Navarr waited impatiently outside Linnayen's room. It was now late afternoon and he had received no word all day about the Ki's condition. Despite ordering his staff to keep him abreast of events, no one, it seemed, knew anything other than she had recovered consciousness and was slowly on the mend. She had intermittently slept for brief periods and had received no visitors other than her immediate family and the old counsellor Sen-Beoraan.

Navarr was not unduly worried. The fact that her husband had been admitted to the room that morning did not cause him any concern. He knew where he stood in the Ki's affections and his grip on her was vice-like. She needed him like a drug and, to his own surprise, he often found that he could command feelings that were almost affectionate once they had taken their fill of each other. Their lovemaking was always passionate. He only had to run his hand along the inside of her smooth thigh and she would be afire for him, soon tearing off his clothing in a desperate race to satisfy herself.

Then he would push her down and force her legs apart, his strong hands kneading her soft flesh and breasts until she cried out for him to enter. That's when he would push deep and hard into her, deaf to her moans, hearing only his own blood rushing through his veins. Sometimes she would almost scream. That made him feel even more powerful. He was the cause of her pleasure – *and* her pain. Him, not her simpering fool of a husband. Him, Durroc Navarr, the boy from the gutters made good. Durroc Navarr was in control of the most powerful woman in the known universe and that was not about to change.

He had become aroused both at the memory of their encounters and at the run of his thoughts and he shifted his position in order to regain his composure. As he did so he saw Evica coming from Linnayen's room and she locked her eyes on his.

'Commander,' she began. 'The Ki is still very tired. I do not expect that she will be up to seeing you today.'

'I am sorry to hear that, my lady.' His tone was as smooth as silk and he dropped his eyes in order to accentuate a humility he did not feel – had never felt. 'I had hoped otherwise.'

'I'm sure. Even so ...' Evica replied haughtily. 'Perhaps tomorrow?'

'Of course, my lady.' His acquiescence was quick and, apparently, sincere. 'But perhaps then you could tell me how my lady is? Is there any change?'

Evica hesitated for barely a moment and her eyes never moved in their gaze. Was it enough for Navarr to have noticed?

'No ... No change,' she said bluntly. The arrogant commander, her sister's secret lover, did not need to know anything. Who knows? By this time tomorrow, with any luck, he'll be back where he belongs in the ranks, from where he should never have left.

'In that case,' Navarr continued, 'perhaps you could let my lady know that I asked after her?'

Evica nodded her assent then turned away from him. She strode purposefully down the corridor. As she reached the end she stopped to see if Navarr had yet left. Only then, under her openly disapproving scrutiny, did he turn and walk away in the opposite direction.

Navarr smiled secretly. What did it matter that the Lady Evica disliked him? What did it matter if everyone hated him? He would soon have things back the way they were. Linnayen could not do without him. He *knew* how she needed him. Only one thought niggled at the back of his mind. She had hesitated. Evica had hesitated. Now why was that, he wondered.

Chapter Twenty-two

True to his word, Jax came to see Linnayen again that evening. She had been sitting with her mother while Nen brushed her newly washed hair when the door slid open and Jax stepped through. Their conversation that morning had been in her thoughts almost continually and she was still confused and concerned that they appeared to have had such a bad marriage. Was it just that they were young, or inexperienced? Or had they had been forced into the union against their will? Whose will though? Had he never wanted to marry her? Perhaps he had been in love with someone else. That would, indeed, build huge resentment. It could explain everything. But no, it could not be that. He had said he thought they could have grown to like each other in time – given the opportunity.

Perhaps *she* had not wanted to marry *him*. But how could that be when her mother and sister explained to her that afternoon, in response to her questions, that the marriage had been her idea in the first place. Maybe they had just not taken to each other. Or maybe the former her, the Linnayen she had been before the accident, was rude and arrogant and not even a saint could have borne being with her. Her thoughts were a maelstrom. She wanted – no, needed – to find out more.

She was tired now, both in body and mind, exhausted with trying to absorb and understand all this new information, and not a little afraid too. Everyone meant well, she could see that. Her mother and her sister were very kind and did not try to foist too much onto her, but it was all a little scary. There would be time enough for her memories to return over the coming days, weeks, maybe even months. The male doctor – the Earthan – had said that it may take many months for her memory to be fully restored, if indeed it ever was. And that thought frightened her even more. What if she never remembered? What if she always felt like this? A stranger in a strange place. Disconnected. Adrift.

She had had enough for now. It was only early evening but she was ready to sleep. The warm bath and Nen's gentle brushing of her long black hair had relaxed her and her mind was wandering when her thoughts were interrupted by Jax's arrival. Not that she minded. She wanted to see him again and it was by her request that he had come back.

'Hello, Linnayen. Hope I'm not disturbing you,' he said. Linnayen was seated on a high stool, Nen behind her. She made to get up in order to greet him.

'Oh, please don't,' he exclaimed. 'I only stopped by to see how you're doing.'

'Thank you, Kevor Jax. I'm much better. The pain in my head has almost gone now,' she remarked, smiling.

'Pleased to hear it. I hope it won't keep you awake tonight. You can always ask the doctors for something to help you sleep, you know.' He could not help himself. He was being genuinely solicitous. This new, helpless, kinder Linnayen was bringing out the old Jax, the well brought up young nobleman. He had to keep reminding himself that she could, at any moment, slip back into her real self and he would have to suffer the same humiliation all over again. It might pay to be a little more wary, he told himself.

'I know,' she replied. 'But I don't think it will be necessary. I'm quite tired already.'

'Oh, my dear! You should have said,' Li-el chimed in. 'Here we are, keeping you up. Come on, Nen. Kevor, you too. We'll leave you in peace.'

Linnayen smiled into Jax's eyes in exactly the way he had always dreamed, hoped, imagined she would. He was struck dumb by the strength of his response.

'Kevor?' Li-el questioned him impatiently with her eyes.

Linnayen's voice was soft as she diverted her gaze to the older woman. 'One minute alone, please ... Mother.' It still seemed so odd to use that word. This woman, who had been so nice to her, was still a virtual stranger. Only with Beoraan had she felt a little more comfortable – and with Jax, the first person she had seen on waking.

Nen gathered up the brush and comb, folded Linnayen's dressing-gown across the end of the bed and, with a brief goodnight to her lady, left the room.

'Very well.' Li-el came over kissed the young woman on the cheek. 'Good night, my dear. Try to rest. And don't worry. It will be better still tomorrow.'

Once she had gone, Linnayen got up from the stool. Jax helped her over to the bed and plumped her pillows to make her more comfortable. Once again, she smiled up at him before she spoke.

'Thank you – and thank you for coming back to see me.'

'It was nothing.' He brushed it off. 'Anyway, I wanted to see you. Wanted to make sure you're not taking on too much.'

She shrugged and sighed. 'That's an understatement! I'm having a hard time understanding *anything*. There's so much I don't know. It's exhausting!'

'I'll bet. And I want you to know that I'm not going to make it worse. I'll get going any time you like. Just say the word.'

'Oh no,' she replied, worried that she might scare him away. 'No, I want you to stay. I wanted you to know that I've been thinking very seriously about our ... predicament, I suppose you'd call it. And I want to apologise.'

'Apologise! What on earth for?' he exclaimed with a look of genuine surprise. He continued in a calmer tone. 'You're hardly responsible for your own accident, a fall that could have killed you.'

'I know,' she began. 'It's not that. It's putting you in this situation. I mean ... All this. The amnesia ... It's hard for me, yes. But what must it be like for you and my family? You must have been so worried. And then, when I finally *do* wake up, I don't know who any of you are and I treat you like strangers. It must be hard for you. That's what I'm sorry about. You didn't ask for this either.'

Jax sat down on the edge of the bed. He took her hand and patted it reassuringly.

'Look, what we've gone through is nothing compared to you. Please don't feel you have to apologise.'

'You're very kind.' She leaned forward and he took her arm in order to help her sit up. Before he knew what was happening, she held his face with her other hand and planted a soft, small kiss on his cheek. Jax was amazed, his deep blue eyes widening with the shock. Linnayen kissing him? Unbelievable!

'Don't look so horrified,' she laughed. 'Or *was* it horrible?'

With a shrug of his broad shoulders, Jax's laughter was obviously self-conscious.

'Sorry, I'm not used to it, that's all.'

'So I see.' She lay back on the pillow and her laughter faded. She looked tired now. 'But perhaps you will be – in time.' The look in her eyes was perfectly serious. Yet there was a softness there, too, a gentle good humour he had never seen before. Linnayen was *so* different. Where was the haughtiness, the pride, the self-containment? Where was the cold formality that had been quintessentially Linnayen? If it were not so ridiculous he would almost have thought that she was flirting with him.

Her tired eyes closed and her shoulders sagged as if the weariness she had staved off was now too great a burden to carry any longer.

'I'll go now,' he said, rising and tugging on the hem of his crumpled tunic.

'You'll come again tomorrow?' Her voice was faint and small. She had opened her eyes again, but in the gathering darkness of the twilight, no emerald shards reflected back at him, only the hazy glow of the bedside lamp.

'I will,' he promised. At that moment, in the silence and stillness, he felt an overwhelming urge to lean down and return her kiss. But something stopped him. Some inner self-preservation mechanism kicked in and held him back. No, he would not be drawn in. Not again.

He turned and walked towards the door and, looking over his shoulder as he left the room, he saw that she was already asleep.

Dinner had been wonderful. The food was truly superb. The wine and aperitifs had been delicious. And the company was, as always, amazing.

Balisel was in a playful mood and had given him more than one reason to spill his wine mid-sip. Luckily, the restaurant had been crowded and no one seemed to be paying much attention to them. They had been able to titillate each other's appetites with growing excitement as the meal progressed until, finally, at the end of the evening, in the privacy of her suite, they had finally consummated their unnatural relationship.

The exhaustion they both felt when it was over was not purely corporeal. The relief of being able to drop their mutual guard, to be completely and openly themselves for one rare moment, was cathartic and left them drained of all strength, both physical and mental. Even breathing afterwards had seemed a struggle and all they could do was lie next to each other, staring at the ceiling while the slow-spreading delight of their shared endeavours passed through their bodies. They had not spoken for many minutes, then Balisel broke the silence.

She rose and leaned on one arm, looking down at his handsome face so like her own, and was consumed by her feelings for him.

'You're so beautiful, Durroc,' she stated simply.

He turned his eyes from the ceiling to look at her and in them she read a look of pure, absolute love. This man, her brother, would do anything for her. She was his life, he was hers.

He smiled slowly, accepting the compliment and returning it in his warm gaze.

'Is it like this with her?' Her question was spoken blankly, honestly.

He shook his head admonishingly, but still smiling. 'You know it isn't.'

Seeing in his face, hearing in his tone what she wanted to know, she relaxed. She had not been worried. Not really. He was always hers and no silly girl would come between them, whatever her status. Linnayen Genara would never see the look of undying adoration that she saw in her brother's eyes. What they had was beyond any power to be broken – not in this life, and not in death either.

Navarr noted the way her head had cocked slightly to one side, almost childlike in the way she received the truth of his words, and he was struck once again at the depth of his feelings for her. Only her.

He got up and went to the bathroom to shower and dress. Balisel did not protest. She, too, knew that their tryst was concluded – for now – just as surely as she knew he would be back, some day and in some other place. She lay back down and snuggled into the pillows, smelling his scent and feeling both comforted and aroused.

When Navarr came back, dressed and looking fresh, she was already sleeping. He draped the covers over her naked body and let his eyes linger for a few minutes before forcing his mind to resume business.

The evening was almost over but he still had one call to make and it needed to be done now, when no one was around, when they would all be asleep.

The hospital was quiet, as he had expected. Only two guards were on duty outside the Ki's room when he arrived shortly before midnight and he had seen only a couple of nursing attendants since passing through ward reception.

Both guards came to attention as he approached, their heels clicking smartly together, breaching the quiet of the long passageway. Navarr raised a hand both to acknowledge them and to order them to be at ease.

'You men need a break,' he said. 'I will stay.'

The two guards looked at each other, the uncertainty clear in their eyes. Their orders had been quite unambiguous. They were not to leave their post under any circumstances. But this was their commanding officer and head of security.

He saw their hesitation and a flicker of puzzlement knitted his brows.

'Well? What are you waiting for?

'Sir …' The first guard cleared his throat and swallowed in an effort to gather courage. 'Our orders are not to leave our post.'

Navarr sighed heavily. The muscles in his jaw contracted ominously. 'And who gave you those orders?'

The second guard shuffled his feet a little and both lowered their eyes.

'That's right. Now take a break, as I have *also* ordered.'

It was clear that the serpentine tone of his voice would brook no further argument. The two guards nodded their assent and walked quickly away.

Navarr's smile was cat-like. Power was so good. Almost as good as … No, nothing was as good as being with his sister. And to make sure that he could continue to have both, he had a job to do. It was time to awaken his Ki and remind her of how good he made her feel.

The door slid smoothly to a close behind him. Detecting his presence, a glow-globe hovered across to meet him and emitted just enough light for him to find his way to Linnayen's bedside.

He looked down at her sleeping figure, loosely outlined by the coverlet. He found himself enjoying these moments as he took in the curve of her slender arm, the shapely rise of her hips and her long tapering legs. The mass of her jet hair sprawled wildly across the white pillow and a few tendrils curled across the skin of her shoulders, which appeared silver in the moon glow. One small dark wisp nestled in the slight crevice between her breasts, its tip pointing like an arrow towards the barely visible outline of a nipple. The picture was both innocent and madly erotic and his silent grin was visceral in its intensity.

He had not been alone with her since before they left Altan, both having deemed it too dangerous to rendezvous privately on board the *Jensa Kadenx*. The plan had been to wait until they were on Earth when he would oversee her appointment schedule and opportunities for sex could be more easily found. Now, of course, with Linnayen's accident, the plans had had to be changed, or rather, postponed. But Navarr had waited long enough. Seeing Balisel earlier that evening had fired his blood and he was ready to rekindle his special relationship with the young Ki. It was time to take back what was his – both the power and the woman.

He pulled back the covers down to her hips. She was wearing a simple white nightgown, trimmed with a floral design in lace. The fall of its neckline revealed her cleavage and Navarr felt the first tremor of sexual excitement in his abdomen. He had always liked her breasts. They were full and round, with well-defined areolae and, usually within seconds of him touching her, the nipples were enticingly erect.

The sudden cooling of the air around the woman caused her to stir. Navarr instantly pulled the blanket back over her, then knelt by the side of the bed in order to bring his face level with hers. He looked intensely at her features. The long lashes, the straight nose and the mouth, its lips slightly parted, behind which he could glimpse her white teeth. He could just make out the tiny scar on her forehead that he knew she had got as a child falling out of a farm wagon one summer in Mayar. In her haste to get back to the homestead for dinner, she had not fastened the back flap properly and, when she had leaned against it, she had tumbled out, going head over heels backwards and hitting her right temple on a sharp stone. She had suffered more from the embarrassment than the injury itself, she had told him, but the cut had been deep enough to leave a permanent mark and a reminder to do things properly in future.

The remembrance of the story brought on a sudden feeling of tenderness and he reached a hand across to stroke her cheek. He was once more surprised that he could, on occasion, feel quite warm towards her. She began to wake and he immediately snapped himself back to the matter at hand. Now was no time for foolish sentimentality.

'Mmm ... What ...?' In the dim light Linnayen could not see who was kneeling at her bedside. She blinked her eyes and tried to bring them into focus.

'It's me,' he whispered.

'Oh ...' All she could discern was a male shape and she instantly thought of Jax. 'What are you doing here? Why ...?' She was groggy and her eyes screwed tightly shut as she started to yawn.

'I couldn't wait any longer.' His reply was low and deep and he hoped it expressed the depth of his craving, the craving she had always returned.

The glow-globe had positioned itself behind Navarr and his face was mostly in shadow as Linnayen looked at him. She could not quite see who it was, but the voice sounded a little like Kevor Jax's. It had to be him. But why would he visit her in the middle of the night? Why not wait until morning?

Navarr slid a hand beneath the coverlet and touched her waist. Her body instantly tensed in response. He caressed her there, then let his hand move down along her thigh. She sucked in her breath and he could see the sudden rise and fall of her chest as her breathing increased.

'What ...?' She began to speak and her voice was high-pitched and nervous. She had not expected this. He may be her husband but he was still a virtual stranger!

'Shhh.' Navarr thought to calm her. In the darkness he slid his hand down to the soft warm flesh between her thighs and, almost as though it had a mind of its own, it travelled ever upwards. He wanted to touch her. He knew that as soon as she felt his fingers caressing that most private part of her she would soon be ready for him. He could tell it was working; she was already squirming deliciously and her breathing was becoming more rapid.

'No! *No* ... Not like this,' she cried. This was not how she had imagined making love would be with him. This was too direct, too intrusive, too quick.

Navarr ignored her protests. He had almost reached his goal. A little further and he would have her gasping. He rose up, not breaking contact, and with his other hand stroked her forehead. Her eyes by now were wide open, searching the shadow for his face, her fear growing. This could not be Kevor Jax! She had not known him long but he had struck her as gentle, kind. Perhaps this was why they had not been happy in their marriage. He must have two very different sides to his character. If this was her husband, no wonder things were bad. She struggled and tried to move her body away from him.

Navarr lowered his head to hers, ready to take her open mouth and stifle her feeble moans. As he moved, the glow-globe followed and took position on the other side of Linnayen's body. Now she could see him! The light fell full upon his face. It was not Jax! This was the face of the blond stranger who had visited her before, with Beoraan. *Not Jax!*

She opened her mouth to scream out her protest, but Navarr was already on top of her, his tongue filling her. She writhed away from his hands, her growing fear giving her a sudden surge of strength. Then she raised her left arm and pushed as hard as she could against his shoulder, further moving his hand away from her.

Navarr was surprised. What was she playing at? Indeed, her body had stiffened. Was she trying to pull away from him? This was not like her. By now her hunger for him was usually intense. Always by now she would be clawing at him, begging him, demanding that he enter her. *Ah! She's playing a game.* Perhaps she wanted to try a new way to excite him. Well, if that's what she wanted, it was working. He could feel blood coursing through his body and his penis swelled under his tunic.

He broke off the brutal kiss, leaving her gasping for breath.

'A new game, my love. I like it.' His words rang like a sickening sneer inside her brain.

My love? What was he talking about? Linnayen's thoughts were a tumult inside her head, but she had enough wits about her to realise that this was her only chance to break free before this went any further – before she would not be able to stop it.

'Get off me!' Her voice rose with every syllable. At the same time, she drew back across the bed, slithering her body as far as she could to be out of his reach.

Navarr was puzzled. What was going on? Linnayen seemed determined to be rid of him. Either that or she was playing the game too well.

'Come now, Linnayen,' he cajoled, still reaching across to touch her arm.

'How *dare* you!' The use of her birth name, by a man who was both a stranger and a servant, was an affront. Instinctively, she knew she should not tolerate such familiarity. Once again she pulled away from him and, reaching the far side of the bed, rose to a sitting position. She was now out of the reach of Navarr's arms, thus forcing him to break off his assault and come to the other side of the bed.

'It's my lady to you – and always will be!' she spat the words at him, her eyes glittering like cold steel, never leaving their target. Then she remembered the guards who would be outside her room. 'Guards! Guards! Come here!'

Navarr's laugh was hollow and nervous. She was taking the game too far – if game it was. He was beginning to have doubts.

'I sent them away so that we could be alone, my sweet.' As he spoke, he walked slowly, ever closer to her. Half of him wanted to believe this was still a game. The other half was becoming acutely aware that this was strange sport and that a change of tack might be called for.

'I am not your *sweet!*' she replied, horrified and disgusted. 'Get away from me!'

He continued to move towards her, like a man possessed of some hypnotic trance. His eyes never left her and, even in the dimness of the stark white room, she could make out the psychotic gaze they held.

Linnayen could see that the gap between him and the door was closing – her escape route. It had to be now. If she didn't make a run for it he might trap her, and she could not afford for that to happen. She leapt up and, keeping her head low, ducked under his outstretched arms and ran towards the door.

The suddenness of her movement caught Navarr off-guard. His brain failed to send out the signal to his arms quickly enough to stop her and she dashed past him.

'What? Linnayen! Enough of this. Come back!'

Too late. Sensing a shape approaching at speed, the door panel opened quickly and the light from the corridor flooded into the room, silhouetting Linnayen as she passed through.

She ran down the long corridor, her fear giving extra strength to her weakened limbs. Over her shoulder she sensed the large blond man following her, gaining on her, and she willed her legs to continue to hold her.

'Linnayen! Come back! What are you doing?' he cried out after her, trying to keep his voice low but urgent. But she ignored his words, determined to reach the foyer where she knew there would be doctors and attendants and safety. Only a few more steps and she would be there.

His heavy hand landed on her right shoulder, grasping her with such force that she flinched with the pain. She sucked in her breath and spun around, her left arm raised, fist clenched ready to strike a blow. He saw it coming and ducked back, placing himself out of her reach.

'Nice try. If I weren't so sure you loved me I'd almost believe you meant to hurt me.' His voice was hard, the words clipped. She tensed every fibre in her weakened body, ready to defend herself if she had to.

Love him! Linnayen could not believe what he was saying. Love *him*? This awful brute of a man – this monster! Not possible. It could not be!

'I don't love *you!*' she yelled, swinging her arm back and clipping his cheek with the back of her left hand.

At that instant, the door to the foyer area opened and Evica and Tariik Min rushed through, weapons drawn.

'You heard my sister, commander.' Evica's voice was a low growl. 'Let her go – now!'

Navarr was still reeling from the slap on the face. What had gone wrong? Why was she behaving this way? He could not take it in. Before the accident, Linnayen had been hungry for him. She had always wanted him. But she had changed – and her sister was about to shoot him if he did not let go of her immediately.

'Commander! Let the Ki go!' This came from a stone-faced Tariik Min, who raised his weapon to take proper aim.

Navarr's instinct for survival took over. The situation looked bad – very bad – but there was a chance to salvage something. He released his hold on her and turned to face his accusers.

'Of course.' He held up his empty hands almost nonchalantly in order to show that he had no intention of harming Linnayen. 'Lady Evica, I was merely restraining my lady to stop her from injuring herself. She woke and was disoriented and fearful. I had to help.'

Linnayen was unable to speak for the moment but was shaking her head wildly from side to side, denying his words.

'Oh, I know exactly what you were doing, commander. The Ki no longer needs your ... *help*.' Evica's lip curled, then she continued, 'Or anything else from you at this time.'

She nodded an unspoken message to Tariik, who stepped forward and stood by Navarr's side to keep a silent guard on the disgraced commander. Linnayen finally regained her breath and with it her composure.

'Get him out of here!' Her voice was shaky but, underneath the tremors, her resolve was clear.

Tariik took hold of his arm and, in genuine surprise, Navarr looked down at the young Dasnirian's hand. He was being restrained. Somehow things had gone terribly wrong. Had he lost his position? *Surely not!* His confusion was evident on his face.

Evica could not hide her smile of triumph. At last! The arrogant commander Navarr had fallen from grace.

'Commander? You seem surprised.' She wanted to string this out as long as possible to better enjoy his humiliation. 'Oh ... but things have changed. Didn't you know?'

'K-know what?' Navarr stammered, trying to shrug off Tariik's restraining hand.

Linnayen's eyes followed her sister as she walked over to stand by her side in an unspoken display of support. Evica finally replied.

'My sister has regained her senses in more ways than one. The fall on the *Kadenx* did wonders for her memory … It helped her to lose it.'

The truth of Evica's words began to register in his troubled mind and his eyes displayed his growing understanding.

'That's right,' Evica continued. She smiled reassuringly at Linnayen, who knew that she needed to do nothing more right now. Her sister – stranger though she was – had come to her aid and was making the nightmare end. She relaxed and allowed Evica to place an arm around her shoulders.

'The Ki does not remember you, Commander Navarr. Nothing about you. But after tonight, I'd say she will never forget you now.'

The promise in Evica's words was clear. His actions over the last minutes had been sufficient to render his career and aspirations at an end and he knew it. His shoulders slumped and his piercing eyes finally dropped their gaze to the floor.

'What is to become of me?' he asked flatly.

Evica was about to reply but Linnayen stepped forward. This man had offended her and she would decide his fate.

'You will learn that in good time,' she began. She wanted to think this through very carefully. Some instinct told her not to make any sudden decisions. Linnayen continued, her voice now steady and measured. 'For now, you will be escorted back to your quarters where you will remain – under guard.'

The look in Navarr's eyes both reprimanded her and pleaded with her to remember what they had once been to each other. Could she not recall the love, the passion they had once shared? His gaze was met by a stone wall. There was nothing for him in her eyes but green ice. He turned away and, as he walked through the doorway to the foyer beyond, Tariik Min at his back, his shoulders suddenly straightened and his neck stretched upwards. He was a proud man and, although it seemed he had met with disgrace and defeat, Navarr knew that this was just a temporary setback. He would be back, and next time he would not be so nice.

'You know your father's name appears on the list of suspected members?' Jax leaned forward as he spoke, hoping that the gesture conveyed the gravitas he felt the situation warranted.

For once Duncan McCrae did not throw back his head and laugh as Jax had expected he would. The sandy-haired actor, whose features were fast becoming familiar to audiences around the world, sat stiffly on the high-backed chair in Beoraan's quarters and scanned the faces around him. There was Jax, his oldest and most trusted friend and confidant, Beoraan, the sharp-eyed alien counsellor, and Tariik Min, the soon-to-be bridegroom, who had not yet spoken and was observing the exchange as he lounged against the far wall.

'Hardly surprising,' Duncan returned with a shrug of his shoulders. 'Those are the circles he used to mix in – until his retirement.' Duncan could not quite fathom what was happening. Was this an interrogation? Did his best friend truly suspect his father of plots and subversion, of being involved with this crackpot organisation, the Order of Sumere?

'Quite so,' chimed in Beoraan. 'But does he still keep in contact with any of them?' The old man's words were delivered as though he were enquiring about the weather. So why did they not seem innocuous? *Or*, thought Duncan, *am I being paranoid?*

'I wouldn't know,' Duncan said, his puzzlement turning ever more towards concern. 'You'll have to ask him.'

Jax could feel more than see the resentment building in his friend. It was time to step in.

'Thought we'd sound you out first, Duncan. You see ...' Jax saw the warning in Beoraan's eyes and tried to convey in his own glance that he knew what he was doing. Tariik also straightened his stance, then came to stand closer to where the others were seated on the couches in the centre of the room. 'Er, how can I put this?' Jax continued, slightly flustered and embarrassed by what he was about to ask. 'We think this Order of Sumere is actively conspiring to destroy the peace treaty we've just signed. That there's some sort of conspiracy –'

'And you think my father has something to do with that? A *conspiracy?*' Duncan's voice rose in consternation. 'You must be joking.'

'Wait,' Jax interrupted. 'Let me finish. If the Order is active – if it exists at all, though we're pretty sure it does – then we want to know what they're planning. With Tariik and Evica's wedding coming up in a couple of weeks … Well, it could be an ideal opportunity to cause havoc.'

'What? An act of terrorism?' Duncan interjected.

'That's correct.' Beoraan's voice punched the air.

The old man rose from the couch and paced slowly across to the wide span of the window that overlooked the sprawling plazas and high-rises of downtown Los Angeles. Aircars and windshifters scurried busily in the cramped spaces between the buildings and, far below, one could make out microscopic figures walking in the concrete canyons. In his mind's eye he saw the destruction that just one fractal blast could cause on a city of this immense size. In less than five seconds nothing would exist here but a flattened, scoured bowl twenty kilometres wide. No debris. No bodies. Anything that remained defragmented would have been shot clear across to the outer rims where it would arrive like a million tiny bullets piercing the flesh of people living even twenty kilometres away from the blast zone. Yes, an act of terrorism on that scale would incontrovertibly return them to a state of war, royal marriage or no royal marriage.

'The wedding …' Beoraan let the words hang for a few moments, then continued gravely. 'The Order of Sumere could do untold damage – if it was allowed to.'

'That must *not* happen.' Tariik Min finally joined the discussion, his words hammering into the air around them. He continued, the urgency apparent in his tone, 'And that's where your father could help us.'

'I don't see how,' Duncan began, the confusion returning to his face.

'He knows these people, Duncan,' Jax explained. 'He meets them socially, he's a member of the same clubs, sits on the same executive committees, attends the same functions. He could help us discover who is really behind all this.'

'You want him to be a spy?' Duncan asked, a hint of a smile creeping into the corners of his mouth.

'A little more than that,' Beoraan answered. 'We would like him to completely infiltrate the organisation – in effect, to become one of them – for a short while, of course.'

Jax took up the explanation again. 'Quite frankly, his outspoken views on retaining independence for Earth could be an excellent calling card. He's a well-known opponent to the peace treaty.'

'Which is why he'd never agree to help you.' Duncan finished the thought that had been at the back of all their minds.

When Beoraan had brought the news to Jax about Navarr's investigation into the Order of Sumere they had been more interested in Navarr's motive for looking into the obscure organisation than the group itself. Upon questioning, Navarr had given no specific reason for his research, merely that the name had cropped up in a standard security scan and he thought it worthy of further investigation. There was no ulterior motive, he had said, and it was too mundane a matter to have bothered Beoraan with it, which is why he had not sought the counsellor's authorisation to commission the research in the first place.

But then, Navarr had not been in a cooperative frame of mind. Since being stripped of his position as head of the Ki's security – a consequence of his dreadful behaviour and repulsive revelations to the young Ki on that fateful night one week earlier – he had been reassigned to the Union's primary resources trade delegation, a group of diplomats that had accompanied them from Altan. He had been allowed to retain his rank but, in this way, he had been swiftly removed from the Ki's immediate presence without causing any ripples in the delicate political pond.

Navarr had been well known and respected among the Earthan politicians and civil servants and, with the arrival of the Ki and her family, they had been happy to have a familiar, if alien, face return to their shores. His sudden disappearance from the royal entourage would have been highly noticeable if he had also been dishonourably removed from duty and stripped of his rank, as Linnayen had wanted. Beoraan, with the help of Li-el Dacas, had persuaded her that it would be far better to place Navarr in a seemingly important yet basically impotent position, as this would give no cause for concern to the Earthans and yet serve the purpose of getting him out of her sight. It would also curtail any hopes and dreams he might still have of holding any power base.

Consequently, Navarr was now relegated to chief of staff to the trade delegation and had already left Amerimex for a series of goodwill meetings in various capital cities throughout Earth. Linnayen was much relieved to be rid of him and had already decided that they would not travel home to Altan on the same spaceliner. In the meantime, Jax was determined that this was the end of his rival. He would be plagued by the arrogant usurper no more and he felt as though a weight had been lifted from his shoulders – until Beoraan had told him about the Order of Sumere. The more he delved into Navarr's research, the more unsettled he became. These people could be highly dangerous, if only because of their unpredictability. However, when he saw Joe McCrae's name on the list of suspected members, he laughed out loud.

'Oh no, Beoraan. Not Joe,' he had assured the counsellor. 'Absolutely impossible. I've known him all my life. So has my father. He hates the Union, but he would never plot and scheme for its downfall once it had been duly approved by the council. Joe is a stickler for the rule of law – in all things.'

'And that, my lord, is why he must be persuaded to help us.' Beoraan had spoken the truth. However much Joe McCrae might hate the peace treaty and Earth's new place in the Galactic Union, he hated a blatant disregard for the principles of democracy even more.

'You may be right, Duncan,' Jax agreed now, nodding his head. 'Maybe we *are* foolish to think he might help us. But for all the times your father has spoken out against the Union, he has never condoned terrorism. And I think – no, I *know* – if he knew he could do something to avert a massacre of innocents, he would.'

'Well, of course he would, when you put it like that,' Duncan was forced to concur. His father had always been vehemently opposed to Earth joining with the other planets, but he had never approved of the use of mercenaries to continue the combat and would rather die himself than see innocent people harmed. Joe McCrae was old school. Armies fought battles using trained combatants, and he preferred that women did not fight, either, although they made up more than forty percent of the armed forces.

'So will you support us? Will you take me to meet your father?' Beoraan asked the final question and Duncan, with a shrug of his sandy eyebrows, returned the old man's piercing gaze. 'When can you be ready to leave?'

Chapter Twenty-three

Linnayen still could not remember Durroc Navarr or anything about the relationship she was supposed to have had with him. He had said they were lovers – that she had loved him. But she found this impossible to believe. She hated his blondness, his tanned skin and the cold blue eyes. The sharp angles of his face were singularly unappealing and, overall, his looks, which she must once have found attractive, now left her not only cold but also nauseated. Similarly, she thought his manner and personality to be quite repellent and was amazed to think that she might at one time have found his haughtiness appealing.

She had broached the subject with Jax the day after the awful incident at the hospital. Was her involvement with the commander the reason their marriage had been less than happy? He had confirmed it, explaining that both before their wedding and after it, she had continued an affair with Durroc Navarr and, as a consequence, he had remained aloof from her; it was what she had wanted, he said, and he had learned to live with it.

'But it was not what *you* wanted?' she had asked.

'No,' he had replied, and his eyes dropped in memory of the pain it had caused him.

This news made her feel terrible. He had obviously had feelings for her, which she – and this Navarr – had managed to destroy. All she could do was apologise, but she was acutely aware of how inadequate it sounded, given the enormity of her duplicity and insensitivity. Whoever she was then must have been unbearable. She had to make amends to this young man whom she had so wronged. She hoped that she had not done so much damage that Jax would not be able to forgive her.

It was increasingly important to her that she sought and won her estranged husband's forgiveness. Although she could still not remember anything about her life with him, Linnayen was quickly growing to like and respect him. He had been kind and solicitous to her in the days after Navarr's attack, although he maintained an air of reserve too. This did not surprise her though and she, rightly, put it down to a defence strategy. After all, she had hurt him badly. It was hardly likely that he would open up to her of all people, even though she did not feel like that person anymore.

As for Durroc Navarr, he was now well occupied elsewhere and, with luck and no small amount of manoeuvring, the chances were that she would never have to see him again. Beoraan and her mother had persuaded her to retain his skills and experience, at least for the time being. But she reserved her judgement on his long-term future. She was not comfortable with the thought that she might have to face him again at some time in the course of her duties. The further away he was from her, the better.

Durroc Navarr let the warm water bead and trickle down his broad, hairless chest. The fine spray of the shower felt good after the sticky warmth of the night. He had overridden the environmental controls for the hotel room and allowed the evening air to enter during the night. For all his travels and knowledge of Earth, he had not appreciated that tropical nights can be almost as hot as tropical days and he had spent a disturbed night tossing and turning under the thin cotton sheet. It was a mistake he would not make again. *Another mistake*, he reflected bitterly.

He finished his ablutions and touched the dry control on the shower wall. Instantly the walls of the cubicle issued jets of warm air that rippled across his naked body. His enjoyment of the sensation was purely physical and, for a fleeting moment, he was reminded of the pleasure he had often taken with the Ki – experiences he was determined to relive.

The loss of his high position and his influence over Linnayen was proving a bitter pill to swallow. He could not believe how badly things had turned out. He had come so close to the ultimate prize: total control – through the Ki – of the whole Union, which now included Earth too. But because of one slip, one stupid mistake, he had lost it all. *For now.*

He berated himself for not picking up the signals sooner. Linnayen's behaviour that night had been odd, different. He had not expected her to be so coy. But it had been so long since they had had sex, he had not thought it strange at the time. Also, she had been deeply asleep and he had woken her up perhaps too suddenly. As the days before he left with the trade delegation passed, he had plenty of time to reflect on his predicament. He surmised that Linnayen's amnesia had been common knowledge in her inner circle. Her mother, sister and Beoraan would surely have known – and her husband, too, of course. So why had he not been informed? Had he been kept in the dark deliberately? And if so, by whom? Could it have been Jax?

The thought that his mistress's husband and former close friend could have been actively instrumental in his downfall rankled and fuelled both his desire for revenge and his determination to reacquire his position. In truth, Linnayen had never loved the boy, he recalled. It would be unlikely that she would even have any affection for him. So why should he tolerate her being with him? Especially if that was not what she really wanted – or *who* she really wanted. He knew her, knew what she liked, and, when she regained her senses, her memories, she would soon realise what she had done and want him back. Of that he was sure. Then he would take care of the bothersome Ki-consort once and for all.

Whatever he did, whatever revenge he took, he knew he would have only one chance. It was important to get it right and that was where his sister could prove her worth. Balisel was good at these things. She had always been the better strategist. She would know what to do to further their cause and, as ever, it was always an excellent experience seeing her. Whatever obstacles life threw up, at least he would always have Balisel, and the thought gave him both considerable comfort and a surge of primal satisfaction.

His thoughts were interrupted by a computerised voice telling him that his breakfast was about to be delivered and that his guest had arrived and was on her way up to his suite. He smiled and strode into the bedroom to grab his robe from the end of the bed, swiftly putting it on to cover his nakedness.

As he entered the lounge, he instructed the door to open, thereby allowing the attendant to wheel in a colourful tray of assorted fruits, juices and spiced pastries along with a steaming pot of hot coffee. Navarr had been pleased to discover the culinary delights of the historic city of Kualalumpur, the capital of the Makassar Republic, where the trade delegation had been for the last two days. The teeming metropolis comprised some twenty-eight million souls packed into an area of little more than three hundred square kilometres, making it one of the densest conurbations on Earth and only achievable due to a proliferation of towering skyscrapers. His hotel was in one of these super-structures and his room on the ninety-fifth floor commanded a stunning view over those parts of the city that were not obscured by similar soaring monoliths.

'Put it on the balcony, thank you.' His voice, usually imperious and rude when dealing with servants, was pleasant, reflecting the happiness he felt at the thought of seeing Balisel again.

The attendant wheeled the trolley steadily towards the doors of the shaded balcony, which opened upon his approach.

'I don't know which sight makes me hungrier, that breakfast or you.' Balisel's languid voice traversed the space between them like a slow bow wave across a still lake.

She stood framed in the open doorway, one hand resting lightly on her hip, her head cocked slightly on top of her long neck. She was dressed in an airy concoction of floral silks that swayed in the light, warm breeze wafting in from the open balcony. As she walked towards him, the silks moulded themselves to her body, displaying virtually every curve. Her breasts rippled enticingly against the fabric and the smile on his face widened with every passing second as, once more, his body responded in a familiar way.

'Well, I know what *I'm* having,' he replied, by now laughing. Balisel threw back her head and chuckled with him as he swept her up in a bear hug. The silent attendant, his eyes now averted, slid past them and out of the room.

'Oh! I can't tell you how good it is to see you again, sister.'

She pulled her head back and focused on his mouth. Her eyes lifted to his and, in them, he saw all he needed to know. But there would be time later to fulfil the unspoken promises they made to each other in their glance. For now, there was more urgent business and Navarr, albeit reluctantly, released his hold.

'I need your advice,' he began, as she slid out of his grasp. 'Since the business of the other week, I have been thinking about what to do to restore the status quo.'

Balisel raised a perfectly waxed eyebrow. 'You think there is a chance of that?'

'Oh yes. Once Linnayen is returned to her usual self – and that is only a matter of time – I have no doubt that she will want my presence once more.'

Navarr's voice contained a confidence that was born more from hope than fact and Balisel knew him well enough to suspect it. She loved her brother, though, and did not wish to see him despondent. He had sounded so dejected – almost crestfallen – when he told her what had happened with Linnayen. Then, as the days passed and he had learned that his fate was to be virtual exile, he had become angry. He had not worked for so long, so hard and at great personal sacrifice to see it all trickle away after one ridiculous incident, he told her. They must meet, he said. Then they would work out how their fortunes could be re-established.

'That's good, Durroc,' she said, then walked towards the balcony, beckoning him to follow. 'Come. Let's talk. But let's not allow this wonderful breakfast to go to waste, eh?'

She made herself comfortable on one of the two padded daybeds and began pouring coffee. Meanwhile, Navarr activated the isolation shield to give them the privacy they needed. A slight shivering of the air above the parapet was the only evidence of the invisible wall that now sealed off both their voices and their bodies to any prying eyes and ears, whilst allowing them to still partake of the view. Not that they were interested in the cityscape below.

Balisel handed a cup of dark, aromatic mocha to her brother and began summarising. 'If you recall, before this situation, we spoke of disrupting the peace treaty by means of a death – apparently accidental, of course.'

'I remember,' he replied. 'The Ki was to be instrumental in the death of her husband, thereby returning us to conflict.'

'And this would have suited both our aims and the Order's.' Balisel cleared her throat before continuing. 'However, now that things have changed, I think we could take a different path. I've been playing with a few ideas …' She adjusted her position to settle herself further back on the couch.

'This is my favourite, so far,' she continued, unable to restrain the glee in her voice. 'How would it be if a band of Earthan rebels were to kidnap the Ki?'

Navarr pondered the idea briefly before working through the scenario. 'The Altanis would be furious. There'd be chaos.'

'Correct. And what if, in the kidnap attempt, the Ki's husband was ... how can I put this nicely?' Her perfect brows furrowed in a show of mock concern, then she shrugged her shoulders. 'Oh, I can't ... Let's say killed?'

He smiled conspiratorially. 'Then the Earthans, too, would be enraged and, of course, baying for blood.'

'Quite so, mayhem all round. Not a great time for a royal wedding, especially an *alien* royal wedding, eh?'

Navarr's mind raced alongside his beautiful sister's as he listed the likely consequences. 'The Altani embassy would be outraged. The Union would demand instant action, reprisals and the like. The Earthans would be grieving for the loss of their favourite prince, why did we ever get involved with these aliens, and so on. There would be utter turmoil.' He spoke quickly, trying to keep up with the thoughts inside his head. 'Opponents in both camps would decry the untrustworthiness of the other. Perhaps the kidnap on Earth and the murder of the Ki-consort might be followed with a raid by Union pirates in kneejerk retaliation for the terrible atrocity? Tempers would be flaring all over the galaxy ...'

She matched his smile. 'Yes, deliciously chaotic,' she said gaily. 'You understand, Durroc, the rebels – kidnappers – would be mercenaries, *our* mercenaries, and they will, of course, hold her somewhere quite safe and impregnable until – and this is the part you'll really like – until *you* come to the rescue! Imagine it: her former chief of security, currently serving his Ki quietly on a trade mission, offers up crucial knowledge about the rebels. He and only he is able to trace them by calling upon an old contact. This he does and then insists on leading the force that rescues her.'

'Yes! Of course!' Navarr's eyes were afire with the whirl of thoughts behind them.

Balisel went on. 'You realise, if the Ki were to be heroically saved by her former chief aide – the only man she had ever been able to trust in the past, now the only man she can trust in the future

– who proves his loyalty by saving her life once again … Well, you can see where this might lead, yes?'

He certainly could. This could be his way back in. Into her favour – and her bed. How could she deny him after that?

Balisel leaned forward and delicately lifted a small glazed pastry from the platter, placing it onto the palm of her fine white hand. She sucked her fingers clean of the sticky honey coating before speaking again.

'Of course, there is another consideration. I'm sure the Order of Sumere would be happy to support if not more actively join in the melee. It rather gives them exactly what they want too.'

Navarr nodded his agreement. 'More importantly, it gets us off *their* hook.'

'And, with your restoration, puts us in a position where they no longer *have* a hook – not one that matters, anyway.'

The corners of her full mouth turned up and the conspiratorial smile extended to her eyes, narrowing the ice-blue slits. She had done it again. He could always rely on her.

Navarr stood up and came around the table. Placing a hand on the back of the couch, he leaned over her long frame. He could see the deep V of her cleavage beneath the flimsy silk. With his other hand he gently brushed one strap of her dress down over her shoulder. She wore nothing underneath. He knelt in front of her, as if paying homage to her beauty and her superiority, then slowly, his eyes never leaving her face, he slid his hand up into the warm space between her legs. At the same time he leaned forward, focusing on the exposed rose-coloured nipple and his mouth opened to suck it greedily.

The fine pastry, so expertly crafted by a young apprentice chef deep below in the hotel's vast kitchen, tumbled from her hand, showering the dark red velvet cushions with flaky crumbs as her hands moved to encircle his head. Breakfast was always one of Balisel Navarr's favourite meals.

As they had done once before, so long ago it seemed now, Tariik Min allowed himself to be pinned to the ground by a laughing Evica. She sat astride him, her wild red hair falling across her face, its strands tangled over her eyes and stuck to the wetness on her lips. He could not imagine any creature more beautiful or more heart-stirring and he still sometimes had to pinch himself to believe it was all real. *Surely no man could be this lucky!*

'You should know by now, my love, never to leave your right side undefended. I'll *always* best you,' she affectionately boasted.

Tariik smiled. 'That's what makes it fun.' He gently brought her face down to his and kissed her. When they finally parted he spoke again. 'Take advantage of me every day, I'll not complain.'

Evica giggled and tussled with him. They rolled around on the floor in a flurry of bedsheets, the squeals of their laughter drowning out the voice emanating from the companel.

'… awaits. Do you permit entry?'

The sheets suddenly stopped moving and the air they contained allowed them to billow silently to the floor, outlining the two entwined figures.

'Did you hear something?' It was Tariik.

'No. You're just trying to distract me …' Again there were muffled chortles of laughter and a quick squeal as Evica continued in her search for Tariik's more sensitive spots. The linens, once more, were on the move.

'Do you permit entry?' The simulated human voice spoke again, this time a little louder.

They both sat bolt upright and turned to look at each other like two small children caught in a mischievous act. Tariik smiled, his raised eyebrow asking the same question of Evica. She dug him hard in the ribs.

Tariik spoke out loud to the comsystem. 'Who is it?'

Evica glared silently at him. He was not supposed to be there. It was unspoken, of course, and although most people accepted that it happened between young couples, it was not still considered proper behaviour in Altani culture to have sex before the couple were married.

From the gauze-covered panel came a clear voice.

'It's me … Linnayen.' It still sounded strange to say her own name, but she persisted. She knew she would eventually get used to it. 'Can I come in?'

'Oh … Yes,' Evica replied, getting to her feet and fumbling to gather the bedclothes around her naked body. 'But hang on a minute. I'm not dressed.'

Tariik, too, jumped up. He was quite naked and Evica happily took in the sight of his taut buttocks and flat, strong stomach. He looked around for his clothes, most of which had been distributed unevenly around the room and across various pieces of furniture by Evica some hours before. Ever the tactician, he began gathering up the garments in a quickly planned circuitous route and, within a minute, he had them all. With a last, lingering glance at the still-naked Evica and a mischievous wink, he ducked swiftly through a door into the dressing-room where he intended to remain until the Ki had left.

She could not help but smile at the closing door. He was her life, all she would ever need. Despite the stories she had heard that marriage eventually became boring and routine, the romance soon fading, she felt certain that she would still be head over heels in love with Tariik even when they were bent with age and comparing wrinkles. She had so much to look forward to and the knowledge made her glow deep down in her very soul.

'Evica … Are you still there?' Linnayen's concerned voice interrupted her reverie and she quickly set about putting on her wrap.

'Yes! Come on in.' The panel slid back. Linnayen, dressed simply in a knee-length green tabard over black leggings, entered the room. She scanned the space and her brows furrowed.

'That's odd, I thought I heard Tariik's voice.'

Evica's eyes creased with embarrassment. 'Well, um, you did. He's just left.'

This news did not seem to have any impact on Linnayen – *the new Linnayen*, thought Evica. The old one – before the fall – would have bristled at her sister's boisterous behaviour.

The young Ki remained placid and open. 'Oh, that's a shame. I wanted to talk to you both about the wedding. I'd like your advice.'

Evica's mouth fell open with surprise. It was not like her sister to ask for anyone's help. She had always been so much in control. Then she remembered. *That was before.*

Linnayen was suddenly and acutely aware that the young woman – her sister – was undressed. 'Oh, I can see you're not really ready. Would you prefer it if I came back later?'

'Oh no ...' Evica was quick to assure her that she was welcome – now and at any time. They were, after all, sisters. 'Please. I'd like to talk. What did you want to ask?'

With that she sat down on the end of the bed and gestured for Linnayen to take an armchair opposite her.

'Well ...' Linnayen sighed heavily before continuing. 'This is all a little new to me – ceremonies and the like. I mean, I know before I used to do them all the time. That's what Beoraan says.'

'That's right,' Evica confirmed with a nod. 'It was a large part of your life. Meetings with officials, dinners, speeches, all sorts of ceremonies, rituals ...' A look approaching sheer horror began to cross Linnayen's face and Evica decided to shut up before she had her sister fleeing the room. 'But that was then. It's all right now. We all know things are different.'

'You mean *I'm* different,' Linnayen cut in, interpreting her sister's thoughts.

'Well, yes. But that's to be expected, and that's fine.' Evica got up and pulled a stool over to sit next to Linnayen. 'You've been very ill. And you're not better yet.'

'The doctors say it will take a long time before I'm back to my old self. But I'm not so sure that I will ever be back to the way I was. I mean – I feel like *this* is me now.' Although she tried hard not to sound pitiful, Linnayen could not hide the despair in her voice. 'It feels like I'll never remember everything again – or everyone. I'm so sorry. I know *you* all know *me*. But you are still strangers to me.'

Her voice rose in desperation and she was close to tears, not for the first time in the last few days. Evica leaned forward and took one of her sister's hands in her own. She squeezed it reassuringly.

'I know ... I know. This must be dreadful for you. None of us can imagine what you must be going through.'

The softness in the woman's voice and the obvious worry in her eyes finally did it. For so long Linnayen had tried to keep it all in, away from the prying, concerned eyes of all these strangers. But now, at last, she could not stop the blissful release of tears and sobs racked her thin frame.

She could not speak. All she could do – all she wanted to do – was cry, to let it all out, and Evica sat patiently next to her, alternately holding her hands and rubbing her arms. The salty liquid in her eyes blinded her temporarily, but she could hear Evica's voice trying to soothe away her pain. It was not really working, but Linnayen appreciated her sympathy anyway.

It was many minutes before the tears subsided. Evica knew then that this was a different Linnayen and that there was no guarantee that the old one would ever come back to them. All the years of preparation for leadership, the training, the memories, especially of their father – all gone, possibly forever. And in their place a new young woman, born into a strange and, at times, frightening new world, one that was not even her home-world. If the person who had been her sister never fully returned then *they* would all have to adjust, she reasoned. They could not – should not – expect her to mould herself according to their expectations of her. But that was what they had been doing, albeit unknowingly. Her mother, Beoraan, even Kevor Jax who, perhaps, had been the most understanding of them all.

Gradually, as Linnayen's spasms lessened and she allowed the air back fully into her lungs, Evica was able to provide the comfort the frightened young woman so badly needed.

'Linnayen, I understand. We've been stupid. Been trying to impose our memories onto you. Wanting you to be who we remembered.' She paused and took a deep breath. 'But you can't be, can you? That's not who you are anymore, is it?'

Through bleary eyes, the raven-haired young woman looked at her, shaking her head.

Evica continued. 'I thought so. I understand.' She patted Linnayen's hand. 'You be who you are – who you *must* be – and leave everyone else to me.'

Linnayen began to object. 'But the ceremonies, my position … I'm expected to do these things …'

Evica brushed aside her concerns with a wave of her hand. 'Don't worry about all that. I'll take care of it. The Ki's sister and mother can do all these things,' she assured her. 'You must rest. Take stock of yourself. Find somewhere quiet where you can gather your thoughts and work out what you want. Would you like that?'

Linnayen stared at the swirling patterns in the deep threads of the floor covering at her feet. *Go away? Away from all these people? Alone?* She was not sure. Hesitantly, she replied. 'That sounds nice. But where? Would I be alone, do you think?'

'I don't know where. This isn't our home planet. Perhaps Kevor Jax could suggest somewhere. And as for alone, no, of course not. If only for security reasons, you should be accompanied. Take anyone you feel comfortable with. Though Nen and Dr Mai should also go with you, just in case.'

Linnayen thought it over. It sounded good. Somewhere quiet. Only now, when the suggestion had been made, did she realise how badly she had wanted this. Time and space and freedom from the noise and the hubbub and the expectations, the responsibilities.

'Yes. You're right, Evica. I need to go away – for a little while.'

Evica smiled. 'I'll make the arrangements. I'll speak with your hus –'

Linnayen prevented her from finishing the sentence with a darting look.

'I mean the Ki-consort,' she concluded. 'I'm sure he'll want to help.'

Evica recalled the last few weeks. Formerly a little distant in his dealings with the Genaras, Jax had been almost friendly to her and her mother. They were all, she supposed, united in their concern for the confused Linnayen, whose body had mended well but whose emotions were still raw and tender.

Jax had surprised Evica by the many small kindnesses he had shown to his wife, like ordering fresh flowers in her room every day and organising a dressmaker to help her choose clothes that she would like, rather than those she had, effectively, inherited. It seemed to him that her old Altani wardrobe did not seem to suit the new Linnayen, who seemed more at ease in casual tunics and leggings rather than the formal dresses and gowns they had brought from Altan. Jax had also arranged that Linnayen's first excursion be a simple walk in the hospital's gardens late at night, in private, rather than with the usual groups of patients and visitors and, of more concern, the prying eyes of the media. He seemed to understand, too, that his wife was not the same person and Evica wondered if he secretly preferred the new version in much the same way she did.

She felt guilty about it but it could not be denied. There was much about the new Linnayen to like. Virtually all the old formality had gone and any reserve she retained was more due to shyness and insecurity now rather than aloofness. Her old businesslike style of dealing with people was gone, replaced by an uncommon politeness and consideration, and Evica had to admit that she was growing to like these new mannerisms. Her mother was not so taken with it though. Li-el was from a different generation, one more steeped in the traditions and behaviours of her forebears. Perhaps, too, thought Evica, she just misses the daughter she once knew. Beneath all her mother's hauteur and bravado, she had a genuine love for her daughters and it was hard for her to accept the changes she now saw had taken place.

Linnayen's words cut into her thoughts. 'But what about the wedding? I want to be here for that. I *must* be here. I imagine it will be expected of me, won't it?'

Evica had to admit she was right. There was no getting out of that ceremony. The Earthans would be mortified if, after having come all this way, the Ki did not attend her own sister's wedding. Besides, whoever this new sister was, she wanted her there to witness her and Tariik's happiness. She nodded her agreement.

'Yes. You must be here. Would you mind?'

'Oh no, not at all. I *want* to be there. In fact, that's what I came to see you about.'

'Yes, of course!' said Evica, remembering now her earlier words. 'You wanted my advice about something?' Evica gave her full attention.

'It's about Kevor Jax,' she began, and the nervousness crept into her eyes once more. 'I know he's my husband and all that. But he is still a stranger – to me, that is.'

'True,' Evica agreed. 'And the problem is?'

'Well, Beoraan tells me that we'll be expected to – well – act married in front of everyone. Be affectionate, if you know what I mean.' She stumbled on through the words, wringing her hands anxiously together as she spoke. 'He said there'll be dancing – although I don't know how to do that – at least, I don't *think* I do. And, well ...'

Linnayen swallowed nervously and her black eyebrows knitted together. She continued nervously. 'He said that we would be expected to be familiar with each other. To touch. Maybe even kiss, in public? Is that so? Will I have to kiss him?'

Evica smiled and a small giggle escaped from her mouth. She fixed on Linnayen's worried eyes.

'Well, that all depends.'

'On what?'

'On whether or not you *want* to.'

Linnayen's eyes travelled back to the pattern in the carpet. She tried to conjure up an image of the dark-haired young man and clearly saw his remarkable eyes looking back at her. They were as she had always seen them since she woke up from the accident – blank, non-committal. She could read nothing in them. No affection, no liking. He treated her with courtesy. Indeed, he had been unfailingly considerate. But there had been barely a trace of natural friendliness or warmth. She knew she had been monstrous to him in the past through her crazy affair with the awful Commander Navarr. But that was not her – not who she was now. She wanted to apologise and had, but how could she truly make amends? It was a continual source of distress for her and the thought forcing him to make a show of fondness for her was only going to rub salt into his wounds. She did not want this any more than she believed he did and, if there was any way of avoiding the predicament, she wanted to know how.

The only problem was that when she thought about him, in the rare, quiet moments she had come to crave, she felt herself softening. He may not want to show affection to her but she discovered to her secret pleasure that she wanted to show affection to him and she wondered, for what felt like the hundredth time, what his kisses might feel like. But maybe he would be repulsed at kissing her and she did not want to give him any more reasons to hate her.

She pulled her thoughts back from their private domain and looked back up at Evica. The laughter still bubbled in her sister's eyes.

'Oh, that's not the problem,' Linnayen said, the anxiety plain in her voice. 'Quite the reverse.'

Beoraan squinted against the glare of bright sunshine streaming in through the windows of the clubhouse. He was trying to focus on the silhouetted figure that was growing infinitesimally larger as it made its way towards him. It was now in the deep shade of a large tree, which in turn was framed by a backdrop of distant pale purple mountains made hazy in the summer glare. *More mountains!* Only these were different. 'Stately' was the word that came to Beoraan's mind. These mountains with their treeless contours were smooth, solid, almost regal in their bearing, not like the harsh outlines of the San Gabriels. These mountains were soft, welcoming. But you could sense their underlying strength and danger and he wondered if the Scottish people were like their mountains and high moors. He would soon find out.

A few seconds later, the figure stepped back out into the sunlight and Beoraan was able to make out his features. Light, sandy hair, broad shoulders, tall – over two metres, thought Beoraan – and long legs, which were clad in trousers of a light check pattern. He wore a short-sleeved, close-fitting tunic that highlighted a well-muscled chest and strong arms. Indeed, for such a big man, he looked very fit. There appeared to be not an ounce of fat anywhere on him. Without doubt, Joseph McCrae, at fifty-four years of age, was an impressive individual.

Duncan left Beoraan and went out through the French doors to meet his father. It had been at least two months since they had last met when Joe had come to see Duncan in a new Vacy Doyle play in London's Soho. Although not his first opportunity to watch Duncan perform, he had enjoyed the experience and was proud of his son's achievements in the theatre. But Joe McCrae would have approved of just about anything his son undertook; his only reserve was that Duncan had somewhat followed in his mother's flighty footsteps, and that was a little worrying.

In the warmth of the afternoon, the two men hugged each other affectionately and Beoraan noted the rapport between them as their heads nodded in instant conversation and their voices raised up in laughter. They had a strong relationship, Beoraan reflected, as it should be between father and son – not like it was between Jax and his father. He had not been the only one to notice the reserve that hung like a sinking fog in the air between the two

Bashir men. There was not the openness, the friendship that these two golden-haired men shared. It was a bond born of unique circumstance as Duncan's mother, would-be celebrity-cum-actress Jemima Heaney, had walked away from both father and son when the boy was only twelve years old. For some few years they lived in hope that she might come back and, more through lack of funds than any sense of duty, Jemima visited from time to time. She would love to stay longer, she always explained, but so-and-so was putting on a new play and needed her for this part or that. The excuses became background noise to Duncan's young ears and, eventually, as could be expected, father and son became closer.

Duncan led his father over to where Beoraan was seated by the window. The old man got to his feet in order to take the outstretched hand that was offered as a greeting by the tall, sharp-eyed man.

'Oh, please, don't get up,' he said with the trace of a lilting Scottish accent.

'Too late,' Beoraan replied with a short laugh.

'Father, this is Sen-Beoraan, privy counsellor to the Ki of Altan.' Duncan gestured towards the old man. 'And, Sen-Beoraan, this is my father, Joseph McCrae.'

'Just Joe will be fine, Mr Beoraan,' he said self-deprecatingly. 'We don't stand on ceremony in these parts.'

The counsellor smiled. 'Then I, too, will have to be less formal. But please forgive me if I lapse. We Altanis are very proper and correct in most things. Perhaps it is a failing.' It was both a statement and a question and Beoraan noticed that Joe McCrae did not rise to the bait but instead sat down quietly.

His eyes locked onto Beoraan's.

'My son tells me you want to ask a favour.'

A waiter arrived with a tray of drinks and small squares of cut bread and dry biscuits upon which sat various toppings. Beoraan held back until the tray was placed on the table in front of them and the waiter had left before continuing.

'That is correct. But it is rather a large favour. And, I must warn you, it could be dangerous.'

Joe McCrae raised his eyebrows and, with a look of amused disbelief, turned to his son. 'Duncan, what is this? Some joke?'

'No, Dad. Hear him out.' Duncan's tone was as serious as Joe had ever heard and there was something in its solemnity that told him he needed to give the old man his full attention.

'Mr McCrae, we need your help.'

Joe looked straight into the old man's red-rimmed eyes. '*You* ... want *my* help? You know how I feel about your lot?'

'We most certainly do. You have often and loudly spoken out against we – as you put it – aliens, and the new Galactic Union. I am sure no one in the council is in any doubt about where your allegiance lies,' Beoraan replied swiftly.

'And you still want a favour from me? You must be mad,' Joe scoffed, pouring some of the dark amber liquid into a fine cut-glass tumbler and adding no ice or water to the whisky. He was enjoying the afternoon. His game had been excellent, he was with his beloved son again and he was having intriguing sport with an alien. He had no intention of ruining everything by diluting the whisky's rich flavour or dulling its warmth.

'He's not mad,' Duncan answered. 'Listen to him, Dad.'

Raising just one sceptical eyebrow, Joe McCrae nodded at Beoraan to continue.

'As you know, there is to be a royal wedding very soon, an event at which many of the most important and influential people from both our planets will be gathered.'

Joe certainly did know about the wedding. He had been invited but he did not approve of the fiasco. He knew as well as the Altani counsellor that it was all a big publicity stunt, the aim of which was to show the aliens in a good light. The Galactic Union may now exist but it still needed selling to the masses, he thought wryly.

Beoraan continued. 'It is possible that certain elements ... certain *groups* may see this wedding – or the wedding day itself – as the perfect opportunity to commit an atrocity.'

'You mean some sort of terrorism?' asked McCrae, now becoming interested in the scenario Beoraan was describing to him.

'Correct.'

Joe shook his head in genuine concern. 'That'd be terrible.'

'Again, correct,' Beoraan concurred. 'And, of course, we are putting in place the most stringent security measures, as you would understand. Believe me, Mr McCrae, it serves neither of our purposes to see our fellow countrymen and women hurt or killed. I think you would agree?' Beoraan was a master of statecraft and knew the importance of establishing the common ground before asking for something that might not be willingly given. He could almost feel McCrae leaning to his way of thinking. 'But even the best security may not be enough, Mr McCrae.'

'I said it before and I'll say it again.' Joe's voice was stern and Beoraan feared he was going to have a harder job on his hands than he thought. 'It's Joe. Call me Joe.'

Duncan smiled across to the old man, who acknowledged his look with relief and understanding.

'Sorry … Joe.' Beoraan was highly uncomfortable with the level of informality but hid it well, resisting the urge to squirm in his seat. 'As I was saying, security will be tight. But the fact is we are still going to be vulnerable – unless we have a little inside information. And that's where *you* might be able to help.'

Joe looked aghast and went to rise from his chair. His voice was a low growl. 'Are you saying you think I'm linked to terrorists in some way? Because if you are, you can get out of my sight and out of my golf club this bloody minute!'

'Dad!' Duncan leaned across and placed a calming hand on his father's knee. 'He's not saying that! Quite the opposite. If you'll let the man finish.'

'I am so sorry, Mr M – Joe. I fear you have misunderstood. I have not explained myself very well.' Beoraan hurriedly continued before he upset Joe McCrae any further. So this is what they mean about the Highland temper, he thought. He had been warned that retired Councillor McCrae was a volatile man, but Duncan had assured him it was largely bravado. 'His bark's worse than his bite,' the young man had said, and now he knew what he had meant.

'What he's saying, Dad, is that they want you to infiltrate these people,' Duncan went on.

'That's right, Joe. We have intelligence that there is a suspected group or terrorist cell known as –' Beoraan stopped himself mid-sentence, more for the dramatic effect than anything. 'Oh, I have to ask that you keep the following information strictly to yourself.'

'Of course,' McCrae agreed, now calm again.

'Thank you.' Beoraan feigned a look of relief. *Of course you'll keep it confidential. And I wouldn't be telling you this if I had not already had you screened in more ways than you would believe could exist.*

'The group we suspect is known as the Order of Sumere. Have you heard of them?' And this was the last test. Beoraan would know from McCrae's reaction whether or not their faith in him was justified.

Joe McCrae looked from Beoraan to his son, then back again. His face gave nothing away. He waited for many long seconds before answering.

'Actually, I have.'

Chapter Twenty-four

Marcus di Luca smiled enthusiastically across the desk to the young Ki of Altan, happy to be included in the discussion.

'I agree with young Jax. Santorini is an excellent location,' he pronounced. 'It will be perfect. And I would be very happy to prepare the villa for your arrival.'

'Thank you, professor.' Jax added his appreciation, although he felt a tinge of embarrassment at the old man's use of the epithet 'young'. He was, after all, twenty-six years old now and a married man.

'Thank you, Professor di Luca.' Linnayen spoke quietly. She had not played much part in the conversation. Two days earlier, Evica had asked Jax for his advice about a possible retreat for Linnayen once the wedding was over. Evica had explained Linnayen's feeling about finding a quiet place to gather her thoughts and continue her convalescence and he had fully agreed. He had not needed to spend much time in deliberation either before recommending his mother's family villa on Santorini, an island of the Cyclades, a jewel of the Aegean Sea and fabled site of the lost city of Atlantis. It would be perfect – remote, beautiful, a peaceful haven.

'Oh, you are most welcome,' the professor concluded, and his eyes shone with pleasure at the thought of returning to the wonderfully serene whitewashed villa atop the high cliffs of the ancient settlement of Neothira.

'I hope you won't mind missing the wedding, professor,' Evica added solicitously.

'Oh, not at all, my dear.'

Jax smiled at the way his old mentor had taken a liking to his sister-in-law and had dropped the last vestige of formality when addressing her.

'If truth be told, I'm not up to grand ceremonies these days – not that I ever was.' Di Luca revelled in his persona as a scholar and a recluse. It was not that he disliked the company of people, more that he was not afraid to be alone. He enjoyed solitude and felt himself fortunate that he had been able to lead exactly the sort of life to which he aspired: one of quiet contemplation and solitary study. He had, of course, had to make compromises from time to time in order to earn a living, such as undertaking the tutoring of the young Bashir prince. But that task had turned out to be more pleasurable than he could have foreseen and it still afforded him plenty of private time for his philosophising and studies – as would hosting the young Ki at the villa. No, he was not at all unhappy to be missing the wedding.

'But I can see that you are excited, eh? As you should be, child, as you should be. Why, I recall my young charge here in the months before his wedding. We never saw him without a smile on his face.' Di Luca laughed fondly at his memories, whilst Jax squirmed. His smile was forced and agonised and Evica responded to the humour in the situation with a restrained giggle. Linnayen, though, lowered her eyes. The poor man was uncomfortable enough without being reminded of unhappy times – times which *she* had ruined for him. The guilt surfaced again and she wondered once more if there was a way she could make it up to him.

'I imagine it was much the same for you, my dear lady, although I don't suppose you remember much about it, eh?'

Linnayen suddenly realised that di Luca's question was directed at her and she struggled to regain her thoughts.

Jax came to her aid. 'No, professor, the Ki cannot remember those events. But she will, in time.' He had meant his words to be reassuring – both to himself and Linnayen – then realised with a start that if or when she remembered, things would quickly go back to the way they had been. A frown crossed his face. He liked the Linnayen she seemed to have become. Without doubt she was kinder and more compassionate, but how much of that was due to her weakened physical and emotional state rather than any new wellspring of formerly hidden character traits he did not know – and he was not sure he wanted to find out.

'Yes, I'm sure I will remember. Especially with everyone being so understanding and kind.' Linnayen turned to face Evica and Jax. 'You really have been so patient. And you've gone to so much trouble for me. Thank you.'

'Oh, there's no need to thank us.' Evica's words were warmly spoken. 'All we want is for you to get better.'

'And we'll do whatever we can to make that happen,' Jax finished for her.

Suddenly, without warning, she was transported back to a room much like this one. A pale roseate sun was shining through an open window. Floor-length curtains of a fine yellow fabric billowed in warm breeze and a man, dressed in a loose robe of some shimmering material she could not place, was sitting cross-legged on a highly polished wooden floor. He was smiling across at her. His face was not old. His skin was olive and his hair was dark like her own and worn long. It was adorned with two long, thin golden ropes that hung on either side of his cheeks and she knew, without knowing how she knew, that they signified his authority, his rank. She could see his lips moving but could not hear the words. He seemed to be urging her to do something – something she was reluctant to do. But there was a fondness in his mannerisms. He was smiling, almost laughing out loud. There was a board game on the floor in front of him and his large hand was drawing away from it as though he had just made his move. Perhaps he was urging her to take her turn. Then his voice burst, as rich and as warm as hot chocolate, into her consciousness.

'… must do whatever you can to make that happen. I know you don't want to. But that's the game, little one, and you must aim to win.'

'I don't want to win – not against *you*. So I won't play it.' Her voice, determined, tinny and small, came from somewhere behind her consciousness and she knew it was her, as she had once been, when she was a child.

'You can't just opt out, Linney.' He was laughing at her. 'There's a puzzle to be solved and, besides, you're not a quitter – not *my* little Ki.' With that he stretched a hand over to her and began to tickle her tummy. She collapsed into a fit of giggles, tightly clenching her muscles in the vain hope that it would stop her from laughing so much.

'Daddy! Daddy!' She squealed with delight. 'Oh, stop it, Daddy! Stop it! Daddeee!'

'Linnayen … Linnayen?'

Evica's calm but insistent tones entered the memory, blocking it out, forcing it to recede back into a smoky distance. Linnayen's eyes brimmed with warm tears and she took a large gasp of air, forcing her eyes to refocus on the room, on Jax, the old professor and the concerned face of her fiery-haired sister.

'Are you all right? What happened?' Evica asked again.

'I saw our father, Evica! I remembered him!' The tears trickled down her cheeks. 'Oh! He was … Oh, Evica! He was so …'

As the tears streamed down her face, Evica cradled her sister's small frame. No one could have predicted that when the memories finally began to return, not all of them would bring joy or comfort. Linnayen's brief glimpse of her father – whilst it was a happy moment – had flooded her with a renewed sense of loss. Her mourning was instantaneous and overwhelming.

Suddenly reminded of Yenshar Genara, their beloved father who had died nearly three years earlier, Evica, too, could not hold back her tears. If only he could have been with them. She also missed him and, as the weeks leading up to her wedding grew fewer, he had been ever more in her thoughts.

The two women, melded together in their sad embrace, sobbed quietly, each taking a measure of comfort from the other. Di Luca and Jax looked on in silence, the one trying to work out what had just happened, the other realising that this was a private moment and that they were intruders. After a few moments, the old professor felt a slight tug on his sleeve as Jax motioned for him to join him in leaving the room.

Balisel had to admit that there were some pleasures this planet had to offer that she could very much get used to. In the last few days, before arriving in the much-heralded city of Athens – apparently the cradle of Earthan civilisation, according to an enthusiastic, rosy-faced hotel clerk – she had experienced scuba-swimming with a piscine species called a hammerhead shark under the crystal waters of the Red Sea. Then she had played the part of an ancient Egyptian queen called Cleopatra in a clever simulation play. The hotel had a library of them. She could have chosen to be a Celtic warrior queen called Boudicca, a French emperor's mistress named Josephine, a twenty-fifth century Luna freedom fighter known as L'abeille Petite, or any one of a hundred famous and infamous men and women from Earthan history. She had settled on the famed seductress Egyptian ruler after reading in the blurb that she had married her brother. It seemed appropriate at the time. But after a day of being bathed, oiled, massaged and partaking of an array of sensual and edible delights, she had been a little upset to discover that the queen's marriage had, after all, been a cold and political affair, holding none of the forbidden pleasures she had been expecting. No matter, she thought, and turned her mind, as the evening drew in, to other more pressing matters and the certain knowledge that any unfulfilled desires would soon be quenched.

It was time to contact Durroc, who would by now be on his way to Athens. He was due to arrive later that evening with a party of twenty senior Union politicians who would be attending the wedding. It was unfortunate, but her brother was not allowed close access to the Ki or any other members of the royal household anymore. Durroc had told her that he had been allocated two new aides, both of whom were selected and trained by Tariik Min who, she might recall, was a weapons expert. Durroc had no doubt, he said, that they had been briefed to do more than assist him in his duties should the need arise and he was quite certain that they would be quick and efficient.

The fact that her twin was being so closely watched did not particularly bother Balisel. The planned kidnap attempt would never be connected to him – or her, for that matter. The mercenaries she had commissioned through the capable Carri Aqua were, even now, standing by, ready to be set upon their target, waiting only to know who, where and when. They would work out the how and, it went without saying, they did not need to know why. The honed skills of the two guards assigned to her brother would never be needed and all he would have to do was play along with the charade. All too soon he would volunteer himself to lead the rescue party and, if need be, Min's buffoons would be disposed of at that time.

It was all a game – a deadly serious one, of course, but that only made it more interesting. Balisel squirmed with excitement. The mere thought of what they were about to do – kidnap the Ki and kill her husband – gave her a deep-seated thrill, and the knowledge that not even the Order of Sumere knew their full intent was doubly delicious. They would, as the Earthans put it, 'kill two birds with one stone', although she hoped they would not have to take the saying too literally. Durroc wanted his regal lover back and for his power to be restored. As for Balisel, it would not be too terrible to lose both the Ki-consort and the Ki. Change meant opportunity and opportunity meant the chance for profit. She and Durroc were a highly resourceful team, the perfect balance with her talent for acquiring wealth and his gift for leadership. Even without the Ki she had no doubt that Durroc would regain his position, if not on Altan, then somewhere else. Earth, perhaps?

Balisel smiled as she pressed the flat touch screen next to the bed. It was time to talk to her brother – to let him know that all the arrangements had been made and to remind him that she was, as ever, looking forward to seeing him again later that night.

Kumiko Toyotomi looked resplendent in an embroidered kimono of gold silk. Her ancient eyes slowly swept the marbled ballroom, stopping every so often to focus on the richly attired men and women as they danced, and of others standing at the edges of the room, huddled together in their self-important cliques, heads nodding, mouths laughing. Dressed in their finery, assured in their movements, unconcernedly comfortable in the knowledge that they were the chosen ones, the privileged few, society's upper echelon. Invitations to the embassy ball had been sent only to the most important and influential members of the government and civil service, although for the sake of acquiring media attention, a sprinkling of celebrities and high-flying business leaders had also been added to the mix. In common with most of the other amalgamated countries, Nippon-ko had chosen to hold a function for Lady Evica Genara and Tariik Min to honour them on the occasion of their wedding. The council had sanctioned the ball, which was yet another attempt to harmonise relations with the planets of the Union.

It was not often these days that Kumiko attended grand functions such as these, but there had been no escaping this one – not that she would have wanted to. There was an undeniable fascination in seeing the aliens at close quarters and it was a chance to watch all the players in action, laid out before her like pieces on her chessboard. She wondered how she would move them or whether she would even need to. She would prefer not to get too involved. She had enough to do already, what with the council and her other interests. No, watching was best in this case. She had to admit to feeling a little tired these days, which was, she told herself, perfectly understandable for someone of a hundred and seven years. Luckily, her mind was as sharp as a blade still, and the knowledge that she could, if she chose, manipulate the thoughts and actions of nearly every person in the room still gave her a ripple of satisfaction.

Just then, amid the whirl of dancers, Kumiko saw them. The female, her dark red hair falling like tendrils of fire past her waist, wore a trailing purple gown. Her arms were painted in intricate patterns of sepia swirls and decorated with glittering gems in the ceremonial Altani fashion. She looked to Kumiko like a primitive heathen. The male, black-haired and blue-eyed, was dressed in a loose shirt of cobalt satin tucked tightly into black dress trousers. His waist was drawn flat by a broad cummerbund of silver cloth. He at least looked more presentable, but, Kumiko remembered, he was still half-fish. The Dasnirians retained a thin web of skin on the lower half of their hands and toes, a remnant of an earlier stage of their evolution. The only sign that she felt and then suppressed her revulsion was a lifting of one perfectly sculpted grey eyebrow.

The couple's dance was more coordinated than that of others in the room, but even from this distance the old woman could see the light in their eyes and the way the bodies seemed to strain to get closer to each other. There was fire between these two lovers and the matriarch concluded that theirs was no political union, unlike that of the female's sister.

The Ki of Altan, leader of the new Galactic Union was not present on this evening, her recent accident and ensuing convalescence having been given as the reason, although Kumiko had her doubts. More likely, she thought, the noble lady would not deign to meet the great-grandmother of a suitor she so blatantly rejected. Her great-grandson James had not been particularly deflated by the incident, but it was still an insult to her family and to the Toyotomi name, made worse because it came from an alien whore. Not that she would have wanted her noble house tainted with the foreigner's blood. Not like the president of the council! How typical, she thought, that the Bashir popinjay would jump at the chance to defile his own family's bloodline in order to further his ambitions. He had damned his son to a life of misery in pursuit of personal kudos and that was something no Toyotomi would ever contemplate – unless the reward was sufficiently pecuniary. But the Bashirs had gained not a cent from the transaction and that was both stupid and unforgivable.

The old woman's thoughts ran on. *Now we are stuck with the barbarian hordes! Ah, but that won't be for much longer.* Ennio had brought her news from the Order. Only he knew of her longstanding attachment to their cause and that underneath the skin of the seemingly liberal council member lurked a very private, very right-wing fanatic. Not even Ennio's wife, her own granddaughter, knew of Kumiko's connection to the terrorist organisation and was certainly not aware that her husband had for nearly three decades been a leading member and financier of the highly secretive group.

Ennio's news spelled the end of the new Galactic Union, hopefully for good! The planned kidnapping of the alien ruler was a brilliant idea, and if the son of the foolish Bashir peacock was lost in the process then so be it. At least there would be no one to follow after the father and that had to be advantageous. She reflected on the years that had been. Kumiko had always spoken out in favour of uniting with the aliens. This had suited her purpose, as it was the ideal cover for her activities within the Order. Meanwhile, David Bashir had been her adversary, holding firmly to the view that to unite with the aliens would mean disaster. If only he knew how closely his views were to her own – but not for the same reasons. He feared the new Galactic Union would dominate Earth and its resources, that any merger would be unbalanced and to Earth's disadvantage. He also truly believed on religious and cultural grounds that the races were too disparate to merge successfully, whilst Kumiko just despised them per se because they were pagans and of a lower order. They were an affront to her lineage. The thought of them interbreeding and mingling with humans made her squirm with disgust.

But for now, Kumiko Toyotomi had to hide her true feelings – at least until the Order assumed power. Only then could she reveal herself. She had discovered long, long ago that in the game of politics, it paid to keep oneself hidden. It was the only way to win. And she felt nothing but derision for soft-headed idealists who played the game with the aim of changing the world for the better. *Idiots! Did they not know that altruism was the most selfish pastime there was? Why does anyone do good deeds if not to feel better about themselves?* At least she was open about her ambitions – or would be if anyone had been allowed to see inside her heart. Everything she did, or would do, was for the advancement of the Toyotomi family, its fortunes, power and status.

Never reveal who you are! Why even Ennio Nori did not really know her, despite their intensely secret relationship. He was entirely loyal to her and the only one who knew of her true leanings. She had taught him the value of presenting one face to the world and another in private. Thus, to his business colleagues and all other members of his family, he was believed to be an ordinary, if somewhat dull man, middle-aged before he was in his thirties. Loyal, good head for business, but essentially dreary and nondescript. In his heart and only ever in the company of his grandmother-in-law was he a proud patriot, and he took a furtive delight in being party to Kumiko's innermost thoughts.

He had attained a high position within the Order and was pleased at Oleander's progress with the alien woman. It had been his idea to pursue the dead ambassador's theories and it seemed that the imbecile Byers had been on the right track. The Navarr woman *did* have something to do with the assassination attempt on Linnayen Genara, possibly even the twin brother too – although he appeared to be of little use to them for now. He was no longer close to the person of the Ki and Ennio wondered why. He had been the Ki's favoured envoy before her wedding to the Bashir prince and had been in charge of her security during the journey to Earth. Now he had been placed at the head of a trade mission when, logically, he should have stayed where he was. Had he fallen from favour? Had people close to the Ki also suspected Durroc Navarr of something underhand and would this impact upon the Order's latest plot?

There were still too many unknowns for his liking. But, if Oleander's hunches and his suspicions were correct, the alien twins were a deeply duplicitous pair and, therefore, easily malleable.

People who had secrets were the perfect tools, thought Nori. After all, what more compelling motive could there be than that of self-preservation, the oldest and strongest of human instincts? The female's proposal to kidnap the Ki and, if possible, kill young Bashir in the process was a masterstroke. It would, within hours, blow apart the peace treaty, thereby returning them all to a state of war and, as Kumiko had endlessly reminded him, present limitless opportunities for profit.

Nori's eyes scanned the ballroom floor to the dais where his grandmother-in-law sat, stiff-backed, unsmiling, unblinking. For the benefit of any eyes that may be watching them, a well-practised look of almost venomous hatred passed briefly between them and the sham that they were mortal enemies was once more reinforced.

'Well, well … Ennio! You're the last person I would have expected to see here.'

A large hand landed solidly on his shoulder. He jumped in response and, fleetingly, worriedly, he wondered if its owner had intuited his thoughts. The voice was deep and accented and familiar. He spun round to see the tanned face and brown eyes of Joe McCrae.

'Joseph! You startled me.'

'Thought as much. You looked a million miles away. And I'd be a liar if I said I wouldn't like to know what you were thinking.'

Nori raised his eyebrows and scoffed at the suggestion that he had any thoughts of any great interest. He hoped his expression hid the knowledge that his thoughts always ran rather deeper than they often appeared.

'Then you'd be heartily bored, old man – unless you have a profound interest in gilts.'

Joe McCrae was not to be put off. 'Oh, come now. I'm sure you've more on your mind than stocks and shares? Like, for example – and harking back to my original comment – what brings a man like you to a gala like this? It's hardly your sort of thing, given your sentiments.'

Nori glared at the Scotsman. 'Surely you would know that Grandmother requested the family to be here – *all* the family. She wants to show the aliens how well she likes them.' His distaste was apparent in the sneer with which he delivered the words.

'But not *you*, eh? Still the same, Ennio?' Joe asked pointedly. As far as he was concerned, it served no purpose to shilly-shally around the matter. They both knew how the other felt about aliens in general and the new Galactic Union in particular. Neither man had any liking for the way recent events were shaping Earthan history and both of them would have preferred a world as it was a decade or so ago. But that was where the similarity stopped. Joe McCrae was prepared to debate and argue the issues in an open forum. He believed in the power and validity of democracy, even when the resultant decisions were not as he would have liked. But he also knew that there were people like Nori for whom the ends justified the means and he disliked them as much as he did alien sympathisers like Nori's grandmother-in-law.

Nori looked up at the tall Scot. 'Well now, Joseph, that would hardly be appropriate these days, would it?' He added with a sneer, 'Given that we are all *friends* now ...'

McCrae laughed out loud. 'Aye, friends.' Then, in a quieter voice, he continued. 'But it's amazing how quickly things change. Friends one day, enemies the next. In a fast-changing world like this, one can never say how things will turn out, or what events might alter the status quo. Don't you think?'

The financier gave no outward sign of his discomfort with the way the conversation was developing. In fact, and to McCrae's surprise, a smile grew across his flat features.

'Joseph, are you trying to tell me something?' he asked wryly.

'Me?' the Scot returned, a look of feigned shock on his face. 'No! I'm just making a general observation. But perhaps you are – or would like to?'

Nori's face remained the same, the smile frozen there as if set in stone.

'Now what could I possibly have to tell you that you would want to hear? If you recall, you were never interested in anything *I* had to say.'

The look that passed between the two was pregnant with the memory of an occasion, many years before, when Nori had tried to persuade Joe McCrae to become involved in – as he had put it – 'a little project'. Joe remembered it well and still fumed in secret at what he had heard that day.

They had been seated next to each other at a London charity dinner for an environmental group. It was a glittering affair to which many business leaders and politicians had been invited, both due to the size of their bank accounts and because of the influence they could wield, if sufficiently pandered to. During the course of the evening the guests had been encouraged to part with their money through a series of party games, performances and auctions and, by the end of the night, the revellers' spirits were high. Everyone had had a good time and the charity had raised a considerable amount of money. It was in such an atmosphere that Nori had fouled the air with his quietly spoken suggestion that if McCrae really wanted to help the world, he might want to stop talking about it and actually do something. When Joe had asked him what he meant, Nori had told him that some people – he would not say if he knew them personally – were keen to take the battle against the alien hordes to a higher level. Instead of the interminable border skirmishes, the people Nori spoke of were investigating how much damage could be done on the aliens' home planets – perhaps with certain chemical compounds fed into essential life-support systems, or strategically placed detonation devices, places where the collateral damage would be deeply felt.

McCrae's good humour had dissipated like the sudden clearing of a morning mist and a chill anger had run the length of his spine. He had fought to remain calm.

'You mean acts of terrorism? Against non-combatants?'

'Don't you think that would give the Union cause to stop and think?' Nori had replied without the slightest trace of emotion. 'Perhaps the cost of colonising us would be greater than they would like to pay. I rather think it might help the cause, Joseph – our *mutual* cause, I should say.'

The financier's smooth voice had droned on a little longer and he had spoken of a group, going by the name of the Sumerians, that had been covertly recruiting all manner of people. He had asked Joe if he knew of them, to which Joe had shook his head, wondering all the while how closely Nori was involved with these terrorists.

Joe recalled how incongruous Nori's words had sounded against the backdrop of people's laughter and the music that filled the room. His expression had been interpreted by Nori to be one more of intrigued surprise than horror. Could it be possible, Joe had wondered, that the man had absolutely no comprehension of what he was suggesting? The wanton slaughter of innocents? The mass destruction, without warning, of ordinary people going about their everyday business. He had no great liking for the superior manners of the Altanis, or the green-tinged, sly-looking Huthons, or the brutal Autabronis, but they were, basically, humanoid and just as worthy to live in peace and happiness as he was. McCrae's anger and dislike was of their politics, not their people – no cause was worth the senseless killing of civilians.

His reply to Nori, when it finally came, had left the man in no doubt of his feelings. His voice was low and as hard as the granite of his mountain homeland.

'Do you honestly think that I would be interested in supporting acts of sheer bloody murder – even against the bloody aliens? What kind of mongrel do you think I am?'

Nori had shrugged his shoulders. He had, it seemed, misjudged the councilman, but he was not particularly worried. In the event that McCrae said something about their conversation, Nori's defence would be that it was all rumour, whispers, nothing that anyone could not have heard about already. Mere speculation.

As it turned out, Joe McCrae *had* said something. He had related the conversation to his friend and occasional supporter David Bashir, the then newly appointed secretary for primary production. However, as time had gone on and the war against the Union of Planets had continued to be waged in much the same way, both men had let the matter drop, preferring to push the information back to a corner of their minds for the time being. Now, twenty years later, it had resurfaced. When the old Altani counsellor Sen-Beoraan had spoken of the Order of Sumere, McCrae had instantly recounted these events and had been quite open about his brief encounter with Nori. As soon as he'd said the financier's name, Beoraan's sharp intake of breath told him it was something serious and, as the old man outlined what they would like him to do, he had had no hesitation in agreeing to help.

Thus it was that, two days before the wedding of the Altani princess and her Dasnirian partner, Joe McCrae was forcing himself to smile and be ingratiating with the despised Nori. *If this is what it takes to put paid to the terrorist bastards, then I'm up for it!*

Joe forced his features to adopt a smile. He had to convince Nori – and quickly – that he was, after all, one of them. Time was short and if there was anything to know he would not get too many chances to find it out.

'As I said, my old friend, times change, and we must change with them. This is not the world I want to grow old in.'

Friend! Nori thought. *Since when?* Whilst it was reassuring to hear that McCrae's views might be coming around to his own, Nori was too wily to believe that he had had an overnight conversion. He remained guarded.

'Really? So you finally want to change the world? By what means, though, Joseph? *That's* the question, eh? By what means?'

All good humour left the two men's eyes as each sized up the other.

'Well, Ennio, perhaps that's something we might discuss ...' McCrae let the thought drift away, but his eyes moved towards the terrace. There was no need to run the risk of being overheard and they had already been seen long enough in each other's company.

With a brief nod, the dark-skinned financier walked in the direction of the tall gilt-edged windows and McCrae, taking a brief glimpse of the room to see if anyone had been watching them, followed a couple of steps behind.

He did not notice Kumiko Toyotomi, still sitting in her armchair on the raised dais at the side of the room. The old woman's head was tilted back and she appeared to have fallen into a light sleep. It was one of her favourite poses, enabling her to watch the room from under half-closed eyelids and enjoy the comings and goings of the throng. She was intrigued to see her grandson-in-law in the company of her old adversary and could not help feeling a spasm of impatience at wanting to know what they were talking about. *Soon,* she thought. *He'll come and tell me everything and then I'll decide what needs to be done.*

The day had finally arrived. Evica, for all her usual exuberance, was feeling calm and at peace with herself. She had not a shadow of doubt about what she was going to do that day. Tariik was the one, her soulmate – a more complete partner she could not imagine and, in a few hours, they would be united forever. It was not, for her, an occasion for excitement but for fulfilment, a closing of the circle, and the knowledge gave her the most intimate feeling of satisfaction and happiness. She knew that Tariik, too, would be feeling exactly the same.

Her only regret was that the ceremony could not have taken place on either of their home-worlds, and she suspected that Linnayen now would not have been so insistent on an Earthan wedding. Since her sister's accident there had been such a change in the once formal, self-controlled young woman. Linnayen seemed to have lost all her guile and she was often confused and quite tearful. That was to be expected. As Linnayen herself had said, there was so much she no longer knew. All the years of training in statecraft and the subtleties of negotiation, all the history of both her own planet and that of the other member planets – all gone now. She was, she felt, an altogether different woman now and had begun to wonder whether she should step down from the Ki-ship altogether.

Evica could not bring herself to tell Linnayen that to abdicate her post would be virtually unthinkable. It had only ever happened once before some three hundred years earlier when one of the Baktanishan Kis had overstepped the bounds of his authority by embezzling millions of keks in a series of trade deals with the Autabronis. Once his crimes had been discovered, he was swiftly impeached and the once noble Baktanishan family had never recovered their power.

If Linnayen were to abdicate, the two houses of Genara and Dacas would be torn apart and there would be a serious power vacuum in the new Galactic Union. At such a time in their history with the unification with Earth still developing, an internal power struggle on Altan could be disastrous, thought Evica. Thus, whilst she sympathised with her sister's predicament, she had counselled her that the position of Ki was much greater than its incumbent and that any change to the status quo could have far-reaching ramifications. Consequently, she asked Linnayen to hold off making any decisions until she had finished her recuperation and, resignedly, she had agreed.

In the meantime, there was a wedding to celebrate and, now that the hour was upon them, Evica and Linnayen put all thoughts of the past few weeks behind them and focused on the day ahead.

The room at the top of the Delphi Tower Hotel was finally quiet. The attendants who had seen to Evica's hair, dress and makeup had all left and only Linnayen and her assistant, Nen, remained. As the faithful attendant tidied, the two women stood quietly together, looking out across the cityscape of ancient Athens, knowing that only a few minutes remained to them before the proceedings would begin. Evica's cool hand touched her sister's shoulder and she smiled as Linnayen's sombre face turned towards her.

'What are you thinking?'

Linnayen's eyes dropped down and studied her tightly clasped hands. Her eyebrows creased in either worry or concentration, Evica could not tell which.

'I was trying to remember my own wedding day,' Linnayen replied quietly. Her shoulders lifted with her sigh and she raised her face to Evica. 'But I can't. There's nothing.'

The catch in Linnayen's voice as she spoke moved Evica almost to tears. So much has been lost, she thought. So many memories not merely faded and remembered as snippets as these things are but all gone, as though there was nothing to remember. As though there was nothing but a black, empty void a few weeks ago and now there was a world crashing in and clamouring all around, demanding to be noticed. She could empathise with her beleaguered sister but felt despondent at her inability to take away some of her pain.

'Don't even try, Linnayen. It'll come back to you eventually.'

'Everyone says that. But what if it doesn't? What if I *never* remember these things?' Linnayen responded plaintively.

Evica had already thought long and hard about the consequences of such an outcome. Indeed, she had thought about little else in the last few weeks and days. If the old Linnayen remained lost to them, would the council demand a new Ki? And, more importantly, would it have to be her? This was not a prospect she or Tariik relished. They had envisaged an altogether quieter life together, one more removed from the Altan court and filled with the simple pleasures of friends, work and, hopefully, children. A scenario wherein she was the Ki and Tariik the Ki-consort, where ceremonies and schedules ruled the day, was not what either of them craved, although, if the task was forced upon them, they knew they would rise to it. Evica prayed, though, that it would not come to that and felt guilty that some of her determination to help her sister stemmed from a selfish desire to protect her own dreams.

'You will, Linnayen. You will. But it'll take time.' Seeing the doubt in the young woman's face, she added a further conviction. 'And we will all be here to help you.'

Linnayen's return smile was faint, offered more to reassure her sister than because she felt comforted. No one knew how this felt inside. How could they? Unless it had happened to them …

'Enough!' she suddenly cried, and a look of resolve settled on her face. 'You're right, Evica. I'm worrying pointlessly and this is a wedding day – *your* wedding day! Time to be happy.'

She grasped Evica's hands and squeezed them affectionately, a broad grin spreading across her features.

'And I am. Very happy,' Evica gently replied.

At that moment, the doors to the penthouse opened. Framed in them stood Li-el Dacas, come to take her firstborn daughter to her wedding.

Chapter Twenty-five

It was not until the next morning, as Jax lay in bed breathing in the warm nutty aroma of freshly baked bread, that he began to fully realise what had happened last night. The delicious smells coming from the antechamber of his suite stirred his stomach into life and, whilst he wanted very much to jump up and eat immediately, he wanted more to continue his reverie in the quiet of his bedroom before the rush of the day's activities began. It was peaceful there, the only sounds being the muted, distant hum of aircars and a low hubbub of voices from the breakfasters in the next room. Duncan and his parents would probably be there, he thought, perhaps Aramikov too.

He wondered what they were all talking about in the next room and decided it was probably a dissection of the wedding and the wonderful party that had followed it yesterday evening. But what they did not know – what only he knew, at least for now – was that Linnayen had changed – *really* changed – and he was beginning to believe it might be for good.

The still fresh memory of the things she had said to him last night, and the way she had looked at him, made it hard to breathe deeply as a lump caught in his throat. He closed his eyes and the image of her face filled the blackness. Her large green eyes smiling into his and her white teeth framed by rose-coloured lips as she threw back her head to laugh at something he said. It was a Linnayen he used to dream about in the days before he married her and now, unbelievably, it looked as though it was becoming a reality. He quickly silenced the nagging doubt that it might all crumble back into the dry bitter dust it had been before and allowed himself to enjoy this one shining moment.

Ignoring the groaning from his stomach, he played the evening's events over in his mind.

First there had been the wedding ceremony itself. Evica and Tariik had looked splendid, he in full dress uniform and she in a sparkling silver gown overlain by a gold filigree tunic woven with Dasnirian sea-pearls. Amid all the formality, Jax recalled how hard it had been for them to keep from smiling and it was obvious how much in love they were. When it came time at the end of the service for the groom to seal the union with a kiss – an Earthan tradition that the couple had specifically requested be included in the ceremony – Tariik had swept back the trailing red tresses, cupped his wife's face in two hands and kissed her for so long that the congregation began clapping and cheering in approval. They had finally emerged, pink-cheeked and with broad smiles across their faces, and they waved enthusiastically to the people. Evica's eyes glistened with unshed tears of joy.

The wedding had taken place in front of one of the oldest structures on Earth, an ancient temple known as the Parthenon. The white columns of the temple had provided a magnificent backdrop to the raised dais upon which the blessings had taken place and the afternoon sun had shone down through the clear domed security shield, suffusing the air with a bright golden glow. The congregation was seated within the shield in a semicircle, whose rows afforded each of the two thousand invited guests a spectacular view. On the dais a little apart from Tariik and Evica were their families and the two Altaniskaran high priests who were to perform part of the ceremony. These priests and some of the other minor Union civil servants who had accompanied them from Altan only a week ago, would be staying on Earth for the next two years as part of a cultural and civic exchange programme. The idea had been Linnayen's long before the accident, and Jax thought it an excellent one. The sooner their people started getting to know each other, the better. He only hoped that the stiffly formal mannerisms of the priests would not irk the more easy-going Earthans.

He had been seated on the dais next to Linnayen, who had looked stunning in a long dress of jade silk. Her hair had been left undressed and fell like a waterfall at midnight to below her waist. Her only decoration was a small bejewelled tiara, which held her hair back from her face, and the Cord of her office, which was draped around her neck. Li-el Dacas, too, had been simply attired in her dowager's purple and made a very imposing figure as she stepped forward to place her daughter's hands into Tariik's. She had not smiled, of course. That was not the Altan way. But Jax was amazed to see that Linnayen, who had caught Evica's eye, was finding it hard to keep from grinning. He could not believe what he was seeing. Linnayen was happy and relaxed and seemingly not bothered about displaying it!

The whole ceremony would have been perfect but for one blemish, recalled Jax. Durroc Navarr! He had been there as ambassador to the trade group. It had been a month since his attempt to rekindle his affair with the Ki. Jax caught him glaring up at the dais, his frost-filled eyes riveted on Jax in a look of unadulterated hatred. His arms were folded across his broad chest and the set of his shoulders was undeniably aggressive. Linnayen seemed not to have noticed him, though, and for that Jax was thankful. He wanted nothing to spoil her apparent good humour – and lack of memory about Navarr.

After the ceremony, they had all retired to the Union legation building for an evening of speeches, dancing and merriment. Evica and Tariik had been pleased to discover that, like the Dasnirian tradition, weddings on Earth were celebrated in high style with a large gathering of revellers, a fact which considerably mollified Evica's original feelings about being married on Earth. Had they been joined on Altan, they would have partaken of a stately dinner at which they would have had to observe customary greetings and interminable speeches. At least here the couple could enjoy their wedding, as could Tariik's many family members, who had – much to their delight – begun to feel distinctly at home on the watery blue planet.

During the evening, Linnayen and David Bashir had delivered a joint speech of welcome before handing over to Tariik's father. The quiet seagrass farmer was quite unused to such large gatherings and began his soliloquy in a halting fashion, peppered with many 'ahs' and 'ums'. But within minutes the friendly faces looking up at him and the general bonhomie in the huge room relaxed him and he began speaking of his son and new daughter-in-law with both affection and overwhelming pride. Even Li-el Dacas was heard clearing her throat and Jax suspected that she was more affected by the outpouring of emotion in the room than she would have them all believe.

Then came the dancing, which was led by Evica and Tariik. The first was a wild stomp reminiscent of the Dasnirian reel they had performed nearly two years ago at Linnayen's birthday party. Jax had never seen anything quite like it, although it reminded him of old gypsy dances. He thought it grand entertainment and he was, yet again, amazed to see his wife smiling, then clapping her hands and stamping her feet in time with the rhythm of the music. Given his history with the inflexible, upright woman who had been his wife, he felt it was almost surreal.

Then his father, who was seated next to him, had nudged him to take Linnayen to the dancefloor. At first he had shaken his head, his eyes saying that it would be too discomforting. But David insisted. Protocol dictated that no one would ask her to dance until she had danced with her husband. Jax saw the familiar set of the bushy eyebrows. This was a matter of duty, they said, and he knew there would be no denying his father. He had tentatively turned to Linnayen, clearing his throat before he spoke.

'Umm … Would you like to dance, Linnayen?'

She turned to look at him and her eyes were sparkling like emeralds in firelight. Her smile was genuine, of that he had no doubt.

'Oh yes!'

He took her hand and they stepped forward to join Evica and Tariik. At their approach, the crowd cheered its approval. Linnayen was taken aback by the response and Jax felt the recoil in her hand. He looked into her eyes and smiled reassuringly. *It'll be fine. Just follow me.* He felt the tension ease as she fixed her gaze on him and they began to pick up the rhythm.

She was a light as down. Her feet spun across the polished floor and the amazement on her face at her own skill was a pure joy to see. She had told him later that she did not even know if she *could* dance. She had no memory of dancing. But he had asked her and the music was so compelling and the melody so strong that she could not help but respond. Before she knew it she was sailing and swirling across the floor, held firm in his arms, and it felt excellent!

Her joy was infectious. The dance seemed to have unlocked the gates of her heart and her happiness burst out.

'Like a cork from a champagne bottle, my old chum,' was how Duncan had put it. They had shared a few minutes about halfway through the evening and Duncan had been more than forthcoming about the newly charming Ki of Altan.

'I have to tell you … When I first met her, I thought she was a stiff as a flagpole. I thought you'd have your work cut out for you.'

Jax had nodded in reluctant agreement. 'You weren't far off. Linnayen was always – well, formal, I suppose.'

'Well, she's not tonight. What's got into her? Did you ply her with a bit of bubbly before you got here?'

Jax laughed. Duncan had already had a few glasses of the very same and was beginning to get a little drunk.

'No, I didn't. And the amazing thing is I don't think I would have needed to. She's been in a good mood all day,' Jax answered as Duncan's sandy eyebrows rose skyward in disbelief.

'Well, whatever it is she's on, save some for me.' Duncan fought hard to hold onto a hiccup but was unsuccessful.

Waving away the returning smell of champagne, Jax giggled back, 'I don't think you'll need any, Duncan, my friend. You're doing just fine.'

Then, remembering their task the next day, he became more serious.

'But take it easy. Remember we're off to the islands tomorrow.'

'No worries, old boy. I'll be fine. The McCrae constitution and all that. Built like an Aberdeen Angus! Bloody unbreakable!'

Duncan had wandered back to a group of fellow actors and their hangers-on and Jax resumed his contemplation of his wife, marvelling once more at her ebullience. Suddenly the memory of their wedding night flared into his mind and he reminded himself not to believe his own eyes – at least, not yet.

Jax shifted his position in the bed and checked the time-screen contained within its headboard. The bed was an antique faux-mahogany four-poster of Makassan craftsmanship from the twenty-second century that had been adapted with a secure-shield and the usual comsystems. It was very comfortable and, as it was still not too late, he decided to linger.

The evening had continued in much the same happy vein

as earlier although, more for the comfort of the tired guests, the dances got slower in tempo. At one point, he recalled, Jax had been deep in conversation with his mother when he suddenly had the feeling that he was being watched. He let his eyes scan the room, but all he could see were the many faces of people in conversation, or laughing, or dancing and even some who were obviously falling asleep. It was only when he looked over his shoulder to look at the people seated at his own long table that he caught Linnayen studying him. On being found out, she quickly looked down at her wineglass. A second later she lifted her gaze to see if he was still looking at her and she gave a small, timid smile – by way of an apology for staring, he supposed.

A short while later, and this time at his mother's urging, he again asked Linnayen to dance. This time the music's beat was slower and he was obliged to hold her more closely to him. At times during the dance – during which they hardly spoke – their bodies touched and, despite his strongest desire not to, Jax felt himself enjoying the sensation. He was conscious that his feelings were being reawakened. God forbid he should be dragged down into loving her again. It would to too much to bear if, after a rekindling of his feelings for her, she was to regain her memory and take up with the despised Navarr again who, thankfully, had been dropped from the evening's guest list.

And his resolve would have held but for the fact that Linnayen seemed to be enjoying the touch of his body, too, and – amazingly! – she did not seem to be concerned about showing it. Jax could have sworn that there was a soft, almost dewy look in her eyes and he was conscious of her efforts to suppress the exaggerated rise and fall of her chest as her breathing became deeper. Then, when the dance finished, she had begged him to stay with her and talk. Talk! She was being inordinately friendly and he found himself more than willing to keep company with her.

Suddenly, he had looked at his watch and realised that more than an hour had flown by and the two of them had not stopped talking. He had not noticed anyone or anything else in the room in that whole time and he suspected the same could be said for her. Indeed, they would have continued had they not been interrupted by a bleary-eyed Beoraan who stopped by to remind them of the travelling arrangements for the next day when Linnayen would depart for Thea Bashir's villa on Santorini.

She'll be leaving in the morning. With a sudden pang, he realised that he was going to miss her. It had been past midnight and, subsequent to being interrupted by Beoraan, Linnayen had had many more dances, although only one more with Jax. That had been even slower and, as the lights had by that time been dimmed, Jax could not see the look in her eyes. She had, in any case, kept her head resting on his shoulder for most of the time. He could, however, feel the pounding of his heart – or was it hers? – and, when she lifted her head at one point to look at him and smile, he had to fight off an overwhelming desire to kiss her mouth.

In the morning light of the new day, he now wondered if he really had detected a look of disappointment on her face when he had cleared his throat in order to break the moment. He had wanted to kiss her but some inner self-preservation mechanism had held him back and he wondered now whether he should have given in. Then he remembered what had happened and what she had said to him before entering her room last night and knew the answer.

The doors to his apartment slid apart and he quickly closed his eyes, pretending to be asleep.

'Come on, Jax! Time and tide wait for no man – or prince. Up you get!' It was Duncan, the only one audacious enough to burst into the Ki-consort's room, Jax thought with a smile.

'Ohhh, do you have to?' he groaned, pulling the covers over his head.

'No!' boomed the ebullient Duncan. 'But I'm going to. We have a queen – or whatever she is – to escort to her holiday. And you can't do that with no clothes on.' Duncan thought for a moment. 'Well, maybe you could. And from what I saw last night, I wonder if the lady might not mind.'

'Duncan!' Jax's indignation was almost genuine, but he smiled all the same. 'You mustn't speak about her like that. She *is* the Ki, after all.'

'Ah, but still a woman, old man, still a woman ...'

Nen placed the small vanity casket carefully on top of the pile of trunks that hovered lightly in front of her. They were not taking too much as Linnayen had told her they would only be away for a couple of weeks at most and, as this was to be a retreat of sorts, there would be no need for gowns or any other finery.

'Just the basics, Nen,' Linnayen had told her before adding, 'and besides, we want to leave some room in case we find something nice to buy. Yes?'

Nen had nervously smiled her assent, but she was unsettled by the familiarity her mistress was employing these days. In truth, Linnayen had always been a little less formal with her, especially when it was just the two of them. But since the fall, it was as though many barriers of rank and class had dissolved and Nen was finding it a little discomforting. She was, though, happily prepared to get used to it in time and quietly counted her blessings.

The palletron moved off slowly to take the luggage aboard the hydroplane, where it would stow itself in the cargo bay whilst she and her mistress's party made its way across a long, carpeted embarkation ramp. First came Sen-Beoraan, his grey head bowed in conversation with Dr Em-sin Mai and Captain Chandra, head of the small security team that was to accompany the Ki and stay with her after Jax and his party had left for the mainland.

Beoraan had suggested early on that Jax should escort Linnayen to Santorini and stay for a day or two until she was settled in. At the time he had not seen any real necessity to do this as di Luca would happily take her under his wing and show her around. But with the worry of what the media might make of it, he had had to agree with Beoraan that it would look better to accompany his wife. He had also felt uncomfortable at having to be alone with Linnayen and had solved the dilemma by inviting Duncan along for the ride. But, now, after last night, he was relieved he had accepted Beoraan's suggestion and was looking forward to the next few days. Thus, it was a lively band of travellers who boarded the hydroplane and their spirits were high.

Linnayen scanned the backs of her fellow travellers as they walked across the bridge onto the vessel, seeking out Jax's frame. Just the sight of him pleased and excited her and, since last night, she was eager to move things along between them. Although she could not be sure, she thought he might even like her. If there was some hope of recreating a friendship or even some affection between them then she wanted to try it. He had been so nice at the wedding. She had enjoyed talking to him and, when they discovered they had spent nearly half the evening in each other's company, they had both become suddenly very self-conscious. *That was a good sign, wasn't it?*

The events of last night played in her mind. They had had a couple of dances and then talked endlessly about everything and anything, both animated and at ease. She had been a little piqued when the old counsellor, Beoraan, had come along and disturbed them.

After that, Linnayen was once more whisked away to the dance floor by a succession of escorts and they had had only one more dance before the festivities came to an end shortly after midnight. She recalled the last dance, when the lights had been at their lowest and the music at its slowest. Their bodies had moved as though they were two halves of a whole, perfectly in sync and without any awkwardness or hesitation. Her mind had been totally focused on the moment and her thoughts consumed by his presence. Now, staring at his back in the light of day, she remembered how his dark eyes had looked at her last night and how she had wanted to feel his lips on hers. Then, too soon, the music had stopped and the dancers were forced apart.

It had been time to bid farewell to the wedding couple and for all the guests to take their leave. She had kissed her sister affectionately and Jax had shaken Tariik's hand. Everyone made their farewells and then Jax had turned to her and offered to take her back to their rooms. During her convalescence and in supposed deference to her illness, they were keeping separate quarters. However, when they had arrived in Athens for the wedding, the hotel had allocated them adjoining suites, each with its own sitting room, bedroom and bathroom. Thus they were apart, but sufficiently together that no one would have cause for comment, and the sham that was their marriage could continue.

They stood in the doorway to her suite. He had been the first to speak.

'Well, it's been quite a day. You must be tired.'

'I am. But I've enjoyed – oh, everything!' She felt her shyness return and was conscious that he, too, had shuffled his feet nervously.

'Yes, me too … Well, we've a bit of a journey tomorrow. I'd better let you get some rest.'

She nodded her agreement. 'And you too.'

'Right.' Jax had cleared his throat. 'I'll say goodnight then.'

It was at that point that he had touched her arm, leaned forward and kissed her lightly on the cheek. It was meant to be a polite gesture, she thought. That's all. But later she wondered if his lips had not stayed on her skin just a fraction of a second longer than they needed to. It did not matter. All that mattered was that he did it and it felt wonderful and she wanted him to do it again. She could not help herself as she replied.

'Goodnight, Kevor. Thank you for a wonderful evening. You were …' She stopped, searching for just the right word, before finishing, breathlessly, 'Amazing.'

His eyes had widened with surprise. He had not expected such an outburst of genuine openness.

'Yes … Um, right,' he stammered, before turning on his heel.

Linnayen had not seen the glimmer of a smile cross Jax's face as he turned and walked to his own room. As it was, she had walked into her room, her parting smile fixed rigidly on her face, not daring to look at him again for fear of seeing his indifference once more.

Linnayen was halfway along the embarkation platform when Li-el Dacas broke into her reverie. 'Evica and Tariik have arrived safely. I still don't understand what all the fuss is about with honeymoons but they seemed happy to fall in with local custom. A little too happy, if you ask me.'

'They're in love, Mother.' Linnayen replied with a shrug of her shoulders as if to say it was inevitable. But Li-el, who had been raised within the bounds of a more austere tradition, was not mollified.

'Love! What should that have to do with it?' Li-el was getting onto what had recently become a favourite topic of hers – these silly emotional Earthan ways, of whose laxity and illogic she heartily disapproved. She continued her rant. 'In my day, marriage was about making the right family connections and choosing a mind-mate, someone who shared your values, had the same opinions, made the same kinds of decisions …'

Linnayen interjected. 'That's what Evica has found with Tariik, only better. They not only think alike, they are soulmates and very much in love. I think they're very lucky.'

'Soulmates!' Li-el sneered at the Earthan term. Then, seeing Linnayen's uninterested expression, she changed tack. 'And I suppose that's what *you* want? With him?' She nodded at the outline of Jax's back, some twenty paces ahead of them.

Linnayen flashed her a look that was both imperious and questioning.

Ah! A touch of the old Linnayen, thought Li-el. *Perhaps the old Ki is still inside her after all.*

Linnayen did not answer her mother and instead picked up the pace to walk a little way ahead. As she approached the vessel, Jax turned from his conversation with Duncan and put out his hand to help her on board. She took it and felt comfort in its warmth, then gave him a silent glance of thanks. Jax's returning smile was both hesitant and genuine.

'The crew's prepared a cabin for you in case you need it. But the journey will only take a couple of hours. So if you want to just relax on deck, please feel free,' he explained.

'Thank you, Kevor.' She paused, unsure of what she wanted to do. The spotlessly white hydroplane was large and impressive and she wanted to explore it. From where she stood, she could see an open decked area in the bow with upholstered couches under sunshades and at the stern she could make out a strip of gleaming blue water. A swimming pool, she supposed. Jax was waiting patiently for her response. She had to decide. 'Perhaps I could see the cabin first – then maybe a swim?'

Jax nodded curtly and put out his hand.

'Let me show you the way.' With that he took her elbow and led her inside. The heat from the sun was already building and she was glad of the cool, darkened interior. Jax had walked a little ahead of her and went to open the door to her cabin. As the doors slid apart, she saw that the cabin was very well appointed, having been furnished with lush fabrics and polished furniture. There was even a bed hidden behind a lace-edged muslin curtain and, at the far end, reflected in a wall mirror, she could make out a white-tiled bathroom.

'This is wonderful. Very luxurious,' she murmured. At times like these she found it hard to accept that her position brought with it great privilege. It felt wrong to have so much opulence. Inside, she felt just like an ordinary person, certainly not a powerful interplanetary leader. She did not deserve such treatment and it was embarrassing. *Something I will have to get used to – again.*

'Well, just make yourself comfortable. We'll be getting underway in a few minutes.' Jax turned to leave and almost collided with the approaching figure of Li-el Dacas. He flattened himself against the wall in order to let her pass. 'Excuse me, Lady Dacas.'

Li-el did not answer, her thoughts occupied by the look of the cabin.

'Hmm … A little cramped, but it will do.'

'Mother!' Linnayen admonished her. 'It's perfect. I like it very well.' She smiled across to the departing Jax who nodded his thanks for her support.

He was about to leave, then thought he had better remind his mother-in-law that she was definitely *not* coming with them. 'Lady Dacas, I'll send someone to escort you ashore in a few minutes.'

Li-el nodded to signify that she had heard, then returned her focus to Linnayen, ignoring the possibility that her behaviour was imperious and rude. She was a dowager Ki-consort, a position of the highest rank, and Jax was merely her son-in-law.

There was a time, Linnayen supposed, when she would have acted in much the same way as her mother. From what she could understand, she, too, had been haughty and arrogant, although she could not now envisage what she must have been like. The prospect, though, that she might one day remember all her former existence presented a dichotomy. On the one hand, she wanted all her memories back. She was desperate to recall the happy times of her childhood and the love her father had for her. His wisdom, his love and his knowledge had all made her who she was and she wanted to discover that again. But on the other hand, if she had been the sort of person her mother was, or who Jax and her sister had described – detached, superior and calculating – then perhaps it was better not to remember. She just could not imagine herself being that way, and the worry that she might revert gave her much cause for concern.

As Jax had said, they were soon underway. Linnayen farewelled her mother, promising to contact her as soon as she arrived at the villa, and it was a somewhat reluctant Lady Dacas who was escorted back to the embarkation platform by Duncan McCrae. His attempts at lightening the mood with off-the-cuff remarks about absence making the heart grow fonder had fallen on deaf ears and Li-el had looked at him stony-faced as though he were a halfwit. Jax later teased him that, finally, there was one female in all the universe who was completely immune to his charms, to which sentiment Duncan, recalling the elder woman's fiery glare, expressed his greatest relief.

The journey to Santorini passed pleasantly enough. After changing into a swimming costume in her cabin, Linnayen went astern to find Duncan already seated at the edge of the pool. They were finally out of the harbour and the pitch of the hydroplane's engines rose in volume as the air was forced under its hull to lift it clear of the water surface. They were airborne in less than a minute and skimming along a metre above the waves. The increase in speed unsteadied Linnayen and she would have fallen into the pool but for a quickly raised hand from Duncan to hold onto.

'The last thing you need is another fall, eh?' Duncan said brightly. 'Or we'll all be back to square one.'

Linnayen saw the joke and laughed with him. She sat next to him, dangling her feet in the cool blue water.

'We haven't really got to know each other, have we?' Linnayen began. 'How did you and Kevor come to meet?

'I was at school with him. He was a runty little thing and I took him under my wing.' Duncan's boast was delivered with an engaging grin.

'He was shy?'

'As a mouse. Luckily, he had me to show him the world!' Duncan noted the drop of her shoulders. 'And you? Who was your childhood friend?'

Without thinking, she replied, 'My father. He was ... He was ...' Just as suddenly, the tears began to well and Duncan laid a comforting arm over her shoulders. 'I can't remember. I get glimpses – feelings, really. But nothing specific.' A sigh escaped her taut chest. 'They tell me it will all come back eventually, but ...'

'And they're right!' Duncan interjected. 'Don't doubt it. Pretty soon you'll be back to the imperious, stuck-up, bossy young woman you were before and we'll all be bloody relieved.'

She looked up stunned, about to object, then saw the cheeky wink he delivered with his words and burst out laughing.

'Now I know why Kevor likes you so much,' she replied. 'But just for that ...'

Without warning, she rammed her hand into Duncan's back and, with a yelp of surprise, he toppled into the pool.

'Hey! I take it back!'

She quickly jumped in after him. The cool water was so refreshing and she gloried in the feel of it on her skin. She plunged under the surface and pushed herself across the width of the pool, stroking easily on one breath.

'Well, you haven't forgotten how to swim,' said Duncan as she turned for another lap.

'For which I'm very grateful, otherwise you'd have to rescue me!' she re-joined.

Duncan guffawed and saluted her. "And that sense of humour ... much appreciated, my lady.'

He swam to the side and clambered out. 'I'm off to change – and maybe get us some food. Will you be all right without me?'

'Absolutely. Thank you, Duncan.'

Now alone and floating peacefully, the coolness of the water was refreshing. It felt good to be relaxed and carefree. Although since the fall Linnayen had not had to deal with any complex matters of state – Beoraan and her mother having taken over her administrative duties – she had still felt the pressure to be the head of state. Now, for a few moments, with her eyes closed and the sun warm on her face as she lay in the blue water, she had no worries. She could just be herself and she allowed her mind to go blank.

She did not know how long she had been floating when the sound of voices interrupted her wanderings. Her eyes opened slowly and she made out a shape through the hazy gauze of her eyelashes.

'... be hungry. So I brought you something.' It was a man's voice.

She was transported in a blinding flash, back to a time and place that was both familiar yet new. There was a pool, a deep turquoise blue and surrounded by lush vegetation and rocks. It was almost circular and she was floating in the middle of it, arms outstretched, drifting, dreaming. Then she got out of the water and, as she stood shiny with the water droplets cascading down her skin, two men approached. One was Beoraan. The other was tall, well-built and strong, his body like smooth rock. She was conscious of a ripple of sexual excitement passing through her body and her loins throbbed with a sudden lightness. Her breath came in shallow gasps. Then she saw his eyes. They fixed on her and she could see nothing else, the background having dissolved into a foggy haze. There was only his eyes and they bored into her, searing her with their icy blue fire.

She floundered in the water and fought to regain her composure. The memory – *was it that?* – quickly receded and the figures of Jax and Duncan took shape. She was back in the present day.

'Are you all right, Linnayen?' It was Jax.

'Yes … I'm fine,' she spluttered.

'We brought you some food,' said Duncan. 'And, seeing as how neither of us had a hand in preparing it, it should be quite edible.'

Pushing away her unease, she smiled at Duncan's joke and swam to the side of the pool. She was getting used to Duncan's easy nature and was growing to like him very much. She could see why Jax was fond of him. They seemed to have a bond borne of complete honesty and Linnayen imagined that Jax might share things with Duncan that he would never share with anyone else.

As she sat in the shade of the awning at the table, she watched the two friends and, occasionally, joined in with their conversation. Duncan's witticisms were nonstop and, as the vessel sped across the deepest azure seas she had ever seen, she was thankful that he was there to lift her mood.

The memory in the pool, although now ended, was not gone. And as she sat, seemingly unperturbed in the company of her husband and his friend, she could not shake off her feelings of fear, loathing and intense sexual attraction to the man in the memory – the man who, she now realised, was Durroc Navarr.

Beoraan had watched the hydroplane depart the harbour before returning to his makeshift office back at the Galactic Union legation building. He was tired. The last few days especially had taken a toll on him – both physically and mentally – and he was almost relieved to see Linnayen depart. *One less thing to worry about. Almost.*

He spent the next hour sifting through a mound of paperwork, making notes on each document before handing them to his assistant, Asud. Finally, on reaching the last document, he sighed loudly and told the girl that he would rest for a little while, but to bring him the news of the Ki's arrival on Santorini when it came. He wanted to be quite sure that she got there safely; only then would he feel that the threat had lifted. Thea Bashir's villa was impregnable – he had seen to it – and mercifully, the wedding, too, had gone without a hitch. Security had been at optimum levels, especially because Joseph McCrae had been unable to learn anything about the Order of Sumere.

As he napped, he recalled the events of the last two days. McCrae had come to see him the day before the wedding and had told Beoraan of his contact with Ennio Nori and how he believed he had convinced Nori that he was now ready to join him. However, McCrae could not press the financier too hard as that would have aroused suspicion and, as it had turned out, Nori had divulged nothing, telling him only that the Order would be in touch. It was not exactly the news Beoraan had been hoping for. Although, he asked himself, what other news he could have wanted to hear? That there was, after all, a terrorist plot to destroy the wedding? No. They had learned nothing concrete, but at least no damage had been done and the events of the last few days had run exactly as planned. Even so, he would feel much happier when this trip to Earth was finally over and they could return to Altan. It was so much easier for him to keep control of things there.

The door to his office slid open and Asud entered. She came quietly over to where he was dozing on the daybed, bowing her head before addressing him with the familiar Altani term, which meant 'elder father'.

'Sen-reb, not wishing to disturb you but the Lady Kumiko Toyotomi asks to see you. She waits without.'

Beoraan's near white eyebrows raised in mild surprise. This was as unexpected as it was intriguing. Now what could the old woman want with him? He was surprised, too, to find that his daydreams had consumed the best part of another hour and, though he knew he must have slept, he felt drained and still very tired. He did not want to be disturbed, but the Toyotomi matriarch was too important to turn away.

'Really? Has she told you the purpose of her visit, Asud?'

'She said only that she was passing and thought to call on you.'

Kumiko Toyotomi did not strike him as a woman who acted on the spur of the moment. But his curiosity was piqued and he asked Asud to show the lady in, with the proviso to interrupt him in ten minutes. He still had a speech to write that afternoon and, with luck, he would be able to finish early and get more rest.

As Asud moved to the door he got up, straightened his grey woollen robe and smoothed his hair. He was still rubbing the sleep out of his eyes as the tiny, stooped figure of Kumiko Toyotomi approached him and bowed. He returned the courtesy.

'Good afternoon, Lady Kumiko. How kind of you to call on me.'

She smiled faintly and bowed her head once more. 'I hope I am not disturbing you. I know what a busy man you must be.'

The old woman, who looked remarkably fit for someone over a hundred years old, was known to be both intelligent and wily, but he was not stupid enough to believe that she had called upon him for no good reason. Beoraan wondered if a subtle game had begun wherein the courtesies would go back and forth like the opening salvos in any worthwhile campaign. But when would the first shots be sent across the bow?

'Indeed. But you, madame, are a pleasant and welcome interruption in the schedule of this busy old man.'

'You are too kind, Sen-Beoraan,' she replied with a silken voice. 'And I will try not to keep you from your duties any longer than necessary.'

Out of Altani politeness, Beoraan offered her a seat, which she gratefully accepted, though he feared that once emplaced, she would be harder to shift.

'Thank you.'

'Now, tell me, what brings you to see me today?' Beoraan, although conscious of the need for some pleasantries, was in no mood for any verbal shilly-shallying. He wanted to get this exchange over and done with.

'As I told your assistant, I was passing and thought to see you to clear up an old matter.' Kumiko's quiet voice was a veil through which her true motive could be concealed. Despite himself, Beoraan was intrigued and he gestured for her to continue.

'If you remember, you prevailed upon me some time ago to raise the suggestion of the Ki marrying the Bashir boy, even though it was at the expense of my own great-grandson's happiness.'

His mind went back to those times when Navarr – captain, as he had been then – had been trusted to lead the negotiations for the Ki's marriage. Kumiko's great-grandson James had been a candidate, but Linnayen had had other ideas. She had wanted Kevor Jax because he was the son of the main opponent to the peace treaty. Marriage with him would have sealed the final breach, which it did, even though it had not been personally successful for the Ki and her husband. He had spoken secretly to the Toyotomi matriarch to broach the subject of a partnering between Jax and Linnayen – to plant the seed of the suggestion – and, as expected, it had taken root.

'I do indeed recall those times, madame. You were very helpful and, for that, the Ki is very grateful,' he replied.

'No thanks are necessary, counsellor. I did it for the cause of peace, as you well know, and I bear no ill will for my family's loss of status. It is of this that I wanted to assure you.'

No, madame, he thought. *You did it to prevent the Ki from marrying your great-grandson. His happiness? Loss of status? Rubbish! Your hidden prejudices betray you. And don't think I don't know of them.*

'And that cause unites us both,' he replied in a flowery voice. 'The marriage has brought our nations and planets together and I am hopeful, as you must be too, of a bright future. Your ... sacrifice has not gone unrewarded.'

He was keen to move the conversation along. *Come on, old woman, what are you really here for?*

'Oh, yes. A bright future,' she repeated, nodding with the apparent wisdom conferred by old age. 'And I wanted to assure you – indeed it is the other reason I am here – that, just as I was instrumental in bringing about the Bashir union, I am fully prepared now to work for its continued success.'

Now Beoraan was intrigued. What *was* she getting at? She saw his brows furrow slightly in confusion.

'I'm sorry, I don't quite understand –' he began, before she cut him off.

'Ah, of course. It is a delicate matter and I shall try to be sensitive to the circumstances.' Kumiko was enjoying the interplay. She always liked being in control, but it felt so much better when one's adversary was a man as intelligent as the respected Sen-Beoraan. She shifted her position a little to ease the strain on her frail back before continuing.

'Sen-Beoraan, I am a very old woman and I have acquired a good understanding of human nature.'

Beoraan could not help but notice the slight emphasis she placed on the word 'human' and he stifled the offence it gave. He was surprised, though, at the slip and wondered if she thought he was dim-witted enough not to notice. The old woman continued.

'I know when a marriage is good ... or bad. And I know, as do you, that this one is floundering. Rumours abound, you know how it is. People talk, others listen, word gets around.'

Beoraan thought he had better put a stop to this line of conversation before it got out of hand. But, so far, the old woman had not actually said anything, and he would neither confirm nor deny the innuendo.

He shrugged his shoulders, a gesture that was entirely noncommittal.

'Lady Kumiko forgive my ignorance. I still do not understand,' he said, hoping that he sounded quite ingenuous.

A smile cracked across her dry lips, which parted to reveal a row of yellowed teeth.

'The Bashir marriage is a sham. It's to be expected, of course. Political marriages nearly always are. Even your own planet's history would have proved that.' Seeing that the counsellor was not going to be drawn in, Kumiko continued. 'And it would be quite acceptable, except that it threatens the new union. If their marriage falls apart before the peace has solidified, we could all be back to square one. Therefore, I propose to place the entire Toyotomi wealth and influence at your disposal. I want you to know that my family will be your ally. There are trade matters we could undertake for you, financial arrangements we could smooth for you. I gave you my assistance before to help create this treaty. I pledge my family's support again to help cement it.'

Beoraan was flabbergasted, although he tried not to show it. He knew Kumiko was a proponent for peace from the old days, but her grandson-in-law was anything but. Could he trust her? Linnayen and he had been reliably informed that she was, for all her talk of peace, a racist, which seemed incongruous. But why else would she have helped make sure that the Ki did not become a member of her family? This did not feel right.

'Madame, I am honoured, and most thankful for your pledge.'

'No need to thank me. This is a matter of duty.' Her words were clipped. He got the impression that she wanted to cut him off before he said anything more.

Beoraan knew he needed time to think and was grateful when the door slid open and Asud stepped forward. He excused himself from Kumiko, walked to where she stood near the door and gave his attention to the girl.

'Sen-reb…' The girl spoke quietly but, in the absence of any other background noises, Kumiko was able to hear her words. 'The Ki and her party have arrived safely.'

Beoraan nodded with a sigh that could have been interpreted either as one of relief or mild despair. He was not foolish enough to believe that the old woman was not watching him even now.

'Thank you, Asud.' He walked back towards the couch and addressed Kumiko.

'Please forgive me. A matter needs my urgent attention. But I would like if I may to talk with you again very soon about your kind offer.'

Kumiko nodded. She was happy, now, to take her leave.

'Of course. I shall inform my staff to expect your call.' With these few words she made it quite clear that she felt the handling of the details was beneath her – but not him – and he was sensitive to the implied insult. It only served to confirm his opinion that she was more arrogant and, perhaps, more devious than he had originally believed.

'May I say again, Lady Kumiko, how generous is your offer. I shall, of course, inform the Ki immediately.'

Her reaction was to brush away his words as though they were too insignificant or too obvious to have needed saying. She had the information she wanted and was ready to go.

Shuffling across the carpeted floor towards the doors, she looked just like any other old woman, thought Beoraan, with hunched shoulders and her remaining vision focused on the ground in front of her. Why then did he feel that somehow, in some way, she had got the better of him?

Kumiko's thoughts had already run ahead and her impression of the meeting had already been put into a compartment of her mind for later reflection. There were other more important matters at hand now.

So the Ki has arrived, eh? Good. Now we can start.

Chapter Twenty-six

arseille Auteuil, known only to her colleagues as Oleander and to the Navarr woman as Carri Aqua, waited patiently while the connection was made via numerous electronic security blocks and scramblers to her handler.

She had spent the morning reading an account of the second Saturn campaign, wherein the ships of the old American Republic had defeated the rebel off-worlders and secured the colonies for its own immigrants in perpetuity. The conflict, although theoretically resolved, had of course left a legacy of hatred between the descendants of the first colonists and the later newcomers, who had been forced upon them. There had been, from that day to this, intermittent flare-ups – some of them quite bloody – and Marseille could not help but wonder at the foolishness of mankind. If the Americans had left well enough alone and pursued a negotiated settlement, she pondered, the situation would have been contained and, ultimately, resolved. Thousands of lives would have been spared and thousands of grieving mothers, fathers, sisters saved the agony of interring loved ones. But then Amerimex would not have acquired the vast gas resources of Saturn. It would not then have gone on to reacquire its position as the planet's largest manufacturing nation and holder of the greatest number of military weapons. No, yet again, and throughout history, some gung-ho nation had taken it upon itself to prove how powerful it was by slaughtering the innocents, or to line its own pockets with stolen wealth. Hypocrisy! That was something she could never be accused of and she was proud of it.

With Marseille, what you saw was what you got. She killed purely for the money and her targets were political – the men and women who had put themselves into the public arena, usually for their own personal gain. She had nothing to feel ashamed about. For the most part her targets were despicable, deplorable men and women who, she reasoned, had set themselves up – usually by treading on innocent toes. They had to accept that assassination was part of the deal. Put yourself out there and you must take what comes. It was an acceptable risk of a high-stakes game and anyone who did not understand that basic fact of life should not play.

Her line of work often gave her pleasure. She felt a kind of satisfaction when eradicating a particularly nasty or arrogant or self-centred individual. Like the stupid ambassador on Altan. Now that had been a peach of a job, foreign travel and a truly great kill too. Imaginative, professional. Just the way she liked it.

Not like this job was shaping up to be. There were too many imponderables and too many people for her liking. She did not like working with mercenaries. Marseille considered them to be relatively stupid, dangerous and far too unpredictable. You never quite knew when they would take it into their heads to storm off and grab whatever was to hand – money, valuables, women. They were, for the most part, animals, and for the purposes of this job she was nothing more than an animal trainer. Still, the money was good and she would have a nice long break after this – perhaps off-world on one of the Jupitan moons or even further afield. She liked what she had heard of Hutho, the green planet. Yes, perhaps there. Trees and fast-flowing rivers would make a pleasant change from the dry, rocky wasteland of north-eastern Anatolia where she was now stationed with Labyrinth's Whip Company in the ancient Ottoman fortress of Guyvar Neref.

The line crackled into life and she placed the micro-receiver into her ear. Her handler's computerised voice passed on the news that the target had arrived at its destination. There had been no change to its itinerary and Whip Company was to proceed according to plan.

At last! By this time tomorrow it would all be over. The target would be secured. And, by this time next week, she would be on her way to the outer solar system, ready to catch a transporter to the lush alien world of Hutho.

Linnayen stared with amazement at the towering grey-black walls of the island of Santorini as the hydroplane, reducing both its speed and height, swung around a rocky brown promontory into the huge inner bay. She stared in open wonder, as had thousands of visitors before her, at the sheer cliffs, which rose out of the pale blue waters. These waters had once been deep and dark. But since the eruption of the island's central volcano in 2643, the island had risen further above the ocean floor, a process which had served both to increase the height of the rock walls and lessen the depth of the water between the still smouldering caldera and the outermost crater. The water, which formed a wide moat around the central caldera, was now relatively shallow and the cliffs, which formed the inner walls of the crater, were over four hundred metres high. They were near vertical in many places, rendering them completely impassable by foot.

But most surprising of all was the sight of the town of Neothira perched high on top of the crater wall in a tumbling cascade of white and pastel buildings. They clung precariously to the rock, seemingly glued to the undulating rim of the crater, and Linnayen wondered if the stunning view the residents must enjoy was worth the anxiety of living on a natural knife's edge.

The hydroplane approached a large floating pontoon that jutted out from the base of the cliff. Upon the burnished steel platform stood two aircars, which had been commandeered to take the royal party to the villa where, Jax expected, di Luca would be waiting to greet them. They swiftly disembarked from the hydroplane and, whilst Linnayen, Jax and Duncan took in the impressive stretch of cliff face above them, craning their necks with the effort, Nen, Dr Mai and a handful of crew saw to the stowing of the luggage on board one of the aircars.

Within a few minutes they were ready for the short flight to Thea's villa and Linnayen thanked the hydroplane's captain for his attendance. Due to the ever-present down draught of air close to the cliff face, the aircars had to firstly fly out across the water towards the caldera before commencing their ascent. This gave the group a chance to see the volcanic vents and fumaroles of the caldera at close range and Linnayen was apprehensive at the sight of the yellowish smoke puffing out of many cracks. Jax noticed her nervousness as she recoiled from the aircar's window.

'Don't worry, nothing will happen.' His smile, which was meant to be reassuring, appeared to mock her slightly and she instantly wanted to affirm herself.

'I'm not worried,' she said, a little too quickly for it to sound convincing.

Jax explained the phenomenon. 'The gas is mostly sulphur – very smelly and poisonous if you breathe too much of it. The molten rock – or lava, as we call it – is trapped far below the surface in a magma chamber. In days gone by, the lava would burst out at the surface every so often – it's under great pressure down there – and there'd be a huge volcanic explosion, much like the one that formed this island.'

He said it all so matter-of-factly, she thought. Yet he was talking about life-threatening, terrible events that must have cost many people their lives. She could not let this go unquestioned.

'But that must have been dreadful! What about the people who lived here?'

'Ah yes,' he began sadly, hanging his head. 'The island has a history of eruptions. The earliest one – although it's more myth than fact – is said to have drowned the ancient city of Atlantis and the thousands of people who lived there. It was the end of one of the most advanced civilisations of its day. But we've since discovered that that was more likely to have happened in the shallow northern waters of the Black Sea where a submerged lost city was found back in the twenty-third century.'

In a slow, sweeping glide, the aircar swung away from the caldera and began its approach to the rock face. It soon began to rise vertically and Linnayen could see, some two hundred metres above the pontoon, what appeared to be the remains of an old track carved into the rock face. It zigzagged its way up until it levelled out and disappeared between the first buildings of the city.

'But what about here? The eruptions?' Linnayen urged.

'Here? There were sporadic eruptions from time to time and, yes, people were killed.' Jax's eyes scanned the barren black walls as he spoke. 'The last one – the one that gave the final push to these huge cliffs – was just over four hundred years ago and nearly two thousand people lost their lives. The old city of Thira was almost completely destroyed. This town of Neothira was since built and there hasn't been another eruption since then.'

'Aren't the residents worried, though, that there might? I don't think I could sleep at nights with that hanging over my head,' Linnayen commented.

'They don't have to worry anymore,' Jax replied. 'The depressure system that was constructed after the eruption in 2643 has taken away that worry.'

Seeing Linnayen's furrowed brow, Jax continued his explanation, one that had been first told to him by his mother.

'Santorini was chosen as the test site for a new geological engineering method. You see, throughout the centuries, people have chosen to live near volcanically active areas because they almost have no choice – the soils produced by the breakdown of the lava and volcanic ash are so rich. Good for farming, you understand. So the geologists and engineers at the Berkeley Institute in Amerimex developed a technique of simultaneously drilling pressure release columns through the mantle rocks and into a magma chamber.'

Linnayen was listening carefully and Jax, encouraged by her interest, went on.

'It was a hugely tricky undertaking for many reasons. First, you had to map the magma chamber quite precisely. Then, because the land surface directly above it would stand at differing heights, the drill speeds had to be variable yet similar enough so that one drill head didn't breach the chamber ahead of the others. That would run the risk of the lava exploding up through the drill channel. So pressure at the drill heads had to match the pressure inside the magma chamber.'

Jax, enthused about his subject now, glanced over to see if he was confusing her.

'Yes, I can see that,' Linnayen mused. 'So each drill head would also have to contain a mechanism for measuring and maintaining the pressure as it descended.'

'Absolutely. You've got it.' Jax was pleased at her response. 'Then, of course, there was the problem of temperature. The heat of the magma was enough to melt any substance on the face of this planet, including anything you could build a drill head out of. That problem wasn't solved until the discovery of couparnium on Mercury, which has the highest known melting point of any metallic compound. But there was still another obstacle.'

'And that was?' Duncan fed the opener this time, a smile widening his face. His old friend Jax was enjoying his role as both tour guide and teacher, or perhaps, he pondered, it was the presence of his disarmingly pretty wife. Whatever the reason, it was good to see him animated and relaxed for a change.

'Once the drill channels released the burden of over-pressure, the magma would naturally want to rise to the surface. Under normal circumstances, as it rises it cools and solidifies –'

'Thus blocking the drill channels,' Linnayen finished for him.

'Exactly. So there had to be holding reservoirs along the route of the drill channels where temperatures could be kept sufficiently hot to keep the magma fluid but stable. There are subterranean tunnels that run horizontally in the strata just above the magma chamber where the temperatures are well over eight hundred degrees Celsius. The magma can spread out, still molten, still under pressure, although much reduced, but it's controlled. If there's a build-up of magma, a pressure wave is sent down one channel to cause, in effect, a fake eruption up another channel – an eruption straight onto the seabed where it's rendered harmless. The top vents of those channels and reservoirs are what you saw before we entered the inner bay of the island.'

Jax reminded them of the strange metal towers they had seen dotted across the blue waters as the hydroplane had neared Santorini, each one emitting plumes of smoke.

'I thought that was gas mining,' Linnayen said.

'Well, it is in a way,' Jax confirmed. 'The gas emitted from the vents turns turbines fitted in the pressure channels, which in turn produces electric power for the island. It's a neat system.'

They turned their attention to the landscape passing below them. The town lay a little way in the distance now and had given way to undulating fields, delineated by lines of stone walls. Some fields were ochre and looked barren while others contained orderly rows of dark green olive trees, or the bright green foliage of vegetables growing under clear bio-domes. It was late summer and the autumnal rains had not yet begun to make their mark on the open fields so the wild grasses remained brown, their meadow flowers having long since died away in the summer's heat.

'Here we are.' Jax indicated the walls of a sparkling whitewashed mudbrick and glass villa set high atop the northern end of the cliff wall. It was on a gentle slope of land that ran downwards away from the rim some metres away. In order to preserve the view, though, the front face of the villa rose in four steps, all facing towards the inland sea and the island's caldera. The villa was surrounded by elaborate gardens that were themselves bordered by tall, thin cypress trees, and Linnayen could just make out a central courtyard where she thought she caught a glimpse of a bright blue pool. At one of the corners stood a high square tower. It had at one time been a church bell tower but it now housed the mounting for the security shield, which had been dropped for the aircars' arrival. The traditional materials of mud and stucco had been mixed well with the newer glass and metal additions. Combined with an innovative design, the overall effect of Thea's villa was one of comfort and solidity but with a hint of opulence, and Linnayen found herself eager to settle in for her much-needed break.

Marcus di Luca was beaming with pleasure as he stood on the rooftop landing platform to welcome the guests. His small, chubby hands were laced together in front of his rotund stomach, ready to receive his formal pupil. He did not have to wait long. As soon as the aircar doors opened, Jax rushed across to di Luca to give him an enthusiastic bear hug. Their greeting lasted only a few seconds before Jax jogged back to the aircar. He put out his hand to help Linnayen, who had been patiently watching the exchange with the old professor. She accepted his assistance and stepped down onto the platform, by which time di Luca had shuffled forward and was already bowing to her.

'Oh, professor, please. There's no need for that,' she said, dismayed at his subservience.

The old retainer lifted his head cautiously and found a pair of smiling green eyes looking into his. He was pleased. He liked that this grand young woman of great rank was pleasant and informal. His two weeks at the villa – and hers, he hoped – would be happy ones.

'I can't tell you, my lady, how wonderful it is to see you again,' he said, warmly. 'I do hope you'll like it on Santorini. Lady Thea's villa is a wonderful home, but you must tell me if anything is not to your satisfaction and I'll see to it at once.'

'Oh, I'm sure everything will be perfect, professor. But thank you for your kind concern.' She smiled broadly and nodded her approval.

She has a smile as wide as the sea itself! My young prince has chosen well, he thought. 'Well, come along then and I'll show you your rooms.' Di Luca said excitedly. Although he enjoyed his own company and the quiet pleasure of his study, it was occasionally rather a treat to be surrounded by so many young people. The hubbub was a welcome change, at least for a day or two.

Di Luca led the way inside and Linnayen immediately felt the pleasure of cool air on her arms and face. It was early afternoon, a time when the sun was at its zenith and the heat outside had become fierce. The old man trundled on ahead of her and Jax, who had come to walk by her side. As they walked, di Luca enquired of their journey and told them that he and the villa's staff had watched the wedding, which of course had been on all the news channels.

'What a delightful ceremony. Your sister and her husband looked as though they were enjoying every minute of it! Charming couple. Charming!'

'They did enjoy it and they are very happy,' Linnayen replied warmly.

'And the wedding reception that evening was truly magnificent,' Jax added. 'Amazing food, great music and ... dancing.'

Linnayen noticed his hesitation and flicked him a glance. It only lasted a split second but it was enough for Jax to spot the amusement hovering around her eyes and mouth. Was she laughing at him? A ripple of anger passed through him. He must remember to keep up his defences, he thought. Funny, he had been almost certain last night that she had changed. Now he was not so sure.

'Ah, here we are,' di Luca said, stopping and pushing open two heavy wooden doors on his right. 'I thought you'd like Lady Thea's room. It's possibly not as grand as the master suite, but it's very comfortable and the views are actually a little better, I think.'

The room was wide and painted entirely in white. The farthest wall and half of the ceiling comprised a curved glass panel that during the daytime was fused with a smoky grey-blue tint to help keep the room cool. The view beyond was, as di Luca had promised, truly spectacular, looking out over the curve of almost the entire island and the blue waters of the inner crater. The large bed, draped in sparkling white sheets and decorated with embroidered pillows, was set on a low dais against the window so that its occupant could look up through the glass ceiling to the stars at night and out across the blue bay in the morning. The room was otherwise sparsely furnished. Two white couches had been placed to one side of the room at right angles to each other and facing a small vidscreen that was set halfway up the wall. On the other side of the room, an arched doorway framed by two deep green fan-palms led through to a bathroom and dressing-room. The only other furniture in the room was an antique writing desk and chair in the opposite corner to the couches, with a view of the room and beyond.

Linnayen's eyes were wide as she took in her luxurious quarters.

'This is wonderful. Thank you.'

'Well, as I said, it's very comfortable,' the old man replied, then turned to Jax. 'And although you won't be with us long, I'm sure you and your wife will make yourselves at home here.'

With that he turned and headed back towards the door. Jax's eyebrows drew together. Did di Luca mean what he thought? Did the old man plan to have them sleep together – in here?

He looked across at Linnayen, who had a similarly confused look upon her face. Here was a dilemma that neither of them had prepared themselves for. The professor had obviously assumed that they slept together. Although he knew that Linnayen had been ill, it had not occurred to the old man, who had been raised with more traditional ways and customs, that they would sleep apart. They were a married couple after all, and married people shared the same room.

Jax was in a quandary. How could he broach the subject with di Luca without embarrassing him or fuelling any more rumours about the state of his marriage? Di Luca was almost out of the door and about to take Duncan, Nen and Dr Mai to their rooms when Jax opened his mouth to say something about the sleeping arrangements. Linnayen's hand on his arm stopped him in his tracks. He looked at her, his eyes forming a question.

In barely more than a whisper Linnayen said, 'It's only for one night.' She nodded her head, then her eyes led his in the direction of the two couches.

He understood. The couches looked comfortable and no one would have to know. But the thought did cross his mind that he would be alone with his wife for the first night since their wedding.

Durroc Navarr looked at the conference hall's gilt antique timepiece and sighed. The hours and minutes seemed to be dragging like treacle through an hourglass. The trade meeting called to discuss the rates and frequency of shipments of refined carbon, magnesium and other Earthan minerals was bogged down in a morass of minutiae and he was by now completely uninterested. Indeed, nearly every aspect of his new role as delegation leader left him indifferent and apathetic. It was all very tedious compared to his former duties and status as head of the Ki's security team, a position he would soon hold again if the next few hours went as planned.

Navarr was quietly anxious about the events that would be taking place but he believed he hid it well. He resisted the urge to drum his fingers on the table and instead turned his mind to the plan for the kidnap, going over, for the tenth time, the proposed sequence that the mercenaries of Whip Company would soon enact.

No one in the conference room had any idea what was going to happen, which gave him a feeling of smug satisfaction. Everyone felt assured that any threats had passed now that the wedding was over. But, of course, Evica and Tariik's wedding was never the target. Even his old superior Beoraan, whose doddering manner, he knew, belied an underlying shrewdness, had given no indication that he was overly worried now about any terrorist plots. Indeed, with the cessation of the wedding's activities, all seemed calm and things were returning to normal. The visit of the Altani royals was fast becoming a standard heads-of-state tour and all the regular safeguards were in place. These, though, would not be adequate to protect and defend the young Ki from the skilled men and women of Whip Company, who, he had been reliably informed by his sister, were the best there was.

By this time tomorrow, thought Navarr, all hell would have broken loose and he would take his deserved place at the centre of power once again. In his mind's eye he saw himself issuing orders at speed to a bevy of flunkeys and assistants, just as he used to – the indispensable commander in charge of events – and he allowed himself a barely noticeable smile.

Not long now. He would have control of the Ki's heart and her mind once more. He would be her consort in all but name. Even the prospect of possessing her body again gave him a surge of physical pleasure that he had not been expecting but welcomed all the same.

All he had to do was wait for Balisel's signal and be ready to move. And it could not come soon enough for the impatient commander.

The local custom in these warmer climates, Professor di Luca had told Linnayen after lunch, was to take a nap in the afternoon and she had duly followed his advice. Although the journey from Athens had not been overly long, the events of the last few days had tired her and she was pleased of an excuse to rest. As she drifted into sleep on the large white quilted bed, her thoughts were of her strange situation and her growing desire not just to make amends to her husband for her past betrayal but to fulfil her role as his wife – and all that it entailed.

When she awoke a couple of hours later, the long, low shadows falling across the polished wooden floor told her that it was quite late in the day. After a few minutes she stood up and stretched her arms above her head, yawning. In the bathroom she splashed cold water on her face to revive herself. Patting her face dry with a soft towel, she heard a murmur of voices and the gentle slapping sounds of flowing water coming through the high window open above the washbasin. Trying to recall what she had been shown of the villa on arrival, she guessed that the window faced towards the inner courtyard and the pool.

The voices were indistinct, although she could hear frequent laughter. Whoever was down there was having a good time and she yearned to be part of it. One of the worst things about her amnesia, she reflected, was the loneliness it brought. She had been truly isolated within her condition and, even with the patience and understanding that everyone had shown her, no one could grasp the absolute seclusion she felt. Friends and family members were to all intents strangers, and however nice and well-meaning they were, she had lost the lifetime needed to know them as intimately as they knew her. They had experiences and memories of her that she now knew nothing about and, thus, all the common ground upon which they should have been able to base their relationships was gone.

Perhaps the former Linnayen could have existed like that, she thought. But not her. She was young – only twenty-four years old – and this was an exciting and fascinating new world, crammed full of interesting new people, and she wanted to experience it all. In time, she hoped, more of her memories would return and would perhaps bring her joy and a sense of belonging. But in the meantime, she had a new life to live. Rather than mope or worry about a past that could not yet be found – or that she may not want to relive – she would look forward to building a future. A future, she hoped, that would include the handsome, sensitive young man who was her husband.

At that very moment, his deep laugh carried through the window on a light, cool breeze and she smiled.

Yes, a swim is just what I need to wake me up! She turned back into the bedroom and began searching the contents of her trunk for a bathing costume.

'Ah, at last! You've had a good sleep?' Duncan was the first to notice Linnayen's arrival and he quickly stood to offer her a chair at the table around which he, Dr Mai, Nen and Jax were gathered.

'Thank you. Yes, I slept well,' she replied with a friendly smile.

'That's good, my lady, because I believe Mr McCrae has a night of revelry planned for us all.' The normally solemn, serene doctor almost smiled.

'And knowing him, that means you'll need your strength,' Jax said fondly, patting Duncan on the back. Suddenly he remembered the reason for their visit to this island and added, 'If you're up to it, of course …'

The look of concern on his face suggested a sense of solicitousness rather than affection to Linnayen. He was, as ever, being intensely polite.

She smiled more broadly. 'Oh yes! I feel fine.'

'Excellent!' Duncan roared. He puffed out his chest and continued, 'For tonight we shall dine on the finest, freshest fruits these fortuitous islands have to offer. We shall feast and frolic with festive abandon and –'

'Oh, Duncan, shut up!' Jax exclaimed, bringing to a sharp halt the actor's stream of alliteration.

Linnayen laughed at the sandy-haired man's pretence at being crestfallen. 'That's a lot of "f" words, isn't it?' she said, still giggling.

Jax and Duncan glanced at each other and burst out laughing. She was confused. She appeared to have said something amusing and a look of puzzlement took over her features. Seeing this, Jax tried to explain.

'Oh, sorry, Linnayen. It's an Earth thing – a joke. We're not laughing at you.'

'Course not,' Duncan concurred. 'I'll try to explain …'

Over the next few minutes, Linnayen received her first lesson in Earthan humour. It was not to be her last.

After a swim with her companions, Linnayen announced that she would return to her room to shower and dress. Jax rose to go with her and she was momentarily surprised. Then she remembered. To their companions, they were very much a married couple. It was natural and normal for her husband to go with her and it felt rather nice. She felt a small glow of pleasure as he took her arm to lead her back into the villa.

Duncan, Dr Mai and Nen held back and, once the couple had gone, their eyes all met in a knowing look.

'Nothing too strenuous tonight, Mr McCrae,' warned Dr Mai.

'Wouldn't dream of it! Besides,' he surmised with a knowing wink, 'I think she'll need whatever energy she has for later.'

The look of complete surprise on Duncan's face was something Dr Mai would always treasure as the unassuming Nen smacked him smartly on his upper arm before stomping off, her tiny chin held high.

Oleander studied the holographic image from all angles as it revolved slowly in the air. It was a diagrammatic representation of the Bashir villa in its situation on top of the cliff walls of the crater rim. Surrounding the villa was a dome of faint shimmering red light which signified the outer security shield. This was purely defensive and designed to repel or deflect any incoming object, be it vehicle or weapon. Within that was another orange-coloured band representing the villa's inner shield, which, in contrast to the outer one, was not defensive in nature but offensive. It was in effect a trigger mechanism that would, if touched, set off an array of target-sensitised weaponry. Thus, even if the outer shield were breached, the inner would destroy everything thrown at it.

There was no way to get past these shields. But then, they had known that. They could, of course, be disengaged from inside the villa, but there had been insufficient time to infiltrate the staff or produce a cybernetic doppelganger to replace one of them, which would have been Oleander's first choice. Thus, she and Whip Company had been left no alternative but to take the villa from the only place where the shields did not reach: below ground.

This, too, had presented some complications. The sloping land surrounding and falling away from the villa was heavily guarded and far too open. The distance to the villa was too great to allow any subterranean tunnelling and, in any case, the noise of such an enterprise might have been audible at the surface. Certainly, the vibrations of tunnelling over a lengthy period would be picked up. No, their assault had to be as quick and quiet as it was possible to be. And this was where the knowledge of Dr Cornelius Pak had proved so invaluable.

Dr Pak, a noted vulcanologist of the early twenty-third century, had mapped and measured the dimensions of some thirty-four volcanoes around the world. His painstaking and often tedious work, whilst not winning him any major prizes or honours in the field of geoscience, had become one of the cornerstones of vulcanology. The millions upon millions of measurements Dr Pak and his students had taken over four decades had produced the finest and most intricate three-dimensional maps of some of the most complex geological systems on earth. In the same way that medical science had long ago mapped the genetic codes of most living organisms on the planet, Dr Pak's work led eventually to geo-predictive intelligence: the understanding of and ability to predict almost exactly how any active volcanic system will react in an eruptive event. His work enabled scientists and engineers to predict exactly where and for how long lava would flow, what the chemical composition of that lava or ash would be and the degree of volatility of any eruption. The only factor Dr Pak's work did not encompass was the frequency of eruptions. But that was adequately handled by seismologists and in no way did it devalue his work.

Whilst Oleander appreciated the volume of Dr Pak's contribution, she cared little for its scope. The larger ramifications of the collection of so much data was of little consequence to her, but the precision of his mapping of the volcano of Santorini was a positive blessing in this undertaking. For without Cornelius Pak, the quiet plodding scientist, the assault on the Bashir villa would be virtually impossible.

His maps provided the key for they showed a long dormant fissure of little more than ninety centimetres in width rising vertically to within six metres of the surface at a point directly beneath the villa's outer garden. This underground wormhole – a natural weakness in the otherwise solid rock – would be their way in. All Whip Company had to do was to wait for cover of darkness, at which time four company members would scale the sheer cliff walls. Once at a point approximately eight metres below the cliff top, they would use a laser drill to cut through the crater walls horizontally until they reached the vertical fissure. The resulting crawl-space tunnels, whilst no more than a metre wide, would be sufficient to allow the men to push through into the villa's grounds well inside the parabola of both security shields. These would then be disabled once the men had made their way into the control room. The rest of Whip Company's force would then descend in aircars ready to fly the captive Ki and their comrades away to the stronghold of Guyvar Neref, where Oleander now waited.

A sudden opening of the door behind her caused Oleander to spin around. Balisel Navarr and Whip Company's commanding officer entered the room. The tall, blonde woman made a striking contrast to the shorter, honey-brown Oleander, yet both were intensely attractive, a fact that had not escaped the lascivious eye of the company commander, Kees Rennick.

A natural fighter, he enjoyed all his missions, relishing in the challenge and the bloodshed. But some had added bonuses, he reflected, as he stared at the two women. These two would make for some memorable fantasies when this mission was over and he could allow himself to sleep again. And who knows, maybe not just fantasies.

'You can wipe that smirk off your face, Rennick.'

Oleander's voice was as sharp and poisonous as her gaze. She guessed what he had been thinking and, in that instant, Rennick knew his fantasies would always be just that. The dark woman's eyes held more than a promise of death. He had heard the rumours. She was said to be a top assassin who worked exclusively for a highly secretive, wealthy group of right-wing fanatics. He supposed that it would not help his career to get either Oleander or her employers offside.

Balisel ignored the exchange, her eyes squinting to focus on the rotating image.

'Everything is ready?' she asked haughtily.

'Yes,' Oleander replied. 'The plan is foolproof.'

'And the equipment?' Balisel queried.

This was Rennick's area. 'The drill is working perfectly and its power cells are fully charged, although we'll be carrying back-up cells just in case. The aircars are fuelled, tested and ready to go. All company personnel are carrying hand weapons as well as the standard micro-mines, phaedex caps and aerotorps. The men are primed and armed to the teeth.' Rennick's confidence in the supreme destructive ability of his troop was obvious in both his tone and bearing. He lifted his chin in a display of strength and infallibility. Balisel Navarr was not impressed.

'All well and good, commander, but do they know where they are going? Do they know how to locate the Ki's bedroom once inside the villa?'

Rennick could not quite hide the glint of derision in his eyes as he forced himself to answer civilly.

'They could find the room blindfolded – *and* the target.'

'They'd better,' Balisel shot back, the ice-blue of her eyes taking on an edge of steel. 'I don't need to remind you that we'll only get one shot at this. And you *will* get it right!'

Oleander joined the exchange. 'Miss Navarr, I assure you we will need only one shot. Nothing will go wrong.' Her voice was slow and calm. Her eyes never left Balisel's, who could not know that the assassin's thoughts gave her all the assurance she needed. *But even if it does go wrong, the Order will still get what it wants – the Galactic Union threatened by the attempted kidnap and you and your twin brother completely in our control, bound to us forever by your secrets.*

'Rennick,' Oleander began, the honeyed voice now abrupt and businesslike. 'Make your final checks. Take your personnel through it one more time. We leave at 7pm.'

Chapter Twenty-seven

Jax could not recall when, in many long months – possibly since before his marriage at least – he had felt so relaxed and at ease. He was having fun! He scanned the faces around the small whitewashed taverna in which they had chosen to dine that evening after strolling through the winding streets of Neothira.

Those who were not laughing were smiling, and those who did not smile were engrossed in apparently enjoyable conversations, judging by the amount of nodding and friendly banter going on. There was Duncan McCrae at the head of one table, arms spread wide, eyes closed and a look of rapture on his face, trying to impress Em-sin Mai with his delivery of a Shakespearean soliloquy. The shy maid, Nen, looked by far the more taken with his recital. Jax suspected that the practical doctor was putting on an interested face out of politeness and, possibly, respect for the actor's obvious enthusiasm for his subject.

Then there was Linnayen and Marcus di Luca sitting closest to him, their heads bowed together in quiet conversation. She was smiling at his words and the old professor was delighted when, every so often, she would interrupt him to ask pertinent questions that drew out his great store of knowledge. From what he could overhear, di Luca was regaling her with stories from Greek mythology. He caught the words 'Perseus' and 'Medusa' and wondered what Linnayen would make of a gorgon's head, writhing with snakes that could turn whoever looked upon it to stone. Jax thought that the old man had not had such a fine audience in a couple of decades; certainly *he* had never been such an attentive student when he was a boy.

The remainder of their party comprised Captain Chandra and four of his men and, although they were officially on duty, Jax had asked that they be allowed enough leeway to join them for a meal at least. After all, as Jax had explained to the captain, they would have to eat anyway, and they might as well all eat together.

With such a lessening of formality and it being their first night on the holiday island, perhaps it was to be expected that the group would be in high spirits. The warmth of the night air, the charm of the old buildings with their white walls and colourful painted balconies under a canopy of clear stars added to the atmosphere. On their way to the restaurant they had passed many brightly lit stalls and small shops and Jax had noticed the enjoyment Linnayen took in inspecting the many souvenirs and embroidered fabrics, chatting about them with Dr Mai or Nen or whoever was nearby, himself included. He had never seen her like this, her face alternately animated or engrossed. Was she finally becoming the woman he had always imagined her to be before he learned the truth of her duplicity? She even tried to buy one or two pieces and had not been embarrassed or offended when the company laughed at her for neither knowing about money nor bringing any with her. She had laughed at her own naivety until Duncan kindly stepped forward to offer his wrist to the shopkeeper to be scanned so that the necessary debits could be made from his reserves.

'Thank you, Duncan, you're very gallant,' she had said warmly. 'But I am sure my husband can pay for this – or are we poor?' Her question went to Jax, accompanied by a mischievous gleam in her eye. He, still reeling from his wife's new-found public informality, had been caught unawares by the question and fumbled a response.

'Oh, um … No, no, of course not. I mean, I'll take care of it.' Linnayen smiled into his eyes and, from over her shoulder, Duncan had raised a questioning eyebrow at Jax. The young Ki was being decidedly flirtatious with her somewhat gauche husband.

Jax had paid the shopkeeper and accepted the wrapped bundle containing the fine table linen that had so taken Linnayen's eye. The group had moved on but Linnayen and a couple of the guards had hung back a little, waiting for him to catch up to them.

'I'm sorry. I didn't mean to tease you,' she said, placing her arm through his.

'Right.' Feeling the lightness of her touch on his arm, he had suddenly felt like a schoolboy, tongue-tied and self-conscious. The feeling was partnered by a slight churning sensation in the pit of his stomach, which he knew had nothing to do with his digestion. No, he well recognised these symptoms – so like those he'd had when he first met Linnayen – and he determined to put a stop to them before they took hold.

He had walked on with her, giving largely monosyllabic responses to her many comments and questions. Linnayen, though, was tenacious, and the more reserved he tried to be, the more determined she became to humour him. Privately, though, she had begun to despair and she wondered precisely *how* awful she must have been before her accident for him to be so defensive now.

Finally they had reached the restaurant, which had been chosen by the old professor. It was a traditional taverna with an open dining terrace that sat close to the edge of the crater rim and, from its parapet, the view out across the circular bay was breathtaking. The sun had just dipped below the horizon and a palette of rich orange and peach colours still emblazoned a corner of the sky even whilst the darker cobalt of the night encroached upon the expanse.

Linnayen had gone straight to the parapet's edge to see the view and, spreading her arms out to support her body, leaned as far into the sunset colours as she could. Jax, fearing she might lose her balance, rushed to where she stood and took a firm hold of her shoulder.

'Be careful! It's a long way down.'

She smiled over her shoulder. 'And you wouldn't want anything to happen to me, would you?' Suddenly her face grew serious. Her gaze fixed upon him in the growing darkness. 'Or would you? Perhaps you'd prefer it if something did.'

'Don't be ridiculous!' he snapped, his surprise and confusion giving way to a growing anger. 'I don't want to get rid of you –'

She cut in before he could continue. 'Why not? Who could blame you? I've not exactly been a model wife, have I? I used you. Cheated on you. I was unkind to you.' Her breathing quickened with every word and her voice grew louder. Her anger, too, was growing. Anger at herself. Anger at her amnesia and the impossible situation. 'Why would any man want a wife like that? Why *wouldn't* you want me gone? Or dead!'

'No! That's the last thing I want. I would never want to hurt you. I …' He stopped the words from coming. This was dangerous ground. He nearly said the one thing he had vowed he would never say to her. His voice regained its calm. 'You are my wife. We are bound to each other. We have a duty.' He snapped the words at her, closing off any retort.

In the look she gave him he saw a trace of the old Linnayen. Scorn, sorrow, distaste. She shrugged her shoulder firmly out of his grasp and turned her head away from him. This was not how she had wanted it to be. Why had she deliberately sparked an argument between them? What devil possessed her?

Then the thought crept into her mind like a frost descending upon the cold earth. Was this the real her? The one she used to be? Perhaps she was regaining her former self after all and, if that was a taste of what she had been like, no wonder he had been so wounded.

He began to turn away as the rest of the party took their seats at the extra tables the proprietor had hastily brought out onto the terrace.

She placed a restraining hand upon Jax's arm. 'I'm … Kevor, I'm sorry. I spoke out of turn. I – I don't know what got into me.'

There was genuine remorse in her expression and he knew he needed to speak, to make his position plain.

'Look … you must know, Linnayen, no matter how things were between us before, I never wished you harm.'

'I'm sure. Perhaps I'm feeling guilty.' She noted the look of surprise on his face. 'I've wronged you so much.'

Jax's head reeled and for the first time he began to believe that she truly had changed and that the nightmare of his marriage might even be coming to an end. But what if her memories of Navarr returned? It was still early days in her recovery and there lay many months ahead in which his taint may yet again stain their relationship. He remembered an adage of his mother's: *actions speak louder than words*. And he resolved to wait a while longer before committing himself again to his beloved but betraying wife.

His reply came short and sharp. 'Then let's hope our future will be a better one. Will you eat?'

Not long after they were seated, a variety of colourful dishes and wines began to appear. The proprietor had suggested that he bring an array of different foods and that they would honour him by sampling them all. This idea was well received by everyone, although Linnayen and Em-sin Mai were curious as to what comprised the dishes and insisted that the proprietor stay close by so that he could describe them. They found that although the flavours were slightly different from what they were used to on Altan, some of the vegetables and fruits used were like the produce of their home planet. The similarities in climate, axial orientation and atmospheric composition of Earth and Altan, Jax explained, were probably responsible, as was their approximate distance from each system's central star. The two planets had a shared astrophysical, chemical and geological history, having been formed at around the same time.

'Give or take the odd hundred million years, of course,' Jax explained, at which Linnayen laughed.

'Of course. A mere nanosecond!'

Jax could not stop himself from enjoying the moment of humour.

'And a little before *my* time, so we'll have to take it on trust.'

Marcus di Luca joined in. 'Well, no. Not really. There's ample evidence in the rocks themselves to prove the chronologic development of both planets. However, I think you'll find that Earth is fractionally the older of the two.'

'And Autabron is the very oldest of us all,' Linnayen added. Then, after a second wherein she registered her surprise at this knowledge, she continued. 'Although I didn't know I knew that – until now.'

Everyone burst out laughing, Linnayen included. Jax felt his heart warmed by this amazing turn of events. Perhaps her memories – certainly her store of knowledge – was returning bit by bit. But if Linnayen could learn to laugh at herself – something unimaginable before the fall on the *Jensa Kadenx* – then maybe she would not regain her old personality. She could even become the person Jax had originally envisioned in those early days when he had made his appraisal of her over a vidscreen.

He realised now how naïve he had been then – had seen only what he wanted to see, perceiving an ideal life partner endowed with the qualities he wanted them to have. He had been an idealistic, romantic fool, forgetting that she, too, was her own person with a personality and traits that he would all too soon discover were not necessarily what he was seeking in a mate. No, he had, he now realised, been a complete idiot, swayed more by the romance of the situation than by logic and he had paid a heart-wounding price for his error.

'What else do you remember of your planetary studies?' Di Luca asked of Linnayen.

She scanned her damaged mind, trying to focus, to bring back some hidden snippet. 'Let me see … I remember that Dasnir is nine-tenths ocean, that on Hutho the average lifespan of the giant nolbuthu tree is three thousand years. I remember that the Ksas on Altan is the longest and highest chain of mountains of any of the known planets and that your planet of Jupiter has the greatest number of moons orbiting it, although I can't remember how many.'

Duncan clapped her performance. 'Nor can any of us. And such matters are the stuff of schoolrooms, not a romantic restaurant on a warm summer's evening under a glorious mantle of stars,' he retorted with a flourish.

Em-sin Mai nodded approvingly. 'This is encouraging. Your personal memories will likewise return, my lady.'

'Do you really think so?' Linnayen asked nervously, wondering if, now that her new life was taking on a shape of its own, she wanted her past to resurface. How, she pondered, would her old memories fit into this new existence? Would they enrich it or push it to one side and force her to become her old self? So much still could not be known.

'I do, my lady. But it will take time,' the straight-backed doctor replied in her usual forthright manner. 'And there is, as you know, no guarantee that you will remember everything.'

Linnayen frowned, accepting the truth of the doctor's words. Seeing her head droop and feeling the need to cheer her up, Duncan added, 'With any luck you'll never remember Jax's habit of sucking the air through his teeth or pig-snorting when he laughs. I wish I could forget.'

The atmosphere was instantly lightened and Duncan quickly suggested to the proprietor that they have some music and dancing. The rotund man rushed away to see to it and Duncan inveigled Captain Chandra and the other guards to help him push back the tables to make room.

The strangest noise assaulted Linnayen's ears and she assumed it was what passed for music in these parts. It issued from a hidden source that must have been fitted into the walls of the building and its strains floated in the air around them. The first tune had a strong regular rhythm overlain with the soft sound of many stringed instruments, pitched both high and low. The words, which were in the local language, sounded lyrical, but of course meant nothing to her. The proprietor told her that the song told a story about a man and a woman who fell in love on a moonlit night when they were both young and beautiful.

'They marry, share a life of joy and pain. Now they are very old and the man is dying. It is another moonlit night and he reminds his wife of how they felt all those years ago, of the passion they had – the great love – and he vows to her that he still feels the same.'

'Even though she is old and wrinkled?' Nen asked, being drawn into the evening's entertainment.

'Ah, the song says that he loves her still *because* she is old and has lived her life with him, helping him, sharing his joys and sorrows,' the proprietor replied. 'It is a song of praise, if you like, for the virtue of a good wife.'

Then there's a song my husband will never sing to me, thought Linnayen wryly.

The next song was faster – obviously a dance – and Duncan pulled a reluctant Nen to her feet to start the fun. Linnayen was delighted at the antics and turned to Jax, a beaming smile on her face.

'Would you like to dance too? You know, this planet is very good at dancing, having happy times. Not like stuffy Altan.'

He was caught off-guard but his surprise at her comment was stopped before it could invade his thoughts too deeply by her insistent tugging on his sleeve to begin. It seemed she had, albeit unknowingly, recalled another piece of information from her past. But the rhythm of the music was omnipresent and allowed his thoughts no space to expand. It was more pressing that he dance, and for once he was glad of the freedom it brought. If only for tonight he would forget his troubles and enjoy himself.

Inside the small tunnel that had been so neatly drilled into the steep side of the crater wall, the air was damp with the exhalations of the lead man. In the pale light ahead of his face he could see his breath condensing on the scratched rock walls, covering them with a fine film of dew. His arms ached from steering the drill for the last twenty minutes. Although its polarised lasers worked quickly, slicing through the tough, volcanic rock like a warm knife through butter, and the drill was mounted on a hoverplate, he still had to take some of its weight when manoeuvring it. He was more than ready for a rest and, at a signal in his earpiece a few minutes later, he sighed in relief. It was the end of his shift and, switching the drill into standby mode, he slid his body backwards down the ten metres of tunnel he and two team members before him had just excavated.

On exiting the breach, he sat down on the small platform that he and the other three team members had constructed against the crater wall following their climb up from the sea as soon as darkness had descended. No one spoke. Another driller entered the tunnel. Only seven more metres and they would intersect with the old fumarole tube. The going would be easier then and they would be able to begin the climb upwards towards the villa itself. He estimated that they would be in the grounds within the next two hours, which would leave them plenty of time to locate and disarm the security shields in preparation for Whip company's main attack in the small hours of the new day.

It was nearly ten o'clock when Marcus di Luca called a halt to the dancing, telling them that he had an announcement to make. The noise of the music and laughter subsided and the old man cleared his throat.

'I have arranged a little surprise for our special guest tonight. An experience that I hope you will find both exhilarating and beautiful.'

Duncan looked at Jax with a puzzled expression. Jax shrugged, just as confounded as everyone else. Whatever his old tutor had planned, he knew nothing about it.

'Here on the island we have a marvellous attraction, an activity that many tourists enjoy and I hope you will like it too, my lady. It's calling cloudsailing and, if I am not mistaken …' The professor looked across to Captain Chandra, who nodded his confirmation. 'It is time for us to cast off!'

The grin on the old man's face was infectious and, despite the looks of surprise and misgiving between them, Linnayen, Dr Mai, Nen, Jax and Duncan arose and followed Captain Chandra out of the taverna to where three aircars stood waiting.

They were taken to a small airdock a few kilometres out of town and, as they approached the dimly lit landing platform, Linnayen made out the silhouette of a craft unlike anything she had ever seen before. Its steel keel rested on the smooth floor of the airdock and rising out of its torpedo-shaped fuselage there stood three tall masts. At first she thought that the upper half of the fuselage was open to the skies. Then, as they parked on the airdock's platform, she caught a reflection of moonlight on something shiny and it became apparent that it was made of some transparent material. It seemed that one could sit inside the body of the craft completely protected from the elements yet feel surrounded by sky. If they were to go flying – or was it sailing? – in this vessel, it would indeed be a truly unique experience.

The party, having been escorted to the cloudclipper by the airdock's ground crew, climbed aboard and seated themselves as instructed by the clipper's first officer. Within minutes they were airborne and the slow hum of engines could be heard straining to lift them into the night sky.

Their seats tilted back with the angle of the rising craft and Linnayen's dark green eyes opened wide to take in the misty filament of stars that comprised the neighbouring suns and solar systems of their shared galaxy. For an instant she was reminded of a similar yet subtly different sight from her home-world where the same stellar strand could be seen every clear night, although in a different configuration to this. It was no less beautiful, however foreign it appeared to her eyes, and she was pleased to suddenly realise that, yet again, she had remembered something of her past.

There was silence for a few minutes as they rose through the air, everyone lost in their individual reveries. When the clipper reached its cruising altitude they levelled off and the low mechanical engine hum of their ascent gave way to a finer hissing noise, over which the vessel's captain began his commentary from the sealed cockpit in the bow.

'Good evening again, ladies and gentlemen. I hope you enjoyed our ascent.' The voice was clear, friendly and reassuring. 'We have reached an altitude of four thousand metres and are now able to cloudsail. The change in noise from our engines is because the clear conditions mean we have to produce our own clouds tonight. If you look below you will begin to see the clouds forming beneath us.'

Everyone shifted in their seats to look down. Linnayen, in a window seat, noticed that Jax was reluctant to lean across her and, with a wordless smile, she took his arm and gently tugged him closer.

'Of course, on cloudy nights we do not have to do this, as nature provides them for us,' the captain continued.

Outside Jax could see wisps of fine white water vapour growing denser beneath them and the silver mirror of the ocean, picked out by the moonlight, beginning to disappear. Suddenly he was aware that Linnayen was no longer staring out of the window but her half-closed eyes were studying him, taking in the line of his neck and his profile. He was instantly conscious that her lips were mere inches from his and for a few brief seconds they both hung there. Even without the rise and fall of her chest indicating to him that she was aroused, the smouldering look in her eyes left no doubt.

She wanted to kiss him. She wanted desperately to know how those lips would feel on hers. And Jax felt himself being drawn in and down towards his wife's moistened mouth. They were so close. One more second.

The captain's clear voice penetrated the stillness like an explosion. 'Once we have built up enough cloud we can begin to sail properly and then I invite you to take the ultimate challenge on our famous cloudskimmer!'

Linnayen caught her breath sharply. Jax sat back in his seat and Linnayen saw, out of the corner of her eye, the movement of his Adam's apple as he attempted to regain his composure. The moment was gone, she thought. Another opportunity lost. But her sadness was at odds with her joy, for she could have sworn that he had wanted to kiss her as much as she had wanted to kiss him. Perhaps there was hope yet.

'What the jolly roger is cloudskimmin'?' This was Duncan from a seat behind them, putting on a pirate's accent, at which Nen giggled and Dr Mai frowned.

'I've no idea,' Jax replied hurriedly. He had an overwhelming need to speak, if only to bring his world back to normal again.

'Aha!' Di Luca cried. 'That's the wonderful part about this experience and I heartily recommend it to you.' He took a mischievous and extreme pleasure in his position of greater knowledge.

'You've tried it yourself, professor?' Duncan asked.

'Oh yes. Last summer, with Lady Thea.'

Despite continued probing from the young actor, di Luca would say no more and further teased and goaded Duncan, saying, 'You just wait.' Meanwhile, the fabricated clouds outside had thickened to the point where they could no longer see any trace of either sea or the island far below.

With yet another shift in the noise of the engine and a feeling of movement outside the craft itself, Linnayen noticed that the three masts protruding from the clear roof of the fuselage appeared to be moving downwards. Their bases had ended within the craft; indeed, they had all had to walk around them when they had taken their seats on embarkation. She was astounded to see that, with exquisite smoothness, the three round structures descended through the floor until they reached their fullest extent. No longer were the three tall masts above them but, she presumed, beneath them and now out of sight. The captain spoke again.

'Thank you for your patience, ladies and gentlemen. We are now ready to unfurl the sails and let them take over the propulsion of the ship.'

Linnayen raised her eyebrows in amazement, and a glance at Jax suggested that he was equally surprised.

'Welcome to cloudsailing!' the captain continued with a flourish. 'This unique and remarkable method of propulsion involves the heating of water to produce vapour – steam – which, of course, rises. These are the clouds you see below us. However, in order to produce forward motion we make a hydro-thermal convection current within the cloud, and this is achieved by warming elements at the tips of the three masts. The masts also contain silkweave sails made of polymer strands and, if you look below, I will now unfurl our sails.'

Once again, the passengers strained to look down to into the swirling mists that had now been spotlighted with a rainbow blend of colours.

'Look, Kevor!' Linnayen could not contain her excitement at the scene that unravelled beneath them. Vast, shimmering, billowing fields of paper-thin fabric had opened below and were swelling with the warm moist air. They took on the colours of the cloud and its movement, so that the travellers felt every gentle dip and sway.

'Now I understand why they call it cloudsailing,' said Linnayen, a look of animated excitement on her face.

'Yes, but are we going to get seasick or airsick?' Duncan asked, gripping the arms of his seat whilst taking a deep breath.

Linnayen looked behind her to Nen sitting next to Duncan and saw her huge grin, and she grinned back. The rise and fall of the ship was a wonderful new motion that felt exhilarating.

'Perhaps cloudsick?' ventured Dr Mai.

'Then I am very glad we have you on board with us, Emsin,' Duncan said with his usual charm and good humour.

The rolling, riding motion seemed to put everyone in a good mood and, thankfully, no one showed any signs of nausea. The engines of the vessel had by now been completely shut off and the only sound around them was a high-pitched whistling as the wind rushed past.

'And now, for the more adventurous among you, I would like to offer you the chance to try cloudskimming.' The captain's smooth voice once again interrupted their thoughts. 'Our cabin staff will take you aft and show you what to do. Andros, Marie, please escort our guests.'

The two smiling crew members stood up from their seats in front of the cockpit and walked towards some steps near the middle of the fuselage that led to a lower deck. They encouraged the passengers to follow them, which, one by one, they did with varying degrees of caution or enthusiasm. Once below, the man, Andros, opened a door that led into another cabin where many pieces of equipment hung, including ropes, harnesses and objects that looked like lifejackets. There were also small oxygen tanks and face masks, and a selection of what looked like rubberised clothing of the type used by underwater divers.

Jax was beginning to get an understanding of what cloudskimming might entail when the hostess, Marie, asked them all to look up at a monitor for a brief visual presentation.

Firstly they were shown how to put on the rubberised thermal suit, then fix a solid plasticised jacket over the torso. The commentary explained that this jacket contained a simple flexichute which would open automatically if they were to disengage from the cloudclipper for any reason; a 'skimmer' could also detach himself manually, but this was only to be used in the event of an emergency. The chute's steering and lift controls were, the commentary explained, to be found on the front chest panel of the jacket. However, as the autonavigator would activate upon detachment, these were purely a back-up system.

Noticing the look of concern that passed across Nen's face, Duncan took her hand and patted it reassuringly. His accompanying fixed smile, though, did not necessarily comfort her.

Next came an outer harness that fitted over the shoulders and between the legs. It was further secured at the waist, where two safety clamps were positioned to receive a rope that ran from a mounting within the cabin. Another rope ran to the cabin mounting from a harness clamp that was fixed on the chest band. Once the participants in the video were suitably kitted out and attached to the cabin mountings, the aft wall of the clipper slowly slid down to reveal nothing but the open sky. A fine-meshed, virtually translucent safety net was also lowered and stabilisers along its length and width seemed to stop it from flapping around in the rushing wind.

'Welcome to the world of cloudskimming!' the commentary concluded. 'Now you are ready to truly fly!'

As the screen dimmed and the cabin lights came back up, the crew smiled at the stunned looks on their faces.

'Yes,' said Andros. 'We're going to fly. Please kit up exactly as you saw in the display just now. Marie and I will help you and check that you are secure before allowing you to exit the clipper in groups of no more than four at a time.'

'We will show you how to do this when you're ready.' Marie took over the instructions. 'But, briefly, you will descend using the net and, once you feel comfortable, you can let go. Your rope will allow you a maximum of seventy metres. You can control its length by means of this pad here on the chest panel.'

Andros took over once more. His voice was the essence of authority and professionalism and was obviously pitched to reassure the passengers. 'Please remember that you don't have to let go of the net if you don't want to and we will be out there with you to assist anyone who needs it.'

Duncan McCrae's face was now a mask of almost sheer terror. He looked at Professor di Luca who was already putting on his thermal suit.

'And you say you've done this before?' he asked incredulously.

'Yes,' returned the professor with a wry smile. 'And so has Lady Thea. Twice!' With this he looked across at Jax, who was already suited up and had heard the exchange. He grinned.

Linnayen watched the friendly banter affectionately, seemingly so much at odds with the more formal manner of her own people. She could not imagine her mother or Dr Mai or Beoraan behaving so informally, although she guessed that Evica would slip comfortably into such a conversation.

Her mind flitted briefly back to the events of yesterday, the wedding and all the celebrating that had followed it. Evica and Tariik had managed to have an enjoyable if not a totally familial wedding. She wondered what they were doing at that moment. Following the Earthan tradition of taking a honeymoon, they had chosen to have their private holiday trekking in the high mountains of southern Amerimex. After this they were to join Linnayen to continue the state visit and its rounds of events before returning to Altan.

Along with her sister, Linnayen was also comfortable with the more relaxed behaviour of the Earthans – since the accident, it seemed. She wondered how much they would both look forward to going home to Altan, and whether her home planet would seem quite foreign. It was strange that her alien husband's planet seemed more her home now than anywhere else, purely because she could not remember anywhere else. It was a beautiful place filled with lush scenery, all manner of foods and sweet-smelling air, and its people were, for the most part, easy-going and friendly. Perhaps, she pondered, this explained why her husband was intrinsically a good man, a kind man, despite his outward reserve. If only she could break down a little of the barrier he had erected around himself and prove to him that she was, indeed, not the same self-serving, political animal he had married. Then she remembered that he was going back to Athens the next day and, with a pang, realised that she would miss him rather more than she had imagined.

Em-sin Mai's voice broke into her thoughts.

'My lady, as your physician I am duty-bound to advise you against participating in this activity. Another trauma to your head could be very dangerous.'

Linnayen had not considered this. The doctor was probably right, but the prospect of cloudskimming was too irresistible.

'You're correct, of course, Dr Mai. And I thank you for your conscientiousness,' she replied, quickly adopting the formal manner of speech, which she had soon realised the Altanis found more comfortable. She noticed a brief look of disappointment on Jax's face. 'However,' she continued, 'I'm going to do it anyway. I feel absolutely fine.'

Em-sin Mai frowned and began to speak again, but Linnayen cut her off.

'I insist, doctor. I am well. I will come to no harm,' she said reassuringly, but emphatically. Lowering her eyes in acceptance of her mistress's command, Em-sin Mai retreated towards the rear of the cabin.

'Then I shall remain here and trust that my services will not be needed,' she added, reinforcing the requirements of her duty without a trace of rancour. She knew that Sen-Beoraan would strongly disapprove of this activity and of Linnayen's part in it, but her duty was clear. She needed to be available and clear-headed to treat any possible injury to the Ki or her consort.

Jax had, like the others, watched the exchange and was pleased that his wife was daring enough to try cloudskimming, although Duncan appeared less than keen. Everyone had finished strapping themselves into their harnesses, but Nen and Captain Chandra also declined the opportunity and joined the dutiful doctor to wait and keep watch over their charges.

Chapter Twenty-eight

alisel Navarr drummed her fingers on the soft mulberry velvet of the chaise lounge. It was just past midnight and, if their calculations were correct, Whip Company and Oleander would by now be within two hours of entering the Bashir villa on Santorini. The actual kidnap was due to take place at 2am and, given that it would take an estimated seven minutes to undertake the abduction and get Whip Company airborne, they would be back at Guyvar Neref by 2.45am, only three hours from now.

It was pointless trying to sleep. She was too keyed up. This was, by far, an audacious act with the highest stakes of any game she had ever played. But if it came off, she and her brother would achieve the ultimate goal: absolute dominion over the Galactic Union. For whether Durroc controlled the Ki by charm or by coercion, control her he *would*. Balisel would make sure of it.

Although her brother was possessed of great magnetism, as she herself knew only too well, the Ki's accident on the *Jensa Kadenx* may have led to permanent and irreversible changes in her personality. Balisel, therefore, had taken the precaution of purchasing a tidy quantity of the infamous Huthon narcotic urthrengo. Quite undetectable in the body, though not strictly habit-forming, its influence was commonly short-lived due to the death of the user. Urthrengo was one of the most powerful mind-altering substances in the known universe, its effect being auto suggestive. A person under its influence could be persuaded to do anything, and that included absolute recklessness and even self-harm. The drug had been responsible for literally millions of deaths as, in earlier centuries, Huthon warlords had fed it to their troops who would then enter battle fearlessly, happy to accept their fate as cannon fodder whilst under the drug's malign influence.

The drug was, of course, illegal. But Balisel's contacts through Gunnashey Kuth and Dor were many and varied and it had not been difficult to acquire some. Indeed, she had first tested it on her lately departed husband and she recalled with fleeting amusement Jeremiah's unstoppable enthusiasm to go for a midnight swim on their honeymoon, even though the water was icy cold and he was a hopeless swimmer. Not that that would have mattered. In the waters of the Floating Ice Gardens of Dasnir he would have had around six minutes – maybe eight at a pinch – before he froze to death. To be on the safe side she had allowed a good half hour to elapse before raising the alarm that her darling husband had disappeared. By the time they retrieved his body, it was far too late. His vital organs had already crystallised and shattered and his fingers and toes had been snapped off as his body had brushed against the delicately carved ice floes in the current.

So, she reflected, if it came to it and if her brother's powers of persuasion proved less than successful on the Ki, Balisel was prepared. She had not brought them this far to fail for want of a little passion. Consequently, if the lady was not willing then Balisel would make her so – and make her brother the most powerful once more.

Her smile as she stared out at the star-laden night sky above the ancient fortress was as cold as the ice of her eyes and her thoughts drifted away into dreams of a future without limits, without constraints, where she and Durroc could always be together.

Duncan McCrae placed his hands and feet carefully in the loops of the skimmer net as he made his way towards its end. Linnayen, Jax and di Luca were already there, their hands stretched forward clasping the last loops of the net, their bodies and legs swinging out in midair, waiting for him to reach them. Linnayen was smiling, looking alternately at Jax, the professor and the view of the moon-bathed sea far, far below them, and it was obvious to Duncan that she was thoroughly enjoying this experience, unlike himself.

'Come on, Duncan. You're nearly there!' Jax called out. Duncan nodded to signify that he had heard, but his throat was too dry to speak. He continued with his manoeuvring and was soon level with the others. His legs were now dangling free, his only contact with the relative safety of the net being his white-knuckled grip on its last loops and his safety line.

'Oh, well done, Duncan!' Linnayen called across to him. 'Isn't this exciting?'

Under any other circumstances her grin would have been infectious. But not now.

'That's one word I *could* use,' he called back, a sick grimace stretching across his features. 'But I'm not going to.'

'Are you going to let go, my lady?' di Luca asked.

'Try stopping me!' she replied with a grin.

Jax could not help but smile at her enthusiasm. He had not realised his wife was such a daredevil. She had certainly never displayed this aspect of her character before – at least to him. This was a whole new side to her. Perhaps it was true that the accident and her amnesia had wrought significant personality changes. If so, he wondered, what else would be in store for him? And how long would it all last until she reverted to type?

'What about you, Kevor?' she teasingly asked. 'Care to join me in a spot of flying?'

The giggle that accompanied the words was infectious and no matter what her past misdemeanours and behaviour had been, tonight Jax wanted to enjoy her company and just have fun.

'Don't mind if I do,' he replied in the same light vein. Then, reaching across and prying one of her hands away from the net, he continued. 'But, of course, ladies first.'

Her scream as she released her other hand and fell away from the skimmer net was more of delight than shock and was quickly replaced by loud laughter. In an instant, Jax released his hold on the net and dived after her, paying out his safety line as fast as it would go. He swung down in a wide lunging arc and, once she saw what he was doing, she tried the same manoeuvre. By contrast, di Luca's descent was a little more sedate and Duncan was still pondering the wisdom of letting go at all. The male steward, Andros, was also on the net, fitted out with a jetpro backpack and ready to give assistance to anyone who needed it.

'Look!' Linnayen called down to Jax. 'The island! See if we can spot the villa.' She drew level with him then stopped the safety line.

The cloudclipper's ascent had steered a course north-west and away from the island. But once they had levelled out and begun skimming, the captain had brought them about so that they would be sailing back towards the island and their home airdock. Linnayen could make out the approaching black outline of the island; its towering walls at this distance, though, were nothing more than a thick jagged line.

'No. We're still too far away,' Jax replied.

'How long do you think till we can?' she fired back.

'At this speed,' Jax looked up at the dark bulk of the clipper above and to their front before continuing, 'about ten minutes, I'd say. But I don't want to get home too soon. I'm enjoying this.'

Linnayen was pleased to see that he was grinning from ear to ear. For the first time since her return to consciousness, he looked entirely at ease in her company. She realised that this must be what he was naturally like – when he was not putting on his polite facade. This was the real Kevor Jax, the man he was for his family and close friends. His smile transformed his face, making him more handsome than she could have believed, and she revelled in both the physical and emotional freedom of these moments. In a sudden release of happiness, she threw back her head and whooped with joy. Jax joined in with her laughter.

Above them, still clinging firmly to the net, Duncan called down.

'I'm glad *you* think this is funny. I, for one, am failing to raise even a titter!'

Duncan had never been terribly gung-ho. All through the long years of their friendship, Jax had always been the one to risk life and limb first, whilst Duncan had preferred to assess the situation before moving. There was no lack of adventure or bravery on his part; indeed, once committed to a course of action, there was no firmer comrade than Duncan McCrae. Jax knew that Duncan would happily face any hardship or danger to help his friends. But he was not a born risk-taker and this evening's rather extreme entertainment was not Duncan's style.

'It's not like you to lose your sense of humour, Duncan!' Jax shouted back, not even trying to stifle the laughter caused by his friend's uncomfortable predicament.

'If that's all I lose during this little adventure, my friend, I'll be very thankful.'

Linnayen joined in the conversation. 'Try to relax a little, Duncan! Don't forget, you can't come to any harm out here.'

'I appreciate the sentiments, my lady, but you'll forgive me if I can't quite bring myself to believe you,' Duncan countered. 'Nothing personal, of course.'

'Of course,' she accepted. 'Even so, Duncan, we're quite safe.'

No sooner were the words out of her mouth than they heard Professor di Luca's cry of surprise and terror as his safety line fell away from the wall mounting inside the cabin of the cloudclipper. The old man's body shot away behind them and suddenly he was free-falling down towards the shimmering expanse of sea beneath them.

Within seconds, the steward, Andros, had released his safety line and powered up the jetpro unit. He darted after the fast-disappearing body of di Luca at top speed.

'You were saying, Linnayen?' Duncan began.

All eyes were fixed on the two closing forms far below and their laughter had long since ceased. In less than thirty seconds – even before di Luca's chute had opened – the steward collected him in mid-air and had begun the ascent back towards the clipper. There was a collective sigh of relief once they saw that the old professor had been rescued and Linnayen was the first to let out a cheer.

'Well done!' she called down to Andros. Then, raising her head she called up to Duncan. 'You see, Duncan … Perfectly safe.'

'Yes, and with hindsight, I think it's best I go in now.'

Jax chuckled and shook his head as Duncan began climbing back up the net towards the open portal of the cabin. He was still a little unsteady and the other steward, Marie, clambered down to help him.

'Well, *I'm* having a good time,' Linnayen called across to Jax. There was a look in her eye that Jax had never seen before. He was amazed. If his eyes were not deceiving him, he could have sworn she was planning some sort of mischief.

'And, if you ask me, I think the professor's had the best time of us all,' she went on. The raising of her eyebrows combined with the wicked smile told Jax all he needed to know, which was why he was quite prepared when, in the next instant, Linnayen disengaged herself from her safety line and, with a peel of laughter, fell tumbling away from the clipper.

The two stewards' faces were masks of horror. Andros was still bringing the professor back to the clipper and Marie was pulling a tremulous Duncan back into the cabin. Neither could leave their duties at that moment.

Seeing their consternation, Jax called out. 'Don't worry, I've got this! I'll call when we've landed.'

With that he too unfastened his safety line and fell away into the darkness. He could easily make out the figure of Linnayen as her flexichute had by now fully opened and she was drifting towards the northern arc of the island. The clipper had travelled almost the whole distance back to the island in the last few minutes and, with the wind behind them, there was enough of a breeze to carry them across the drowned caldera to land on the leeward slopes. It soon became apparent that the chutes would need little manoeuvring as they were headed to the area around the Bashir villa and, if the wind direction held, they would land within a kilometre or two. Thus assured, Jax concentrated on catching up to Linnayen and, by tacking across the breeze, he soon managed to draw level to her.

'Linnayen, you shouldn't have done that.' There was no response to his gentle admonishment and he wondered if she could not hear him. He spoke again, this time a little louder. 'Are you all right?' He barely needed to call out though. The night was silent and his words travelled the short distance between them easily. But there was still no response.

'Linnayen?' he repeated, his concern growing by the second. 'Linnayen?'

It was all coming back to her now. *Falling. Falling fast.* The water spray in her face. Her arms outstretched, her legs spread wide to catch and keep the updraft. There was another with her. In her mind's eye, she saw herself turn her head to look across at him. She smiled … No, she laughed. He was handsome beyond belief. His smile took her breath away. She glowed under his gaze and an exciting warmth spread through her body.

'Linnayen! What's the matter?' Jax's voice was urgent and he quickly steered the chute to get as close to her as he could without endangering them.

Finally his voice penetrated the fog of remembrance and she was suddenly aware of where she was and what they were doing.

'Oh … Kevor. I – I'm fine. I'm okay.'

'What happened? Why didn't you answer me?' he demanded.

She shook her head to clear the mist of the unbidden memory. 'I'm sorry. I didn't mean to worry you. I was confused.' She stumbled through her words.

'You recalled something, didn't you?' Jax asked, remembering that it was still only a few weeks since her fall. Perhaps cloudsailing had not been such a good idea after all.

'Yes … But it was nothing. I remembered fall-flying once – on Hutho – with … with my sister.' This was not the time to remind him of the man who had been her lover. That was all in a previous life. That was a different woman – a girl who was foolish and proud and self-centred.

'Fall-flying?' repeated Jax. 'What's that?'

She smiled and shrugged her shoulders.

'Like this. A lot faster … Maybe not as enjoyable.' A little of her former good humour was returning as she put the memory of Navarr out of her mind. 'Perhaps I'll show you one day.'

Jax raised his eyebrows in mild surprise. She was assuming that they would have a future together and it was an issue he had not yet fully considered. The last few weeks had been spent living from day to day. He had – perhaps deliberately – not wanted to reflect on what would happen as the days, weeks and months progressed. He had been so inured to their former life together that he had not speculated on how things might be in a future that did not contain the hated Navarr – a future where it was just the two of them.

'Yes, perhaps,' he replied a little hesitantly, then looked away. Suddenly self-conscious, he did not want her to see the confusion in his eyes.

They were approximately five hundred metres above the caldera, slowly approaching the north wall of the crater's rim. The moon, which had lit their descent for most of the way, slipped behind a small high cloud but they could still make out the shapes of houses and stone-walled fields in the distance behind the crater wall. The Bashir villa would be one of these, but they were still too far away to make it out clearly.

The breeze was holding and Jax estimated that they would make landfall in a few minutes. The flexichutes held them well and it was just a matter of enjoying the slow ride down. Once on the ground, Jax would make a call to the villa and a member of the house staff would come and get them.

'Jax … That's what they call you, isn't it? Your family and friends?'

'Yes. It's a nickname – an inherited one – from my great-great-grandmother,' he replied. 'We share the same eye colour apparently.'

'Ah yes,' she returned. 'Your eyes. I noticed. They're quite an unusual colour. That's natural then?'

Jax laughed. He was well aware of the Altani practice of eye colouration, as was Linnayen, it appeared. Unknowingly again she seemed to have remembered something of her home planet.

'Yes, I haven't had pneumo-shots in my iris to change the colour, if that's what you mean.'

She smiled across at him. *Then our children might inherit the trait.*

'Did you see that?' Jax's voice broke her train of thought. He was pointing at something away in the distance. 'There, on the cliff face.'

She searched the area of crater wall he had indicated, which was about three hundred metres away and almost directly below them.

'See what?'

'A light … or something. Metal maybe,' he replied.

Linnayen shook her head whilst continuing to scan the black wall of the crater.

'Sorry, no, I can't see anything.'

'There, I saw it again! Something reflected,' he called out, but Linnayen had seen nothing and, by now, it was too late to look again as they had sailed over the top of the crater rim.

'I saw nothing, Jax.' Her inability to support his testimony felt strangely like betrayal.

He frowned and although he said nothing more, it was obvious that the incident troubled him. He was positive he had seen something metallic and shiny on the surface of the crater wall but he knew that could not be. The crater walls were virtually perpendicular, too steep even to contain pockets of volcanic debris, let alone a piece of equipment. The rocks there were sharp and angular. There were no roads or tracks at this end of the island either, so it could not have been a vehicle.

But he *had* seen something. He was sure of it. And whatever it was, it was close to the Bashir villa.

Oleander checked the time: just after midnight. The drill leader had just reported back that they had less than five metres to go now and were already well inside the old fumarole and heading straight up. The drilling had been much easier since they entered the cavity and the drill leader estimated that they would be inside the villa grounds within the hour.

Things were going well. In fact, they were ahead of schedule, so much so that they might have to slow things down. Oleander was enough of a professional to know that it was always better to follow the pre-set plan, no matter the temptation to divert or jump ahead. They had said 2am for the kidnap to begin and 2am it would be, not a minute before. If they had time to spare she would instruct the company to go over the plan one more time, check their weapons, check their communications, check their transportation. Nothing could be left to chance. The plan would not fail because of a technical hitch, of this she was certain.

And in the meantime she would use the time to think. Think about Balisel Navarr and how she would try to wriggle out of the Order's hold over her and her conniving brother. Oh yes, she was not so naïve that she did not imagine the Navarr woman was up to something. There had to be a reason behind her willingness to execute the kidnap at such close quarters *and* to accept the partnership between her and the Order without putting up more of an argument. Sumere was, in effect, blackmailing the Navarr twins. But some inner disquiet told Oleander that the woman had been a little too quick to accept their situation, a little too ready to fit in with the Order's wishes. Balisel had an agenda of her own, of that she was sure. But it was something more than a fondness for her brother and a desire to see his advancement. Was she overlooking the obvious, she wondered. Balisel was very defensive whenever her precious brother was mentioned. Perhaps the Order's blackmail was less of an incentive than they imagined and the Navarrs had had something like this planned all along. After all, they were behind the assassination attempt on the Ki of Altan and it *had* been Balisel's idea to stage the current kidnap.

The darkness encouraged her mind to explore such curling thoughts and she was grateful for the time of quiet – the calm before the storm. In the dark of the tunnel entrance her liquid brown eyes scanned the calm sea far below. She pondered the nature of love and power and what drove some people to risk it all to have one or both. The force – at least in Balisel Navarr's case – was inordinately strong. She had seen the look in her eyes – a look of complete focus, diamond-hard, hungry and unwavering – and thanked her lucky stars. People like Balisel Navarr kept Oleander in business, and they were making her very rich too. At least she would never have to take up her mother's profession and the humiliation that went with it. After tonight's little escapade, she would have enough money to take a step back from the business – perhaps even retire altogether. Just a few more days and she could disappear into the real world, the ordinary world of ordinary people and go back to being simple Marseille Auteuil once more, just like she'd always dreamed.

'Look, Jax, the villa! I didn't know we were so close.' She looked across to him, obviously pleased by her discovery. 'We'll be home well before the others.'

The white stucco and glass structure of the Bashir villa passed a mere two hundred metres below them. Much of the building was in darkness apart from a couple of outside spotlights and the glow of underwater lamps in the pool. Jax put the business of what he had seen on the cliff out of his mind and responded to Linnayen's enthusiasm.

'We can steer ourselves home,' he said. Linnayen looked down to the controls on her chest panel. Suddenly Jax remembered that the security shield would automatically repel them if they tried to land within the villas bounds.

'Wait, Linnayen. First I'll have to get the shield dropped. Just hold on before you go diving in.'

She nodded that she had understood and continued to drift patiently beside and a little below him. Jax loosened the neck of the jumpsuit and spoke into the small communications button on his lapel, reeling off his personal call-sign. The security staff inside the villa had already been alerted by Captain Chandra that the Ki and Prince Bashir had left the cloudclipper and that they should be ready to deactivate the shield and its defence systems on Jax's command.

'Okay, Linnayen, it's clear now. The shield's down.'

It was trial and error at first with no small amount of laughter as the flexichute, responding to Linnayen's use of the controls, swung her this way and that before she finally managed to steer herself back towards the villa at a steady rate of descent. Jax found the whole process a little more straightforward as he had had the benefit of using flexichutes at the military academy. He called out advice to Linnayen but was unsure how much of it she heard because she was laughing so much.

He was still having a hard time coming to terms with this new side of her personality. Her new-found enjoyment of life was quite irresistible and try as he might, Jax could not resist being drawn into her good humour and bonhomie. With a final whoop of delight, Linnayen landed squarely on both feet in the gardens of the villa. The house staff had already come out to welcome them and offer assistance and within minutes they were both out of their safety harnesses and made their way up to their room.

Linnayen flounced through the door and, with an exaggerated sigh, flung herself down on the huge bed.

'That was fun! Did you know the old professor had arranged it?'

He shook he head and smiled. 'No, he dreamed it up all by himself. But it didn't surprise me. He was always up to something when he was my tutor.'

Linnayen sat up sharply and began to remove her shoes. 'Like what?' Her eyes focused on him and her interest was plain to see.

'Oh, like the time when I was six and I scoffed at him when he told me milk came from cows.' Jax smiled at the memory of the precocious, black-haired, tree-climbing tearaway that he had once been and the patient but much-tested professor. He continued under Linnayen's warm gaze. '"Rubbish!" I told him, very imperiously. "Milk comes from water and clouds and toothpaste and they mix it up at the swimming pool."'

Linnayen giggled at his imitation of himself as a know-it-all six-year-old.

'Ah, so you already had a fine grasp of chemistry?'

Jax smiled back, enjoying the telling of a story he had almost forgotten. 'I knew everything – I was six. But di Luca had a surprise in store for me the next day.'

Intrigued now, Linnayen's eyes widened and Jax took a moment to pause and recapture the breath he had almost lost at the sight of her.

'Go on,' she urged.

'He woke me while it was still dark. It must have been about four or five in the morning. "Come on," he said. "Don't believe me about cows and milk, eh? You'll see." And he took me off to the aircar. My mother was there, very sleepy and still in her dressing-gown. She gave me a kiss goodbye and we set off. I kept asking where we were going but he wouldn't say.'

Linnayen giggled again, then stifled a yawn. The evening's adventures had begun to take their toll on her energy, but she was having such a good time that she did not want it to end yet. Besides, she enjoyed watching Jax's face as he spoke. His natural good looks came to life as he dropped his guard and she devoured every moment, trying to memorise his features.

'Finally we landed in a paddock in the middle of nowhere. Di Luca gave me a pair of rubber boots to put on and we walked across the fields to a large barn. It was still dark so I couldn't tell much. We went inside. It was filled with all sorts of machinery and hoses and a raised central dais with fenced off sections. The lights were very bright and a woman in overalls saw us and waved. Then she nodded to someone in the back and a door in the far wall cranked opened.'

Jax was well into his stride now and his own enjoyment of the story animated his face, expressing a range of emotions.

Linnayen was entranced by him and instinctively keep quiet as he continued.

'That's when I heard them – the shuffle of hoofed feet and the hum of mooing. Cows! Heaps of them. All black and white and noisy! They entered the stalls on the milking platform – that's what it was, you see. And, as the platform slowly rotated, a robot clamped a milking apparatus to each cow's udder. By the time a complete rotation had been done, every animal had been milked and it was time to come off and let another one on.' Jax laughed and shook his head as he walked over to sit next to Linnayen on the end of the bed.

'I was amazed! For one thing, I had never even *seen* a cow – only the picture di Luca had shown me the day before, which I had rudely disbelieved. So *they* were amazing enough. But when I saw what looked suspiciously like milk flowing along all these clear hoses into big metal vats ... They let me taste it. It was creamy and yellow and I hated it. But di Luca was right, of course. And I learned that day that the old fellow knew everything. And anything he didn't know, he knew that as well!'

Linnayen laughed out loud. 'You must have been very sweet when you were six,' she said warmly.

'Not on that day,' he replied wryly. 'As punishment for my disrespect I had to help wash down the milking shed. You'd be surprised how much waste comes out of an animal that size.'

'Yes, I remember,' she said, wrinkling her nose and laughing. 'Evica and I used to help with milking the akus when we were little. They're a little like cows.' The memory had slipped so easily into her consciousness, and with it she felt a flood of sensations from her childhood suddenly bubble up. Sounds, smells, feelings, especially the feeling of solitude. She had been a lonely child. She knew that now and it felt both sad and incongruous, given who she seemed to have become. It was overwhelming and it left her shocked and speechless and a little breathless.

Jax noticed her sudden silence followed by a gasp and he realised what had just happened. He stared at her, face full of concern.

'That was another memory, wasn't it? Are you all right?' He could not help himself. She looked so lost, so alone. It was the most natural thing in the world to place his arm around her shoulder. He argued with himself that he would have done it for anyone who was in such obvious distress.

Her voice was still and small. 'Yes ... I'm ...' She let out a long, low sigh that seemed to release more than just stored air. Her body shrunk a little and her muscles finally relaxed. Then, without warning, tears welled at the corners of her eyes and a small, soundless sob made her slim frame tremble.

He sighed, drawing her closer. 'It's all a bit much, eh?' He stroked her head softly with his other hand, trying to reassure her. 'It's all right. Everything will be all right.'

Over and over again, as her sobs continued, he comforted her. She was exhausted and he knew innately that she needed to be held. She just needed a friend – someone to lean on. As the minutes went by in silence, he held her and her thin arms went around his waist, clinging weakly.

He could not recall the exact moment when his natural outpouring of comfort and kindness turned from an act of friendship and concern to one of passion. One minute he was holding the quietly sobbing woman in his arms, stroking her long, soft hair. The next, while his mind twisted through a maelstrom of thoughts and feelings, he was touching her cheek, fingertips gently exploring the line of her jaw, then her mouth, wiping away the salty wetness.

She shivered almost imperceptibly, then lifted her head to look up at him. Her eyes were still wet, though she had stopped crying now and, in the dim light of the room, they appeared like two deep pools of green ocean into which he was uncontrollably sinking. Her lips, too, were moist and parted and he could feel her small shallow breaths warming the air between them.

There was no holding back from then on – he could not fight it anymore. His resistance left him and suddenly he felt her hand caressing his face and her lips touching his cheek. He knew that within seconds they would have found his mouth and he would be totally lost, again addicted to this woman as he once had been. He had a spilt-second left in which to act, to stop the madness from happening all over again.

He drew back. He needed to see her face, to read her eyes. Was it real this time? Did she love him? Or was he being made a fool of once more?

Linnayen's eyes lifted slowly and in their dark pools he saw her confusion and her hurt – and something more. He knew then, once and for all, that this was no charade, and a long-held dream was finally coming true.

'Whip One, fifteen minutes to completion. Awaiting command.' The drill leader's voice was little more than a whisper inside her earpiece. Oleander checked the time: 1.20am. They were early and this pleased her. They would use the time wisely.

'Whip Two, upon completion, institute systems check nine through twenty-eight – repeat, nine through twenty-eight. Whip Falcon, report recon status.'

From her vantage point in the small cradle high on the crater wall, Oleander's sharp eyes scanned the vista of the water far below. They then turned heavenward as though able to see the two airtransporters that hovered some seven thousand metres above them and would be monitoring any comings and goings at the villa.

The commander of Whip Company's airborne division responded in a bland monotone. 'Target remains inside the building, main bedroom, upper level. Two guards, main gate. Two guards, inner court. All house staff retired. No other persons at this time.'

They were there, the Ki and her consort, virtually alone and unguarded. Now would have been the perfect moment to attack whilst the main guard was still en route to the villa from the cloudsailing adventure. Whip Harrier's reconnaissance had been tracking the royal party since it had left the villa earlier that evening and noted it was already on its way back. This would give them more of an opposition. But it could not be helped. She did not want to rush things and they would not be beaten anyway. Whip's personnel outnumbered the royal bodyguards four to one, so success was certain no matter when the attack took place.

In twelve more minutes, the drill team would break the surface then withdraw back along the shaft to where it levelled out. There they would wait until she gave the signal to enter the villa compound. Their priority would be to deactivate the security shield at the villa's entry lodge so that the armoured transporters could drop the rest of the company's personnel, a handful of whom would go directly to the targets' location within the main building. The assault would be 'quick, quiet and slick', as Rennick had said in his many briefings to the company. They had seven minutes to finish the job before the downed shield, if not reactivated, would emit its emergency signal and override the block, thus trapping them all inside the villa compound.

All Whip Two had to do now was finish the last couple of metres of drilling and bide their time. Oleander reflected that in less than an hour all hell would have broken loose. Their mission would be accomplished and they would be on their way to the fortress of Guyvar Neref where the Navarr woman was waiting. It was at that exact moment that Oleander entertained the possibility that she may have to undertake one last commission for the Order and, when she remembered the arrogant, acid-tongued alien, she could not in all honesty pretend that the job – her last job as Oleander – would be distasteful.

Chapter Twenty-nine

They were in another place and time – a place where only they existed and time did not pass. From the moment when Jax returned her kiss they had begun a new existence and there would be no turning back from here.

There had been no coyness, no fear and no holding back. When they kissed it was as though his love poured into her and she responded, eager to drink it down. Her lips roamed over his mouth and neck. His skin tasted of the night air and, in his dark hair, she could smell the ozone from the sea, fresh and salt-laden. His physicality was overpowering, blocking out all other levels of awareness and, when she felt him open the front of her blouse, she surged forward to meet his touch. It was both the most natural and the most exhilarating gesture either of them could have imagined.

Their lovemaking was unhurried yet, with every passing minute, as their senses became more keenly aroused, there came an urgency. For Jax it was as though these moments might be a dream, an illusion that would suddenly fade and dissolve into mist. Thus, in an effort to hold onto the dream, he blocked out all sensation and all knowledge except that of her. It was not a hard task. Her body was soft and warm and undulating and she responded to his caresses by forcing herself ever closer to him.

Still seated at the end of the large bed, they pulled and tugged at each other's clothes until they were mostly disrobed. Then, for a few moments they pushed away to study each other in the soft golden light of the glow-globes that swayed in the air above them. The shadows fell on their honeyed skin like a sunset over the desert. But the desire to touch and to taste soon rose again and, with renewed passion, Jax pulled her towards him and lowered his mouth over one breast. Linnayen shivered. His tongue was firm and insistent. She lay back onto the white coverlet of the bed, drawing him down on top of her, one long leg cupping his torso, inviting him to explore further.

Jax needed no encouragement. The sight of her virtually naked and the feel of her skin upon his own were sparks that kindled an explosion of desire – desire he had always felt but had never truly fulfilled. He remembered now a night that seemed so long ago, when he was a young, immature newlywed, little more than a boy, and he had made love to Linnayen in much the same way as he did now. Only now he was a man. Life's hard lessons had wrought a new maturity and understanding. Then he had seen only a beautiful girl and had endowed her with a personality as loving and as open as his own and a passion as strong as his. He had not wanted to believe that she could feel otherwise, much less that she could love another man.

But now, tonight, everything was changed. It had to be, he thought. Surely her responses were not a sham? Surely she could not falsify the look in her eyes? And even if she could, her body was not lying. She wanted him as much as he wanted her and, after all these months of hoping for her love then turning to others for affection, he could not refuse her – or himself.

He slid off the end of the bed and removed her loose linen pants, slipping them down her smooth legs. Linnayen's breathing was deep and heavy and, as he looked up, he could see her small stomach rise and fall with the effort to keep it steady. Jax pulled himself back onto the bed and gently pushed her legs apart with one knee. He covered the mound of her crotch, still hidden beneath her flimsy cotton panties, with his hand and felt the tremor of her gasp. Then he lowered his head and placed his lips over hers. Her hands took his face and stroked the line of his jaw, then moved to feel the muscles in his brown back.

Their kiss was long and slow, each trying to hold back the urgency that grew with every passing second, each wanting to make these moments last. Finally he could hold back no longer. Neither could she and, with movements that were both graceful and unstoppable, Linnayen gave herself completely to her husband and allowed him to truly make her his wife.

'Home at last!' Duncan stretched out his arms as they walked across the inner courtyard.

It was nearly two in the morning and they had sailed home in the cloudclipper rather leisurely once the excitement of losing two of their passengers died down. Captain Chandra had contacted Jax while he and Linnayen were still airborne and, as he knew they were safe, there seemed no reason to hurry back to the villa. As soon as they arrived, Chandra went to check with his staff that all was secure.

'Does anyone want a midnight swim?' Duncan tried to sound encouraging, but even he had to stifle a yawn.

'Oh, Mr McCrae, I'm too old for that,' Nen giggled in reply.

'As am I,' di Luca concurred. 'And I need sleep.'

The party could not be persuaded. So, with a drop of his shoulders and a wave over his shoulder, Duncan finally gave in and bad everyone a good night.

'Goodnight, sweet ladies … and professor.'

Di Luca's scowl was cheerfully long-suffering and Nen once more giggled happily. The party dispersed to their rooms and the sensor lights began to dim.

The sounds of the homecoming rose into the warm night air of the courtyard and drifted in through the bedroom window. It stirred the lovers, alerting them that they were no longer alone.

They laughed quietly. In her happiness, Linnayen's face lit up like sunshine reflected on a morning sea and Jax was, once more, overcome with the desire to kiss her – and more. He stroked her fine hair, which spread like folds of silk across the white sheets, then leaned down to cover her mouth once more. He could not get enough of her. They had made love with a passion and a depth neither could have believed possible and the climax, when it came, left them shuddering and weak, with hearts pounding and gasping for breath.

Once had not been enough and within minutes he had begun to kiss her again, starting with her lips, then her breasts, her arms, stomach. Every touch brought a reaction that Linnayen could do nothing to stop. She burned for him and she knew now, without any doubt, that this was the man for whom she was meant. This was the man with whom she would spend the rest of her life, and she glowed with the knowledge. No doubts, no fears, no more lies or deceit. Theirs would, at last, be a real marriage – a union of love and respect and trust, and she was excited about their future.

Suddenly Jax broke off his kisses long enough to look at Linnayen's smiling face. She pulled him down to her once more and, rolling over on top of him, she studied the midnight blue eyes fondly, then caressed his cheek.

In the quiet stillness she spoke simply and directly. 'Jax, I love you.'

He had waited so long to hear these words. This was his dream coming true and he would never have believed that a moment could contain such happiness as this.

'Oh, Linnayen … My love.' He struggled to speak as his emotions overwhelmed him. 'I can't tell you what that means to me …'

She placed a finger to his lips. 'I think I know. It means the same to me too.' She dropped down to lay by his side, propping her head up on one hand while she stroked the dark hairs on his brown chest with the other.

'I was such a fool before. I'm so sorry for what I did to you.'

It was his turn to hush her and he did so with a light kiss on her lips. 'That was a different you. It's not who you are now. Now you're the woman I first fell in love with.'

'But I was cruel, so manipulative. How could you love me?' Her face creased with distaste at the reality of what she had once been like. 'How could you even *like* me?'

He smiled. 'I didn't! You were horrendous. But I couldn't stop myself from being in love with you. That's what hurt so much.

That's why I kept away from you – it hurt too much to see you every day, especially with ...'

He did not want to besmirch these moments with the mention of Navarr and so he left the name unspoken. But they were suddenly keenly aware of their past and the scars it had left.

'That will never happen again,' she said, and there was a firm edge in her voice as though the promise was being made as much to herself as it was to him. 'From now on, there is just you and me. That's all I will ever want – or need.'

Jax smiled at the resolve etched onto her stern features. 'I can't think of a better way to start this marriage – again.' He rolled her onto her back and swept her hair away from her face, the better to kiss her. As he lowered his head, he finished his thoughts. 'But now, I think that's enough talking.'

They were in. Oleander had made her way along to tunnel to join the six members of Whip Two as they exited the shaft into the courtyard. Two men moved to the entry lodge where they promptly slit the throats of the two guards before disconnecting the security system. The shield and all inner alarms were now offline. Above them, Rennick and the armoured aircars were descending.

Exactly at 2am the first paratrooper swung down to the ground and within ten seconds, he had been joined by forty others, all armed to the teeth. They swept through the villa's spaces like a tidal surge, twisting and curling into every nook, silent and unstoppable.

It was Marcus di Luca who sounded the first alarm. His advanced years, whilst affording him much wisdom, gave him little comfort through sleep and, despite the evening's earlier excitement, his thoughts were keeping him awake. Instead he had taken down a small volume of poetry and settled himself comfortably on the daybed on the balcony under the light of a tiny hovering glow-globe. He was used to the night noises or, sometimes, the lack of them. Thus, when he heard a faint thumping noise coming from the room below his where some of the guards were billeted, he knew something was not right. He got up and walked to the end of the balcony in order to lean over and hear better what might be going on. And, although he did not know it then, it was an action that saved his life, for at that very moment one of Whip Company's paratroopers entered his room. He made a quick scan with the night-search eyepiece that was clamped on one side of his head but, finding it empty, the trooper moved on towards his next scheduled target.

From the dark corner of the balcony where he stood, di Luca had heard the door panel slide open and, instinctively sensing danger, shrank further into the shadow. He saw the glint of the intruder's weapon as its reflection was caught briefly in the pale blue light of a small clock above his bed. At the same time he was aware of a flash of red light that illuminated the space below the balcony for a few seconds. He reckoned that a silenced weapon had been discharged and it was probably in the main foyer. Did this mean that all their guards had been overpowered? He had to assume this might be so. Obviously they were under some sort of attack and di Luca knew he had to act quickly.

All the household staff, himself included, carried transmitters which, when activated, emitted a signal to an alarm receiver. This in turn sent a message to the main barracks – a temporary structure adjacent to the villa's external walls. Although the intruders seemed to have bypassed the shield and their other alarm systems, di Luca hoped the personal relay, which was on a separate circuit powered from the barracks and therefore outside the field of attack, would still be operational. He depressed a grey pad set into the control array on his wrist and the resultant green glow told him that the signal had been sent. Thank God, he thought. Help would come soon, but would it be soon enough?

In the meantime, he had to get to Jax and Linnayen for, without doubt, they were the targets of this night's attack. He prayed he would not be too late.

Jax felt rather than heard the noise. A scraping that sent a shivering sensation along his spine was coming from the direction of the door and it was enough to warn him that something was not right. His kiss with Linnayen was frozen and, placing his finger to his lips, he climbed off the bed and quickly slipped on his shorts. He searched through his clothes, which had been so quickly and pleasantly discarded less than an hour earlier, for a weapon. Although he did not often have to put it to use, his training at the academy and the regular refresher courses he had had to undertake in the diplomatic corps now stood him in good stead. He knew never to be more than a couple of metres from his firearm at any time and tonight was no exception.

After a second's confusion, Linnayen, too, gathered that there was something amiss and she jumped up as silently as she could and threw on her blouse. Even as she dressed, she ran lightly across to the table where her sidearm lay in its holster. Jax had already found his laser cannon. It was unsheathed and ready and Linnayen watched as he advanced towards the door. He had closed about half the distance when it slid open to reveal the silhouette of one of the masked mercenaries. Jax fired immediately and the shape collapsed. Although it slightly blocked the doorway, it was not enough of an obstacle to stop the rest of the mercenaries from rushing through the aperture.

Jax continued to fire as the dark soldiers advanced on him. But their personal shields had automatically realigned to the frequency of his laser cannon and, apart from one insignificant hit to the second guard's shoulder, the rest of Jax's shots were useless, their impact being absorbed by each shield's magnetic field.

At the other side of the room, Linnayen had managed to get a couple of shots away with her weapon, wounding two of the attackers. But the impact of such a small sono-blaster, though it could penetrate personal shields, was not enough to disable her attackers and she was quickly overpowered.

As the first guard took hold of Linnayen, Jax was hit in the leg and tumbled to the floor. He sucked in a breath with an agonising rasp and his eyes closed ominously. Linnayen saw him go down and, as her captors tried to drag her away, she screamed.

'Jax! Jax! No, let go of me!'

Struggling and kicking all the way, she heard him take another shot from one of the mercenary's weapons and, with a quick glance over her shoulder as they pushed her through the door, she saw his torso covered in blood.

'*No!* Jax!' Her scream came from a deep pit in the darkest reaches of her consciousness. It was a primal sound and it tore through the silence of the night attack like a thunderclap.

Duncan ran to the door of his room. The muffled noises and scuffling sounds had already alerted him to the fact that something was not right and, although he had never received military training like his best friend, he had been briefed on security and knew how to use a sidearm. He took a pistol from the wall-mounted rack and, as he opened the door, he heard Linnayen's terrible scream coming from the other side of the villa, across the gallery. It was quickly followed by the rushing and zipping noises of various weapons as they discharged. In the pale pool-lit glow of the central courtyard he could see the flashes of gunfire and human shapes running this way and that. Everywhere was chaos and moving shadows. The house guards, many still dressed in their nightwear, were obviously battling a group of soldiers who seemed heavily armed and highly competent, judging by the way the guards were falling.

From where he stood on the gallery looking down into the melee, Duncan selected a target, took aim and fired. He missed and the darkly clad intruder turned to locate him, but the low stone wall offered him some protection. After the first shot was fired back at him Duncan remembered to switch on his personal shield and kept firing. He thought he had taken one of the aggressors when he saw a shape drop to the ground, but when another human form fell he noticed the shot had come from somewhere below and to his right. So they were not completely defenceless – someone else on his side of the villa was putting up resistance. However, he could tell that they were vastly outnumbered as for every one of the mercenaries that fell, another two took his place. This slaughter could not go on for much longer or they would all be wiped out.

Suddenly, above the noise of the battle, Duncan heard the whine of a turbine and the air around him was stirred and sucked in a powerful updraft. Long ropes dropped from a large blue-metal transporter that had swung quickly down into the space above the courtyard. It hovered noisily over their heads, its high-pitched whine drowning out the sound of weapons fire. Some of the house guards began to shoot at it but its shield absorbed or deflected everything that was thrown at it.

Then, in the space below, Duncan saw two mercenaries carrying the limp form of Linnayen as they ran towards the swaying ropes. Linnayen was bare-legged and half-clothed and Duncan realised that she had been disturbed in her bed. But where was Jax? There was no sign of him and this worried Duncan more than if he had seen his old friend also being taken away.

Within seconds the mercenaries had hold of the ropes, which were swiftly lifted into the body of the transporter. Others joined them and soon all the ropes, each carrying their human cargo, were winched into the transporter. The last mercenary was not even inside the craft before it had swung away and began its fast climb. What Duncan did not know was that Whip Company had less than fifty seconds left before the villa's back-up shield would become operational, trapping them all inside.

The firing had lessened now and it was becoming easier to raise his head above the parapet to see what was going on below. Many of the mercenaries had left with the transporter that now carried Linnayen and the few remaining were fighting only a rear-guard action, waiting for a second craft to swing down and take them to safety.

Just as the noise of its engines could be heard entering the airspace above him, Duncan, out of the corner of his eye, saw old Professor di Luca alone on the villa's flat white roof. He seemed to be manoeuvring a large, heavy object, but Duncan could not make out what it was. Then another silhouette appeared – perhaps this was Jax, he thought. Between them the large object was positioned onto the low roof wall. It was then that Duncan saw what it was: a xelex-cannon – possibly the only weapon that might stand a chance of penetrating the transporter's shield.

More ropes had swung down from the second transporter to hoist away the last of Whip Company's personnel. Duncan fired again and managed to bring down another two – one as he ran across the courtyard and the other as he was pulled up through the air. The second body fell from the rope and into the pool where his feeble movements signified that he was still alive. All was chaos as the few remaining mercenaries returned shots over their shoulders while they dashed towards the swirling ropes. A warning siren issued from the craft and cracked the air like a whip. Those mercenaries still on the ground – some half a dozen or so – instantly redoubled their efforts to reach the ropes. They stopped shooting and made a run for it and Captain Chandra's house guards felled a couple more. But the rest made their destination and the transporter's winches began hoisting them aloft even as it began swinging its nose away from the villa, out towards the caldera's rim and the open sea.

It was at that very moment that Marcus di Luca fired the first shot from the xelex-cannon. The noise was deafening – a boom that picked up the air around it and sucked it skywards. The ensuing rip of green fire sailed past the departing transporter and evaporated into the black night. But di Luca had not waited to see if his shot had found its mark. He unleashed another round and, this time, the green burst enveloped the transporter and brought it to a shuddering stop in mid-air. Green electric flame pulsed over the metal hull and, as if it were happening in slow motion, the nose of the vessel tilted down and it began to sink. Its forward motion had by this time carried it out over the edge of the crater rim and it plunged, inevitably, towards the dark, silver-flecked waters of the flooded caldera. At the first touch of metal on saltwater, the whole erupted in a ball of rainbow-coloured flames and explosions, and behind the noise of the explosions could be heard the faint cries and screams of the men and women trapped on board.

Duncan arrived on the rooftop just in time to see the huge transporter hit the water and explode, and in the light given off he made out the identity of di Luca's assistant. Nen was still puffing and panting from her exertions at hauling the heavy cannon, then helping the professor position it. There was a faint smile of satisfaction at a job well done on her face but it could not hide the concern in her eyes.

All three stood in silence for a few moments watching the death throes of the vessel as it sank beneath the water. Then, as one thought entered their minds simultaneously, they all turned and ran towards the stairs to see what had become of their friends and charges. They knew Linnayen's fate, as everyone had seen her carried away in the first transporter. But what of Dr Mai and Captain Chandra? Then, of course, the most obvious question of all: what had happened to Jax?

'Damn! Forty of my best men and women! We should have found and killed the old man – killed all of them.' Rennick's words were sharp and he clearly felt Oleander's plan was flawed. After all, she had been the one to insist that they kill only as necessary. Old men and women would be no obstacle to their goal, she had argued. Yet here they were, one ship down and, in total, nearly forty personnel lost when the enemy had lost only a quarter of that. It was a disaster as far as Rennick was concerned.

'Shut your mouth!' Oleander spat back from the shadows of the transporter's main cabin. 'We got what we came for and you'll be well paid for this night's work.'

'That's not the point. We should have known about the cannon. *You* should have known,' he insisted venomously. She had failed them and he was not going to let the woman forget it – or get away with it.

Oleander did not reply immediately. He was right. She should have known.

'It was not there yesterday. They must have brought it with them,' she replied coldly, as if this could justify the situation.

'We still should have known. Your recon was shit and you know it.' Rennick barely controlled his rage. He did not like losing such good fighters. His people were the best, supremely well trained. It took months if not years to get them to this level. The rewards for this job, he mused darkly, had better be well worth it for it would cost a fortune to train replacements.

Oleander deflected the conversation with a shrug of her shoulders and spoke to one of the mercenaries who had carried Linnayen into the craft.

'How is she?'

'Out cold. Undamaged,' he replied curtly. Linnayen's screams at seeing Jax's demise in the villa had been quickly curtailed with a shot of a fast-acting sedative. It was always going to be easier to deal with an unconscious captive rather than a kicking and screaming one who might be injured in the melee.

'And Bashir?' Oleander turned again to Rennick. 'Are you sure he's dead?'

He looked at her scornfully. 'What do you take me for? An amateur?'

She was not impressed – and he still had not answered her question. Her tone was testy. 'I'll ask again. Did you kill him?'

Rennick's reply was swift. 'Of course. He'll never see another sunrise.'

Oleander nodded her satisfaction. 'Then we've achieved our mission.'

'Good,' said Rennick uncomfortably. 'Because I've had enough of it. It's time I took my people home.'

'Not so fast, Rennick,' she retorted quickly. 'If you recall, the capture and killing was only half of the deal. We'll need you to guard the target for a while yet – until the decision is made what to do with her.'

'You won't need all of us for that,' Rennick argued.

'*I'll* be the judge of that,' she fired back. 'And besides, you're being paid handsomely for your *full* services, not part, and not just when you feel like it either. Oh, and if I were you, I wouldn't even begin to think about reneging on our deal. You have no idea how serious the consequences would be.'

Her tone matched the content of her words sufficiently to cause Rennick to reconsider his position. He shifted in his seat, the better to see her in the cabin's gloomy light. His eyes riveted on hers.

'Very well,' he said tersely. 'But this better not go on too long. I've had enough of you – and that bloody ice queen too. I have other clients, you know.'

'Double-cross us and you won't – ever.' Oleander could see that she had won the round for the time being, but she knew it would crop up again. Rennick was uneasy, nervous, and that could be fatal in this game. She hoped that she would not have to attend to him in the same way she would to Balisel Navarr. Given the man's fine, strong body, she would much prefer to have sex with him than kill him. She was a woman, after all, and in her prime. In the dim light, a slow smile spread across Oleander's face. Rennick was confused. What did she have to smile about? There was nothing amusing about their situation and it was going to get worse, with half the world's security forces looking for them in the next few days.

'Okay, we'll stay, but not for long. So you'd better tell our mutual friends to decide fast. Oh, and if you want my professional opinion, I'd kill her rather than keep her.'

Linnayen lay on the floor of the cabin still as the grave, wrapped in a blanket with her head supported by a pillow. Only her eyes betrayed the fact that she was alive as they swung back and forth under her heavy eyelids. Her dreams had taken over the depths of her mind.

She saw herself standing in a beam of light, dressed in her finest clothes. She wore a golden gown decorated with diamonds, crystals and pearls, and a headdress of spun silk entwined with fine gold ribbon. She could see nothing beyond the light – did not even know if solid ground existed beyond the brilliant shaft. There was neither sound nor echoes to help her sense how large or small was the space around her. Then, when she tried to lift her arms to stretch them out in front of her, they would not move. They were as heavy as lead and it was as though they were taped to her sides. She opened her mouth to speak and moved her mouth to form words, but no sound came out. All she could hear was the steady deep rhythm of her breath – sucking in, then out – filling her ears with its rush. She was trapped, a living corpse.

Her anxiety grew with every passing second as she struggled against her confinement. Her eyes widened with her mounting fear. She was totally unable to move or speak and she could think of no way to end her captivity.

Then, like the touch of a feather on the skin at the back of her neck, she felt a presence drawing her towards itself. She could still see nothing beyond the brilliant light but the black void, but there was something there, she knew it. Then she felt it and the effect upon her was electric. It was a kiss on her lips of such passion and longing and love that for a moment she could not breathe. And she knew whose kiss it was. She could feel his arms around her now, supporting her, caressing her face. Suddenly love for this man surged through her body like a warm fire and she knew that she was safe and cherished. This was where she wanted to be – always.

Finally, the dark veil lifted and she saw his face and drank down its image greedily. She began to feel the torpor lift from her limbs and the sound of her breathing subsided. Her freedom was close at hand. Then, without warning, a terrible vice-like force took hold of her around the waist. It was like a steel clamp, encircling her and dragging her backwards, out of the light, into the black void. She called out for him to take her hands but it was all too quick and, before he could grasp her fingers, he fell away into the shadow and was lost.

Em-sin Mai took one look at the stricken body on the floor and sprang into action. There was not a moment to spare if she was to have a chance of bringing the young man back to life. Her first duty was to protect the life of the Ki. But as soon as she had entered the bedroom, running and ducking low to avoid being either hit or spotted by the attackers, she quickly realised that the Ki was already gone. Then she had seen the body of the Ki-consort slumped in a bloody heap and her professional duty soon replaced her dismay at finding Linnayen missing. She could do nothing for the Ki, but she might be able to save the Ki's beloved husband.

Jax was not breathing and he had no heartbeat. There was a gaping wound at the top of his left leg from which blood seeped thickly and another slightly smaller but equally bloodied opening just above his stomach. He was, to all intents and purposes, quite dead. But Em-sin Mai was not about to give up. She reasoned that he could not have been down for more than a few minutes and, if she could get his heart and lungs working again, she could treat the wounds. Her only worry was that his brain might have gone without oxygen for too long and that could have disastrous consequences. Still, it was worth trying and she reached into her case to pull out the necessary equipment.

First came a heart-starter, which she fixed to Jax's chest by means of its adhesive backing. The small device emitted a constant and powerful electromagnetic pulse that caused the heart muscles to expand and contract. In this way, Jax's heart was forced to pump again. Within seconds the blood began to flow from Jax's two wounds and, although it would soon be imperative to get blood back into his system, for now his circulation was restored. Her next priority was to get air into Jax's lungs.

Dr Mai grabbed a clear breathing mask from the bag and strapped it onto Jax's face. She then fitted a small capsule of compressed oxygen to a pump mounting on the outside of the mask and left it to do the work of forcing air into Jax's empty lungs. There was enough of the life-giving gas in the capsule to last for many minutes, which would, she estimated, give her enough time to treat the two major wounds.

Over her shoulder, she was vaguely aware that the battle continued. Flashes of weapon fire were reflecting on the far wall of the room and her ears picked up the sound of the engines of a large transporter. But all that was of no consequence right now and she assessed that the battle was elsewhere and she was in no danger.

Jax's femoral artery had been severed. Em-sin Mai took a pressurised medicator from the bag and shot a small amount of haemo-nanobot into both ends of the torn arterial wall, then formed a bridge between the two ends of the now pumping artery with a small strip of adgel. Within seconds the nanobots went to work and, with miraculous ease, began rebuilding a highly serviceable artery wall. After a minute the microscopic bots had completed a join that was firm and strong and, in time, Jax's own cells would superimpose themselves over the artificial wall.

Dr Mai repeated this procedure on the ruptured veins and arteries within the stomach wound and, similarly, after another couple of minutes, the bleeding was also stopped. Though not so severe, this wound was actually more worrying because of the likelihood of damage to Jax's internal organs, the full extent of which she would not know until they could get him to a hospital. For now, she had limited any further deterioration in his condition. The heart-starter would be good for at least three hours unless his heart started beating again under its own steam, in which case it would automatically shut itself off. But she would soon have to find another oxygen micro-cylinder if Jax did not start breathing naturally again very soon. There was also the matter of getting extra blood into him to make up for what he had lost.

A huge boom shook the walls and a faint green flash filled the room for a couple of seconds. Dr Mai ignored it and put aside any nervousness she felt. Her work was all-consuming at this moment and her face was stern as she concentrated on the job at hand.

She dived into the bag once more and searched for a small phial containing concentrated artificial blood, which she delivered via the medicator straight into the vein running down the inside of Jax's left arm. Judging by the pools of blood on the floor, most of which she rather hoped was the Ki-consort's and not his wife's, she estimated that he had lost around a litre. The compound was fast-acting and soon she could see a faint pink colour returning to Jax's pale cheeks, but he remained unconsciousness.

There was another booming noise and green flare from outside, followed by the sounds of straining engines and air being whipped and thrashed in some ghastly death throe. The noise faded away and it appeared that the shots and firing had ceased. The battle was over but her work was far from done. There would be casualties – many of them – and she allowed herself a large sigh to release her tension and refocus her mind.

At that point she heard a commotion in the hallway and Duncan McCrae's voice calling out for the Ki and her consort.

'In here!' she called back.

Duncan crashed into the room, followed by Nen. He was dirty and bloodied, but he appeared to be uninjured. He took one look at Jax, lying still on the floor in a dark puddle of now cold blood, and rushed over to kneel beside him.

'Is he …?' he began shakily.

'Too soon to know, but I think not,' Dr Mai replied in her usual clipped tone. 'Where is the Ki? Have you seen her?'

Duncan was dazed. His eyes were glassy as they gazed down at his best friend's stricken form. This could not be happening. He could not lose Jax.

Em-sin Mai's urgent voice interrupted his thoughts. 'The Ki! Where is she?'

Duncan shook himself and swallowed before replying. 'Gone … They took her. She was alive though – I think.'

Dr Mai knew then that, with her first duty clearly removed from her sphere of responsibility, her next task was to administer to everyone else, and she was anxious to get on with her work. She spoke quickly and efficiently.

'Stay with him. Do not move him. I'm going to get some more oxygen.'

She departed the room while speaking into her personal communicator, feeding instructions to some distant emergency service operator. Help would soon be on the way. But would it come soon enough to save the life of the Ki-consort?

Chapter Thirty

eoraan could have kicked himself. He knew something like this would happen. Why had he not listened to his inner voice? He should have insisted that if the Ki were to go anywhere to recuperate, he must be with her – *and* a small army. That was the trouble with being away from home. On Altan he could have insisted that she stay somewhere safe and within his control. But here on Earth it was hopeless. She had been allowed too much freedom. There were too many enemies and protest groups, both secret and otherwise. And there were too many other voices speaking in her ear, leading her to believe that she would be in no danger. Now look what had happened. Disaster! The Ki kidnapped – possibly even dead by now, though he prayed to all the gods of Altaniskaran – and the Earthan ones too – that this were not so. Worse still, the life of the Ki-consort hung in the balance. Things could not be worse – not in any way, shape or form.

It was nearly four o'clock in the morning. Thirty-five minutes earlier, Asud had crept into the darkened room in the Athenian palace where the Altani party were being housed and woken the old counsellor with the news that something terrible had happened on Santorini. He was needed urgently.

As soon as he entered the library that had been sequestered as his office and saw the rows of lights flashing on the companels and the frowning faces of the embassy staff, he knew the situation was grim indeed. Asud had briefed him as they had made their way down the grand central staircase from his room.

Terrorists or mercenaries – they could not yet say which – had attacked the Bashir villa, kidnapped the Ki, then shot the Ki-consort. He was being kept alive purely by heart and lung machines at that moment. One airtransporter had been brought down, but the other one, containing the Ki, had got away and had been lost by all the tracking stations. Twelve of Captain Chandra's guards had also been killed, but they had taken at least forty of the mercenaries. At least they had acquitted themselves well. Two of the attackers had been injured and were being questioned, even as their wounds were being attended to.

Beoraan barked out questions as he took his seat at the desk. Had anyone been to tell the dowager Ki-consort yet? Where was the president of the council, Sheikh Bashir, and his wife? No! Do not put a call through to the Ki's sister – yet. They needed to wait and confer with Lady Dacas. Had the medical team arrived yet to treat the wounded? Dr Mai could not cope alone. And had anyone thought to get a forensic scientist to the island? There was so much to think about, so much to do.

At that moment, David Bashir and Lady Thea burst into the room. They, too, had been woken in the middle of the night. They had dressed hurriedly and a staff aircar had brought them at top speed to the palace from their rooms in the council's embassy.

Surprisingly, given the seriousness of the situation, David Bashir was very restrained. Beoraan had expected the mountainous man to be angry and demanding. Although he had never experienced it, he had been warned of the man's temper and fully assumed that the council president would be explosive by the time he got to them. But he was quite the opposite. Perhaps because his son's life stood on a knife-edge and his daughter-in-law had been abducted – maybe even killed – the harsh realities of the situation and the need to think clearly were paramount. Bashir's long years of experience stood him in good stead in these moments. He knew that nothing would be achieved by ranting and raving and, if his wife's sallow, drained face was anything to go by, he needed to stay calm for her sake too.

All Thea could think about was Jax and if he was going to live or die. No! Dying was out of the question. She would not let herself go down that dark path. He would live and, although she knew she was being selfish, she could not help but be relieved that at least she knew where her son was, and that he was still – if barely – alive. Unlike Li-el Dacas, who must, she thought, by now be distraught.

'Any news, Beoraan?' asked Bashir, the suffering in his tone more than obvious.

'All we know at present, sir, is that the Ki-consort is stable. He is alive – albeit with assistance. It is perhaps too soon to know how he will progress …'

'Or if,' Thea Bashir finished the thought.

'Now, my love,' David said gently. 'There's no if about it. He is young and strong. He will pull through – have faith.' Bashir moved over to his wife and put a large arm around her shoulders. The tiny woman seemed to disappear into his overwhelming frame.

Beoraan was more than a little moved by this open display of emotion. It was uncommon for Altanis to show such fondness in public although, of course, many relationships contained more than a modicum of affection in private.

'I am expecting to hear from Dr Em-sin Mai at any moment. We will know more then,' Beoraan said.

He stood up from his desk and, sighing, walked over to the window. The rooftops of the ancient city spread out below him, bathed in the quiet, pale darkness of the early dawn. Not yet morning, no longer night, the city slept on, unaware of the traumatic events unfolding far off to the south in the Aegean Sea. Beoraan – not for the first time in his later years – envied the sleeping people whose lives never held these horrors or heavy responsibilities. People who never had to bear the burdens of state, of decisions that seemed so right at the time but proved so wrong in retrospect when lives were lost, or families torn apart. Although they, too, faced their everyday dilemmas and moments of crisis, nothing they would face would be as dangerous or as influential as the decisions people like him had to make every day. He envied them their peace of mind and their simple lives.

He sensed a presence by his side and looked out of the corner of his eye to see the dark profile of David Bashir.

'Yes, they're lucky, eh? Those who do not bear our burdens?' Bashir reflected solemnly.

'It is better so,' Beoraan answered honestly. 'We are the protectors and the pilots, we guard and guide. It is our duty and, for me, a birthright. I serve as my father and mother served before me.'

'Is that how you see it? Duty?' Bashir's question was rhetorical. 'It is a noble view of civil service, one I fear not shared by all. At least, not here on Earth.'

Beoraan allowed the trace of a smile to lighten his eyes. 'You think we are not also stained by flagrant ambition and avarice on Altan?' The old man sighed and shrugged his tired shoulders. 'How I wish it were so. This will never be a perfect universe. There will always be evil and greed – and plain stupidity and ineptitude. There will always be poverty and hunger and terror. All we can do is try, by our very best efforts, to minimise it, to promote a philosophy that despises it and, at all times, protect the innocent. This is what we do.'

'And I, for one, am thankful we have people like you who are not afraid to meet the challenge.' Thea Bashir's quiet voice entered the space behind them and they turned as one to include her in their reverie.

A few moments of silence passed during which they turned their thoughts and prayers to the dead and the injured – and the missing.

'Sen-Beoraan.' It was Asud. She lowered her head in deference to the old counsellor. 'Lady Dacas is on her way.'

Beoraan nodded and his sigh was imperceptible. Li-el Dacas was not an easy woman at the best of times. The coming interview would be one of the hardest meetings he would ever have to undertake and, before the maelstrom hit, he allowed himself one small moment to wish that he had been born any other man at any other time and in any other place.

Wedding ceremony over, Commander Navarr's trade delegation was preparing to move on from Athens. There were still three more cities to visit in the next ten days and the off-world delegates were eager to set up more deals with their Earthan counterparts. It was an undeniable fact that the Earthans were as well versed in the art of trade and negotiation as the Altanis, Autabronis and the Dasnirians and this had made for some stimulating exchanges. The Huthons, as could be expected given their preoccupation with more spiritual matters, were not ideal traders and, in return for copious quantities of the magnificent green-marbled ru-hoku timber, the Autabroni delegates acted as their representatives.

Navarr's initial boredom had worn off and he had begun to take an interest in the comings and goings of the negotiation processes. He could see the great potential for personal wealth in some of the trades that were being made and appreciated now what Balisel saw in all this – and how she had become so very rich. The game of barter with its sudden twists and turns, its play-acting, its bluffs and bravado was all rather good fun. But to Navarr it was still a longwinded means to an end and for him the sport was not worth playing unless he knew he was going to win.

Balisel had contacted him shortly before four in the morning to say that everything had gone according to plan. The Ki had been delivered safely and unblemished to the fortress of Guyvar Neref, the upstart Bashir husband was dead and soon the Galactic Union would be in disarray with accusations and counteraccusations flying back and forth. Everything was working out just as they had envisaged and all that was left to do now was to wait for the news to break. Then Navarr would step forward with the secret information about who had kidnapped the Ki. It was hinted at in the file he had on the Order of Sumere – the file Beoraan had found at the time of Navarr's disgrace – but now he had more information, of course. Now he would be able to tell them of how the Order had tried to recruit his sister and how they had taken Balisel to where they were holding the Ki, and how Balisel had seen the Ki – alive, but held captive. It would then be up to him to convince Beoraan to let him lead the search for the Ki and he was confident of his ability to do this. The old man still had faith in his abilities and, despite his fall from favour, he was still one of the best heads of security there had ever been in the royal household. Even Beoraan would have to admit that.

But that was for later. Right now, all he needed to do was to consume a hurried breakfast and leave a note for the chief Altani delegate that he was spending some time with his sister who had unexpectedly arrived on a brief holiday. He would join them tomorrow, he wrote, although of course he had no intention of doing so. Ah, but it would be good to have some free time with Balisel and to hear all about the death of his rival. He had been working too hard lately, he reasoned, and besides, he could do with a little diversion.

The doors to the library slid apart and Li-el Dacas glided into the room. As ever, she was dressed magnificently. Her outer nightrobe rippled as she moved, its velvet folds cascading like a deep blue waterfall, and her hair was swept back neatly from her face with a jewelled silver hairband. It was obvious that she had taken a little time to adjust her appearance before coming to them, as befitted someone of her station.

Beoraan bowed low before her, as did all other Union staff in the room. In the absence of the Ki she *was* the Ki, no longer the dowager. But, for a variety of reasons, all hoped that that would not be the situation for much longer.

'Well, Beoraan, what news?' Her voice was calm, clear and authoritative.

'Our lady remains missing, seemingly abducted. All efforts are being made to trace the airtransporter that removed her from the villa.' Beoraan paused to clear his throat before going on. 'The condition of your son-in-law is that he is alive and stable. He is not conscious. A medical team has just arrived at the villa and we should know within minutes the status of all the injured.'

She nodded curtly then turned to the Bashirs, who still stood close to the window.

'My heart goes out to you both. Your son lies in mortal danger. But I assure you that Em-sin Mai is the best. Doctors of her order are trained to the highest degree. She will not cease in her efforts to restore him.'

Tears welled in Thea Bashir's almond eyes, more in response to the kindness of Lady Dacas's tone than her words.

'Thank you, my lady,' Thea replied. 'And I am praying for Linnayen too. I know it is hard but we must trust that God is keeping her safe.'

Li-el Dacas's stare cut through the space between them like a rapier and her response was almost scornful. 'I have no need of blind faith. My daughter lives.'

'Yes, of course,' David Bashir interjected. His manner implied that he was encouraging a false hope and Li-el picked up on it.

For no more than a split-second her face was as stone before her mouth opened wide in a warm smile. There followed a bubble of laughter, which amazed the Bashirs and Beoraan.

'No, you don't understand,' she began. Her smile softened and she placed a soothing hand on Thea Bashir's and stared into the woman's worried eyes. 'I *know* my daughter is alive.'

They understood. She was a mentante and had obviously detected her daughter's mind.

Li-el did not expand on her statement; they did not need to know that Linnayen was unconscious. That knowledge would worry them as much as it did her.

Just as quickly as the comfort and relief had come, Li-el's face suddenly darkened like approaching storm. 'But we have to find her – and the people who have done this. I want them all, and I want them dead.'

His clothes were bloodstained and filthy, and under any other circumstances he would have been horrified at his appearance. But not on this morning. Duncan leaned his tired body against the roof's parapet wall and looked out across the caldera's silhouetted rim to the eastern sky. Thin, filmy clouds lay parallel to the horizon, tapering strands of peach and gold lit from below by the rising sun. The deep cobalt of the night lay behind him and his sweat-stained face shone in the morning light. It was an incongruously beautiful sunrise. It did not seem right that it should be so beautiful when everything was now so awful. In a matter of minutes, the world had turned terribly, horrifically upside down. His best friend was a whisper away from death and Linnayen had been taken.

How would he tell Jax about Linnayen? He had never felt so alone, or so grown-up. In the space of the last couple of hours he realised he had truly become a man, and not just because di Luca and Nen and Dr Mai, even Captain Chandra, had looked to him for leadership. In the confusion and near panic that had followed the mercenaries' attack, and more by a process of elimination than through any merit he possessed, he had become their leader. But he also felt that he could not have survived these hours without their unflagging support.

Slowly he became aware of a presence, an unmoving silhouette in grey. She coughed and instantly he knew it was Dr Mai. There was news, but good or bad? He walked towards her, trying hard to straighten his back and steady his gait.

Her features were in shadow, not that he might have learned anything from the Altani's habitually serious face. His eyes asked the dreaded question and she responded without hesitation.

'Sir, the Ki-consort is asking for you.'

The morning sun shone brightly through a lead-lighted window of the tower room in the castle of Guyvar Neref and, even though it was only nine o'clock, the day promised to be hot and unyielding. The temperatures in this part of northern Asia Minor could soar to over forty degrees Celsius at this time of year and the fortress was far enough inland to receive no relief from any sea breezes. In the winter, of course, the reverse was true. The snows whipped in, borne across the Black Sea from the icy wastes of the Ural Mountains far to the north, and the land became a frozen, treeless wasteland, ugly and forbidding. Hardly a land worth fighting over. The region's poor, thin soils were wracked by too-frequent earthquakes and its extreme climate had never attracted permanent settlers for long. No, Guyvar Neref had not been built for settlement.

It stood squarely at the entrance to a high pass near Abbasgol in the Ararat Ranges, nestled between the rich trading ports of the southern Black Sea and the high plains of Kurdistan, a natural short cut that had saved many ancient merchants' precious days of travel and hardship. In its dark history ownership had changed many times, each landlord extracting ever-higher tolls for safe passage through the pass. Depending on the despot in charge at the time, some would demand terrible and painful prices, and many travellers were maimed or had their families held hostage on the whim of the landlord. Thus, the castle's fearful reputation grew and only the most foolish or desperate of merchants would brave the wardens of the pass of Guyvar Neref.

The ancient edifice had been largely unoccupied for over seven hundred centuries and, as such, had never been refurbished or repaired. The Order of Sumere had put a small army of workers through the place in the days before the kidnap to clean a few rooms, add security controls and make the place serviceable, albeit barely so. It was no palace. There was no air conditioning and the small portable solpower unit packed only enough energy to run basic life support and communications systems. They would not need the place for more than a day or two, though, so it was hardly worth going to too much trouble.

In the tower room, with its sweeping views across the baked and dusty foothills, colours from the leaded glass dappled the pale grey stone slabs of the floor, brightening the otherwise drab interior. Balisel Navarr waited impatiently for the door to open, drumming her tapered nails upon the slick steel surface of a table in the centre of the room. Oleander sat quietly on a couch apparently reading a book, although her thoughts were more focused on the tall blonde woman and the obvious anxiety she displayed. Suddenly, the heavy door swung open and Durroc Navarr walked briskly into the room.

'Durroc!'

Balisel's smile was broad and transformed her face, making her frozen beauty suddenly thaw with a rosy blush. There was an uncommon softness in her eyes also and, as she allowed herself to be enfolded in her brother's muscular arms, her body visibly relaxed.

Oleander was not slow to notice the interaction between brother and sister. Indeed, one would almost have thought they were lovers. *Was this the key to their ambition, their single-mindedness? No, surely not ...*

His smile was slow and sensual and Oleander could see how many women would fall under the spell of those crystal blue eyes. His presence was powerful, dominating with a natural assumption that he owned or controlled everything around him. Even she felt a little overawed at first, but she soon regained her control and remembered the job at hand. This was no time for flights of fancy, sexual or otherwise. They all had a job to do and she was intrigued as to how the alien twins wanted to handle it. Of course, whatever they wanted was immaterial. The Order had long since decided how this game would be played and what the result would be. Still, it would be interesting to watch the interplay between these two and their reactions when her strategy was finally revealed.

The tall man released himself from his sister's embrace and came over to where Oleander sat on a low couch, her shapely brown legs crossed in an overtly feminine manner. She held out her hand for him to shake and he took it firmly in his two whilst his eyes locked onto hers.

'I can't tell you how much I have looked forward to meeting you, Miss Aqua.'

There it was again, that slow smile accompanied by a piercing look, designed to melt any resistance. Oleander wondered if he used these techniques on everyone he met – men as well as women – or was he genuinely unaware of his power?

'And I you,' she replied, raising her free hand to enclose his. The gesture was, as Oleander intended it to be, openly inviting, pulling him down and encouraging him to sit with her. He responded by sitting close enough for her to feel the warmth of his thigh against hers and his look told her that he knew perfectly well what sport was taking place between them.

From across the stone-walled room, Balisel's stare was as sharp as a cat's claw. She hated them both at that moment – but she hated the woman more. She was used to Durroc being manipulative. Without it, she assured herself, they would not have got where they were today. But that was all it was. If ever it became serious and she ran the risk of losing her brother then playtime would most certainly be over – for everyone.

'The operation has gone well, I hear?' Navarr said, looking hard into the dark woman's eyes.

'Yes. Linnayen Genara is safely under lock and key and her husband is very, very dead.'

Navarr grinned and threw a conspiratorial look across to Balisel.

'Unfortunately, we lost over forty personnel,' Balisel cautioned, in an effort to dampen her brother's approval of the assassin. 'Kees Rennick is not a happy man.'

'He's being well paid,' Oleander scornfully replied. 'And he knows the risks we run.'

'But we have enough guards left?' Navarr asked. If things went his way then an attack would come next to free the Ki, and he wanted at least a token show of resistance. Otherwise how could he appear to be the hero of the day, the Ki's saviour, and win his way back into her favour?

'Enough guards for what?' Oleander asked, her suspicions alerted.

'Why, to protect our charge, and us,' Navarr replied. 'In case we should be found.'

A frown crossed the dark woman's face. Something felt wrong. 'But we will not be found.' Her tone was both puzzled and guarded. 'I made sure our transporters left no trace. And all

Rennick's people are either dead or here. We are quite secure – unless you have reason to think otherwise?'

'He doesn't,' Balisel interrupted. 'My brother is being cautious, and rightly so.'

Oleander raised an eyebrow, the gesture intended to show her scepticism. *No, there's more to this. But what?*

'And speaking of our … What shall we call her? Guest?' Navarr's smile was brittle. 'How is our guest?'

'Still unconscious, but otherwise unharmed,' Oleander replied. 'Rennick's men have her under guard in the old dungeon, as it happens. Very appropriate, eh?'

Navarr laughed. He liked the woman's attitude. At any other time she would be worth cultivating. It was a shame that their acquaintance was likely to be so short.

'Yes, you picked well. This is indeed a godforsaken place and suitably equipped. The dungeons – now that's a nice touch. The Ki will be mortified to wake up there. Not at all what she's used to.'

Navarr was pleased with the way this was shaping up. The worse her plight, the better it would be when her loyal commander and lover came to rescue her. *How great will be her gratitude then,* he assured himself.

'You sound almost pleased to see her suffering,' Oleander said thoughtfully.

'It won't do her any harm to see how the other half live for a while,' Balisel snapped, deflecting the potential inquiry away from her brother.

Oleander understood now. She knew their history – had made it her business to know. The Navarrs had struggled to get where they were. They had had to live off their wits and their cunning. Nothing had been handed to them and they had never known even affection, let alone love. This was where the drive came from – the desperation to win. They needed to get to a place where no one could touch them and where they had absolute control. She knew that feeling. She shared some of it too. But with the Navarr twins it was different. They were cold and methodical, almost brutal, and she knew that somehow they got a warped pleasure from all this.

Durroc Navarr suddenly stood up and walked back over to his sister. Placing an arm around her waist, he kissed her on the cheek.

'But now, to business. My time is short and I have much to do.'

His smile was broad and engaging. Despite her misgivings, Oleander could not help but be charmed by this man.

'Take me to my mistress.'

'I am impressed, wife. Only *you* could have thought to do that.'

Tariik Min stroked Evica's cheek fondly and she looked up into his blue eyes with a sad smile.

'I could not risk him being free to roam at will without some sort of safeguard. I know how devious he can be – maybe even dangerous,' she replied.

'Well, it looks as though your caution has paid off. He's obviously up to something and, no doubt, we'll soon know what it is.'

Evica's wide eyes narrowed as a frown settled across her brow. 'But if he has harmed her in any way …'

'We don't even know if this has anything to do with Linnayen's kidnap yet.'

Tariik tried to sound reassuring. But in their hearts they knew that it must have. For weeks Durroc Navarr had done nothing and gone nowhere. He had behaved himself perfectly and had been fulfilling his duties as head of the trade delegation to the letter. He had been the epitome of contrition. But Evica had not been convinced and nor had Beoraan. Between them, they had ensured that Navarr would be tracked wherever he went by means of a haemo-worm that had been injected during a medical examination administered to him after his displacement from the Ki. Although the Earthans were not aware of his status, he was officially on probation, awaiting an investigation into his behaviour. Once they were back home Navarr would probably end up either in detention or exiled, so it had made good sense to implant a tracker into him whilst they were still so far from home. The haemo-worm was both undetectable and highly effective, even over distances of up to a thousand kilometres. And today it had proved its worth. Navarr had broken with his routine and changed his schedule only hours after the Ki's kidnap and the attempt on Jax's life. It could not be mere coincidence.

Evica stared unseeingly at the landscape passing far below, sandy brown lands interspersed with shining golden streaks as the early morning sunlight reflected on the many twisting ribbons of water they flew over. They had just crossed over into Eurotanian airspace but the country below still retained its old name, Espana, despite having long since amalgamated with sovereign states to the north and east. In twenty more minutes they would be making their descent to the Athens airdock and, finally, Evica would be able to *do* something. This sitting around was infuriating and frustrating.

Tariik felt it too. He was trying hard to be reassuring and doing a passable job at it, but he was as anxious as she to arrive in Athens and get moving on Linnayen's rescue. It was a sudden end to their honeymoon in the Andean Mountains, a time of privacy and intimacy that had been wonderful, albeit very brief. But he reminded himself that they could always go back to that once Linnayen was safe and Kevor Jax restored to good health.

The news had reached them shortly after they had taken off that Jax had been badly wounded and still unconscious, although this was due to a drug-induced sleep brought on by Dr Mai's remedies rather than his injuries. Jax was going to be all right. But there was no news of Linnayen and that was more than worrying.

It was true that Commander Navarr's sudden departure from Athens might have nothing to do with the kidnap. But in his heart, Tariik did not believe it. He had never liked the smooth, ambitious commander and trusted him even less. And Navarr's excuse to the trade delegates that he was taking the opportunity to visit his sister for a few hours while she was on holiday in the area seemed very thin. Tariik could not believe that Navarr would take off for a break knowing that the Ki had been kidnapped – and he would have known. Of that Tariik was sure and so was Evica. Navarr had his sources, even since his disgrace. No, there had to be more to it. Navarr was up to something and he and Evica were going to find out what it was.

He patted his wife's limp hand once more, then took hold of it and raised it to his lips. His kiss was soft and he followed it by placing his cheek on the back of her hand as he looked up into her eyes.

'Don't worry,' he spoke quietly. 'We *will* find her, and she will be well.'

Evica smiled back weakly. She was thankful to have this man by her side right now. His love gave her strength. She knew Linnayen was alive; she too had reached out with her mind and found her sister's life force. But she also knew, as did her mother, that Linnayen was unconscious, and unless she woke up they could have no clue as to her whereabouts. Without Linnayen's eyes they were blind.

Evica nodded to her beloved husband. 'Yes, I know we'll find her. But will we be in time to save her?'

Chapter Thirty-one

Navarr had been waiting for this moment for many long weeks. Since the Ki's fall on the *Jensa Kadenx* there had been only the one chance to get close to her and that had proved disastrous. The sight of her now, lying on the thin pallet in the corner of the dim, stone-walled room, both intrigued and excited him. She was completely at his mercy. The most powerful woman in the known universe was totally under his control and all that was left to decide was how he would take his pleasure. What would give him the most enjoyment, he wondered. To have her simpering thankfulness once he had rescued her from her terrible torment? Or to have her as she had once been, imperious, sometimes demanding? Until he wrestled her down and gave her what she craved.

The thought aroused him. He remembered fondly the many nights – and days when they felt like it – when they had coupled with frenzied impatience. Nights when she had sometimes pleaded with him to go more slowly, to take more time, when all the while he knew what she really wanted was more. Well, now she would get her wish.

Balisel stood in the open doorway, the light behind her casting a long silhouette across the broken flagstones. Her hands rested impatiently on her hips.

'Well? As you can see, brother, she is fine. Quite unharmed. Can we go now?'

Navarr ignored her. His mind was still elsewhere, in a past that had been filled with lust and power and control – absolute control – in his position as the Ki's lover. It was a time when he had felt completely safe from harm. Nothing could touch him then. Not hunger or poverty or dirt or hate-filled faces. And it was all because of her. She – the Ki of Altan – had brought him all that he had ever dreamed of and he wanted it back.

'Durroc? Did you hear me?' Balisel was getting annoyed and bored. He had seen his precious Ki. What more did he want?

'I heard you,' he replied, somewhat absently. 'Now, what is it you knocked her out with?'

'Oh, nothing too terrible. Well, nothing she won't recover from,' Balisel said. 'I spiced it up with a little urthrengo so that she'll be docile. Don't want her screaming.' Balisel's beautiful face screwed itself up with distaste.

'The Huthon drug?'

'Yes. It worked well for dear Jeremiah, as you know. Couldn't teach him to swim, though.' Her face took on a look of mock-sadness that could not stop the smile in her eyes.

Navarr removed his fixed gaze from the sleeping Ki for a few moments to join in with his sister. He stepped towards her and stroked her cheek with affection.

'You've done well, my love. As always.'

He adored her. But he wanted these moments alone – had dreamed of these moments – and now he wanted her to leave.

'But go now.' Seeing her look of surprise, he quickly moderated his tone. 'I'm hungry, that's all. Go and get me some breakfast … please.' He smiled fondly, then kissed her cheek. 'I'll be a few minutes.'

Reassured, Balisel departed and, as soon as her shadow had disappeared from the end of the passageway outside the stone room, he closed the door behind him. The room was darker now, its shadows even more pronounced as the only light came in the form of a single bright shaft from a high barred window.

A sudden deep sigh broke the stillness. In a flash, all his attention returned to Linnayen's supine body. She lay on her stomach, one knee splayed out, her profile sunk into a coarse cotton pillow. He covered the space between them in swift, quiet steps and knelt at the side of the white-sheeted pallet. He studied her features, taking in the full lips and the fine straight nose, before letting his gaze travel down the length of her body, which was covered by a thin blanket. It was too thick, though, to properly allow him to see his prize. He wanted to see her – all of her – again, just as he used to.

He pulled the cover off. Linnayen was wearing only a silk blouse that was crumpled and dirty, but it did not detract from her beauty. Her legs were bare and, with the change in temperature, she shivered. The movement caused her blouse to rise, revealing the tops of her thighs.

Navarr sucked in his breath. He lifted the smooth fabric. She wore no undergarments. Tiny motes of dust sparkled in the shaft of light above the bed before falling onto the smooth mounds of her honeyed flesh. He could not stop himself from reaching out to touch what he had once possessed and, at first, he was gentle. He stroked the soft skin, relishing the privacy of these moments. All this belonged to him again – her skin, her smell, her hair, every curve of her body – and he became heady with the desire that grew deep inside. His hand moved to the cleft between her thighs. She sighed again and another shiver took her body.

He could feel her now. She was warm and wet – ready for him, just like old times. Should he take her now? His body responded to his thoughts in a delicious rush. He was hard, harder than he could ever remember. It was almost painful – a sweet pain that he knew could only be relieved in one way. Why not now? She was his prize. He had worked hard to get her, risked everything – career, status, even his freedom. He *deserved* her. So, why not take what was his?

He removed his tunic. His bare chest was already warm and glistening with fine droplets of perspiration from the morning's early heat. Then he lowered his pants. Naked, he climbed onto the miserable low bed, straddling her still sleeping frame. Gently he lifted her waist and buttocks and placed her on her back. He did not want to take her like an animal – well, not this time, anyway. No, he wanted her to see his face. He wanted her to know who owned her now, who was having her purely because he could, not because he wanted her or loved her, like that fool of a husband. But he did not matter anymore. Now there was only Commander Durroc Navarr, and the proud Ki would soon know who her true life partner was, for he would make it so.

There was a moment just before Linnayen woke up – or thought she woke up – when she sensed someone else inside her mind. It was a woman – maybe two women, she could not be sure. Their thoughts got tangled up and twisted, tripping over themselves in a hurried rush to get to her. She sensed their anxiety but could decipher nothing of their content. All she was left with before consciousness returned was a feeling of warning.

They did not need to worry though. She was safe and warm and loved – *being* loved. He was here with her now, right now. She could feel the warmth of his body on her and the touch of his hands, stroking her, caressing her. And more … Yes, much more. He was at one with her and the fullness of the love she felt for him flowed out of her like a brilliant light piercing the dark shadows. She could even see the light. It was above her head, slanting away to a distant corner. She could see tiny dancing specks of dust in it and, all the while, there was his warmth filling her and surrounding her. His love was part of her now – the two had become one – in a heady confusion of passion and desire. Her contentment was complete. She wanted no other happiness but this – except to tell him so. And she spoke his name.

'We tracked him to an area in northern Anatolia, sir, where he stayed for just over an hour before travelling – now in the company of his sister – to the city of Odessa. He was observed having a brief lunch at a local restaurant with Ms Navarr. They left the restaurant together then walked in a local park before going to the Hotel Pushkin, where they remained for two more hours. He then returned here.'

'Thank you.' Beoraan smiled at the intelligence officer who had brought him news of Navarr's travels that day. The young man nodded his head smartly then turned and walked away. Meanwhile, the old counsellor stared at the floor, trying to compile his thoughts.

Evica sighed. 'I'm not sure this tells us anything,' she said despondently.

'You are sure Navarr knew of the Ki's abduction before he left this morning?' Beoraan asked.

Tariik Min responded. 'Well, no. But if *you* got the news before 4am, it's my bet that Navarr knew soon after. He still has influence among the ranks and Evica believes he has spies everywhere.'

'You may be right. But knowing the commander, I very much doubt that he would leave on such a ...' Beoraan searched for the word, then continued. 'Such a frivolous mission, and at such a time of crisis. He just wouldn't do it.' The old man shook his head, his disbelief obvious.

'He would – if he were trying to fool us, or if he already knew where she was.' Evica bristled with the force of her words.

Beoraan was not convinced. 'Lady Evica, I am sorry to disagree with you but I just can't believe it. So few people knew what happened on the island this morning and I'm certain none of them would have said anything. And, despite his past behaviour – which, I hasten to add, I loathed as much as anyone – his loyalty to the Ki is unquestionable. I've observed him with her many times; he is quite dedicated to her. He would not harm her.'

'So you think he has nothing to do with this?' Tariik finished.

Beoraan exhaled loudly and his shoulders slumped. He was so tired. He hung his head.

'I do not know. I'll reserve judgement until I have more facts – or until the commander himself proves me wrong.'

At that moment, Asud entered the library apologising for the interruption. Beoraan smiled kindly at her.

'Sir, Commander Navarr wishes to see you. He says he has important news.'

They all looked at each other in mute surprise, eyebrows raised. The very devil they had been tracking was outside their door.

'Well, counsellor, perhaps you will get your proof sooner than you think,' Evica said acidly.

Beoraan asked Asud to ask the commander to enter and a few seconds later a flushed Durroc Navarr rushed into the quiet room. Noticing Evica and Tariik, he remembered the protocols of rank.

'My lady, lieutenant, Sen-Beoraan. Thank you for agreeing to see me.'

He lowered his head as he spoke but was bold enough to lock eyes with all three of them as he continued.

'I have just returned. The news ... terrible. My lady, I cannot tell you the depth of my despair and concern.' He spoke quickly and earnestly, giving all appearance of the devoted servant. 'I want to help. I assume you are already working on a rescue attempt? I realise my position but I want to offer my services, my skills ... And I know something about it.'

At these words, all three pricked up their ears.

'What could *you* know?' Evica spat the words out.

Navarr turned his gaze towards her. 'I think I know who took her – who's behind *all* this, even the assassination attempt back on Altan before the Ki's marriage.' He coughed and lowered his head, acknowledging the sudden death of the Ki's husband. 'Oh ... My condolences.'

Navarr chose this moment to display the sorrow he did not feel for the death of Jax. In his enthusiasm to lead the rescuers to the Ki, he had not taken the time to update himself on how the day's events had progressed. He was, therefore, quite unaware that Jax, although still weak, was now recovering in an Athens medcentre.

Evica placed a restraining hand on Tariik's arm. There was no need to give the commander any more information than he already had.

'Thank you. It has been a terrible night.'

The silence in the room was deafening and he felt all three pairs of eyes upon him, like hot branding irons waiting to strike flesh.

'They're called the Order of Sumere,' he began. 'A radical right-wing group whose aim is to keep Earth free of alien influence. They are fanatically anti-Union, highly secretive, well-funded and it is believed that their members come from the very highest echelons of Earthan business and political society.'

Beoraan was the first to break the following silence. 'Yes, we know of them. If you recall, I questioned you about the dossier you made on them.' Finding the file about the Order of Sumere in Navarr's things after his downfall had led to their request for Joe McCrae to do a little digging, but there the investigation had stalled for now. *So it was significant after all.* 'But what makes you think it was them?'

'Ah … Here I have a confession to make.' Navarr looked sheepish and embarrassed. 'There's something I should have told you.'

It was working. His show of contrition was well rehearsed and he thought he was doing rather well on the whole. Navarr had them all believing that he was, indeed, the once proud, now humbled commander, anxious to do the right thing – to come clean. Only then would they believe the web of lies he was spinning. He paced a small area in front of Beoraan's desk, behind which the old man had retired.

'I began looking into them following the death of the Earthan ambassador on Altan, Byers. You remember him?'

They did indeed and Evica grimaced at the memory of how the poor man had died. Beoraan's eyes tightened as they focused in on the blond man before him. What was Navarr getting to? What did the ambassador's murder have to do with this?

'The Order was just a name on a list of suspect organisations and I could find no link between them and the ambassador's death. There were so few Earthans on Altan at the time that it was easy to eliminate any potential killer. I know better now. There was one

Earthan on Altan who I have since discovered is a member of the Order. But I'll come to her later.'

Evica shot a glance at Tariik. *What's happening here? What does he know?*

Navarr cleared his throat and continued. 'I looked at the organisation again after the attempt on the Ki's life. But since the assassin, Delgar, was killed at the scene ...' Navarr paused long enough for them to remember how he had saved the Ki's life and slain her would-be killer.

'Yes, I remember well your efforts, Commander Navarr,' Evica interrupted. *And it was after that night that my sister became your lover. Coincidence?*

Navarr took the interjection as a compliment and nodded his thanks before continuing.

'When we investigated Delgar, we could find no links to anyone. Besides, he was an Autabroni, not an Earthan. So I had no reason to suspect the Order.'

Tariik, who was perched on the arm of Evica's chair, shifted his position. He was getting tired of this delay and wanted Navarr to get to the point instead of singing his own praises. Navarr picked up on the body language and hurried on.

'Then, a week before the Lady Evica's wedding, my sister told me that the Order had tried to recruit her.'

There was a general stunned silence at this announcement and Navarr paused for the effect to register.

'That's the confession I had to make. I should have told you, Sen-Beoraan, of this at the time – I realise that now. But I wanted to see what I could do to make amends for my past behaviour. So I asked my sister to play along with them and spy for me.'

'Wait a minute,' Evica interrupted. 'Why would the Order of Sumere contact your sister? Surely they would know of her relationship to you and of yours to the Ki? It doesn't make sense.'

Navarr could sense Evica's antagonism but it did not worry him. He had his story worked out and it was perfect. She would find no flaw or loophole.

'It does when you know my sister's political leanings. We may be twins but we do not think alike in all matters. Sadly, I had been unable to persuade her of the advantages of Earth entering the Union. She always saw it as a threat to her company's business interests – especially on Autabron – and has made no secret of the fact either. Now, though, her feelings have changed due to recent events in her life.

'As you may know, my sister tragically lost her husband some months ago and has inherited his investments here on Earth. She can see many advantages now of amalgamating her business ventures. We believe the Order was not aware of the shift in her views and sought to recruit her. It has been searching for new members from Altan and the other planets to join its ranks –'

'Thereby giving it a foothold on other planets of the new Galactic Union to continue causing its havoc,' Beoraan finished for him.

This was going very well indeed, thought Navarr smugly. He even had the old man filling in the story for him.

'Exactly. Balisel came straight to me. I advised her to be wary – especially for her own safety. But she was keen to help. She may not yet fully believe in the Galactic Union but she has no desire to get involved with fanatics either.' Navarr was building to the climax now and delighted in seeing the studious attention on their faces. He had them hooked. *Just a little more. Not long now.*

'Please, commander, get to the point.' Tariik was obviously losing patience and his dislike of the blond man was beginning to show openly.

'Well, my sister went back to them, hinting that she would be keen to join them, but that she wanted proof of their capability. She was told by a go-between known as Oleander that proof would come very soon – within days, in fact. Something big was going to happen. And sure enough, they have just proved their point,' Navarr concluded with an audible sigh.

Evica's eyes narrowed in concentration. Navarr's words were plausible, but still her distrust of the man drove her to find something that did not fit.

'But how do you – or your sister – know that this attack and kidnap is the work of the Order? Where's the proof?' Evica asked.

'I was coming to that,' Navarr began, clearing his throat. His enthusiasm for his subject grew noticeably as he spoke. 'In the early hours of this morning, my sister called telling me that she had been taken in the middle of the night from her hotel in Odessa by this Oleander. Virtually kidnapped! She was told she would come to no harm – they wanted her to witness their capability. They took her to an aircar and, once they were underway, she was made to wear an incom-mask that blocked her vision. When they arrived at their destination the mask was removed and she found herself sitting behind a viewing panel. On the other side of it was the Ki. She appeared to be asleep and all Balisel could make out was that she was lying on a small bed in a dark room with stone walls. She said it looked very old.'

Evica gasped and jumped up out of her chair. She crossed the space between them to stand squarely in front of Navarr.

'Where is this place?' she demanded.

Navarr shook his head sadly. 'I don't know. Balisel and I made a search of the area she thinks she was taken to but we found nothing. Remember, she was kept incommunicado. All she could remember was flying over what she thought was a large expanse of water. This was at the start of the journey. They went for approximately twenty minutes before making landfall. She thinks they crossed onto land because she noticed the aircar rise suddenly when it hit a thermal up-flow. They flew for a few more minutes before landing. We plotted possible landfall destinations, given the average speed of an aircar, and met this morning in northern Anatolia. As I said, we searched, but soon realised we would need more resources.'

Tariik looked at Beoraan and Evica. The same thoughts were passing through their minds. This all fitted in with the intelligence report they had received earlier about Navarr's movements.

'What happened to your sister after she saw the Ki?' Beoraan asked, prompting Navarr to finish the story.

'She was put back into the mask and taken back to her hotel. The female, Oleander, told her to say nothing of what she had seen.' His reply was swift and delivered with just the right amount of openness, he thought. 'Oh, and there's something else. My sister secretly photographed Oleander. Balisel's a resourceful woman ...'

These words were said with no small amount of genuine pride, which gave the whole story an edge of credibility. Navarr almost had himself believing it.

'That's when I recognised her as the same woman who had been on Altan at the time of Ambassador Byers' death. She was listed as a journalist on her ship's manifest and, when she was investigated at the time, her identity checked out. But she's our link to the Order of Sumere, and it probably clears up the mystery of the ambassador's murder too. The Order would have had much to gain by the ambassador's death.'

At any other time, Evica would have found this information of great interest. But not now.

'My sister? Was she injured?' Evica's voice faltered and her shoulders visibly sagged. The effort of these moments was beginning to wear her down.

'No.' Navarr's tone was soft and kind, the only time any of them could remember seeing him like this. 'My sister said that she seemed to be unharmed, my lady. She was only sleeping.' It was at that point he remembered how Linnayen had looked when he had left her.

She had opened her eyes only once whilst he had been with her, right at the end. But she had not seen him. She was woozy and had spoken his rival's name in a voice thick with the effect of the sedatives. How strange, he thought, that the one time when he had made love to her and actually felt something akin to the emotion was the one time when she was not aware of it. He had been surprisingly gentle. She had stirred a little and moaned all the while and moved her deliciously smooth body beneath him, which had excited him even more. When, finally, he had climaxed, he could have sworn that she did too, even though she was still apparently in a drug-induced stupor. The moment was almost precious and he was amazed to find his feelings bordering on tenderness.

There was a natural silence while everyone made the effort to gather their thoughts and think of what needed to happen next. Tariik was the first to break into their collective thoughts.

'Are we likely to hear from the kidnappers soon, do you think?'

Ah, this was more like it. A little bit of deference. Navarr liked being back in control, if not quite yet in charge.

'Impossible to say, I think. But my sister expects to hear from Oleander again. She was told they would be back in touch. Balisel is smart. She will try to find out whatever she can, I promise you.'

'Not good enough,' snapped Beoraan. 'We cannot wait. Anything could happen to the Ki in that time. We must make a detailed search of the area. Stone walls imply an older building. We'll explore them all.'

The old man had sprung to life. Now at last they had something to go on. At least they knew where to begin the search. And although he still did not trust the commander, he was thankful for his loyalty. Despite Navarr's disgraceful past behaviour, Beoraan knew they could depend on him to help them find the Ki.

'Lieutenant, my lady, perhaps you could make a start?' He looked across to the newlyweds, who instantly moved in the direction of the companels and began to punch keys to access the relevant databases.

'Commander Navarr, come with me. You need to tell your tale to Lady Dacas.'

Navarr bowed to Evica and Tariik, who barely noticed his departure with Beoraan. They had work to do. It seemed that Commander Navarr had meant well after all and their suspicions were temporarily – if unfortunately – allayed.

Jax felt terrible. His mouth was parched and he turned his head to look for something to drink, grimacing with the pain the movement brought. He did not recognise the room he was in but knew it was not the villa. Noticing the plasma screens and instrument panels at the side of his bed, he guessed he was in a medcentre and probably back in Athens.

The rustle of the crisply laundered sheets as he moved roused Duncan who had been sleeping in a large armchair at the side of the bed. He opened a bleary eye before quickly sitting upright.

'Thank God, you're awake! How are you feeling?'

Jax took a few moments to study his friend's face, which was both more anxious and dirtier than he had ever seen. Then his gaze dropped to take in his clothes. Duncan was filthy! It appeared that he had not left Jax's side since they had returned to Athens from Santorini and the destruction at the villa.

'Sore, thirsty,' Jax croaked. 'But what happened to *you*?'

Duncan looked down and shrugged it off. 'Oh, nothing. The fighting …'

Jax winced as he tried to lift himself higher up the pillow.

'Pain?' Duncan asked. 'Can I get you anything?'

The young man nodded carefully. 'In a minute. Tell me… Linnayen? How is she?'

Duncan hesitated for a second. 'I'm sorry … She's gone.'

Jax sucked in a breath and tried to get out of the bed. Duncan laid a calming hand on his shoulder.

'Oh, no – don't worry, she's alive. Taken by those bastards. I saw her being lifted into their transporter. She was out cold but I don't think she was hurt.'

He tried to sound as reassuring as he could, but Duncan realised only too well how grim things were. It was as much as his acting skills could do to keep the worry out of his eyes. The stunned look on his friend's face told him that the full horror of Linnayen's plight had registered.

'But you don't *know*, do you?' Jax grimaced again as a stabbing pain passed through his chest.

'Hey, take it easy, old man. You've had a narrow escape. You almost died on us back there. It was that doctor who got you through. She was bloody marvellous.' Duncan's voice firmed by the second. He had come so very close to losing his friend and he was not about to let him do any further damage to himself. 'Now lay still, and that's an order.'

Jax nodded weakly. 'Why, Duncan? Do we know why? Has there been any demand yet?'

'Not as far as I know. It's only been twelve hours since the raid so there's time for that still.' Duncan shrugged his shoulders as he continued. 'And as for why, your guess is as good as mine. Terrorists? Criminals? I guess we'll find out soon enough.'

Jax tried to swallow but his throat was dry. 'Could you ...?' He gestured to a flask of water that stood on the side table.

'Of course,' Duncan replied, dropping a long straw into the neck of the flask. Jax sipped greedily at the water. At this moment, nothing had ever tasted so sweet, but the joy he found in slaking his thirst dissipated when he remembered what had brought him here. Linnayen kidnapped, perhaps hurt. It was too cruel after all they had been through. She had said that she loved him – *loved* him! He would not lose her again.

Duncan continued the sorry saga. 'We lost twelve guards and another ten are injured, but everyone else is unhurt. In fact, Professor di Luca and that little maidservant Nen are heroes. They brought down one of the airtransporters with a xelex-cannon. It was quite a sight.'

Jax was still in shock from the news of Linnayen to register much interest in what Duncan had to say. The thoughts roiled through his mind like churning storm clouds. *Linnayen gone.* Then, in the quiet that followed as Duncan's words receded into the distance, anger grew inside him, surging up like a tidal wave, gathering mass and strength with every minute. He vowed that this crime would not go unpunished. He would save his wife – and he would do so with his own hands.

The darkness when she woke was absolute – or so it seemed at first. As the seconds passed and her bleary eyes widened, she began to make out areas of shadow and greyness. But the overwhelming sensation was of silence. She had never before experienced such quietude. Nothing moved to disturb it, not even the wind. So when she shifted her body on the hard bed, the noise of the coverlet seemed to deafen her and she instinctively tried to smother the sound.

She reached out a hand and felt and felt the chill on her palms of old stone and the dry crispness of lichen blooms. For a moment she wondered where she was. *This was not the villa!* Snatches of memory crept into her consciousness and, as she sat up, she hung her head and let the tears flow. But reason soon overcame her sorrow. She needed to get her bearings – to know her prison and discover, if she could, its weaknesses. There had to be a way out; she just had to find it. Besides, keeping herself occupied would help to push away the agony.

She could not bear to think about him – not now. She did not want to remember the terrible scene of her beloved Jax on the floor of the white room in Santorini. He could not be dead! It would not be fair. It must have been a dream, she reasoned. She would wake up from all this soon and find that he was not dead, only injured. Or maybe he did not fall at all. Maybe she only thought she saw him fall. Everything had happened so quickly. There was no way of knowing what was real and what was imagined. *Better not to think about it. Can't think about it! Must find a way out!*

She stood up slowly and stretched her back and shoulders. Her joints were stiff and she winced with the pain. Feeling her way around the entire perimeter of the room, she discovered a door. It was made of wood that was heavily pitted and it possessed an opening or hatch at head height and a large, square lock plate. There was no handle. Her eyes were by now accustomed to the darkness and she could see that there was also a window high up in the wall facing the door through which she could see a multitude of stars. They were very beautiful and she wished with all her heart to be up among them and out of this awful place.

Then she realised that she needed to relieve herself. The knowledge gave her only one choice: she would have to call for help. Perhaps this would give her a chance to see the faces of her kidnappers, and her husband's murderers. *No! He is not dead!*

Her yells and cries for attention pierced the night, ripping through the dreams of the guard who slept outside. He stumbled up and pressed the communicator pin on his chest to alert Captain Rennick and Agent Oleander.

'All right! All right! Calm down, I'm comin',' he grumbled. As he moved a glow-globe came to life and its beams trickled through the window in the cell's heavy door. At once, Linnayen spun round to take in the extent of the room and was dismayed to find it was as she had imagined. There was nothing but stone walls and a dowdy pallet for a bed in the corner.

'What ya want?' The guard's harsh voice was rough with having been woken too abruptly.

'I need to relieve myself,' Linnayen answered.

'Is that all?' The guard was obviously not impressed with having been woken in the middle of the night for such a trivial matter. 'Use the bloody bucket.'

She looked over her shoulder to the dim corner he had indicated and curled her lip. 'I need *proper* facilities – if you don't mind.' She tried to keep her voice simple and calm, figuring that the more reasonable she appeared to be the more likely her chances of getting out of the cell, from which it would be impossible to break out. She needed to be moved to somewhere else to stand even a chance of escaping.

The guard sighed resignedly. 'Hold on. I'll have to clear it first.'

Linnayen did not want anyone else to come along. She could take one guard, but two would be difficult. Evica had always been the one who shone in military training, but she had enough skill to acquit herself well when the situation demanded it. She had to stop him.

'I only need to … you know. I wouldn't be more than a minute,' she pleaded sweetly. 'You could come with me. Just turn your back.' Her voice was soft and seductive. She was not above using her charm on such an oaf as this when it suited her purpose.

The guard laughed out loud. He had still not made any move to open the door.

'Nice try.' He leered at her through the window, licking his thick lips and very obviously staring at her cleavage and bare legs. 'Perhaps another time.'

'Haneef!'

The guard sprang back and away from the door as the mercenaries' leader, Rennick, walked smartly down the passageway.

'She wants to pee, sir,' the guard said with a sneer in his voice.

Rennick stepped over to the hatch in the door and studied the captive in the pale light of the glow-globe. Linnayen stood still and tall with straight shoulders and her chin lifted proudly. She did not meet the man's gaze – why should she? He was far beneath her, both in rank and human dignity.

'Very well. Take her,' Rennick pronounced. 'Use restraints.'

The guard unlocked the door and entered the room. Linnayen stood staring ahead at a point high above Rennick's head while the guard placed a flat metal band around her neck and tightened it.

'Don't even think about escaping,' Rennick warned. He had done his research; Oleander had insisted on it. The Ki of Altan may be only a girl of twenty-four years, but she was fit and had been trained in hand-to-hand combat, just like her elder sister. One should never be complacent, he reminded himself. 'The choker delivers an unpalatable shock, even at its lowest setting. And I assure you there's more than one hand on its control, even if you could get it away from me.'

Linnayen glared into Rennick's hard eyes, but her anger made no dent in him. Not that she expected it would. Even so, she wanted to wipe the arrogant smirk off his face.

'You know,' she began, as menacingly as she could muster given her weakened state, 'If I were in your position I would think very carefully about what you say to me. One way or another I *will* get out of here and, when I do, you'd better hide.'

Rennick smiled and raised his eyebrows, demonstrating his appreciation of her performance. 'Yes, I can see how that might intimidate others. But you have much to learn if you think it's going to scare me.'

Linnayen shrugged to show that she did not care about his opinion. 'Oh, I have no intention of scaring you, I just made you a promise. You *will* pay for this – you and whoever is pulling your strings.' She spat the last words out with contempt. She had guessed that he was not the brains behind this operation and his flicker of anger in response confirmed it. Linnayen decided to push in the knife a little further.

'So what orders have you had from above? Keep her in good health? Don't damage her? Don't mark her?' Linnayen's disrespect was apparent in every syllable. 'And how long will you have to look after me? Do you like being a nursemaid? Must be quite a comedown given your level of skill and training ...'

'Shut up, bitch! You don't know what you're talking about,' Rennick barked back.

'Really? I think I know when I'm dealing with a lackey instead of his master.'

Rennick raised his arm as if to strike her across the face with the back of his hand. A piecing look from the guard who still stood behind Linnayen stopped him short, reminding him that his orders had, indeed, been unequivocal. He was not to harm her in any way or the penalty would be more than just a cut in his fee.

'That's how much you know!' he returned, snapping his fingers in front of her face. 'I answer to no man! Now – do you want to pee or not?'

Her silence was answer enough. Rennick nodded at the guard to move her forward out of the cell and along the passageway. She stumbled a little but soon found her footing. Then she smiled, for in the fleeting moment when Rennick had gone to strike her she had been able to use her mentante ability – an ability she had all but forgotten she possessed – and she had glimpsed his thoughts. It gave her two useful pieces of information.

Firstly, it *was* possible to read Earthan minds after all – apparently when they were in a heightened emotional state. She recalled now that Altani mentantes had never had much luck in penetrating Earthan psyches, but this experience proved that it could be done. One just had to enter when they were angry or, perhaps, when they were feeling other emotions strongly.

And then there was the clincher. She had seen in Rennick's mind the face of her abductor – and it was a woman.

So it had been true when he said that he did not take his orders from a man. There was something else though. A trace of what she had seen lingered and nagged at her, tugging at her mind's sleeve. There was something about the woman, something familiar. But what? Who was her captor and why had she been taken?

Suddenly, breathlessly, like being plunged into icy water, the scenes of last night came back to her and she saw Jax fall once more, a look of intense agony twisting his handsome features, and it was all she could do to keep walking. All thoughts of the strangely beautiful woman she had seen in Rennick's mind instantly flew away and she was left with nothing but bleak emptiness and abject misery at the thought of her dead husband.

Chapter Thirty-two

It's remarkable – you're almost as good as new!' David Bashir cried.

It had been just over thirty hours since the attack at the villa and through the medcentre's window Jax could see that the Athenian sun was already high in a cloudless blue sky. Jax had had a good night's sleep, thanks to a compound administered by Dr Mai, and physically he felt a hundred times better than the day before. The pain in his heart, though, had not been so easily relieved and the signs of it had left their mark on his face, which was haggard and drawn.

'Hardly that, David!' Thea interposed. Her look would have withered a less resilient man. 'Can't you see how weak he is? My poor boy. How are you coping? How is the pain?'

'Mother, I'm fine. Really.' Jax tried to calm her fears. Thanks to the nanobots, his body was fast repairing itself, but the ache in his heart was unrelenting. He patted his mother's hand as she took a seat at the side of his bed. 'They've given me a shot for the pain and actually I don't feel too bad.'

Thea gave a short snort. 'Rubbish! You're in pain. I can tell. I'm your mother. I know these things.'

'Thea, if the boy says he's okay, he is. Leave him alone,' Bashir countered, shaking his head.

'Don't be silly, David. He's been through a terrible ordeal and he needs to be looked after.' Thea was insistent. She did not get too many chances these days to be a mother – not since Jax had left home – and she was not going to miss this opportunity. 'Kevor, is there anything we can do? You only have to say.'

Jax looked down to gather his thoughts for a moment. He did not want to betray his emotions but the fact was that, inside, he was torn apart. Linnayen was gone. None of them could know what she had suffered – was still suffering. Evica had been to see him late yesterday afternoon and had told him that both she and Lady Dacas had sensed Linnayen's presence, that she was still alive, but how much faith could he place in their mentante abilities? He wanted to believe them but he had to be honest. None of them really knew if Linnayen was alive.

Jax kept his voice calm and steady. 'I'm fine. And in a few hours, with all this new blood pumping around me, I really will be as good as new, just like you said, Father. But in the meantime, what you can do to help me is tell me what is happening. What's the news about Linnayen? Does Beoraan have any leads? Have we heard from the kidnappers yet?' Jax's tone became more urgent as he spoke.

David Bashir nodded solemnly and began to summarise the situation.

'No, we've had no demands so far. But that doesn't mean we won't. And, as for leads …' Bashir paused. He did not want to upset his son by flattering someone he knew his son despised, but Jax had to know that the disgraced Commander Navarr had proved his worth and come to their aid. 'Well, we are on to something. Commander Navarr's sister has seen Linnayen. She was taken to witness her incarceration.' Seeing the puzzled look on Jax's face, Bashir tried to explain. 'It's too long to go into now, son. But Balisel Navarr saw her and said she was alive, though unconscious and being kept prisoner by these people, a terrorist group calling themselves the Order of Sumere. She doesn't know exactly where but we're whittling down the options and we should have it pinpointed within a few hours.'

'She's alive? Definitely?' There were smiles of reassurance on his parents' faces. 'But what's all this about Navarr and his sister? What do they have to do with it?'

At a small sound behind them – the merest rustling of rich fabric and a quiet cough – they all turned to see Li-el Dacas standing at the back of the room.

She answered Jax's question. 'They have everything to do with it, my son – everything. But in what way I cannot yet tell. There is something though ...' Her voice trailed off as her thoughts searched for the key to unlock the puzzle in her mind.

Jax frowned. There was much to do. A rescue party to put together, maps to be studied and a plan of action to decide. But he found it hard to organise his thoughts. Every time he came close to making some sense of it all, images of Linnayen lying still and cold and lifeless came into his head, flooding the order with a swirling tide of chaos. As if she knew of his inner turmoil, Li-el Dacas spoke again.

'Don't worry, Kevor. She is well, although her quarters are appalling!' She said these last words with outraged dignity. Treating a Ki of Altan in such a fashion was intolerable – a pitiful, squalid jail. When she got her hands on these people, she vowed, they would pay for this atrocious behaviour.

The Bashirs gaped at her, open-mouthed and questioning.

'Let me get this straight: you have *seen* where she is being kept?' Jax asked tentatively.

'Why yes,' Li-el confirmed. 'And I have to tell you, it is not a palace by any stretch of the imagination.' Belatedly she registered the effect her words were having on Jax and his parents and realised they did not understand.

'My apologies, that is what I came to tell you. Linnayen has regained consciousness. I have seen what she has seen. She has allowed me to enter her mind.'

It took a few moments for the full import of this news to sink in.

David Bashir was the first to speak. 'Oh, thank God! Is she well? Has she been harmed?'

Li-el looked fierce. 'No – I hope even these despicable brigands would not do such a thing to the Ki of Altan, although their crimes are already too many to count.'

Jax finally found his voice. 'Lady Dacas, please tell me what you saw. Can you identify where she is being held?'

Her eyes closed the distance between them and her concern was evident.

'I cannot. But who knows? Linnayen may be able to get it out of them and then we'll know.'

Thea Bashir was confused. 'I'm sorry, I know you have telepathy but how will you know? How can you *see* what she sees?'

'They're mentantes, Mother,' Jax explained. 'They can read each other's minds, understand each other's thoughts. So if Linnayen finds out where she is being held, she'll be able to transmit that thought to her mother.'

Li-el held up a hand. 'I'm afraid it's not exactly like that. Indeed, sometimes people's thoughts are well hidden from us. Then, of course, the mentante protocol forbids us from entering without the host's permission – you can understand why. But being a mentante is also much simpler than that. It allows us to actually see what another is seeing and understand their thoughts, if they are willing.'

Thea nodded. 'So when Linnayen woke up, wherever she is …'

'That's right. I had a good look around. But there was nothing much to see, just an ancient stone cell. Earlier, though, she met two of her captors, but they did not seem to be the ones in charge.'

'And when will you next get … in touch with her?'

At first Thea thought Li-el had not understood her question as a puzzled expression crossed her regal features.

'Ah, no, I won't be getting back "in touch" with her. I don't need to.' Li-el glanced around at the looks of worry, confusion and, from Jax, plain frustration. He was clearly losing patience – he wanted answers and action and he wanted them now.

Li-el continued swiftly. 'No, Linnayen has made the supreme sacrifice, something virtually unheard of among mentantes. She has allowed *jaaseyan* to take place. Only mentantes know what this is and I must ask you not to speak of it outside this room. You would understand it to mean "attachment".' Li-el struggled to find the words to explain what this meant and its importance in Altani culture. 'My mind is even now grafted onto hers. In effect, at least for the time being until we detach, our minds are as one, sharing everything.'

A few moments passed in which the Bashirs took in this new information. It was Jax who broke the silence.

'And does it work both ways? Can she see us too?' he asked. His mother gripped his hand a little more tightly.

Li-el's smile was almost mischievous. 'Correct. I am *her* eyes just as she is mine. It's a little something that our enemies are unlikely to know about. Rather gives us an edge, I hope.'

Li-el's understatement brought a smile to every face in the room. It was the best medicine Jax could have had at that moment. Not only was he now certain that his wife was alive but also that she could see him and know he was safe. This was an opportunity he was not going to miss.

'Lady Dacas, would you mind very much telling your daughter how much I love her?'

Li-el's smile broadened. Jax saw now the older woman's resemblance to her daughter and for the first time in many hours, Jax allowed himself to feel happiness.

Her reply a second later was accompanied by a brief laugh. 'She says: prove it – come and get me.'

Kumiko Toyotomi looked out across the vast expanse of conifer trees that swathed the steep hills surrounding her summer home on the island of Hokkaido. The blue-green hue was deep and rich, almost black, and their silhouettes against the pale blue early morning sky were as jagged as a saw's teeth. She reflected that all beauty contained such dark truths – that nothing can exist without its opposite – for how can we know light without darkness? Or hunger without satiety? Or love without loathing? These northern trees proved the point, so sublime in their symmetry but with needles sharp enough to draw blood from a careless finger. In all beauty there hides pain. *As it is in nature, so is it in life – and death.*

She bore no animosity towards the captive alien queen. Indeed, from what she knew of the girl and what she had heard about her, she seemed to be regarded as a good leader. She was intelligent, skilled and thoughtful, supposedly with a keen grasp of politics, too, which was a trait Kumiko found quite admirable, given her own interests. Under any other circumstances she would have welcomed the girl into her fold and enjoyed developing her obvious diplomatic skills, but needs must. However promising the girl might be, she was a pawn in much larger game and she would have to be sacrificed. Perhaps she should have allowed her great-grandson to marry Linnayen Genara after all – she could have controlled her then, used her to the Order's advantage perhaps. Kumiko had always enjoyed puppetry, and the playing of a naïve child-ruler might have proved highly amusing. It would also have avoided the necessity of killing her, of course.

But it was too late now. The course was set and the game must be played out to its inevitable conclusion. The death of the Ki of Altan would set back planetary unification for a good decade at least, as the recriminations would fly back and forth. Nothing like an important, high-level murder to fuel a feud, she thought. It was a shame too that the Ki must not die swiftly or cleanly – that would be too easy to forgive. No, her body must be seen to have suffered the most heinous torture, an act so despicable that the very thought of peace between the Union of Planets and Earth would be buried deep – as deep as the child's poor, broken body.

Indeed, this girl's death would be a terrible loss, but what a boon for the Order! In a single stroke she would have secured a lasting discord, she reflected. *A fine legacy!*

Kumiko closed her tired eyes and tilted her head back. The pale rays of the sun penetrated the papery skin of her eyelids and she could not endure the brilliance of the light for more than a few seconds. Still, there was the enjoyment of the sweet-smelling mountain air left to her. The warmth of the sun encouraged the trees to release their sharp pine perfume and the air was refreshed and glorious. *Magnificent! There can be no finer world than this. And, though I will soon leave it behind, I have kept it free and untainted for my heirs.*

Her work was almost done. There was only one thing left to do – after a short nap. As she allowed her mind to relax, the old lady reminded herself to call her grandson-in-law, the ever-faithful though sadly unimaginative Ennio Nori, and he would soon see that her orders were carried out.

'I think I have it.' Navarr spoke the words with just the right degree of sudden awareness, he thought. He didn't want to sound too confident. It had to appear that he had worked his way through the intelligence and arrived at the conclusion after much effort. The illusion that he was, once again, merely a loyal security chief, sincerely concerned for the welfare of his Ki, had to be maintained if he was to win the confidence of these people.

Already he was aware of Tariik Min's hostility, and Lady Evica had little time for him too. As for the old man, Beoraan, Navarr believed he was completely won over; he had him just where he wanted him.

All around the room, heads looked up. They had been scanning virtually every ancient stone construction in north-eastern Anatolia and cross-matching them with suspected trace emissions from airtransporters for close to twenty-four hours without success, mainly because of the huge volume of each. The area was both filled with antiquated buildings and experienced a large volume of air traffic due to the many geothermal energy plants that dotted the region. Orbital surveillance had picked up multiple signals of occupation and, one by one, these had been investigated by airborne response teams. So far every occupant they found had a legitimate reason for being there. They could not even be sure that it was an old building they were searching for; all Balisel and Li-el Dacas had seen were stone walls. In theory, the Ki's prison could be underground, making detection by an orbiter even more difficult, especially given the geological profile of the area. Past seismic events had left the rocks of the northern sierra splintered and fractured and the minerals they contained played havoc with the detection equipment.

Navarr, Evica and Tariik had also been searching the databases of such institutions as land registries, civilian councils and utilities providers, whilst Beoraan and his staff scoured the historical record for archaeological sites and buildings of architectural antiquity.

Finally, and figuring that they had been kept on the baited hook long enough, Navarr led them to the ruins of Guyvar Neref. It was time to bring the sequence of events to a close – time to rescue his Ki and reassume his position by her side.

'This could be it,' he said hesitantly as Evica and Beoraan came to stand behind him. He worked the controls on the smooth metal console and a three-dimensional image of the ruined fortress sprang out into the air in front of them. 'We are picking up life signs in the tower room – there.' He pointed out the position of two glowing blips in the topmost room.

'Only two?' Evica snapped.

'Wait ... No, there are more. Here – and here.' Navarr pointed out other rooms in the castle and a large central hall where small clusters of lights could be seen.

'What do we know of this place?' This was Evica.

Navarr tapped a key on the console and Guyvar Neref's location with reference to key landmarks was also displayed. Beoraan punched the castle's coordinates into a tablet and began to read out loud a summary of the fortress's dismal history. Tariik Min, meanwhile, crosschecked it against his database and added the latest information regarding its ownership.

'Ah, now this is interesting,' Tariik began. 'The fortress is on land owned by a weapons development outfit called Nemeses, which is a contractor and supplier of xelex missiles and other heavy armaments to the Eurotanian government.'

'Judging by the state of the place, they appear to be using it for target practice,' Evica said with a wry smile.

'Storage, actually,' Tariik continued. 'But Nemeses is – surprise, surprise – one of the companies listed in the directorships of one Ennio Nori.'

'Who has links with the Order of Sumere,' Beoraan finished for him.

A few seconds passed, time enough, Navarr thought, for them to register the information and decide their responses.

'I'll alert the response team in that area. If the Ki is there, we'll soon know. We'll have proof within thirty minutes,' Navarr concluded, then moved quickly on. 'And in the meantime, I'll organise the recovery force. We will need to act swiftly and quietly if we are to rescue the Ki.'

Evica's brow furrowed and she glared across at the ice-blue eyes. Who did he think he was, she wondered angrily, dishing out orders and issuing instructions? He needed to be reminded of his place.

'Commander Navarr, the recovery force is not your concern. I believe you have a trade delegation to rejoin.' Her voice was acidic. Evica was determined that Navarr should not get the upper hand ever again. Her sister had been better off without him and his overbearing ways, as had they all. If anyone was going to take charge it would be her or Tariik, not the jumped-up commander.

Navarr hung his head in the face of her reproach, a touching display of humility, he thought.

'I apologise, my lady. I did not mean to overstep my authority.'

He could feel her hackles subside as the apparent sincerity of his words hit home. It was important now to make every word count. His delivery was crucial. Whatever happened, Navarr knew he would have to be in the recovery force and he could not afford to slip up.

'Although I know I have displeased my lady, my eagerness to help overcame me. Please forgive me.'

'Your apology is noted,' Evica snapped back.

'However, Commander Navarr, your thinking is good,' Beoraan interjected. The old man turned to Evica with a look that begged for her tolerance. Whether they liked it or not, Navarr was a professional and his organisation and combat skills had never been more needed than now. He took up where Navarr had left off.

'Get an airborne response to this Guyvar Neref. See if they can pick up any trace of recent airtransporter activity. In the meantime, Lady Evica, my lord Tariik, perhaps you could brief the recovery team. I believe Captain Chandra has his personnel on stand-by.'

Evica and Tariik nodded their agreement and walked away to attend to their duties. Navarr quietly sighed and shook his head the barest inch. The movement was enough to gain the old counsellor's attention.

'What's this, commander? Disapproval?'

'No, sir. It's just that Captain Chandra is the one who lost her in the first place.' His tone contained enough contempt to warrant Beoraan's full attention and Navarr knew how to make the most of the opportunity. If he could persuade Beoraan then the old man could turn Lady Evica.

'Please, hear me out.' He spoke humbly, quietly and it was as though a whole new Navarr had been born. 'Don't allow your personal disapproval of me to get in the way of good judgement. *Use* my skill, my training. Whatever else you may think of me, I am still loyal to my Ki and I'm the best security chief she ever had. If anyone can get her back, Sen-Beoraan, I can.'

Beoraan stared into his eyes. Could he trust this man? Heaven only knew how much he wanted to, but Navarr – once so promising – had let him down badly by inveigling his way into the Ki's affections and assuming a power to which he had not been entitled.

Navarr persisted. 'Please. Give me this chance to redeem myself. To prove to you – and Lady Evica – my loyalty. And if that means nothing then think on this. Why waste me on a trade delegation when I'm a fully trained and highly skilled combat expert? Let me help.'

The old man said nothing but his eyes bored into Navarr's. He had to admit to himself that the commander's argument was convincing. Navarr was good – the best combatant they had – and his tactical skills were without comparison. Beoraan wanted the Ki back safe and sound, and not just because she was his ruler. He was worried for the young woman, the little girl he had watched grow to womanhood. Although the dowager Ki had made contact and assured Linnayen that she would soon be safe, she was still so young and Beoraan surmised that she must be frightened. On balance, he finally reasoned, Navarr was right. He had to go with the recovery team and Beoraan would persuade Lady Evica. But Navarr would not have it all his own way. Evica and Tariik, at the very least, would be there to keep a close eye on him.

'Everything you say is true. Very well, commander. Make your apologies to the delegation secretary and be ready to depart for Guyvar Neref within the hour.'

Yes! Navarr's eyes glittered with triumph. It was happening. He was on his way back – back to the pinnacle of power where he belonged.

Good news, daughter. We think we've found you. We'll soon have you out of there.

Her mother's words stole quietly into her mind, but the only outward sign she gave that she had received them was a low sigh. It had been part of her training since childhood to suppress externalised emotion, a useful if not vital tool of statecraft. Besides, her mind was fully engaged elsewhere currently and she could not afford to be diverted. She knew her mother could see what she saw, but not what she heard. And it was at that precise moment that she heard voices – one male, one female – coming towards her along the dark, tunnel-like corridor that led to her cell.

The man's she recognised as the mercenaries' leader, Rennick, her main captor, or at least the only one she had met so far except for a couple of slow-witted guards. But the woman's voice was unfamiliar. Could this be the woman she had seen yesterday in Rennick's mind when she had made him angry? Was this the woman from whom Rennick received his orders?

For so many hours nothing had happened. Since the day before yesterday she had been brought food and water, the latter both to drink and for washing. And though she had wrinkled her nose in disgust, the guard, Haneef, had insisted on leaving a bucket for her toilet. On seeing her reaction, the guard could not resist sneering.

'How the mighty are fallen, eh? Reduced to pissing in a bucket.'

Linnayen had glared at him, trying not to give in to the rising anger and loathing she felt.

'And how, exactly, have I offended you?' she had asked shortly. 'You don't even know me.'

'I don't need to know you. It's *what* you are, not who. Had everything handed to you on a plate. Never had to work a day in your life. Never been hungry. Never been thirsty ...'

Apparently Linnayen's question had incited Haneef to vent steam and it looked as though he would be pleased to continue in much the same vein for some time.

'That's not true,' she had interrupted. 'Not all of it.' Suddenly the memories came flooding back with the full force of a tidal wave. 'I worked hard from childhood. I trained for years to take on the responsibilities of leading my people with honour, skill and compassion. I had it drummed into me every single day what my duty would be and how, if I failed, peoples' lives would be at stake. If you get your work wrong, you might get a reprimand. If I get my job wrong, people die. Try living with that!'

Haneef had scoffed. 'Oh, my heart bleeds.' He threw the bucket into the corner of the cell where it clanged noisily against the stones. 'And you try living with *that*, miss high 'n' mighty.' He had laughed loudly at his own joke then closed the cell door behind him, still chuckling as the key had turned in the lock.

Listening now to the slowly approaching voices, Linnayen glanced down at the torn and filthy blouse she still wore from the night of her capture, but yesterday she had at least persuaded the man, Rennick, to give her a pair of combat pants to cover her bare legs. Not that she had been cold – far from it. The temperature in the cell had risen steadily since daybreak, but the stones had remained a little cool to the touch, which brought some relief.

Since Haneef's last visit with her yesterday morning, she had received only one more visitor – in the flesh, – another male guard who had that morning brought her some bread and a fresh jug of water. This one had said nothing at all and barely made eye contact with her, despite her questions. What was happening? How long would she remain here? When could she go home? Nothing. The tanned face held barely concealed contempt as he picked up her old tray and left the room, locking the door behind him.

It had been a few minutes later that she had first become aware of her mother's consciousness in the space inside her mind and it filled her with a sudden warm glow, like the sun's rays falling on cold skin. She was thankful at that point to be alone. Had her guard been there he would have seen the incongruous smile on her face, followed swiftly by the tears in her eyes, and his suspicions might have been raised. She was quite sure that most Earthans did not know about mentantism and she wanted it to stay that way. She did not want to lose the only advantage she had.

Her mother's inner presence gave her the measure of comfort and reassurance that she desperately needed. It also gave her the knowledge that her husband was not dead. When Li-el had first mentioned his name in her train of thought, Linnayen had winced with pain. There had not been a moment since she had woken up that she did not recall the events at the villa and the sight of his bloody chest as he had fallen to the floor. The thought of having now to go on living without him so soon after they had come together was unbearable. No one could have survived a hit like that – or so she thought.

Li-el had felt Linnayen's reaction to the image of Jax that she had transmitted and marvelled at the depth of her sorrow. Surely her daughter had not been that close to her consort? He was a political tool, nothing more, and there had never been any love or affection involved – nor should there be, thought Li-el, in a good political marriage. So why did Linnayen suddenly feel so distraught – no, devastated – at the news of his injuries? There was no understanding it and Li-el was confused.

Injury? Had she understood correctly? Had her mother indicated injury – *not* death? The joy and relief Linnayen felt were almost overwhelming. *He's alive!*

It was at that point that her mother suggested *jaaseyan* and perhaps it was because she was so happy and emotional that she readily agreed to a bonding that was virtually a complete invasion of her inner self. This was not a process that, under normal circumstances, she would have ever considered. But she had to acknowledge the wisdom of it, given her situation. Any information her mother could glean through her would bring rescue a little closer, of that there was no doubt. It made good sense, but she did not have to like it and she made her mother promise to sever the attachment as soon as she was safe. Li-el, in her usual haughty manner, was indignant at the thought that she would stay in *jaaseyan* with her daughter any longer than was strictly necessary. That would be unthinkable. Every mentante knew the dangers of staying bonded for any length of time – of how the individual life essences would begin to combine and exchange, making disassociation both difficult and incomplete. One could lose a part of oneself forever and gain characteristics from the *jaaseyan* partner that would more than likely be quite unwanted.

The night had passed slowly and she slept fitfully. Her mind would not allow her to rest as it turned and twisted, trying to make some sort of order out of the chaos. Images of Jax's soft smile swam in and out of focus, then Navarr's image would appear, though why she should think about him she did not know. Since his disgraceful behaviour weeks earlier she had hardly spared a thought for him. But now, in the stone-walled darkness, his face, laughing one minute, lust-filled the next but always intensely compelling, danced behind her closed eyes and she was ashamedly conscious of her response. If she hated him so much, why could she not dispel his image? It was almost as though she desired him sexually and she squirmed with the awful feeling. She did not love Navarr. How could she? *Surely no!* The very idea was hideous.

Navarr was a monster and he would never change. *Would he?*

Finally the morning had come and any gentleness it contained was soon beaten down by the growing heat. Today the flagstones seemed warm to her bare feet, whereas yesterday they had felt cool. It was soon obvious that the day would be scorching and Linnayen had resolved to remain as calm and still as possible to conserve what little energy she had left. Sleep had not revived her – far from it – and she felt drained and lethargic. Her only comfort was knowing that Jax was alive. She had something to fight for now. Despite her fatigue, she had steeled herself to get through another day and, if possible, try to help her mother to find her.

Then, at the very moment that her mother's words had reached her, confirming that she had been found, she heard the voices in the passageway. She could not make out what they were saying, but they seemed to be raised slightly. There was definitely some disagreement taking place between Rennick and a woman.

Their footsteps drew closer and soon she was able to understand the odd word of what had become a heated exchange.

'… had our orders …' This was the woman.

'… know that's crazy …'

'Who's paying you? Do as …'

'… wrong … bad decision …'

And so it went on. It seemed to Linnayen, from the little she could hear, that Rennick was objecting to the orders he had been given. But she was now not certain that the woman was in fact Rennick's boss, having referred to 'their' orders. So someone else was in charge? She speculated that it was the white-blonde woman whose face she had glimpsed inside Rennick's mind.

'Do it now!' The woman's voice, now only on the other side of the door, barely concealed her anger and impatience. Oleander had just about had enough of Rennick's whining. What was the man's problem? Given that Linnayen Genara had already seen his face, he would be much better off once she was dead. His objections were infuriatingly stupid. Besides, he was being paid well for his handiwork and she knew he was no stranger to torture. Surely he could not be squeamish?

'And she's okay with this?' He wheedled at her resolve. 'No, I didn't think so. She wouldn't want this, would she? Have you even told her what you're up to? Well, have you?'

Rennick did not like the idea of killing the alien queen. She was too valuable a piece of property alive. They could make a small fortune from her – far more than he was getting from Oleander's paymasters. It was insane to kill her off without even demanding a ransom. What was the point of taking her if not to make themselves rich? Surely that was what the Navarr woman was in it for and he did not think she would take too kindly to her prize being destroyed.

'This is not her project. She was just a necessary accomplice. Her part in this is finished. But ours is not.' Oleander spat the words out through clenched pearl-white teeth. 'We have our orders and, trust me, you do not want to cross our employers. They can make your life a living hell. You'll do as you are bid, take the money and get the hell out of here if you have any brains.'

He knew that what she said made good sense but Rennick's inherent greed was like an itch that would not be scratched. She was such a prize. They could make so much more money. It was madness to do away with her and, given their specific orders, especially in such a gruesome way. Oleander said that the order had come from the highest level – use extreme methods, the suffering must be real in order to enhance the political statement. Even to such an old hand as Rennick, this seemed harsh. After all, she may be an arrogant little rich girl, but she was harmless. It was one thing to inflict pain and suffering on those who deserved it, or those who engaged willingly in war. But the outright brutal execution of a young woman who had committed no crime was different and, for the first time in his career, he felt mildly uncomfortable with what he was being asked to do.

Linnayen, on the other side of the thick door, listened to the exchange and tried to find a weakness in the resolve of either of them that she could exploit. The man had referred to another woman and, from what Rennick had said, she seemed to be in a position of authority.

The key began to turn in the lock and, with the speed of a cat, Linnayen stepped away into the shadow of the cell's corner, slid to the floor and closed her eyes in a pretence of sleep. Rennick was the first to enter. He quickly scanned the room and found her, then kicked at her outstretched feet.

'Get up. Come on.' He was in no mood for niceties given that he faced a task that was best over and done with quickly. At her slow response he kicked her again and raised his voice. 'I said get up!'

'All right, give me a moment,' Linnayen replied groggily, adding enough thickness to her voice to make it sound as though she had just woken from a deep sleep.

Rennick leaned over and roughly grabbed her arm to pull her to her feet. His fingers dug into the thin flesh of her upper arm and she winced with pain.

'Ow! There's no need for that.'

He ignored her and pulled her up anyway. Suddenly their eyes connected in a shared look of concern and puzzlement. The ground beneath their feet trembled slightly and, as if from a far-off place, there came a low, grumbling sound and a sudden hollowness in the air. This was followed by a moment of pure silence. Then the ground heaved again, this time with a larger, more rhythmic motion, as though a wave was passing through the point where they stood.

Linnayen and Rennick stumbled a little before finding their balance. Small clouds of rock dust puffed out from the ground and walls around them, but they soon settled as all became calm once more.

'Earthquake,' Rennick said to her, as if explaining a local phenomenon to a tourist.

'I know,' Linnayen returned with no small amount of contempt. 'We have them at home too.' A sudden pang of homesickness wrenched her heart. It was all coming back to her now. Out of the mists of her amnesia she saw the towering snow-capped peaks of the Ksas, draped in the pink and gold folds of a winter sunrise. The Genara family had a lodge high up on Mount

Ypraan and she vowed that, once she was out of this and back on Altan, she would take Jax there. They would finally have a proper honeymoon and she would leave him in no doubt of her love.

Oleander stood in the doorway, hands on her hips and a frown creasing her brow. There was an air of nervousness about her and she appeared to have been unsettled by the earth tremors.

'Come on! Let's get on with it.' Her voice was urgent. Her instinct for self-preservation niggled at her with increasing force. If there were going to be more tremors she did not want to be underground with the weight of the fortress above her. It made sense to get above ground. 'Bring her upstairs to the main hall.'

Rennick's surprise at Oleander's instruction was plain on his face. Moving her was not necessary, Linnayen suspected. That had not been the initial reason they had come for her. So why? Why *had* they come? To interrogate her, perhaps? But then why would they have waited over two days to ask her any questions? It did not make sense.

'Come on,' said Rennick and he dragged her towards the door.

This was only the second time she had been let out of the cell but the passageway was not much brighter in the morning than it had been two nights ago. It was not until they reached the stairwell that a few straggling beams of sunlight penetrated the gloom.

Whatever her captors had planned for her, she knew that these next few minutes would be vital. Here was a chance to see the full size and scale of the place in which she was being held and Linnayen took comfort in the knowledge that her mother – and her rescuers – would now see inside the enemy camp. It was the only help she could give them and she prayed that it would be enough. She prayed too that they would come for her soon – very soon. She did not like the look in the woman's hard eyes and she suspected that her time was running out. That's it, she thought with growing trepidation. *They are going to kill me.*

Chapter Thirty-three

Evica, Tariik and Captain Chandra sat nervously in the crew anteroom. They had spent the last twenty minutes fitting themselves out with a variety of weapons and armour before checking that Chandra's team members were equally well armed. Now, at last, everything was ready. All they needed to know was whether the target location was confirmed by air reconnaissance and until then, all they could do was wait.

There was no need to speak. The plans had been made and they all knew what was going to be required of them. The pilots who would fly them into the rescue zone were huddled together around a corner console, staring intently at maps and three-dimensional projections of the area around Guyvar Neref. Being at the head of the pass and encircled by jagged mountain peaks, there was little cover around the castle and, if the mercenaries had air cannon, they would be extremely exposed as they made their approach runs. Their only chance was in the element of surprise and, hopefully, their sheer weight of numbers.

The doors slid apart and Jax, Duncan, Nen and Dr Mai walked into the room. Evica's eyes widened in surprise. She had not expected Jax to be up and about so soon; after all, it had been only two days since he received his injuries. But all she could detect was a little stiffness in his gait as he walked towards her. The bindings around his chest, the blood transfusions and, more importantly, the painkilling drugs Dr Mai had supplied were obviously doing a good job. Even so, his face was drawn and pale and the furrow between his dark brows was clear evidence of his worry over Linnayen's capture.

Evica stood up quickly, as did Tariik and the captain, and her words of welcome were heartfelt.

'Kevor. It is *so* good to see you. How are you feeling?'

He smiled weakly and took her hand in his two. 'I'm fine. Thanks. And thanks to you too, Tariik, for keeping me up to speed on our progress.'

'It was nothing, Kevor Jax.' Tariik had made it his business to update Jax of their search results virtually every hour since he had regained consciousness. His logic came straight from the heart – if this had happened to Evica he would want the same consideration shown to him. He could not imagine what Jax must be going through right now, but he could certainly empathise with him. Were he ever to lose Evica, he would be devastated. Thankfully, they knew Linnayen was alive and this fact had brought them all much comfort and a renewed determination to find her quickly and bring her home.

'It meant a lot, believe me,' Jax replied. He scanned the faces around the room and noted that everyone was dressed in combat suits. Only their oxygen packs and helmets were missing. These would be picked up from the airdock hangar on the way to the various aircraft that were now assembled and being fuelled, ready for take-off.

'Well, I see you're ready.' As Jax spoke, he looked to Duncan, who immediately moved off to the side of the room.

'Yes,' Evica responded. 'As soon as we have confirmation that Linnayen is at Guyvar Neref, we'll be off.'

He nodded that he understood.

'And we expect that any minute,' Tariik concluded, almost enthusiastically. 'It won't be long now.'

'Of course. Then I'll be quick.' With these words Jax turned to Duncan, who had returned carrying two combat suits.

'These should fit,' he said somewhat brightly. Duncan was pleased to be doing something useful after two days of inaction. Jax's idea to go along with the rescue team had been just what they both needed – both physically and to relieve the torment they were going through. And although Duncan was no fighter, he hoped that his support and encouragement would be enough to help Jax through this ordeal. Whatever happened today, he reasoned, he would be there to help his friend and, maybe, he would in some way make amends for not being of more use at the villa.

Evica and Tariik looked at Jax and Duncan, then at each other, their eyes wide open in amazement.

'What do you think you are doing?' Evica asked of Jax.

'Coming with you, of course,' he replied matter-of-factly.

'Er, do you think that's wise?' Tariik questioned hesitantly.

'Given that you were almost dead only two days ago?' Evica finished, the concern rising in her tone.

'I'm perfectly well. A little stiff, but more than able to fly.' Jax's words were clear and relaxed. 'You forget. I'm a first-class fighter pilot – probably better qualified than most of the pilots in this room. And the more of us, the better. After all, we don't know yet what we're up against – or how many of them there are.'

'Even so, Kevor. The effort will be –'

But he cut Evica off in mid-sentence. 'Manageable. Dr Mai has attended me supremely well.'

He turned and nodded his appreciation to the grey-suited doctor who stood a little way behind him. She rolled her eyes in response.

'And I am feeling fine. Trust me.' Jax smiled at Evica and once again he cupped her hands, his voice quiet and sincere. 'If I didn't think I was up to it, I wouldn't put myself forward. I would do nothing to jeopardise this mission or Linnayen's life. So, Evica – sister – like it or not, I'm coming with you.'

She knew then that any further words would be wasted and shrugged in acquiescence. There was no denying it, her brother-in-law, who had seemed so ineffectual and naïve when she had first met him, was now a force to be reckoned with. Even though his body and mind had been through hell in the last few days, he stood proudly, his shoulders straight and square, and his chin held high. His whole demeanour had changed. He was a leader from top to toe, more than fit to be a Ki of Altan. Her sister, whether she knew it or not, had chosen well.

'Then you'd better be quick – brother,' she said with a wry smile. Her eyes were focused on a point over his shoulder. There stood the team's ground commander who was in the process of nodding to his pilots, confirming that Guyvar Neref was their target. 'Looks like we're off. See you there!'

Jax spun around, taking in the flurry of activity as pilots and crew members rushed towards their crafts.

So it was true: Linnayen had been located. As Evica, Tariik and Captain Chandra jogged towards the airdock, Jax moved over to where the ground commander was briefing the last of the pilots.

'Are we clear? Rapier Wing on main approach, Sabre on left, Pike on right flank. We'll only get one chance at this, so let's get it right.' The half-dozen heads gathered around him all nodded, then the pilots walked smartly in the direction of the airdock.

'Commander,' Jax began, 'is it true? The Ki at this fortress?'

'Yes, sir. We received confirmation from the recon team a few minutes ago.'

'And the kidnappers? How many are there?' Duncan asked.

'We couldn't tell exactly. Heat sensors picked up around thirty bodies, but the walls were mostly too thick to penetrate. There's also a shield, so we have no precise knowledge of their heavy armaments or their G2A capability,' the commander replied, the doubt evident in his voice. 'We're going in with gas, of course – and sonics. We want everyone alive.'

'Of course,' Jax agreed. He could think of nothing more devastating than the thought of Linnayen being killed during her rescue attempt. They were so close now – nothing could be allowed to go wrong.

'I'm coming along, commander. I'll take one of the Sprints if that's okay?'

A mingling of surprise and concern passed over the commander's face.

'Are you, um …?' he began falteringly.

'My son is quite sure. And more than capable.'

David Bashir's strong voice filled the void. He knew he would find Jax up here, knew he would not be kept out of this. He was, after all, a Bashir – a fighting man. Their Pathan blood ran deep in their veins at times like these; indeed, it was all he could do to stop himself from joining Jax. But he did not want his boy hurt either.

He walked over to his son and placed an arm around his and Duncan's shoulders.

'But you'd better take more care of yourselves this time, eh?' he said. His eyes twinkled with mischief, but his heart hammered with both pride and fearfulness. Behind the bravado, David Bashir secretly prayed. *Let no harm fall upon them. Bring them all home.*

'We will, Father. Don't worry,' Jax reassured him and, for the first time in more years than either of them could remember, he hugged his father.

The sight that met Linnayen's eyes when they reached the top of the narrow stairwell was both unexpected and uncomfortable, and she squinted to adjust to the brightness. The main hall, hewn of ancient stone blocks, was as tall as it was long and the far wall rose some twenty metres to an open sky. The worn remnants of two huge stone buttresses sprang out from its sides like clawed feet and at its top was a high arched window, long since devoid of any glass but with surrounding carvings that suggested it was once a striking feature. Perhaps there had been a grand banqueting room up there, Linnayen thought, and she imagined a gathering of dancing men and women swirling around the room whilst music trilled across a sea of soft glow-globe light. A sudden wistful longing that she could be in such a place right now, in Jax's arms, filled her.

A roof only partly covered the hall at the end where they stood but a bioskin had been rigged up from the old roof to a point about halfway up the far wall in order to keep out the elements. The translucent sheeting allowed in the light while the skin's environmental controls kept the searing heat of the morning at bay.

There were a handful of mercenaries milling around. Two were sat at a small control panel and were each monitoring a vidscreen. Another was holding a tablet and checking settings on an upright array of switches, lights and touchpads. Linnayen wondered if this was some sort of weapons system and gave it careful study. Anything she saw could be of use to her mother and she was aware of Li-el's presence inside her, watching everything. She was obviously excited to be seeing something useful after so long of nothing but grey, bleak stones. Li-el had also felt her daughter's anxiety over the earth tremor and this gave her another reason to urge the rescue team to make haste. Her daughter was surrounded by enough danger without adding to it.

'We can't do it here,' Rennick said to the woman.

'Do what?' Linnayen jumped in with her question, which she hoped might trick them into giving something away that she might use to her advantage.

'Shut up!' Oleander spat back.

Linnayen glared at her. This was not the woman she had seen in Rennick's mind and the knowledge that there was some higher authority spurred her on. She needed to find out as much as she could and there was always the chance that this other woman – the pale blonde one – might be the key to unlock her prison.

'I will not! I demand to speak to your superior. There's clearly someone else in charge. You two would not be capable of organising this operation.' She tried to sound as imperious as she knew how and it felt surprisingly comfortable. The old Linnayen, she thought. *Yes, that's how I must have been.*

Oleander and Rennick looked at each other questioningly, their eyes sharing the thought. What did she know? How could she know?

'You know nothing,' Oleander finally replied in a low growl. 'You're just a pawn in a game – and your usefulness is coming to an end.'

Despite the implied threat in the woman's words, Linnayen was unbowed. 'I know that I am useful to you as long as I am alive. I am worthless if I'm dead.'

'Oh, I don't know,' chimed in Rennick. 'Your husband would have been worth more, if only he wasn't dead already. People only have to *think* you're alive for us to get what we want.'

He doesn't know that Jax is alive! Too many thoughts were clamouring inside her brain. She needed to calm herself in order to think all this through. She took a deep breath.

'And when they find me dead, what do you think they'll do to you? I can tell you now that you'll be hunted to the ends of the universe. There will be no place for you to hide. No sanctuary.' Linnayen's words of warning rang in the air, causing a couple of the mercenaries to turn around from their tasks to see what was going on. 'Oh, and my people *will* find you. There are things about us you don't know. Special powers that make us different from you Earthans. You will all be found and killed before the month is ended. What good will riches bring you then?'

'Rubbish!' Rennick dismissed her speech with a sneer then laughed. 'Special powers! That's a good one. What are you then? Shapeshifters? Mindbenders? Give me a break.'

'Rennick, shut up!' Oleander barked at him. 'She's just stalling for time.' The honey-dark woman indicated with a nod to a doorway in the corner of the hall, hidden in the shadows behind where they stood.

'Take her to the tower room.' Oleander was aware that whatever Rennick had planned for Linnayen Genara did not need an audience. She moved closer towards him, placing an arm on his, and lowered her voice. 'Do it there.'

Jax settled himself into the pilot's seat of the Sprint and began checking the controls. Next to him Duncan studied the array of lights and screens, his face a study of wonderment. Sitting quietly behind, hands clasped in their laps, faces calm and serious, were Em-sin Mai and Nen.

Jax smiled to himself, remembering the little maidservant's behaviour a few minutes earlier in the airdock. He had expected that Dr Mai would insist on coming with them and that made perfect sense; Linnayen could be hurt and they might need her services on the spot. But Nen? He had questioned her gently, having no wish to offend her.

'I appreciate your loyalty, Nen. But it could be dangerous,' he had said.

'That's why you need me – why my lady might need me.' She had planted her feet firmly in front of him, hands on hips. Her tiny frame was as immovable as a slab of granite.

'Your lady *will* need you – here, when she gets back,' Jax insisted.

'Ah, you forget, sir. I'm good with cannon.'

Over his shoulder, Jax heard Duncan chuckle. He looked back at Nen and detected a mischievous glint in her eye.

'I see. Want to get another transporter, eh?'

'A woman's work is never done, sir.'

They were all smiling as they made their way across the airdock to board the Sprint-16 fighter craft. In the cockpit Jax switched on the companel and spoke with the flight commander as he ran through the systems checklist.

'For the duration of this mission, sir, your call sign will be Rama. Rapier Leader is already four hundred klicks from target and expects you to rendezvous with them at coordinates alpha-three-nine-sigma-four-one.'

'Understood. ETA to rendezvous will be twelve minutes.'

Jax completed his pre-flight checks and announced that he was ready for take-off. On obtaining the all-clear from flight command, the craft slowly rose into the air and Jax swung it about so that its nose pointed towards to the airdock wall, which was already nearly fully open. As soon as it cleared the internal space of the dock he applied full power to the ion-drive and the vessel shot forwards and upwards.

Inside the cockpit, a broad grin stretched across Duncan's face as he revelled in the speed of the ride. But Dr Mai and Nen remained impassive; they were more used to travelling in such vehicles back home on Altan and the exhilaration of the experience was nothing new to them.

They sped across the sparkling waters of the northern Aegean Sea at a mere five thousand metres. The random outlines and tiny outcrops that made up the many islands of the region flashed beneath them in a blur of shape and colour as their speed increased. Jax had to make up time as the main rescue party was already well ahead of him.

His face was a stone wall. Ignoring the tightness in his chest, all his thoughts and feelings were focused on the place where Linnayen was. He could see the irregular shape of the ancient fortress in his mind and tried to imagine in what part of it they would be holding Linnayen. *Below ground, probably. That would be the most secure.* That's where he would begin looking. They needed more information from recon. He did not like that they were going in almost blind, but at least they had appropriate weapons. The sonic blaster and gas torpedoes were designed to immobilise, not kill.

It all seemed straightforward. He had run simulations just like this in his student days many times. All he had to do now was to recall his training and rely on his gut instinct, that insubstantial but imperative trait that had never let him down before. He had no doubt about his skills. But, as they rushed towards the dismal fortress of Guyvar Neref, he prayed that they would arrive in time.

'What was Beoraan thinking!' Evica cried. She had just heard the despicable Navarr's voice over the companel. It appeared that he had been given the job of tactical officer with Sabre Wing. 'He should have cleared this with me first.'

Evica was fuming. She did not want Navarr anywhere near her sister ever again. He had done enough damage and she was fearful that his star might rise once more if he was seen as the hero of this mission.

Tariik tried to calm her. 'Beoraan was probably only doing what he thought was right – and you have to admit, Navarr is extremely good at what he does. Perhaps we should wait and see how he performs.'

'If we do that he may try to win back his position with my sister. I couldn't stand it if she were to take up with him again. It would be too …' Evica stumbled over her feelings, searching her brain for the appropriate epithet to express the level of her loathing. In the end she finished with an exasperated sigh. 'Oh, I don't know. Just awful. We must not let it happen. Do you hear me, Tariik? It mustn't happen.'

Tariik, who had been holding her hand, stroked her face. 'Don't worry, my love. It won't. Beoraan will be having him watched even as we speak – he's not a fool. But if Navarr can bring Linnayen back to us then I, for one, will thank him.' He looked into her defiant eyes in a silent plea for her tolerance.

Tariik also hated that Navarr was with them. But the commander was cunning, strategic and ruthless and these attributes would be very much needed today. Their discussion on the matter of Navarr's presence in the mission was suddenly interrupted by a transmission from flight command.

'Rapier One, be aware that seismic activity recorded in target region. Highly local epicentre. Initial readings have ground quakes building to R6.8 with possible volcanic activity too.'

Captain Chandra responded. 'Thank you, flight command. We copy and understand. Please keep us posted.'

He swung round in his seat and smiled at the worried faces of Evica and Tariik.

'Looks like we have an earthquake in progress at Guyvar Neref,' he said, rather too brightly for Evica's liking. 'That should keep them occupied.'

Evica's face fell. *He thinks only of the enemy and the destruction this might bring to them. What about my sister? She's down there.*

What good would any of them – even the great Navarr – be to Linnayen if she were to be killed in an earthquake before they even got there?

The door swung shut behind him, its lock clicking into place as Rennick pushed Linnayen into the tower room. They were in the highest level of the old fortress. Linnayen guessed it was about fifty or so metres above ground level, judging by the number of steps they had climbed. The staircase rose in sections of about ten steps each, then turned at right angles. But with no banister of any kind, the depth of the central stairwell had made Linnayen dizzy as they climbed and once or twice, due to Rennick's heavy-handedness, she had stumbled worryingly close to it. Only his firm grip on her tangled hair as he pushed her along had kept her from tumbling over the edge and Linnayen thought it very odd that she should feel gratitude to her would-be executioner for keeping her alive, even if it were for only a few more minutes.

Once in the room and momentarily free of his hold, she rushed towards the far window, navigating her way past a pair of couches and a low table. She held a faint hope that there might be a way out through it. But her spirits sank when she saw the drop below, for the tower sat atop a precipice whose height she could not even estimate. The smooth stone walls of the castle melded almost seamlessly into flat plates of grey-brown rock that plunged vertically down for many hundreds of metres towards a narrow chasm. She did not know it but Rennick had brought her to the favoured spot of many of the castle's old warlords where, in times gone by, a wooden platform extended out from the rock walls. It had amused many to have enemies prodded and poked towards the edge until they confessed their supposed crimes. As soon as the victim had relaxed and begun to shuffle back to safety, a lever in the tower's wall was released. The floor of the platform would fall away and the poor, tortured soul would drop into the abyss, his screams fading with every passing second until there was nothing but silence.

The wood of the old platform had long since rotted away and all that remained of it were the weathered stubs of two timber battens. There was no escape possible that way and, on quickly scanning the rest of the room, Linnayen realised that she was indeed trapped. The door was the only way in or out and the huge, square frame of Rennick stood between her and it.

Through her daughter's eyes, Li-el saw these events with growing alarm and, as quickly as she could, she relayed them to Beoraan, who in turn passed on the information to flight command and the squadron leaders. Linnayen was in the tower room. They knew exactly where she was now. Unfortunately, it did not help them much as getting to her was going to be nigh on impossible.

In Sabre One, though, the newly appointed tactical officer already had the makings of a plan. The recon team had spotted two aircars at the castle, parked on the ground a few metres from its main entrance. If he could get to one of these he could fly to a point close above the tower, fire a line and grappling hook through an upper window, then abseil down into the room. Yes, it sounded perfect. Just him and Linnayen. The old counsellor had communicated that there was a man in the room with her – large build, dark hair – and he guessed that this must be Rennick. Well, he would have to go, of course. The rescue not only had to be perfect, it had to look it too, and that would mean losing Rennick. His death would make the rescue much more authentic, thought Navarr, with no small amount of satisfaction. One had to appreciate the beauty in how it was all coming together. Not long now. Only a few more minutes and Navarr would be back where he belonged.

Linnayen's fears mounted with each passing moment. She had placed herself at the farthest point from Rennick with her back against the glass of the window. As he approached, she moved swiftly to her right. There were no obstacles along this side of the room to trip her up. But he matched her movement, forcing her to go back the other way.

There was no mistaking the leer on Rennick's unshaven face. She knew what it meant. Her death, obviously, was not going to come until he had taken his pleasure with her. Linnayen knew that whilst she could hold him off for a few minutes in a struggle, his size and weight would win out eventually. Although her heart was pounding with fear, she calculated that these few minutes might be just enough time for the rescue team to get here. She had to do anything she could to stretch them out, to give them more time.

That's right, my girl. Do whatever you can to stall that monster. Li-el was encouraging her on. She had picked up on Linnayen's reasoning and knew, like her daughter, that whatever time she could buy for herself and the rescuers was going to be very precious indeed.

An imperceptible change came over Linnayen's face, fear replaced by caution. Suddenly, she allowed her glance to sweep up and down Rennick's body. She saw the shape of his erection and returned her gaze to it, making sure he saw where she looked.

He smiled.

'Yes. It's all for you.'

She said nothing. She tilted her chin up in a pose of apparent arrogance and disdain. But the gesture merely allowed Rennick – as she knew it would – a better view of the rise and fall of her breasts as she breathed deeply with a mixture of fear and anticipation. The response was as expected and his eyes narrowed in mounting desire. She was conscious of the need to drag this out as long as possible. It was time to speak.

'You can't do this,' she said, shaking her head at him. 'You'll get into trouble – with her.'

Rennick's eyebrows rose in amused surprise. 'Oh will I? You think Oleander cares what happens to you?' He laughed cruelly.

'No, not her. The other one. The blonde. She's the important one – the one who's really in control here. You know it. And so do I.'

A look of genuine puzzlement flickered across his craggy features before the leer was restored.

'Now how do you know about her?'

'Wouldn't you like to know.' It was not a question. The challenge was there and Rennick was nibbling at the bait.

'Yes, I would – and I'm going to find out because you're going to tell me.' The threat was plain and he made it clear that he would enjoy making her talk. He moved a step closer. Linnayen pushed her body into the wall and tried to decide which way to run. She went right, sprinting, and Rennick, who had moved to grab her, was left clutching at the air.

'Come here!'

Linnayen got a hand on the doorknob but it did not move. In those few seconds Rennick covered the space between them and took hold of her long hair. Linnayen cried out in pain as the strands were tugged from her scalp. She bent her head back and Rennick pulled her towards the floor.

The angle at which she went down revealed a fine view of her cleavage and he smirked with the additional pleasure it gave him.

'Now there's a pretty sight.'

Linnayen could feel his breath on her exposed neck. It stank and her stomach heaved.

'Not for the likes of you, filth!' She sensed that her reaction was stimulating him and, with the hope of dragging the time a little further, she persisted. 'Get away from me, you animal! Pig! Scum!'

'Oh, you're good … I like that.' Rennick's voice had lowered. He was obviously enjoying their exchange.

Still holding a clump of her hair, he moved his left hand down into the dark, warm cleaved area he so admired. Linnayen felt his hand on her bare breast and recoiled. The sensation of movement only seemed to excite him more and he laughed again.

'Very nice. I can see you're going to make me a happy man before you die.'

At this moment, Linnayen stretched up her right hand and tore at his face. Her nails went down deep into his rough flesh and the blood oozed up almost immediately. Rennick cried out, letting go of her hair as he placed a hand to his cheek.

She scrambled to her feet and tried to put as much distance between them as possible, given the confines of the room. She had almost made it out of his range when she felt his hand grip her ankle. Although it was firm, she felt that she would have wriggled free but for a sudden lurching of the ground, which threw her completely off balance. A silent, fluid tremor rippled through the stones and walls of the tower room, and the last thing she saw as she fell hard towards the stone flags was the edge of the low table fast growing within her field of vision.

In Athens, Li-el Dacas winced and cried out her daughter's name. She could not feel the pain of her fall but knew the agony in her heart. She found strength enough to cry out to Beoraan and the Bashirs, 'Hurry! We must get her now!'

Chapter Thirty-four

The silence was more than total, the emptiness complete. All sound drained away, like the sea before a tsunami, leaving a numb void that was thick and tangible. Oleander's keen senses had only just become aware of the change in the atmosphere before the first shock slammed through the rocks underlying Guyvar Neref.

'What the …?' Oleander sprang up from her seat at the control panel and tried to steady herself. She had been examining the manifest for their remaining airtransporter, making sure they had enough fuel and supplies to get them to the Order's secret base in Antarctica. The intention was to leave as soon as Rennick had finished his work. He had gone upstairs with the girl a few minutes earlier, but she expected him to take a little time. After all, they had had their orders and Rennick would need time to fulfil them adequately – she understood that. He would probably take some pleasure in it, though. For her it was just a job. Whereas for Rennick …

She looked around the quivering hall. The empty silence was now replaced by a grinding and straining noise as the stone slabs of the walls and floor rasped against each other, forced into an angry embrace. Stone-splitting cracks began to pierce the air and the ground beneath her feet tilted and swayed in an unstoppable ripple. She rode the wave of energy, arms stretched out wide to steady herself.

The shield! The thought came suddenly that quake would have breached the force field's integrity. This might make them detectable, certainly vulnerable. That was her priority – as soon as the ground stopped shaking. She had to check that it was secure.

Then, Rennick's people. She saw that some were running mindlessly, dodging tumbling debris as if there was somewhere to hide from this. Others were crouching under consoles, chairs or the two buttresses. Every face was scared. And who wouldn't be, thought Oleander. She realised that they had to get out of there and, if Rennick had not already finished his work – if he was still alive – they would have to take the Ki too. Her body could not be found to have died in an earthquake – that would be a tragedy that might strengthen the fledgling bond between Earth and the Union, exactly what the Order of Sumere did *not* want. And if the Order did not get what it wanted, her life would be forfeit. She knew how they operated. They would send someone after her – someone just like her.

The far wall shuddered ominously. It was going to collapse and fall. Oleander called out to the men who had taken refuge under the buttresses to get out from their hiding place. Although her voice was virtually deadened in the thick air, her frantic waving caught their attention and they ran out towards her with only seconds to spare. Suddenly the central arch of the glassless window at the top of the wall cracked and, with what seemed unusual slowness, it crashed down into the hall, bringing a swathe of stones with it. The cascade of rubble tore through the roof of the bioskin as though it were tissue paper.

As if it was a signal to the force that had brought about its destruction, the falling of the upper wall brought the tremors to a sudden stop. Oleander quickly took stock of the hall. The rest of the walls in the hall were still standing, although she guessed that they would have to be unstable, to say the least. Rock dust was falling and swirling still and the taste of it was stale and musty inside her mouth and nose. They had to move fast and she began barking out orders.

'Haneef! Check the shield! Arkan! Get the transporter ready. Evacuate on my signal. I'll get Rennick and the girl.' With that she bounded across the hall towards the tower stairs. Amazingly, the tower still stood. But she had not taken more than a dozen steps when a massive sonic blast ripped through the fortress, stopping her dead in her tracks.

Captain Chandra in Rapier One had calibrated a non-specific frequency for the blast so that the shield's underpinning matrix – the sonic code that kept it in place – would be destabilised. Sabre and Pike Wings would then have a few only a few seconds to measure the echo and determine the frequency needed to completely break through the force field. It would have to be precise though. The slightest miscalculation would render the blast ineffective and the mercenaries' shield would hold. This would make the possibility of a prolonged exchange more likely, thus increasing the risk to the Ki. But once the shield was down they could land the transporters and the ground troops could move in quickly.

Rapier One, like Navarr, had received the information that the Ki was in the tower room and Evica and Tariik wanted to be put on the ground as soon as possible in order to get to Linnayen. Captain Chandra was apologetic.

'I'll get you in as soon as I can. But we must wait for Sabre and Pike to complete their runs and make sure the shield is down. Any sooner and we could be fighting all morning. Don't forget, this place is a weapons' store.'

Evica knew that what he said made sense. But she was almost frantic with worry and anxious to get to Linnayen. She bit her lower lip and studied the fortress through narrowed eyes as they circled it, taking position for the next bombing run.

In Sabre One, Navarr prepared to depart from the craft's lower bay, where the rear portal doors were already open. The leached brown landscape passed by only a few hundred metres below but at this speed he could make out nothing of the landforms. It was all a blur.

He had already decided not to wait for the shield to be taken out as he wanted to be ready to fly the aircar straight to the tower room and claim his prize. He had divulged his plan hurriedly to Sabre Wing's commander and Navarr had been authorised to proceed on what the commander thought was a dangerous part of the mission, but a necessary one. If the alien tactician could pull this off, she thought, they would have the Ki out of there in less than three minutes. It was worth trying.

Navarr gripped the handle of a small one-man proglide. Although unfamiliar to him, the ship's weapons officer had quickly run him through its controls and these had been straightforward enough. His main concern, the weapons officer told him, would be to clear the wake of the craft as he descended. Thus, he would need to boost to full power as soon as he left the portal and dive groundwards towards the aircars.

He nodded his understanding to the officer and powered up the unit. In one fluid motion, Navarr steered the proglide to the portal and, without a backward glance, dropped away headfirst into the empty space below. He straightened his body and stretched out the unit's handles in front of him, diving through the air in a perfect arc. At any other time he would have taken time to enjoy the experience, so much like the fall-flying he had done with Linnayen nearly two years ago now. He remembered that day and recalled the way her laughter and excitement and flashing green eyes had made him feel. The memory made him smile. There was no doubt about it, Linnayen Genara stirred him and always had. Perhaps it was the unique mix of power, naivety and beauty? Whatever it was, it excited him and he was looking forward to experiencing it all again.

'Look over there!' Duncan watched the plummeting form with amazement and horror. 'Someone's fallen out!'

Jax had flown the Sprint-16 at top speed and they had finally caught up with the main force. He had kept the communications channels open the whole time so that they could all hear how the assault was progressing. Thus, they knew that the first sonic blast had affected Guyvar Neref's shield and that, so far, there had been no return of fire. But there was nothing about this. Jax felt sorry for whoever had fallen, but his thoughts went swiftly back to Linnayen.

'Wait! No … He's not falling. He's flying!' Duncan cried.

At that moment, two massive sonic blasts were unleashed at the castle, followed within seconds by a stream of fluorescent green laser fire ripping through the air, which was aimed at the aircraft passing along the ruined castle's flanks.

Jax's Sprint swept low and as slow as he dared take it past the fortress. He was looking for somewhere to land. With the unleashing of the sonic blasts the air attack would soon be over – certainly once their shield was disabled – so his Sprint was not going to be needed to fight and they could concentrate on getting to Linnayen. Luckily, most of the firepower was being aimed at the aircraft ahead of him and he was able to take a good look at the area and the castle's crumbling walls.

As he took their second fly past, all the time dodging the castle's returning fire, he saw that the proglide flyer had landed and made it to one of two aircars, which was now rising and heading towards the tower. If he could get the Sprint down close to them he could take the other one. Whoever the flyer was, Jax thanked him for having the foresight and guts to ignore the danger and go straight to Linnayen. He would give the man a medal if he succeeded in rescuing his wife before he could get there himself.

'Sir! There's a place we can land.' This was Nen who, for the entire journey, had sat still and quiet in a seat just behind him. She indicated a flat patch of land in a dry gravelly riverbed that ran below an old road leading to the front of the fortress. The patch held a few clumps of brown grasses and weeds but otherwise it was clear and, though tight, appeared to have just enough space to land the Sprint. Best of all, the spot was a mere two hundred metres from the remaining aircar and the line of the road would give them cover as they ran for it.

Jax indicated that he could see it and turned the Sprint towards the riverbed, bringing it ever lower.

It was obvious now that the sonic weapons had taken out the

shield as the first of the gas torpedoes was released by one of the Rapier craft. It took a path towards the centre of the fortress and had already pushed past the boundary of where the shield would have been if it had still functioned. But, with only a few metres to go, the torpedo was hit by a blast of green laser fire and exploded in a huge crimson burst. Its contents, a fast-working soporific compound, were now being carried in a pink cloud by the wind towards the south in the direction of Jax's Sprint.

'Masks, everyone!' Jax shouted, and within seconds, Nen, Em-sin-Mai and Duncan had affixed metal masks to the lower half of their faces with only their eyes still visible. Despite the whistle and whizzing of weapons fire all around the vessel as it descended, Jax could see no fear in any of them. Dr Mai and Nen were particularly cool and calm and he found himself even more admiring of these two Altani women than ever. His wife was lucky to have them, and it would not be long now before they would all be reunited.

This is almost too easy.

Navarr was more than pleased with the way things were going. Swinging the aircar into a position where it hovered just outside the window of the tower room, he switched the controls to remote. He had expected to abseil down into the room, but the upper half of the window and part of the roof seemed to have crumbled into the chasm below following the last big tremor. Now he could easily jump across and into the room which would give him a little extra time and, judging by the condition of the tower, he figured he would need it.

Clouds of dust were billowing through the hot air and there was no way of knowing how much longer the structure would hold, or if the earthquake had finished. He could barely make out the figures of Linnayen and Rennick lying prone on the stone floor.

Navarr took stock of the situation and prepared to make his jump. He slid open the aircar's side doors and, taking a couple of steps back to run up to the gap, he easily crossed the two metres between the hovering vessel and the floor of the room. Linnayen was lying on her side the first stirrings of consciousness beginning to move her limbs. There was an ugly gash on her forehead, which was seeping blood. Rennick was across the room in a sitting position, his back against the door. He was rubbing the back of his neck with one hand and his face was twisted with pain, presumably from being thrown into the wall . He looked up at Navarr's silhouette against the cobalt sky, now visible through the damaged window.

'What are *you* doing here?' he asked groggily.

'I could ask you the same question,' Navarr replied. He glanced again at Linnayen to check she was still not conscious before continuing. 'Because if you have damaged my prize in any way, your death will be both certain and painful.'

Rennick scoffed, his contempt he plain.

'*Your* prize? No one gets her, she's to die. Didn't you know that? Orders from above,' he smirked.

'What orders?' Navarr snapped back.

'She got them this morning,' Rennick responded, nodding his head backwards towards the stairs and the unseen assassin. 'So you'd better bid farewell to the lovely lady, commander. You won't be seeing her again – not in this life, anyway.'

Navarr's smile was sardonic and his eyes narrowed menacingly.

'Ah, can't do that. She's mine; she always has been. Anyway, the orders have been changed.'

'Yeah? Who says?'

'This.' With not the slightest hesitation, Navarr raised a palm-sized disc laser and shot a stream of bright orange liquid light directly at the crown of Rennick's head. The heat of the beam melted the flesh, cartilage, bone, even brain tissue, right down the centre of Rennick's head, which immediately cleaved in two. The outer dermal layers, their edges blanched by the laser, curled apart like tomato skins and the innards of his cranium oozed out. Navarr grimaced at the sight of his own handiwork, then shrugged apologetically. It was a necessary part of the plan – *his* plan, anyway

– and had to be done, but he was thankful Linnayen was not awake to see it.

The business with Rennick now concluded, he turned his attention back to Linnayen. She lay still and he presumed that she had slipped back into unconsciousness. He needed her awake now to witness his daring rescue. This was going to be the moment when all his and Balisel's scheming would come to fruition. His Ki would be saved and she would be eternally thankful to her loyal and, from then on, indispensable commander, whom she would welcome back to her side – and her bed.

Suddenly the ground heaved, throwing him off balance, and as he toppled backwards towards the gaping window he fought to steady himself. He must not falter now, not when he was so close to getting it all back. *It will not end like this!*

Oleander saw what was going on. The cameras that had been secreted around the fortress were programmed to detect ground movement of any object larger than a domestic cat. Thus, as soon as Jax and his team began their run towards the other aircar, she saw them on the control panel screen in front of her.

The last few minutes had been fast and furious. Since the second and third sonic blasts had taken out their force field, her time and that of the weapons officers had been spent both in returning fire to the attacking aircraft and in trying to take out the incoming gas torpedoes. So far, only one torpedo had hit the ground, but it had fallen short of the castle and the prevailing wind had carried its payload away from them. She knew what the gas would do and wondered academically whether they had gone for tithium or a zelentek compound. They would certainly not risk using anything lethal, not while the Ki's life was at stake.

However, she knew that they could not hold out for much longer. In sheer numbers their opponents would soon overcome them. The only decision she needed to make now was about her future: the rest of her life spent in an off-world penal colony or death here, now, today. She had to make the decision. Should she continue the fight? Should she try to stop the rescuers from taking the aircar? And if she did not stop them and her employers discovered her treachery, how long would she have anyway before they found and killed her? And they would kill her, of that there was no doubt. But life always presented opportunities. While one lived there was always a chance.

There were four of them. Scurrying little figures, running like hunched dwarves across a stubby brown landscape towards the aircar. One press of a switch on the companel to activate the external xelex cannon and she could kill them all. But then, the other man had already taken one of the aircars. She had been too busy locking in on two gas torpedoes and had not seen his aerial descent, missing the chance to fire on him before he snatched the aircar away. So perhaps they already had the girl. There had been no word from Rennick and she did not know whether their hostage was alive or dead. Surely he had had time to kill her? The girl must be dead, in which case, she reasoned, her own life might not be forfeit. Oleander knew that if their instructions had been carried out, the Order might leave her to her fate. And if they had not …

'Incoming torps! Engage. Fire on lock!' The weapons officer at her side looked too young to be doing this. He was fresh-faced, eyes clear and sharp, and his skin was smooth. He was a handsome young man and Oleander had always enjoyed male beauty. She would miss all that.

She turned her attention back to the screen. The rescuers had reached the aircar and she could see clouds of dirt being pushed into the air as the vessel lifted skywards. The trace of a smile flitted across her face as she watched its ascent and felt the ground rumble and stir yet again beneath her. The tectonic upheaval was not finished with them and, however powerful the Order of Sumere believed itself to be, it could not compete against such an unstoppable force as an earthquake. She continued to smile. This was pure irony. She had always said this would be her last job and, as she saw the fast-approaching slab of masonry from the collapsed castle wall, it looked like she would be right.

Linnayen could hardly believe it. She knew he was a low creature, but that he would stoop to collusion with her kidnappers – a commander of the Union of Planets – was too much.

It had been hard to keep still during the exchange between Navarr and Rennick. It had lasted no more than a minute and then what followed had been unbelievably gruesome, although Navarr had not even blinked from what she could see through slitted eyes. The terrible sound alone of Rennick's demise would be with her for many weeks and months to come, if not longer. But the worst of it was that Rennick had known Navarr and, by that association, she now knew who her kidnappers had been – and who was behind the attack at the villa that had so nearly resulted in her husband's death. Even the renewed trembling and shuddering of the castle's stone floor and walls was not enough to distract her from an utter loathing and hatred of the man who now staggered towards her.

'Don't worry, my lady. I'll soon have you out of here. Lay still.' He fought to be heard against the backdrop of grinding rock and splintering stone.

'Don't come near me!' she cried, her voice still weak, her throat clogged with dust.

'It's all right,' he assured her. 'I have an aircar. I'll carry you to it.'

'No! Leave me alone.'

Navarr frowned. She must be disorientated from her fall in the earthquake. It had obviously left her confused. No matter, he would keep playing his part, just as he had rehearsed in his mind many, many times.

'Please, don't be frightened. You are safe now.' He made his voice soothing and reassuring, a voice one could trust. He moved to her side and quickly knelt, the better to lift her. 'I have come to rescue you, my lady. Let me carry you now.'

The look on Linnayen's face was one of pure horror. He could not understand it. Perhaps she was hallucinating?

'Don't touch me,' she said. Her voice was a low growl. 'I know what you did.'

Navarr thought quickly. Had she seen what he had done to the unfortunate mercenary?

'Well, of course. He was going to kill you. I had to kill him to protect you.'

'Not that. I know this is all your doing. You planned the attack at the villa and my kidnap. Though I don't know why.' The floor shook again and Linnayen prayed that the tremors would soon stop. While it continued she could see no way of escaping from him.

Navarr shook his head. She was slipping away. He had to put a stop to this.

'No, my lady, you're quite wrong. I've saved you. I will look after you, my Linnayen, be by your side, just like before. You remember?' He smiled. Memories flooded back of the nights of fierce passion. The moments of stolen touches and arousing caresses, even in front of the old counsellor. It stirred his blood. He needed to touch her again and he leaned across to cup her cheek in his hand.

Linnayen shrank back, a gesture helped by the sway of the floor. Using the tilt to her advantage, she rolled away towards the door, forcing Navarr to stumble on his knees. There was a glassy intensity in his eyes like glittering marbles. *Madness? Was that it?* She recoiled even further but he came after her, all the while calling her name.

'Linnayen … Linnayen, come back!'

She lifted her head, attempting to judge the distance between them, and there framed in the light behind the grotesque figure of Navarr stood the man she loved. A small, noiseless gasp escaped her lips and a smile of both relief and love grew.

Navarr's concerns were alleviated. *At last! She remembers …* But within a second he realised that she was looking over his shoulder. He turned his head slowly to see who or what was behind him.

No – impossible! He's dead! Oleander had assured him of it. Yet here he was. The Ki-consort stood tall, his silhouette casting a shadow over the disbelieving Navarr. Kevor Jax was alive and apparently unharmed. *This cannot be!* He could not lose everything he had worked for. Not now, when he was so close. With the stealth and speed of a cheetah, Navarr planned his next move. He needed no more than a moment to reorganise his facial expression and get the pitch of his voice just right.

'My lord! Jax! You have come just in time. I was helping my lady to safety when the quake struck again.'

His voice was smooth and glib. Jax marvelled at how naturally the lies fell from his mouth, like the untrammelled flow of a spring stream.

'But we must be quick. This structure will not hold much longer,' Navarr warned.

Jax glared at him with a strange mixture of sorrow and loathing. This man had been his friend. His mind flashed to the day they had stood, brothers in arms, on the edge of the precipice in the high Himalaya having just defeated the terrorist assassin Visnivic. On that day they had each saved the other's life. Now here they were, implacable enemies. Navarr had taken his wife and, thanks to the information he had received only moments before he left the aircar from Li-el Dacas, Jax also knew that Navarr had been involved in the kidnap and the attack at Santorini.

Jax's team had reached the aircar and were quickly ascending towards the tower room when Li-el's voice had burst into the earpiece of his communicator, reporting what she had seen through Linnayen's half-closed eyes as she pretended to be unconscious.

'It's Navarr. He's the kidnapper. He's just killed his accomplice. Get to my daughter now!'

The aircar ascended in a tight arc. Navarr's vessel had blocked any purchase they might have had close to the tower room's open window so Jax was forced to hover slightly above it. Duncan had taken the controls and, wishing him good luck, watched as Jax had leapt down onto the wing of the other aircar, then bounced off that into the tower room. Although he landed on his feet, he had almost stumbled due to the still shuddering floor surface and the sudden shock of pain in his chest. It reminded him that there was more than one good reason to get Linnayen out of there – Navarr was not their only danger.

'It's over, Navarr. Step away from her.' Jax's voice cut through the tumult.

'Jax! It's him. He's the one!'

'I know. We saw.'

Navarr shook his head, refusing to believe that his grand conspiracy was all but over.

'We'll deal with him later,' Jax said. 'But let's get you out of here first.'

Linnayen pushed up off the debris-strewn floor and, almost leaping over the still kneeling Navarr, ran towards Jax, who quickly took her in his arms. They turned towards the gaping hole of the window and, steadying themselves, prepared to leap across the gap and into the cabin of Navarr's hovering aircar. Linnayen could not resist taking one last look at the face of the man who had been both her lover and tormentor, the man who had schemed and plotted – since when, she wondered – to use her purely to further his own ends. He remained on his knees, chest heaving as his breath came in hard. His blond head was turned towards them, watching them go through two ice-blue slits.

'Wait!' he cried. 'You have to know, Linnayen.' His voice suddenly broke. 'You were ... special.'

The look she returned was both pitying and scornful.

'As my husband said, you will be dealt with.'

'No! You loved me! I *know* you did!' Navarr rose to his feet, anger filling him, and Jax knew that if they did not go he would be upon them in seconds.

'Linnayen, jump! Now!' He took her hand and pulled her with him as they ran towards the breach in the window, which had begun to crumble under the strain of the continuing tremors. Linnayen felt fingers brushing her ankle as she passed over the space between the window and the vessel and it was enough to cause her to lose her balance. One foot slipped off the shiny metal floor of the aircar and she fell heavily on her stomach. The sudden weight tipped the vessel and, had it not been for Jax's firm grip, she might have slid completely out and into the void. Instead only the lower half of her body hung over the edge and Jax was already pulling her back in towards the interior and safety.

Then, with not even a warning shout, Navarr too made the jump. He caught Linnayen's flailing ankles and the sudden additional weight almost tore Jax's shoulders from their sockets. His chest pounded and he felt the seep of warm blood under his bandages. As he was pulled towards the opening, he jammed his feet up against the doorframe and gripped Linnayen's painfully stretched wrists. She screamed and tried to kick off her tormentor but Navarr held on, pulling her body down as he struggled.

'Jax! Help me!'

But at that precarious moment he could do nothing but hold on with all his might. His chest wound oozed warm sticky fluid as the damaged flesh was pulled apart. Linnayen's face was distorted with fear and pain, and he felt the agony of helplessness. If Navarr made it into the cabin using Linnayen as a ladder he would face that hurdle then. But until then he would not let her go, no matter what.

'Hold on!' he called out, looking around desperately for something to help.

A deep rumbling sound suddenly split the air around them, followed by a loud crack. Jax scanned the landscape and saw that it was again shaking violently. The tower room, only metres away, finally began to crumble and, with a drunken stagger, fell away. All around the ground heaved and tore itself apart, ripping deep cavernous wounds into its flesh.

'Hold on, Linnayen! Hold on!' Jax's voice was desperate.

Linnayen felt a sudden shift of weight on her leg followed by a loud scream. She looked down and saw Navarr had let go of her right leg and his face was contorted with pain. Then she saw why. His left arm was gone and only a bloodied, ragged stump remained, from which rich red blood was spurting. His remaining arm still gripped her ankle. From the corner of her eye she saw the flash of a silver aircar dash by and in its open door stood Nen, steady as a rock, taking yet another shot at Navarr with a high-powered ion-laser.

Linnayen smiled grimly at her maidservant's handiwork, then looked up at Jax. He, too, had seen Nen's shot meet its mark and it gave him renewed determination to get Linnayen into the aircar and free of Navarr's clutches.

Nen took a third shot, her second having missed, and this one hit home, striking Navarr in his chest. With a gurgling shriek he let go of Linnayen's ankle and fell away from the hovering aircar.

At that moment a tumultuous crack split the air and a column of hot, sulphurous gas shot up from the depths of the abyss below. It was followed in an instant by a writhing funnel of orange flame, a fire spout, and at its summit, swathed in its fiery caress, was Durroc Navarr, buoyed up by its hot gases. His mouth was open in a terrible, silent scream and his eyes, frightened and pleading, were fixed on Linnayen.

The upward force of the gas column combined with the release of Navarr's weight caused the aircar to tilt and veer away. Linnayen tumbled into the cabin, legs flying wildly, and landed on top of her husband. Jax groaned with the impact but immediately clasped her to him. There was no time to embrace though – the aircar's autopilot had been shaken by the combined impacts of the rising superheated gases and flame, and Jax staggered up to the control panel to fly them out of danger.

Linnayen, breathless and trembling, gripped a rail at the open doorway and looked down. As they rose skywards away from the devastation below, she watched Navarr's body fall back into the now fast-receding fingers of fire. The flaming spout disappeared almost as quickly as it had shot up, taking with it the piteous, charred remains of her one-time lover. She was grateful that her husband was so preoccupied with the flying of the aircar that he did not see the tears well in her eyes as the memories returned in a sudden rush. Navarr was right. She had loved him – once.

'Remind me never to get on the wrong side of *you*.'

Everyone laughed as Jax put an arm around Nen's narrow shoulders and gave her an affectionate squeeze. Already word of Nen's prowess with an ion-laser had got around and she was shyly receiving the many looks of approval.

'I dread to think what they'll let you loose on next, mistress Nen – and how much will be left standing afterwards.' This was Duncan.

'You didn't do such a bad job yourself, Duncan,' said Jax. 'That was a fancy piece of flying for an actor!'

They had all arrived safely back at the airdock in Athens, having elected to fly straight back and leaving Captain Chandra's men to round up the now unconscious mercenaries. The gas torpedoes had finally found their mark during Jax's rescue of Linnayen in the tower room and it had been a simple matter after that of waiting for the quake to subside before going in to pick up survivors.

Linnayen could hardly believe it was all over. She stood silently, drinking in the sight and sounds of the people around her – people she held dear, people she loved. She smiled. It was wonderful to be alive, and safe and loved. She looked up at the animated face of her husband as he talked with her sister and the others, going over the last forty minutes. He was full of life and excitement and, at that very moment, she wanted nothing else but to be with him for the rest of her life – and she knew that he wanted it too.

She squeezed his hand to get his attention and he looked down into her emerald eyes. As their eyes met there was no other sight or sound – they had entered a space and time which was their own, and they knew that this was how it would always be.

'Husband, I think we have some unfinished business.' She spoke quietly so that no one would be able to hear her words. But there was no doubting her determination. 'At the villa, you said something about starting our marriage anew.'

The power of Jax's smile warmed her body to its core and she felt a surge of love and passion.

'Is now good for you?' he asked, raising an eyebrow.

Without waiting for her reply, he encircled her with his arms and kissed her deeply and longingly. They were not aware of the looks and smiles of everyone gathered around them as their kiss went on and on.

Suddenly, Linnayen broke off.

'Excuse me,' she said to Jax and pulled away from him. She stood still and quiet with her eyes closed. There was a slight shuddering of her body before she became still once more.

'That's better,' she said, returning to Jax's embrace.

He was puzzled. 'What was that about?'

'Well, unless you want my mother with us …'

'Oh. Right.'

Their lips met again and, from then on, there would be no more interruptions.

Epilogue

In the Beshwuk Highlands on Autabron, the pre-dawn air in the Rakuum Settlement hung still and lifeless. Through a rudely carved stone window there was no sound and no movement on the dry plains far, far below. Not that Denkau expected any at this time of the morning, or on this day. Even the ore miners took a few hours break on the morning of Grunkaar, one of the holiest of days for the Guznon people. The observations would, of course, be subdued and respectful and, no matter the time they took, the rituals would be both precise and complete. Nothing would be allowed to impinge on their worship this day, not even the heathen woman and her sorry business.

Denkau was sure he had done the right thing in locking the witch away, despite his wife Mira's suggestion that she be allowed to watch. No, it wouldn't hurt her to be restrained until she was needed. The witch had interfered too much already. Besides, it was a bad omen for outsiders to witness the rites of Nuonabat. It was none of their business and, while he was leader of Rakuum, no female foreigner, or 'ko-kura', would ever observe their ceremonies, even those who brought great gifts.

The sky was finally turning a deeper red and, in the distance, the sharp outlines of the Beshwuk Mountains were slashed and cut by the bloody colours. Denkau knew that in a few more minutes, the orange orb of Lau, the first sun, would erupt above the horizon and the peace of the day would be broken by the calling of the Tamuns, the holy men and women who would lead them in prayer and sacrifice. Then there would be many tasks and observances to perform before the mighty golden Uzno joined his brother in the heavens and their fiery dance began.

Two suns, twin spheres that slowly spun around each other, dancing across the skies in a sombre waltz. Their world was unique. Their people were unique. The Guznon were the chosen, favoured by the gods, endowed with massive strength and endurance. None knew this better than he, though it brought bile to his lips when he remembered how they were forced to deny their religion and kowtow to the miners. They thought the old ways were nothing but quaint customs and that they had died out. But Denkau – and others like him – had long ago made a solemn promise to keep the faith pure and unsullied by so-called progress. The miners may have brought them wealth. Indeed, many Guznon now lived in fine homes surrounded by the trappings of indolence. But they had not brought enlightenment and they did not understand the spiritual needs of the Guznon.

They trample upon our beliefs and mock our faith. The souls of our young people are fading before the excesses of this new age.

It was time to act – decisively. Lau and Uzno needed to know that the Guznon had not forsaken them and that those who had strayed would be returned. And before this day of Grunkaar was done, they *would* know.

'Damn you! You can't do this to me!'

Balisel Navarr's words fell on deaf ears. Denkau had given the orders last night that she was to be kept inside the catacombs for the time being. She must not be allowed to gaze upon the ceremonies this day. Like them, she would be served neither food nor drink, but locked away until it was time for her release.

The two huge Autabroni guards, nearly three metres tall, their armour glistening dully in the rays of the lamplight, guided her inside the rock-hewn chamber and closed the door. She heard the bolt being hammered into place on the other side of the door and knew that any more protest would be useless. What was in Denkau and Mira's minds she did not know, but she consoled herself with the sad look on Mira's face when they had taken her from her bed only minutes earlier.

'Don't worry, little witch. It is better this way,' Mira had assured her.

'Kalik? What about Kalik?' she had cried, trying to keep the fear out of her voice.

'He is well.' Mira had stretched out and patted one of Balisel's hands in a gesture of comfort. 'I will take good care of him.'

'Why can't I be with him? You must bring him to me.'

There it was again, thought Mira – that attitude. The little witch is always so arrogant, so demanding. *She has brought us great gifts, of course. But at what a price! Having to put up with her overbearing ways, day in, day out. Still, our sacrifice will be worth it. We will be as one with the twin spheres. All our people – and the lost souls – will be shown a path home.*

It was time. Mira left the inner chambers and went to join Denkau on the high parapet to greet the first sun, Lau. She climbed the stairs quickly, still so sure-footed after all these years. Working in the ore fields – whatever the drawbacks – kept the Guznon fit and she was glad of the strength in her limbs today.

Denkau had arrived a few minutes earlier and had already taken his place at the very edge of the vast parapet, so close that his bare feet were less than a metre from the lip of the flat rock. He was unmoving as Mira crossed the huge space and silently moved up to stand beside him. When he became aware of her presence he turned his head and stared into her dark eyes. She returned his gaze and saw in it the tangled forces of love and joy and faith. This was a day they had awaited all their lives, dreamed about for an eternity, and it was about to begin.

Suddenly Lau's fiery fingers erupted above the horizon and the perfect silence was shattered by the sounds of horns and the shrill wails of the Tamuns, calling all Guznon to prayer and worship. There would be no excuses upon this day. Attendance on the high parapet of Rakuum was mandatory and, amid a barrage of lowing and mumbled prayers, the people of Guznon came forth. As though in a mass trance, men, women and children shuffled forward out of doorways in the rock walls and made their way towards the edge of the high cliff. Clouds of dust kicked up by the thousands of feet rose in the cool morning air and hovered about the bodies before settling back to the ground once the multitude had stilled.

At the sound of silence behind him, Denkau raised his arms and began the chant of Lau, the song that began the day of Grunkaar and was the first of its many rituals. His voice was strong and deep, reverberating through the air, its chords almost tangible. And, for the first time since he had learned the words to the chant of Lau as a young shaman, he knew that they would not go unanswered. Not on this day.

Down below in the rock chamber, Balisel Navarr heard it all. The prayers of the multitude and Denkau's chant, although she did not know it was him, her protector.

She had been surprisingly lucky, she thought, to have found Denkau and Mira, and that they had taken her in so readily. Not many people would have been interested in hiding the despised sister of Durroc Navarr in the aftermath of the Ki's kidnapping. Indeed, Linnayen Genara Bashir had not been slow to issue a warrant for Balisel's arrest and she had had to pay big money to get away from Earth less than twenty-four hours after her brother's demise.

Sometimes it was hard to believe that he was really gone. She still could not bring herself to think let alone say the word dead. His image still filled every void in her mind and she wondered if there would ever come a time when she would stop grieving for him. She did not think so. After all, she only had to look at her beloved Kalik to see his face.

The Guznon had given him the name after his birth, as was their right, and she had no objection. Kalik Navarr sounded right. It meant 'bring to the light' they told her, and her name, Ko-Makum, a term of both affection and respect, meant 'little witch'. They had given her this name because of her eyes – the crystalline blue of legend, the eyes that her son had inherited. Mira told her that the Guznon had many fables and legends, but that there was one about the Ko-Makum of Rundak who brought life to her tribe amid a terrible drought and famine. The Guznon were close to death but were saved by the magic of the ancient witch who brought life-giving rain and, because of her, the Guznon survive to this day. The ancient Ko-Makum, it was said, had eyes the colour of the sacred mineral zorcuum, just like their little witch. So this was a great and wonderful sign, Mira said, and Balisel had been accorded many privileges since she had arrived at Rakuum. That she also carried a child in her belly was a blessing beyond hope or dreams.

Not that she was going to hang around much longer, thought Balisel. Pretty soon, once the fervour for her capture had died down, she would take Kalik and get out of these godforsaken catacombs the Guznon called a settlement once and for all. She had enough money, after all. The Galactic Union's investigators could not possibly have traced all of it, of that she was certain.

Despite her change in status, she was grateful to Mira and Denkau. They had taken her in when she most needed help and least expected to receive it. She had travelled to Autabron on an ore trader that she picked up at the busy Nova Ryka Transit Station in Saturn orbit. The captain was a fellow that GKD had used a few times and, with her promise that he would both earn himself a sizeable fee for carrying her and guaranteed shipments for the next five years, he was willing to turn a blind eye to her unfortunate status. After all, he reasoned, what were a little conspiracy and kidnapping compared to the millions of keks he would be getting?

When she finally got to the plant at Euta Makaan, it did not take her long to infiltrate the GKD purchasing department's comsystem and instruct the programme to give priority selection to the rogue captain. Although the access codes had been changed, she had been one of the designers of the back-up coding procedures. It had taken her little more than five minutes to download the codes and work out which ones would have been initiated to replace the old access details.

Whilst she was in the system, she also set up a few relays to transfer the odd asset to selected accounts and operational interests around the Union – some hers and some GKD's own. But she was clever. None of the transfers were large and there were just too many to arouse suspicion. Once her resources were in place, it was time to disappear.

Without doubt, no one in their right mind would choose to hide out in the bergussian ore fields, a deadly wasteland encompassing nearly a third of the planet's surface. These plains were nothing but arid, rock-strewn deserts where nothing grew. There were few landmarks to speak of, apart from the incision of the Beshwuk Ranges, and those that did exist were merely the processing plants – squat, blocky structures whose location could only usually be picked out by their tall, spindly comtowers. These were lit up at night, thus giving the evening landscape an ethereal beauty that, with the morning suns, was soon shattered.

The secret of the ore fields was below ground. Whilst the trawlers scraped off the precious ore above, the miners and plant employees lived in an array of underground cities. It had to be so, for life on the surface was unsustainable. The heat of the two suns fried the dusty soil and the resultant thermal currents hoisted vast spiralling columns of dirt and rock high up into the atmosphere. These hot whirlwinds were death to any trawler caught in their grip as even so large a piece of machinery could easily be sucked up into the draught and lifted for kilometres before being dropped like a stone when the column tore itself apart. The comtowers, anchored into the bedrock many hundreds of metres below, monitored atmospheric conditions and gave warning of imminent whirlwind activity. Indeed, without the sensitivity of their instruments the ore could not be mined, for once the warning went out, the trawlers had to get back to the nearest hangar at top speed. In the early days this had happened all too frequently and many lives had been lost.

These incidents and the tough regime of mine life on Autabron had given the planet and its people a reputation for fierceness and fortitude. You had to be almost indestructible – or very greedy – to work in the ore fields and it was no surprise that some of the prime mining sites were harvested by prisoners under sentence of hard labour.

And that was what had attracted Balisel. Who would think of looking for a criminal inside a virtual prison? It was in the underground city at the Zaz-Rakuum field that she met the tall, flame-skinned, white-haired Denkau, local leader of the tribe of Guznon, the most ancient and proudest of the tribes of Autabron. She had done her research well and knew that this man had power over ten thousand ore miners who looked to him for their spiritual guidance.

When she went to see him she was only mildly surprised at his reaction to her, staring open-mouthed and speechless for some minutes. Balisel assumed that he had seen few Altanis in his lifetime and passed off his fascination as no cause for concern. She boldly asked him outright for protection, explaining that her twin brother's plot had failed and that she was under somewhat of a cloud with the authorities. But she would make it worth his while, she had said. Whatever he needed – for himself or his people – she would gladly give. She had great wealth and, even if she used most of it now to secure her future, she had the skills and talent to build it all back up again.

Though her eyes were striking and she professed to be a twin, Denkau had not been impressed and was about to dismiss her. He did not like this woman or her arrogant ways. She was too hard, too brittle, like the very rocks themselves, and his instincts told him that she would bring them nothing but trouble. But Mira, sitting in the shadows behind her husband, had seen something more and had coughed to attract his attention.

Denkau knew his wife well enough to know that she needed to speak with him and, making his excuses, he withdrew into the next room, taking Mira with him.

'Well, wife, what is it?'

'She said she would give us anything, yes?'

Denkau was irritated. He wanted to get back in there and get rid of the wretched woman. Her hair and eyes were abnormal, the signs of a witch. But not a good witch, like their famous ancestor Ko-Makum. This one stank of evil and he did not trust her.

'You know she did,' he responded curtly. 'But it's not enough. We're better off without her.'

Mira shook her head. 'No, husband. We must keep her. She carries a gift, a prize beyond imagining.'

At Denkau's puzzled expression, Mira's eyes became crafty. It was an expression he rarely saw in his normally kind wife and it shocked him.

'The little witch is pregnant. She may not be a Ko-Makum but she bears a child who may bring us to the Light, just as it was foretold.'

The prophecy! Ko-Makum had wielded her magic and saved them all with the life-giving water from the skies and then she passed into the realm of Lau and Uzno, never to be seen again. But her magic was said to live on and would come back to the Guznon in times of great trouble and need, borne by another such as her – a twin – just as Lau is to Uzno.

No one knew more than Denkau how great was their need in these troubled days. The Guznon were drifting away from the faith of the ancients, meandering in a desert of indolence and despair, existing without hope. The miners had brought them nothing but unrest and disquiet as their young men and women fell into gluttony, covetous behaviour and waywardness. *The little witch must be the sign.* Mira was right. They had to keep her.

Denkau and Mira had assured her that they would hide and protect her. They wanted little in return, too, just the naming rights to her unborn child. It amazed her that they knew she was pregnant. How could they know? She was barely eight weeks into her pregnancy. Mira explained that she had a gift for these things – prescience, one might call it. Whether it truly was foresight or just a lucky guess, Balisel thought that the giving of a name to her baby was such a strange request – almost inconsequential – that she found herself agreeing. She could not be hidden in the city, though, Denkau explained. That would be too dangerous. They would have to take her to the catacombs of the settlement, their ancient home before they came to live below the ore fields. Balisel agreed again. This place was even more remote and inaccessible and, with the spending of a little of her money, she was able to provide for herself a few home comforts.

Mira herself looked after Balisel's needs and, when the time came for her baby to be born, she acted as the midwife. Only a handful of the Guznon came with them. Even Denkau stayed in Zaz-Rakuum for most of the time. As the months passed, Balisel grew used to the quiet of the high cliffs, although the solitude often galled her. The catacombs ran along and into the rock for many kilometres and, as they had the place to themselves, it was easy to believe that the world and all its troubles and her raw grief for the loss of her beloved twin were part of another lifetime. So passed the days of her pregnancy with her brother's child and, in the midst of her acute boredom, she vowed that as soon as Kalik was old enough and they did not need Denkau's protection anymore, they would get out of this place.

Kalik's birth had been mercifully swift, but not without intense pain. Balisel had lost a lot of blood and was weak for a couple of days after the birth. But Mira had insisted that the baby suckle, despite Balisel's obvious tiredness and revulsion at the process. She was too weak to argue and allowed Mira to bring the child to her. Only then, when she saw his white blond hair and his too-pale blue eyes, did she begin to fall in love with him. The tiny face, the perfect fingers, the smoothest of skin. He was so like Durroc – and her, of course. He was the best of them both and he would grow strong and clever and, most important of all, one day he would avenge his father's death.

Balisel had not forgotten. She would never forget. Linnayen Genara had taken him away from her and Balisel cursed her, her Earthan husband and all her family. Whatever it took, however long, she would see the Genara line torn apart, and Kalik would be the instrument of their undoing. She would see to it.

Suddenly, she became aware of a change. The chanting and the low hubbub of muffled voices had stopped. What was going on now, she wondered. It was bad enough that she had been forced to stay locked away today, but to keep her uninformed was unforgivable. She could see the logic in being kept locked up like this once Mira explained it to her. Grunkaar was a big day for the Guznon. Many thousands would be making the long climb up to the catacombs and it would be better if she were not seen. Whilst it would be highly unlikely that any of the Guznon would tell the authorities about the strange blonde Altani woman living in the old settlement, it was not worth taking any chances, Mira reasoned, was it? Balisel understood. She just wished Mira had given her something to eat and drink before she left. The Guznon may be required to fast on the day of Grunkaar but she did not see why that should apply to her. She was not of their faith and she confessed to knowing little about it and caring even less.

With no warning, the bolts of the door slid back and Mira stood framed in the doorway. She was dressed in bronze and gold ceremonial robes and wore a metallic headdress sculpted to look like to two suns. She smiled at Balisel and beckoned her to come out.

'At last! I thought you'd abandoned me.'

'Oh no! We would never do that, Ko-Makum. You must know how very precious you are to us,' the priestess replied with sincerity.

Balisel shrugged her indifference and spoke again, quickly and sharply. She had had just about enough of this. 'Where's Kalik?'

'He's up on the parapet with his wet nurse. I've come to take you to him.'

'About time,' Balisel replied testily, and she pushed forward towards the stairs ahead of Mira and the men who had accompanied her.

Balisel was amazed at the sight that met her eyes. There were thousands of them, men and women, young and old, all the Guznon tribe gathered on the flat expanse of the parapet, hundreds of metres above the Rakuum plains. The twin suns were low in the morning sky but the heat was already building. Denkau and his people had rigged a vast linen shade at the edge of the cliff to give them all respite from the heat and the suns' rays. Even so, Balisel thought, one would not want to be out here any longer than was strictly necessary. Even the ore trawlers, with their environmental controls, could not work much beyond midmorning here, for fear of their hulls melting.

Denkau stood near the edge of the parapet, his silhouette framed against the horizon by the parted crowd. He beckoned her to come to him. He was holding Kalik out in front of him, a tiny bundle, as though offering the baby to her to take. She walked briskly forward and, as she passed through the throng, they bowed their heads to her, which she thought was as it should be. It had been too long since she had been accorded any respect; it was one of the aspects of her former life that she rather missed.

When she reached Denkau, he handed Kalik to her. The crowd suddenly cried out in a rhythmic chant, to which they also stamped their feet. The noise was deafening, so much so that it woke the sleeping two-month-old, who instantly cried out in distress. Balisel tried to calm him by bouncing him a little and cooing, but no one, not the wet nurse or Mira, seemed to pay any attention to the wails of the infant. Finally Denkau led her to a splendid chair, which was more like a throne. It was draped with a heavy tapestry that was very new and very colourful. Indeed, the work that had gone into weaving the tapestry had taken many months, as it had had to be done in secret in Zaz-Rakuum before being brought to the high settlement for this special day.

'Be seated, Ko-Makum. Rest from your burden.' Balisel did as she was bid. She had no desire to stand in the growing heat holding her son.

Then Denkau turned to face the gathering of his tribe and began to half-speak, half-chant to them. He made slow, solemn gestures with his arms and Balisel gathered that he was leading them all in some sort of prayer.

After a few minutes Denkau's chant stopped and Mira took over. Once again her words were mostly a song and she, too, made many sweeping hand gestures. It all looked very impressive, thought Balisel, and she was glad that they had changed their minds and let her see their sacred ceremonies.

Finally, just as Kalik stopped crying and looked as though he might settle back to sleep, Mira finished her chant and came over to Balisel.

'I will take the child now, Ko-Makum. It is time,' she said, and her tone was suddenly very formal and serious. Balisel was intrigued.

'Time for what?' she fired back as she handed her baby son to the woman.

Mira passed the baby to one of the Guznon servant women while Denkau came and stood beside her.

'Ko-Makum, the time has come for us to receive your great gift.' Denkau's words were delivered with solemnity, as though this was all part of the ritual rather than a simple answer to her question. 'We thank you in all humility and offer you our eternal devotion. Your sacrifice is the greatest gift you can make and your name will live on in Guznon history from this day forth.'

Balisel frowned. What was going on? What sacrifice? This was not the first time she had heard them use that word. And where had they taken Kalik? Then it hit her. *Oh no! Not him. Not Kalik!* It was all she had left of Durroc.

'What do think you're doing?' she spat back. 'Don't start playing games with me. Bring my son to me – now! This instant!' She began to rise out of the chair, ready to go after the servant who had taken her son away. From behind, the massive red hands of the two Autabroni guards grabbed her wrists and, in a few swift movements, bound her to the chair. She struggled, kicking out with her legs and narrowly missing Mira. But it was useless. Once her wrists were tied the guards did the same to her ankles, and then her waist.

'No!' she screamed. 'Give me my son. Don't hurt him!'

'Your son is quite safe and will remain so here among the Guznon. We will cherish and nurture him for all the days of his life. He is a most wondrous gift and we are honoured to receive him into our tribe.' Mira spoke quietly and clearly. She felt it was important for the little witch to know that the child's future was assured, for she had given the impression of truly caring for the babe whilst she had cared for no others.

Denkau continued. 'And we thank you, Ko-Makum, for your gift too. Your sacrifice will appease the wrath of Lau and Uzno who, even now, anticipate your coming and greatly welcome it. Before the dusk of this day there shall be water upon the plains and in the reservoirs and in the rivers far below. This will be so only through the grace of your passing.'

'No ...' Balisel's voice was a whisper. She was beginning to understand. Sacrifice, they had said. Not her son but *her*. They meant to kill her. These savages intended her death.

'You can't do this. It's – it's barbarous. You can't do this! Let me go!' Her voice grew louder, the panic and the fear tearing at every syllable. She struggled again with the ferocity of a lion, screaming and crying out for Denkau to release her.

'Ko-Makum. Be still. You yourself said that you would gladly give whatever we needed to obtain help for you and your child,' said Denkau, and the look he gave her was both pitying and scornful. 'But your wealth is nothing to us. The only thing we need from you, little witch, is your life essence. And, in return, our twin gods will favour us with water from the heavens. Thus it was in the past for Ko-Makum of Rundak, your namesake.'

'But I am not her! I'm not a witch. I have no magic!' Balisel shouted back.

Mira looked stunned at these words and strode boldly up to stand before Balisel. She looked deep and hard into the frightened woman's eyes.

'Oh, Ko-Makum, you are so wrong. Look at your hair, your eyes.' She stretched out a hand and gently stroked the fine blonde hair. 'Just like the ancient one. And you are a twin! Your magic is more powerful than you know.'

'Most important of all,' Denkau cried out, as much for the benefit of the crowd as for Balisel, 'you brought the child, the one who will return us to the ways of our gods. The Bringer into Light, our saviour, our prince.'

'Kalik?' Balisel shook her head violently. 'No. You're wrong. He is *not* those things. He's just a little baby – and an Altani. He's not even Guznon. You can't do this! Let me go! Let me go …'

Her struggles were futile, as were her protests. The straps around her body held firm. At a signal from Denkau, the two guards lifted the chair and turned it around to face out across the plains of Rakuum. But Balisel was unable to see the spectacular view through the tears that had filled her ice-blue eyes.

So this was how it would end. No way out. Less than a year after the death of her beloved brother, she would follow him. There seemed a strange simplicity and harmony in the thought. They had always been together in life, much closer than two people could even dream of being.

The silence of the crowd behind her was oppressive and she wished now that they would just get it over and done with. If there was no escaping her death then let it be swift, let it be merciful.

She tried to see his face in her mind's eye and there he was, grinning, throwing back his beautiful head as he laughed. Then, as the softness stole over his eyes – the softness given only to her – he leaned down to kiss her.

Suddenly the cloth shade fell to the ground and billowed loosely in the updraught at the edge of the cliff. The full power of the twin suns was unleashed on the expanse of the parapet and, instantly, the temperature rose. Where it had been hot before was now scorching. Already the superheated air burned her windpipe and she was forced to close her eyes to stop them from dehydrating.

She could hear the gathering behind her turning to walk back into the cool shadows of the catacombs. But Denkau and Mira held back, bearing the heat for a little while as best they could.

'We know you are scared. But know this,' said Denkau. 'Whatever else you did in your life, whatever your sins, whatever shame you carry – all is washed away on this day. Your sacrifice is a gift beyond all thanks.'

Balisel heard his words though she could not see him. She wept, but her tears dried immediately on her cheeks. Then she felt Mira's hand on her arm, stroking her hot skin.

'Be brave, little witch. It will be over very soon. And know that your legacy will live on in your son.'

Balisel almost laughed out loud. My son, *his* son.

'You'd better be right, old woman,' she croaked 'Or I'll come back to haunt you to your grave. My legacy *is* my son – and he will avenge his father's death!'

These were the last words of Balisel Navarr. Mira transcribed them precisely once she was back inside the settlement as well as documenting the morning's glorious events. Her son would want to know of them when he was grown. After all, they would be his destiny.

The dance of the two suns came to a close and, with their passing, a cool wind swept over the barren red plains. In the distance a roiling wave of clouds formed and grew ever larger. Like a tsunami, they sucked the air towards them and, in a sudden lurch, spilled their abundant moisture onto the dry dirt for the first time in over twenty years. Mira and Denkau sighed and smiled at the tumbling, swirling rains and gave thanks for the sacrifice of the little witch. Thus ended the day of Grunkaar and all was renewed on Autabron.

My beautiful daughter – our beautiful daughter – Setiyan celebrated her second birthday today. She is absolutely wonderful! Full of life and mischief and happy giggles. We sometimes wonder what we did to deserve such a lovely child. She still has those amazing eyes – lighter than Jax's, but not as green as mine – which I thought she'd lose as she got older. And her mop of floppy blonde hair is just like Jax's grandmother's, I have been told.

Jax and Evica planned a party for her. Most of the palace children were there – and little Odar, of course, my handsome nephew. We had musicians, too, and a wonderful troupe of magicians and clowns came to perform. Of course, Setiyan did not really appreciate the cleverness of the performers, but she loved all the noise and hoopla and people making a fuss of her. Jax won her heart completely – as he always does – when he took her for a ride on a miniature jenka, holding her very tightly, of course. Her eyes twinkled like two perfect little blue stars and it was all I could do not to pinch her fat cheeks with pleasure. She just adores him – as do I.

Then Nen scolded us both for overtiring her when she began to get niggly, so we wound things up and sent everyone home. Evica and Tariik stayed on for some afternoon tea and we watched Duncan in his new vidisk, playing a hard-hitting fighter pilot who rescues a politician's daughter, then falls in love with her. I'm afraid I didn't much like it – it all seemed a bit far-fetched – but Duncan was excellent, and we cheered him on.

I was glad of the early night, though. Pregnancy tires me, just like it did with Setiyan. Luckily I've not been getting those nightmares about Navarr this time around, so I'm sleeping much better.

Now, when I think about those days, it's as though it was all some terrible dream. How could I have even looked at that man! Thankfully, much of my memory of those months seems to have gone for good. And in the end, I suppose it all turned out for the best, although we never found Navarr's sister, and the captives from the fortress could tell us nothing about the Order of Sumere either. Jax says we'll work it all out eventually and I suppose he's right.

We must be up early tomorrow morning for a meeting with the Dasnirian senators to discuss the proposed changes to the shipping networks, followed by a visit to Sen-Beoraan's new School of Interplanetary Communications at Jinkat'naru University. It will be good to see my old counsellor again; I miss him so much since he gave up his position to set up the school. But, as Jax says, he is never far away – unlike Mother, who is having a wonderful time on Earth. She has discovered a place she calls 'the southseas' and swears that the warm water lagoons have special healing powers. Jax seems to think it is more to do with the healing powers of something called 'cocktails', although he will not tell me what these are. Sometimes he gets that mischievous look in his eye and I know he is teasing or making fun of me, but it gives him so much pleasure that I can't be cross. We are both so happy. I can't believe I was once so horrible to him. I must have been mad.

I looked in on Setiyan before sitting down to write this. She was untroubled and peaceful. She sleeps so perfectly, as if she knows that she is completely loved and that we will always love her, of course, no matter what her future brings.

GLOSSARY of TERMS

CHARACTERS

The Altanis

Linnayen Genara	Daughter to Yenshar Genara, leader of the planet Altan
Yenshar Genara	Leader of the planet, Altan, father to Linnayen and Evica
Evica Genara	Linnayen's older sister
Sen-Beoraan	A member of the Union Forum and counsellor to the Kis of Altan. 'Sen' is an honorary title showing respect.
Nen	Maidservant to Linnayen Genara
Dr Em-sin Mai	Physician to the Genara family
Lady Li-el Dacas	A noblewoman of the House of Dacas, consort to Ki-Yenshar Genara, mother to Linnayen and Evica
Durroc Navarr	Army officer and senior diplomat, special envoy to Linnayen Genara
Balisel Navarr	Twin sister to Captain Durroc Navarr and financial director of mining conglomerate, GKD
Captain Tejarc	Captain of the spaceracer, GU *Jensa Kadenx*
Asud	Female assistant to Sen-Beoraan
Sen-Kilas'ab	Manager of the Cadal'baran Lodge on Hutho

The Earthans

Kevor Jax Bashir	Only son of Sheikh David and Lady Thea, known as 'Jax'

Sheikh David Bashir al Fahrazad — President of the Council of the United Democratic Nations (UDN) and father of Jax

Lady Thea Bashir — wife of Sheikh David and mother of Jax

Professor Marcus di Luca — Tutor to the young Jax

Duncan McCrae — An actor and Jax's best friend since childhood

Joseph Connor McCrae — Duncan's father and retired member of the UDN Council

Harriet Whitton-Blake — Student at the UDN Diplomatic Corps and Jax's first girlfriend

Hal Byers — Earthan ambassador to Altan

Count Josef Aramikov — Aide to Jax

Marseille Auteuil — Female assassin, code-named 'Oleander', also known as Carri Aqua

Kees Rennick — A mercenary soldier, accomplice to Oleander

Jeremiah Danforth — Assistant to Balisel Navarr

James Toyotomi — A scientist and suitor to Linnayen Genara

Kumiko Toyotomi — Great-grandmother to James and member of the UDN Council

Ennio Nori — Grandson-in-law to Kumiko Toyotomi and member of the Order of Sumere

Captain Chandra — Leader of Linnayen Genara's bodyguards on Earth

Milos Visnivic — A mercenary pilot

Celeste Malone — A senior pilot for the UDN Special Services Corps

The Dasnirians

Lieutenant Tariik Min — A weapons instructor in the Union of Planets army

Bedarek Min — Tariik's grandfather

<u>Autabronis</u>

Margog Delgar	An employee of GKD at the Euta Makaan ore processing plant
Denkau and Mira	Husband and wife, high priest and priestess of the ancient Guznon faith, leaders of the Guznon tribe

PLACES AND LOCATIONS

Adhana Island Hotel	A luxury hotel in the city of Genkarah on the planet Altan
Altan	One of the four planets in the Union, circled by three moons, home and birthplace of Linnayen and Evica Genara
Amerimex	A nation on Earth comprising the old countries of the United States of America and Mexico
Antipodea	A nation on Earth comprising the old nations of Australia, New Zealand, New Caledonia, Papua New Guinea and Micronesia
Arbour of Serenkiraah	Home to a reclusive order of priests and priestesses living in seclusion in the high Ksas Mountains on Altan
Autabron	One of the four planets comprising the Union of Planets, an arid planet with vast reserves of bergussian ore. Autabron is unique in that it has two suns, Lau and Uzno, which revolve around each other. Autabronis are generally red-skinned with white hair.
Bargassi Demi-galaxy	A distinct arm of the Milky Way galaxy and the location of the planet Autabron
Bastimi Falls	A spectacular waterfall on the Bastimi River on Altan
Bast-ra	A tourist town near the Bastimi Falls

Beshwuk Highlands	A range of steep-sided mountains that rise above the Rakuum Plains on Autabron
Cadal'baran Lodge	The holiday lodge of the Genara family on Hutho
Carissian Basin	A marine depression on the planet Dasnir that contains some of the planet's richest srif farms, home to Lt. Tariik Min and his family
Dasnir	One of the four planets in the Union, where 9/10ths of the surface is water. Dasnirians have remnants webbed skin between their toes and hands
Debenka	The first of Altan's three moons, the others being Onuak and Revishankan
Elidian	A floating city on Earth, main home of the Bashir family
Eurotania	Comprises the old countries of Europe including parts of ancient Russia and the Balkans
Euta Makaan	A large bergussian ore processing plant on Autabron
Floating Ice Gardens	A tourist attraction on Dasnir, featuring wind and water sculpted icebergs of unusual beauty
Genkarah	A large city on Altan, traditional home of the Genara family
Gutokuroc Falls	A series of four major waterfalls on the Utieku River on the planet Hutho
Guyvar Neref	A ruined 13th century fortress in northeast Anatolia
Hashaniq	A grain farming region spanning a large part of the southern hemisphere on Altan

Hutho	One of the four planets of the Union, heavily forested and with a green sky. Huthons have evolved to have a pale green skin.
Hutoriaku Plains	An expansive, deeply forested lowland region on Hutho
Jarunei Strand	An arm of the Milky Way galaxy that exhibits a natural phenomenon of electromagnetic wave-pulses used by spacecraft to vastly accelerate propulsion
Jinkat'naru	An underground city in the high northern Arctic region of Altan
Kalinbi-Makkar Dam	A dam holding back a huge reservoir of water that supplies the city of Silbaraz-Re on Altan
Ksas Mountains	The highest mountain range on Altan
Kushaan Canopy Park	A leisure complex built in the treetops of the Kushaan Forest on Hutho
Lau	One of the twin suns of Autabron
Makassar Republic	A nation on Earth comprising the ancient empires of Malay and Indonesia
Mayar	A rich farming region on Altan famous for its extensive grasslands
Mulakush	A city on the planet Hutho, headquarters of the company GKD
Ngoro Strand	An arm of the Milky Way wherein lies the Earthan Solar System
Nippon-ko Republic	A nation on comprising the free nations of Japan and Korea
Onuak	The largest of the three moons encircling Altan
Pillar of Peyjaan	A unique geological feature; a 60-metre high pillar of pale blue ambicinite rising from the ground at the Arbour of Serenkiraah

Rabakaran	One of two high Arctic underground cities on Altan
Rakuum Planis	An extensive area of desert on Autabron famous for its bergussian ore deposits
Rakuum Settlement	An ancient city of caves, catacombs and tunnels carved into the Beshwuk Ranges on Autabron, the original tribal home of the Guznon people
Revishankan	The smallest of the three moons of Altan
Seta Ridges	A ridge of low-lying ice hills in the high Arctic region of Altan
Silbaraz-Re	The largest city on Altan, birthplace of Durroc and Balisel Navarr
Solab 3	A space station situated between the planets of Mars and Jupiter
Utieku River	One of the largest rivers on the planet Hutho
Uzno	The name given to the second sun of Autabron
Zaz-Rakuum	An underground city, home mainly to miners and processing plant workers on Autabron

VOCABULARY & OTHER NAMES

Aircar	A small solar-powered, airborne craft used on Earth for personal transportation
Airdancer	A brand of two-seater aircar
Altaniskaran	The main religious group on Altan
Altan-Re	An annual ceremony on Altan celebrating the elements of life
Altek	The highest-ranking priest or priestess in the Altaniskaran faith
Astrometallurgy	The science of the behaviour of metals in space

Baktanishan	A formerly noble family of Altan, now disgraced
Bergussian	A valuable mineral ore found in large quantities on Autabron
Braup-AG	A GKD subsidiary, gas platform operators on Autabron
Dar-aak's Comet	A comet which approaches the planet Altan once every 534 years
Dirratin gas	Found primarily on Altan and Hutho, used as a propellant in fuel systems of inter-planetary craft
Fractal blast	The blast from a fission-pulse weapon which disintegrates molecular linkages
Fre'gath	A non-addictive drug used in ceremonies on Altan to reduce inhibitions and promote relaxation
Galactic Union	The name given to the combined political entity of the Earthan UDN and the Union of Planets
Gerantel	An addictive drug that produces hallucinations
Grunkaar	A holy day for the Guznon people of Autabron
Gunashey Kuth and Dor (GKD)	A multi-planetary business enterprise involved in mining and processing of bergussian ore and dirratin gas
Guznon	Name given to one of the oldest tribes on Autabron
Guznonabat	The religion of the Guznon people
Haranshay Systems	A large ore-processing machinery and operating systems manufacturer
High Altek	The central authority of the Altaniskaran religious order
Hitarr palm	A rare poisonous plant, native to Altan
Jaaseyan	A state of absolute mind linkage, only achievable by the most skilled mentantes

Jekarion gas	A gas found in the atmosphere of Altan, which has the property of refracting light in the red wavelength, responsible for the rose-coloured skies of Altan
Jenka	A small horse-like creature, native to Altan
Jensa Kadenx	A Galactic Union spacecraft
Kalendarium	An opaline crystal mineral mainly used to decorate buildings, found only on Altan
Kareek	A small dog-like animal with scaly skin, very loyal, kept as a domestic pet on Altan
Kek	Monetary unit of all the four planets in the Union
Ki	The highest-ranking secular individual of the planet Altan, male or female. The title which has 'royal' status is attained through birthright and training, but can be changed by vote of the Altan Council
Klik	A measure of distance in the Union, a little under a kilometre
Ko-kura	'little infidel' in the Guznon dialect on Autabron
Ko-Makum	'little witch' in the Guznon dialect
Ksarpi trees	A species of rainforest tree found mainly in the high glades of the Ksas Mountains on Altan
Kuttashansi	A spaceliner of the Union of Planets fleet
Labyrinth	A secret militia organisation on Earth
Lady/Lord of Light	Honorary title given to the reigning Ki of Altan
Latis-Mei	A race of indigenous people on Altan
Magori	A climbing shrub with brilliant orange flowers

Mentante	A person with telepathic abilities; most usually a genetic trait passed down within families
Nuonabat	Special rites and ceremonies performed on the Day of Grunkaar
Order of Sumere	A secret group of well-funded political dissidents that seeks to keep aliens out of Earth society
Palletron	A hovering pallet used to transport heavy objects
Pystro-ion stream	An unusual cosmonic phenomenon where super-charged ion particles align themselves in the same plane and can penetrate metal
Pulsor	A small, high-powered electronic emitter
Pyro-cannon	A lightweight, laser-like weapon mounted on UDN battlecraft
Reassigner	A specialist in physical reconstruction using archaic cosmetic surgery methods, an outlawed occupation
Sen	Title denoting honour acquired through service to the community
Serenkiraah	The name of an Altani former high priest and recluse who 'abandoned' his body by taking poison to free his spirit in order to attain holy enlightenment
Sestriarch	The head female of noble families on Altan
Sinnsey	A flowering shrub, indigenous to Altan
Sonochip	A transceiver worn under the skin near the ear
Spaceliner	An interplanetary passenger vessel
Spaceracer	A super-speed spacecraft

Srif	A seagrass indigenous to the planet Dasnir, used to make high-protein food additives
Sur-Dacas	A Union of Planets battlecraft
Sur-Kabanash	A Union of planets spaceracer
Sur-Lenes	A Union of Planets battlecraft
Tamuns	Priests and priestesses of the Guznonabat faith
UDNS Lennox-Mayn	An Earthan long-haul spaceliner
United Democratic Nations Council (UDN)	A forum comprising elected representatives from all nations on Earth; the governing body concerning matters of trade, defence, human rights and communications amongst others
Union of Planets	The trade and legislative organisation of the four planets, Altan, Dasnir, Autabron and Hutho, though each planet retains its own sovereignty
Urthrengo	A Huthon-developed drug that renders users highly compliant
Vatortube	An air-pressurised elevator
Vidisk	A data storage chip
Vidlink	A compact visual and audio communications system
Windshifter	A small personal airborne vehicle used on the four Union planets
Zorcuum	A pale blue calcitic mineral found in the Beshwuk Highlands, much valued by the Guznon

ACKNOWLEGEMENTS

Although the writing happens alone, because of the help and encouragement of some wonderful people, this was never a lonely enterprise. My thanks to my lovely, talented editor, Simone Ford, whose fine-tuning and amazing eye for detail got this manuscript to the perfect read it is today, despite the anxiety caused by bushfires surrounding her small community in country New South Wales. Thanks also to Rob Williams, trapped in South Korea by the virus-that-changed-the-world, yet who still produced such a beautiful cover for me. They are special people. As is Debbie Young who gave so freely of her expertise and support – many thanks indeed.

To all those who gave me encouragement and support, especially my much-loved daughter, Caroline, my amazing and beautiful 'eggies', Chloe and Amelia, and my wonderful son-in-law, Jesse – thank you for making me smile. I am so proud of you all.

Thanks also to Fiona and the team at Serendipity for cheering me on. Also, to my special Coffs Harbour friends, Lyn and Wendy, for putting up with my excited waffling and not shutting me up and old Coramba pals, Jen and Andy, who were my first guinea-pig readers – thanks to one and all.

Across the oceans, huge thanks to the Old Blighty crowd: my very smart, whisky-loving pal Ian Gill, his smart and thoughtful wife Michele, my animal-loving, globe-trotting buddy Jane M and my darling Holleys of Uley. If it were not for Belinda who nagged me and had faith in me, I would never have published this book. Everyone should have a 'Belinda' in their life and know the blessings it brings. Thanks go beyond words.

ABOUT THE AUTHOR

576

Penn Adams is originally from London where she worked on two national newspapers and a women's magazine before going to London University to study geography. After five years in public relations, she left the UK in 1989 to backpack around the world and ended up staying in Australia. Here, Penn worked in conservation and not-for-profit organisations, all the while writing – both commercially and for fun. She trained as a teacher in 2008 and now lives in the paradise of northern New South Wales encircled by rainforests, beaches and the glorious Pacific Ocean.

BOOK TWO of the MALIGN SERIES

Twenty-five years have passed since the fateful royal marriage between Linnayen Genara and her Earthan husband, Kevor Jax Bashir. While peace has settled upon the five planets, it faces a new threat from an inspirational new leader of the tribes of Autabron. Linnayen and Jax unknowingly risk the lives of their two daughters, the high-spirited Setiyan and the questioning Calin, in a mission to quash fanatical plots and return peace and productivity to the fractured planet.

At times like these, new heroes are needed desperately. But can Decker Finn be the one man to succeed where the forces of the Union have failed? Or must he lose everyone he cherishes to save another's love?

Follow the story in *The Malign Legacy* out December 2020.

www.pennadams.com